Richard Laymon wrote over thirty nov[...] May 2001, *The Travelling Vampire Show* [...] Best Horror Novel, a prize for which [...] shortlisted with *Flesh*, *Funland*, *A Good*, [...] and *A Writer's Tale* (Best Non-fiction). [...] works include the books of the Beast House Chronicles: *The Cellar*, *The Beast House* and *The Midnight Tour*. Some of his recent novels have been *Night in the Lonesome October*, *No Sanctuary* and *Amara*.

A native of Chicago, Laymon attended Willamette University in Salem, Oregon, and took an MA in English Literature from Loyola University, Los Angeles. In 2000, he was elected President of the Horror Writers' Association. He died in February 2001.

Laymon's fiction is published in the United Kingdom by Headline, and in the United States by Leisure Books and Cemetery Dance Publications. To learn more, visit the Laymon website at: http://rlk.cjb.net

'Stephen King without a conscience' Dan Marlowe

'In Laymon's books, blood doesn't so much as drip as explode, splatter and coagulate' *Independent*

'A brilliant writer' *Sunday Express*

'No one writes like Laymon and you're going to have a good time with anything he writes' Dean Koontz

'Incapable of writing a disappointing book' *New York Review of Science Fiction*

'A gut-crunching writer' *Time Out*

'This is an author that does not pull his punches . . . A gripping, and at times genuinely shocking, read' *SFX Magazine*

Endless Night

and

Midnight's Lair

headline

ENDLESS NIGHT first published in Great Britain in 1993
by HEADLINE PUBLISHING GROUP

MIDNIGHT'S LAIR* first published in Great Britain in 1998
by HEADLINE PUBLISHING GROUP
*Previously published as MIDNIGHT'S LAIR under the
pseudonym Richard Kelly

First published in this omnibus edition in 2006
by HEADLINE PUBLISHING GROUP

A HEADLINE paperback

2

0 7553 3176 1 (ISBN-10)
978 0 7553 3176 5 (ISBN-13)

Typeset in Janson by Avon DataSet Ltd, Bidford on Avon, Warwickshire

Printed and bound in Great Britain by
Mackays of Chatham plc, Chatham, Kent

Headline's policy is to use papers that are natural, renewable and recyclable
products and made from wood grown in sustainable forests. The logging and
manufacturing processes are expected to conform to the environmental
regulations of the country of origin.

HEADLINE PUBLISHING GROUP
A division of Hodder Headline
338 Euston Road
London NW1 3BH

www.headline.co.uk
www.hodderheadline.com

Endless Night

This book is dedicated to our friends:
Larry Mori & Joan Parsons,
Curators of the Mori-Parsons Museum
of the Weird and Wonderful
where they dwell

PART ONE

Someone in the House

Chapter One

Jody came awake moaning.

'Wake up!' The whisper sounded urgent. 'Jody, wake up! Please!'

The voice belonged to Evelyn. Probably so did the hand shaking her shoulder.

She thought, Oh, yeah. I'm at Evelyn's. Sleeping over. *Trying* to sleep over, more like it.

She opened her eyes, rubbed them, yawned. The room was dark, but she could see Evelyn looking down at her from the bed. The girl's face was a dim blur smudged with shadows. Her arm, darker than the white sheets, was stretched toward the floor where Jody had settled for the night in her sleeping bag. Her hand had a tight grip on Jody's shoulder.

Jody moaned again. 'What is it this time?'

'I heard something.'

'Gimme a break,' she murmured. 'You messed up a really neat dream. I wanna get back to it, if you don't mind. Jeez.' As she yawned, Evelyn shook her shoulder again.

'I mean it. I'm not kidding. I *heard* something.'

'So?'

'I'm scared.'

So what else is new? Jody thought. She didn't say it, though. Evelyn had a way of blowing just about everything out of proportion, making big deals out of nothing – but she was Jody's best friend. They'd been best friends since kindergarten, so Jody'd had about ten years of experience with her histrionics.

'It probably wasn't anything. Just go back to sleep.'

'It was somebody breaking one of the windows downstairs.'

'Uh.' Jody yawned again. Now that she'd been awakened, she felt too hot inside her sleeping bag. Had Evelyn's father shut off the air conditioner before turning in? 'Breaking glass?' she asked. 'Maybe one of your parents is up and dropped something. What time is it, anyway?'

'One-fifteen.'

'Jeez.' She found the inside zipper tab up near her left shoulder. The hand on her other shoulder flinched when she slid the zipper down. 'That was just me,' she explained.

'What're you doing?'

'Melting.'

'We've gotta *do* something.'

'Yeah. Let's go back to sleep.' She swept aside the stifling thickness of her sleeping bag. From the knees down, it still buried her. She freed her legs and stretched out, uncovered. That felt better, cool and nice except where her nightshirt kept the air away. If she were at home, she could simply take it off. Not here, though. 'Does your dad turn *off* the air conditioning at night?'

'My God, Jody.'

'Can we open a window, or something?'

'They don't open.'

Remind me never to live in a state-of-the-art house, she thought. 'That's probably why somebody broke one.'

'I don't find any of this amusing.'

Jody felt her nightshirt glide up her body, giving her a momentary, soft caress as she raised her arms and folded her hands beneath her head. Now, she could feel the air's touch higher on her thighs. She eased one leg sideways.

4

A lot better.

Just gotta get back inside the sleeping bag before daylight. Wouldn't want either of the guys to see me like this. God, that'd be embarrassing. I'd never be able to look Mr Clark – Charles – in the eye again. It'd be even worse if Andy got a look. A lot worse. Him and his major-league crush. The poor tyke might throw a heart attack, be the first twelve-year-old in history to drop dead from over-excitement.

'Do you think we oughta take a look around?' Evelyn asked.

'All you heard was a little breaking glass?'

'Yeah.'

'That could've been anything. It probably came from outside. Maybe somebody dropped a bottle.'

'What if it's a robber?'

'If it's a robber, I don't think he would appreciate a visit from us.'

'Ha ha.'

'Anyway, the burglar alarm would've gone off.'

'Maybe not.'

'Your dad *always* sets it before he goes to bed.'

'I don't know about that.'

'My God, Ev, every time your folks turn in before us, your dad *always* warns us not to touch any of the doors. Or does he only do that when *I'm* staying over? Does he think I'm a bad influence and'll talk you into sneaking out to get wild?'

'No. He thinks you're great.'

'Very perceptive man.'

'But the alarm doesn't *have* to go off, you know? Not even if it *is* set. Criminals have ways . . .'

'Sure. Real pros do. But pros try not to go busting into houses when people are in them. They like to go in when nobody's home. For one thing, it's less of a hassle. For another, it's a much lighter sentence if they get caught. It's only burglary, if nobody's home. Boosts it up to robbery if anyone's there, *armed* robbery if the bad guy has any kind of a weapon. That's what Dad says.'

'He always carries a gun, doesn't he?'

'Most of the time.'

'I sure wish *he* was here right now.'

'Oh, for Pete's sake, Ev. If you're this worried, maybe we'd *better* take a look around. Or maybe you'd rather dispense with the preliminaries and just dial 911.'

'I'm thinking about it.'

'Oh, your parents would love that. Look, why don't we go and wake up your dad?'

'Sure. He'd kill me.'

'Not if there's a bad guy in the house.'

'But what if there isn't? What if I wake him up, and it's all a false alarm?'

'You woke *me* up.'

'That's different.'

'Yeah, it's okay to wake *me* up.'

Evelyn was silent for a few moments. Then she said, 'Maybe I'd better.'

'Better what?'

'Tell Dad.'

For the first time, Jody felt a slight tremor of worry. Even though Evelyn's father seemed like a really nice guy, the poor girl had always shown major reluctance to disturb him. If she was ready to wake him up, she *must* be seriously concerned about the noise she'd heard.

Evelyn swung her legs down from the mattress. She stood up and took a long stride to step over Jody's chest.

'You're really going?' Not waiting for an answer, Jody said,

'I'll go with you.' As soon as Evelyn was out of the way, she sat up. Evelyn kept walking. 'Hold it. Jeez.'

She stopped and waited.

On her feet, Jody asked, 'Do you have a robe I can wear?'

'I thought you were supposed to be hot.'

'I am hot. But what if Andy's up and around?'

'Don't worry, he's not. Nothing wakes him up.'

Evelyn pressed a shoulder against her bedroom door and turned the knob. When she stepped back to pull the door open, Jody did a quick shuffle to avoid being stepped on.

Evelyn swung the door open wide.

And grunted.

Jody heard a quick, wet punch.

Something poked her belly. She sucked in her breath, drawing in a stench like week-dead rat, and stumbled backward as Evelyn seemed to leap straight up in the middle of the doorway. But it wasn't a leap. On her best day ever, she couldn't have leaped so high. Her head struck the top of the door frame.

This isn't happening, Jody thought.

No.

Huh-uh.

No way.

But she could feel a small trickle of blood sliding down her belly. Untouched by her loose hanging nightshirt, it dribbled on downward to her groin. It felt very real.

So did the blood she heard *splashing* as it fell from Evelyn. Very real.

And the stink of rot was real, too. For a few days last summer, Jody had smelled much the same disgusting odor after a rat had died behind a bathroom wall at home. Dad hadn't been willing to demolish the wall to retrieve the carcass. So they'd had to wait it out.

This smells just like death.

This *can't* be happening.

Evelyn hung there limp, head dropping sideways, bare feet nowhere close to the floor, a blob of darkness growing on the back of her nightgown. From the middle of the blob protruded a pointed silver tongue.

Before Jody could make sense of what she was seeing, Evelyn glided away from the doorway and vanished into the corridor.

Jody stood frozen.

She couldn't move or scream. She couldn't breathe.

The shape in the darkness looked like a man. A big man. An obese man. His pale head was smooth, probably hairless. Though somehow he didn't seem to be naked, every part of him that Jody could see had the same gray hue as his head.

The act of swinging Evelyn's body away from the doorway had turned him sideways.

Jody couldn't see the shaft in his hands. She knew it had to be there, though. Maybe six feet long.

Her best friend was hoisted on its point.

As she watched, numb, the man marched off.

He didn't see me!

Oh my God, oh my God! He doesn't know I'm here! Evelyn was standing in the way, and . . .

I've gotta get out of here!

But then she wondered if it might be safer to hide. No. Maybe he'll be back. Maybe he'll search the whole house. Maybe he'll set it on fire before he leaves.

Gotta run!

Get dressed first? She *wanted* to get dressed. In just the nightshirt, she felt exposed and vulnerable.

But what if he comes back while I'm . . .?

Besides, there was money in a front pocket of her jeans – a

whole handful of coins. Bound to jingle if she picked up the jeans.

Gotta just go. The hell with my clothes.

She crept forward. Crouching, she peered around the doorframe.

The man with Evelyn was halfway to the end of the hall, framed by a yellow glow that came from the lighted doorway of the master bedroom.

The rotten odor had faded, but still hung in the air, sweet and filthy.

It's him, Jody realized.

How can he smell like that?

I don't want to know, she told herself.

He looked as wide as a refrigerator. He seemed to be dressed in shaggy scraps and tatters that swayed with the motion of his lumbering walk. He carried Evelyn in front of him, on the end of his spear, her head near the ceiling.

As he neared the lighted doorway, he lowered her slightly. He swung her to the right. He marched her into the bedroom, followed and disappeared.

They're all dead! Evelyn, her mom and dad – Andy? What about Andy?

The boy's door, straight across the hall from Jody, was shut.

She glanced both ways, then scurried for his door on hands and knees.

He would be no help to her. She knew that. What help could a twelve-year-old kid be in a situation like this? Especially a kid Andy's size. But she didn't want his help. She wanted to get him out of the house.

A terrible thing to wake him, though. It might be a kindness to let him sleep, safe from the knowledge that his family had been destroyed.

She would be waking him up into something too horrible to understand.

She knew that she might not be able to save him, anyway.

They might both end up getting killed.

She would stand a better chance of survival, herself, if she let him sleep and made her break alone.

What the hell, she thought.

A voice inside her head, sounding very much like her father, told Jody, *Go for broke, honey*.

Reaching up, she gripped the door knob. She turned it. The latch gave out a *tunk* that made her wince. She pushed the door. As it swung inward, she crawled into Andy's dark bedroom.

She got to her feet and eased the door shut.

Leaning back against it, she tried to catch her breath.

In this room, the curtains were shut. Blurred smears of light glowed along their edges. Jody could see little more than the vague shape of Andy's bed. She couldn't even be sure the boy was in it.

She listened. She heard the wild pounding of her own heartbeat. And she heard Andy breathing.

Slow, easy breathing.

He's either asleep or faking it, Jody thought.

From somewhere in the distance came a sound of quiet music. The main song from *Cats*. Was it coming from Mr and Mrs Clark's bedroom? Had that monster turned on their radio?

What's he doing in there?

'Andy?' she whispered.

No answer.

She didn't dare turn on a light.

Bending over and sweeping her arms from side to side, she made her way carefully toward the bed. Her bare feet pushed into a soft heap of blanket on the floor. Her hands found the top sheet. Following the edge of the mattress, she sidestepped along the end of the bed, then up its side.

She sat down on the mattress. She reached toward the middle and lowered her hand. It settled on warm, bare skin.

Andy's chest. She felt it rise against her hand as he inhaled. She felt his heartbeat.

What if it's not Andy? What if it's someone like . . .

Of course it's Andy, she told herself.

'Andy?' she whispered. She jostled his chest.

'Mmmm.'

'It's me. It's Jody. You've got to wake up.'

'Hmmm?'

She found his lips with her other hand. 'It's all right. Just don't yell or anything.'

'Jody?' His voice sounded husky. 'It's you? It's really you? Oh, man.'

'Somebody's in the house.'

'What?'

'We've gotta get out.'

'Who's in the house?'

'Some kind of – I don't know. A maniac.'

'We've got a *maniac* in the house?' He sounded more astonished than alarmed. 'You mean like Freddy or Jason or something?'

'I mean the real thing.'

'Where?'

'Never mind. Let's go.' She gave his chest a gentle slap, then stood up.

'Jody?'

'We've gotta hurry.'

'Before the *maniac* comes for us?' She couldn't see his face.

From his tone of voice, however, she suspected that his initial confusion was gone. He sounded as if he might be aiming a sneer at her.

'I'm not kidding, Andy.'

'Yeah, sure. Man, you had me going for a second. Just for a second, though. Man. Thanks a lot. I'm really amused.' And then he bolted upright on his bed and shouted, 'REALLY AMUSED, EVELYN. HA HA HA!'

Jody felt as if she had been kicked in the heart.

'Shut up!' she cried out in a hoarse whisper. 'What're you *doing*? You just got us killed!'

Chapter Two

'Oh, come on,' Andy muttered. 'You can quit your little game. I'm used to Evelyn pulling junk on me, but I thought *you* were better than . . .'

His voice stopped when Jody slapped the light switch. She whirled around.

Andy squinted against the brightness from the ceiling bulb. 'Hey.' He was sitting cross-legged on his bed, covered to the waist by a white sheet.

'What've you got?' Jody asked.

'Huh?'

'A knife? You got a pocket knife or . . .?' She spotted a baseball bat propped against a corner near his window. She ran for it.

'Jody!'

'He's coming!' Unless maybe he didn't hear Andy's yell. With the bedroom door shut and the music going down in the other room, maybe . . .

'Who's coming?'

'The killer!' She grabbed up the bat with both hands. A Louisville Slugger.

'Hey, come on. Cut it out.'

As she rushed for his bedroom door, she warned, 'You'd better get up.'

'Oh, sure. I'm not *wearing* anything, in case my dumb sister forgot to tell you.'

She swiped at the switch. Darkness clamped the room.

'Thanks,' Andy said.

'Shhhh.' Jody raised the bat overhead. It was a good, solid bat, but not awfully heavy. Certainly not heavy enough to make the muscles of her arms tremble and flutter this way.

She listened.

To her heartbeat and fast breathing. To a sigh from Andy. She heard no sound of music. She heard no footsteps.

Maybe he left. Maybe he left before Andy shouted.

But she didn't think so. That would be too good to be true. Like waking up and realizing all this had been a nightmare. *You're not gonna get off that easy.* This was bad stuff, worse than she had ever imagined possible, and she knew somehow that the worst was ahead.

If only I had my pistol. Just a little .22, but . . .

'Evelyn's gonna bust through the door in a mask, isn't she? That spooky one she got last Halloween.'

What'll it feel like, getting a spear through the guts?

This is what I get for trying to help someone, she thought. And then she felt ashamed of herself.

Dad does this stuff every day.

God, if only he was here now!

13

That's just what Evelyn had said, she remembered. And a couple of minutes later, the spear had picked her up.

It got me, too, she realized. The same point.

Just a little poke. She could feel the wound now, a small sore place just below her navel and a little bit to the right.

Got me after going all the way through Evelyn.

'Jesus,' she murmured.

'What?'

'Nothing. You'd better get dressed.'

'I'm not moving. If I start to get dressed, you'll turn the light on. Where's Evelyn? What's she doing, hiding someplace with a camera?'

He'll lose his attitude fast, Jody thought, if I tell him she's dead.

No, he'll think it's part of the gag.

Besides, she couldn't tell him. She knew she couldn't force herself to say the words.

What's taking the goddamn monster so long?

Maybe he isn't coming. Maybe he's gone.

Fat chance.

What am I doing here?

Waiting and bleeding, she thought.

Correction, not bleeding. From the feel of things, the wound had quit leaking. There seemed to be a single strip of blood, no longer going anywhere but making her skin itchy underneath it. The strip went down from the wound to the hollow at the top of her leg, then ran along the hollow at a downward angle to her groin.

Now that she was thinking about it, the itch got worse.

She wanted to rub it and wipe the blood away.

Her hands were busy holding the baseball bat overhead.

Just my luck, the second I let go . . .

The door swung slowly inward.

Jody caught a whiff of the death stink. She held her breath.

As the door opened more, a dim mist of light spread across the room. The edge of light found Andy's bed, crept toward him, revealed him sitting cross-legged.

His mouth fell open.

His back straightened.

He began to make a quiet, very high-pitched humming sound, a soft whine of panic as if he ached to scream but didn't dare.

A shadow blotted out the fan of dull light.

A floorboard in front of Jody creaked.

Go for broke, hon!

She chopped the Slugger down with all her might.

She'd played enough hardball with her dad to know the sound and feel of a good hit with the fat of the bat. This was a very good hit. This was a home run.

The *thock* of the blow was followed by a grunt, then muffled thumps which Jody figured were the man's knees hitting the carpeted floor, then a softer sound which had to be his torso landing, then another thump – his face making contact.

Jody swept her forearm up the wall until it flipped up the light switch.

The man lay face down, motionless on the carpet. The top of his hairless head was a collapsed, bleeding gully.

Jody shut the door fast.

'Oh, God!' Andy blurted. He was standing near the foot of his bed, prancing on the mattress to keep his balance, clutching a pillow to his groin. 'Oh, God, what's going *on*? Look at him! Look at him!'

Jody stood over the intruder, holding her bat high, ready to strike again if he should move.

He had come in with a machete, not a spear. It was still in his hand. Its blade was smeared with blood. Blood also speckled and smudged both his arms, his back and rump and legs.

'Hit him again,' Andy said.

'Shhh.'

'What's wrong?'

'Everything,' Jody whispered. 'It isn't him.'

'Huh?'

'It isn't *him*. This guy's skinny.'

'Look at his butt.'

'You look at his butt.' She stepped toward the machete. 'The other one's still out there. The fat guy.'

'It's sewed shut.'

When Andy said that, she had to look. She looked as she crouched to pick up the machete, and saw a crosshatch of stitches up the center of the man's rump. She thought, How does he poop? And then she saw the rumbles in his buttocks and the backs of his legs. Then the ragged edges hanging around his ankles.

The rope of braided hair around his waist wasn't merely an ornament. It was a belt.

She looked up at Andy.

'They're pants,' he whispered. 'They're *pants*!'

Still prancing on his bed with the pillow clutched to his groin, Andy suddenly rushed to the end of his mattress, bent over and vomited.

The thick gush missed his bed, but splashed down on the head of the intruder. Jody stumbled backward to get away from it.

Suddenly, she was having a very hard time catching her breath.

Bat in one hand, machete in the other, she turned toward the bedroom door. She felt as if her heart and lungs were being squeezed by fists. She gasped for air.

Behind her, Andy coughed and sniffed. 'Where're Mom and Dad and Evelyn?' he asked.

'I don't know.'

'You said about another guy. A fat guy.'

'Yeah.'

He'll smash through the door right now and pick me up with his spear.

She wished that the door had a lock.

Bedroom doors always have locks. In the movies.

Some bedroom doors in real life probably had locks, too, but she'd never seen one.

'Do you think . . . Do you think they're all right? Mom and Dad and Evelyn?'

'No.'

'Oh, God. Oh, Jesus.'

Jody turned around. Andy stepped to the floor and sat on a corner of his bed and hunched over, hugging the pillow, head down. 'We've gotta get out of here,' Jody told him.

He looked up at her. His face was red, eyes squeezed almost shut, teeth bared.

'The other's gonna come,' she said.

Lowering his head again, he muttered, 'I don't care.'

'He'll kill us.'

'So?'

Jody went to him. She stepped between his knees. The hanging front of her nightshirt enfolded the top of his head. She moved forward until his head pushed against her. It pressed her lower than she had expected.

An odd bit of her mind thought how embarrassing this would be under other circumstances.

But she didn't feel embarrassed at all.

With the knuckles of the hand that held the machete, she

17

gently caressed the back of his head. His hair was dripping wet.

'We're gonna get out of this,' she whispered.

'Is everybody dead?'

'I don't know.'

'I'm so scared.'

'Me, too. It'll be all right, though.'

Andy lifted his head, but didn't move it away. She felt the rub of his hair through the thin jersey fabric, then the pressure of his face. His face was so low that she couldn't feel the push of his chin. 'What'll we do?' he asked. She felt his lips move. His breath was like hot steam against her skin.

Can't believe I'm letting him, she thought. If Rob had ever tried to put his face there, much less his hand . . .

This isn't Rob. This is Andy and he's just a kid and his family's been wiped out and we're probably gonna die . . .

How do we not die?

There has to be a way.

Standing here with Andy's face buried in her wasn't accomplishing a thing.

Yes, she realized. It calms him down. Calms me down, too.

Her heart was no longer slamming. She could breathe almost normally.

'We'll be okay,' she whispered.

He didn't speak. His face moved from side to side. Maybe he was telling her no. Maybe he was just doing it to feel her.

'I sure wish you had a phone in your room,' she whispered.

'Mom and Dad have one.' His voice was muffled, his breath very hot.

'I know. But it's in their bedroom. I'm pretty sure that's where the fat guy is.'

If he isn't about to crash through the door.

'Maybe we'd better jump out a window,' she said.

18

'They don't open.'

'I know. We'd have to break one.'

His head shook again. This time, Jody was sure he meant no. 'It's awful far down. And it's cement. We'd bust our brains out.'

That might be better than meeting up with the fat guy, she thought. Anything might be better than that.

'I wonder what he's doing,' she said.

'The other one?'

'Funny he hasn't come to check on this one.'

'Maybe he's busy . . . stealing stuff.'

'If he is,' Jody said, 'maybe we can sneak right by him. All we've gotta do is get downstairs and outside, then we'll be okay.'

'That'd be better than trying to jump.'

'Let's do it.'

'Okay.' He nodded, his head rubbing up and down against her. And then he kissed her through the nightshirt.

The kiss made her squirm. 'Hey!' she gasped, and back-stepped away from him. 'Jeez!' Then she saw the look on his face. 'Never mind. It's all right. Let's go.'

'I've gotta get dressed.'

'Do it quick.' She turned away. She glanced at the corpse just to avoid stepping on it or in the thick mat of vomit. The sight of the body made an icy snake come alive in her guts. She stepped past it and carried her weapons to the bedroom door.

She leaned her back against the door.

Andy, standing beside his bed, bent over to pull up his jeans. He hadn't bothered with undershorts. His rump looked very white and smooth.

He didn't know she was watching. When he started to turn around, she elbowed the light switch.

'Let's go,' she whispered.

'I'm not done . . .'

'All you need are your pants. Let's go. Be careful you don't trip.'

'Do you think he's dead?'

'If the bat didn't kill him, I'm sure your puke did.'

A strange, hushed laugh came through the darkness. 'You're weird, Jody.' He said nothing for a few seconds. Jody could hear him sneaking closer. 'Maybe we can kill the other one.'

'We might have to try. Do you want the machete or the bat?'

'You keep the bat. You're good with it.'

'Fine.' She lifted the machete up from her side, moving it slowly until it was straight out in front of her, its blade upright. 'I'm holding it out,' she said. 'Don't cut yourself.'

Something in the darkness bumped her outstretched arm just below the elbow.

I hope that's Andy.

'That you?' he whispered.

'Yeah.'

Both his hands found her arm. One held on while the other fingered its way to her hand. Jody let the machete go. When he released her arm, she reached out. Her hand met bare skin. She stroked him. His side, she guessed. Just a little down from his armpit.

'Are you ready?' she whispered.

'Not really.'

'Yeah. Me neither.'

'What'll we do?'

'Whatever we have to,' she said. 'We'll sneak out if we can. But if he sees us, we'd better run like hell.'

'What if we can sneak up on him?'

'I don't know. Depends, I guess. If it really looks like we

20

have a good chance of taking him by surprise, I guess we should try it. The thing is to get out of here alive. That's the only thing that matters, okay?'

'Okay.'

'Ready?'

'Will you hug me?'

'Geez, Andy.'

'Please? Everybody's dead.'

'Okay. But watch the machete.' With her hand on Andy's side to guide her, she stepped forward and pressed herself lightly against him. He put an arm around her back. It hardly touched her, though.

'I've always wanted . . .' He went silent.

'What?' Jody asked.

'Something like this. To hold you like this. I mean, it really . . . it's really nice.'

She kissed his forehead.

'I sure love you, Jody.'

'Hey.'

'I do. I love you so much.'

'Hey.' She bent her knee enough to slide her down to where Andy's mouth was. Then she hugged him hard with her free arm, squeezing herself against him, kissing him.

With his free arm, he hugged her fiercely.

When she finished kissing him, he said, 'I won't let anybody hurt you, Jody. Not ever.'

She patted his side. 'Just you 'n' me, kid.'

'I'm ready when you are.'

'Okay. Follow me.'

'No. I'll go first. I'm the guy.'

'You're the guy, fine. But I'm in charge. You follow me.'

'But . . .'

'Shhh.' Taking his arm, she pulled him away from the

21

door. She squatted at its edge herself, and rested the bat against her right shoulder. 'Get behind me.'

She felt one of his knees nudge her rump.

'Here goes,' she whispered.

Reaching up with her left hand, she found the doorknob. She turned the knob and swung the door inward.

Chapter Three

Nobody stood waiting on the other side of the door.

Jody lowered her knees to the carpet and shuffled to the middle of the doorway. There, she leaned forward and glanced both ways.

The corridor looked deserted.

Light still glowed from the master bedroom near its far end, and the music had resumed. Now, the song was Billy Joel doing 'Goodnight Saigon'.

Dad's favorite song, Jody thought. And again, she wished he were here.

He'd been a platoon leader in Vietnam. Now, he was a sergeant with the LAPD. Out on the streets somewhere, right now, protecting the civilians.

Here's a civilian who could really use you, Dad.

Jody got to her feet and stepped into the corridor. She walked slowly toward the lighted doorway, Andy following with his hand flat against her back.

No way to avoid the open door. Not if she wanted to use the stairs. They were on the other side.

22

She could only think of two alternatives: jump from a two-story window, or hide. Getting hurt was a sure thing if they jumped. They might not break their heads open as Andy had suggested, but the impact was likely to disable one or both of them and keep them from running away. Hiding wasn't the answer, either. The very idea of hiding gave Jody the creeps. As a kid, she had played hide 'n' seek enough to know that you usually get found. Besides, the guy might be in the house for hours. He might set it afire before leaving.

Hiding seemed like crawling into a dark trap to wait for the slaughter.

We won't be safe till we're outside.

Which meant they had to use the stairs. Which meant they had to pass the lighted bedroom doorway.

'Goodnight Saigon' grew louder with every step Jody took.

She didn't like the part about all going down together. Not at all. It meant getting killed together, didn't it?

We're not gonna get killed. We're gonna make it.

If we can just make it past the door . . .

She wanted to warn Andy against looking into the room. She didn't dare make a sound, though. And she knew that he would have to look, no matter what.

As she neared the doorway, she gripped the bat with both hands and switched it to her left shoulder as if she were stepping up to home plate.

She had always batted lefty.

Hitting baseballs was the only thing she did left-handed. She didn't know why. Dad *claimed* not to know why. Sometimes, she suspected that he'd pulled a fast one when he'd shown her how to swing.

Bet he never thought I'd have to bust a guy's head.

I might have to do it again.

Oh, Jesus.

Only a few steps from the doorway, Jody felt her terror surge. She ached to scream. She ached to break into a sprint and race past the door.

Slow and easy, she told herself. Easy does it. If we can get past the door without being spotted, we're home free.

She wondered if they should crawl by, or squirm past the opening on their bellies. They might be less noticeable that way. But they'd be exposed for a longer period of time. Besides, it would be a tricky maneuver with their weapons. And if they did get seen, they'd be down on the floor, unable to defend themselves or make a quick run for it.

We'll stay on our feet, she decided.

Scoot right by, silent and fast.

She didn't know which side of the corridor might be best. It seemed that crossing close to the doorway would give them the briefest exposure. She couldn't do that, though, just couldn't. What if the guy was right inside? He'd be able to grab them as they went by.

Or skewer them.

Anyhow, the top of the stairway was on the left side, away from the door.

She angled to the left, Andy's hand still pressing against her back.

The wood of the baseball bat felt slippery in her sweaty hands.

She stepped into the spill of light.

Don't even look, she told herself. You'll hear it if he spots you.

She kept her eyes straight ahead.

And spotted the dim shape of the newel post at the top of the stairway. Eight or ten feet away, no more.

We're gonna make it!

That's what she thought until Andy's fingertips dug into her back and he let out a moan that made her skin prickle.

She snapped her head to the side.

She looked through the doorway.

Standing near the bed was the fat man who'd killed Evelyn. But he wasn't alone. There were others. Five, six? More?

They were silent in there. Not laughing or growling or discussing matters or kidding around. They were silent and busy. The only sounds were Billy Joel on the radio singing about the Vietcong, bedsprings squeaking, rough breathing and wet noises.

Jody couldn't recognize Evelyn or Mr Clark or Mrs Clark.

She supposed they must be in there, though, in the middle of things.

All she saw were men, bare skin, weapons and blood.

She looked in at it all for only a second, not even long enough to see what they were doing, but more than long enough to know that she didn't *want* to see.

At the same instant she began to turn her eyes away, one of the men swiveled around.

He'd probably heard Andy's moan.

He was hairless. He wore blood. He held a hatchet in one hand, a severed head in the other. He held the head upside down by the red mess in the stump of its neck. Its hair hung swaying. Jody couldn't tell whether the head belonged to Mrs Clark or to Evelyn.

'Run!' Andy yelled.

Jody ran. The first stride rushed her past the far edge of light.

Behind her, Andy yelled.

She glanced over her shoulder in time to see him throw the machete. The moment it left his hand, he lunged sideways and raced after her.

Jody made it to the stairs and charged down them, sliding her right hand down the banister rail, holding the Louisville

Slugger with her left, the bat bumping her shoulder as she bounded toward the bottom.

'They're after us,' Andy gasped.

Jody swerved to the left. Her shoulder skidded against the wall. 'Go by! Get in front! Get the door!'

She slowed her descent. Andy was at her side for a second or two. Then he was ahead of her. She crossed over to the railing just in time to bump her hand on the newel post at the bottom.

Staggering, she whirled around.

Somebody was halfway down the stairs. A quick black shadow.

More than one? She couldn't tell.

'Get the door!' she yelled.

'I'm trying.' She heard a rattle of chain. 'Almost . . .'

'Leave us *alone*!' Jody shrieked as the shape leaped at her from the stairway. It flew, airborne, arms stretching out for her. She thought she glimpsed a hatchet in its right hand. She swung.

Her bat smacked flesh.

The attacker grunted.

The blow knocked him crooked. Instead of coming down on Jody and slamming her to the floor, he hit the floor alone.

The front door swung open, letting in enough light from the porch to show the man sprawled on the floor. One quick step, and Jody was standing over him. She raised her bat high.

And heard footfalls thundering on the stairs.

'Jody!'

She gave up every thought of finishing him off.

She lunged for the doorway. Andy waited. Her foot no sooner touched the welcome mat than the door crashed shut.

Side by side, they dashed across the porch. They didn't

bother with the steps; they simply leaped and hit the walkway running. Jody shifted the bat to her right hand and grabbed its middle and pumped her arm just as if she weren't clutching it. Almost.

'Where to?' she gasped.

'I don't know!'

For now, it seemed almost good enough to run for the street.

The street in front of the house looked crowded. With parked cars. Five or six of them, all different from each other. And a dark van.

They just drove up and parked right in front of the house! Like a caravan, or something! Jesus!

What if they left someone behind to keep watch?

Jody quit worrying about that when she heard the house door swing open. She glanced over her shoulder. Men rushed out. She moaned and faced forward and tried to run faster.

'Head for a house!' she gasped at Andy.

Andy, at the sidewalk, cut hard to the left. Jody followed.

He's little, she thought, *but he's sure fast.*

At least we're outside.

If only a car would come along!

The bat weighted her down. It interfered with her arms. Without it, she could duck into the wind and pump for all she was worth and pick up some major speed. But she didn't dare get rid of it.

She remembered her first home run. She'd been so excited seeing the ball sail white and clean over the distant fence that she'd forgotten to drop the bat. She'd rounded the bases just like this, clutching it like a nutcase.

It had darn near killed Dad laughing.

But he'd been awfully proud, too.

Jesus, am I ever going to see him again?

She looked over her shoulder. The men were cutting across the grass.

This time, she really looked.

She wanted to see them well and know what she was up against.

Three of them.

The fat guy with the spear wasn't among them. Must've stayed behind in the house. Others must've stayed, too.

Three had come out to tie up the loose ends.

To kill us.

The guy in the lead was fast. He had nothing in his hands, but there was a belt or something around his waist, so he probably had a sheath knife. The guy behind him carried a sword – a *saber* that he waved overhead, flashing moonlight. The third was having trouble keeping up. Maybe because the ax he carried was too heavy and awkward. Maybe because he was huge.

Jody couldn't tell what they were wearing. Skin, she supposed. Their own and other people's, like the man she'd killed. Skin, and lots of blood. Blood from Evelyn and Mr and Mrs Clark. Blood that looked black in the night.

What are these guys?

They seemed too awful to be real.

She wished they would at least yell. People *always* yell when they chase someone, don't they?

What's the matter with them, afraid they'll wake up the neighbors?

At the end of the line of parked cars, Andy leaped from the curb and ran into the street.

Jody leaped. She glanced at the rear of the last car.

Always get the license plate, Dad had told her many times. If anything ever happens involving a motor vehicle, make sure you get the license plate. 'But that'd be stealing,' she had supposedly responded one time when she was about four years old. 'You don't *take* it, you get the number. Remember it, write it down.'

She wanted to get the number now.

The license plate was easy to see in the pale glow of the streetlight. It looked black and shiny. Paint? Tape?

She didn't pause to investigate, but veered away from the rear of the car and stayed on Andy's tail. He was dashing at an angle toward the other side of the street, seemed to be heading for a massive, two-story brick house.

Its shrubbery was bright with spotlights. The walkway to its front door was bordered by footlights. The porch light was on. The area of pavement in front of the three-car garage looked like a tennis court illuminated for night games.

Lights everywhere except in the windows of the house.

All of them looked dark.

Who's gonna be up at this hour?

She wondered why Andy had picked this house. The one next door to his own place had to be closer. Maybe he knows these people, or . . .

She took a quick look back.

And glimpsed a For Sale sign on the lawn of the house beside the Clark home.

So maybe this *was* the nearest house with people in it.

It'll do a lot of good, she thought, if they're asleep.

Twisting further around, she saw the leader of the bunch leap off the curb. The other two seemed to have fallen behind him a little, but not much.

Are they gaining on us? she wondered.

Doesn't matter. They're too close.

'Help!' she shouted as she ran. 'Help! Police!'

Andy took up the cry.

Jody started shouting, 'Fire!'

Andy called out 'Dr Youngman!' as he left the street in his wake and sprinted up the lawn. 'Dr Youngman! Help! Please! Dr Youngman!'

Jody joined in.

The grass was cool and very wet. Dr Youngman must've watered his lawn tonight.

'Dr Youngman!' Andy yelled. 'It's Andy! Andy Clark! Help! Open up! Help!'

Jody scanned the house front, watching for a window to fill with light.

All the windows stayed dark.

A hot night. If the windows were shut and the air conditioner running, nobody inside the house was likely to hear their shouts.

But maybe Dr Youngman *had* heard them. Maybe he just wasn't turning on any lights. Maybe right now he was heading for his front door. Maybe he would swing it open wide just in the nick of time and say, 'Hurry inside, kids. Quick!'

Oh God, if only.

'Forget it!' Jody gasped. 'They'll kill us on the porch!'

Andy didn't hesitate. Maybe he'd already reached the same conclusion. 'Porch' was coming out of Jody's mouth when Andy broke to the left.

Jody made her turn away from the porch as fast as she could, and yelped as her feet skated out from under her.

She seemed to take a long time going down.

An endless sideways glide, her body sinking closer and closer to the ground, finally touching down with her left hip, then a smooth slide over the soft wet grass.

Sliding in.

Stealing second.

Jesus! They're gonna get me now!

Chapter Four

The slide through the grass shoved Jody's nightshirt halfway up her back.

She sat up fast.

The guy came in grinning. He dropped and skidded on his knees. He didn't smell like the others, didn't stink of rot.

'*Gotcha* now, babe,' he whispered. Grabbing the short hair on the back of her head, he jerked her backward. His face came down at her. 'You're a real beaut.'

She pounded the top of his head with the Louisville Slugger.

An upward swing from the ground, one-armed and without much power behind it.

She didn't wait to see its effect, but rolled hard to the left. She felt a tug at her hair. Then she was free, scuttling over the grass on knuckles and knees, hanging on to the bat.

The guy with the saber was running straight at her.

He was only a few strides away when Jody burst to her feet and took off. He twisted and slashed. The saber made a quick *whewww* as it whipped past her back.

Then he gasped.

Jody glanced around in time to see him slip and tangle his legs and land on his rump. The guy who'd caught her on the ground was on one knee, ready to stand. One hand was clamped to the top of his hairless head; the other pulling a knife from the sheath at his hip.

The man with the ax had done a lot of catching up.

Can't forget about him, Jody warned herself.

He was tall and broad and muscular. And he had that ax.

He looked unstoppable.

He'll just keep coming, no matter what.

But he sure wasn't fast. He was still in the middle of the lawn, jogging toward her, when Jody dashed onto the warm, dry pavement of the driveway.

Andy waited for her, bouncing, shaking his arms and legs like a relay runner anxious for the pass of the baton. The instant Jody reached his side, he pivoted and ran.

Side by side, they sprinted across the driveway.

They ran for the hedge. It stretched the length of the driveway, a wall of green squared off at the top. Higher than Jody's head.

'Under,' Andy gasped.

A cinch we can't go through – or over.

Jody saw what he meant. Though the bushes appeared to be a solid mass, there were open spaces near the ground, gaps between the trunks.

She took a glimpse back. The guy who'd caught her after the slide had again taken the lead. He was almost to the edge of the driveway.

She and Andy dropped to their knees.

She thrust her bat through the gap, flung herself flat and squirmed into the bushes. Squirmed in fast and frantic. Ready to feel a hand grab her ankle and drag her out.

Or maybe the guy with the ax would chop . . .

It's taking for ever!

The bushes and the ground itself seemed to be alive, clutching at her, clawing her, pushing her back.

And then she scampered free.

Andy was beside her, pushing himself up. He was whimpering and gasping.

'It'll be all right,' Jody whispered. On elbows and knees, she turned herself around and peeked under the bushes.

She searched for feet and legs.

She saw only the driveway and the lawn beyond it. Pulling back, she snatched up the bat and got to her feet. 'Let's go.'

'Where are they?'

'I don't know.'

She guessed that the men must be on their way to the far end of the hedge. It would take them a while to get there. Ten or fifteen seconds, maybe.

If only we could disappear!

Crawl back through to the other side? Right. It wouldn't take a genius to leave the ax-man behind, just in case.

Andy suddenly clutched her short sleeve and tugged at it. 'I know! You go back and try and get Dr Youngman to open up. I'll lead those guys on a wild-goose chase.'

'That's nuts!' Jody blurted.

'It'll work! I'll circle around and meet you.'

'No. We'll . . .'

'Go back through.' He tugged her sleeve, stretching the neck of her nightshirt down off her shoulder.

'Hey.'

He kept pulling. 'Get down. Go back through.'

No time to argue. She sank to her knees.

'See ya.' Andy whirled and sprinted off across the lawn.

The stupid jerk! she thought. He's acting like it's a *cowboy* movie!

She started to get up, intending to go after him.

He was already halfway to the next driveway.

She was on one knee, ready to stand, when the first of the pursuers raced past the end of the hedge. He slowed. He turned his body. Jody froze, knowing he was about to face her. But he spotted Andy first and lurched into a run.

Jody dropped flat on the grass just as the man with the

saber appeared on the sidewalk and joined the chase. A moment later, he was followed by the ax man.

They all cut across the grass, going after Andy.

Just the way he'd figured.

They think I'm with him. Probably think I'm up ahead somewhere.

'Go, Andy, go,' she whispered.

Then she turned herself around and squirmed back through the gap at the bottom of the hedge. At the other side, she sprang to her feet. She switched the bat to her left hand as she sprinted across the driveway. She wondered if anyone could hear the slap of her bare feet. They sounded even louder on the painted concrete of the walkway curving from the edge of the driveway to the porch. She leaped the porch stairs. She flung herself against the front door and crashed her fist against it.

She pounded on the door with all her might, eight times, nine, ten. Then thought, *My God, what if they hear me knocking?*

So she quit and slid herself across the cool wood and jabbed the doorbell button again and again and again. Each time she poked it, she heard a faint chime from inside the house.

'Come on, come on, come on,' she whispered.

Continuing to jab the button, she twisted her head away from the door and peered over her shoulder. She saw no one. Just the broad lawn, the driveway and hedge, the empty street. Empty except for the vehicles in front of the Clark house. Five cars, one van.

'My goodness, hold your horses!'

Jody flinched. She dropped her hand from the doorbell. 'Help! Please! There're men after me.'

'I'm coming, now.'

Jody pushed herself away from the door. She turned all the

way around. *Still okay.* Facing the door again, she bent down and braced her elbows on her knees. An awkward stance, particularly with the bat in her hand, but it helped her breathing.

With a quiet squeak, a hatch in the door swung inward. It was just the size of the thin, wrinkled face behind it. A nose jutted out between two upright wooden bars. But the bars got in the way of the woman's eyes, so she tilted her head sideways. She wore glasses with bright red frames and lenses the size of hockey pucks.

'Now you tell me what's going on, young lady. What's this about being chased?' Her gaze roamed past Jody as if searching for pursuers.

'You've gotta let me in,' Jody gasped.

'I've got to do nothing of the sort. Are you one of those loudies that was doing all the yelling a while back that woke me up?'

She *had* heard them. 'Yes! It was me and Andy Clark.'

'Andy Clark? That's a fine lad. What's he doing out and about this time of night?'

'He's *with* me!'

'I don't see him. You *are* a sight, girl. Whatever *have* you been up to?'

Jody stood up straight. She took a few quick breaths. 'They murdered everyone. All the Clarks but Andy. I'm a friend of Evelyn's. She's been killed. They've all been killed. You've got to let me in. We've got to call the police before they get *us*, too! Please!'

The old lady blinked behind her enormous glasses. She shook her head. 'This is all terribly confusing.'

'It's simple!' Jody blurted. 'It's simple as *hell*! There are maniacs out here with swords and axes and knives and running around like a bunch of fucking refugees from *Lord of the Flies* and they want to kill me and Andy! What could be simpler than that? Damn it, open the door!'

'Young lady!'

'Don't you *get it*?' She whirled around. Still, nobody was coming. She turned to the old woman again. 'Please. We're going to get killed.'

'I can't just let any old stranger into the house,' she said, continuing to shake her head. 'I have responsibilities. It isn't my house, you understand.'

'I don't care *whose* . . . Where's Dr Youngman? Who are you?'

'I'm Mrs Youngman.'

'Is your husband home?'

'My husband passed on, I'm afraid.'

'I'm sorry.'

'He's been gone these nine years.'

'Please open the door. Please!'

'This is my son's house. Dr Ernest Youngman.'

'Is *he* home?'

'I wish he were. I'm sure he would know precisely what to do in this sort of predicament. But he simply isn't here. He's off to Big Bear for the weekend with the whole kit 'n' kaboodle. Everyone but me, that is.' Her face lit up. A bony old hand with liver spots appeared in front of her face, and snapped its fingers. 'I'll call up Ernest right this very minute and . . .'

Jody swung the Slugger hard with both hands.

Its fat end struck the door just below Mrs Youngman's face.

The blow sounded like a shotgun blast.

The old lady jumped.

'Open the door or I'll break it down!' Jody shouted.

The face vanished.

Oh, God, now I've done it.

Lowering the bat, Jody rushed forward and pressed her face to the bars. She couldn't see Mrs Youngman.

'I'm sorry,' she said. 'Please. I'm so scared. If they get me, they're gonna chop me up and . . . Please!'

'You made me pee myself!'

'I'm sorry. I'm so sorry. Really.'

'You're a vicious child!'

'I'm not. Really. I'm sorry.'

'A juvenile delinquent, that's what you are!'

'Jody!' Andy's voice. Calling from somewhere not far away.

His voice thrilled her with joy; he'd made it. The creeps hadn't caught up with him. But his voice also shot terror through her; he was on his way, and they were sure to be close behind him.

Jody whirled around and spotted Andy as he dashed past the end of the hedge by the driveway. She waved her arm.

'Where are they?' she called.

'Coming,' he yelled. Changing direction, he raced straight toward her. Apparently, he could see that the door's spy hatch was open. 'You got him!'

'Afraid not. He's at Big Bear. Nobody's here but his mother, and she won't let us in.'

'Mable!' Andy shouted as he ran closer. 'It's Andy! Mable, you've gotta let us in!'

Hearing metallic rattles and clacks, Jody turned to the door. It swung wide open.

She lunged over the threshold. Mrs Youngman, behind the door, scowled at her. The old woman's eyes were red and full of tears.

'I'm sorry,' Jody said.

'The damage has been done, you mean thing.'

Andy charged into the foyer. As he flopped onto the marble floor, huffing, Jody took the door from Mrs Youngman.

She gazed past its edge as she swept it along.

Out on the sidewalk, the man with the knife ran into view from beyond the hedge.

Jody finished shutting the door very fast.

But not fast enough, she was sure of that. He'd been looking at her.

She groaned as she twisted the deadbolt lock.

'What?' Andy gasped.

'I think he saw me.'

Chapter Five

'They'll be coming in,' Jody said.

Andy, still gasping on the floor, shook his head. Sweat dripped off his hair as if he'd just stepped out of a shower. His jeans hung low, showing where his tan ended. The skin of his back was ruddy and wet, criss-crossed with welts and scratches. 'Maybe not,' he gasped.

'We're witnesses. They've gotta kill us.'

'Nobody's going to kill anyone,' Mrs Youngman said. Sniffing, she wiped her eyes with the back of her hand. 'The both of you come with me. We'll call the police this instant.'

Andy pushed himself off the floor. He backhanded sweat out of his eyes. His chest and belly looked worse than his back.

'What happened to you?' Jody asked.

'Went through some bushes. Fell. Couple times.' He grinned. 'Really gave 'em a run.'

'Let's not dally,' Mrs Youngman said. She led the way. She

wore a pale blue nightgown. Jody, hurrying after her, saw that the back of it had a wet place down below her rump.

'I'm really sorry I scared you that way.'

'Hush about it.'

'I'm not a jerk. I don't do stuff like that. I just . . . I kind of went nuts for a second. You know? Those guys, they're like . . . Do you have a gun?'

'I most certainly do not.'

'Does your son? Does he keep one around for . . .'

'Guns are for killing, young lady. My Ernest is a healer.' She stepped through an archway into a dark room and reached toward the wall. A moment later, a chandelier bloomed light.

Following Mrs Youngman alongside a big oak dining table, Jody looked for a telephone.

She didn't see one.

Who ever heard of a phone in the dining room, anyhow?

'Where is it?' she asked.

The old woman turned around. 'Don't you listen? You should *listen* when you're spoken to.' On the second 'listen', she pecked Jody in the chest with her forefinger.

'Hey,' Jody said.

'Don't you "hey" me.' Two more pecks. Her fingernail was long. Jody could feel its curved end jabbing through the thin fabric of her nightshirt. She knew it must be making little crescent dents in the skin between her breasts.

This is crazy, she thought.

'I'm sorry,' she said.

'You young people think you're so smart, you never listen to anyone.' She pecked Jody again. 'What did I tell you?'

'About what?'

Another peck.

'Mable,' Andy said. 'Quit doing that to her.'

39

Mrs Youngman ignored him and jabbed Jody four more times as she explained, 'I *told* you. I think I made myself *quite clear* on the matter. My Ernest doesn't *keep* guns in his house.'

'I know!'

'If you know, why did you persist in asking me where . . .?'

'The telephone. The *telephone*! I wanted to know where the telephone is!'

'*I* know where the telephone is. That's where we were going before you began pestering me.'

'I'm sorry,' Jody said. 'I won't pester you again. But we'd better hurry.'

Mrs Youngman turned around and resumed walking. 'There's no call to hurry,' she said. 'The house is all locked up safe and sound. We'll be perfectly fine until the police arrive.'

'The police,' Jody said, 'don't actually show up the instant you call.'

Mrs Youngman scowled over her shoulder.

If she stops again, I'm gonna knock her down and find the phone myself.

She kept walking.

'Are you being smart with me, young lady?'

'No.'

'Her dad's a cop,' Andy explained.

'That explains a great deal,' Mrs Youngman said, and stepped through a doorway at the end of the dining room.

The light came on, and Jody followed her into the kitchen. She walked close behind her. She had an urge to smack the back of her head, just a quick swat with her open hand.

'There's nothing wrong with my dad,' she said.

'I'm sure.'

Jody saw Mrs Youngman's reflection off to the right in the glass of the sliding door beyond the breakfast table. First a side view, then a front view. The image of the old woman was very distinct, but had a depth that showed darkness through her.

A phone was mounted on the wall just to the left of the door.

Mrs Youngman stopped and reached for it.

Jody wondered if the sliding door was locked.

Then she saw herself in the glass. She stood just beyond the kitchen table, the bat hanging from one hand while her other hand squeezed the back of a chair. It was like looking at a stranger, a haggard and terrified urchin who resembled Jody only by coincidence and who happened to be wearing a red jersey nightshirt just like Jody's, with Winnie the Pooh hugging a honey pot on its front. She knew this wasn't a stranger, though. She could feel the nightshirt hanging against her skin, feel where it was so wet that it clung to her. She could also feel the curved wood of the chairback against her thighs, the slippery handle of the bat, the floor under her bare feet, and places all over her body that felt as hot as burns where she'd been scraped, scratched and poked.

In the reflection, Andy was just behind her and off to the side a little. Still trying to catch his breath.

Mrs Youngman plucked down the handset and frowned at it.

Jodie saw that it had an antenna and no cord.

'Do you know how to work it?' Andy asked.

'Certainly.'

'It's a remote phone,' he said.

'I know, I know.' Mrs Youngman sounded peeved.

'You've gotta flip that little switch up near the top. Push it all the way over to where it says talk.'

'Which switch?'

'Here, I'll do it.' In the glass, Jody watched Andy step past her. He looked skinny and fragile, hardly more than a little boy. 'I've worked these things a lot,' he said. 'They've got one just like it that they take out by the pool.'

As he turned and took a stride toward Mrs Youngman, he changed. The boy in the glass transformed, grew in size and bulk and breadth. His face turned heavy and mad. He lost his jeans. His hands, empty an instant ago, now clutched an ax.

Jody's confusion didn't last long.

She shrieked, 'No!' and grabbed Andy's shoulder and jerked him backward as the sliding door exploded. She glimpsed the ax swinging sideways through a swarm of tumbling fragments – on a course toward Mrs Youngman's belly.

She turned away, ducking and flinging up an arm to shield her face.

Through the clamor of shards falling onto table top and floor, she heard the *fump* of the ax chopping into its target.

Glass nipped Jody's rump and the backs of her legs. She staggered forward to get away, then twisted around and looked and saw that the ax had actually struck Mrs Youngman higher than the belly.

It had burried its head between her breasts, deep into her chest. The blow had apparently slammed her back against the wall. She had a shocked look on her face. The phone was just beginning to fall from her hand.

The man who clutched the handle of the ax didn't so much as glance at Jody or Andy as he stepped through the destroyed door.

Jody swung Andy by the arm, propelling him toward the dining room. As she raced after him, she swatted the kitchen switch and killed the light.

Behind her, someone muttered, 'Fuck.'

On her way through the dining room, she snagged two chairs away from the table and flung them backward as she ran by. The switch for the chandelier wasn't within reach, would require a slight detour, so she made an instant decision not to bother with it.

The foyer was lighted, anyway.

She thought Andy might go for the front door, but he didn't. Good. One of the other guys might be right on the other side.

She followed Andy across the foyer to the stairs. He started racing up them. So did she.

Going upstairs didn't seem like a great idea. But neither did going outside.

It was obvious, though, that Andy had spent some time at this house. He and Mable knew each other. He knew how to work the phone and had mentioned something about a pool. Probably came over to swim with a Youngman kid, or something.

He'd been here before, so maybe he knew of something upstairs that would help. Maybe Ernest the healer had a firearm, after all.

Her own dad kept plenty of secrets from Grandma Fargo, things that Jody knew about and sometimes revealed to friends.

So maybe Andy knew where to find a gun.

Oh God, please!

Hearing quick footfalls from below, she glanced over her shoulder just in time to see the ax man hurry out of the dining room. He jogged through the archway, looked toward her from the foyer but didn't react or slow down.

Andy had already reached the top of the stairs.

Jody, taking three at a stride, sprang to the top a moment after him. There, she turned around and saw the ax man jerking open the front door.

He's leaving?

He didn't spot us after all?

He thinks we ran outside?

Right at the start of all this, the guy who killed Evelyn hadn't noticed Jody standing just behind her in the dark room. Maybe this guy had no better eyesight than . . .

He didn't run out into the night, but whirled away from the open door and rushed for the stairs as his friends with the knife and saber charged into the house.

Andy grabbed Jody's sleeve. He pulled it hard, stretching the neck of her nightshirt down off her shoulder. The pull sent her stumbling toward him, and a wall blocked her view of the three intruders.

'Come on!' he gasped in a whisper.

'They got a gun?'

She heard a thunder of footfalls on the stairs.

'Phones. Almost every room has a . . .'

'It's too damn late for 911.'

'We can . . .'

'Let go my sleeve.'

He let go. The ruined neck still drooped off her shoulder.

'Get ready to run.'

'What . . .?'

She leaped sideways. The ax man was in the lead, rushing up the stairs like a crazed lumberjack. When Jody loomed above him, he hefted the ax.

Jody hurled her Louisville Slugger like a short, stubby spear. She'd aimed for his forehead.

That's where the bat struck him, its fat end clouting him above his eyebrows, bashing his head back.

The moment she saw the bat hit him, she sprang sideways past the wall and gasped, 'Go!' and hoped Andy would lead them to someplace with a lock.

From the sounds of thuds and slams and outcries she heard as she lunged after Andy, she guessed that the ax man must've gone backward down the stairs and knocked into one or both of his buddies.

He's gotta be out of the picture, she told herself.

But that leaves the other two.

Two against two. Now the sides are even.

Right. Even, my butt.

They'll kill us.

'Where're we going?' she blurted as she dashed down the corridor on Andy's heels.

'Jim's room.'

'He got a lock?'

'A phone.'

'Does his *door* lock?'

'Don't know.'

She heard the men behind her.

'Johns got locks,' she gasped.

'No phone.'

A glimpse back showed her two dim figures rushing side by side.

'The parents' room,' she said. 'Where?'

Andy's vague, pale arm swung up and pointed to a gray rectangle just ahead – a doorway perhaps a shade less dark than the corridor.

'Go there!'

He cut across the corridor. So did Jody. 'The door, the door, the door!' she yelled.

She followed him through the doorway. They both skidded and staggered, stopping fast, reversing direction. Andy grabbed the door by its edge and slammed it. They threw themselves against it.

Shoulder to the wood, Jody reached out and swept her open hand down the wall. She found a light switch. She flicked it up and the room filled with light that made her squint.

The muffled thud of footfalls rushed closer.

Jody looked down at the doorknob. No lock.

No mechanism at all for securing the door.

Great.

She flipped herself around. Back to the door, she scooted her feet over the carpet and bent her knees and braced herself for impact.

Andy did the same.

She felt his arm against her arm.

The bedroom was very large. It did look like the master bedroom, but it also looked as if the old Mrs Youngman had been sleeping in it.

With permission? Jody wondered.

Shades of Goldilocks.

She's dead. Dead. Jesus.

The covers were folded at its foot, the top sheet twisted over to one side, the bottom sheet rumpled. The old woman must've been too hot.

The doorknob turned very fast and the door shoved at Jody's back. The pressure only lasted a second.

Guy must've just pushed with his hand.

Beyond the bed, open draperies showed a sliding glass door. Only half the expanse reflected the room, and Jody realized the door had been left open.

Mrs Youngman must've wanted fresh air.

Maybe didn't like air-conditioning. Or didn't know how to work it.

Jody saw a lawn chair and a railing beyond the open part of the door.

A balcony.

Between her and the balcony stood the bed. It had an elaborate wooden headboard and nightstands on both sides.

A white telephone sat on the nearer nightstand, probably fifteen feet from Jody.

The door slugged her back.

She and Andy both grunted. Their knees bent. Their feet skidded on the carpet. The men must've thrown their shoulders against the door, met more resistance than expected and failed to follow through, because after the burst that nearly threw Jody and Andy off their feet, the door banged shut.

Jody ached to make a run for the telephone.

By himself, though, Andy wouldn't stand a chance of holding the door shut.

'Yes!' she suddenly said. 'Yes, it's an emergency. We've got killers in the house. Dr Youngman's. On Laurel Lane. Hurry! They're trying to get us!'

Andy met her eyes. Though he looked ready to scream, he said, 'How long did they say it'll be?'

'A couple of minutes. They said there's a unit real close to here.'

From behind the door came a hissing of quick whispers.

Jody ran for the nightstand. She snatched up the handset of the phone and heard a dial tone.

She tapped the numbers 911.

Andy stared at her.

She waved him to step toward her.

With a nod, he moved silently away from the door.

The phone rang once in her ear.

She pulled open the top drawer of the nightstand, hoping for a handgun.

Another ring.

No gun. A flashlight and address book and . . .

The men came in.

Chapter Six

Without either Jody or Andy trying to brace it, the bedroom door sprang wide when the two men struck it.

'Andy!'

Andy didn't need the warning. Even as they stumbled into the room, he took to his feet. He raced past the end of the bed while Jody dropped the phone, dived onto the mattress and scurried across. She was still on her hands and knees when Andy got to the open glass door. Speeding through, he grabbed its inside handle. The door shook, but yanked him to a halt. Jody flung herself off the bed. She staggered past Andy. He hurled the sliding door shut. As it rumbled behind her, Jody thrust her hands against the balcony's toprail to stop herself. Her arms bent. Her belly shoved at the railing with enough force to bow her.

Below was a concrete slab, pale gray in the moonlight.

Beyond the edge of the concrete was a massive rectangle of black with ripples that glinted silver.

The pool.

But straight down was the concrete. Six feet of it between her and the pool? Or maybe ten feet. Or maybe twelve.

'You go first,' Andy gasped. 'I'll hold the door.'

Go first? Jump? Of course, jump. There's no other choice.

She looked back. The saber man was reaching for the door handle. The other guy was jogging across the bed – must've paused to do something – like check the phone.

'Forget the door!' Jody yelled. 'Jump!'

She heard it starting to rush open as she hopped and caught

the toprail under her right foot and thrust herself up. Her leg was still bent when she found the rail with her other foot.

She glimpsed Andy off to the side, using both hands to vault over.

Maybe he's got the right idea, she thought as she sprang up and forward, away from the balcony.

Oh Jesus! I'm so high! Jesus!

She heard a sword cut the air behind her. It didn't seem to cut her, though.

The hot slipstream raised her hair and nightshirt. She tried to see straight down, but the shirt blocked her view.

She was sure she must be dropping straight for the concrete.

Would've taken a magnificent leap to clear it and reach the pool.

Maybe it won't be so bad, she told herself.

Bend your knees and . . .

Andy cried out. A quick, harsh cry of pain.

Jody's feet smacked down. The impact stung. Her knees folded. As she tumbled forward, she flung her arms up, hoping to protect her face from the concrete. But didn't get them high enough in time. They were only halfway up when she slammed and splashed.

Water surged into her mouth, rushed up her nostrils.

Made it!

She blew out air to clear them, emptying her lungs but getting rid of the water fast before it could trigger a choke or gag.

Then she clawed for the surface.

She was amazed that her leap had carried her all the way to the pool. Andy hadn't even tried for the pool. Maybe he'd *known* it was too far away, so he'd vaulted the railing instead.

From the noise he'd made, he must've gotten hurt.

Breaking the surface, Jody sucked air and blinked water from her eyes. She twisted around. Both men were looking down at her from the balcony.

They could jump right on me.

Neither looked ready to try it, though. Maybe they didn't want to risk the concrete.

She watched them as she breast-stroked toward the side of the pool.

If they were planning to jump, she thought, they would've done it by now. But they know I'm coming for Andy. Maybe they'll throw their knife and sword at me.

They won't do that.

Where's the ax man?

The ax man vanished from her concern when she reached the side of the pool and both men suddenly bolted into the bedroom.

'Oh, God!' she gasped.

She jumped and shoved at the edge and burst from the water. She got a knee onto the tiles, flopped forward, squirmed and scrambled up and ran for Andy, her drenched nightshirt glued to her skin, her feet smacking the concrete.

He was sitting up, clutching his right knee and gasping and sobbing.

'They're coming,' Jody said.

He looked at her. He shook his head.

Jody scurried around behind him. Squatting, she clutched him under the armpits.

'Don't,' he said. 'Get out of here.'

'We're gettin'.' She hoisted him. Stood him upright and balanced on one leg. 'Try to stand on . . .'

He tried and cried out and hobbled and fell backward against Jody. She stumbled away under his weight, but stayed up. Arms wrapped around his chest, she squeezed him against her.

'Put me down,' he gasped. 'Drop me. My knee's busted.
I'm done for. Please! Get out of here while you can.'

'Not without you, pal.'

She hustled backward alongside the pool, hugging Andy to
her chest. He tried to help by hopping along with his good
leg. The injured leg hung limp, heel dragging.

'Any ideas?' she asked.

'They're gonna kill us.'

'Have to catch us first.'

'Leave me here. You gotta. You can get away if you . . .'

'Hey, shut up.'

She scanned the rear of the house. So far, nobody was
rushing out.

At the end of the pool, she stopped. 'Which way? You've
been here. Where can we . . .?'

'Back there. The fence.'

She swiveled her head and saw a block wall a few yards
beyond the side of the pool. It looked like it might be seven
feet high.

'Great,' she muttered.

She put her back to it and made for it, towing Andy.

She watched the house.

What'll I do if they come?

If I drop him, I can make it over the wall easy.

*Dad would never drop him in a million years. Not even if it
meant dying.*

'Maybe they won't come,' she said.

'Why wouldn't they?'

'The cops might be on the way, for one thing.'

'How do you figure that? You faked the call.'

'Maybe they don't know I faked it. Besides, maybe the cops
picked up when I made the real call . . .'

'Did they?'

'Don't know.'

'Anyway, you didn't tell 'em nothing.'

'Didn't have to. You call 911, the computer gives 'em the address. They'll send out a car.'

'Do you think they will?'

'They might. If those bastards *think* they're coming, that's what counts. They don't wanta be chasing us around if cops're on the way.' Seeing that she had passed the corner of the pool, she glanced over her shoulder. The wall was only ten or twelve feet away. 'We're gonna make it,' she muttered.

'Here they come,' said Andy.

The words turned her insides cold and squirmy.

They were coming, all right. The two from the balcony – silhouettes backlit by downstairs windows, one waving his saber overhead, the other sprinting ahead of him. The one in the lead must've put away his knife, maybe so he could run faster. They raced toward the pool from off to the left.

At least it's between us.

At least the ax guy isn't with them.

Things could be worse . . .

Jody's back hit the wall. She twisted around, swinging Andy, then shoved him at the gray barrier, lifted him, rammed him upright against the blocks. His body shuddered and he cried out. She grabbed the waist of his jeans, stuck her other hand under his crotch and heaved him upward.

He seemed to spring into the air.

He flung his arms across the top of the wall.

The moment Jody saw that he had a purchase, she leaped clear. He kicked up his good leg. She looked back and saw the one guy – the one who'd caught her in the front yard – tilt sideways as he rounded the pool's corner. He was *way* ahead of the saber man.

Jody flung herself at the wall. Leaping, she grabbed its top.

Her body made a smacking sound as it struck the blocks. She pulled with her arms, climbed with bare toes digging at the vertical face. Higher, higher, the rough blocks scuffing the bottoms of her toes, snagging her nightshirt, and then the edge of the top row scraping the undersides of her breasts and moving down her ribs and belly like a rasp file.

'Hurry!' Andy gasped.

He was sprawled along the top of the wall, his face only inches from Jody's right wrist.

In front of her, just beyond the wall, she glimpsed dark limbs and leaves.

Good. Not just somebody else's back yard or pool. A field?
Maybe we can lose them in the trees.

'Go!' she told him. 'Don't wait.' She threw her left leg high to the side and caught the edge with her foot.

Her right leg still hung down, knee and toes against the wall.

'Watch out!' Andy cried.

And Jody cried out, herself, when her ankle was grabbed.

'*Gotcha!*'

First one hand, then two. One clutched her ankle while the other rubbed upward on the side of her leg, stopped only a bit below her groin and squeezed her thigh so hard that tears flooded her eyes.

She knew that wasn't where he wanted his hand to be.

Just couldn't reach any higher.

'Leave her alone!' Andy yelled.

Jody looked at the boy. He was blurry through her tears.

He was pushing himself up. And she knew that he meant to leap on the man and save her.

She shot out her right arm and shoved the side of his face, ramming his head away. His body twisted, started to tumble off the wall.

Without her arm to prop her up, Jody plunged forward. The hands tore at her leg, trying to jerk her down, but all her weight and the momentum of the push at Andy's head threw her toward the other side of the wall.

Probably snap my leg off.

She tensed every muscle in her right leg.

Down below, Andy crashed through foliage, thudded and grunted.

The edge of the top row of blocks dug hard into Jody's thigh.

And into the fingers clutching her there. The man yelped and the hand let go.

The edge acted like a fulcrum.

She felt her leg shoot backward and up, ripping her ankle from the man's grip. The heel of her foot pounded him somewhere. An instant later, her leg flipped high and cleared the top.

She was upside-down, dropping headfirst, her face only inches from the back of the wall. Then her legs started coming down behind her. The rate they were moving, she figured her heels might be the first part of her body to strike the ground.

But her legs kept dropping even after she sensed that her body was stretched out level. They swept lower and lower. Then her rump smacked the steep ground, mashing crisp and prickly weeds, bouncing, throwing her forward in a headfirst somersault down the slope.

A tree pounded her shoulder, knocking her sideways, turning her tumble into a quick, wild roll. She flipped and flipped. She tried to spread-eagle, hoping that outstretched arms and widespread legs would stop her, but the ground battered her arms out of the way and knocked her legs together and she kept on spinning downward like a log. Once, she grabbed a handful of weeds. Their roots popped from the soil. Later, something gouged her side. Finally, the ground dropped out from under her.

A freefall made her heart lurch with dread.

But the fall only lasted a moment. She landed on her back on a bed of rocks that rolled and clattered as Jody's momentum slid her across them and flipped her over one last time.

For a while, the world seemed to go on tilting and swaying. Then it settled down.

She lay there, huffing, her heart slamming.

I've gotta get up, she told herself. Gotta get up and run. They're gonna be coming. They'll kill me . . .

She didn't hear them coming, though.

The wall's way up there, she thought. Way, way up there. If those guys didn't have the nerve to jump off the balcony, what're the chances they'll make a try at this?

Who knows?

If I hear them coming, I'll get up and run. But not till then.

For now, she didn't want to move. Not even to fix her nightshirt.

The fall had twisted her nightshirt and rucked it way up, leaving her naked below the midriff. She didn't like it. Bad enough that her butt showed, but she didn't enjoy having her bare front against the ground. God-only-knew-what might be there. Bugs, spiders, worms, snakes . . .

All she could feel under her body, however, were rocks. Some small as marbles, some big as baseballs, some round, some blocky, some pointy – each of them pushing against her someplace. They were under her legs and groin and hips and belly and ribs and breasts and arms and face. In some places, they hurt more than in other places. Nowhere did they feel good.

With an effort that made her dizzy, she moved her arms

away from her sides and folded them under her head. She pillowed her cheek on a forearm.

Better.

But she still ached everywhere. The rocks weren't the worst of it, either. Her skin seemed to burn with countless hurts. Beneath her skin, her muscles everywhere quivered and jerked and flinched. Under the muscles, her bones seemed to ring from the pounding they'd taken.

Just to make sure her legs weren't broken, she moved them slightly. The rocks beneath them rolled a bit. Some scratched her skin. The movement hurt her in many ways. It convinced her, though, that she'd broken no bones in her legs.

Broken bones.

Andy! Where's Andy?

Slowly, Jody lifted her face off her crossed arms. She swiveled her head.

The area was very dark, but specks and patches of moonlight glowed here and there. She seemed to be lying on a path of rocks. Its sides were bordered by steep banks a few feet high.

A creek bed. A *dry* creek bed.

Up ahead, where she could see over the banks, the place looked like a jungle.

This is okay, she thought. This is really good.

They'll never find us here.

She knew that she had to find Andy, though. Lowering her head, she rested for a while longer. Gradually, her breathing and heartbeat calmed down.

While she waited, she listened. She heard birds twittering and squawking, cars passing on a distant road, the faroff hum of a prop airplane, a door banging shut, a dog yapping, music and voices that apparently came from a television.

She did not hear anyone crunching through the foliage on the hillside.

That was a very good thing.

It was also good that she could hear a television. Though sounds might carry long distances on such a quiet summer night, the TV meant that a house was within a reasonable distance. She could probably get to it if she needed to.

She didn't want to think about going in search of a house. Maybe later.

For now, she was well hidden and safe. She felt very lucky to be alive. She sure didn't want to jeopardize herself by venturing out into an unfamiliar neighborhood.

The thing to do is find Andy, she decided.

Gritting her teeth, Jody pushed herself up to her hands and knees. Though her hurts flared, she didn't allow the pain to stop her. On her feet, she pulled at the twisted damp rag of her nightshirt, unwound it, and drew it down her thighs.

To her right, she saw the hillside that slanted up, heavy with trees and bushes, toward the rear of the Youngman house. She couldn't see much of it. She certainly couldn't see the wall at the top. But nothing seemed to be moving down toward her through the darkness.

To her left, she saw more trees and undergrowth. Splashes of moonlight, but no light from houses or streets. How odd. They *had* to be there. She'd visited the area often enough to know that every hillside had a road curving around its base, that every such road was lined with houses.

Houses on the hillsides always had houses somewhere below them. Being at the bottom of a hill, she must be fairly close to the back of someone's place.

So where are the lights?

Maybe a power failure, she told herself.

She didn't like the idea of that. Not one bit. A power failure might've been caused on purpose by those men to give them darkness.

What if it wasn't just the guys I saw? What if they're all over the place? Hundreds of them. Like The Night of the Living Dead, *or something.*

No, that's crazy.

This whole thing's crazy and sick. I don't need to make it worse by going nuts with my imagination.

She knew there hadn't been a power failure as of five or ten minutes ago; the Youngman house had still been lighted up the last time she'd seen it from over by the wall. Besides, if that bunch had wanted to knock out all the lights in the area, they certainly would've done it *before* starting their attacks.

I bet there isn't any power failure, she thought. I just can't see the lights because of all the trees and stuff. Fences, too. Almost every house was likely to have a solid fence of wood or cinderblocks to protect it from the wilds at the base of the slope.

Probably no way to reach a street *without* running into a fence.

More climbing.

I'll need to give Andy another boost.

Have to find him first.

She listened again for sounds of anyone approaching.

They're long gone. They've gotta be.

'Andy?' she called softly.

She stood motionless, listening. No answer came.

'Andy!' she called more loudly.

She waited.

Maybe he's out cold.

He had dropped from the same wall as Jody, must've tumbled down the same slope. Even though they'd started at almost the same place, however, he certainly hadn't ended up in the creek bed with her.

It seemed likely that he'd stopped short, somewhere up the slope.

How far up?

She hadn't seen or heard him rolling down the slope. Maybe he'd landed by the wall and *stayed* there.

What if they got him?

'Jody?'

She whirled toward the slope. 'Andy?'

'Where are you?' The faint, fearful voice of the boy came from above and off to her left.

'I'm on my way,' Jody called.

Chapter Seven

It took only a few minutes to find Andy. He lay in the darkness beneath an overhanging lip of rock. Jody could only see the dim gray of his torso and face. His jeans made him invisible below the waist.

As she approached him, he propped himself up on his elbows.

'Are you okay?' she asked.

'Yeah. What about you?'

'Fine.' She sat down beside him. The ground was springy with weeds. They were damp and soft. They felt a lot better than the rocks of the creek bed. She leaned back, bracing herself on stiff arms, and stretched out her legs beside Andy's. 'You didn't tell me there was a *cliff* behind that wall,' she said.

'Yeah, well. They didn't get us, did they?'

'Not so far. Have you heard anything from up there?'

'No. You?'

'Huh-uh.'

'I think they went away.'

'Sure hope so,' Jody said. 'I think we'd better stay here, though. How's the old knee?'

'I don't know. I'm not so sure it's broken anymore.'

'What, you think it *healed*?'

'I don't think I broke it. Maybe it's just twisted.'

'It *better* be broken after you made me *drag* you all over creation.'

He was silent for a few moments. Then he said, 'You saved me, Jody.'

'Yeah, well. Glad to be of service. You were pretty good yourself, pal.'

He sank against the ground and rested his hands over his hips. He sighed.

'Are you okay?' Jody asked again.

'Sure.' A while later, he said, 'They got everyone, didn't they?'

Jody lay down beside him. She pulled his arm and he rolled onto his side. They scooted toward each other until their bodies met. She held him. 'It's all right,' she whispered.

Like hell, she thought. They killed them all. His mom and dad, Evelyn. His whole family.

'Everything'll be all right,' she said.

Andy didn't say anything.

After a while, he began to cry.

Jody squeezed him tight against her while he wept with his face pushed against the side of her neck.

Soon after he stopped crying, the sirens began. There seemed to be one at first, then many, their wails rising and overlapping and dying.

The night was still filled with sirens when Jody murmured, 'Good God. I haven't heard anything like this since the riots.'

'Sure sounds like a lot of cops,' Andy said.

'Not just cops. Fire trucks.'

'Do you think so?'

'Yeah.'

As the noise of the sirens diminished, Jody heard car doors thudding shut, voices shouting, other voices tinny and amplified by loud speakers, others broken, crackling with static.

'Do you think my house is burning down?' Andy asked.

'It might be. I hope not, but . . .'

'Do you think they're in it?'

'Oh, Andy.'

'They are, aren't they?'

'I don't know.' She pressed her mouth against the side of his head. After a while, she said, 'We oughta get up there. The sooner we tell the police what happened, the better.'

She started to ease away, but Andy tightened his arms around her.

'Come on,' she whispered.

'I don't wanta.'

'I'll help you walk.'

'That isn't why.'

'What do you want to do?' she asked.

'Stay here.'

'Do you want me to go up and bring someone . . .?'

'No! You've gotta stay, too.'

'Andy.'

'Please. We gotta just stay here.'

Jody relaxed in his arms. She gently stroked the back of his head. 'Are you afraid those guys might be up there?'

His head moved beneath her hand, nodding.

'They didn't come down after us,' she said.

'They might be waiting.'

'I don't think so. They probably started the fire on purpose, you know? It's a great way to destroy physical evidence.'

'Fingerprints and stuff?'

'Yeah. All kinds of things. So they probably started the fire and then took off. They sure wouldn't want to be here when the fire trucks and cops showed up. They're probably miles away by now.'

'Maybe.'

'They'd be nuts to stick around.'

Andy was silent for a few moments, then said, 'You think they're *not* nuts?'

'Okay. I should've said "stupid". They're nuts, all right, but they aren't stupid. Those two didn't jump off the balcony, for instance. They knew they might get hurt. And they didn't come down here. Must've figured it'd be a waste of time, and too risky. Or maybe my trick with the phone worked. If they really thought I'd gotten through to 911, they had to figure the cops would be showing up in five or ten minutes. They *didn't* want to be around when the cops arrived.'

'I guess not,' Andy admitted.

'Which means they're gone, right?'

'I guess so.'

'They're gone.'

'Okay.'

'So let's get out of here.'

He shook his head and hugged her very hard.

'Andy.'

'What if they're waiting for us?'

'They aren't. Come on, we just went through this.'

'Maybe they all took off like you said, but maybe they left

just one guy behind to hide and wait for us and ambush us when we come out?'

Jody hadn't thought of that. 'That's crazy,' she said.

'Yeah.'

She could *see* the ax man crouching in the dark. Waiting. Knowing she and Andy would be drawn up the hill by the promise of safety in the hands of the police.

They knew it'd be awfully tough to find us down here.

One guy could stay behind easily enough. The rest of them drive off, and he stays. Millions of places to hide. He hides and waits and just when we think it's all over he jumps us and that's all she wrote.

Oh, man. It made sense.

'I don't know,' she whispered.

'Remember what you said to Mable?' He must've detected that Jody was starting to see the matter his way. His voice sounded quick, almost eager, and he relaxed his hold on her. 'You said they had to kill us because we're witnesses.'

'Yeah. I know.'

'They aren't gonna just let us get away. They'll leave a guy behind to jump us the minute we show ourselves. I know they will.'

'I guess . . . they might.'

Right now, she thought, there must be bunches of cops up there. Cops and firemen. We'll be fine once we get to them. If we wait too long, though, they'll be gone. Then we'll be on our own.

'I don't know what to do,' she muttered.

'Let's just stay here.'

'We can't stay here for ever.'

'Till morning. If we wait till morning, nobody can sneak up on us. We can see him coming, you know?'

'He might see us before we see us. And by then, the cops and firemen might not be around anymore.'

'We oughta wait till morning.'

'I don't know.'

'Let's stay.'

'I've gotta think about it.'

Andy snuggled against her.

She stroked his hair and caressed his back and tried to think. She wanted very badly to *be* with the cops who were probably all over the place in front of the Clark house. As much as she wanted that, however, she hated to do what would be necessary to make it happen.

Waiting for dawn would be a mistake, though.

She asked herself what her father would do in a situation like this. And the answer came fast.

She didn't have to wait long for Andy to fall asleep. As soon as his breathing changed and his body relaxed against her, she began to ease away from him. She moved very slowly. She paused often. At last, their bodies were untangled. She rolled over, got to her hands and knees, and stood up.

Andy lay on his side, head cushioned on one bent arm, his other arm resting along his side, his legs back.

Definitely asleep, Jody told herself.

But she feared that he might wake up the instant she looked away – as if her gaze was the only power that kept him sleeping. So she watched him while she crept sideways.

What if this is the last time I see him alive?

What if I come back with a cop and he's dead, all bloody and hacked and . . .

He'll be okay.

She began to climb straight up the slope.

After making up her mind to go for the police by herself, she had considered the best way to do it. The sensible course would've been to make a major detour – head off to one side or the other, or actually move away from the hillside, climb whatever fences might be in the way, and cut through someone's yard to whatever road might be down here.

A lot of directions to choose from. One crazy lunatic, left behind to finish the job, couldn't cover everyplace.

A detour might be safer than the direct route, but it would sure take longer.

She wanted to reach the cops fast and get back to Andy fast.

So she had decided to charge straight up the hillside.

Maybe not *charge*. Sneak.

Sneak so Andy doesn't wake up, sneak so the bastard waiting at the top, hunkered down with his back against the wall, won't hear me coming.

If he's even there.

Maybe nobody had stayed behind, at all. Maybe they'd all raced off in their cars after setting Andy's house on fire.

If one of them *had* stayed, he might be anywhere.

The climb wasn't easy. Several times, Jody's feet slipped out from under her and she landed on her knees. In places, the hillside was so steep that she had to crawl. Here and there, she was forced to grab weeds or bushes or tree roots to keep herself from skidding backward.

After an uphill struggle that seemed endless, she made her way past a tree, got above it, and leaned back against its trunk. The way the tree slanted out from the slope, it took much of the weight off her feet.

She gasped for breath. Her heart thumped madly. Her skin felt very hot, and she seemed to be sweating everywhere. She wiped her eyes with a moist, slick arm. She blinked.

Almost there.

And then she saw thick piles of smoke clotting the night beyond the top of the wall. The smoke shimmered with a red glow.

It's the Youngman house, she realized. That's the one they set on fire. Not Andy's place, after all.

Unless maybe both.

Probably both.

No wonder all the sirens.

The ruddy light did nothing at all to illuminate Jody's side of the wall. The top of the wall was a straight edge, the night glowing above it, nothing but blackness below.

Nobody's there, she told herself.

Yeah, right.

He could be standing with his back to the wall, straight above her, staring down at her right now.

But the wall, Jody guessed, was probably at least a hundred feet long. He could be waiting anywhere along it. (Or be long gone.) If he hadn't spotted her yet, and if he was a fair distance away to one side or the other, and if she was very quiet and very quick . . .

She bent her knees. She started to scoot down the trunk, but its bark scratched her back and snagged her nightshirt, so she had to push away from it. Squatting, she scanned the slope and wall.

Probably no one's even there, she told herself.

She leaned forward. On hands and feet, she crept higher.

Really ironic if I get myself killed at this stage of things. Made it through so much, only to get nailed when I'm almost to the cops.

She had learned about irony in her English class last year. Her English teacher, Mr Platt, had explained that it was the flipside of poetic justice.

She believed in God.

She wasn't too sure about his merciful side, but one thing was very clear: God delighted in irony.

It would probably tickle him, she thought, to see me catch an ax just when I get to the wall, just when I think I'm home free.

Please, don't. Okay? It'd kill my dad. You already got Mom in one of your irony binges, so just try to control yourself this time, okay? Please? Amen.

The prayer had no sooner taken flight from Jody's mind than she thought, Oh, great way to talk to God. Now I've probably pissed him off and he'll kill me for sure.

She stopped.

Poised on her knuckles and the balls of her feet, she stared straight ahead at the black wall. It was probably no more than two yards away, though she couldn't be sure. Too dark to be sure of anything.

She glanced both ways, but saw nothing.

Might as well get it over with.

The way her muscles were jumping and jiggling, she wondered if she would have enough strength to make it over the wall.

I'll make it, she told herself.

On the count of three.

One.

Two.

Three!

She sprang up and forward like a sprinter leaving the blocks, churned up the final piece of hillside, hurled herself toward the wall and leaped.

Even as her hands clamped the top, she heard quick footfalls rushing at her from the left.

PART TWO

Simon Says

Chapter Eight

He blamed me. Mitchell, that is. It was just after the girl and the kid got away from us. I'd gotten a hold of the girl's leg when she was trying to go over the wall, but she broke loose. That's when my troubles really got started last night, so that's where I might as well start this off.

It *was* my fault. I should've had her. What messed things up was that I had a hand way up high on her leg, and she wasn't wearing any panties. All she had on was this red nightie that was like a really big T-shirt. I got distracted, so then it took me by surprise when her leg suddenly kicked back. I lost hold of her ankle, and my other hand got mashed between her leg and the wall. So I lost her.

It beat up my hand pretty good, by the way. Raked skin off the backs of my fingers and knuckles. I even bled, but not much.

Anyway, I lost her. I should've had her twice last night, when it comes right down to it. The first time was in the front yard of the old bag's house – the house she and the kid finally got into. She'd tried to make a turn, but didn't slow down enough and ended up taking a slide across the grass instead. Which gave me the chance to catch her. I did, too. She tried to get up and get away from me, but I yanked her down by her hair.

I had her flat on her back. Her nightie'd gotten shoved up, so it was rumpled around her chest. I couldn't see her tits, but the rest of her was all laid out in front of me. That's when I first saw she didn't have any panties on. She was real slim, but not skin and bones. Her skin looked smooth and nice. She didn't look like she had any muff at all, not till I was on my knees by her head, and then I could see how she had some hair, but it was so fine and wispy that you could look right through it.

I held her down on the ground by her head hair. What I wanted to do more than anything was . . . a lot of stuff. For one, I wanted to give her a feel. I wanted to run my hands all over her. I wanted to get that nightie off her, too. And believe it or not, I wanted to take a good look at her face. I'd only caught a glimpse of it, and the light hadn't been any good, but what I'd seen gave me the idea that she had a real knockout of a face.

Anyway, those are things I *wanted* to do. I knew better, though. She wasn't here for me to play with, she was here for me to kill. And the quicker, the better. No time to enjoy her, just get it done. So I didn't touch her except to hold her down on the ground by the hair while I went for my knife.

Before I could pull my knife, she clobbered me with her fucking baseball bat. It wasn't hard enough to knock me out, but hard enough to hurt like hell. I couldn't help but let go of her.

That's how she got away the first time.

The second time was when she was on the wall and I had her by the leg.

It was my fault that she got away both times.

When I lost her at the wall, Mitchell said, 'Damn it!'

'Don't worry about it,' I told him. I jumped and boosted myself up. From up there, I saw what was on the other side – namely, a very steep slope – and that's when I knew we were in for real trouble. I jumped back down and shook my head at Mitchell.

'What's that supposed to mean?' he asked.

'It's a big drop-off back there. They're probably still falling.'

'A cliff?'

'More like a hillside.'

'The fall gonna kill 'em?'

'I doubt it.'

'Shit.'

'We can't go down there, Mitch.'

'Can't let 'em get away.'

'I know, I know,' I said.

That's when he told me to stay behind. He and the rest of the guys, he said, would take care of the exit routine: loading up the bodies and torching the houses and hitting the road. I should stay here to kill the girl and the kid.

For about half a second, the idea excited me. Without the others in my way, I'd be able to do everything I wanted with the girl.

Then the other half of the second hit and gave me an idea I didn't like at all; if they left me behind, the cops would get me. Almost for sure.

There I'd be, cops crawling all over the place, me on foot and miles from home, with nothing on except my shoes and my Connie kilt.

That'd sure be a sweet fix to be in.

It'd be especially sweet because of the fact that we aren't allowed to let the cops take us alive. If we get caught, we might talk. That's the problem. So we can't let ourselves get caught. We've either got to commit suicide or go down fighting.

The penalty for getting taken alive . . . never mind, I'm getting sidetracked. The thing is, Mitch wanted me to stay and take care of the witnesses.

'You wanta leave *without* me?' I said.

He goes, 'Somebody's gotta stay.'

'Then let's *all* stay. Go on back and get the others, tell 'em what happened. If we all search, we might stand a chance of finding those two before . . .'

'All right,' Mitch said.

He'd said it awfully fast, as a matter of fact. But I was too relieved, just then, to let it worry me.

'You stay here,' he said, 'and start looking.'

He turned away and started walking.

'Can you hurry?'

He twisted sideways and raised his arm and shook his old Rebel saber at me. 'You better find her, man. You better find 'em both, or you're . . .'

'Just get the others over here, okay?'

'Tom's gonna have your ass.'

'Oh, fuck off. I'm the only one who even got close enough to *grab* her. You and Chuck were useless.'

Just when I said that, Chuck came out a back door of the house. He had his ax propped up against one shoulder and the old lady's body hanging over the other. He was bloody all over.

Mitch saw him and picked up his speed a little.

When they met, they said some things I couldn't hear. Then they turned around and went into the house.

I perched myself on the wall. Sitting up there with a leg hanging over each side, I'd be able to watch for the others to come, and I could also look down the hillside.

Nothing showed down there, just bushes and weeds and a lot of trees. The moon made some things look dirty white. A lot of places, shadowy places, were just plain black. At the bottom, the ground leveled out for a while. Then came a row of houses with big, fenced back yards. Plenty of the back yards had pools. Most of the houses were dark, but a few had spotlights. The pool of one house was all lighted up, but I couldn't see anyone swimming in it. Fact is, I couldn't see anyone anywhere.

Out past the fronts of the houses, there were some cars parked in driveways and also on the street. I could see a long stretch of the street between the ending places where it curved around the hill and vanished. Not a single car was moving on it. Not a person was walking on it. I did see a cat scurry across and hide under a parked car. Nothing else, though.

I sure couldn't see any trace of the girl or the kid. Couldn't hear them moving around down there, either.

Maybe if I kept still, though, they might do something to give themselves away. That's what I hoped for. Because if they didn't, our chances of finding them were slim to zilch.

The girl'd put in a call to 911, but she hadn't gotten through. She'd tried to fake us out, but Mitch checked the phone in the bedroom and it was still ringing at the cop end of things. So we're okay on that score.

Which didn't mean that *somebody* hadn't called the cops.

But it was a good sign that none had shown up yet.

Sitting on the wall, I tried to put myself in the girl's shoes. (Not that she was wearing any, because she wasn't. Had nothing on at all but that loose nightie. All bare underneath it. Bare and smooth and slim and – couldn't have been any older than fifteen, sixteen. Young stuff. Young, fresh stuff. Maybe even a virgin. Right. Not hardly likely. I don't think there *are* any virgins anymore. We live in crummy times. Nothing crummy about this gal, though. I can't wait to get my hands on her – my cock *into* her. Oh, shit, where was I? Better rewind a little.) Okay. Put myself into her shoes. Right. What I figured was that she might lay still, either because of getting hurt in the fall or maybe because she decided that hiding was the safest thing she could do. If she did keep still, we might stand a good chance of finding her if we fanned out and searched down there.

Or she might try to reach help.

So I kept a sharp eye on the back yards of the houses down there.

In a way, I almost hoped the girl and the kid *would* make a dash for one of those houses. They'd call the cops the minute they got inside of one, and we wouldn't have any choice except to bail out.

That gave me an idea.

Just suppose I ran and *told* the others that those two had made it into a house?

There'd be hell to pay if they found out I'd lied, of course.

Hell for me and some others.

But how were they ever gonna find out?

It seemed like a terrific idea. And even if it *was* a lie, it might save us. It struck me as awfully risky to stick around this place and search for those two. After you've done a massacre, you don't *want* to linger around. You want to get out and far away as fast as you can.

If we carried out a hunt, we might have to stay another hour. Or even longer, depending on how it went.

Tom might even keep us here till daybreak.

He wouldn't let us leave, not while there was any chance at all of laying our hands on them.

It isn't just because they might be able to identify us. *I* sure don't want them alive to pin any of this on us – especially since I'm the one the girl got her best look at – but Tom's big concern is keeping everything quiet. The last thing he wants is for things to get spread around on the news so we wouldn't be a secret society anymore.

He's very big on this secret society stuff.

According to him, it'd ruin everything if people found out about us and what we're up to.

We call ourselves the Krulls, by the way. (Or Krullers, when we're feeling whimsical.) Tom came up with the name for us, right at the start of things. He found it in a book. That was back when we were in junior high. Tom was always reading these trashy slasher books, and this one had to do with a group of people called the Krulls who ran around the woods like savages doing all sorts of weird shit. They were a bunch of real sick puppies. They loved to torture and kill people. They ate people, too. A lot of them just ran around naked, but some of the others wore clothes they made out of human skin. This one gal wore a bikini top that was made out of the faces peeled off two dead babies. We all thought that was pretty cool.

Maybe the guy that wrote about Hannibal Lecter read the same book we did way back then. Or maybe both those writers got their ideas from Ed Gein in Wisconsin, who did some of those things for real.

Anyway, Tom was really turned on by all that Krull stuff. The book was like his *Bible*. He made us read it, and he went around all the time quoting from it. Whenever we got together, we used to talk about the Krulls and how much we'd like to be running around in the woods that way, killing and raping and having a great old time.

It was just something we got a kick out of going on about, though. I don't even think it was all that abnormal. I knew plenty of other kids who weren't part of our group, but who also got turned on by stuff about perverts and psychopaths and ax murderers and the Nazi death camps – about *any*thing that had to do with brutal, sadistic slaughter.

One guy I knew, George Avery, always carried around this

paperback that had about fifteen pages of photographs near the middle. The pictures were in black and white. They weren't very clear, either. But two of them showed naked dead women who'd been found in the woods. You couldn't see whether the gals were pretty or not. The shots were so pale and blurry that you could hardly even see their tits. Their nipples were good and dark, though. And so were their muffs. You could see *them* great. And you could also see their stab wounds, which looked like dark slots all up and down their fronts. I don't know why, but neither of the gals was bloody. Maybe the cameraman cleaned them off so they'd make better pictures, or something. I don't know.

That kid, George, always had his nose in those pictures – at least when he wasn't showing them around to impress the rest of us, that is. And he was not a particularly screwy guy. In fact, he was a model student. Straight As, the whole nine yards.

What I'm getting at, we *all* basically enjoyed that kind of stuff back when we were in junior high. It wasn't just Tom and his little clique of future Krulls.

This other kid, Harold . . .

Wait. I'm running off at the mouth again. The thing is, I'm stuck here for a while and I've got this tape recorder and enough tapes to recite *War and Peace or The Tommyknockers* or something. It's a real temptation to blabber everything under the sun.

I *do* want to tell everything, that's the problem.

The problem in more ways than one.

Where was I? Am I gonna have to rewind again? No. I was on top of the wall. Right.

I was telling about how Tom wants to keep the Krulls a big secret, and that's why he'd take all sorts of big risks just in order to kill the girl and the kid.

I'd just come up with the idea of lying, saying I'd seen them run into a house.

A stunt like that might get us moving quick.

I decided to give it a try.

Just when I was about to jump down, though, here come the sounds of a skidding roll and thud.

That's okay, I thought. It's the side door of Tom's van sliding shut. They'd gone ahead and tossed the bodies in, so now they were about ready to come over here to help me search.

But then car doors started thumping shut. They went fast: thump thump-thump thump thump thump. Then engines sputtered and zoomed.

My stomach dropped like a ton of lead.

I jumped off the wall and ran for the house.

Ran for about five seconds before two more things happened: the noise of the car engines faded out, and I saw flames behind the big picture window of the old bat's house.

None of that stopped me, though.

The fire kept me from taking a shortcut through the house, so I raced around the side and had to waste time fooling with a gate. By the time I got out front and had a view of the street, my *friends* were gone.

We'd come up here in the van and five cars, and some of us had doubled up. I'd driven Chuck. I'd picked him up at his house in my Mustang. (Plates covered with masking tape.) We'd passed my flask of rum back and forth along the way, and we'd smoked a couple of his cigars. We'd had us a fine old time, joking around and stuff even though we were feeling pretty tense. As per standard operating procedure, I'd left my key in the ignition before Chuck and I climbed out and headed over to the van.

Now, everything was gone.

Including my Mustang.

There's an old John Wayne movie called *They Were Expendable*. It's about PT Boat guys in World War Two. (It's been colorized now, so you can see how Duke looks with black lips.) Anyway, I was just a kid the first time I saw it, and had to ask my old man what it meant, expendable. He told me, 'It means nobody gave a rat's ass if they lived or died.'

It means more than that, though.

You're expendable when the mission's more important than your life. More important to *someone*. That someone isn't likely to be *you*.

Those guys, Tom in particular, had decided I was expendable. No matter what the cost – to me – I'd have to stay behind, hunt down the girl and the kid, and kill them.

I muttered, 'Thanks a heap, motherfuckers.'

Then fire blasted through a downstairs window of the big house up the street where we'd staged our raid.

SOP: take the stiffs, burn the houses, beat it before the fire trucks show.

We'd never left a man behind, though, until now. Lucky me.

I ran like hell, going back the way I'd come – through the gate, along the side of the house, past the pool to the blockwall.

By the time the first sirens sounded in the distance, I was crouched down on the dark side of the wall.

Chapter Nine

I stayed there at the top of the slope with my back to the wall for a long time, listening to all the noise. There were sirens, doors banging shut, guys shouting, loud-speakers, fire truck radios, cop radios. I heard water shooting out of hoses, hissing and splashing. And I heard snaps and crackles and crashes and exploding glass, all sorts of noises the house made as it got chewed and crunched by the fire.

My recently departed 'pals' obviously hoped I'd be sneaking down the hillside to hunt out the girl and the kid and kill them. That was my mission, after all. That was why they'd abandoned me.

So it gave me a lot of satisfaction *not* to go down there.

You don't treat a guy like that – desert him – and really expect him to go out of his way for you.

Anyway, I was tired. I'd been up all day and most of the night. Not only that, but our little foray had taken a lot out of me. That sort of thing is such a rush! But tiring. Really wears you out. You go into a house not knowing what'll happen. It'd be safer if you did some planning, but we don't. We just pick a place at random, so we don't know who might be in it. That way, we get more surprises – good and bad. And a lot more fear. Going in, you're so scared you want to piss, but you get a hell of a charge out of it. And then *they're* the scared ones. They're fucking terrified. They've never been so scared in their lives, they're just praying it's a nightmare they'll wake up and escape from, and it's all because of you. They're in your power. They know it, you know it. You're in charge. They can't do a goddamn thing about it except maybe beg and scream and cry. And then you get wild, and do anything you want to them. Anything. They're getting it from every side at once.

By the time it's all over, you're so wiped out you feel like a zombie.

That's when everything goes the way it's supposed to.

This time, we're right in the middle of our party when we suddenly find out we've got survivors. They really took us by surprise. Just a while before they turned up, Ranch had brought in a fine example of teenage girl on a stick. Brian got inspired. Probably hoped she had a sister hiding somewhere. So after a while, he took off to go looking.

Brian, otherwise known as Minnow, has the worst kill record in the whole bunch, so none of us thought he'd come back with anybody. I sure didn't. But the last thing I expected was to see a couple of kids staring in at us.

How come Ranch didn't find them? How'd they get past Brian?

Anyway, there they were. I was worn out *before* they showed their faces. So then we had to chase them.

Shit, I oughta kill both the little creeps just for making me run so much. And for getting me into this mess.

Which I might never get out of alive, goddamn it and them and Tom and Mitch and all the others straight to hell!

At least I'm okay for now.

I was basically okay last night, too, hunched there against the wall, but I was dead tired. Way too tired for climbing down that hillside.

If they wanted me to climb down and hunt around for those two, they were stupid to drive away like that – they should've stayed to help.

So fuck them.

I quit squatting, and sat on the ground. I leaned back

against the wall, stretched my legs down the slope, and shut my eyes.

It felt great to relax and shut my eyes.

But this didn't really seem like a good place to sleep. A fireman or even a cop might decide to take a look over the wall. Or a helicopter might show up with its spotlight.

Down the slope somewhere, in the trees and bushes, I'd be a hundred times safer.'

But I couldn't make myself move.

In my *head*, I did it. I crept down the hill, looking for a safe place to hide, and crawled into a nice little gap with thick bushes all around. Well, well! The place was already occupied. By who else but the girl. What a surprise! (My surprise might've been due to the fact that I'd drifted off to sleep. She'd been put there by my dream.)

She was too scared to move. She stayed on her back, all stiff and whimpering, while I crawled onto her. Then I tore the neck of her nightie. Stretched it till it ripped. She put up a little fight. Not much, just enough to make it fun. I smacked her hard across the face. After that, she quit struggling. She cried when I tugged the nightie off her shoulders and dragged it down, all the way down and off her.

'Please don't hurt me,' she whimpered. 'Please. Please don't hurt me!'

So I hurt her.

Hurting them is the best part.

I hurt her with my fingers and teeth. She bucked and screamed. I sucked her blood. I bit in deep.

I was *so* glad the others had ditched me. If they'd stayed, I would've had to share.

She was all mine!

I grabbed her by the shoulders and rammed my cock into her all the way up to the hilt, and it was great. She was wet and tight, so wired with fear and pain that she was a mass of twitches and tremors. Each time I thrust in, it made her tits jump a little. The harder I pounded, the more they jumped. They were small, but not too small. They were shaped like cones. Their nipples as dark as chocolate.

I couldn't stand much more. I was plunging and ready to explode. I shut my eyes to make it last longer, because the sight of her under me was too much – how she was pale in the moonlight, crying, tits jerking. That stuff turned me on more than how she felt, probably.

Then suddenly she laughed. It was a cold, mean laugh. It made me feel like I had icy worms wiggling under my skin.

The laugh got me to open my eyes.

It wasn't *her* under me anymore. It was Hester Luddgate, from way back in the eighth grade when she was thirteen and so were we.

At her best, Hester'd been a disgusting pig: tiny pink eyes, a wide nose, a sunken chin that made her upper teeth loom out moronically, and boobs like swollen bags of pudding. And that was when Hester was at the top of her form.

The girl underneath me was Hester at her worst.

Hester the way she'd looked after we got finished with her. After we'd cut off her eyelids, nose, lips. After we'd done all the rest. But before she'd actually died.

She wasn't a pleasant sight.

I lurched away from her, bumped my head on something awfully solid, and woke up fast. No Hester, after all. She'd been a figment of my dream.

A great dream for a while there, till Hester reared her ugly head and grossed me out.

What a relief to find myself still sitting in the dark with my back against the wall! I took some deep breaths and tried to calm down. My heart was pounding like a madman's. I had a huge boner from the earlier parts of the dream.

Dreams are supposed to mean stuff.

I wondered what my dream meant.

Well, I figured it meant one thing for sure: I wanted to fuck that girl.

And maybe the dream was telling me that I'd get to do it if I tried.

One thing my old man taught me: you don't accomplish anything sitting on your duff. You've gotta work for what you want, get your butt in gear, put your nose to the grindstone. In other words, haul your ass down the hillside and hunt for that girl till you find her.

In my dream, she'd turned into Hester on me.

She wouldn't do that in real life, though. She'd stay the same girl all the way till I finished with her. Well, not *exactly*. There'd be some changes. The changes would be done by me, though. By me and my knife.

Without any help from my friends.

So I got to my feet, brushed off the seat of my Connie kilt, stretched. Even though the dream had taken a nasty turn, I felt pretty good. I felt like the sleep had drained out all my tiredness. The stretching was great. I had to moan because my muscles felt so tight and strong.

If she's down there, I thought, I'll find her.

I started picturing her again in my head, and what I'd do to her.

Then I reminded myself not to forget about the kid. He had to be nailed, too. That wouldn't be any great thrill, but it needed to be done.

Maybe the girl knows where to find him, I thought.

I thought, I'll make her talk.

I'll make her talk, then I'll make her scream, then I'll make her plead and weep, and then I'll make her die.

Yes. Mmmmm.

All these thoughts were getting me pretty excited again.

I was ready.

I took about two steps down the hillside, then heard a quiet, sneaky sound. It came from over to my right, and a ways down the slope. Standing frozen, I heard a soft crunch of weeds, the snap of a twig, another crunch.

Oh, God, I thought, please let it be her.

Sort of a laugh, really, asking God favors that way. Like I'm sure he'd be eager to lend a hand and toss me the girl so I could get my jollies demolishing her.

Somebody answered my prayer, though.

Because I stood there and didn't move a muscle and before you know it, the girl climbed into sight. Just as I spotted her, she stopped moving. She was about fifteen feet over to my right, and almost at the top of the slope.

The only reason I could see her was because she'd stopped where there happened to be a gap in the bushes and trees between the two of us. The gap framed her. It probably framed me for her, too, but that didn't worry me. I hadn't been moving, so she hadn't heard anything out of me and didn't know where to look. Besides, I was standing in the wall's shadow, and she was in moonlight.

I could *see* her because of the moonlight, but it wasn't enough to show me much. I could just barely make out a dim, blurry face. And one arm. And legs from pretty high on their thighs to about the ankles. The rest of her was mostly invisible.

Her head turned. The way it moved slowly from one side to the other, I knew she was checking to make sure the coast was clear.

A time or two, she stared straight at me.

Her head didn't stop, though, so I guess she didn't spot me.

After looking all around, she stood still for a while. Then she crouched lower, holding herself off the slope with her arms, bending her legs. I figured she planned to crawl the rest of the way to the wall.

But suddenly she seemed to explode off the ground. No more sneaking around. No more caution. She just plain went for it hellbent.

And I went for her.

I dashed along the wall, and she threw herself at it and jumped. Her body whomped it. She caught the top and scurried up. Then she flung her right leg out to the side and kicked it up and caught the top with her foot.

But I had her.

I *had* her.

She was quick, but not quick enough. I was quicker, and close, and I had her.

Her left leg was mine.

I'd grab it and jerk her off that wall, and then she'd *all* be mine. Not just one leg, both legs – and everything that was between them, everything that was above them.

Mine!

One more stride was all I needed. Both my arms were out, ready to grab her leg. I was paying attention, too. It wasn't like last time when I let myself get distracted. My mind was on my job, not on her snatch. Only one thing mattered – getting a good hold on her ankle.

But something grabbed my ankle, first.

A root, a weed, some damn thing. Whatever it was, it looped my left foot. The way it felt, you would've thought a goddamn cowboy had lassoed my foot and yanked it back.

One of my hands actually did make it to the girl.

But only my fingertips. They sort of brushed the side of her foot.

Then the ground slammed me. I kept my head up, at least. Would've been worse, except for that. As it was, the bellyflop punched all my air out. For a while, I couldn't move at all, not even breathe.

When I got my wind back, I rolled over.

The wall was dark. The sky was red and shivery with firelight. The girl was gone.

The girl being gone didn't surprise me. The ground being gone did.

I must've been stretched out at the edge of the drop-off when I rolled over.

Once I started rolling, I couldn't stop until a tree finally put the brakes on me. By then, I was almost at the bottom of the hill. Every part of me felt scratched and bumped. I wasn't sure I could move.

I got up anyway, and started to run.

Speaking of which – gotta run right now. My teeth, so to speak, are floating.

Chapter Ten

Hello. It's me again. I'm back. Not only relieved of my bladder's burden, but now equipped with a bottle of Beck's Beer. The dark kind.

My hosts, Mr and Mrs Benedict Weston, are nothing

if not hospitable. Their casa is my casa.

I was gone a while. Had to check around. Glad to report that all is quiet on the Weston front.

So. Where was I?

Oh, yeah. The girl'd just gotten away from me.

You'd almost think she was meant to escape, the way I got tripped just when I almost had her.

There's a Paul Newman movie, *Somebody Up There Likes Me*.

Somebody up there must like that girl, or she wouldn't be so lucky. That's not a happy thought, is it? If somebody likes *her*, it stands to reason he must be against *me*.

The thing is, luck hasn't gone south on me. Not yet, anyway. Which makes me think maybe God isn't necessarily on her side, after all.

Things've gotten hairy now and then, but so far I remain unshafted.

Of course, I'm not outa here yet.

I seem to be fairly safe, but it ain't over till it's over. Won't be over till I've removed myself from this neighborhood.

If then.

When is anything *really* over?

I'll tell you when it was over for Mr and Mrs Benedict Weston. It ended for them when I tripped by the wall. They were killed by the root that saved the girl.

That's right.

The girl lived, so it's the farm for them.

Funny how things work out, though I don't suppose the Westons would find it all that amusing.

Here's the thing – because I tripped, she made it over the wall. And right on the other side, the place just had to be crawling with firemen and cops. And they had to be awfully curious. Two houses that close together, burning like hell, wouldn't look like an accident to anyone but a moron.

So they're all wondering what's going on, and suddenly a gal comes running and blurts out how one of the bad guys made a grab for her about thirty seconds ago. Where? Just the other side of that wall.

Cops were probably doing sprints for the wall before I even stopped rolling.

My only chance was to run like hell and hope for the best.

I chugged to the bottom of the slope, jumped off some sort of a bank, and ended up in a ditch with rocks at the bottom. The ditch didn't have much of any undergrowth. Mostly it was just a rock bed. Instead of cutting across it, I followed it off to the right.

For one thing, I could make better time on rocks than battling through bushes and that sort of crap. For another, the cops were probably gonna concentrate their search on the area straight downhill from the wall, so a veer off to one side or the other was bound to give me an edge.

You know, it takes the cops a while to get their shit together.

Right off the bat, probably a few of them – two, maybe even four – would've jumped the wall and started searching for me on the slope. But it might be ten minutes, half an hour, who knows how much longer, before a chopper shows up, or before they can get a whole fleet of squad cars out here to hit the area in a big way.

All I had to do was stay away from the first bunch of hot dogs, then make myself invisible for the reinforcements.

That's all.

I figured I didn't stand the chance of a snowman in hell. And my chances, they'd melt down to zilch in about five or ten minutes.

My big plan to go sideways at the bottom of the hill had

started out as a good idea, but it was turning into a bad one fast. So I ran up the bank, put my back to the hillside, and went through the goddamn heart of darkness till I ran smack into a chainlink fence. It went *chinnggg* and bounced me right off it. I landed on my butt, then got up and rushed the fence. Jumped, caught hold, dug in my toes, and climbed it like a chimp.

I was wearing shoes, by the way. We all wear shoes. Nikes, Reeboks, British Knights, L.A. Gears, Converse, and even Keds. We shave all the hair off our bodies (except for our eyebrows and lashes), dress up in our favorite skins, and generally make like a bunch of wild maniacs. But we always wear shoes. You'd be nuts not to.

Going up the fence, I couldn't see anything but darkness in front of me. That didn't make sense. When I got higher, though, I saw a house. Its windows were dark, but that wasn't what had blacked out my view. The thing is, there was a wooden fence about three feet past the chainlink. My guess is that the chainlink was there first, and the Westons (or someone) decided they didn't like being able to see a place behind their house that hadn't been tamed by bulldozers. Maybe it gave them ideas that creepy things might sneak out of the night to come and get them.

Creepy things like me, maybe?

Nah.

In their worst moments, they never imagined someone like *me*.

Anyway, the fences hardly even slowed me down.

I'm no acrobat, but I'm not any slouch, either. At the top of the chainlink, I stood on the iron rail and planted my other foot on the wooden fence. Then I jumped. All of six feet down to the grass on the other side.

I crouched there and wondered what to do next.

Obviously, I wanted to get inside the house.

When we make a foray – that's me and the guys – getting into a house is simple. Tom knows everything there is to know about home security. He checks for alarm systems, then deactivates whatever he finds. Minnow gets us in. Usually, that's a matter of using his glass cutter on a window. It's simple and quiet. (Except when there's an accident, like last night, for instance, when Chuck wasn't paying attention and his ax handle knocked a drinking glass into the kitchen sink – crash!)

Normally, it all works great.

But what I needed to do was disappear, not put a hole in a window for the cops to find.

I could try running around the house and checking all its doors and windows. Some people in L.A. *don't* keep everything locked tight every moment of the day and night. About one in a million, maybe.

Ringing the doorbell wasn't gonna do the trick, either.

The fact is, I couldn't think of *any* way to get inside the house without drawing attention to myself.

For a minute there, I actually considered smashing my way in just so I could get my hands on some car keys and beat it in one of their cars. (A family with a house in a neighborhood like this was bound to have at least two.) I could just see myself roaring away down the road, cop cars coming at me from everywhere. I'd be lucky to get a mile.

Escape by car was out. Hiding in the house was out.

Panic was starting to creep in.

Panic *crashed* in when I heard the helicopter.

Thup-thup-thup-thup.

Maybe the greatest sound in the world if you've been lost at sea for two months in a life raft, drinking nothing but piss and eating your maties.

When you're a killer and you know it's gotta be a cop chopper, the sound cramps your guts. It makes you want to grab your knees and assume a fetal position. Or maybe weep.

Fear is a pretty interesting thing, I've noticed. Some kinds are a great rush. Other kinds are the shits. I'm no expert, but my guess is that it has to do with how much control you've got over the situation. The more control, the better it feels.

When you're me with a cop chopper heading your way, you don't get a dose of the fun fear. You get the bad kind.

Anyway, I looked toward the noise and spotted the chopper. It was cruising low over the crest of the hills, maybe half a mile away, heading for the fires. Its spotlight was white and sent a bright blade slanting down at the ground.

So far, it didn't seem to be searching for me.

That was bound to change fast.

I had to get out of sight.

In the middle of the yard was a lemon tree. The yard also had a patio with a plastic roof, a picnic table, and a couple of lounge chairs where you could sunbathe if it was daylight. I could duck underneath any of those things and hide from the helicopter.

If I wanted to get found, that is.

By this time, the chopper was hovering over the hillside behind the old bag's house.

Looking for me.

I let out a noise like a sick cat and made a dash for a wooden building off to my right. When I got past its corner, I saw the driveway leading up to it from alongside the house. A nice, wide driveway.

This was a two-car garage. Its main door was shut, of course. But over near the corner was a normal, human-sized door.

It swung open without so much as a squeak. I slipped into

the dark and shut it. This place was a lot darker than the night outside. It had windows along one wall, though, and they let in some light. Not much. Dim, gray light that looked dirty. But it was enough to let me see that this was a utility room. It was part of the garage, but separated from the rest by a wall.

The room was sort of long and narrow. Next to me, just inside the door, was a boxy thing that looked like a refrigerator laid on its side. A freezer chest.

I felt around, found its handle, and lifted its lid.

A glare came out that made me squint. Vapor curled up like white smoke. Cold air hit my skin.

I shut the lid fast to cut off the light.

Then I just stood there for a while, nothing to do except listen to the helicopter while my eyes got reacquainted with the dark. Finally, I could see again. There were a couple of wash basins under the windows, plus a washer and drier in the darker area beyond the basins. I headed that way.

Looking for a place to hide.

Could I fit inside the clothes drier? I'm not a big guy, so maybe.

As a last resort, I might've given it a try.

Past the drier, at the very end of the room, a water heater was braced up in the corner. Next to it was a cabinet about five feet wide, with double doors. I tugged the doors. They each gave off a quick little chirpy noise and swung open.

I'd been hoping for an empty space like a closet. What I found were shelves loaded with all kinds of stuff.

What I might do was unload one of the shelves and crawl into the cabinet and shelve *myself*. To make a trick like that work, though, I'd have to pile stuff back up in front of me once I'd gotten inside, or else hide on a shelf above the eye level of the cops who were pretty sure to come looking.

Might work. I stretched up to do some exploring, then stepped on the bottom shelf to give myself more height. And that's when I discovered that the cabinet didn't go all the way to the ceiling.

I climbed higher.

Hanging on with one hand, I used my other hand to explore.

Between the top of the cabinet and the ceiling was a two-foot gap.

Nothing was stored up there. It was empty.

Until I crawled in. (Used the shelves like ladder rungs, and luckily they held. Maybe somebody up there *does* like me.)

Once I got on the top, I curled on my side, reached down and swung the cabinet doors shut. Then I scooted myself back until the rear wall stopped me.

I'd found my perfect hiding place.

It was perfect in terms of hiding, not in terms of comfort. In terms of comfort, it was the shits. Remember, I was naked except for my Reeboks and my little kilt of Connie's hide. For a place like that, I should've been wearing coveralls. Or maybe one of those big white suits that guys wear when they have to mess around with toxic wastes. But all I had was my bare skin and Connie's. Webs clung to me. Spiders dropped on me out of the dark and scurried up my legs and back. They crawled on my face. They got under Connie's skin. It was awful. Spiders give me the creeps, give me goosebumps.

I went to work slapping and rubbing the damn things to oblivion. That was disgusting, too. You could hear them go crunch and feel them turn wet. When you went to brush a body off your skin, it rolled like a booger. Sometimes, it stuck to your finger and you had a hard time flicking it off.

Anyway, I kept busy destroying the spider population while the search went on. Except for the sounds I made, the only other noise came from the helicopter. There were probably *plenty* of other noises, but nothing you could hear. The chopper's roar would fade out, then grow and grow until it shook everything. Sometimes, I thought the damn thing was about to land on me. But then it would fade out again.

It was circling.

Circling and circling and circling. I couldn't see it with my eyes, but in my head I sure could. I saw it circling and circling, the whole time shining its big white beam down at the hillside and the wilds at the bottom of the slope and the back yards and side yards of every house around.

Looking for me, just for me.

The noise alone was enough to drive you crazy.

By now, everybody in the neighborhood was probably wide awake and staring out their windows. They might've slept through the sirens, but you can't sleep through a cop chopper, not unless you're drunk or deaf. Not when it stays and stays, circling and roaring like that.

If you're a regular person, you're pissed because it woke you up. More than pissed, though, you're worried. Because you know it's up there for a reason. You know it's hunting a bad guy.

Which means a bad guy's running around somewhere near your house.

You look out your window. Just how close *is* that chopper? Just how close *is* that bad guy? You pretty much expect to spot somebody running across your yard and you just hope he doesn't try to come in your house.

It sure gives you the creeps.

But hell, you oughta be the guy the chopper is *looking* for.

When you're the one it's after, it stops being anything as normal as a police helicopter. It's more like some kind of monster-machine, like maybe a UFO getting jockeyed around by a team of bozos from outer space that are so mean they'd make your basic Gestapo psychos look like Mary Poppins – and they *know right where the fuck you're hiding*.

Even tucked away in my snug little nook on top of the cabinet where the spotlight had no chance at all of finding me, the chopper made me want to shrivel up and disappear every time it came close.

You won't get away from me! You can't get away from me!

Man!

Anyway, it was kind of freaking me out up there. So sue me. I'd had a hard night.

When all of a sudden a light beam flicked across the ceiling, I thought for a second that the chopper'd found me.

I thought, How'd it get in here?

I almost screamed.

Then someone said, 'Think he's in the freezer?'

'Would *you* hide in a freezer?' the other guy asked.

'Yeah. A night this hot? You bet.'

One of them opened the freezer. I heard it.

The guy who'd said, 'You bet,' said, 'Hey, look. They've got Dove bars.'

'No kidding.' This one sounded like he didn't give a hot hoot for Dove bars.

The chopper was off at a far end of its circle, so I could hear the noises that cops make when they walk. Jostling, squeaking, rattling noises. Their gunbelts are just loaded with every kind of shit imaginable. A walking cop sounds more like a saddle horse than a person.

'Do you want one?' asks the Dove Bar guy.

'No. And neither do you.'

'I want one. They're a lot better than Eskimo . . . Nobody's gonna hide in a washing machine, Pat.'

'No?' I heard a lid squeak open.

'See? Told you.'

'The way that freezer's lighting you up, you'd better hope this lizard doesn't try to cap you.'

'He's not armed. He woulda used it on the kids.'

'You never know. Just shut it, okay?'

'You sure you don't want a Dove bar?'

I heard a quiet grunt. 'Not in the drier.'

'I could've told you that.'

'Oh, you could tell me a lot of things, Hank, but more than a few of them might be wrong. Matter of fact, my second collar was a weenie-wagger I found inside a clothes drier.'

'He fit?'

'Sure. He was a little fella. In every way.' The cop walked closer to me. He sounded like he was almost right underneath me when he stopped. Then the cupboard doors gave their chirping sounds as they came unclamped. 'He'd been entertaining all the gals at the laundromat.' The doors bumped back shut. I heard Pat walking away. 'I just so happened to have a quarter.'

The other cop, Hank, laughed.

'Seemed like a great idea, give him a little spin. But then about two minutes after I dragged him out, he blew his supper all over my back seat.'

'Aw, shit!' Hank went.

'Not shit, puke.'

These guys were a barrel of laughs.

Then they were gone.

I stayed put. Eventually, the helicopter went away. The silence was great. I couldn't feel anything crawling on me. I relaxed and fell asleep.

And slept until Hillary Weston showed up in the morning to do her wash.

Chapter Eleven

When I woke up, a woman was humming in the room down below me. I couldn't see her, though. The edge of the cupboard top was in the way. All I could see was the ceiling. It was sunlit and painted yellow.

I wanted to know what she looked like.

From the sound of her humming, she seemed to be near the washing machine or drier. If she was facing either of those machines, she wouldn't have a view of the cabinet.

So I scooted forward and looked past its edge.

She stood in front of the washer, at an angle that showed me her side and her back. Unless she had tremendous peripheral vision, I was out of sight.

By the time I saw her, she'd already finished throwing in her laundry. She was busy sprinkling detergent powder into the hole at the top of the machine.

She looked good. Slim and not too old. You can't always tell with women, but I'd say she was under thirty by at least a couple of years. She had thick brown hair. Her face had points and corners – cheekbones that stuck out too much, too sharply. A nose and jaw like that, too. Not exactly pretty, but unusual and what you might call 'striking'.

In fact, her whole body was like that.

She wore a bright yellow tank top and red shorts. Her shoulders were bare except for the straps. They had a deep golden tan but looked rather bony. Her butt made me think of the word, 'pouting'. Maybe because it stuck out like the lower lip of a bratty kid. It was small but prominent, and looked solid. Her legs looked hard and glossy as if they'd been carved out of wood.

You don't get a body like that without working for it.

Which meant she was tough-minded, determined, proud. Just my type.

But it also meant she'd be fast and strong.

Taking her would be a risky job, but I knew she'd be worth it.

When she was done with the detergent, she set the box out of the way and shut the top of the washing machine. She turned toward me just a little bit as she reached her right arm across the machine and turned the dial. Her left breast pushed at her tank top. It was like the rest of her – small, compact and pointed.

All of a sudden, I was thinking about the girl from the house. You know, the one that got away.

She was built a little like this one.

She was younger, of course. And much softer, and miles prettier. But the size was about the same.

And I thought how badly I wanted her. I remembered the look and feel of her. And how much trouble she'd caused. And I wondered how to find her.

I was still thinking about those things when water started gushing into the machine and Hillary turned away and walked to the door.

After she was gone, I climbed down off the top of the cabinet. I hung by my fingers, then dropped. Then I hurried and crouched at the end of the freezer.

And waited. You wouldn't believe how hot it was in that place. Sweat dribbled all over me. It tickled. I felt like my whole body'd been oiled, then rolled in a pile of dust and webs and bugs. There were dead spiders smeared all over my chest and arms and legs. Some old blood from the folks last night, too. Plus, I was dotted with lots of red bumps. I itched like crazy.

I could smell my sweat, too. My sweat, and the stale blood.

Usually, I do like the others and lather up. I didn't do it last night, though. A good thing, too. For one, the cops – Hank and Pat – would've caught a whiff of me the second they came through the door.

Maybe I'd better explain. Lathering up is one of the things we do before we start on a foray. It's like actors putting on their makeup before the curtain opens on a play. We do it in Tom's van. That's where we change into our skins, where we arm ourselves, and where we lather up.

We don't lather up with soap. We scoop the stuff out of a big jar and smear ourselves with it. Tom labeled the jar, LUCKY STIFF STUFF. It's just his sense of humor. Inside the jar, what we've got is a portion of someone we've killed.

Killed a while ago.

The stuff is slimy and ripe.

Some of us dab it on like after-shave. Some like to really pile it on. It's pretty disgusting what some of them do with the stuff.

I use it sparingly, myself. A touch here, a spot there.

We do it for good luck. And because the death stench instills fear in the hearts of our enemies. And we also do it just because it's so fucking weird we get a kick out of it.

Anyway, I didn't lather up last night because the trots hit me. Tom's got a toilet in the van. That's where I sat while the others were doing their bit with the jar. By the time I got finished and came out, they'd already left.

Hey, what do you know? I never thought of this till just now – the jerks had gone on ahead to the house to start without me, and then later they drove off without me and left me in this fix. So this was like a preview of coming betrayals.

Anyway, all I wanted to do was catch up. I didn't want to miss out on any of the fun. So I didn't bother gooping myself.

Maybe that saved me.

In fact, I'm sure it did. Those cops that came looking for me in the utility room would've smelled me. I'd be dead right, now if I'd used the Lucky Stiff Stuff. Dead and soon to become my own brand, my own flavor of the week. Simon Scent.

Great. I'm starting to get morbid.

Probably the beer.

Anyway, the thing is, I *didn't* use the stuff, so I didn't stink, so the cops didn't nail me. So there I was hunkered down in the utility room this morning, waiting for Hillary Weston, sweaty and itchy – but stinking of nothing much worse than my own BO.

I sure wished she would hurry back.

After a while, I started thinking about what I'd like to do to her. That got me pretty excited, so basically I forgot about how hot and itchy and miserable I was.

Finally, she came back.

When she walked past me, I stabbed the top of her foot. She wasn't wearing shoes or socks or anything, so my knife went right into her bare skin. She sucked in a big, surprised breath and tried to jump back. Her foot actually jerked up off the floor. It didn't get away, though. All it did was slide a few inches up my knife blade.

Then it was *me* who jerked her foot up. I pulled out the knife while my other hand clutched her ankle and yanked her leg forward and shoved it really high.

She was letting out a squeal until her back slammed the floor. Which knocked her wind out. After that, all she could do was wheeze.

I landed on top of her, sat on her chest, grabbed a handful

of hair to keep her head pinned down, and pushed my blade against her throat. Hard enough to hurt, but not hard enough to cut her.

Next, I asked who was in the house.

She shook her head. She tried to talk, but only choked out some noises. Her chest was pumping fast. It felt good, going up and down under me that way. And I liked how I could feel her shaking.

After a while, she whimpered, 'Please don't hurt me.'

'I don't want to hurt you,' I told her. 'You'll be okay if you do everything I say.'

She nodded hard. She was crying, of course, which didn't improve her looks. I didn't much mind the tears or her red eyes, but the snot sliding out of her nose was pretty gross.

'For starters,' I said, 'who else is in the house?'

She waited too long before answering. Also, during the wait, a change came into her eyes as if a good idea had struck her. 'My husband,' she said. 'He's ... he's home sick from work. He's right inside. He'll be coming out here in a minute. He's a policeman.'

'Liar, liar, pants on fire,' I said.

Then I took my knife away from her throat and jammed it crosswise between her teeth and slashed down, opening both her cheeks with one quick swipe.

She grabbed her face and didn't even seem to care I was stripping off her clothes. She had an all-over tan. Personally, I like finding fresh, white places on a gal. The white shows modesty, a sense of privacy. When I see it, I know I'm being treated to secrets.

There's something hard about an all-over tan. On Hillary Weston; it seemed appropriate.

I would've preferred some pure, white places, but I did enjoy the polished, glossy look of her tan. And the way she squirmed on the floor. And how her tits jiggled. They were small, with brown nipples that reminded me of the suction cups that came on toy arrows when I was a kid.

I used to pluck them off, and whittle points on the arrows with my knife.

I shot a cat named Mickey in the eye with an arrow like that.

You could lick the suction cups and make them stick to your forehead. These looked like they'd been licked and stuck on to the front of Hillary's tits. Neither of them had a socket for the arrow shaft, though; these came to a blunt point instead.

Her skin was hot and smooth and slippery.

She flinched and writhed each time I hurt her.

When she started to scream, I stuffed her panties into her mouth.

It'd take me an hour, maybe, to tell everything I did to her. I know I'd get a kick out of talking about it. Talking about these things is almost as good as living through them again. But a lot needs to be told about other stuff.

I'll cut to what I found most interesting.

Normally, I'm completely focused on the person I'm with. I'm into the moment, you know? I'm not daydreaming. While I did Hillary, though, I made believe she was the girl.

You know, *the* girl. The one who got away.

Hillary vanished. The girl was under me, and I loved every minute of it, every inch of her.

Afterward, I perched on top of the freezer and ate a Dove bar. Then I put Hillary in the freezer.

As much as I hated to expend the effort, I mopped the mess off the floor. Then I left the utility room. The room had been *horribly* hot and stuffy. Outside, the summer breeze felt cool and soft and wonderful.

The back yard was fenced in, completely enclosed and private. Hillary's tan should've been a clue to that. Too bad I hadn't made the connection earlier. I could've dragged her out into the fresh air before indulging.

Oh, well. No great loss.

It would've been much nicer, is all.

While I headed for the back door of the house, I made myself a mental note to do the girl outside. If at all possible.

Even if it required some extra efforts.

The perfect surroundings for the perfect treat.

I entered the house. It was as chilly as a refrigerator. I shivered and got goosebumps. But I took comfort from the knowledge that Hillary in the freezer had it worse than me.

I was fairly confident that her husband was *not* at home, but I went looking anyway. The search turned up nobody. From the looks of things, they didn't have children, either.

I learned their names from subscription labels on magazines in the bathroom.

Benedict and Hillary Weston.

I wondered what the girl's name might be.

Maybe Traci? Kimberly? Lynn? Joan?

I'll find out.

I took a very long, hot shower. The mess sluiced off me. Soaping down, I closed my eyes and pictured myself in the utility room. Not with Hillary, of course, but with my girl.

I wished she was with me in the shower.

And she *will* be with me in a shower. Maybe not today. Maybe tomorrow. We'll take a nice, long shower together *before* I take her outside to do her. That way, she'll be squeaky clean.

She shouldn't be difficult to find.

The way I had it figured, our friendly folks in the news media were sure to give the whole story a big play. They'd tell me the names of the two kids who'd survived last night's ordeal. With a little bit of luck, they might even say where the kids have gone to.

Only one problem.

My 'pals' might get to the girl before me.

Chapter Twelve

It made me sick to think of the others getting to her first. They could have the boy. I didn't give a hot hoot about him. But I wanted the girl for myself.

I *had* to have her, but they'd kill her if they got the chance.

Suddenly, I felt like time was running out. I told myself to calm down. Even if Tom and the others had found out where the kids were, they wouldn't rush into anything.

They're nuts, but they aren't fanatics. They don't want to die for any cause. They just want to enjoy the thrills of making *others* die.

So I tried to calm down. I stayed in the shower, soaping and rinsing, until I felt completely clean. Then I stepped out and dried myself on a thick, soft towel. It was a little bit moist when I pulled it off the rod. You'd think it would've gone into the wash with the other stuff. But maybe Hillary'd planned to wash it in the next load.

I hoped she'd been the one who made it wet.

The idea of rubbing myself with her towel was kind of appealing. What part of herself had she wiped with this section of the towel – with this?

It was disgusting, though, to imagine it might be her husband's towel. What if he'd dried his cock or ass with the same part of it I was using on my face?

Not a pretty thought.

I searched the towel for clues. Sniffed it, studied it for telltale hairs.

Wherever we go, we leave pieces of ourselves behind.

That's why the cops go over crime scenes so carefully, gathering up everything, even vacuuming. They're looking for what we've left of ourselves. Not just fingerprints or footprints, but bits of us. They want shreds of fabric from our clothes. They want samples of our spit, blood and semen. They want the specimens of our skin scraped off by the fingernails of our prey. And, oh yeah, they very much want our hair.

It's all physical evidence, and physical evidence is what makes convictions.

Our little gang wants to avoid being identified, much less convicted, so we do our best not to provide any physical evidence. Even though we don't wear gloves (they're like condoms and screw up the feel of things), we're very careful to wipe whatever we touch. We leave our civilian clothes in the van. Except for our shoes, we don't wear anything into the house except whatever we've tailored out of someone else's skin. The outfits *always* include scalp or pubic hair of the person who originally wore the skin. Like I said earlier, we go in with no hair of our own except our eyebrows and lashes. So any other sorts of hair we leave behind won't belong to us.

To protect ourselves against traces of us we might deposit on or inside the bodies of our victims, we simply take the bodies away in the van. We have other reasons to take them. But the effect is the same: they aren't left behind to give away information about us.

Last but not least, we burn the scene of the crime. We use delaying devices to start the fires. That way, we've got time to make a getaway ahead of the fire trucks.

Nothing cleans like fire.

But just in case the fire might go out or be extinguished too fast, or otherwise not destroy the area, we leave little or nothing of ourselves behind. What we leave, if anything, is more likely to confuse the cops than enlighten them.

For instance, strands of hair from the head of a drifter we picked up on Mulholland last year. Or fingerprints from the pretty young kindergarten teacher who was last seen going to her car after a midnight showing of *The Rocky Horror Show*. (The trick's in Tom's Fabulous Fingertip Gloves.)

You can see, we're like NASA. We've got loads of backup systems, failsafe systems – *redundancy!*

We leave behind nothing to incriminate us.

Except this time a couple of witnesses!

Oh, well, they'll be taken care of. By me, I hope. The girl, at least. Like I say, they can have the boy. A couple of the guys would *prefer* him, if you know what I mean. No sexual discrimination here. We're equal opportunity killers.

Anyway, to get back to the point, I found a curly brown pubic hair on the towel I was using after my shower. It matched Hillary. Unfortunately, though, I didn't know Benedict's hair color.

And didn't want to know, frankly. I told myself that this was Hillary's pubic hair and her towel. Then I finished drying.

After that, I cleaned off my Connie kilt. I hadn't worn it into the shower. You know, you don't want to wash fine leather with hot water. I'd previously treated it with a conditioner and water-repellent lotion, so a damp washcloth took off most of the blood and grime.

I didn't put the kilt back on, of course. To get home without being stopped, I'd need to wear something just slightly less conspicuous.

Conventional clothes. And hair, if possible.

The cops had to know, by now, that my head was shaved. There was probably an APB – 'Be on the lookout for chrome-domes.' They might even have roadblocks.

You might think this head-shaving thing is pretty stupid. We're so careful not to leave traces behind, but then we go wandering around with bald pates, and you can't make yourself much more conspicuous than that.

Actually, though, there's a much more basic reason for shaving our heads. The reason has nothing to do with being careful about physical evidence. I'll get to it later, if I have time. It would take a lot of explaining.

For now, let's just say that having a bald head usually presented no problem for us. That's because we always made sure nobody saw us during a foray and survived.

We sure had survivors this time, though. So my bare crown could get me killed.

I went searching through the master bedroom. I wanted to find a wig. No such luck.

In a drawer of the bedstand, though, I did find a .45 caliber Colt Mark IV. It was the government model, a black (actually, they call it Colt blue) semi-automatic. Two loaded magazines were in the drawer with it.

I would've preferred finding a wig.

Firearms make too much noise. And killing with a gun – it's interesting and not entirely bland, but it doesn't give you the real joy and satisfaction that you get from using other means.

We all have our favorite methods. Only Dusty prefers guns.

I figured this was an emergency, though. I was in sort of a fix, and a .45 might be my ticket out.

If only I had a good head of hair to go with it . . .

I'm not a great original thinker, but all of our bunch read horror novels. Generally, they aren't very scary. They're just pretend, after all, and we've done stuff for real that makes most of the fiction seem pretty tame. But we get a bang out of them for a lot of other reasons, and we study them for new ideas. Like I said earlier, the whole idea for our gang came from some old horror novel. Today, a book I'd read last year is what gave me the answer to my hair problem.

The answer, of course, was Hillary.

Me and my knife paid a visit to the freezer.

She hadn't frozen yet.

I took her scalp along with the hair, so I could wear it like a cap.

Then it was time for another shower. I took my new wig in with me, and shampooed it. After drying it a bit with a towel, I tried it on. Too small. But a couple of cuts up the sides loosened it. I put it on again. It was maybe a little *too* loose, but it would have to do.

I kept it on and used a blow drier on it. I brushed it, fluffed it up. In no time at all, the hair looked great.

It would've looked great on a gal, anyway. It made *me* look like some sort of a fruitcake – like a rock star or one of those 'shock radio' freaks.

People were bound to stare at a *guy* in this sort of hair.

Well, I would be wearing Hillary's hair so why not wear her clothes, too?

The cops certainly weren't looking for a woman.

I would transform myself from Simon into Simone.

Even though the wig felt rather nasty on my head, I kept it on while I went hunting for the proper attire. The hair was dry, but not the scalp. It felt like I'd peeled the skin off a raw chicken breast and slapped it on my skull. Not very pleasant. But I was afraid that if I took it off, it might dry and shrink, and maybe even stiffen in a way that would screw up its fit. Besides, I was Simone, now. Simone had lush, brown tresses.

Soon, she'd be gorgeous. Or at least not so obviously a man.

As it turned out, Benedict's clothes wouldn't have fit me anyway. He was a lot bigger than Hillary, whereas she was just my size.

I found a most alluring pair of panties. They were royal blue and shiny, with little more to them than a stripper's g-string. Wearing those and the hair and nothing else, I looked positively alarming.

The addition of pantyhose made me look like a fellow I'd seen one night when an old girlfriend dragged me to *Swan Lake*. Oh, how merrily he'd leaped and pranced!

I wanted to throw a chair through the bedroom mirror. But broken mirrors are supposed to bring bad luck. This particular mirror was the size of the closet door, so it'd probably bring more than the usual seven years. I needed all the luck I could get, so I let it alone.

I could've just turned away from the mirror, of course. I didn't. As much as I hated the ludicrous images it tossed back at me, they intrigued me.

When I put on the bra, the mirror suddenly became my friend. The bra matched the panties. I wadded tissues into balls, and stuffed its flimsy cups. No longer did I look like a dancing fairy. Now, I was a woman.

Simone.

For a while, she turned me on. Why not admit it? Hell, I've admitted a few other things this afternoon, huh?

I loved the look of her. I posed, studying her from every angle. I caressed her. She was me, of course – I'm not crazy.

But I do have a pretty good imagination, so I found it easy to pretend she was a stranger. A beauty, too.

When I squeezed her tits and the nice pert cups of the bra collapsed, the feel of the mashing wads of Kleenex put a damper on my excitement. I got on with business.

I went looking for a skirt.

Young gals in LA hardly ever wear skirts. They wear shorts or jeans or sweatpants. Which is fine with me. I'm not one of those ancient farts who thinks a gal isn't feminine except if she has a skirt on. The trend makes me curious, though. I like to wonder about the whys of things.

The real difference – the *central* difference between pants and skirts – probably the only difference that counts in a sunny climate – is that skirts are open between the legs, while pants have a cloth barrier there.

Are skirts avoided for no other reason than because they don't have that barrier?

And what would that mean or signify?

Do the gals feel safer, more protected, when access is restricted? I know I feel vulnerable when I wear my Connie kilt. That doesn't bother me, though. It adds to the thrill. But maybe on a day to day basis, you'd rather have the safe, sheltered, enclosed feeling you get with pants.

Anyway, who knows the real reasons for anything?

What I knew was that I wanted to wear one of Hillary's skirts or dresses. Maybe for a lot of reasons. But it would've been dumb for me to pose as a female – hair, pantyhose, bra, etc – only to face the world in a pair of jeans or shorts.

I needed the total, complete effect.

Nobody seeing me should have to wonder even for an instant whether I'm a gal or just a long-haired geek.

I finally chose a pale blue, denim skirt that hung loosely to mid-thigh, and a bright yellow blouse. The blouse had sleeves that ended at my forearms with wide, floppy cuffs. It buttoned up the front. I left the top buttons undone to catch the eyes of the fellows. In the mirror, I actually appeared to have cleavage – an effect of the bra, maybe. The bra, by the way, could be seen through the fabric of the blouse.

My Adam's apple was so insignificant that I didn't bother tying a scarf around my neck. Cross-dressers *always* try to hide their throats. It's such a giveaway. But then, it's probably necessary if you look like you've swallowed Mount Shasta.

I used an electric shaver to take a day's growth of whiskers off my face, then added a few touches of makeup.

Last but not least, I slipped my feet into a pair of bright, white tennis shoes.

Then I checked myself out in the mirror. Terrific! Simone was a masterpiece. She looked cute, confident, carefree, casual but well off. The sort of woman who maybe had played some tennis this morning, and was now on her way to run a few chores before lunching with 'the girls' at the club.

She didn't look like a Simone, though. More like a Doris or a June. Which was no problem at all.

Happy with my new appearance, I loaded the Colt. I carried it and the spare magazine into the kitchen. Earlier, I'd spotted Hillary's purse there on the counter in front of the radio.

Her car keys and billfold were inside the purse. I added the gun and magazine, slung the leather strap over my shoulder, and went out the back door to the garage.

The garage door didn't have any remote control opener that I could find. But it slid without any trouble when I dragged it sideways by the handle.

Hillary's car was not inside the garage.

In fact, the two-car garage looked as if it was being used to store everything *but* cars.

No car was parked in the driveway, either.

That's all right, I told myself. It's probably on the street.

I went through the house and looked out its front window. The Westons had a very large lawn, all neatly trimmed. Beyond the lawn was a stretch of curb long enough to hold four parked cars. And four cars were parked there. The curb on the far side of the street was empty – a sure sign that this was street cleaning day for that side. Everyone had scrambled for places over here.

Great.

Four cars in front of Hillary's house.

One or more of them almost *had* to belong to the Westons.

Likely just one, though. The others probably belonged to neighbors.

It would behoove me to approach the right car on the first try.

The key ring from Hillary's purse held eight keys, including two sets of car keys. The car keys were branded with the manufacturers' names: Chrysler and Jaguar.

From the window, I could see that none of the four in front of the Weston house was a Jaguar. So the Jag would have to be Benedict's car, which he'd driven to work.

I recognized one of the four as a Porsche, another as a Volvo. The remaining two looked nondescript. I'm no car expert, but I figured one of them almost *had* to be Hillary's Chrysler.

I hurried outside and across the lawn. From the sidewalk, I checked out the two mystery cars: a Honda and a Toyota.

The nearest Chrysler vehicle was parked on the other side of the Weston driveway, beyond not only their driveway but past a Toyota, a VW Rabbit, and a Ford pickup.

The shiny, blue Chrysler Imperial was parked with its bumper no more than a yard short of the neighbor's driveway.

Would Hillary have parked *this* far from her house?

Not damn likely.

Especially not when she and her Benedict owned a perfectly good, empty driveway.

This was almost for sure *not* her car.

It was the only Chrysler anywhere near their house, though. Maybe Hillary had a reason for parking it here. She might've picked up something at the store for her neighbor, parked here to drop it off, and then walked home instead of bothering to move the car.

Something like that. Life is odd. Who knows?

If this *was* her car, I could be on my way in a few seconds. If it wasn't, then somebody might see a woman trying to unlock a car that didn't belong to her. Or an alarm might start blaring.

I decided to take the risk.

Keys ready, I stepped around the rear of the Chrysler, walked on the street to its driver's door, and plugged a key into the lock. It slid right in. But it wouldn't turn. I tried the other Chrysler key. It also fit into the slot, but refused to budge when I tried to twist it.

So far, no car alarm had killed the morning quiet. Nobody had yelled at me, either.

I pulled out the key, stepped back, then frowned and shook my head for the benefit of anyone who might be spying on me from one of the houses. Then I stepped around to the back of the car, peered at the license plate, shook my head again and walked away, trying to look puzzled.

I returned to the Weston house.

And that is where I still am.

Chapter Thirteen

Where the hell is Hillary's car?

In the shop? Maybe it'd gotten recalled for faulty brakes or something. Maybe somebody stole it. Maybe she'd loaned it to a friend.

Maybe God, wanting to shaft yours truly, had DISAPPEARED the damn thing!

Anyway, wherever it might be, I couldn't find it.

So I sat on a sofa in the living room and did some thinking.

I wanted to get out of the neighborhood. I wanted to track down that girl, beat the others to her. But most of all, I wanted the cops not to get me.

If they got me, I was a dead man.

Not that they'd shoot me down in cold blood, nothing like that. No matter what everybody says, the LAPD doesn't go around murdering people or beating them up for no reason. If you don't try to fight them, they take you into custody without roughing you up at all.

I would have to *make* them shoot me.

If I shoot, they'll shoot.

You see, the main rule of our little group is that we do not get taken alive. There's a simple reason for that: anyone taken into custody might squeal on the others.

Nobody wants to get squealed on.

So nobody gets taken alive. If we can't escape from the cops, we're obligated to shoot it out to the end, or commit suicide.

There's too much of a penalty for being taken alive.

It's a death penalty. You give yourself up, everybody in

your family dies. Your parents, your wife, your children. Your girlfriend, if you're not married.

In my case, they would kill my fiancée, Lisa; my sisters, Sandy and Dora; probably their husbands, Steve and Gary; and most definitely my niece, Sue, and my two nephews, Randy and Dan.

Sounds a bit extreme, huh?

It's supposed to be. It's supposed to make us die if we have to.

On the bright side, though, it has never been done.

So far, the threat's been enough.

Because you know they'll do it. They'll *enjoy* it, too. You know damn well what they do to people and how much they enjoy it (because you've done it yourself), so the idea that the object of the fun might be your mother, your girlfriend, your child – is just really appalling. You *would* rather die, yourself, than put someone you love through anything even close to such horrors.

Bill Peterson is the only guy who's had to make the choice.

It happened a few years ago, over in New Mexico. The rest of us got away clean, but Bill got caught. He was cornered in an alley, and he'd lost his weapon. So the cops just cuffed him and read him his rights. I was hiding across the street, and saw him get put into the car. It gave me a sick feeling. But it also made me hope that he *wouldn't* make the sacrifice. Because if he failed, I'd get to do things to his sister, Donna. Things I'd wanted to do for a long time.

Bill made the right choice, though. When they uncuffed him at the station to fingerprint him, he went crazy. He grabbed a cop's gun and got himself pulverized.

After his death, I ended up spending a lot of time with Donna. You know, comforting her. We went together for a while, and I finally got to screw her. It was no big deal, though. It never is. There has to be the rest of it, or it's just pretty much of a bore.

Anyway, Bill's the only one of us who ever had to take the hard way out.

I've got no intention of being number two.

Which means I've got to stay clear of the cops.

With Hillary's Chrysler gone, things didn't look tremendously bright for my future.

I sat on the sofa and went over my options. Here are a few of them: I could walk away, call a taxi, or steal a neighbor's car.

Any of those choices, though, would expose me to a lot of risk.

If I hiked out of the neighborhood, I'd be in public view for a long period of time. People would see me. People might even talk to me. Up close, somebody might just notice that I'm not a woman. Walking was out. Too much could go wrong.

A taxi ride would expose me too much to the driver. The cops were sure to track him down, sooner or later, and ask him about me. Of course, I could kill him after we get where we're going. In broad daylight in LA? Thanks, but no thanks.

If I tried to hotwire a car, somebody might report me to the cops. Hotwiring wasn't my style, anyway. No. What I would do, instead, is ring a neighbor's doorbell, pass myself off as Hillary's sister, get myself inside, and let some blood. Drive off properly, with a key in the ignition. Once again, though, the risk outweighed the gain. When you enter someone's house with murder on your mind, you're walking into a minefield. No telling how many people might be inside, or how they might explode. Great if there's six or eight of you. Not so great when you're just one guy.

When it came right down to it, I actually had no safe course of action.

But my instincts told me to sit tight. Sooner or later, Benedict Weston would be swinging his Jaguar into the driveway, home from a hard day at the office. He'd walk into the house. I'd kill him with my knife, take his keys and drive off into the sunset.

That was my plan.

It's still my plan.

I'm still waiting.

Once I'd made up my mind to stay, I turned my attention to matters that didn't have anything to do with escaping. First, I searched for *The Times*. Couldn't find it, though. The newspaper must've gone the way of Hillary's Chysler.

So I made coffee, then threw together a breakfast of bacon and eggs (over medium), and English muffins. While I ate, I listened to the radio.

News on the hour gave a report of last night's adventure. And what a report!

Basically, it said that two house fires, late last night, had claimed the lives of four people in the Avalon Hills section of Los Angeles. In one house, a family of three had perished. The family of six that normally lived in the other house had been vacationing at the time, so the one fatality at that place had been the elderly mother of the owner. According to the reporter, arson investigators had gone to the scene.

Nothing about two kids surviving.

Nothing about murder.

Nothing about *us*.

At first, I thought maybe the kids hadn't talked. They'd talked, though. Otherwise, why would the report tell about people perishing? Without help from the kids, nobody would know anyone had been inside either of the houses last night.

Tom and the guys did *not* leave any bodies behind. That just wasn't the way we did things. Even though I hadn't been there to see it, I *knew* they'd taken the bodies. So the kids had told, all right.

Probably told everything they knew.

And the cops must've decided to keep the truth to themselves.

Maybe they figured it might start a panic if people found out a group of wildmen was breaking into homes and committing wholesale slaughter.

Maybe they planned to hide the facts till after they caught us.

Or maybe they hadn't believed the kids. Would *you* believe a wild story about a neighborhood in LA getting invaded by a pack of half-naked, hairless men with knives, spears, axes and sabers? The cops might even think the kids made up the whole business to save their own hides. Maybe they thought the kids were the ones who'd burnt the houses.

If the cops had already searched through the rubble and not turned up any bodies, they might not know *what* to make of the whole deal.

Then again, maybe they'd believed every word spoken by the kids, and had given the news folks a twisted version for the sake of protecting them. You don't want to go around advertising that you've got eye-witnesses to a mass murder. Not when the killers are still at large. Not if you want to keep your witnesses alive.

Who knows? All sorts of possibilities.

To me, though, there were two really major things about the news story. First, it hadn't alerted the whole world to be on the lookout for bald-headed maniacs. Second, it hadn't given me the name of the girl.

It hadn't given her name to me, and it hadn't given it to *them*, either.

Every so often, I've taken breaks from taping these memoirs, and listened to different radio and television stations. Instead of expanding as more details became available (as reporters snooped), the stories shrank. Very strange. Very suspicious. For whatever reason, it looks like a lid has been clamped down on the story.

Just a few minutes ago, the five o'clock news on KNBC said only that arson was suspected in a pair of house fires that occurred overnight in the exclusive Avalon Hills section, taking four lives.

Thanks to the lid, there's been no mention at all of the boy or girl. No mention of butchery or a gang of ruthless cut-throats.

This is good, but also bad.

I might still have a chance to find the girl first.

If Benedict ever gets home from his damn job!

I've decided to hang around here till nine. If he hasn't shown up by then, too bad. It's *adios*, anyway. I'll go ahead and phone for a cab.

In the meantime, it's just me and Mr Sony. That's my brand of cassette recorder. Not *my* brand, theirs. The Westons'. I've been giving it quite a workout today with this little adventure in oral history. My memoir, my confession, the true account of my dastardly deeds.

Why am I doing it, you might ask?

And who are you, you that's right now listening to this? A cop? A court reporter transcribing it for the prosecutor? Maybe you're Tom or Mitch or all the boys at once, listening in unison in Tom's garage. Maybe you're me. Maybe no one will ever hear these tapes. Are you no one?

If you're someone – and you must be, or you wouldn't be

listening – then you might be wondering why I made these tapes at all.

Why am I telling?

Why oh why oh why?

Why is Hillary's Chrysler missing?

Why did that fucking root trip me when the girl was in easy reach?

Why anything?

To be less obtuse and more to the point, however, why did my fellow Krulls drive off and abandon me?

Ah, yes, that might be the rub right there!

If I'm expendable, maybe they are, too.

Maybe this is how I protect myself and my people. I hide these tapes somewhere, then let it be known that they'll end up in the hands of the cops if any reprisals are made.

Works in the movies all the time.

Just for the hell of it, here goes a membership list. This is it – the Club, the Secret Society, Our Gang, the Krulls – the name of everyone who's ever been one of us:

> Tom Baxter – our fearless leader
> Charles 'Chuck' Sarnoff
> James 'Mitch' Mitchell
> Terrance 'Ranch' Watkins
> Brian 'Minnow' Fisher
> Clement Calhoun
> Lawrence 'Dusty' Rhodes
> Bill Peterson (the late)
> Dale Preston (the late)
> Frank 'Tex' Austin (the late)
> Tony 'Private' Majors (the late)
> Simon Quirt (yours truly)

That's us. The full complement, the roll call, the living and the dead.

Quite a few of us have bit the dust along the way, it seems. Good fellows, all. Good and perverted.

Uh-oh.

I hear something.

I hear a *car*!

There is a powerful, grumbly engine on the beast.

Sounds like the car might very well be a Jaguar.

Hmm. Silence.

Hear that? A car door going thud.

Benedict is here, I do believe.

Just for laughs, I'll leave the recorder going. Maybe it'll pick up the fun and games.

Shhh.

I hear footsteps. A key is going into the front door.

Stay tuned, folks.

'Oh, hello. You must be Benedict.'

'Uh, yes. Uh . . .'

'Doris. Doris Knight. Hillary mentioned that you might be along any minute.'

'Oh? Where is she?'

'Oh, she's indisposed at the moment.'

'Indisposed?'

'The little girl's room. *You* know.'

'Oh. Yeah. Well . . .'

'I just stopped by to chat for a while. I'm so new on the block, and I said to myself, "Self, you ought to go around and meet your new neighbors." So here I am. Hillary was just telling me about her car troubles. Horrible.'

'Yeah. The thing was supposed to be ready yester . . . Hillary . . . she has a blouse just exactly like that one.'

'Really? Did she buy hers at Nordstroms?'

'That purse is just ... What's going on here? That *is* her purse. Hillary! *Hillary!*'

'It is her purse, Benedict. It's her blouse, too. And her skirt. Her *everything*. For heaven's sake, this is even Hillary's *hair!* Catch!'

'*Ahhhhhh! Ahh! Ahhhhhh!*'

'Hey, shut up!'

'*Ahhhhh!*'

'Simon says "shut up". And so does Samuel Colt.'

'*Uh. Uh-uh.*'

'Shhhhh.'

'*Uhhh.*'

'Okay, that's better. Now pick up the hair and bring it back over here ... Thank you. Now, get down on your knees.'

'*Puh – pleeeeze!*'

'Simon says get down on your knees.'

'*Don't shoot me. Pleeeeze!*'

'Oh, I wouldn't do that. Too noisy. And not much fun, really. I'll do you with this little baby here.'

'*No. No! Put that ... Don't! I'll do anything. Pleee ...* EEAWWWAHHHH! BLUHHAWWW! EEEEEEE! EEEEEEEEEEE! EEEUHGGUG! UH.'

'Shit. Now I have to change my clothes.'

PART THREE

Witness Protection

Chapter Fourteen

Jody woke up in her own bedroom. She wasn't under the covers, though. She lay on top, dressed in shorts and a blouse instead of her nightshirt, warm rays of sunlight slanting across her legs. The light was golden, afloat with drifting motes.

She knew it must be late afternoon.

Suddenly, she remembered Evelyn getting hoisted high in the dark doorway.

On the edge of remembering more, she sat up fast. And groaned as a legion of sharp pains and dull aches scaled her body. She hurt *everywhere*.

At least I'm alive, she thought.

With that, she fell off the edge, plunged into an abyss where images of slaughter flashed through her mind.

To stop them, she scurried off her bed. She winced when her feet hit the floor, and realized they were bandaged beneath her white crew socks. She dropped backward onto the mattress to get the weight off her feet. And her *rump* sang with pain. It wasn't a terrible pain, but a peculiar sort that gave her a lump in the throat and made her eyes water.

When the hurting faded, she took a deep breath and wiped her eyes.

'You must be a hell of an engineer,' the ER nurse had told her. He was a nurse, but a man. He had reminded her very much of Mr Rogers. Fred, not Roy or Will. Fred Rogers, who always had beautiful days in his neighborhood. The nurse had the look, and also the sing-song voice.

'A what?' she'd asked. 'An engineer?'

The nurse gave her a big smile. 'Because you're such a ramblin' wreck.'

'Oh,' Jody had said.

That was somewhat later, of course. The doctor had already been in, by then, and left. There'd been nothing at all cheerful or dopey about the doctor. He'd reminded Jody of Mr Green, her social studies teacher. He'd scowled at her chart, then scowled into her eyes, then said, 'Let's have a look at the damage, young lady.'

Time to get naked. Dad, obligingly, made himself scarce by swaggering to the other side of the partition.

'Let me see, now,' the doctor had said. 'What have we here?' He'd then commenced to do more than simply look at the damage. He'd prodded it, stroked it and squeezed it, muttering all the while. 'Uh-huh. Uh-huh. Hmmm. Does it hurt when I do this? Uh-huh. Yes. Hmmm.' And finally, he'd pronounced, 'Well, you'll live. I'd say you've got nothing more serious here than your standard, garden-variety assortment of nicks, scrapes and bruises. I'll have a few words with your father. In the meantime, we'll have Nurse Gumbol in here to patch you up, then you'll be free to go.'

Exit the doctor. Enter Nurse Gumbol, who was pretty handsome, actually, even if he did remind Jody of Mr Rogers. Handsome *and* young. Enough of both so that her skin flushed red all the way down to her toes. He'd said, 'Oh, please, don't be embarrassed, deary. I've seen it all, if you know what I mean. Though you *are* my first engineer of the day. I can see just by looking that you must be a *hell* of an engineer.'

'A what? An engineer?'

'Because you're such a ramblin' wreck.'

Then he had gotten to work with antiseptic and bandages. First he'd done her front. Then she had rolled over so he could patch her back. He'd saved her feet for last. He'd never stopped talking.

Jody couldn't remember much of what he'd said, but did recall that it had mostly been cheerful and fairly lame. A nice guy, but *gosh*.

One thing he had said was, 'Next time you go up against Green Bay, wear padding.'

In the car on the way home, she and Andy in the back seat, Dad behind the wheel, she'd asked, 'Hey, what's Green Bay?'

'A city in Wisconsin. I suppose it's on Lake Michigan.'

'The nurse said I should wear pads when I go there. Or something like that.'

At that, Dad had looked over his shoulder and smiled. 'Back in olden times, when I was just a kid, the Green Bay Packers under Vince Lombardi was the best football team in the world. I believe the nurse was making a joke about the vast extent of your injuries.'

'Doesn't he *know* what happened to me?'

'He knows you were fleeing assailants. That's all we gave out about either one of you.'

'Did you have the guy that looks like Mr Rogers?' Andy had asked her.

'Yeah. He was nice, wasn't he?'

'Yeah.' Then, as if the simple idea of someone being nice was too much for him to bear, Andy's face had crumpled. Jody had put her arms around him and embraced him while he cried.

He'd been asleep by the time they'd reached home. Instead of waking him, Dad had come around to the car's back door and lifted Andy out and carried him into the house.

Jody hadn't planned to take a nap, herself. She'd been very tired, but what she'd really wanted was to change into normal clothes, then go to her father and be with him. Sit with him and maybe have some breakfast, and talk, and look at him, and just *be* close to him where it was safe.

She must've stretched out on her bed, though, and shut her eyes.

And then she must've slept for hours and hours.

No wonder, she thought. I sure didn't get much sleep last night.

Last night. The hallway. Her glimpse into the master bedroom. All those men. All that blood. The upsidedown head . . .

She sprang up and hurried across her bedroom, grimacing, gritting her teeth. The bottoms of her feet felt raw, but the padding of bandages and socks helped. Her good Reebok running shoes would cushion her feet even more.

In her closet, searching for them, she remembered that she had worn them to Evelyn's house.

They'd been brand new. Bright white with pink laces, so soft and squishy and cozy inside, and it had been wonderful how they made each step feel springy.

Gone. Burnt.

She felt the loss as a tight lump in her throat.

Silly, she told herself. They're just shoes.

She slipped her feet into her moccasins, instead. As she left her room and walked down the hallway, she realized she had also lost her Eeyore socks.

My Eeyore socks.

Losing them hurt. Her eyes stung. She knew it was silly to cry over lost socks, but they'd been a gift picked for her specially by Dad and they'd been Eeyore, Pooh's poor, melancholy friend who always, always seemed to be the victim of life's unfairness. You had to feel sorry for him. You wanted to comfort and protect him.

If only she'd worn her Tigger socks to Evelyn's yesterday. She wouldn't have minded – not much, anyhow – Tigger getting burnt. But poor Eeyore . . .

She stopped thinking about her socks when she found Andy asleep on the living-room sofa. He was covered to the shoulders with a blanket. All she could see of him was the shape of his body curled under the blanket, and the light brown hair on the back of his head.

He looked very small.

He looked very alone.

He's got me, Jody told herself.

I saved him. All by myself, I saved him. He's only alive today because of me.

She realized he wasn't just Andy, Evelyn's pesky little brother, anymore. Because she had saved him, he was now a lot more than that.

Like my own brother.

That's what she thought for a moment as she stared at him. She had no brother, so she didn't know how she might feel toward one. But the notion that he was now like her own brother seemed off. Somehow wrong.

Not like he's my brother, like he's my child.

The idea seemed outlandish. But somehow right. This was probably nothing at all like being a real mother, but she was the *cause* of Andy being alive just as surely as if she *had* given birth to him.

Whatever might happen to him from now on, whether good or bad, would only occur because she had led him out of the house last night.

How weird.

Weird, but nice.

Jody went to him. She bent over him and looked down at him sleeping. His breath made quiet sounds. Gently, she stroked his hair.

'You and me, kid,' she whispered.

'Careful you don't wake him,' came a whisper from behind her.

The voice in the silence startled her, but it was a good and comfortable voice. She looked around and saw her father under the arched entryway to the dining room. A corner of his mouth was stretched sideways. His usual smirk, but not really a smirk. Not a reflection of his attitude, at all, but the permanent effect of his encounter with a .22 caliber bullet that had penetrated his skull. The bullet had done remarkably little damage. Its scars were hidden under his hair. On its way through his brain, however, the little slug had rewired the right side of his face. When he was serious, he seemed to be smirking. When he was happy, his face wore a big, lopsided grin that made him look quite goofy.

To Jody's way of thinking, the bullet had improved her father's appearance.

According to a book she had read, everyone in the world looks like either a pig or a weasel. One or the other. But her father didn't fit the pattern. The animal he resembled was a gorilla.

Before the shooting, he'd looked less like a cop than like a creep you might see on the television show, *America's Most Wanted*.

Which had never seemed fair at all.

Though he'd looked downright thuggish, he was more sensitive and compassionate and gentle and sweet than any man Jody had ever known. So the bullet had come like an artist from God to correct a mistake, to give his mouth a cheery upward turn.

Some people seemed to think that the constant smile made him look eerie. Not Jody, though. She considered it a major improvement.

The street lizards had dubbed him 'Smiley'. His nickname among the boys at the station was 'Kong'.

He was standing under the archway with a can of Bud in one big hand.

He wore baggy, tan shorts, white crew socks, and blue Nike running shoes. His T-shirt was neatly tucked in beneath the waistband of his shorts.

Yosemite Sam, emblazoned on the T-shirt, had both sixguns drawn and blazing. Parts of the *hombre* were hidden from sight, however, by the leather straps of a shoulder holster. The holster, flat against the left side of his ribcage, held his 9 mm Browning.

The sight of the Browning gave Jody a hot, squirmy feeling.

Normally, she felt comfortable about firearms. They were part of her father's job. No big deal. She even had her own .22, and loved to go out shooting with it.

But Dad didn't normally carry while having a beer in the late afternoon in his T-shirt and shorts in his own home.

That was eerie.

She reached down to pat Andy's hair again, then thought better of it. Let him sleep. The more he slept, the better.

She turned away from him and walked slowly toward her father. She tried not to hobble. She tried not to wince. Dad couldn't stand pain – not when it belonged to Jody.

'We can talk in the kitchen,' he whispered.

She walked behind him through the dining room and into the kitchen. She walked; he swaggered. The swagger, like his smirk, had nothing to do with a macho attitude. The swagger had a lot to do with a high-speed chase that had ended in a collision. Though he'd regained full use of his legs, the nature of their stride had been changed for ever.

'Get yourself a Pepsi,' he said.

She opened the refrigerator door. 'Want another beer?'

'Sure, why not?'

She pulled out a cold Pepsi for herself, a Bud for him. She carried them to the table, where Dad had already seated himself with his back to the wall.

He *always* sat with his back to a wall.

In college, he used to sit with his back to the wall. Jody's mother had often told about it. The first time she'd seen him, he'd been sitting with his back to a wall in the student union, drinking a Pepsi and reading an 87th Precinct novel by Ed McBain. Here was a guy who looked like a grouchy ape, and was therefore no doubt a mindless jock, reading a book. Not a textbook, either. A mystery. Reading it, seemingly, for the joy of reading. Intrigued by the shocking contradiction between his appearance and behavior, she'd gone to his table, sat down, and introduced herself.

Kate Monroe.

Jack Fargo.

Jack Fargo. Who had, among other things, two lists of heroes. Fictional heroes and real life heroes. At the top of his fiction list was Steve Carella. His real life list was headed by James Butler Hickok.

Hickok, who always sat with his back to the wall.

Except once. Once in Deadwood, while playing poker, while holding aces and eights, he'd violated his rule. Jack McCall had plugged him from behind and killed him.

According to Mom, Dad had actually said, 'If Wild Bill had followed his own rules and kept a wall to his back, he'd be alive today.'

'But he might be too old to know the difference,' Mom

had quipped, and they'd both suddenly cracked up laughing. By the time the laughter had stopped, according to both of them, they knew they were in love.

The 'back to the wall' principle had been so much a part of Jody's life that she'd gotten into the habit, herself. Except when Dad was around. Then, he got the wall seat. And that was fine. Jody never felt the need to have her back protected when he was nearby.

She sat down, slid the Bud across the table to him, and snapped open the top of her Pepsi.

'Did you sleep all right?' he asked.

She nodded.

'How's it going?'

'Okay, I guess.'

'You got banged up pretty good.'

'I'll say.'

'The doctor says you'll be fine, though.'

'Yeah, he told me.'

'Anyway, we still need to keep an eye on things. You've got to let me know if anything's wrong.'

'What do you mean?'

'Like if you get dizzy spells, blurred vision, headaches, any sort of unusual pains or bleeding. Just don't keep something like that to yourself.'

'Okay.' She took a drink of the Pepsi. It was cold and sweet, and tasted great.

'And if you remember anything else about last night, tell me right away. I know we gave you a pretty good grilling, but sometimes people remember little details later on.'

'They haven't caught anyone yet, have they?' She knew it was a stupid question. If suspects had been taken into custody, Dad would've told her so immediately.

'I'm afraid not, honey.'

135

'*Anything?*'

'Not yet. So far, about all we've got is what you and Andy told us.'

'Is his uncle still coming?'

'He's on his way.'

Jody tried not to let the hurt show. From the look on her father's face, however, she did a lousy job of it.

'I know you went through a lot with him, honey.'

'I don't want him to go away.'

'You want him to be safe, don't you?'

'Sure. But why does he have to go to *Phoenix?* It's so *far*.'

'He'll be a lot safer there. And he'll be with family.'

'What if they're not nice to him?'

'The guy sounded fine on the phone.'

'He might be a child-beater, or something.'

'I'll check him out.'

'Check him out how? You mean look him over?'

'That, too. But I'll put in a call to the Phoenix PD and see if they've got anything on him. Just to be sure, all right?'

'Okay.'

Dad took a swig of beer. He stared into Jody's eyes. 'It sounds like you saved Andy's butt, honey.'

'Yeah, sort of. But we sort of helped each other, too.'

'Your mother would sure be proud of you.' As he said that, his eyes filled. 'So am I,' he added, then quickly turned his head away. 'Why don't you go and get Andy up? Maybe he oughta take a shower or something. And we oughta eat. I don't know. Go on.'

Chapter Fifteen

In the living room, Jody gave Andy's shoulder a gentle shake. He rolled onto his back. He yawned and blinked up at her, looking groggy and peaceful. Then, he remembered. Jody *saw* him remember, saw his eyes change.

She almost told him, 'It's all right.' But that would be a lie, so instead she crouched down beside him and kissed him under the eye.

'Why don't you get up, now?' she whispered. 'Dad thought you might want a chance to take a shower before your uncle gets here.'

'The nurse said to leave the bandages on for a day or two. Didn't he tell you that?'

'Yeah, guess he did.'

'They'd get all soggy if I took a shower.'

'Well, do you want to wash up? You can wash *around* the bandages.'

'Yeah, okay.'

Jody eased the blanket away, and he sat up slowly. He was bare to the waist of his jeans. He had bandages on one shoulder, both arms, his chest, his belly, his sides and back. Where there were no bandages, he had plenty of bruises and scrapes. Still, he looked only about half as damaged as Jody. She supposed his knee made up for that, though. X-rays at the emergency room had shown no fractures, but the twist to his knee was a lot more severe than any injury Jody had sustained last night.

She helped him up, and hung on to him. He stood on one leg. Carefully, he lowered his other foot to the floor. He put some weight on it. 'Oooo.'

'Bad?'

'Not real good.'

'Maybe we should've got you some crutches.'

He reached up behind Jody's back and clamped a hand on her shoulder. 'You're better than some old crutch.'

'Okay, let's go.'

Side by side, they made their way across the living room and down the hallway to the bathroom. She lowered him onto the toilet seat. Stepping back, she said, 'Just a second.' She left him there, took a washcloth and towel from the hall closet, and returned. 'Can you get around well enough to . . . take care of stuff?'

He looked up at her and blushed. She felt her own skin go hot. 'Gosh,' he said. 'Don't worry about it.'

'Well. No. But if you need help, yell. Okay? And you can specify whether you want me or Dad.'

He was still red, but now he laughed. 'Okay.'

Jody left him in the bathroom and shut the door. Then she went to her bedroom and made a selection of clothes: plain white socks, white cotton underpants, and a pair of faded blue denim shorts that she'd worn almost daily for two summers, but which were now too snug and ought to fit Andy just fine. With a quick search of her closet, she found the bright red blouse that always went so great with the shorts. It had been slightly too large for her, last summer. Now, it would probably fit just right. But she wanted Andy to have it, even though it might be a bit too large for him.

She had to crouch and scurry around at the back of her closet to locate her old pair of Keds. They'd been white and beautiful, once. Now, they were grimy but otherwise okay except for a broken lace on the right shoe. She remembered when it had snapped. She'd done a quick fix with a square knot, but never gotten around to replacing the lace.

She took a package of fresh white laces from her bureau drawer, then sat on the edge of her bed and stripped out the old laces. While threading a new one through the eyelets, her gaze wandered over to the collection of clothes beside her.

Dad shouldn't mind, she thought. It's mostly old stuff except for the socks and undies.

Undies! Oh, my God. What was I thinking of?

She knew what she'd been thinking of; she'd seen Andy last night pulling up his jeans and glimpsed his bare butt. So she knew he wasn't wearing undershorts.

But he doesn't know I know, she told herself.

It would embarrass the daylights out of him, me giving him some, undies to wear. Especially a pair of *mine*.

Jeez!

She snatched them off the bed and hurried to her bureau. As she stuffed them into the proper drawer, she heard the bathroom door open. She pushed the drawer shut.

'Andy? In here.' She suddenly remembered his knee. 'Wait. I'm coming.'

Before she could take a step, he called, 'No, I'm okay. I'll make it.' She heard him hobbling up the hallway.

'Are you sure?'

'I'll make it. You stay there.'

'Okay.' Jody went to her bed, sat down and resumed lacing one of the shoes.

Seconds later, Andy stopped just beyond the doorway and pushed a hand against the frame to hold himself steady. His hair was matted down, dark and slick. Where he'd been smudged and streaked with filth, he was clean. He looked in at Jody. 'See? Made it. All by myself.'

'The champ.'

'Yep.' He smiled, but it only lasted a moment. Then

he looked grim again, as if he'd again remembered last night.

Jody finished with the laces of one shoe and started on the other.

'What're you doing?' Andy asked.

'I've got some stuff for you to wear. If you want it, anyway. Come on in.'

He looked uncertain. 'You sure it's okay if I come in your room? I mean, your dad won't yell at me or something, will he?'

'You've gotta be kidding.'

'I mean, you're a girl.'

Jody rolled her eyes upward and sighed. 'Jeez, kid. Sure, I'm a girl. But you're *twelve* years old.'

'Twelve and a half.'

'Oh. Okay. Anyhow, Dad isn't gonna care. Just leave the door open.'

Andy nodded, then stepped into the bedroom. He glanced from the clothes to Jody, then returned his gaze to the clothes. 'I don't get it,' he said.

'They're for you. You don't have anything to wear but those jeans. All your other stuff is . . . you know. Anyway, my dad's clothes would all be way too big for you.' She shrugged.

'But these're *yours*.'

'Hey, who's gonna know they're girls' things? Nobody'll know if you don't tell.'

His upper lip lifted slightly. He kept staring at the clothes. 'Don't worry, they're clean.'

He met her eyes, and let out a soft laugh. 'It isn't that.'

'You mean you're not afraid of my cooties?'

His smile widened. 'No.'

'Don't you like the stuff?'

'Yeah. Sure. But it's *yours*. I saw you in this red shirt last summer. And in the shorts, too. You looked so . . .' He stared down at the clothes and swallowed. 'You can't just give them away.'

'Okay, I'll lend 'em to you.'

'Lend them?'

'Sure. You keep them till the next time we see each other.'

'What if we never . . .?'

'Hey, don't be a dope. We'll see each other again. So you can have the stuff till then.'

Frowning, he picked up the blouse. He studied it. 'Are you sure? It's such a neat shirt. You're the one who oughta be wearing it.'

'Put it on, Andy.'

He swung it behind his back, wrestled his arms through the sleeves, and pulled its front together. He started to work on fastening the first button. And stopped. And ducked his head for a closer look. 'Hey, something's wrong.'

'What?'

'I don't . . . Is it inside out?'

Jody could see that the big, twin pockets were exactly where they belonged. 'No, it . . .'

'The buttons are on a funny side.'

'They are?' She got up from the bed, stepped closer to Andy, bent down and studied the situation. 'No, they're right where they always . . . Oh. Woops. I forgot. Guys wear their buttons on the wrong side.'

'Huh?'

'Girls' shirts have their buttons attached to the left side, but guys' shirts have them on the right.'

'Well, that's sure dumb.'

'Sure is, You still want it, though, don't you?'

'Sure I do.'

'Here.' Jody began to fasten the buttons for him.

'Thanks.'

'No big deal.'

'They'll probably buy me some new clothes pretty soon, anyway. Or at least let me wear Gary's old things. He's my cousin. He's in high school.'

'Is he all right?'

'He's okay. Sort of a geek, is all.'

'How are your aunt and uncle?'

'Oh, they're okay.'

'They're nice?'

'Sure. Uncle Willy's sort of weird, but . . .' He shrugged.

Jody finished with the top button, but she didn't step away. She put her hands on Andy's shoulders. 'Make sure you give me their phone number before you leave. And I'll give you mine. I'll call you every so often. And you call me. Call collect. You know, reverse the charges. Then they won't have any reason to not let you do it. We've got to keep in touch. I have to know that you're all right and they're treating you good and everything.'

Andy nodded. 'I sure wish I didn't have to go.'

'Me, too. But they're your relatives. You could probably stay here with us, but they want you with them, you know? Besides, Dad says you'll be safer there.'

His face contorted. 'What?'

'Safer. You'll be all the way in Phoenix. Those guys won't stand a chance of finding you there.'

'They're still *after* us?'

'Of course. What do you think?'

He looked stricken. 'Can they *find* us?'

'They'll have trouble finding you, that's for sure. Your aunt is your mother's sister, right? So her name wasn't even Clark to begin with, and on top of that she got married to

142

your uncle. So they'd have two name changes to get through. Unless they found an address book before they . . .'

'What about you?'

'I'll be fine.'

'Are you sure?'

'Dad won't let anyone hurt me.'

'Do they know who you are?'

'They might. Or they might not. It depends on whether they found my purse.'

'Where was it?'

'In Evelyn's room. Same as my clothes and stuff.'

'Wow. It had your name?'

'It had the whole sheebang. My brand new driver's license was in it. So if they got their hands on my purse, they know right where to find me.'

'Oh, man.'

'It's all right. Dad knows.'

'That doesn't make it all right.'

'You don't know Dad.'

Andy shook his head. His face was very red.

'Calm down,' Jody told him. 'They won't get me.'

'How do *you* know?'

'I know.'

'Oh, God, I don't like it. They're gonna come after you, I know it. And I'm not gonna be around to . . . I've *been* to Phoenix. Do you know how far away it is?'

'It's not all that far.'

'It's like *eight* hours on the freeway.'

'It isn't that far.'

'Oh, no? I don't want to be in Phoenix when they come after you.'

'I told you, everything will be all right. My dad can handle them.'

'He's just one guy.'

'Yeah. But he's Kong Fargo. Besides, he's got the whole LAPD with him. They're probably just *hoping* those creeps will make a move.'

'I've gotta be here when they do.'

'No you don't, either.' She turned Andy around by his shoulders and eased him backward. He hopped on his good foot, then dropped to the mattress. Jody picked up the shorts and tossed them onto his lap. 'Put these on. I'll throw your jeans in the wash so they'll be good and clean before you leave.'

'I'm not leaving.'

'You have to, Andy.' She turned her back to him. 'Off with them.'

'Don't peek.'

'Why would I?'

He didn't answer. Jody heard the zipper slide down, then a soft sound of rumpling denim.

'Maybe you could hide me,' he said.

'I'm not going to hide you. You'll be a lot better off in Phoenix.'

'Why? If it's safe here like you said.'

'It might not be *that* safe.'

'See? See what I mean?'

She heard another zipper. 'Have you got the shorts on?'

'Yes.' She turned around. His legs were bare below the cuffs of the blue shorts. The right knee was wrapped with an Ace bandage, but both legs had their share of bandages, bruises and scratches.

'Nice gams,' she said.

'Huh?'

'Gams. Gams are legs.'

Andy's eyes lowered to *her* gams.

'Let's get done in here,' she said. 'See if the shoes fit.'

'See if the foo shits.' Andy grinned. Then his mouth shook and twisted, his face went red, and his eyes flooded.

If the foo shits, wear it.

One of Evelyn's favorite sayings.

Andy hunched over his knees and hid his face behind both hands. His shoulders jumped as he sobbed.

Jody sat beside him and rubbed his back. She felt bandages through the shirt. She stopped rubbing, and kept her hand on a place that didn't have a bandage underneath. She drew circles there with her fingernail, hoping to distract him so he would quit. If he didn't stop soon, *she* would start bawling, and she didn't want that.

'Hey, come on,' she said after a while.

'I'm sorry.'

'Here. I'll help.' She picked up the socks. When she knelt on the floor in front of him, Andy sat up straight. He stopped looking tortured, and looked puzzled, curious.

Jody drew his right foot slowly toward her. She rested its bandaged heel on her thigh, just below a bandage of her own, and began to work one of the socks over his toes. 'Whew.'

'Ha ha.' He sniffed. 'Jody?'

'Huh?'

'How are we gonna see each other again?' He sniffed again. He wiped his eyes with the back of his hand. Jody finished with the first sock and eased his foot away. 'I mean it. I don't think they mean to just keep me for a week, or something. I'll be *living* there.' She lifted his other foot onto her thigh. 'It'll be . . . like *permanent*. It's not like a vacation or something.'

'I know.'

'What if we never see each other again?'

She pulled the second sock over his foot and up his ankle. 'Then you can keep my clothes.'

'I mean it.'

From the sound of his voice, Jody suspected he was about to resume crying. 'We'll get together again. You can count on it. You and I are . . . I don't know . . . tied together. Because of last night, you know? We'll *always* be like that, no matter how far apart we are. No matter what.'

'Really?'

'You bet.'

'But when'll we get together?'

Jody shrugged. 'I don't know. But we've got all summer before school starts, and you're only gonna be a day's drive away. We'll work out something.'

'If they let me come, can I stay here?'

'Sure.'

'Don't you have to ask your dad?'

'I know what he'll say. He'll say you can stay here any time you want. That's what we've got the guest room for.'

He let out a long, heavy sigh. 'I *want* to stay here right now.'

'I wish you could.'

He looked doubtful. 'Really?'

'Of course, really.'

'Then help me hide.'

'Hey.'

'Why not? I can hide in your attic, or something. You can tell them I ran away.'

Jody shook her head. She cupped Andy's unhurt knee with her hand. 'Hey. No. For one thing, if you go and pull a disappearing act, everyone'll think the creeps from last night got their hands on you.'

'Not if you tell them I ran away.'

'It won't work, Andy.'

'*Sure* it'll work.'

'No, it won't. I'd have to lie.'

'So?'

'I'm not going to.'

'Why *not*?'

'I'd have to lie to Dad. I won't do it. And you shouldn't even be asking me to do something like that.'

He stared at her. He looked confused, betrayed. 'I thought you *wished* I could stay. Isn't that what you said?'

'Yeah. And it's true. I'd like it very much. But there are right ways and wrong ways to do things. I might want to – I don't know – maybe spend a week at Disney World, you know? But I wouldn't rob a bank to do it.'

Now, he was scowling. 'Nobody's asking you to rob a bank. Cripes! All it'd take is a little fib. *I'd* tell a fib for *you*, you know.'

She let go of his knee and stood up. 'It'd never work anyway, so forget it. Even if I did lie – and I won't – you're crazy if you think your uncle's gonna drive all the way out here and then just turn around and drive home without you. Just forget it. It's not gonna happen.'

'You probably *want* me to go away with him.'

'I do not.'

'Yeah, sure.'

'Just shut up and try on the shoes, okay?'

'Who wants your stupid old shoes, anyway?'

Jody kicked her right foot high and flicked off her moccasin. It jumped at Andy fast, tumbling, and its soft leather sole smacked his forehead. The moccasin dropped to his lap. He gaped at Jody.

'Why'd you do *that*?'

'Felt like it.'

'Well . . .'

She kicked her other moccasin at him. His hand swiped through the air and caught it in front of his face.

'Jody!'

'Ta ta for now,' she said, grabbed his jeans off the floor, and hurried from the room.

Chapter Sixteen

Jody entered the garage through its rear door off the hallway, and tossed Andy's jeans into the washer. She dumped some detergent in, started the machine, then returned to the corridor.

The door to the guest room stood open, as usual.

We've got plenty of room for Andy.

If only he could stay with us . . .

Forget it. Won't happen.

Passing the open door of her bedroom, she glanced in and saw Andy had his head down. She decided not to intrude on him.

She went ahead to the kitchen.

Her father was still there, but no longer at the table. He stood at the counter, shaping hamburger into patties.

'I just put Andy's jeans in the washer,' she said. 'Don't worry, I gave him some of my old stuff to wear. I mean, you know, he's not running around the house in his birthday suit, or anything.'

'Well, lucky us.'

Jody laughed. 'Do you have anything you want me to toss in?'

'Don't think so. I did a load this morning. Including your nightshirt.'

'Winnie? How'd it come out?'

'Not bad at all. At least it's clean. Or *looks* clean. If there's still any blood, it doesn't show. The only problem is, there are some snags and minor rips.'

Jody wrinkled her nose. 'Oh.'

'It isn't bad. Really. I don't think we'll have to consign Winnie to the rag bag. Maybe a few patches here and there . . .'

'Where is it?'

'I hung it out on the line to dry.'

Jody went for the back door.

'No you don't. Halt right there.'

She stopped.

'You can't go outside.' He set down a gob of ground beef and started to wash his hands. 'You finish making the patties, I'll go out and see if it's dry.'

Jody wrinkled her nose. 'Is our *back yard* dangerous?'

'Probably not. Basically, we're surrounded. But you never know who might be up on a hillside with a good rifle.'

'Maybe you'd better not go out, either.'

'They aren't after me, hon.' He dried his hands, then swaggered over to the back door. 'You might wanta pass the word to Andy about staying in.'

He left. As the door bumped shut, Jody stepped to the counter. She picked up the moist, greasy ball and began shaping it into a patty.

Basically, we're surrounded.

By cops, she supposed. That had to be what he'd meant.

Where were they, in the neighbors' houses? On the rooftops?

Jody flinched and yelped as something whapped her rump. She whirled around.

The second moccasin had already been launched. It flipped

end over end. She tried to catch it, but missed. Its sole smacked the underside of her right breast.

Andy, standing in the doorway, bared his teeth in a grimace. His face went scarlet. 'Oooo.'

'Neat play.'

He looked agonized. 'I'm sorry. Did it hurt?'

'Yes, it hurt.' One hand held the meat and both were greasy, so she used the back of her wrist to rub the injured area. 'I'm scraped up there already from the wall last night.'

Andy watched her, his eyes very wide. 'I didn't mean to hurt you,' he muttered.

'Yeah, I know,' she told him, and quit rubbing. 'Besides, I got you first.'

'I didn't know you were gonna turn around.'

She toed the moccasins closer, flipped one rightside up, then slipped her feet into them. She turned again to the counter and worked on shaping the sides of the patty. 'We're having hamburgers, by the way. Is that okay?'

'Sure.'

'We usually do them on the barbecue. Maybe not tonight, though, seeing as how we're surrounded.'

'We're what?'

'Surrounded. By cops. But Dad's afraid of snipers, so you and I have to stay inside.'

'Snipers?'

'He's just playing it safe. I guess they've got things really tightly controlled right here, but there's nothing much they can do about people who might be up in the hills. With a good rifle, you know, you can hit somebody from like a mile away.'

'I know that.'

'See how lucky you are to be going away?'

'Maybe I'll get shot going to the car.'

The words made her stomach hurt. 'Cut it out,' she said. She set down the thick disk of meat and faced him. 'Nothing'll happen. So quit worrying, okay?'

Just then, Dad came in. 'Still pretty damp,' he told Jody. 'We'd better give it a couple more hours.' Then he gave Andy a big, crooked grin. 'Good looking outfit there, pal.'

Andy made a face. 'It's weird, wearing girls' things.'

'Long as you don't enjoy it too much, you're in good shape.'

'Real nice, Dad.'

'Did Jody warn you about going outside?'

'Yes, sir.'

She went to the sink and turned on the hot water faucet. As she washed her hands, she listened to her father say, 'We should all try to stay away from the windows, too. I've shut the curtains, but if these fellows are desperate enough, they might just throw some wild shots at the house and hope for the best.'

'Wouldn't it be better if you and Jody just left town, or something?' Andy asked.

Jody rinsed the soap off her hands, turned the water off, and reached for the towel. Wondering why her father hadn't answered yet, she looked over her shoulder.

He was leaning back against the counter beside the refrigerator, scowling at the floor. Whenever he scowled, he looked murderous.

Jody turned to face him.

'It goes against my grain to run from trouble. But my grain be damned. Honor doesn't matter squat to me when it comes to Jody's safety.' He glanced into her eyes, then quickly returned his scowl to the floor. 'The deal is, what's best? Which comes down to this: what's safest for my girl? We *could* take a long trip, but what happens when we come home again? Or we could move to the middle of nowhere and change our names and start all over like different people.'

'No way, Dad. Huh-uh. Not me. I'd rather take my chances.'

'Yep, I know that, all right. But we'd do it, anyhow, if I figured it was the safest thing. I don't think it is, though. There's no such thing as real safety until those men have been taken off the streets. The sooner that happens, the better for everyone.'

'So you're hoping they'll come here,' Jody said.

'Yep. Only I'm just not sure I want you to be here if they do.'

Andy brightened. 'Maybe she could come to Arizona with me.'

She felt like pounding him. 'I'm not going anywhere.'

'The jury's still out on that, honey.'

'*What?* You *can't* send me away! I won't go! Besides, you need me here. *I'm* the witness, you know.'

'We both are,' Andy reminded her.

'Well, you *are* going. But *I'm* not. Dad! You can't be serious. What kind of trap would it be if you sent your damn bait out of town?'

He aimed the scowl at her.

'I mean it!'

'Settle down, honey. And watch your language.'

'Well, really! You *can't* send me away. It wouldn't be fair.'

Dad stretched an arm in her direction. His open hand gently patted down the air. 'Easy, easy. The deal is, I'm the only one I trust to watch out for you.'

'It's settled, then, isn't it?'

'For now. But let's just say the situation's fluid.'

Fluid. Jody didn't care for the sound of that. She pictured

a puddle on a table top. If the table didn't move, fine. But the slightest bump might send the fluid spilling off its edges.

What would it take, she wondered, for Dad to send me packing without him?

A bullet through a window, maybe.

The phone rang. Its sudden jangle made her flinch and started her heart thudding hard. But she was glad to see Andy jerk. *He's as rattled as me.*

Dad went for the phone, right arm raised away from his side as if rowing the air, the way it always did when he was in a hurry. On a forward swing, he wrapped his big hand around the phone. 'Yellll-oh,' he said, then listened for a while. 'Gotcha. Thanks.'

As he hung up, Jody lifted her eyebrows.

'Nick Ryan,' he explained.

'Ah.' She knew Nick well. He'd gone through the academy with Dad, and was one of his oldest friends.

'He's running the show.' Dad turned to Andy. 'Your uncle's coming up the street. Looks like he made it in time for supper.'

Andy didn't look pleased. 'Oh, great.'

'He's early. Traffic must've been light.'

'Are they sure it's him?' Jody asked.

'A spotter verified the Arizona tag. What I want you to do, Andy, is grab a look at him just to make sure. Let's go.' Dad led the way.

Andy and Jody followed.

On both sides of the front door were long, narrow windows draped with yellow curtains. The first week after moving into the house, Dad had called in a man to have the glass replaced with thick, transparent acrylic slats. The man was missing two fingers of his right hand. Jody, four at the time, had asked, 'Why don't you have more fingers?' He'd smiled and said, 'I got hungry and had to eat 'em. Now, I've got me half a mind to nibble off some of yours. They sure look tasty.' It was one of Jody's earliest memories. Mom had been alive then, had overheard the conversation from the kitchen, and been aghast: first at Jody for asking such an embarrassing question; then at the worker for his reply; then again at Jody. She'd expected Jody to run away screaming. Instead, the toddler had said in a tough little voice, 'You just try biting me, bozo, and I'll knock your head *cleannnnn* off.' Jody didn't remember saying that, but Mom used to tell the story to just about everyone, and Dad even repeated it whenever one of his friends pointed out that it wasn't a good idea to have windows within arm distance of the door. His friends were all cops, of course. And they all got a big laugh out of Jody's encounter with the finger eater.

Until remembering the story again right now, she'd assumed almost from the day it happened that the man had been teasing her. After all, people don't eat fingers.

It occurred to her now, however, that he might've been serious.

After last night, *nothing* would surprise her. In fact, eating someone's fingers seemed almost normal compared to wearing pants made out of somebody's butt.

Dad stepped to the window on the right side of the door and hooked the curtain aside.

What had the front of the pants looked like? Jody wondered.

I don't want to know.

Dad waved Andy over to him. 'Come and take a look. The car's just pulling into the driveway.'

Andy stepped up beside him. As they both peered out the window, Dad put a hand on the boy's shoulder.

A car door thudded.

'It's him, all right,' Andy said.

'Okay.' They stepped away from the window. 'Both of you stand back,' he said. He watched them until they'd retreated a fair distance into the living room. Then he turned to the door and swung it open.

Stopping at the threshold, Andy's uncle smiled nervously and ducked his head forward. 'Jack Fargo?'

'That's me.' He took a huge step forward and swung out his right hand.

'I'm Wilson Spaulding, Andy's uncle.' Wilson's head bobbed continuously as he spoke, and didn't stop bobbing when he finished. He had a nasal voice, droopy eyes and almost no chin at all. He was short and gangly. His chest was as sunken as his chin, and he seemed to be hunching his shoulders forward as if trying to conceal its absence. Perched on his head was a white cap with an emblem including crossed golf clubs. He wore a blue polo shirt, white shorts, knee socks that matched his shirt, and big, black leather lace-up shoes.

Man, Jody thought.

'Glad you made it here so fast,' Dad said, towing him into the house.

Wilson grinned and bobbed. 'I'm nothing if not prompt.'

What a goofball, Jody thought.

'And there *you* are,' Wilson said. He pointed a finger at Andy and shuffled toward him.

Andy stiffened a little as if determined to stand his ground. 'Hi, Uncle Willy.'

The skinny arms wrapped around him. Wilson started slapping his back. 'What a terrible, terrible thing. You poor boy, you poor boy.' Wilson turned toward Dad, still hugging Andy and maneuvering him like a dance partner. 'We were devastated by the news, Jack. Devastated. Absolutely terrible.'

'At least Andy made it through,' Dad told him. 'And my Jody here.'

'So *this* is Jody.'

He let go of Andy and scuttled toward her, arms out, a weird, sad grin on his face. 'I know all about *you*, Jody. Yes, I do.'

She stood her ground.

Andy gave her a look. It seemed to say, *Now let's see how you like it*.

Wilson flung his arms around her and pulled her against him. He felt all crooked and bony. He patted her back and rubbed it. 'Jody Jody Jody. *You're* the one. We might very well have lost our Andy if you hadn't been such a little hero.' He pushed her away and clutched her shoulders and bobbed his head in front of her nose. 'I thank you. My wife thanks you.'

'And I thank you,' Andy called out.

She wanted to pound him.

Wilson's eyes, already red and bulging, seemed to swell even further out of their sockets. 'And I understand it on good authority that you actually *dispatched* one of the murderers.'

'Sort of,' she murmured.

'What a *charmer*! What a little *charmer*! Oh, Jack, you're such a lucky man to have such a daughter.'

'Yes, sir. I know it.' He suddenly appeared beside Wilson, wrapped a hand around the man's skinny forearm, and led him aside.

Thank you, Father!

'Would you like to stick around for a while and have some hamburgers before you start back?'

'I'd be delighted, Jack.'

'How about a drink?'

'*Double* delighted.'

Dad walked him toward the kitchen. 'Name your poison, Wilson.'

'Call me Willy, Jack. But not Wee Willy – I hate that.'

Jody and Andy looked at each other. Andy swung his eyes toward the ceiling. Jody shook her head. They followed the two men, keeping a distance.

'Wee Willy,' Wilson said. 'That's what they always called me. I bet you got a lot of that yourself.'

'Wee Willy?' Dad sounded confused. 'Me?'

'Ha! No! Wells Fargo. Didn't they always call you Wells Fargo? Or maybe Stagecoach? Or maybe Banker? Or Piggybank?'

Jody elbowed Andy. Andy looked as if he was pained by the notion of being related to such a man.

'They never called me anything like that,' Dad said.

'Well, I can't understand why not, with a name like Fargo.'

'Maybe they didn't figure it'd be *safe*.'

'Safe! Ho! Very good.'

Jody took hold of Andy's arm. She stopped walking, and halted him beside her. 'Hey Dad, if you don't need us right now, would it be all right if we leave?'

'Fine,' he called back. 'Just remember what I said about windows.'

'Okay,' she called to him. Then she pulled Andy after her. 'Let's get out of here.'

Side by side, they limped to her bedroom. She led him in, then shut the door. She pressed her back to it. 'I don't want to speak *ill* of your relatives, Andy, but that *guy* . . .'

'You oughta be glad he didn't do *this* to you.' Andy caught her cheek between his thumb and the side of his forefinger. Then he squeezed it and shook it.

'Hey.' She knocked his hand away. 'What is he again? Your mother's sister's husband.'

'Right.'

'Good. That's lucky for you. He's not a *blood* relation, so there's no chance your *kids* might turn out like him.'

'No way.'

'Thank God.'

Andy leaned in toward her. 'What's your big interest in how my kids'll turn out?'

'Oh, give me a break.'

'Huh?' He pushed his hands against the door on both sides of her head, then leaned even closer. His head was tilted back so he could look her in the eyes. 'Do *you* have any weird relatives?'

'No Wee Willy.'

'Then we don't have to worry, do we?'

'Worry?'

He winked at her twice with his right eye. 'About our kids being freako nerds.'

'*Our* kids? You're twelve years old, hot shot.'

'I won't always be.'

'Don't count on it.'

The wild silly gleam vanished suddenly from his eyes.

'Hey,' Jody said. 'I'm sorry. I was just kidding around. You *won't* always be twelve.'

'I might be. They might kill me before my birthday.'

'Nobody's gonna kill you.'

'Maybe it wouldn't be so bad,' he muttered.

'What? Being killed? Don't count on it. For one thing, it's gotta hurt.'

'Maybe for a while. Then it'd be over, though. You know? And then *nothing* would hurt anymore. Not ever.'

'Hey, cut it out.'

'And I'd be with Mom and Dad and Evelyn.'

'Yeah, I guess so.' She put a hand behind his head and eased his face toward her. His forehead pushed lightly against the tip of her nose. His breath felt hot on her throat. 'Do you know what happened to *my* mother?'

'Just . . . you know . . . that she's dead.'

'She got killed when I was in second grade.'

'Was *she* murdered?'

'She got run over by a car.'

'Yuck.'

'It was so weird. It was all because she went to a place called the Longlife Health and Nutrition Center. She was a real health nut, and this was where she always bought all her special vitamins. She came out with a whole bagful of stuff. But she must've wondered about something, because they said she was reading the label on a bottle of pills when she stepped off the curb. The heel of her shoe got hung up and she tripped. She stumbled past where our car was parked and . . . She ended up falling flat right in front of a moving car. That's how *she* got killed.'

'That's awful,' Andy said in a small voice.

'Yeah.'

'Were you there? Did you see it?'

'No. I was in school.'

'Oh, man.'

'I just wanted you to know. Things happen, you know? Really bad things. But . . . like . . . I still miss her and everything, but not all the time. Things'll getbetter for you, Andy. It won't always be this bad. So don't talk about crazy stuff, okay? You don't want to die. *I* don't want you to die. It'd wreck me.'

He raised his face, looked her in the eyes, blinked. 'It would?'

'Sure.'

'Why?'

'Because.'

'You *do* love me, don't you?'

She thought about it for a moment, then answered, 'Sure I do. Now, let's get out of here before you start in on kids again. Because I'm *not* having kids with you, so you might as well forget it.'

'If you say so.' He made a sad attempt at a smile. 'You can always change your mind, though. Know what I mean?'

'Don't hold your breath. Come on, let's see how Dad's coming with the burgers.'

Chapter Seventeen

Dad used the back-yard barbecue, after all. He and Andy's uncle were both outside, but soon came in with a platter full of hamburgers. Dad carried the platter and a Pepsi can. Willy had a glass containing a crushed wedge of lime and the remains of several ice cubes.

'Can I get you a refill?' Dad asked.

Good idea, Jody thought. Get him plowed, so then maybe they'll have to stay.

Not that she wanted Willy to stay.

She just didn't want Andy to go.

'Don't believe so, Jacko. Thanks all the same, but I've got a mighty big drive ahead of me. I believe I'll have a soda, instead.'

'Pepsi okay?' Dad asked.

'Would you have any sort of a diet cola?'

'I'm afraid not.' Dad gave the man an odd look. With good

reason, Jody thought. *Diet* cola? The guy was as skinny as a worm.

'Well, I don't suppose one *real* soda will kill me.' He bobbed his head a few times and winked. 'Just don't tell the wife. She's after me to trim down, you know.'

'Mum's the word,' Dad said.

They sat around the dining room table, each with a hamburger and potato chips on a plate, and either a can or a glassful of Pepsi. For a while, nobody spoke as they customized their burgers with various combinations of mustard, mayonnaise, lettuce, freshly sliced tomatoes, pickles and thick slabs of onion.

'Mmm, good,' Willy said after his first bite. 'Absotivly posa-lutely delicious. My compliments to the chef.'

Quickly, before a conversation could get a chance to start, Jody asked, 'Do you think you'll be able to let Andy come and visit us?'

He tilted his head sideways. 'Why, we aren't even out the door yet, and you already want him back! Jacko, you'd better watch out! I think your little lady might have her *eyes* on young Andy here.'

'She could do worse, I guess.'

'*Dad!* It's nothing like that, and you know it.'

'Oh, I know. The thing is, Wilson, they went through a lot together last night. Looks to me like it turned them into a team – and when you're on a good team, you don't like to break it up.'

'Yeah,' Andy pitched in. 'It's like we're partners.' He frowned at his uncle. 'So you've *gotta* let me come back and see her.'

'Now, don't go aiming gottas at me, Andy. I don't respond well to gottas. However, I imagine we'll be able to arrange something along the lines of a visit. After you've settled in, and your aunt's had time to accustom herself to the situation.'

'He's welcome any time,' Dad said.

'Splendid. Of course, any consideration of a visit will absolutely have to wait until the culprits have been apprehended.'

'But Uncle . . .!'

'Annndrewww?' Willy tipped back his head as if hoping to make his point by showing Andy the interiors of his nostrils. 'We don't argue.'

'What if they *never* catch those guys?'

Jody opened her mouth, but a quick look from her father stopped her from speaking.

'This is not a safe place,' Willy explained. 'I left my job at eleven o'clock this morning and spent my entire day on the road to come here and take you away *because* you're in danger here. In fact, it's gone against my better judgement even to stay for supper – which puts us both in needless jeopardy.' He smiled and bobbed vigorously at Dad. 'Not that it isn't a luscious supper, because it most certainly is. But *you* tell him, Jacko.'

Dad rubbed his left cheek and settled his gaze on Andy. 'You'll be a lot safer in Arizona, that's for sure.'

'That's coming from a police officer,' Willy pointed out.

Jody felt as if she might explode. 'Dad! What if the guys don't *ever* get caught? Does that mean Andy and I never ever get to see each other again in our whole lives? *That* isn't fair.'

Even before she'd finished, her father had begun to pat at the air with his open hand. When her last word was out, he said, 'Settle down, honey. I'm not saying that. What we'll do is play it by ear. We can ask Andy to come for a visit as soon as things look stable around here.' He faced the boy. 'How does that sound?'

'Okay, I guess.'

'And I'll call you on the phone tomorrow,' Jody told him.

'Will you give them your number, Uncle Willy?'

'We've already got it,' Dad explained.

Not much was said during the rest of the meal. Jody worked on her hamburger. She supposed there was nothing wrong with it – that it was probably as tender and juicy and tasty as Dad's barbecued burgers always were – but it filled her mouth with heavy, dry lumps that were hard to swallow. After eating less than half of it, she gave up. She nibbled a few potato chips and sipped her Pepsi.

Andy seemed to be having trouble with his burger, too. He didn't quit, though. He never set it down, but held it over his plate with both hands and stared at it and every so often took a small bite.

He's trying to make it last, Jody thought. He knows he'll have to leave when we're done eating.

Just as Andy finished his burger, Dad asked, 'Would anyone like some ice cream?'

'Sure!' Andy blurted. A reprieve.

'I'm afraid we'd better pass on that, Jacko. Much obliged, anyhow. I'm afraid we've already dallied way too long. We've got that big drive ahead of us.' He winked at Andy. 'Don't we, young fellow?'

'I guess so.'

'You're planning to drive all the way through?' Dad asked.

'That's the thing about me, I never do anything halfway. It's whole hog or nothing. I believe if you're going for it, you should go full steam ahead, come hell or high water, torpedoes be damned!'

'Give me liberty,' Jody muttered, 'or give me death.'

Her father and Andy both looked stunned: Dad shocked by her rudeness, Andy delighted.

But Wilson Spaulding bobbed his head at her, shook a

crooked finger, and blurted, 'Abso-tivly! Preeeecisely! Give me liberty or give me death! That's the sort of gung-ho spirit we like to see. Damn the torpedoes!' He turned to Dad. 'You've sure got yourself a charmer, here.'

'Or something,' Dad muttered.

Andy laughed, but Willy didn't seem to notice him. 'We should take her with us. By force, if necessary! How would you like that, young lady?'

The eagerness that suddenly brightened Andy's face killed her urge to make a crack. 'Thank you for asking, Mr Spaulding. I can't, though. I've gotta stay here with my dad.'

You didn't mean it, anyway, you jerk! You got Andy's hopes up for no good reason at all.

'I'm sorry,' she told Andy.

'It's okay. I know you can't come.'

Her throat tightened. 'I think you oughta have some ice cream.' To Willy, she said, 'We can make up some cones, and both of you can take them with you. We've got chocolate chip, and Ben & Jerry's Heath . . .'

'Oh, I don't think so,' Willy said. 'Cones can be so messy, and . . .'

Her chair crashed to the floor as she sprang up.

'You ignorant son-of-a-bitch! His whole family's been wiped out and you're not gonna let him have a goddamn ice-cream cone? What the hell is the matter with you!'

Even as she yelled, a small voice in Jody's mind was warning, 'My God, listen to you! You've lost it! You've flipped out!'

In spite of the small voice, she blurted it all out, shouting it at the man, spit flying from her lips, tears pouring down her cheeks.

Andy looked shocked, at first. Then he was crying, too.

Willy sat very stiff and still in his seat and blinked at her.

Dad lunged up, rushed around the table, took Jody by the arm and towed her into the hallway. There, away from the others, he hugged her and stroked her hair, 'Oh, honey,' he whispered. 'Oh, honey.'

'I'm sorry.'

'It's okay, it's okay.'

'I just wanted him to get his ice cream,' she blubbered.

'He'll get it, he'll get it. Jesus, honey. Are you okay?'

'No.'

'I know, I know.'

'He's an *awful* man.'

'He's just odd, that's all. He means well.'

'He does not. He's a creep. Oh, Dad. Can't we do something? Can't we stop him from taking Andy?'

'Andy'll be fine with him.'

'No, he won't.'

'Honey, honey. They're his relatives. They'll take good care of him. I know you'll miss him, but . . .'

'*GOODBYE!*' Andy yelled. '*GOODBYE, JODY!*'

'What the . . .?' Dad suddenly muttered.

'*DON'T FORGET TO . . .*'

'*Come on.*' Uncle Willy's voice, quick and harsh.

'Andy!' Jody shouted.

And heard a door smack shut.

'Dad, we've gotta . . .'

'Shhhh.' He stood rigid, holding her tightly.

He's listening.

Oh my God, he's listening for gunshots!

'Dad!'

'Shhhh.'

When the noise came, she flinched. Dad didn't. He stood solid and whispered, 'Just the car door.' Moments later, a second thud came. An engine whinnied. 'They're in. They should be all right.'

The sound of the engine faded. 'Dad, they're leaving!'

'They're past the risky part.' He talked in a whisper, almost as if thinking out loud. 'I'd planned to have Wilson pull his car into the garage so Andy wouldn't be exposed. Never expected he'd run off like that.'

'It's my fault. It's because I went nuts.'

He smoothed her hair. 'You're gonna have to watch that temper.'

'I know.'

'And that language.'

'But he made me so mad. It's like he doesn't have any *feelings*, you know? How could he *not* let Andy have a cone? He's supposed to be Andy's *uncle*, you know?'

'The world's got a lot of jerks in it, honey.'

'That's for sure.'

'When one happens to be a guest in our house, though, you should try to be reasonably polite.'

'I know. Jeez. He only left because of me.'

'He would've left anyway. Your behavior just speeded him along some.'

'I didn't even get to tell Andy goodbye.'

'I know, honey. I'm sorry. But look, you can call him tomorrow and tell him goodbye then. Goodbye and hello. Talk to him as long as you want. Remind him he left his jeans here.'

Jody gasped. 'He did! I forgot all about his jeans!'

'Maybe you can hold them for an exchange of hostage clothes.' After a pause, he added, 'That was one of my favorite outfits you gave him, by the way.'

'The shorts don't even fit me anymore.'

'I know. You've gotten so big. You used to be so cute.'

'Dad!'

He whopped her on the bottom, then headed for the kitchen. 'Come on, *we'll* have some of that ice cream.'

They both decided on Heath Bar Crunch. Jody scooped it into bowls. They ate at the kitchen table, and were almost finished when the ringing phone made Jody jump.

Dad picked up. 'Yelll-oh.' He listened. His face showed no expression except for the usual, one-sided smirk. 'Real good,' he finally said. 'Thanks.' He hung up. 'So far, so good. We've got a couple of units keeping tabs on Willy's car. It doesn't look like he's being tailed by anyone but the good guys.'

'You've got their *car* under surveillance?'

'Sure. What do you think we are, a bunch of chimps?'

'No, but . . . That's pretty cool. So, it's like Andy and his creepy uncle have bodyguards.'

'For the time being.'

'But not the whole way?'

'Only as far as the county line. That should be far enough, though. If they haven't picked up a tail by then, we can be pretty sure they're clean.'

'What if they *do* pick up a tail?'

'Then we're in luck. We'll pounce. We'll grab 'em. We'll convince 'em to cooperate, and next thing you know, we'll have the whole gang.'

'That'd be great,' Jody said.

'It'd be great, but it won't happen. The way these guys acted last night, they don't look like your typical, dumb criminal types. They might not be geniuses, but they aren't morons, either. They know what they're doing. They're careful. They're gonna be hard to catch.'

Jody curled her upper lip. 'They aren't good enough to get *us*, are they?'

'Nobody's that good, honey.'

'Oh, yeah. Right.'

'What, you don't believe me?' He tried to look offended. 'Do *I* look like a chimp?'

He nodded. 'Daughter of Kong.'

'Thank God I got my looks from Mom.'

He laughed and shook his head.

Jody took their ice-cream bowls and spoons to the sink. 'Why don't you go relax or something?' she said. 'I'll do the dishes.'

'Nope. What we'll do right now is slap together about a dozen or so hamburger patties. I'll take 'em out and grill 'em, then hand the things around to our team of vigilant protectors. They'll love us for it. After that, they'll defend us with their very lives.'

He removed extra packages of ground beef from the refrigerator, then worked at the counter with Jody. When six patties were shaped, he said, 'Might as well get these started,' and took them outside. Jody pulled off more chunks of meat, made them into balls and mashed them flat.

She was glad her father had thought of this. Preparing hamburgers for the cops seemed like a nice thing to do. Also, though, it kept her mind off the killers, off Andy, and off Uncle Willy.

Soon, she had six more patties ready for the fire.

Dad hadn't come back inside, yet. She supposed he was probably standing over the barbecue, spatula in hand, keeping his eye on the burgers. 'You know how a watched pot doesn't boil?' he'd asked her – more than once. 'Well, an *un*watched barbecue burns your burgers.' Burgers, or chicken, or steaks, or whatever he happened to be preparing at the time he was imparting his wisdom.

But Jody knew him. He didn't stand watch on the fire to save the food from burning. That was just his excuse. In fact, he did it because he liked to be outside in the early evening, liked the scent of the smoke, liked hearing the meat sizzle and spit, liked to watch the flames leap. He'd never admitted any such thing, but she could see it in the way he behaved. She supposed maybe it took him back to his Boy Scout days, or to his backpacking trips into the mountains with Mom when they were young. Or maybe cooking his meat over a real fire, outside, had an appeal that went beyond nostalgia – maybe it was more basic and primitive, had something to do with 'man the hunter'.

Jody loaded the raw patties onto a plate and headed for the back door.

She remembered how Dad used to stand over the grill with a squirt gun of clear yellow plastic. That was when she'd been very young. He used the gun to shoot down flames. Sometimes, he squirted Jody. That usually made Mom yell at him.

Sometimes, Jody used to take drinks out of the squirt gun.

The water would shoot out of a hole no bigger than the tip of a needle. It would make a hissing sound. Sometimes you shot it at the roof of your mouth, and that tickled. Sometimes, you sucked the water straight from the muzzle. You could always get more water by sucking than by shooting. The water always tasted funny. Like rubber or plastic.

She stepped outside, and the screen door banged shut.

Dad's head snapped around. 'Jody! I told you to stay in the . . .'

First, the bullet hit.

The noise of the shot came a few moments later.

Chapter Eighteen

The bullet smacked the concrete patio far enough in front of Jody so that the platter didn't block her view. She saw a quick spout of chips and white dust, heard a *whing*, felt a tug on her shorts and a sting.

Then came the crash of the shot.

Jody realized she had forgotten to stay inside.

Flinging the platter of burgers, she whirled around and reached for the door handle. She tugged. The screen door started to swing toward her.

A bullet slammed it shut.

She saw the hole in its aluminum frame – a hole the size of a dime. The slug must've passed within an inch of her shoulder.

'Down!' Dad yelled. 'Hit the deck!'

Ducking, she twisted around and looked back.

He was charging at her, gun still holstered, spatula dropping from his hand.

Off beyond him and over to the left, someone with a rifle was standing on the roof of their garage.

How'd they get so close? There were supposed to be cops!

That is *a cop!*

He was facing the hillside, rifle shouldered, eye to the huge scope of his rifle.

The third bullet slammed a bar of hot wind against the side of Jody's head, the top of her ear.

Then her father's body blocked her view of everything. He clutched her, lifted her, swung her. A strange growling sound came from him. Then a grunt as he crashed through the door screen.

Inside the kitchen, he didn't stop, but dashed with Jody through the dining room and into the hallway as if his goal was to get her into the very center of the house where there would be the maximum number of walls between her and the world outside.

There, he pushed her away from him and lifted her up in front of him. Checking her back? Then he lowered her to the floor. He eased her down on her back, and knelt beside her.

They were both making gaspy, whimpery noises.

Jody couldn't catch her breath.

What if I'm dying?

She knew she'd been hit at least once. High on the leg. The wound hurt, burned. But maybe she'd been hit worse, and just didn't know it yet because it was a very *bad* hit, so bad it was numb. So bad it would kill her.

She pushed her elbows against the carpet and raised her head. Just as she did that, Dad yanked her shorts down.

She saw no blood on the front of her blouse.

But her right leg, now minus shorts, was a bloody mess a few inches below the crotch of her panties.

'Oh, my God,' she said.

'It's all right,' Dad muttered. He folded her shorts to make a pad, and pressed the pad to the side of her thigh. After holding it there for a moment, he lifted it away and bent lower. He let out a soft whistle.

'How bad?'

He shook his head. 'It damn near missed you.'

'It didn't *miss* me, Dad! Look at all the blood!'

From somewhere out of sight beyond Jody's head came sounds of quick, heavy footfalls. Dad dropped the shorts, snatched the Browning out of his shoulder holster and leveled it down the hallway.

'Sergeant Fargo?' A woman's voice. It sounded forceful, but calm. 'I'm Officer Miles. Was she hit?'

'Nicked by a ricochet.'

'How about you?'

'Nothing touched me.'

'We've got units going up to look for the shooter.'

Miles sank to a crouch. Her hand went directly to Jody's shoulder and squeezed it gently. 'How you doing there, champ?'

'Not great.' Miles was younger than Jody had expected from the sound of her voice, and prettier.

'You don't *look* too bad for a young lady who's just been shot up.'

She winced as Dad mopped the wound.

'It's not much more than a scratch,' he said.

Miles looked, and nodded. She turned her eyes to Jody's face. 'Are you hurt anywhere else?'

'Almost everywhere.'

Miles curled up a corner of her mouth in a way that reminded her of Dad's usual smirk. 'I'm mostly interested in *tonight's* installment on your injuries.'

Braced up on her elbows, Jody inspected herself. Blood from the wound on her thigh had dribbled down the side of her leg, painted red streaks on the backs of a few small bandages, and soaked the top of her sock. Her other leg looked fine except for its assortment of scrapes, bruises, scratches and bandages.

Above the waistband of her panties, her blouse hung open almost to her chest. She supposed the buttons must've come undone when Dad grabbed her and hauled her into the house. The open area of the blouse showed more bandages than skin.

For a moment, her gaze stayed on the patch of gauze

between her navel and the top of her panties. That was where the spear had poked her last night. The spear that had gone through Evelyn first.

She grimaced.

It's not over. Still not over. Maybe it won't be over till they get me. Me and Andy. Not till we're as dead as Evelyn.

'What is it?' Dad asked.

'Nothing. I was just thinking about Evelyn.'

Dad shook his head. 'Yeah,' he muttered. 'It's tough.'

'Just the single wound?' Miles asked, then added, 'For tonight?'

'Yeah. I think so.'

Miles cocked her head slightly. Her light brown hair was even shorter than Jody's, probably shorter than the hair of half the men on the force. She had a small, puffy scar under her chin. 'What do you say, Sergeant? Should we bring in an ambulance?'

Jody grimaced. 'It'd take me back to the emergency room, wouldn't it?'

From the look on her father's face, she knew the answer.

'I don't want to go. Please. I'm not hurt that bad. You *said* it's only a scratch. I don't want to go anywhere. I want to stay here.'

To Miles, Dad said, 'I'm sure she's at least got a mild case of shock. Hell, so have I, and I wasn't shot.'

'It's just a *scratch*, remember? Don't make me go. Please.'

He looked at Miles.

'It's your call,' she said.

'Please, Dad.'

He seemed to be thinking about it.

'Besides,' Jody pointed out, 'I'm safer here. What if there's another sniper outside? Maybe there's one in front of the house, too.'

Dad shook his head. 'One in front would've tried for Andy.'

'Maybe. Unless he wasn't ready yet. Anyway, I'm safer here than someplace else like an ambulance or the emergency room, don't you think so?'

'Probably,' he admitted. 'Okay, you win.'

Miles gave her shoulder a squeeze. 'If you want to check on the situation outside, Sergeant, I'll take care of Jody . . . patch her up.'

'Would that be all right with you, honey?'

'Sure, I guess so.'

'Hold this right where I've got it,' he told her.

He moved his hand away, and Jody took over pressing the pad of shorts against her wound.

Then Dad helped Miles carry her into the bathroom. They sat her on the edge of the tub, her feet on the floor.

'I'll be back pretty soon,' he said, and left.

'Let's have a look there.' Miles bent over Jody and lifted the pad.

They both studied the wound.

It didn't seem to be bleeding much anymore.

Now that Jody could get a good look at it, the injury *did* seem pretty minor. The side of her thigh looked as if it had been scraped by the tip of a knife – a dull tip that had opened a furrow and hadn't gone in very deep.

'I'd say you're very lucky,' Miles told her.

'Yeah.'

'Let me see if these are salvageable.' She took the shorts to the sink, unfolded them, rinsed out a lot of blood, wrung them out, and shook them open. She whistled softly.

'What?'

She turned around and held up the shorts for Jody to see.

The bullet hole wasn't much more than an inch below the bottom of the zipper. It looked larger than the hole she had seen in the door frame. And rough around the edges, not perfectly round.

'Came out here,' Miles said, and showed her the rear of the shorts. This hole was higher than the one in front. 'Awfully close.'

'It was close, all right. It *hit* me.'

'It could've been a whole lot worse.' She turned to the sink, dropped in the shorts, let water run onto them, and said, 'We can let 'em soak. You might at least want to keep them as a souvenir.'

'Thank God for lousy shots,' Jody said.

'He's probably a terrific shot, or he wouldn't have tried it in the first place. Firing *down* at a target can be awfully tricky. Where do you keep the first-aid stuff?'

'Behind there.' Jody nodded toward the larger of the two mirrors, the one above the counter to the right of the sink.

Miles stepped over to it. 'Your father probably saved you.'

'He got me inside awfully fast, that's for sure.'

'Didn't even bother to open the screen door,' Miles said, and swung the mirror open. 'From the look of the thing, he must've barreled straight through it.'

'That's what he did, all right.'

'You've got yourself quite a father.'

'Yeah, I know.'

She had her back to Jody as she gathered what she needed off the cluttered shelves of the medicine cabinet.

From behind, she looked fairly large and heavy, but not fat. She was broad across the shoulders and back, had wide hips, and a rump that filled the seat of her Wrangler blue jeans. What with the jeans, her plaid shirt and her cowboy boots, she might've been stopping by the house on her way to a rodeo.

When she turned around, her hands were full with a tube

of antiseptic cream, rolls of adhesive tape and gauze. A pair of toenail scissors dangled from her pinkie finger.

'We'll have you fixed up in no time at all,' she said. She knelt in front of Jody.

'Did you know Dad before tonight?'

'Nope.' Arranging the supplies on the floor beside her knee, she said, 'I'd heard of him, but never met him.'

'He's stationed at the 77th.'

Nodding, Miles took the moccasin off Jody's right foot. Then she peeled off the bloody sock. The way she was hunched over, Jody could see down the front of her blouse. She had *major* cleavage. She had a *ravine* between her breasts. Her bra was black and lacy, which seemed like an odd, sexy sort of thing for a policewoman to be wearing on duty, even if she was working plainclothes.

Jody wondered what her father might think of such large breasts and such a bra.

Then she found herself blushing.

Miles rinsed the bloody sock under the bathtub faucet, then crouched and began to clean Jody's leg with it.

'How come you'd heard of Dad?' Jody asked.

'Everybody's heard of him. Kong Fargo. You know about the tape, don't you?'

'Which one?'

'The one they show at the academy.'

'They show a tape of my *dad* at the police academy?'

'You bet. It's used for training in how to deal with armed suspects.'

'Oh! It isn't the weirdo with the machete, is it?'

'That's the one.'

Jody had seen it once, during a party at the house. The guys were showing a lot of video tapes – pretty rough stuff, mostly. Trying either to impress or gross out their girlfriends and wives, she supposed. She had crept in from her bedroom and watched from the rear. Dad had been fairly soused by then, so he never caught on that she was there.

On the tape, a man charges at him, waving a machete. It is night. They are on a sidewalk in front of a store that has big, lighted display windows. The man wears sunglasses, a black goatee, a gold necklace, and briefs that have a leopard skin pattern. He yells, 'Dust the pork!' as he races at Dad.

Dad is in full uniform. His Browning stays in his holster as the maniac runs toward him, shouting, but he is holding his PR 24 side-handle baton.

The guy seems to take a long time arriving.

Jody later realized that she'd been watching the tape in slow motion.

But slow motion or fast, Dad had plenty of time to pull and fire. He'd chosen not to shoot the man.

Finally, the nut arrives and is swinging the machete down and sideways as if he intends to chop Dad's head off.

Dad catches the guy's forearm with a full power stroke of the baton. The machete flies and crashes through the store's plate glass window. While the glass is shattering, Dad is ducking low and bringing up the baton hard and fast between the assailant's legs. It strikes the thigh just to the side of the leopard skin pouch. The man cries out, hops, and plunges sideways through what is left of the disintegrating window.

'They show *that* at the academy?' Jody asked, astonished.

'They sure do.' Miles tossed the moist sock into the tub.

'The creep *sued* us. He and his slimy lawyer wanted three million bucks! Can you believe it? Three million! I mean, Dad had every right to shoot the dirtbag. He risked his life by not shooting him, and the bastard turns around and files a goddamn *lawsuit*!'

Miles gaped at her. When Jody was done, she pursed her lips and blew softly. 'You've got a temper.'

'Yeah. Well. Anyway, the suit was dismissed, but . . . Some things make me mad.'

'Obviously.'

'Yeah. Sorry.'

'Do you know what they call a thousand lawyers at the bottom of the ocean?'

'No, what?'

'A good start.'

Jody started to laugh, but quit when she saw Miles squeezing the tube. A white worm of cream squirmed put onto the cop's fingertip.

'That's gonna sting, isn't it?'

'I doubt it.'

'I'd really rather not have any more pain today, if it's all the same to you.'

'It won't hurt. It's just antiseptic. You don't want to get infected, do you?'

She thought about that one for a while. Finally, she answered, 'I guess not. But take it easy, okay?'

'Easy does it.' Miles gently spread the goo over the raw wound. The white cream turned pink as blood mixed with it.

'Yuck.'

'Does it sting?'

'Feels pretty good, actually.'

Miles wiped her fingertip with a bit of gauze, then unrolled a long strip and folded it into a pad about two inches long. She smoothed the pad against the side of Jody's thigh. It stuck to the ointment. While she taped it in place, she said, 'Anyway, that video was my introduction to your father. I think he became an instant hero to just about everyone who saw it. Of course, we all wish he'd smashed the guy in the nuts, but that would've been out of policy. The brass just loved it that he showed so much restraint and still managed to demolish that scumwad.'

'He's done some other stuff.'

'Don't I know it.'

Jody grinned. 'So, you think he's pretty cool?'

'Cool?' Miles let out a small laugh. 'Something like that, I suppose. He does seem to be an interesting fellow.'

'You don't think he's funny-looking, do you?'

'Jody! That's a terrible thing to say.'

'Well, he doesn't exactly look like Tom Cruise, you know.'

'He looks just fine.'

'Do you really think so?'

'Sure.'

'I figure the reason he doesn't have hardly any girlfriends is because of how his mouth is kind of crooked and how he walks funny. Not to mention that he looks like he's all set to rip off somebody's head.'

'Oh, he does not.'

'I don't think women want to go out with somebody like that.'

Miles looked annoyed. 'Wouldn't *you* go out with him?'

'He's my *dad*. What do you think we are, perverts?'

Now, she laughed. 'I didn't mean it that way, and you know it. I mean, if he was some guy your own age, and not related to you, and he asked you out.'

'Dad doesn't allow me to go out.'

'But if he did.'

'Would I go out with a guy who looks like that?'

'Yeah.'

'Well, sure. Except it'd be weird going on a date with a guy who's the spitting image of my dad. Weird going on *any* date, for that matter. But what do *you* think? Would you go out with a guy like him?'

'You better believe it.'

Jody smiled over Miles's shoulder. 'Hear that, Dad?'

Miles jerked her head around. After a glance at the empty doorway, she scowled at Jody. Her scowl trembled, then cracked into a grin.

'Gotcha,' Jody said.

'I oughta smack you.'

'Anyway, can we get out of here, now?' She stood up and slipped her bare right foot into her moccasin. 'I don't want to sit around all night in my undies.'

'Let's go.' Miles went ahead of her. And looked both ways before stepping into the corridor.

Jody felt her stomach plunge.

What if they're here!

The whole bunch from last night!

Don't be ridiculous, she told herself.

Miles gestured for her to come ahead, then led the way, Jody giving directions to the bedroom. After a quick check of the room, she posted herself at the door.

Jody put on a pair of tan shorts and white socks. She was just stepping into her moccasins again when Dad called, 'Jody? Miles?'

'Down here,' Miles called. 'Did we get the shooter?'

'Found the house he fired from. He was long gone. Left behind a firebomb, but our boys got to it with a couple minutes to spare.'

Miles sidestepped into Jody's room. Moments later, Dad came in. He looked angry, grim. 'A crime scene unit's on the way up there now. They've got a couple of bodies to deal with. The owners of the house, apparently. I want to run up there and have a look for myself.'

'I'll look after Jody till you get back,' Miles said.

'Appreciate it.' To Jody, he said, 'How you doing, hon?'

'Not bad. Officer Miles patched me all up. The guy who shot at me, he killed people up on the hillside?'

'It sure looks that way. Don't worry about anything, though. Nobody can get to you.'

'I'm not worried about that.'

'Just stay inside and keep away from windows.'

'I'll see to it, sir,' Miles said.

He gave her a thumbs up, winked at Jody, said, 'I'll try not to be gone long,' and left.

PART FOUR

Simon Says

Chapter Nineteen

Hello again. Here I am, settled in a rather scabby motel, my hideout till I can get a few things taken care of. It's still Saturday, by the way.

Okay, where to start?

Got it. Here goes . . .

We'll start with the refrigerator.

It was a big white Amana with a major collection of cutesy magnets stuck to its door. The magnets mostly showed imitation food: a banana, a slice of watermelon, a taco, a grilled cheese sandwich, that sort of crap. Benedict's mouth was open, so I shoved the grilled cheese sandwich in it.

A little late for his last meal, huh? Couldn't have been very tasty, anyhow. It was made out of foam rubber and plastic, and had this magnet glued to the back.

While I worked on unloading the refrigerator, I helped myself to another bottle of Beck's and some snacks. Crackers, salami, and cheese.

Tossed most of the stuff into cupboards. Anything that might rot and stink ended up in the freezer compartment or down the disposal. Once the shelves were empty, I pulled them out and stuck them out of sight in the broom closet.

Benedict went into the refrigerator upside-down with his head shoved sideways and most of his weight on the backs of his shoulders. That's the best way to put people in refrigerators. You want their center of gravity to be low, so they're not as likely to topple and fall out the door. It works better if you cut off the head first. That way, the shoulders fit nice and snug against the bottom corner. But I didn't want to mess with it, so I left his head on. Once he was arranged in a way that looked fairly sturdy, I shut the door. Then I shook the whole refrigerator a few times and stepped back. The door stayed shut.

With that chore done, I hurried back into the bedroom. My blue denim skirt and lovely yellow blouse were ruined with blood. I tossed them on the floor. In the bathroom, I washed the blood off my skin. Then I found a faded blue sundress that was sleeveless and had a zipper up the back. Had a lousy time with the zipper, but finally got it up.

I picked up Hillary's hair and put it on, adjusted it in the mirror, and decided that I looked utterly ravishing. Then I gathered my purse and headed for Benedict's Jaguar.

I turned heads.

It was a convertible, of course. And there I sat behind its wheel, naked-armed, gorgeous, my thick brown hair flowing in the wind. (Hillary's scalp made my head itch, but it was sticky so it clung fairly well. A few times, when an odd gust of wind got the upper hand, I needed to clap a hand down to stop the hair from flying off. Mostly, though, it worked fine.)

Within about a mile of the Weston house, I drove past three cop cars: two black and whites, and one 'unmarked' maroon job with a couple of plainclothes guys inside. I figured they were in the neighborhood looking for me.

Well, they sure saw me, all right.

Of the six cops, five were men and one was a gal. They each gave me a good, long look. I had a real urge to smile and wave, or blow them some kisses. But I pointedly ignored them, instead, figuring that's how Hillary would've behaved, seeing as how she was probably a stuck-up rich bitch who considered it beneath her dignity to be friendly to the peons.

Luckily, I didn't need to grab my hair while any of the cops were admiring me.

The cops weren't the only people who checked me out. Men of all ages, shapes and colors gaped at me as I passed. Instantly smitten. Instantly desiring me. One fellow, jogging beside his girlfriend or wife, latched his eyes on me and turned his head to keep watching and stepped off the curb. In the rear view mirror, I got to see him stumble into the street. He flopped and skidded.

I laughed, but then I got pretty excited because his fall made me think about the girl last night – the way she'd slid on the wet grass, the way she'd looked with her nightie up.

Such a beaut, that girl.

I quit paying attention to how guys were staring at me, and spent a while enjoying thoughts about what I would do with her when I got her.

It was great to think about for a while. But after I was clear of the neighborhood, I had to start wondering what to do next.

I couldn't go home. Home is an apartment in West LA where I live alone. For one thing, my keys were gone. I'd left them in Tom's van along with my clothes, and no telling where any of that stuff might be by now. For another thing, some of my neighbors would see me if I went home. My disguise might work fine on strangers, but it wouldn't fool anyone who knows me. And the last big reason for staying away from my apartment was that some of my 'friends' might be there waiting for me.

Naturally, they know where I live.

And they had to know that I'd botched the job. The witnesses I was supposed to have killed had gotten away and told on us. I'd have to be punished one way or another.

Maybe with their own brand of 'the final solution'.

Or maybe not.

One thing was for sure: I'd blown it. The guys couldn't possibly be happy about it.

The best thing I could do, I figured, was to lay low until I could find out how things stood.

That's why I ended up here at the Palm Court. It's the dumpiest motel I could find after cruising up and down La Cienega a couple of times. It looked like a good place for pulling a disappearing act.

The guy in the office looked young enough to be in high school. He had a face so greasy you could fry eggs on it, and a big juicy whitehead at the corner of one nostril. He kept staring at my chest and sliding his tongue across his lips while I filled out the registration card.

I used the name Simone De Soleil and gave an address in Deland, Florida.

I paid with cash, compliments of Hillary and Benedict, for three nights.

The kid had a weird, scratchy voice. 'My name's Justin, ma'am. If there's anything I can do for you . . .'

'I'll be sure to let you know,' I told him.

The plastic tab dangling off the room key was so slippery that I wondered if Justin had been rubbing it on his nose. It showed that I'd been given room eight.

Palm Court has about twenty units, all of them facing the court – which is really nothing but a driveway wide enough for parking spaces in front of the rooms. From the looks of things, the place must've had about fifteen vacancies when I checked in.

My room was at the end. I parked in front of it. My Jag *can* be seen from La Cienega, but just barely. A cop driving by would have to be very lucky to catch a glimpse of it back here.

The room isn't much. But it seems to have everything I need – if you don't count sanitary conditions.

The first thing I did was shut the curtains. Then I turned on the air conditioner. Yes, even a dump like this has air conditioning. It's a window unit that wheezes and clumps and groans . . . I'm sure you can hear it on the tape. Hear it?

Anyway, I don't mind the noise because it'll keep anyone from catching what I say in here.

Before getting started, I peeled off my hair. Or Hillary's hair. Whose is it, anyway? The question of ownership becomes rather fuzzy sometimes, doesn't it?

Whatever. It's mine now.

And I was enormously relieved to free my bare head from its moist, tacky grasp. As soon as it was off, I bent over the bathroom sink and washed my pate with soap and water. Not because I felt *dirty*, mind you; emotionally, the contact with her skin gives me real pleasure. It's the *itchiness* that drives me up the wall.

While I scrubbed my head, I decided I'd better lay my hands on a wig. A wig, not somebody's scalp. Hillary's hair had done a fine job in helping me escape from her cop-infested neighborhood, but now I would need something better. Besides, hers wasn't likely to improve with age.

Her mop of hair is within easy reach, right now, just in case Justin or someone should happen to come to the door.

I've kept my clothes on, of course. God knows, I wouldn't want my skin to come into contact with the chair. The nubby brown upholstery looks anything but clean. I haven't even taken off my shoes, though I'd like to except for the fact that they protect me from whatever gobs and tidbits and sharp objects reside in the carpet.

Okay, I think that brings me pretty much up to date.

The room does have a telephone.

It sits on a small table beside the bed. It's pink, and smudged.

I know Tom's number by heart.

I know I've gotta phone him. And the sooner, the better.

It makes me feel sick to think about doing it, though. Not just because I'd need to touch the filthy phone, though the idea of that is fairly disgusting.

I don't want to talk to him.

He left me out to dry.

No, that's not it. That's part of it. He stabbed me in the back. They all did. And that has to be part of it. But the real thing is that I'm scared.

It'd be like phoning a doctor to get the results of a lab test when you just know he's gonna say you've got cancer or AIDS or something.

Tom is gonna tell me I blew it. If he's feeling generous, he'll spare my connections – Lisa and the others.

But you've gotta go, Simon.

All the pleading in the world won't change a thing. It won't matter that we've been buddies forever. Nothing will matter except that I let the witnesses get away from me, and they told.

I can't make that call. Not right now, anyway.

Fact is, I don't feel like doing anything. I want to just sit here and talk and nothing else.

Maybe I *can* use the tapes for leverage.

I already told who all the members are, so that's taken care of. Now let's give out some real goodies, some really *incriminating* stuff that the cops can sink their teeth into if they ever get hold of these tapes.

Let's start at the start. With the first killing.

Chapter Twenty

It didn't start out to be a killing.

This was when we were in junior high, about twelve years ago. Tommy, me, Ranch and Brian were in the eighth grade together, and we'd been best friends for ever.

Brian's last name was Fisher. That's why we called him Minnow. Because of his name and size. He was a skinny little guy and still is.

Anyway, he developed a bad case of the hots for Denise Dennison. Easy to understand why. She was so cute it almost hurt to look at her. Her hair was like gold, her skin like honey, and she had eyes like the sky on a hot summer morning. If that wasn't enough, she had great tits and never wore a bra, so you could see them every once in a while when she bent over.

I guess maybe we *all* had the hots for Denise.

The rest of us were smart enough to know we didn't stand a chance with her, but not Minnow. He was, is, and always will be a nerd, a klutz, a doufuss, and a complete optimist. In other words, a real loser.

'I think she likes me,' he told us one day after school.

'Bull,' I said.

'What's there to like?' Tommy said.

'Your silken tresses?' Ranch asked. We always liked to rib Minnow about his hair. He wore it down to his shoulders – not real smart when you're a thirteen-year-old wimp. He thought the long hair made him look radical, but it didn't. It just made him look dopey and clued in everyone that he was a self-destructive nitwit.

191

So I said that maybe he could go out with Denise and she could braid his hair for him.

'I'm *gonna* ask her out,' he said.

'Don't waste your time,' I told him.

'She'll dump all over you, man,' Ranch said.

'Maybe, maybe not.'

'Hey, give it a try,' Tommy said. 'You got nothing to lose. The worst that can happen is she says no.'

'And maybe makes you feel no better than a worm,' Ranch added.

'A worm's even lower than a minnow,' I pointed out.

'Ha ha.'

It turned out that when we talked about the 'worst that can happen,' we had no idea.

The next day at school the three of us watched Minnow when he walked up to Denise in the lunch line. From where we stood, we had a good view. We just couldn't hear anything.

She looked great. She had her hair in a pony tail. She wore a pleated skirt that was hardly long enough to hide her butt. She also wore a white blouse, and I can still remember how you could see the pink color of her skin through its back – and no straps.

Minnow stopped right beside her.

'He's really gonna do it,' Ranch said. He sounded amazed by Minnow's audacity.

While we watched, Denise swung her head sideways. She seemed to be gazing straight into Minnow's eyes. She nodded a few times, and had this alert, open look on her face. Then, he must've reached the main part of his speech where he asked her to go ice skating with him at the rink on Friday night. All of a sudden, her face went funny. She tried very hard to keep on smiling, but the smile squirmed into what amounted to a pitiful grimace while she turned him down.

He told us later what she'd said. 'Thanks for asking, Brian. Really. It's very nice of you. But I'm sort of going with someone, you know?'

'I'LL GO WITH YOU! I'M HELL ON SKATES!'

That came from Hester Luddgate, who happened to be standing right behind Denise in the food line, and must've been listening in on the whole conversation.

I've already talked a little bit about Hester. She turned up in that little dream I had last night. The dream where I was having a great old time till the cute gal suddenly turned into an ugly, mutilated thing. That was Hester.

Hester didn't just look like a pig. She smelled like a sock after you've worn it all day – a very hot day, and maybe you'd hiked through a swamp. Basically, she always smelled like that.

Anyway, Hester blurted out, 'I'M HELL ON SKATES,' and then grabbed Minnow's arm. She grabbed it hard. I could see his body go stiff, and later he showed us the bruises her fingers had made.

She gave up her place in line, and hustled Minnow away.

We lost track of them because we were pretty much doubled over laughing and had tears in our eyes.

What we found out, though, was that Hester had gone and dragged him around a corner of the building so they could have some privacy. Minnow'd tried to worm out of the skating date, but she'd used all her charms on him: a combination of tears and threats.

He finally agreed to meet her at the rink on Friday night at eight o'clock.

But when eight o'clock on Friday night came around, Minnow was with us in Tommy's house. It's a mansion up in the hills above Sunset. His mother actually owned the place, but she had no say in anything. Tommy ran her. She was scared to death of him, and never got in our way. She used to hide in her bedroom, and we'd have the rest of the house to ourselves.

So that's where we were when Minnow was supposed to be having his big date with Hester. We had a poster cardboard, and we all sat around it on the floor of Tommy's recreation room (or 'wreck room') and worked on our collage. We called it, 'Death by Torture'. We used pictures of knives and hatchets and arrrows and stuff that we snipped out of sports magazines and a Penney's catalog, plus pictures of naked babes we got from magazines like *Playboy* and *Penthouse*. It was great. We had a terrific time deciding on how to combine the weapons with the gals – where to stick them. And we cut ourselves and used real blood to mess things up right.

At one point, Minnow stabbed his scissors into a closeup shot and said, 'Take that, you stinky swine.'

'She never looked that good,' Ranch told him.

'Poor bitch is probably crying her eyes out,' Tommy said.

I checked my wristwatch. Minnow was already two hours late for his date. 'She's probably quit crying and gone home by now,' I said.

'You really showed her,' Ranch said.

Minnow grinned. 'Taught her not to mess with me, huh?'

That was Friday night. On Sunday afternoon, Minnow was left at home alone while his folks went to watch a celebrity tennis tournament.

He was in the den watching TV. All of a sudden, Hester stepped through the doorway and pointed a .22 pistol at him. She said, 'Where *were* you, Brian? You promised you'd come, and I waited and waited and you didn't come.' She started out cool, smirking, real superior. But pretty soon she was bawling. Minnow figured he was dead meat. 'I *waited* and *waited*!' she kept crying. 'You had no right! You liar! You dirty rotten liar. You *promised*!'

Then she stepped up to Minnow and told him to open his mouth. He did, and she stuck the gun in.

He was still sitting on the easy chair, never had a chance to get up. And now this big stinky slob has a pistol in his mouth. And she cocks it.

'You think just 'cause I'm not pretty like Denise you can treat me like poop! Well, you can't! You can't! So maybe I'm not real pretty, but I got feelings! You had no right! You had no right!'

Then she pulled the trigger.

There was nothing but a click.

The pistol was a semi-auto. It had a full magazine up its handle, but the chamber was empty. We never did find out whether it was empty on purpose – and she only meant to scare Minnow – or if she'd really tried to shoot him but was just too stupid to work the gun.

When it went click, Minnow thought for a second that he'd been shot. Then he realized the thing hadn't gone off, after all. So he grabbed the barrel and shoved it away from him and jerked his head back till the muzzle was out of his mouth. They both wrestled for the gun. She kept trying to re-aim it at him. She was bigger and stronger than Minnow, so she ended up pulling him out of the chair, right onto his feet in front of her.

Big mistake. He pumped a knee up into her fat guts. Totally demolished her, took out every inch of fight. She let go of the gun and went to her knees.

After that, he worked her over pretty good.

Then he called up Tommy, and Tommy phoned me, and I

phoned Ranch. It took us about ten or fifteen minutes to get there.

Hester was sprawled on the floor of the den, lying real still but moaning and whimpering.

We dragged her out to the garage. We used the remote to open the garage door. Tommy pulled his Mercedes in. Then we shut the door and loaded Hester into the trunk.

Back inside the house, we checked around the den to make sure it looked okay. Hester had left nothing behind except her sour stink and some slobber. We figured the smell would go away on its own. But we cleaned up the slobber, then wiped places where Hester might've left fingerprints.

Minnow wrote a note for his parents. It said he'd gone over to Tommy's to 'fool around'.

True enough.

Ranch and I had both walked over, so we had no bikes to deal with. After Tommy had backed his Mercedes out of the garage and the door was shut again, we all piled in. He drove.

Tommy was only thirteen, so it wasn't especially legal. He wasn't the sort of guy to let that stop him, though. This wasn't the first time he'd borrowed his mother's car and tooled around in it.

The whole thing was nuts, really.

Tommy was mature for his age, I guess. Mentally. Physically, though, he looked thirteen. Any cop catching a glimpse of him behind the wheel would've pulled us over and pulled us in – and would've found Hester in the trunk. Of course, she was still alive at that point. They couldn't have gotten us for murder.

Anyway, it didn't happen.

We were all pretty tense, but we lucked out. Maybe everyone in LA – cops included – was over at the celebrity tennis tournament.

We relaxed as soon as we got through the security gate at Tommy's.

He's got a very long, winding driveway. We stopped before the house came into sight. By this time, Minnow had fiddled with the gun and pumped a round into its chamber. He used it to make Hester do what we wanted.

We made her climb out of the trunk and walk ahead of us into the trees. She was shaking and blubbering a lot. Pretty disgusting. But she didn't try to scream or run away. I guess she was afraid Minnow might shoot her.

It was really a beautiful autumn afternoon. Some people say Los Angeles hasn't got seasons, but it does. On autumn afternoons, the sunlight gets a mellow, dusty look. It's more reddish than usual, and throws a soft golden haze over everything.

The afternoon was hot, but had a good breeze – a wonderful breeze that blew my hair and fluttered my clothes. It felt even better when my clothes were off.

Like I said a while back, it didn't start out to be a killing.

I don't think so, anyway.

The way I looked at it, we planned to teach her a lesson – teach her not to mess with any of us, and also give Minnow a chance to get even for the grief she'd caused him. Not kill her.

I guess I thought we might rough her up a little. Nothing serious, though.

That was before we started following her into the trees. Somehow, it all changed, then. For all of us, maybe.

The thing is, nobody knew we had her and nobody could see us.

We could do *anything* to her.

I suddenly knew it, and I could tell by the silence and the way we all gave each other nervous, eager looks that Tommy and Ranch and Minnow knew it, too.

We could do whatever we wanted, and nobody would ever find out.

Even Hester caught on.

She looked over her shoulder at us. All sad and pitiful and pouting. For about two seconds. Then she must've noticed the change in us. She suddenly had panic in her eyes. She gasped and ran.

Minnow shot her.

The pistol made a *bam* not much louder than the sound of an enthusiastic clap.

I heard the bullet smack her. Then she made an 'Oof!' noise and fell to her knees.

The bullet had hit her behind the right shoulder. I saw a dot of blood on her white T-shirt.

She twisted her head around and tried to see the hole. She reached over with her left hand. Her fingers wiggled against her shoulder blade, but couldn't get down to the hole.

We started walking toward her. 'You shot me!' she cried out. 'What's the matter with you? You *shot* me! Are you nuts?'

'Yeah,' Minnow said. 'How did you like it?' He took aim at her.

'Don't shoot me again! Please! No! It *hurts*! Jesus!'

He was all set to shoot her again, anyway, but Tommy whispered, 'Don't. We don't want her dead. Not yet.'

Ranch rubbed the back of his hand across his mouth. 'What're we gonna do with her?' he asked. His voice was shaking.

'Everything,' Tommy said. 'First we strip. Don't want to get any stains on our clothes.'

We stripped. We piled our clothes out of the way so they wouldn't get messed up. We always carried pocket knives, so we took them with us.

It felt great being naked. The sun, the breeze. The way the twigs and leaves crackled under our feet.

Hester didn't put up any fight.

She just cowered on the ground, crying and begging, while we ripped her clothes off.

Man.

She was a pig, but she was naked. For me and Ranch and Minnow, it was all brand new. (No telling what Tommy'd been up to before Hester, but I have the feeling that he was pretty experienced.) Anyway, we were so excited we hardly knew what to do.

We were all over her.

After just studying her and feeling her up for a while, we took turns fucking her.

She didn't move at all while we did it. Just sobbed and stayed limp and still.

Sort of by accident, we found out that it made things better if we hurt her. She'd flinch and jerk and tighten up. So we started pinching her and biting her and poking her with our knives. The worse we hurt her, the better it got.

Then we found out it felt great to hurt her even when we *weren't* fucking her.

When it got really rough, we stuffed her panties in her mouth to muffle her screams and we had to hold her down.

I think, we were at her for about three hours before she died. What gave it away was when she just stayed limp when any normal person jabbed the way Ranch had just jabbed her would've jumped and shrieked.

'What's the matter with her?' Minnow whispered.

'You want a list?' I asked him. I can sometimes be a real wit.

'She's dead, you dorks,' Ranch said.

'Maybe not,' Tommy said. 'Let's see if her heart's still beating.'

Things got *very* messy.

Pretty soon, Tommy was holding her heart in his cupped hands. 'Is it beating?' he asked, grinning at it.

'Beats me,' I said.

He laughed and threw it at me. It bounced off my shoulder. I went after it and threw it back at him. He snatched it out of the air with a neat, one-handed grab. Then we all kind of played catch with it for a while. Made sort of an odd picture, four naked guys, drenched with blood, standing in a circle around Hester, tossing her heart around while Ranch whistled 'Sweet Georgia Brown', the Harlem Globetrotters' song.

Anyway, that's how our first kill happened.

We figured that Hester's body was hidden just fine where it was. It couldn't be seen from the air because of the trees, and it was a good, safe distance away from the driveway and house. Also, the property was walled in. Tommy never allowed his mother to hire any workers, so there was no chance of a landscape guy stumbling onto her.

The upshot was, we didn't cover her or bury her or anything. Just left her sprawled on her back on the ground.

We hiked the rest of the way to Tommy's house. On the front lawn, we hosed ourselves down. (Tommy's mother watched us from an upstairs window – which seemed weird, and also kind of excited me. Tommy wasn't worried. He laughed and waved at her.) The water was horribly cold. I still remember how it made me flinch and shudder, and gave me goosebumps.

After washing off all the blood and stuff, we went around to the back of the house and fooled around in the swimming pool. We raced and played tag. Then we climbed out and sprawled on lounges, shivering until the sun warmed us up.

'Your mom won't tell on us, will she?' Minnow asked.

'You've gotta be kidding.'

'What if she finds the body?' I asked.

'She won't. But even if she does, she won't do anything about it. She knows what'd happen to her.'

After the sun had dried us, we walked back through the woods and found our clothes. We didn't say anything while we were getting dressed. We all kept glancing over at the body, which was about twenty feet away. Some flies had found it.

Minnow handed the pistol to Tommy. 'You'd better keep it. If I took it home, my mom'd find it. Then I'd be in for some real trouble.'

Tommy stuck the gun into his front pocket.

He's the one who wanted a closer look at Hester.

When we were all dressed, we walked over to her.

'I guess that's what she gets,' Minnow said. He didn't sound very cheerful.

'I sure do wish we could bring her back to life,' Tommy said.

'What?' I asked. I couldn't believe my ears. 'Bring her back to life?'

'Yeah. So we could do it to her all over again.'

We all laughed at that one.

Later on, Tommy drove us home. Mom and Dad were out back, having cocktails. I helped myself to a handful of peanuts. 'Did you have a good time over at Tommy's?' Mom asked.

'Yeah! We played catch, swam in the pool . . . It was great!'

Later, Dad did shish kebabs on the barbecue.

Speaking of shish kebabs, I'm starving. Haven't had a bite since the sandwich I ate while I was unloading the fridge for Benedict, and it wasn't much.

Problem is, I can't go out bald and I really don't feel like sticking Hillary's clammy old scalp on my head right now. I've *got* to get my hands on a decent wig.

But first I've gotta eat.

Ah ha! I'll phone in for something and have it delivered right here to my room.

It'll mean touching that grimy phone, of course.

Guess I'll clean it first.

Anyway, that's it for right now. We'll continue my adventures after I've put some chow inside me.

Chapter Twenty-one

Okay. All set. I ordered Chinese, by the way. Sweet and sour pork.

Hester was such a pig. Maybe all that talking about her is what made me hanker for pork.

It was very tasty, by the way.

Before the delivery boy arrived, I wrapped a bath towel around my head – the way some gals do when their hair is still wet. Seemed to work fine.

Anyway, back to my history of our nefarious deeds.

What we did to Hester pretty much changed everything. For starters, it was just incredibly exciting, sexually and every other way. Doing her that way was the biggest thrill I'd ever had. The rest of the guys felt that way, too. I know because we talked about it. A lot. Hell, we couldn't *stop* talking about it.

Mixed in with how great it had been, there was a kind of sick feeling. We all had the sick feeling. It was partly fear that we might get caught and convicted of murder. Being only thirteen years old, though, we wouldn't have had much to worry about from the California legal system. A couple of years in juvenile hall, maybe. But the notion that everybody would *find out* about what we'd done to Hester was enough to give me a yucky stomach. Mom and Dad, for instance. Talk about embarrassing.

I mean, this wasn't like we'd shoplifted an album or smoked dope. This was serious stuff that could basically ruin our futures.

Nothing about Hester showed up in the newspaper or on the television news. Around school, rumor had it that she'd run away from home. She'd run away before, a year earlier, and had actually disappeared for a whole month. So nobody suspected foul play.

That was good news. But we figured it would all change if her body got found. Each day for the first week after the murder, Tommy checked to make sure her body was still where we'd left it. He tried to calm us down by saying it would never be found, impossible.

'And even if it is,' he said that Thursday, 'the cops won't have any reason to think we had anything to do with it.'

'She's on *your* property,' I pointed out. 'And what if we left fingerprints on her.'

'You can't leave fingerprints on skin,' he said.

'Are you sure?'

'Well . . . I don't know for sure, but . . .'

The next day, at lunch, Tommy had news for us. 'I went to the library after school and checked out some books on criminal investigation techniques.' He wrinkled his nose. 'Man, I had no idea. It's a lot worse than I figured. There's no telling what sort of stuff the cops might get on us if they find Hester: how many of us were there, our blood types, hair color, height and weight, not even to mention what they might find out about our clothes and shoes.'

'Just from her body?' Ranch asked, his nose wrinkled.

'Yeah, from her body, plus everything they'll figure out when they study the crime scene.'

I suddenly felt like I might throw up.

Ranch and Minnow looked sick.

'What'll we do?' Minnow asked.

'It's no big problem,' Tommy said.

The big problem was waiting twenty-four hours without going nuts. On Saturday morning, Dad gave me a ride to Tommy's house. He identified himself into a speaker on the gate, the gate swung open and we went up the driveway to the house. Dad mussed my hair. 'Have a good one, pal,' he said. 'If you won't be home for dinner, give us a call.'

After everyone was there, Tommy equipped us with a couple of shovels, a pick, and a rake. Then he led us straight through the trees to Hester.

Man, what a mess. And what a stink.

I won't go into that, though. Don't want to make anybody sick.

Our job was to bury the body.

And what a job it was. Even with four of us taking turns at it, the digging was brutal.

Tommy did his fair share. He was still annoying, though. It seemed like all he could say was, 'Not deep enough. It's gotta be deeper. Deeper. Deeper.'

I was standing at the bottom of the grave when Tommy finally decided it *was* deep enough. 'Just even out the bottom a little,' he told me.

So I bent over with my shovel to put in the final touches,

and those sons of bitches tossed Hester down on me.

Hilarious. They thought so, anyhow.

She dropped onto my back and knocked me flat, and the *stink*! And she was slippery, like her skin had turned to goo. For better or for worse, I was naked (because of the heat, and so my clothes wouldn't get filthy from the digging). That saved my clothes from being wrecked by Hester. But it meant there was nothing between her and me. Talk about revolting!

I guess it was pretty funny, throwing her on me like that. At the time, though, I was anything but amused. I had an awful time getting out from under her. The way her arms and legs wrapped around me, it was like she wanted to *keep* me down there with her. When I finally managed to squirm free, she rolled onto her back and her knees flopped apart till the sides of the hole stopped them. 'Fuck me again.' That's what I heard, and it damn near turned my bones to ice before I realized Tommy was the one who'd said it. He was up above with Ranch and Minnow staring down at us.

So then I boosted myself out of the grave. 'You guys are a riot,' I said. 'Somebody else can fill in the . . .' Then I attacked, pretty much taking them by surprise. Before they had time to react, I shoved Minnow into the grave. Tommy dodged away from me and ran. Ranch stayed to fight. We wrestled, but I wasn't any match for him. He pinned me down. Even though I couldn't throw him into the grave, he ended up nicely slimed from squirming around with me.

Only Tommy got away unscathed.

He always does.

Anyway, Minnow finally climbed out of the grave. He looked gory, but he was grinning. We gathered up Hester's clothes and tossed them in with her. After that, we filled in the hole, then scattered leaves and twigs over the dirt until it looked the same as everywhere else.

Tommy reminded us of the .22 shell from the bullet Minnow had fired at her. He said we shouldn't leave it behind. So we spent about half an hour searching, and I finally found it.

Tommy put it in his shoe. 'I'll get rid of it later. The important thing is that it doesn't get found near the body. Maybe I'll throw it in the trash at school, or something.'

When we started picking up the tools to leave, he said, 'Wait. We've gotta take care of one more thing. Come here.' He held his hands out away from his sides, the way people do when they want you to form a circle and join hands.

We did it.

He said, 'As long as Hester stays here where we put her, nobody can ever touch us.'

'The cops, you mean?' Minnow asked.

'Yeah, the cops. The thing is, nobody will ever find her unless they know where to look. And they won't know where to look unless one of us blabs.'

We all pretty much at once promised we'd never blab.

'We've gotta make a pledge,' Tommy said.

Nobody had any objection to that.

'Repeat after me,' he said. 'I, Thomas Baxter . . .'

We all substituted our own names. As the pledge went along after that, Tommy waited after each phrase so we'd have time to say it. Mine went like this:

'I, Simon Quirt, a full-fledged member in good standing of the Killer Krulls [this was the first I'd heard of our name, though I knew the book where he'd picked it up], do hereby swear on pain of death to myself and my entire family that I shall never betray any secrets of the club to any soul. I also swear to forfeit my own life to prevent the cops from ever taking me alive. I also swear to kill any fellow Krull who breaks this oath, and also to kill his mother and father and sister and brother and dog, if he has them. Amen.'

I almost laughed a couple of times, including when it came to the 'amen'. But I held it in because Tommy seemed pretty serious about the whole thing.

He'd probably been up all night, thinking it up.

Back at his house, the garden hose wasn't good enough to get rid of Hester's aroma. So we went into the house. Tommy only had to wash his hands. The rest of us, one at a time, took hot showers while he went out to get our clothes.

It felt pretty good to be clean and dressed again. We got together in the den and had Pepsis and potato chips. Tommy told us that, with the body buried and everything, the cops wouldn't stand a chance of nailing us for what we did to Hester.

I don't think any of us really believed it.

There would *always* be a chance they'd get us.

For a few weeks, I worried about it all the time. I had plenty of nightmares, too. As time went by, though, it seemed less and less likely that we'd get caught. I quit feeling sick every time the phone or doorbell rang or I saw a cop car.

My nightmares eased off, but they've never gone away completely. I have some real doozies. Nightmares are supposed to be manifestations of unresolved shit in your unconscious mind, or something. I don't know, though. I've got this theory that maybe there really is such a thing as ghosts, but they aren't what people think. They don't creep through haunted houses. What they do is creep into your head. Maybe through the mouth, when you're sleeping. Or maybe through the nostrils. They get in there when you're zonked out, and make nightmares happen.

It's just a theory. Maybe I'm nuts. But I think somebody should look into it. Maybe scientists can figure out a way to stop the ghosts from getting in. Maybe something along the lines of a gas mask you wear when you go to bed. Call it a 'ghost mask'.

Anyway, where was I?

Okay.

What it boils down to is that nothing ever happened. We did all that to Hester, and got away with it.

We talked about it all the time, at least when nobody was around except the four of us. It was like reliving a championship game where we'd demolished the other team. 'Oh, man, did you see the look on her face when . . . I *meant* to shoot her there, you dork . . . How about when I took my knife and . . . Talk about dead, man, was she dead or what . . . How about that stink?' We'd go on and on.

Sometimes, we talked about doing it to someone else. We even made lists. Denise Dennison always topped the list, by the way. It was like a game, though. We had no intention of going after anyone, mostly because we were pretty sure we couldn't get away with it a second time. So we were just playing with our fantasies.

Four years went by, and it looked as if Hester Luddgate would forever be the one and only victim of the Killer Krulls.

The next killings happened during the summer before our senior year of high school.

By then, Tom had a driver's license so he could operate his Mercedes legally. He came up with the idea of taking a trip up the California coast and going all the way to Salem, Oregon. He wanted to check out Willamette University before deciding whether to apply for admission there. He thought it would be a kick if the whole gang went on the drive with him.

My parents agreed to let me go, even though they knew we'd be traveling without any adult supervision. For one thing, they trusted Tom. (He's handsome, polite, intelligent, witty, and rich – what's not to trust?) Also, they figured it would be a good experience for me.

I'm sure the parents of Ranch and Minnow also would've been glad to let their sons go on an adventure like that. Problem was, Ranch and Minnow were out of town on family vacations.

We'd gotten to know some other guys, though. Two of them, Clement Calhoun and Tony 'Private' Majors, joined us for the trip.

We had a blast. Clement was sort of dumb, and always up for anything. Private was a goofball. I could go on for ever about the stuff we did, but there's no point. It was all just dumb teenage junk, and pretty harmless. Like mooning a couple of old farts having a picnic by the roadside, that sort of thing. Also, we got drunk quite a few times.

Sometimes we stayed at motels, and other times we slept in our sleeping bags.

We'd been on the road for a few days, and were driving through a forest of giant Sequoias up above Fort Bragg, when we met up with the bicycle riders. Two of them. It was raining like mad, so they wore bright yellow slickers with hoods covering their heads. They were pedalling along single file, heading north just like us.

In the middle of our lane.

Coming down the other lane was a logging truck.

The bicyclists were going about half as fast as us. Tom couldn't swerve around them because of the truck, so he had to hit the brakes. 'Bastards!' he shouted at the windshield.

Those two freaks just kept doodling along as if nothing had happened. They didn't move over to the side of the road. They didn't even look back at us. Just stayed hunched over their handlebars and ignored us and pedalled up the middle of our lane.

Truck after truck came along, heading south. We had no choice except to stay behind the bikers – or run them down.

'Fuckers,' Clem muttered. 'What's the matter with 'em?'

'They all act like that,' I said. 'Plant somebody's ass on a bicycle seat, they think they own the road. You ever notice that?'

'I've noticed,' Tom said. 'I oughta drive right through 'em.'

'Not a bad idea,' I said.

Private was behind us with Clement. He leaned forward and peered over the top of Tom's seat back. 'Do it,' he said. He sounded very eager. 'Plow right through 'em. Go on. We Won't tell. Will we, guys?'

Tom and I glanced at each other.

'You don't really mean it,' Tom said.

'Sure I do. It'd be a gas. Slam right through those two fucks. It'd be a *gas*.'

'It'd probably kill 'em.'

'Big loss. Right, Clem?'

'Road hogs like them,' Clement said, 'they'll probably get run over sooner or later anyway.'

I smiled over my shoulder. 'You guys are *really* cold-blooded.'

'I'm not gonna run over them,' Tom said. 'It'd mess up my car.'

'Chicken,' Private said.

'Just give 'em a little bump,' Clement said.

About that time, we reached the top of a rise. Another logging truck roared by, throwing a shower of water at us. Then the road was clear all the way to the crest of the next hill, probably a mile away.

Tom could've swung around the bikers, now. Instead, he tooted his horn.

The one at the rear still didn't so much as glance back, but swung an arm in a gesture for us to go around them.

'How thoughtful,' I said.

So then Tom really laid on the horn and sped toward the rear bike. At the very last second, he swerved to the side. We roared by them both. Still, neither of them lifted a head to look at us. Like they were in their own little world.

We got about a couple of hundred yards ahead of them, and Tom pulled off onto the shoulder of the road.

'What're you doing?' Private asked. He sounded real excited and curious.

'Everybody out,' Tom said.

'Fan-fucking-tastic,' Clement said. 'We gonna pound 'em?'

'Something like that,' Tom said.

He popped the hood. Then we all climbed out and stood in the rain just in front of the car.

'What're we gonna do?' Private asked for the second time.

'Just do whatever I tell you,' Tom said.

We checked around. The road was still clear – just us and the bike riders. They came at us single file, hunkered down over their handlebars, their heads down so nothing showed except the tops of their yellow hoods.

Tom had been keeping Hester's old .22 pistol under the front seat, just in case. We all knew about it. Hell, you wouldn't want to take a long drive without some sort of a gun.

What we didn't know is that Tom had picked it up before leaving the car.

We didn't know it until he swung his right hand out from under his jacket, aimed and fired. *Bam bam!* Very quick. The rain was coming down hard, so I couldn't see where the bullets hit. But the bike in the lead took a quick swerve, skidded and flipped, tossing its rider toward the pavement.

Number two biker looked up. He had a black mustache. *Bam bam bam bam bam!*

He flung up his arms and tipped his face toward the sky and fell backward. He hit the rear tire of his bike, which made the bike flip and land on him.

'Let's go, let's go!'

Clement and Private, who both looked pretty shocked, bolted for the car doors.

'Morons!' I shouted. 'Come on. Quick!'

Tom and I dashed past them. He took the first biker and I took the second. While we dragged them toward the side of the road, we gave the other guys orders to bring along the bikes.

We had the road empty with at least half a minute to spare before anyone came along. We ducked in some bushes and watched a big old Winnebago roll by.

Then we dragged the bikers and bikes deeper into the woods. Mine, Mr Mustache, was deader than shit. One round had punched a hole in his chin, another had caught him between the eyebrows, and another had demolished his right eye.

Tom's biker was alive, but unconscious. She was still out cold when we got to a clearing and gathered around her. She had two nicely spaced holes in her left shoulder. We found them when we pulled off her rain slicker. One hole was in her bare skin. The other, half an inch away, had poked through the strap of her tank top. Her tank top was white except for the blood, and very tight. Like it was glued to her. You could see every curve and slope. She wasn't wearing any bra. Instead of normal shorts, she had on a black number that looked like bikini pants.

'Holy shit,' Private said after we'd taken off the gal's slicker.

'Man,' Clement whispered. 'She's hardly got anything on.'

'We'll fix that,' I said.

It was pretty funny, the way they acted while Tom and I stripped her. Like the old saying goes, they didn't know whether to shit or go blind. They just watched and kept their mouths shut. Actually, their mouths hung open. They didn't say anything, though.

She was nothing at all like Hester. She was damn cute. In fact, she looked a little like my friend from last night. Older, though. This gal was probably in her early twenties. Cute and slim, and shiny all over from the rain. She had very short hair that was wet and matted down. She had firm little tits. I watched the raindrops splash them. Her nipples were puckered up hard.

Gets me horny just thinking about her.

The one last night looked like she was maybe fifteen or sixteen. Man, I wish I had her with me right now, right here.

Anyway, we started messing around with the bike gal. Clement and Private got right in with the program. Probably because of how everything had gone crazy, anyhow, with Tom popping Mustache Boy the way he'd done. When you've been part of a deal where a stranger gets shot dead in cold blood, you figure anything goes. You've done the worst and you've got nothing to lose.

And also we knew the gal would have to be finished off so she couldn't tell on us. It was like she was dead already. But she wasn't really.

We were just starting to feel her up and hadn't even started getting drastic when she came to.

She was a hell of a scrapper.

Good thing *she* didn't have a Louisville Slugger.

Private sat on her face.

Uh . . .

I think I'd better try giving Tom a call.

I'd rather not, but . . .

Hell, we've been buddies for ever. What's he gonna do to me? It isn't my fault those two got away. If Tom and the guys had *helped* instead of running away and leaving it all to me, we would've nailed . . .

I mean, how can he blame *me*?

Anyway, the longer I wait the worse it's gonna get.

And what if they go ahead without me and take care of the girl?

Chapter Twenty-two

I picked up the phone to call Tom, dialed 9 for an outside line, then chickened out and punched in Lisa's number, instead. It was partly a way to procrastinate. Partly, too, I wanted to hear her voice. She loves me, which at times can be pretty annoying. On the other hand, though, it can sometimes be nice to know there's at least one person who isn't gonna turn on you, who'll probably stick by you even if things get bad.

I figured that talking with her might cheer me up. Also, I was curious to find out if my recorder could pick up the other side of a phone conversation.

After a few rings, Lisa's answering machine started talking to me. 'I'm not available to answer your call right now, but if you'll leave your name . . .' All that. After the sound of the tone, I told her it was me – in case she was home, after all, and just using the machine to screen her calls.

She still didn't pick up.

All of a sudden, I got a very bad feeling about things.

It's not that Lisa sits around her apartment all the time waiting for me to call or show up or something. But this is Saturday night. We always get together on Saturday nights. We don't arrange anything, I just show up and we do stuff. We eat, maybe take in a show, or maybe we just stay at her place and watch a couple of movies on her VCR and mess around. Normally, I would've been there by about seven, and it was a little after nine when I phoned. She should've been there to answer.

I told myself to stay calm.

A lot of good that did.

Anyway, the tape recorder didn't pick up shit. Oh, it got what I said. But Lisa's voice didn't come through at all, even though I'd held the thing right up tight against the phone's earpiece. You've got to have special equipment, I guess.

I figured the Target store in Culver City might still be open. It had an electronics section. I could drive out there and maybe buy a speaker phone or an answering machine. Either of those might let me record Tom's side of a conversation. But the last thing I needed, with nothing to wear except Hillary's clothes and hair, was to go wandering around in a crowded store.

Besides, I didn't have much confidence in my ability to hook up any sort of telephone equipment.

On top of which, anybody who isn't deaf can tell by the sound of his own voice if there's a speaker phone at the other end of the line. It sounds like you're talking with a metal waste basket on top of your head.

It probably took me about one minute to think about all

those angles and decide to forget trying to tape Tom's side of our conversation.

I know his number by heart. I know it even better than Lisa's. That's because he lives in the same big old mansion where he's always lived, and its phone number hasn't changed in at least fifteen years.

He picked up after three rings.

Here goes the conversation. It isn't exact, since I couldn't tape his side of it, but it's close. I've got a good memory for what people say, even when it happened years ago, and this was only a little after nine o'clock tonight.

'Hello?' Tom answered.

'Hey, man. It's me.'

'Well, well.'

'I guess you're pissed, huh?'

'We were counting on you, Si.' He sometimes calls me that. It's short for Simon, of course. It sounds like sigh.

'I could've used some help,' I told him. 'You all bugged out on me. There's only so much one guy can do, you know?'

'They're kids, Si.'

'Hey, I couldn't find 'em.'

'Kids. And you let them get away.'

'I didn't *let* them get away. You sound like I did it on purpose. Christ! I did everything I could to . . .'

'They're eye witnesses.'

'I know. I know that.'

'They could foul up everything for us.'

'I know.'

'Do you also know they murdered Minnow?'

'What?'

'Minnow. They bashed in his head.'

'You're kidding.'

'We found him in the boy's bedroom.'

'Shit.' Minnow had been an okay guy, but I hadn't loved him or anything. I didn't like hearing he'd been nailed, though. It made things worse for me.

'And you let them get away,' Tom said. Which is how it made things worse for me.

'Which one did it?'

'Which one had the baseball bat?' Not as if Tom didn't already know the answer. Even if he hadn't seen her with it, himself, Mitch and Chuck must've already filled him in on our chase.

'The girl,' I said.

'Jody.'

'You know her name?'

'Jody Fargo.'

'How'd you find out? The news hasn't been . . .'

'The news is lying about everything. The girl is Jody Fargo. The boy is Andrew Clark. His sister's the one that Ranch brought in, just before the shit hit.'

'Shish ka-sister.'

'Knock it off. If you think there's anything funny about this situation, you'll be changing your mind very soon.'

'Sorry,' I told him.

'Jody wasn't part of the family. From the look of things, she was nothing but a friend of the Clark girl, spending the night. We found some of her things in the girl's bedroom.'

'What sort of things?'

'Her clothes, her purse. And her driver's license.'

'A *driver's license*?'

'She turned sixteen last month.'

'It has her home address?'

'What do you think?'

'Shit! Let me have it!'

217

'You'll get it.' He meant that both ways. I could tell by the tone of his voice.

'Look, give me her address. I'll take care of everything. I'll take care of her tonight.'

'You're so full of shit.'

'I'll nail her. You think I won't?'

'I think you'd *better*.'

'So, where is she?'

'Safe at home. That's 2840 Shadow Glen Lane.'

'Got it.'

'Do you know where that is?'

'Sure. Just below Castleview, right?'

'Right.'

'I can be there in twenty minutes.'

'Where are you calling from?'

Nice question. It felt like a hammer pounding me in the heart. 'Nowhere,' I said. Great answer.

'Tell me.'

'Why do you want to know?'

'You don't have a car, do you? I'll have one of the guys pick you up.'

'I don't think so. Thanks, anyway. I've got a car. I can get to the gal's house on my own steam. Anything else?'

'I don't want you fucking up again.'

'I won't.'

'You'd better not. But when I said she was "safe" at home, I meant it. You'd think she was the President, all the security she's got. Dusty already put a try on her.'

I was shocked to hear they'd gone after the girl. It must've been a failure, though. 'He missed? Dusty missed?'

'He missed, all right.'

'Shit,' I said. I'd never heard of Larry Rhodes missing a shot with that .30–30 Winchester of his. That's why we called him Dusty. Anyone he ever shot at, he dusted. Except for Jody, obviously.

An omen, maybe.

Nothing short of a miracle could save a person from Dusty, but my Jody had survived him.

'Is Dusty okay?'

'He got away, if that's what you mean. Which is very lucky for you.'

I didn't want to ask why.

But Tom told me anyway.

'I wouldn't be in any mood to give you a second chance if you'd gotten Dusty killed tonight.'

There was good news in with the bad.

'Thanks, Tom. I mean it. I'll take care of everything.'

'Both of them.'

'What?'

'Jody and the boy, Andy.'

'Where's he?'

'That's for you to find out.'

'You don't know, or you won't tell me?'

'We don't know. He might be on the way to Arizona. Someone with Arizona plates picked him up at the girl's house . . .'

'She'll know where he is,' I said.

'More than likely.'

'No problem. She'll tell me.'

'You know your problem, Si?'

'You mean there's only one?'

'Your *main* one.'

'What's that?' I asked.

'You don't know your own limitations.'

'*Magnum Force*, right? The second Dirty Harry movie.'

'Fuck you and your movies.'

'Take it easy, huh Tom? My Christ, we've been pals since dinosaurs ruled the Earth. I screw up just one time – which by the way wasn't even my fault, if you want to know the truth – and by the way, I'm lucky to even be alive after the way you guys *ditched* me last night – so I mess up just once, and it's like I'm suddenly dirt. You're talking to me like I'm some kind of worthless fucking loser. *You don't know your limitations?* Man, that's lousy. That stinks.' I knew I sounded whiny and pathetic, but I couldn't stop it. 'So maybe I missed those kids last night, I'd like to see you do any better. I'd like to see *anyone* do any better.'

'None of us could've done much worse.'

'Yeah, sure. Nobody else even got close to 'em.'

'Well, you didn't get close enough.'

'I'll take care of them. Don't worry about it.'

'*I'm* not worried, Si. Do you know who *is* worried?' He said, 'Bring her over here,' to someone else.

'Hey,' I said.

My stomach was suddenly taking a nosedive. I'd half expected something like this, but expecting it and getting it are two different things.

'It's Simon,' I heard Tom say.

Then he must've stuck the phone in Lisa's face. 'Simon?' she asked. She sounded pitiful.

'It's me, babe.'

'Goddamn you!' she shrieked. More than once. She really sounded crazy and scared.

'Calm down,' I told her.

'Go to hell!'

'I'm on your side, babe.'

'Oh, really? Oh, really? I know these guys. I know *all* these guys. They're all your good old buddies, you bastard! Why are they *doing* this to me?'

'Doing what?' I asked.

Instead of answering, she yelled, 'Make them let me go!'

'I will,' I told her. 'Don't worry. I'll take care of everything.'

Tom's voice came back. 'We won't hurt her if . . .'

'Sounds like you've *already* hurt her.'

'Not much. But tomorrow night at ten we're gonna start on her in earnest. Unless we've got the kids by then. You bring us Jody Fargo and Andy Clark, and they'll get it instead of Lisa.'

'Hey.'

'We want them both alive. Right here, alive, ten tomorrow night.'

'If you wanted them alive, how come you sent Dusty to . . .?'

'Good question, Simon. The answer's simple. Dusty says the girl's a fox.'

'What, that comes as a surprise?'

'Matter of fact. None of us saw much of her last night – unless maybe you did. So we didn't know she was such a fox. Not till Dusty got back. He got a good, close look at her with his scope. Fact is, he's the one suggested we try to get her alive. Said it'd be a waste of fabulous pussy just to pop her off at a distance.'

'What did he do, miss her on purpose?'

'Do you think he'd admit it, if he did?'

'Well, shit.'

'Looks like he's got the hots for her. And now he's got the rest of us interested. So bring her in alive, Si.'

'All by myself?'

'Hey, we already lost Minnow. I don't want to risk anyone else.'

'Just me.'

'That's about the size of it.'

221

'It really sucks.'

'Tell you what. I'll make things easier for you. I won't insist you bring Andy in alive. Mitch and Chuck'll be disappointed, but what the hell – I don't want to make things *impossible* for you. So it'll be enough to put Andy down. Do that and bring us Jody, and everything'll be cool.'

'How about giving me a couple more days?'

'No way. You've got till ten tomorrow night. One minute after, we start working on Lisa.'

Just then, I almost told him about the tapes I'd been making all day. Something made me hold off, though.

'Any questions, comments, suggestions?'

'I'll take care of it,' I said, and hung up.

Right after that, I turned my recorder on and started playing catch-up, telling about the calls. I've been talking into this thing for fifteen minutes or so, I guess. It's given me a chance to calm down.

At least Tom's giving me a second chance.

And he really did give me a break, allowing me to kill the boy, Andy. If I get a chance to take him alive, I will. It'll earn me some Brownie points from Mitch and Chuck. But now I won't have to worry about it. I'll drop him at a distance if there's no easy way to snatch him.

Everything might turn out fine, after all. If I take care of business, Lisa'll get released and I'll be back in everybody's good graces. Probably.

Which makes it a smart play to keep quiet about these tapes. They're like dynamite – they'll blow up the bridges behind me. One mention of these things, there won't be any going back. It'll be them or me.

And there are a lot *more* of them.

I really want Jody for myself. That's the problem.

One of the problems. Another might be getting my hands

on her, if she's 'got more security than the President' like Tom says.

A guy could get hurt.

If I don't get her, though, things will take a very nasty turn. The guys won't stop with Lisa. They'll go after my sisters, and so on. They'll go after me, too.

Anyway, I *want* to get her.

Tom said I've got to deliver her alive, but he didn't say she has to be in mint condition. So, basically, I'll be able to do *almost everything* to Jody before turning her over tomorrow night.

I'd better quit gabbing, now, and get to work.

Man, I'm starting to get excited.

Ready or not, here I come.

PART FIVE

Missing in Indio

Chapter Twenty-three

The phone rang three times while Jody rushed to get it. She half expected the caller to be Rob. They hadn't seen each other since the day before yesterday when they met at the mall, and she missed him. But what would she say? Should she tell him about the murders and everything? Probably better not to. Dad might not like it if she . . .

'Hello?' she asked into the mouthpiece.

'Wilson Spaulding here. Let me speak to your father.' The odd little man's bluster was missing. He sounded angry. Or scared.

'This is Jody, Mr Spaulding. Is something the matter?'

'You're double-damn right something's the matter. Now, call your father to the phone.'

'What happened?'

'Do like I say, young lady.'

'Dad's not here.'

'Don't lie to me.'

'I don't lie, Mr Spaulding. Dad had to go out for a while. Is Andy all right?'

'I'm sure I wouldn't know. I can't believe Jacko left you alone tonight. You're supposed to be *under guard*. This doesn't make any . . .'

'I'm not alone. Now what do you mean, you don't know if Andy's all right? You don't *know*? How could you not know if he's all right?'

'He's gone, that's how. Gone, vanished, *poof*!'

'What!'

'The little shit absconded with himself!'

'He's *gone*?'

'Are you deaf?'

Jody felt as if she might blow up. *Don't!* she warned herself. The jerk'll hang up and I'll never find out anything. 'Dad will want all the details,' she said, trying very hard to sound polite. 'I need to know what to tell him, Mr Spaulding. He gets really mad at me when I don't take good messages for him.' A total lie, but Willy had no way of knowing. 'Please?'

'When do you expect him back?'

'Any time. I don't know for sure, though. He might be away for another hour, or something.'

'I might very well not *be* here an hour from now. My patience, such as it is, has very nearly run itself to the end of the line.'

'Where are you calling from, Mr Spaulding?'

'A Texaco station. In Indio.'

'*Indio?*'

'Not India, Ind*io.*'

That's what I said, you creep. 'Oh, Indio. Okay.'

'A little burg on Interstate 10 . . .'

'Yeah, over near the Salton Sea. We've been there. And you're calling from a Texaco gas station. And you say that Andy is gone.'

'He certainly isn't *here*. That adds up to gone.'

'Dad'll want to know when you first noticed he was missing.'

'About twenty minutes ago.'

'Around nine?'

'Give or take. I spent quite some time running myself ragged, looking for him. With no success, I needn't add.'

'Where did he go?'

'If I knew that, young lady, he wouldn't be lost.'

'Gimme a break,' she snapped. Right away, she regretted it. 'I'm sorry. I'm just trying to find out what happened.'

'Isn't it obvious?'

'Not to me, sir.'

'I was obliged to stop for gas.' He said it slowly, clearly, as if trying to make himself understood by a moron. 'Andrew-was with me up to that point, sitting in the passenger seat, pouting.'

Pouting. His whole family was slaughtered last night, you bastard!

'I stopped my car at a self-service island. Are you following this?'

'Yes. Thank you.'

'As I began to fill the tank, Andrew opened the door and asked my permission to use the men's room. The John, he called it. I gave him permission. The last I saw of him, he was walking toward the station's office.'

'You let him go by himself?'

'Of course. He's not a baby.'

'He's only twelve.'

'I'm aware of that. And I don't believe I appreciate your attitude, young lady.'

'I'm sorry. I'm just trying to do the best I can.'

'You're insinuating that I'm somehow at fault in this situation.'

'I didn't mean to insinuate anything. Really. I just want to get this information for Dad, that's all. Okay?'

'All right, then.'

'Good. Thank you. Now, when did you realize that something was wrong?'

'When I went to the men's room, myself. That was after I'd finished pumping my gas, and after I'd gone to the office to pay for it. As a matter of fact, I didn't think much of it when he wasn't in the restroom. I thought he must've gone back to the car while I was in the office. So it wasn't until I returned to my car that I realized he was actually gone.'

'You looked around for him?'

'Of course.'

'Did you call the police?'

'Your father *is* the police, young lady. That's why I phoned him.'

'Dad can't do anything officially. I mean, not in Indio. What you need to do is call the Indio police and have them search for Andy.'

'I certainly enjoy receiving instructions from a fifteen-year-old child.'

'Sixteen,' she corrected him.

'I am not about to get the local gendarmes involved in this matter. Andy wasn't kidnapped. He *ran away*.'

'How do you know he wasn't kidnapped?'

Willy didn't answer right away. Jody heard the empty sounds of distance. She heard the faint noise of a truck's horn. 'Isn't it obvious?'

'Why?'

'He didn't want to leave your house in the first place. He didn't want to go *anywhere* with me. So the first chance he got, he ran off. He probably intends to hitchhike back to your house. I wouldn't put it past him.'

It sounded plausible to Jody. More than plausible – likely. The little twerp. She sighed. 'That's all the more reason to find him.' She grimaced at Miles. 'There's a police officer here. Maybe you'd better talk to her.'

She passed the handset to Miles. After identifying herself, Miles leaned back against the kitchen wall, listened and nodded. She didn't listen for long, though. 'Mr Spaulding, you should've notified the local police the moment you realized Andy was missing. Give me your number there.' She pulled a pen out of her shirt pocket, and jotted down the number on the note pad they kept by the phone. 'Okay, Mr Spaulding. I'm going to hang up, now, and call the locals myself. You stay right where you are.' She listened for a moment. Then her eyes widened and her face grew red. 'You will *not*. That boy is your responsibility, and I'll see to it that you're prosecuted if you leave the scene. Is that understood?' She nodded. 'Very good. See that you do.' She hung up.

'You were *great*!' Jody blurted. 'He is *such* a jerk.'

'He's Andy's uncle? Doesn't even sound like he *likes* the boy.'

'I don't think he does. I think the only reason he came to get Andy is because his wife made him.'

Miles nodded, then lifted the phone and tapped in the number for directory assistance.

'What gives?'

Jody swiveled sideways and saw her father swaggering through the dining room. She met him before he reached the kitchen. 'Andy's disappeared,' she said. 'We just got a call from his uncle. Miles is calling the Indio police right now.'

He leaned and glanced past Jody, apparently confirming that Miles was on the kitchen phone.

'How did it happen?'

She told him about the stop at the Texaco station and how Andy had made a solo trip to the restroom while Uncle Willy was busy filling the tank. 'He never came back from the John,' she concluded.

'When did this happen?'

'Around nine.'

Dad checked his wristwatch. 'Great. With that kind of headstart . . .' He shook his head.

'He might be trying to come here.'

'Andy?'

'He didn't want to leave in the first place.'

'You're assuming he wasn't grabbed.'

Dad's words made a cold place in Jody's stomach. 'But nobody followed their car out of here. You said they got clear all right.'

'We thought they did. I don't know. You can't be a hundred percent sure about a thing like that. Anyway, all we can do is guess about what might've happened to him. If Willy thinks he ran off, maybe that's what happened.'

'I sure hope so,' Jody muttered. 'It'd still be awfully dangerous for him, but . . .'

'A lot better than if he got snatched.'

'But what if he tries to hitch his way here, only he gets a ride from some sort of a pervert?'

'I'd hope that Andy would be smarter than to hitchhike.'

'How else can he get here?'

'Sergeant?' Miles asked.

Dad gave Jody's arm a squeeze, then stepped past her. She followed him into the kitchen. Miles was off the phone.

'Did Jody explain the situation, sir?'

'I've got a rough idea.'

'Well, I just contacted the Indio police department. They've got a unit on the way to the scene. Also, they're passing on word about the boy to the Highway Patrol.'

'What's your take on the deal, Miles?'

'It looks like the boy took off on his own.'

'What makes you say that?'

Miles leaned back against the wall. She folded her arms beneath her breasts and tilted her head sideways. 'Well,

Sergeant. From what I heard about last night, he's a game kid. Also, he's gone through an incredible emotional trauma. A shock like that can distort your perspective, so you do crazy things like run away in the middle of nowhere. Another thing is, he found a degree of safety and calm while he stayed here with you and your daughter. I think there are strong bonds between him and Jody. And finally, his uncle is a complete asshole. The boy probably couldn't *wait* to get away from him, and fled the moment a chance presented itself.'

'That's how it looks,' Dad said.

'There are other possibilities, but . . .'

'Let's hear them.'

'Well, the bad guys from last night might've grabbed him. Or he might've run afoul of someone in the gas station toilet. And there's one other possibility that's occurred to me. It's unlikely, I suppose. But we've only got Spaulding's word about how things went down. He might be lying through his teeth.'

'Oh, Jeez,' Jody muttered.

'You're suggesting *he* got rid of Andy?'

'It's just a thought. Adding a kid to the family can be an expensive proposition.'

'You think he *murdered* Andy?' Jody blurted.

Miles grimaced. 'I don't mean that at all, honey. Maybe I shouldn't have brought it up . . .'

'No,' Dad said. 'It's worth considering.'

'I honestly think Andy *probably* ran off.'

'More than likely,' Dad agreed.

'What'll we *do*?' Jody asked. 'This is awful. He might be . . . he might need help, or . . . Do we just have to *wait*?'

'Let's drive out there,' Dad said.

Jody couldn't believe her ears. 'Really?'

'Yeah. We might not accomplish much, but who knows? Better than staying here.'

'It sure is.'

'We were going to be pulling out, anyway. I just talked to Ryan about it. It looks as if our little "trap" got two civilians killed. Three, if you count fetuses.'

Miles winced. 'The woman was pregnant?'

'Looks like our shooter performed a quickie Cesarian on her and . . .' He glanced at Jody and stopped in mid-sentence. 'We don't want to risk anyone else. The guard's being pulled off as soon as we can get out of here. I'd thought we might try Big Bear, but now with this . . . We'll head out to Indio, for starters. Maybe we can find out something about Andy.'

'We can help look for him,' Jody said.

'Pack enough for a week,' Dad told her. 'If we have to stay away longer, we'll deal with it when the time comes.'

'I'd like to go with you, Sergeant,' Miles said. 'On my own time, of course. To provide some extra security for Jody.'

Dad looked surprised.

'That'd be great,' Jody said. 'Can she?'

'Well . . .'

'My shift's about over, anyway,' Miles said. 'All you've gotta do is square it with Ryan so I can leave early. After that, I'm off till Monday night. What do you say, Sergeant?'

'Come on, Dad. We might need her, you know? And besides, she's really nice.'

Dad eyes Miles. 'You sure you wanta?'

'Yes, sir.'

The upturned corner of his mouth stretched its way higher. He stuck out his big right hand. 'Okay.' As she shook it, he said, 'What's your name, Miles?'

'Sharon.'

'Okay, Sharon. Good to have you aboard. I'm Jack.'

234

Chapter Twenty-four

Jody was left alone to pack for the trip. She felt excited, but scared. This was almost like embarking on a vacation. Different, though. Awfully different. There were killers lurking around, somewhere, who wanted to murder her. And maybe they'd already gotten to Andy.

Nobody thinks they got him, she told herself.

Or if they do think it, they're not saying so in front of me. *He might be dead right this very second.*

No, she told herself. He ran away, that's all. That's what Dad and Sharon both think. And it's *not* that they're just saying it to protect me from the truth. Dad wouldn't lie to me. I don't think Sharon would, either.

She's really coming with us.

Dad had no sooner made arrangements with Nick Ryan for Sharon to come along, than she had hurried out the door saying she would be back in half an hour.

'We wanta be ready to hit the road the minute she gets back,' Dad had said.

'No problem.'

That was about twenty minutes ago.

Standing at the foot of her bed, Jody stared at her big cloth traveling bag and wondered what she was missing.

I've got a week's worth of panties and socks, she thought. Plus bras, blouses, T-shirts, shorts, jeans, sweats, swimming suit, moccasins, nightshirt, bathrobe. No skirt or dress. Dad won't be happy about that, if he finds out. I'll just play dumb. Besides, he won't find out unless for some reason we end up going to a fancy restaurant – or to church, God forbid.

235

Sorry about that, God. Didn't mean it.

Anyhow, You don't care what I wear to church, right? If You even exist at all.

Sorry about that, too, God.

So, she wondered, have I got everything?

She had already changed into sweatpants, a T-shirt, and Nikes. She would wear them in the car, along with her jacket and cap. That should take care of clothes.

In the side pockets of her bag, she had tucked a few paperback books, a note pad and pen, a deck of playing cards, and her tiny Kodak camera. Her toilet kit was in with the clothes. Meow, her stuffed kitten, gray and worn and earless with age, was tucked in there, too.

Jody felt sure that she was forgetting something. But what?

Maybe nothing.

She suddenly thought about all the things that she'd left behind at Evelyn's house. Maybe *they're* what I'm missing, she thought. My good old purse and billfold and everything in them. My brand new white Reeboks with the pink laces. *My Eeyore socks.*

All gone. All burned.

They're just things, she told herself. They aren't important.

But I miss them, anyhow. They were mine, and . . .

Sharon's going to be here any minute.

'What do I need to get?' she muttered.

Did she have enough first aid supplies?

Probably not.

She'd taken everything she could find in the medicine cabinet, though.

Enough to last a normal family for a year, she figured.

Enough to dress all *her* wounds about one more time.

Most of them should be able to go without bandages in another day or two.

236

We'll cross that bridge when we come to it, she decided.

You can buy bandages just about anywhere. Even in Indio, probably.

She slid the zippers shut, then hefted her bag with one hand and swung it off her bed. With her other hand, she put on her cap, then picked up her bright nylon jacket. At the door, she used an elbow to hit the light switch. The room went dark behind her.

In the hall, she saw light coming through the doorway to the garage. 'Dad?' she called.

'Out here, honey.'

She carried her things into the garage. There, Dad was standing behind the open trunk of their car. He had changed into blue jeans. Over his Yosemite Sam T-shirt, he wore a Kelly green chamois shirt, unbuttoned and hanging open like a jacket.

'Have you got everything?' he asked.

'Hope so,' Jody said, and handed the bag to him.

He set it inside the trunk. His suitcase was already there.

'Do you need to go to the bathroom or anything?' he asked.

'Nope. I'm all set. Do you want me in the back seat?'

His lopsided smile stretched upward. 'Even better than that – on the back seat floor. At least till we're out of the neighborhood.'

'Oh, terrific. Does that mean there's gonna be more shooting?'

'I doubt if anybody's still around to try something, but . . .' The doorbell rang. 'That's probably Sharon. You go on and get in.'

As he left the garage, Jody swung open a rear door of the car and climbed inside. She sat down. No point in hunkering on the floor any longer than necessary. On the seat beside her was an old blanket that usually stayed in the trunk. It looked rather carefully heaped. She lifted enough to uncover the pistol grips of Dad's 12-gauge Mossberg pump shotgun.

'Nothing like a little firepower,' she whispered.

She'd fired the shotgun herself last summer. A couple of weeks after Dad brought it home from the store, they'd driven out to the desert with all their weapons. With the Mossberg, Dad had blasted apart several four by four blocks of wood and more than a dozen Pepsi cans. Jody had tried it only once. The gun had bucked up hard, almost kicking free of her hands. Though she'd managed to keep her hold on it, one try had been more than enough for her.

It had also been more than enough for her target, splintering the hefty block of wood and hurling it into the air.

If Dad's bringing this . . .

She suddenly knew what she'd neglected to pack – not her toothbrush or deodorant, but her Smith & Wesson: the nice little eight-shot .22 semi-automatic that Dad had given her last Christmas.

Dumb *not* to bring it, she thought.

She opened the car door. As she swung her legs out, Sharon entered the garage ahead of Dad. Sharon hadn't changed clothes. She still wore her western boots, jeans and plaid shirt. But she had put on a faded denim jacket that reached down only to her waist and hung open. The jacket wasn't large enough to hide the holster on her hip. Also, it looked too small to be pulled shut and buttoned – at least across her chest.

She wore a black and gold NRA cap. Its visor, pulled low, had bright gold doo-dads and made her look like a rear admiral.

In one hand, she carried a soft travel bag similar to Jody's, though Sharon's was blue instead of red. In her other hand, she carried a rifle case of tooled leather.

Dad, following her, was empty handed.

Knowing her father, Jody was sure he must've immediately offered to carry Sharon's things. He had kept his chivalry in spite of feminism. So Sharon must have insisted on handling the baggage herself.

'You're right on time,' Jody told her.

'Tried to make it quicker.' To Jack, she said, 'All right if I stow my rifle in the back seat?'

'It won't do us much good locked in the trunk.'

Jody finished climbing out of the car. She stepped out of Sharon's way. 'Dad, shouldn't I bring along my twenty-two? Just in case we get separated, or something?'

'Definitely. Run in and get it. Bring along the extra magazine, too.'

Jody hurried into the house. In her bedroom, she slid open the nightstand drawer and picked up her pistol. She kept it there fully loaded, a round in the chamber, ready to fire except for the safety. She checked the safety to make certain the red dot didn't show, then dropped the weapon into the side pocket of her jacket. She searched the drawer until she found the other magazine. It was loaded, giving her a total of sixteen shots.

You never know, she thought.

She picked up a full box of .22 long rifle cartridges. On her way out, she slipped the box and magazine into the other pocket of her jacket.

Normally, the jacket was almost weightless. Now, its heavy pockets swung every which way as she walked. The pistol and ammo bumped her hips and she could feel the jacket pulling down on her shoulders.

'I guess we're off,' Dad said as she entered the garage. 'Did you remember to turn off your light?'

'Of course.'

He shut the house door after her and locked it with his key. He gave her time to reach the car, then flicked off the garage light.

The car's courtesy light was on. Climbing in, Jody saw the blanket covering the shotgun. Sharon's rifle case was propped up at the far side, behind the driver's seat. She smiled at Sharon, then shut her door and got down on her hands and knees.

'How is it back there?' Sharon asked.

'At least the floor's clean. Sort of.'

The car rocked as her father climbed in. His door thumped shut, and darkness closed down on Jody's nook. She heard the rumble of the garage door rising. Then the car engine started.

'How you doing, champ?' Dad asked.

'Me?' Jody asked.

'Yes, you.'

'Doing okay.'

'Stay down till I tell you different.'

'Okay.'

'I'll leave the headlights off for now.' From his tone of voice, Jody knew he was speaking to Sharon.

'Good idea,' Sharon said.

The car began to back up, its motion nudging Jody toward the front. Her right shoulder and hip pushed against the backs of the front seats. She felt the force shift when the car reached the bottom of the driveway and swung onto the street. Then she found herself being thrust against the edge of the back seat.

'So far, so good,' Sharon said.

'They've probably cleared out of the neighborhood,' Dad said. 'But you just never know. We've gotta be ready for anything.'

'That's probably Simmons back there.'

'Simmons your partner?'

'Yeah. Good guy. But he said he'd give us a flash with his brights.'

'How forgetful is he?'

'There they go.' Sharon sounded relieved. 'He should be staying with us, now, till he's sure we haven't picked up a tail. Maybe you'd better put *our* lights on.'

'Hmm. Yeah.'

Jody heard a couple of quiet clicks as he pulled out the headlight knob. Then came the pinking sounds of the turn signal. She swayed toward the front as the car slowed, felt as if her rump were being shoved during the turn, and then found herself being pressed against the seat cushion.

'How's it going, Jody?' Sharon asked.

'I guess it's better than getting shot.'

'Just a few more minutes,' Dad told her.

'Take it easy on the turns, please.'

'It's a straightaway for a while.'

'Thank goodness.'

Finally, he told Jody that she could get up. Raising her head, she recognized the Laurel Canyon onramp to the Ventura Freeway.

'Looking good,' Sharon said.

Jody twisted around and peered out the rear window. Except for one car, the onramp behind them seemed to be deserted. 'Is that Simmons?' she asked.

'That's him.'

Dad picked up speed and eased into the flow of eastbound traffic.

'Here he comes,' Jody said.

The unmarked police car sped closer, then swung to the left and eased up alongside them. The driver's right arm reached out. For an instant, Jody thought he was pointing a gun at Dad. Her stomach plummeted. But then she saw the man raise his thumb.

Dad returned the thumbs-up signal. Sharon leaned forward a bit and waved. Then Simmons's car shot forward and was lost in the traffic.

The radio suddenly blasted. Before Jody got a chance to recognize the tune, the volume faded. 'Jody's station,' Dad said. 'K-Noise.'

'Very funny, Dad.'

'Let's see if we can't find us a li'l ol' country station.'

'Is that what you like?' Sharon asked.

'I reckon it's what *you* like.'

'How'd you guess?'

'They don't give sergeant stripes to dummies, ma'am.'

Sharon laughed softly. 'Do *you* like country?'

'Reckon I'm ambidextrous.'

'It's fine with me,' she said, 'if we keep on Jody's K-Noise.'

'No,' Jody said. 'That's okay. I like everything, mostly. Except Willie Nelson.'

'You don't like Willie?'

'I think it's his headband,' she said.

'When Jody was eight,' Dad explained, 'she got car sick while Willie was singing "Always on My Mind" on the radio. Ever since then, she thinks about him every time she loses it. And vice versa. That's the *real* reason she can't stand him.'

'Very nice, Dad. Tell everyone about me throwing up.'

'I've done it myself,' Sharon said. 'In fact, I toss my supper every time I see a dead body.'

'Every time?' Dad asked.

'Well, only the ones I meet on duty. I don't usually throw funerals.'

'partners must love that.'

'They've been okay about it. As long as I miss them.' Dad started laughing. He laughed hard.

'They find it amusing, too.'

'What is it, the aroma?'

'Jeez, Dad!'

'It gets me even when I *can't* smell 'em.'

'Knowing how they're *gonna* smell,' Dad suggested.

'Hey, maybe so. I never thought of that.'

'Oh, my God,' Jody said.

'What?' Dad asked. Sharon looked around at her.

'I just remembered. Last night at Evelyn's, the place smelled like something dead. Remember the rat that died behind the wall, Dad? It was that sort of smell. The killers smelled like that. A couple of them did, anyway. The fat one who got Evelyn, he had that smell. And so did the little guy who came to Andy's room.'

Even in the dark, Jody could see the look of revulsion on Sharon's face.

'If you were right about that guy's pants,' Dad said, 'the stink probably came from them.'

'I don't think so. They didn't look ... rotten.'

'Pants that rot?' Sharon asked.

'I can't believe it,' Dad said. 'You mean the word hasn't gone through the whole department by now?'

'I was briefed on last night's homicides, but ...'

'You know about Jody killing one of the perps?'

'Sure.'

'Well, according to Jody and Andy, that guy was naked except for a pair of trousers made out of human skin – somebody's butt and legs.'

'Holy shit.'

'But they looked sort of normal,' Jody said. 'I mean, not *normal*. But we both thought the guy didn't have any pants on, at first. Until we started to notice things. But anyway, what I'm getting at is the skin looked regular. The color wasn't funny. There might've been some kind of preservative stuff on it, but it wasn't brown like leather usually is. And it sure didn't look like it was going bad. I mean, it wasn't slimy or green or moldy, or . . .'

Sharon turned her head away, gagging. More choking sounds erupted from her as she rolled her window down. Quickly, she tugged off her NRA cap and stuck her head out. Her short hair blew in the wind.

Jody reached over the top of the seat and put her hand on Sharon's back. 'Jeez, I'm sorry. I'm really sorry.' Sharon pulled her head in. 'That's all right.' She glanced sideways toward Jack. 'I just needed a little fresh air. I'm okay now.'

Dad looked over at her. 'How long have you been on the job?'

'Six years.'

'And you're still this squeamish?'

'It looks that way, doesn't it.' She sounded defensive, slightly annoyed.

'You must spend half your life throwing up.'

'Come on, Dad. Anyway, she *didn't* throw up.'

'That's right, I didn't.'

'And it's not as if *you've* never done it. Remember when you found that mold on the bread after you'd already eaten half the sandwich, and . . .?'

'Okay, okay,' he said. 'Nobody wants to hear about that.'

'Let he who never vomits cast the first . . .'

'Cut it out, now, Jody.'

'To get back to the point,' Sharon said, 'some of the men who invaded the Clark house last night smelled like dead rats. Is that right?'

'That's right,' Jody said. 'And I don't think the stink came from the skin pants. I don't even know *what* the fat guy was wearing. He looked all shaggy, like his clothes were tattered, or something. He smelled the same way as the little guy, though.'

'And you don't think it was the clothing?' Sharon asked.

'I don't think so.'

'Then what could account for the odor?' she continued, as if determined to show that she could function in spite of the disgusting subject matter.

'I don't know. Unless they're zombies.'

'They're not zombies,' Dad said.

'I know,' Jody told him. 'But why *would* they smell like that?'

'When we get our hands on one, we'll find out.' He drove in silence for a few seconds. 'I didn't smell anything like that tonight at the Zoller house. Just the usual. Nothing like a rotten carcass.'

'The shooter had to be one of the guys from last night,' Sharon said.

'Maybe I just didn't pick up on it. The place was pretty whiffy. Or maybe the stink the kids noticed was a fluke and they don't always smell that way. They might've just finished disposing of an old body, or something, before they paid their visit to the Clark house.'

'Or maybe they hadn't disposed of it,' Sharon said. 'Maybe they had it with them. Maybe they were keeping it.'

'Why would they want to keep a body?'

'For a mascot?' Sharon suggested.

Dad laughed.

'You cops are all a bunch of psychos,' Jody said.

'Ain't that the truth?' Dad said.

'Hey,' Sharon said, 'did you know Psycho Phelan?'

'Are you kidding? Psycho? Man, what a lunatic. Did you hear about the time . . .?'

And so it began.

They started telling war stories.

Jody listened eagerly to their tales of Psycho Phelan, then to one story after another about busts that went awry, amazing goofs, tight scrapes, practical jokes played on fellow cops, bizarre civilians they'd encountered, peculiar deaths that were awful but often hilarious.

To hear what they were saying, though, Jody had to sit on the edge of her seat and lean forward, bracing herself with her arms stretched atop the seatbacks. That way, she could keep her head in the middle of things and catch both sides of the conversation. After a while, however, the muscles under her arms began to feel the strain of holding her up. Her back and neck started to ache. All over her body, nicks and scratches, cuts and scrapes and bruises seemed to come awake and hurt her.

Finally, with a moan, she succumbed. She eased herself backward and settled down in her seat. She wanted to stretch out. 'Okay if I put the shotgun on the floor, Dad?'

'Sure. Just don't fire it.'

'Once was once too often,' she said. She slipped it out from under the blanket and set it carefully on the floor.

'Is my rifle in the way?' Sharon asked, looking back at her.

'No, I think it'll be fine. Gotta get rid of this stuff, though.' She dug her hands into her jacket, pulled the pistol out of one pocket, then removed the loose magazine and box of cartridges from the other.

As she set them on the floor with the shotgun, Sharon said,' 'You like guns?'

'They're okay.'

'She loves her little Smith & Wesson,' Dad said.

'I don't love it. Jeez. It's just a gun.' To Sharon, she said, 'I do get a kick out of shooting it, though. I think that's a lot of fun. I really like shooting – as long as I don't have to shoot some sort of big old cannon. It sort of hurts to shoot the big stuff.'

'Yeah, I know what you mean.' She smiled. 'I've got a Parker-Hale .300 Winchester magnum at home. Every time I fire it, I end up with a big ugly bruise on my shoulder.'

'Why do you fire it, then?'

'I like it.'

'The power,' Dad said.

'That's it.'

'I knew there was something I liked about you,' he told her.

She let out a gruff laugh. 'Glad there's something, Jack.'

'Maybe a few things.'

'My goodness.'

'You guys,' Jody said, and surprised herself by yawning.

'Someone's sleepy,' Sharon said.

'Yeah. I'm gonna stretch out.' She lay down on her back and raised her knees slightly to allow her legs to fit on the seat. Her feet went nicely into the space underneath the tilted rifle case and pressed against the door.

'That looks comfy,' Sharon said.

'It is.'

Dad glanced back.

'Jeez, Dad, watch where you're driving.'

'Okay. Sleep tight, sweetheart.'

Sharon's hand appeared above the seatback and waved. It was a very dainty wave, hand open, closed fingers dipping downward a few times. The way a shy little girl might wave goodnight or goodbye.

Chapter Twenty-five

Jody opened her eyes, found herself on the back seat of the car, wondered for a moment where she was going, then remembered about Andy's disappearance. Though she still felt groggy, she struggled to sit up.

Dad was behind the wheel. Sharon sat in the passenger seat, looking out the windows. From the radio came the quiet sound of Garth Brooks singing 'The Dance'.

There wasn't much traffic on the freeway. They seemed to be in a desert area, a few buildings off to the sides, but not many. This certainly wasn't the outskirts of a city, but it didn't look completely desolate, either.

'Where are we?'

'Coming up on Cabazon,' Dad said.

'Really?'

'You were out for a long time.'

Sharon said, 'We were just talking about whether to wake you up. You wouldn't want to miss the dinosaurs.'

Sharon was right; she would've hated to be asleep when they drove past the dinosaurs. 'Oh, they're cool,' she said.

'Have you ever stopped at them?'

'Yeah. A couple of times. We went into one of them.'

'You can go inside?' Sharon sounded surprised.

'Yeah. I don't know if you still can. Didn't they shut it down, Dad?'

'I think so. Seems to me there'd been some vandalism.'

'But we got in once, maybe about five or six years ago. There was a little souvenir shop right in the stomach of the apatosaurus. You could buy dinosaur coloring books, and rocks, and stuff. It was pretty junky, actually, and the guy who ran it was sort of funny.'

'It sounds neat, though,' Sharon said.

'Yeah, it was. You know, *knowing* you were way up high inside this gigantic monster.'

'There they are,' Dad said.

Off to the left, not far beyond the westbound lanes of the freeway, the two towering concrete creatures stood brightly lit against the night. They looked as if they might have wandered out of the desert and halted in shocked amazement to find themselves confronted by Interstate 10. The apatosaurus with its humped back and long neck looked gentle and perplexed. Maybe it wanted to turn around and hurry back into the wilds. The Tyrannosaurus rex, huge teeth bared, looked savage – looked ready to head for the freeway and tangle with the big rigs.

'Awesome,' Sharon muttered. 'I remember how really weird it seemed, the first time I saw them. I couldn't believe my eyes.'

'They look like they belong in a place like this,' Dad said.

'Yeah,' Jody said. 'But like they're out of place, too. Like they're surprised to find themselves here.' She turned her head and watched the creatures shrink into the distance.

She realized that Andy must've come by here in the car with his uncle. Had he noticed the dinosaurs?

He could hardly miss them, she thought.

Being a guy, he was probably *into* dinosaurs and stuff like that.

Maybe they outgrow it, though, by the time they hit twelve.

She tried to remember if she'd seen any dinosaur models or pictures or books in his bedroom last night.

But when she thought about Andy's bedroom, she could only see the door creeping open and the guy sneaking in, feel how the baseball bat had landed solid, see the awful way it had caved in the top of his head, see him sprawled on the floor wearing somebody else's butt and legs, watch Andy barf down on him from the bed.

God, Andy, where are you?

Just a few hours ago, he'd been right here. Right where we are now, she thought. Except maybe in a different lane.

Unless Willy's lying about everything.

But that doesn't make sense, does it? The guy is a doufuss, but he's not one of the killers.

What makes sense, she told herself, is that Andy couldn't stand him and used the first chance he found to escape.

Unless the killers got him. Followed their car until it stopped, followed Andy into the john . . .

That didn't seem very likely. Why would they waste time tailing the car for like a hundred and fifty miles, then wait for it to stop at a gas station and then make off with Andy when he went to the men's room? That'd be ridiculous.

Doesn't mean it didn't happen that way.

It didn't, Jody told herself. Andy saw his chance to ditch Uncle Willy, and he took it.

'How far are we from Indio?' she asked.

'Maybe thirty-five, forty miles,' Dad said. 'We'll be there in half an hour or so.'

'I sure hope Andy's okay.'

Sharon looked over her shoulder at Jody. 'He's probably turned up already.'

'I don't think he'll get found unless he wants to be.'

'I wouldn't count on that,' Dad told her.

Jody remembered how Andy had tricked and out-maneuvered the killers last night while she'd been trying to get the old woman to open her door. 'He's pretty sharp for a little kid.'

That old woman is dead. She got killed because she let us into her house. If I hadn't gone to her door . . .

'Well,' Dad said, 'if Andy's trying to get back to LA, he can't just lay low and hide. If he tries to thumb a ride, there's every likelihood he'll be spotted by the Highway Patrol or the local cops. He won't last long.'

'What happens if they *do* find him? Will he still have to go and live with his jerky uncle?'

'I don't know, honey. The way it looks, his jerky uncle might want nothing more to do with him. But that remains to be seen. Once he's had some time to consider how his wife is likely to react, he might change his tune.'

'I hope he *doesn't* want Andy.'

'Well, there's no point in worrying about it. Let's just worry about finding him, okay?'

'Where do you think we might find him?' Sharon asked her. 'After what the two of you went through, you must have a fairly good idea about how he reacts to things.'

'I guess so. Let me think for a minute.'

Jody settled back against her seat, rested her hands atop her thighs, and stared forward. She pictured herself in Andy's place, sitting next to Wilson Spaulding as he steers his car into a filling station. Willy climbs out of the car. She waits until he sticks the gasoline nozzle into the tank. Then she opens her door and says, 'I've gotta use the John, okay?' He says something like, 'Go ahead, but make it snappy.' So then she walks fast to the restroom.

Did Willy say it was on the side of the gas station? Or in the rear? Whichever, she would go to it. But not go in. After making sure that no one was watching her, she would bolt.

Bolt where?

That would depend on what was around.

Maybe you run away from the gas station, run across the

street, drop down and hide in a ditch or duck behind something or keep running until you're a few blocks away.

Or maybe there's a truck, something like that, stopped at the gas station. And you can sneak aboard and hide when nobody is watching. And it drives away with you.

That'd be the best thing. Especially if it happened to be going in the right direction. How would you know where it's heading, though? You stow away on a truck, no telling where you might end up.

'He might've just run for it,' Jody said. 'I don't think he'd be dumb enough to stow away on a truck, though. He wouldn't know where it might be going.'

'What about asking someone for a ride?' Sharon asked.

'He wouldn't. Not at the gas station, anyway. He's a kid. People are gonna wonder why he isn't with an adult, so he'd be afraid they might turn him over to his uncle.'

'What about thumbing a ride later, once he's clear of the station?'

Would he try that? Jody wondered. *Would I?*

'I guess it'd depend,' she said. 'Normally, I bet he wouldn't. I mean, I *know* Evelyn would never try to hitch a ride in a million years. We used to talk about stuff like that, and she thought anyone who hitchhiked was an idiot just begging to get raped and murdered. She must've gotten that from her parents. So that'd mean Andy got the same sort of lectures, so you wouldn't think he'd try hitching a ride. But on the other hand . . . His whole family's dead and he's out in the middle of nowhere trying to get away from his creepy uncle. I guess maybe he might try *any*thing. He might not even care how dangerous it is, you know?'

'Well,' Dad said, 'assuming he doesn't want to take up permanent residence in Indio, he's either got to find himself a ride, or start walking.'

'If he decided to walk,' Sharon said, 'he's probably already been picked up by the cops.'

'God, I hope so,' Jody muttered.

'Do you have any idea how much money he's got?' Sharon asked.

'On him?'

'Yeah.'

'Jeez, I don't know. None.'

'He has twenty,' Dad said.

'He does?' Jody asked.

'I sort of slipped it to him. It didn't seem like a good idea to let him go off without any cash.'

'So he has the means to pay for a ride,' Sharon said.

'Afraid so. Twenty won't get him far in a taxi, though. And any cops with half an ounce of sense would've checked out the bus station first thing. If there is one. If any buses are running. Wouldn't be a bad thing if he *did* get onto a bus. At least he'd be fairly safe as long as he stays on board.'

'Andy wouldn't even know how to find a bus station,' Jody pointed out. 'Not unless he asked someone. I don't think he would go around and ask anyone anything. He'd be afraid of getting caught.'

'With twenty bucks,' Sharon said, 'he could bribe someone to give him a lift.'

'That wouldn't be much different from hitchhiking,' Dad pointed out.

'It's a little different,' Jody said. 'I can see him trying something like that. It's still awfully dangerous, but it's not the same. It's like paying your own way, you know? Instead of begging. He wouldn't try that at the gas station, though. He'd want to get away from there. I think.' In the silence that followed her words, a new thought occurred to her. She grimaced. 'What if he *did* get a ride? He could be back in LA right now.'

'It's possible,' Dad admitted.

'Oh, man.'

'Where would he go in LA?' Sharon asked.

'To our house.'

'Do you think so?'

'I know so. He hated the whole idea of leaving.' Jody groaned at the thought of Andy arriving at the house, only to find it deserted. What would he do? 'I'm beginning to wish we'd stayed home,' she said.

'You'd be going crazy at home,' Dad said. 'This way, we're doing something.'

'I know, but . . . Is anyone still watching the house?'

Dad shook his head. 'I doubt it. Ryan was awfully eager to free up the manpower.'

'But Andy won't know where we are, or anything.'

'He'll be all right,' Sharon said. 'If he's the sort of kid who can make it back to your place in the middle of the night, I bet he'll find a way to get inside. Then he'll just settle down and enjoy himself.'

'I don't know. I sure hope so.'

Chapter Twenty-six

Jody woke up. She'd heard something.

Though her eyes were open, the room was very dark.

For a moment, she thought she was sleeping over at

Evelyn's house. But she wasn't in her sleeping bag on the floor of Evelyn's room; she was in a real bed.

Then she remembered what had happened at Evelyn's.

She remembered everything, and finally knew where she was.

Indio. This is that motel – the Traveler's Roost across from the Texaco.

But what had woken her up?

She lay on her back, gazing at the dark ceiling, and listened. She heard the loud hum of the air conditioning unit. Nothing else, though. Dad usually snored, which could drive her crazy when they stayed at motels, but tonight he was quiet.

Thank goodness for that, anyway, she thought.

She was sure there'd been a noise, though. Something loud enough to ruin her sleep.

Maybe a door had slammed or someone had yelled or . . .

Probably nothing important.

Last night, Evelyn heard breaking glass. And I didn't think it was anything important.

The sheet covering Jody suddenly seemed heavy and hot. She flung it aside. Better. She would feel even better without her nightshirt, but she couldn't take it off with Dad sharing the room. At least her arms and legs felt cool, now.

Whatever I heard, she told herself, it probably wasn't breaking glass.

We're safe here. Nobody followed us all the way to Indio. Nobody knows where we are.

She folded her hands behind her head. The short hair back there was damp with sweat. She shut her eyes.

And jerked quick and hard as someone pounded the door.

Three sharp raps.

Maybe it's not our door!

It is our door.

'Dad!' she gasped. 'Dad! Somebody's at the door!'

He didn't answer.

She swung her feet to the floor. Ignoring the pains, she stumbled through the darkness toward the other bed.

Maybe it's Sharon, she thought.

What if it's not?

She bent over the bed and reached for her father. Her hands found the rumpled blanket and sheet on an expanse of flat mattress.

He's gone?

Staggering sideways, she searched for the lamp fixtures on the wall between the two beds. Her fingers bumped a cool, metallic shade. Moments later, she found the switch. She jabbed it inward. Sudden light rammed the darkness away. She groaned and squinted.

Dad's bed was empty, just as she'd thought.

Is he in the bathroom?

'Jody?' The voice came from outside. It was hardly more than a whisper.

She sighed. What a relief! 'Jeez, Dad.' Hobbling toward the door, she realized that he must've gone outside and forgotten to take his key.

Dumb.

He almost never goofed up.

Jody found herself smiling.

He'll never hear the end of this.

'Neat play, Dad,' she said, and swung the door wide open.

And knew she had made a mistake. A big mistake like walking outside with the platter of burgers, completely forgetting Dad's warning to stay in the house.

She should've *made sure* it was him before opening the door.

A mistake like this can get me killed, she thought.

Not this time, though, thank God.

It wasn't her father on the other side of the door, but it wasn't a killer, either.

'Andy!'

She gasped and leaned out and grabbed him by both his arms and pulled him inside fast. Then she leaned out again. She checked both ways. The motel's long balcony looked deserted.

'Nobody saw me,' he said. 'I was extra careful.'

She shut the door and locked it. She faced him. He was grinning.

'You creep!' she blurted.

'Me?'

Then she grabbed him and hugged him.

Hugged him hard, mashing him against her body with all its scrapes and cuts and bruises. It hurt her, hugging him this hard. She knew it must also be hurting him; he'd been banged up awfully bad too, last night.

Good, she thought. I hope it hurts a lot.

But he didn't protest. He kept his face pushed gently against the side of her neck, and moved his hands slowly up and down her back. He didn't try to get funny, though. He never let his hands stray lower than her waist.

'You little creep,' Jody whispered.

'Aren't you glad to see me?'

'I oughta . . .' She almost said, 'kill you,' but stopped herself in time. 'Man, you're gonna be in big trouble.'

'So what?'

She eased herself away from Andy and held him at arm's length. His face looked flushed and dirty. The red shirt that she'd given to him was unbuttoned and open. His chest and belly were shiny with sweat. Jody could see where he had lost a couple of his bandages. The exposed wounds looked raw, but not bloody.

The blue denim shorts hung low on Andy's hips, lower than his tan line, and Jody blushed as she remembered that he wasn't wearing undershorts.

His right knee was still wrapped with an Ace bandage, and he still wore the white socks and Keds that she had given to him. The brand new laces on the Keds were now almost as dirty as the shoes themselves.

'You're a mess,' Jody said.

'You should've thought of that *before* you hugged me.'

She glanced down at herself. Her nightshirt had been spotless white. Now, its front was grimy. 'Doesn't matter,' she said. 'We've gotta figure out what to do with you before Dad gets back. I don't know where he . . .'

'He went to room 238.'

Sharon's room. 'When?'

'A few minutes before I started knocking. Boy, you sure are hard to wake up.'

'He went to *Sharon's* room?'

Andy shrugged. 'I don't know. A big gal, and I mean *big*. Stacked, you know?'

'Cut it out.'

'Her hair's even shorter than yours. Short like a guy's hair. But man, what a babe!'

'It was Sharon. She's in 238. She's another cop. She drove over with us. She's really nice. Dad went to her *room*?'

'Yeah. That's what I said.'

'And she let him in?'

'Sure did.'

'Did she look like she was expecting him?'

'How would I know?'

'What was she wearing?'

'Some kind of robe. It was blue and shiny. Pretty short, too.'

'My God.'

Andy raised one side of his upper lip. 'Is this good or bad?'

'It's good,' she said. 'It's great. I think.'

'You think he went over there to boink her?'

'Jeez, Andy!' She gave his shoulder a rough jab, and he laughed.

'He's probably boinking her right now.'

Jody tried not to laugh, but couldn't help it. 'You've got such a dirty mind. Now, quit it or I'll throw you out of here. I'd forgotten what a pain in the butt you can be.'

'Did you miss me?'

'We thought you might've gotten kidnapped or something. Or even murdered. How could you do a thing like that?'

'I hate that guy. Is there something around here to drink?'

'Just water.'

'That's okay.' He hurried past Jody, limping slightly – not much, though. Apparently, his knee had improved during the past few hours.

Jody followed him past the ends of the beds, toward the long counter adjacent to the bathroom door. When he flicked a switch, bright fluorescent lights came on above the counter.

In the mirror, he looked very small and young and filthy and vulnerable. Like some sort of street urchin out of a Dickens novel. Jody looked so much more adult and . . . she'd known that her white nightshirt was too small. But when she'd stood in front of the mirror earlier to brush her teeth and wash, she'd been wearing her robe over it. Now, she was without the robe. The mirror reflection showed her nightshirt to be horribly short and tight: so short that she could see the bandage Sharon had used to cover the bullet scratch high on her thigh; so tight that it grasped every mound and hollow. She could even see the darker color of her skin where her nipples pushed against the fabric.

Oh, wonderful, she thought. Andy's been getting a real eyeful.

Her face flushed to a deep shade of red.

As Andy bent over the sink, she hurried to her travel bag. Her robe was draped over the top, where she'd tossed it before getting into bed. She put it on and tied its sash.

'You're gonna get hot in that,' Andy said.

'I'll manage, thanks.' She stepped into her moccasins.

'Shoot.'

Hearing him say the word, Jody was tempted to tell him about the sniper who'd murdered those two people (and a baby, a baby that hadn't even been born yet) and then shot at her.

But Andy would want to see the wound.

She could tell him about it later, maybe. Sometime when she was dressed.

She watched him drink some more from the faucet. For a while, he remained bent over the sink, cupping water into his mouth.

At last, he shut off the faucet and dried his mouth on a towel. 'Anything to eat around here?'

Jody shook her head. 'You can't be that hungry. You ate the same time I did.'

'It takes up a lot of energy, being a fugitive.'

'Boy, Andy. They've got cops out looking for you.'

'You're telling me.'

'You must've lost *all* your marbles.' She sat down on the edge of her father's abandoned bed. 'I mean, running away from your uncle.'

He grinned. 'It was easy.'

'Jeez.'

He dropped onto the edge of the bed across from her. 'Wanta know how I did it?'

'I know. You pretended like you had to take a leak. When you got to the john, you ran off.'

'Oh, yeah? Where'd I run to?'

'I don't know, but . . .'

'That's because I didn't run.' He leaned forward, planting his elbows on his thighs, and gave her a sly grin. '*I climbed.*'

'What?'

'I climbed up onto the roof of the gas station.'

'You're kidding.'

'I thought I'd just run away, you know? Run off and hide, just to get good and far away from that turkey, then figure out some way of getting back to LA after he gave up looking for me. Maybe hitch a ride or buy a bus ticket, you know? But what happened, I saw how the door of the john was propped open and it looked like it was just begging for me to climb it.'

'You climbed the door?'

'Sure. What you've gotta do, you hang on to its edge and get your knees on the handles. Then you stand on the handles and grab the top and boost yourself up. Once you're on top of the door, you can reach the roof easy.'

Jody shook her head, amazed. 'You were on the roof the whole time?'

'Yep.'

'And nobody ever saw you?'

'It's got like a wall around the top. A couple of feet high, you know? So as long as I stayed low, nobody could spot me from the ground.'

'Wow.'

'I really thought I'd had it when all those cops started showing up. Man, I never figured ol' Willy would call the *cops*.'

'He didn't, exactly,' Jody explained. 'He called Dad. But Dad was gone, so I talked to him. Then I put Sharon on the phone. Willy wanted to just leave, but . . .'

'That's what I was *hoping* he'd do. I thought he'd be glad to have me out of his hair, and he'd just boogie on home, you know?'

'He sure wanted to,' Jody said, 'but Sharon made him stay. Then she was the one who got the local police into it. They were *all* looking for you. The Indio police, the Highway Patrol, Willy, *us* . . .'

'I know, I know. And *nobody* got around to looking on the roof. Not even you.'

'Did you see me?'

'Sure. What happened, I heard your dad talking to Wee Willy. That was after I'd been up there a *long* time. Hours. I couldn't make out what anyone was saying, but your dad has a really different sort of voice and I knew it was him. So I peeked down and saw both of you. You were almost right under me. Man, I couldn't believe my eyes.'

'Why the heck didn't you just come down?'

'Yeah, sure, and have Willy take me away.'

'He left right after we got there.'

'He did?'

'Weren't you watching?'

'No! Somebody might've looked up and seen me. All I did was take a little peek down every once in a while. I never even saw that woman . . . Sharon?'

'She was with us the whole time.'

'Couldn't have been.'

'Well, she wandered around some. And went to check the bathroom and stuff.'

'I never saw her till your dad went to her room.'

'So what did you do, follow us over here to the motel?'

'Yeah. I heard a car start and thought it might be yours, so I took a chance and looked down and saw it drive off. I thought I'd really blown it, you know? Because Willy'd taken off by then – I couldn't see his car anywhere. And all the cops were gone, too. I almost wanted to jump down and run after you . . .'

'Good thing you didn't. Probably would've crippled yourself.'

'Yeah. I've done enough jumping. But anyway, I kept my eyes on your car and watched where it went. I couldn't believe it when you guys pulled into this motel right across the street. It was like a miracle.'

'We did it on purpose in case you might be hiding somewhere nearby and see us. But jeez, I never thought you'd show up. You were right there the whole time? Man! Right under our noses.'

'Above your noses.'

Jody smiled. 'I *told* them you wouldn't get found unless you wanted to be.'

He wiggled his eyebrows at her.

Her smile faded. 'I guess now we'd better tell Dad and Sharon that you've turned up.'

Andy bared his teeth. 'Ewwww.'

'We've got to.'

'Can't it wait?'

'I don't think so. There are still a lot of people looking for you and it isn't fair to let them keep on wasting their time.' She stood up. 'Come on.'

Andy looked agonized. He didn't move.

'Let's go.'

'They're gonna hate me.'

'No, they won't. They're on your side. Why do you think they drove all the way out here in the middle of the night?'

'Maybe they want a promotion for busting me.'

'Oh, bull. Come on.'

Andy shook his head.

Jody grabbed his arm and pulled him off the bed.

'Okay, okay, I'm coming.' He quit struggling, and walked beside her to the door. 'You don't have to hang on. I'm not going anyplace.'

'You're going someplace, all right. To room 238.' She opened the door. They stepped out onto the balcony.

'Your dad isn't gonna like this. You know what he's doing in there, don't you?'

'Nope.'

'He's boinking that Sharon babe.'

'Maybe he is and maybe he isn't.'

They walked past several rooms before they came to 238. The curtains were shut. And dark. There seemed to be no lights on inside the room.

Uh-oh, Jody thought.

She stopped at the door.

'You'd better not,' Andy whispered. 'You'll be sorry.'

Jody realized that her heart was thumping fast. She had a nervous feeling in her stomach.

This could get awfully embarrassing, she thought.

What're we supposed to do, wait till they get done?

She went ahead and knocked.

Before her knuckles could strike the door a second time, it flew open. Light suddenly filled the room.

Dad smirked out at them.

He wasn't wearing his chamois shirt. But he still had on his

Yosemite Sam T-shirt, jeans and shoes. He even wore his shoulder holster.

So much for him boinking Sharon.

'Welcome back, Andy,' he said. 'Glad you dropped by. Come on in.'

He stepped backward. Jody and Andy entered the room, and he shut the door.

The back of a chair was only inches from the door. He must've been sitting there in the dark, on his side of the small round table, his shoulder only inches from the window curtain. His glass held an inch of amber liquid. In the middle of the table stood a bottle of Irish whiskey. There was no glass on the other side of the table. That glass was in Sharon's hand. She was settled back in her chair, one leg crossed over the other, her slightly disarrayed robe showing a hint of cleavage and a lot of thigh.

She raised her glass as if ready to propose a toast, and said, 'Andrew Clark, I presume.' She winked, then took a sip of whiskey.

Andy blushed.

'Officer Sharon Miles,' Dad introduced her.

'I'm very pleased to meet you,' Andy said.

Dad resumed his seat and picked up his glass. 'Make yourselves comfortable,' he said, gesturing toward the twin queen-sized beds. One of the beds looked as if it had been slept in.

Andy sat on the end of that one, Jody on the other.

She watched her father take a sip of whiskey. 'What were you two doing in here?' she asked. 'Drinking in the dark?'

'That's right,' Dad said.

'It's been very pleasant,' Sharon added.

'Is that *all?*' Jody asked.

The side of Dad's mouth climbed his cheek. 'It worked, didn't it? I hadn't been over here for five minutes before Andy showed up at your door.'

The boy's mouth fell open. 'How do you know?'

With the back of his hand, Dad patted the curtains by his shoulder. 'Watched.'

'Besides which,' Sharon said, 'the whole motel must've heard you trying to wake up Jody.'

'Oh, boy,' Andy muttered.

'He thought you were over here . . . fooling around.'

'He was supposed to,' Sharon said.

'Oh, boy,' Andy muttered again. 'I like walked into a trap.'

'Sort of,' Dad said.

'Very much so,' said Sharon.

'Did you know where I was all along, or . . .?'

'Oh, hell no,' Dad told him. 'After we'd gotten done exploring all the possibilities, though . . .'

'With which Jody was very helpful,' Sharon added.

'We figured you might still be in the neighborhood, probably hiding somewhere. If that was the case, you might be near enough to spot us when we showed up. So we took the rooms here, and I left Jody by herself.'

Sharon set her empty glass down on the table. 'You made a bee-line for her, buddy.'

Andy grimaced. 'Now what happens?'

'Is anybody else hungry around here?' Sharon asked. 'There're a couple of vending machines downstairs with all sorts of good stuff.'

'Fine idea,' Dad said. He polished off his drink, and stood up. 'Why don't you kids come with me so you can pick what you want?'

'Let's all go,' Sharon said.

'You aren't dressed,' Dad pointed out.

'Sure I am.' She carefully adjusted the front of her robe as she stood up. 'I'm perfectly decent. Nobody but me knows I'm butt naked under here.'

'Nobody at all,' Dad said, and laughed. 'Okay, let's go.'

PART SIX

Simon Says

Chapter Twenty-seven

Guess where I am.

Give up?

I'm in Jody's house.

The only problem is, she isn't.

After I got off the phone last night, I was all hot to rush right over here and grab her. For one thing, taking her to Tom and the guys was the only way to set things right. I'd be saving a lot more than Lisa – including my own skin. That wasn't any reason to rush, though. I've got till ten tonight for that. The reason for the rush was just so I could get my hands on Jody and have her all to myself for a while. I mean, I *wanted* her. I could *taste* her.

Tom had warned me, though. He'd said she had more security than the president.

I figured he was exaggerating. But still, there were sure to be bodyguards. Cops all over the place.

In other words, it didn't sound like a great idea to storm the house.

The situation called for caution and smarts.

It also called for a wig. I took Hillary's hair with me, but didn't wear it. The scalp was starting to 'turn,' as they say. A couple of miles from the motel, I swung into an alley and tossed it into one of the garbage bins behind an apartment house.

Then I ran over Engineer Bill.

I don't know what the fuck his name was. He was a bum. I

call him Engineer Bill because he was pushing a train of shopping carts down the alley. This was a few minutes after I'd thrown away Hillary's hair, and I was staying in alleys.

I like the way they are at night. A lot of them are pretty well lit, but they've got dark places, too. There are usually buildings on both sides. The alleys are like secret canyons through the city. Nobody's usually in them except a bum, now and then.

LA's got bums up the wazoo, in case you haven't noticed.

You're not supposed to call them bums. They're the 'homeless'. A bunch of fucking crazy assholes is what they are. And always in your face. Begging. You can't go anywhere without one of them stumbling after you like some sort of damn zombie out of *The Night of the Living Dead*.

They're enough to make you nuts.

My flesh crawled when I spotted Engineer Bill. He was up ahead of me, hobbling along behind his shopping carts. He had long white hair that stuck out all over the place, but I figured him for a man because he was wearing a suit coat and trousers.

He must've heard my car coming. He didn't look around, but he pushed his train over to the right to make room for me to pass. His train was made up of four shopping carts, all of them full of stuff. I guess, by bum standards, he must've been rich. I mean, it took *four* shopping carts to hold all his wealth.

I've heard that the carts go for about a hundred and twenty bucks each, so he was pushing close to five hundred bucks' worth of stolen property.

He wasn't just a bum, but also a thief.

Those are a couple of pretty good reasons to kill a guy. They aren't really why I did it, though. The main thing was because I wanted to see it happen.

He was off to the right, leaning way forward to get his

weight behind the carts. They were rattling and clanking along in front of him. I gunned the Jag. At just the last moment, I swerved. I smacked him behind the legs. He sort of sat down very fast on the hood and I plowed him into the caboose of his train.

The idea was partly to see how far I could shoot the carts. You should've seen 'em go!

It turned out they were lashed together. They went flying down the alley in a straight line for a while, then curved off to the left and flipped over sideways and skidded on their sides. By the time they stopped, Engineer Bill's goods were scattered all over the place.

He was still on my Jaguar. His legs hung off the front, and the rest of him was sprawled on top of the hood. He wasn't dead. Not even close. He whined and flapped his arms and tried to sit up.

I was worried all the noise from the crashing train might get people in the apartment buildings to look out their windows, so I drove off. I drove for about two blocks with Bill on the hood. He kept trying to sit up, which was pretty funny to watch.

I stopped in another alley. There was a box of old newspapers next to a garbage bin. On top was a Metro section of the *LA Times*. I took a few pages from that so I wouldn't have to touch Bill. I spread them against his side and pushed and shoved him off the hood.

A wind sent the newspaper pages tumbling off through the night.

I got into the car and backed away in order to get a good start. Then I sped at him and ran over him. The front and back tires on the left side got his head.

It was like driving over a speed bump. A big one.

Anyway, then it was back to business.

I left the alleys behind and cruised down Pico Boulevard. Traffic was pretty light. Some fast food joints and convenience stores and bars and gas stations were still open, but most places were closed for the night. I kept my eyes on their display windows.

A place called Nuances had windows full of female dummies. The store was closed, but the dummies were nicely lighted so people passing by could admire their underwear. I pulled over to the curb and shut off my headlights.

Cars were going by, so I sat there for a while and enjoyed the view.

Some of the dummies wore skimpy little negligees. Some wore bras and panties. The fabrics were shiny and clinging, or lacy, or see-through. Everything was cut to show plenty. For instance, there were bras and panties with open fronts. One dummy wore a black garter belt and fishnet stockings, and that was it.

They all wore wigs.

There were blondes, brunettes, redheads. A dozen different styles of haircuts.

Every so often, even on a main drag like Pico, you get a break in the traffic. I was waiting for one of those. It came along after about five minutes. Cars were still coming from both directions, but the nearest of them were still a few blocks away.

I jumped out of the Jag, ran to the big plate glass window to the right of the entrance, and smashed the glass with the barrel of my Colt. The whole damn window caved in. Most of it, anyway. There was enough noise to wake the dead, all that glass exploding and crashing down. Not to mention the burglar alarm.

As soon as the glass stopped falling, I climbed in and snatched the wigs off the heads of four of the dummies.

Tugged them off with my left hand, tucked them under my right arm.

Then I hopped down to the pavement and walked to the Jag. The nearest car was still two blocks away.

I just hoped it wasn't a cop car.

I tossed my wigs onto the passenger seat, climbed in behind the wheel, stuffed the Colt into my purse, and took off.

At the end of the block, I made a right. It was a residential street. I drove past a few houses, then swung to the curb and watched Pico in the rearview mirror. A few cars went by, but none of them turned. So I started moving again and put my headlights on.

Sticking to the back streets for a while, I tried out my wigs. They all seemed to be about the same size, which was just a teeny bit too small for my head. Better too tight than too loose, I guess. They went on just fine, but felt a little uncomfortable.

Not as uncomfortable as Hillary's scalp, though. They were dry, for one thing. And they weren't sticky or slimy.

I decided to wear the blond hair. It was full and shaggy, the sort of hair you'd expect to see on a bombshell bimbo.

Just the thing for Hollywood.

That's where I was heading, for Hollywood.

This was Saturday night, so the main drags were jammed with traffic and the sidewalks were mobbed. I made one pass down Hollywood Boulevard, mostly just to get my bearings.

It was enough to turn a girl's head.

My Jag was a red convertible, remember? And there I was, tooling along the boulevard in my flashy blond wig and sleeveless blue sundress, my bare arm resting on the window sill. There were whistles and hoots. A lot of people stared at me. They probably figured I was a famous movie star or a whore. Not wanting to disappoint anyone, I waved and blew kisses.

Face it, as a woman I'm dynamite.

But I had a job to do, so after a while I got away from the crowds and cruised sidestreets where there were houses and apartment buildings and only a few people roaming around. Some of the people were on the way back to their parked cars. Others just seemed to be out for a stroll. There were also some speed-walkers and joggers out for exercise. And a few people walking their dogs.

Dog walkers fall into two categories. There are those who are taking *themselves* for a walk, and have the dog along for protection. Then there are the ones whose alleged purpose is to give their dog a taste of fresh air and exercise – but whose real purpose is to have the dog take its shit away from home, on somebody *else's* property.

Dogs are man's best friend.

They bark at one end and shit at the other.

I'd like to kill them all.

I do kill them pretty often, if you want to know the truth. It's not like killing people, but it's a good way to eliminate the nuisance factor – and it's good practice.

Any time at home when I hear a dog start barking after dark, I get into my black 'nightfighter suit' and go out hunting. Sometimes they're strays, but usually I find them fenced inside a back yard. I never use a gun. I've used just about everything else, though. I've shot them with arrows, hit them with spears and poison darts and boomerangs. I've pounded some to death with a baseball bat or hammer or rock. I've strangled some. I've hacked some with hatchets, meat cleavers, and machetes. Butchered some with knives. Killed plenty with my feet, kicking and stomping.

I could go on and on about dogs.

We have a very special relationship.

Anyway, I saw a lot of people walking their dogs, so it was

mostly a question of choosing which to take. I wanted something like a toy poodle. You know, a sissy type of thing. A woman's dog.

The nearest I could come was a little white Maltese. It had a pink bow in the hair on top of its head. It was prancing along at the end of a leash, stopping at every tree and bush. Such a cute little thing. But not half as cute as its masters.

They were a matching set, slim and pushing forty, with hair as short as Marines. One had a mustache and one didn't. They both wore tan walking shorts with cuffs turned up. And sandals. One wore a fishnet shirt. You could see his hairy chest through its netting. The other didn't wear any shirt at all. He had a pierced nipple with a gold ring in it.

Of course, I didn't see all this from the car. At first glance, all I noticed was the little Maltese being walked by a couple of fruits. I didn't get a good close look at them till after I'd driven around the block, parked and got out and met them on the sidewalk.

I squatted down and intercepted the dog.

He liked me. He wagged his tail and licked my hands. 'Oh, he's such a little cutie,' I said. I smiled up at the boys. 'What's his name?'

The one with the shirt answered, 'Henry Wadsworth Longfellow the Third.'

'Well, hello, Henry, hello.' I rubbed him under the chin.

They both watched me. They looked wary.

I picked up the dog and cradled him against my bosom and kept on petting him. 'My name's Simone,' I told the boys.

Ring-in-the-tit folded his arms across his chest, made muscles and cocked an eyebrow at me. 'Isn't it a trifle early for Halloween, guy?'

'Are you looking for tricks or for treats?' the other one asked me. Then he smiled at his friend. 'What do you think?'

'Most assuredly straight.'

'Straight but definitely warped. More than slightly askew.'

'A cop?' asked Ring Tit.

'Oh, don't I wish. I *adore* cops. He's not one.'

'No, I'm sure you're right. He doesn't have the eyes. Cops have such marvelous eyes. So cynical, and yet amused.'

'You boys are funny,' I said.

Ring Tit lowered his arms but kept his muscles bunched. 'Put Henry down now,' he told me. 'We've got to be on our way.'

'We don't want any trouble,' said Net Shirt.

'Me neither. I'll pay you for Henry,' I said. Holding the dog against me with one hand, I reached into my purse.

'He's not for sale.'

'You're *giving* him to me? Why, thank you so much!'

Ring Tit reached behind his back. His hand came forward with something in it that turned out to be a flick knife. The skinny blade snapped out and locked.

'There's no need for that,' I said, and looked around. Nobody was nearby.

'Put down Henry right this instant,' Ring Tit warned.

Out came my Colt. I jammed it at his chest and pulled the trigger. Man, you should've *heard* that gun go off. A huge BOOM, and down he went. He hit the sidewalk flat on his back and skidded. His pal in the net shirt had time to look shocked and let go of Henry's leash before I put a slug in his chest. He flopped on the sidewalk, too.

They were stretched out next to each other, and Net Shirt had enough oomph left in him to take hold of his buddy's hand. How very touching.

I shoved the pistol into my purse and bent down and helped myself to Ring Tit's ring. It wasn't so much that I wanted the ring. It was just something I wanted to do, you know? I slipped my finger through the hoop and pulled. You should've seen how it stretched out his nipple before the flesh split open and let it go.

People gotta be careful what they go around and pierce.

This was my first pierced nipple, but I've ripped rings out of lots of earlobes, a few out of nostrils, and even an eyebrow once. Can you believe someone piercing her eyebrow? Hell, can you believe a guy piercing his nipple? I'd sure like to find myself a *gal* with a ring in her nipple. Or a twat ring. I've seen stuff like that in pictures, but not in real life. Not yet.

Gives me something to look forward to.

Anyway, I stuck the ring on one of my fingers and ran for the car. I could hear some people yelling.

Needless to say, I didn't get caught.

Something was wrong with the pooch, though. I knew he was limp even before I got to the car and tossed him onto the passenger seat. While I sped away, I worried he might be dead. Like maybe his ticker had quit on him.

But pretty soon he came to.

The damn thing must've fainted when I plugged the pretty boys.

I've never heard of a dog fainting. It happens, though. You can take my word for it.

I was a couple of blocks away from the scene of the shooting before Henry came to. A minute after that, a cop car raced by with its siren blaring and lights flashing. The two cops in the front seat didn't even glance at me.

It's easy to get away with murder.

I'm telling you, it's *easy*.

All you've gotta do is leave before the cops show up.

And only kill strangers. And try not to leave incriminating evidence behind, like a driver's license. One, two, three. Rules to kill by.

I know, I know, I'm oversimplifying.

But you know what? Most of the high-tech forensic shit that scares everyone to death (my former friend Tom included) is of damn near no use at all unless the cops have a suspect to match things up with. Which means they've gotta know who you are in the first place.

Follow my three rules, and you'll be home free.

Anyway, the dog was okay and the cops weren't on my tail, so I went on and headed for Jody's house over on Castleview. That's about a twenty-minute drive from Hollywood.

Chapter Twenty-eight

It was on a quiet street full of one-story stucco houses that had probably been built in the twenties or thirties. They were kept up, though. This looked like a nice, middle-class neighborhood. Not half as nice as the section where I'd grown up, but not bad.

It was three or four miles from Avalon Heights. Jody must've gone to school with shish-ka-sister, and that's how she knew her and ended up at the house Friday night. Just like I went to school with Tom and spent so much time at his mansion, even though we lived pretty far away from each other.

That's one of those things about LA. You don't make friends with your neighbors. If you've got friends, they live five or ten – or maybe thirty – miles away. Which isn't so bad if you're a grownup with a car. When you're a kid, though, it means you spend a lot of time by yourself.

Where was I, anyway?

Oh.

Okay, I was driving past Jody's house. I did it without slowing down.

In fact, I couldn't even be sure which house was hers. I caught an address on the block before I got there, then again on the block afterward. So I could tell that I'd gone past it.

I hadn't slowed down to look for the exact address because I didn't want to appear suspicious. What I did look for was evidence of cops.

Cars were parked on both sides of the street and in some of the driveways. None of them looked much like a cop car. You never can be too sure, though.

I turned onto a sidestreet and parked at a curb in front of a dark house. Then Henry and I took a walk.

Henry was such a character! He pranced along, all dainty and chipper at the end of his leash, just as if he didn't have a care in the world. But each time he hoisted his hind leg by a bush or tree, he stared over his shoulder at me. He never peed, just raised his leg and gave me a dirty look before prancing off again.

With all the stops he made, I had plenty of time to check around.

I checked inside most of the cars parked on our side of the street to make sure they weren't occupied. Also, I watched out for vans or service trucks that cops might be using to stake out Jody's house.

The area looked safe.

Jody's house was in the middle of the block. Its porch light was on, but its windows were dark. No cars at all were parked in its driveway or at the curb directly in front. Nobody seemed to be peering out any of the windows.

If the place was under surveillance, though, I was being watched whether I knew it or not.

So I tripped and fell. Henry had to scoot, or I would've mashed him. Unfortunately, I went down harder than I'd planned. I'd wanted it to look good, but I hadn't wanted to crash my damn knee against the sidewalk. It hurt like a son-of-a-bitch, and I let go of the leash.

You know how it feels to bang your knee? It *hurts*. It's almost as bad as catching a shot to the nuts. Well, maybe that's going overboard. But it's sure no picnic.

So I rolled onto my back and grabbed my knee with both hands.

Even with all my pain, there was a part of me that was glad I'd taken such a bad fall. It was bound to do the trick. If cops were watching, they would've seen this gorgeous blond babe strolling along the sidewalk with her cute little dog. Maybe just when they were starting to worry about her – it being after midnight, after all, and *no place* in L.A. is safe for anyone, much less a sweetie like me, all alone late at night – just when they were starting to worry along those lines, they would've seen me stumble and nail my knee. Then would come a delicious view of my bare legs and panties while I'm squirming on my back.

Cops are all a bunch of horny bastards.

They also think they're God's gift to the safety of mankind.

I'm a beautiful babe and in need of help. In other words, for any normal cops, I'm irresistible.

They'd have been on me like Boy Scouts on a blind cheerleader stumbling across a freeway.

But nobody came to my assistance.

While I was still on my back, Henry came sniffing up to my face. It seemed very sweet of him. I was touched. I thought to myself, This dog is all right.

Then the fucker bit my cheek and ran like hell, his little leash dragging behind him.

I'll kill him if I ever get my hands on him. I'll gouge out his eyes and chop off his little feet and skin him alive and barbecue him and eat him.

I would've shot him on the spot, but that would've been stupid. By then, I was pretty sure no cops were watching me. But firing off my Colt would've blown any chance of getting my hands on Jody.

Anyway, my face was *bleeding*!

The fucking little faggot dog broke my skin, would you believe it?

Blood was getting all over me.

I sat up and held on to my cheek and had a real strong urge just to limp on back to my car and drive to the motel and forget about Jody. Call it a night, you know? Maybe hit the road tomorrow for parts unknown, the hell with Jody, the hell with Lisa, the hell with Tom and the guys.

It's hard to care about much of anything when you've just bashed your knee and gotten bit in the face. All you want to do is quit. Quit and go home.

I no sooner made it to my feet, though, than I suddenly realized the dog had given me exactly what I needed – an excuse to go to Jody's door!

I'd thought for sure that a cop or two would come running out when they saw me fall, and I'd take it from there – either talk my way into the house or shoot them down, then run in and snatch Jody. Maybe use her family car for our getaway.

But no cops had shown up.

Which meant none had seen me fall or get bitten.

Which meant Jody and her family weren't being guarded at all.

Which meant all I had to do was go through the door.

Who could resist opening the door to a woman with blood all over her?

Nobody, that's who.

And nobody is just who opened the door.

I stood under the porch light for about five minutes, ringing the doorbell. I could *hear* it ringing inside, so it wasn't broken. But nobody came.

Were they just heavy sleepers, or were they in there listening and lying low?

Maybe nobody was home. They might've decided to split after Dusty's muffed try at sniping the girl. It'd be a natural reaction: somebody takes pot shots at you, you go someplace where maybe they can't find you.

Anyway, I didn't know. But I wasn't about to leave.

There were glass panels on both sides of the door. All I had to do was bash one, reach inside and unfasten the locks. I didn't do it, though. I didn't want there to be busted glass right out in front where anyone could see it.

So I went around to the back of the house. It had a nice concrete patio with lounges and a barbecue. On my way to the door, I had to step over some dark gobs. No telling what they were. There wasn't enough light to see much. I didn't see the broken glass, so I ended up walking through it. I crunched some pieces and kicked others, making them skitter and clink across the concrete. Made a real racket. A dog started barking, but it was far away and it sounded too big to be Henry.

Walking through the mess, I realized somebody must've dropped plates or something back here. The dark gobs were probably food.

Then I came to the screen door. It was just an aluminum frame without any screening in it.

I swung it open and blocked it there with my back while I

tried the wooden door. You never know about people. Sometimes, they don't lock up. The knob wouldn't turn, though. The door felt stout, and had a deadbolt lock, so I decided not to monkey with it.

I went in through a window, instead. None at the back of the house had been left open, so I just picked one at random. I stood on a patio chair. It was redwood, so it was sturdy enough to hold me up. (Aluminum chairs half the time bend and collapse when you stand on them.) The screen window was attached pretty good. I couldn't pull it off, so I gave the screening a smack with the butt of my Colt. It gave, and the glass behind it shattered.

More barking from the unknown dog.

Aside from that, nothing happened.

So after waiting a while, I bashed in the screening with my pistol. I basically tore my way through it, ripped it out of my way. The window was double hung. I reached in and unlocked it and slid it up. Then I used one of my shoes to brush the broken glass off the sill. Then I climbed in.

Underneath the window was the kitchen sink. I've had to crawl over worse obstacles from time to time. It took a while and a lot of effort, but I finally got myself to the floor.

Then I searched the house. After all the noise I'd made, I was ninety-nine percent sure it was empty. Even so, I kept the gun in my hand, ready for surprises.

I checked inside every room. Just a quick look, but enough to make sure nobody else was around. The last place I checked was the garage, which was attached to the side of the house. You could get to it through a door in the hallway. There were all sorts of tools and appliances inside the garage, but no car. The space where the car belonged was empty.

Which made me fairly sure that Jody and her family had driven somewhere.

It was a relief, but disappointing.

I went into the bathroom, locked the door and turned on the light.

You should've seen me.

When I saw myself in the mirror, I didn't know whether to scream or laugh. My wig was twisted crooked and half my face was a bloody mess. The blood had come from tiny rips in the skin over my left cheekbone. That whole side of my face was smeared and stained with blood. It had run off my jaw and down the side of my neck. It had soaked the collar of my sundress and even spattered the front.

The bleeding had stopped by that time.

Later, I went around the Whole house and cleaned off every place where I could find bloody handprints or drops of blood.

You can't get it all, though.

I'll probably burn the place, sooner or later. But I can't burn the patio or lawn or sidewalk, so the cops are sure to find my blood.

Thanks a lot, Henry.

It's almost like he bit me on behalf of all his brother bow-wows I've dispatched over the years. Payback, you know?

I'd *love* to get my hands on him.

I guess it doesn't matter, though. About the blood. It won't do the cops any good without me. And they won't get their hands on me. Cops are the least of my worries.

Anyway, all I really cared about right then was fixing myself up. I straightened my wig and washed the blood off my face and neck. Then I checked inside the medicine cabinet. What a waste of time that was. I couldn't find any sort of antiseptic or any Band-aids, not even gauze or adhesive tape. Don't these people ever hurt themselves?

I ended up folding some toilet paper into a pad. I held that against the bite, and taped it there with some magic transparent tape I found on the desk in Jody's bedroom.

It is definitely Jody's bedroom, by the way. There had always been the possibility that I'd gone to the wrong house, but her room removed any doubts.

On a shelf were some big wooden blocks that spelled her name. Her name was all over the place, on pencils and stickers and a little fake California license plate, not to mention on pages of school work I found inside a loose-leaf binder. I also found some pictures of her.

There were a few framed photos on top of her dresser and desk. One showed her with shish-ka-sister. They looked maybe seven or eight years old, and were at Disneyland hanging onto the arms of some dopey yellow bear in a red T-shirt. There were also pictures of Jody with her folks. The gal I figured for her mother only showed up in pictures when Jody was pretty young. She's out of the picture now, so to speak. She either dumped the old man, or kicked the old bucket. Either way, she isn't in any recent pictures and she doesn't have clothes in the master bedroom. It looks like Jody lives alone with her father.

And here's a good one: her father's a cop! She has pictures in her bedroom of him in his uniform. There's one where she's real little and sitting on his knee and wearing his cop hat which is about a hundred sizes too big for her.

A cop!

Life is sometimes just one big jolly surprise after another.

Of all the cute little sixteen-year-old babes in the world, I just happen to be after the daughter of a cop.

He looks like an ugly, mean son of a bitch, too.

How did Jody turn out so beautiful with a gorilla like him supplying half her chromosomes? Amazing.

No doubt, though – she's his kid.

She probably inherited the part of him that bounced a fuckin' baseball bat off my head the other night.

Anyway, I did more than just look at her pictures. I went through her drawers and closet. The closet had a few empty hangers, and the drawer where she kept her panties and bras had a lot of vacant space. In fact, there were only two pairs of panties and one bra. The hamper next to the dresser had nothing in it.

So, did she keep extra hangers just for the fun of it? Did she have a big shortage of underwear?

Not real likely.

I went out to the garage and looked inside the washing machine and drier. Only thing I found was a pair of jeans in the washer.

I added things up.

One, Jody and her old man are gone. Two, the car is gone. Three, it looks like Jody has clothes missing.

You add that stuff up, and they give you an answer. Which is that Jody and her old man must've packed a few things and lit out.

Probably planning to lay low for a while.

Not a bad idea when you know you've got killers after you.

Which *I'll* probably have, myself, if I don't turn Jody up in time for the big ten o'clock deadline.

Deadline's a good word for it.

It's three o'clock in the morning right now. I had the cassette recorder in my purse, and fortunately it didn't get broken when I fell. It was starting to sound funny, though, so I put in some fresh batteries. Found them in a kitchen drawer where there was a lot of stuff like strapping tape, glue, and about five different sizes of new batteries.

Anyway, I've been talking into it for a while now, since

right after I checked the washing machine and drier. I'm on a sofa in the living room.

And dead tired.

I've gotta flake out for a while. Might not be a brilliant idea to do it in the living room, though. No telling when somebody might show up. There's a guest room way at the end of the hall. That wouldn't be much fun, would it?

I think I'll try Jody's bed.

Yeah.

I'm sure I'll enjoy lying in her very own bed. I'm sure I'll like that a lot.

Maybe it'll help me have sweet dreams.

Chapter Twenty-nine

I'm back.

Maybe it wasn't such a great idea, trying to grab some z's on Jody's bed. I couldn't get her out of my mind. I kept remembering everything about how she'd looked and felt the other night. And I kept thinking about how this was her bed, how she gets into it every night, maybe naked sometimes, and how my skin was pressing against the same sheets that had been rubbed by Jody's body. It made me hard and achy and a little nuts.

I also spent a lot of time imagining what I would do with her. I thought about ways I might like to tie her up, and how I would hurt her, and the different ways I would fuck her.

And those were the *good* things that ran through my head.

There were also times when I worried about never being able to find her, what the guys would do to Lisa if I screwed up, what they might do to my sisters down the line and what they might do to me.

I spent part of the time horny, part of the time scared. And my face hurt from the dog bite and I had a headache.

It made for a very long night.

I slept just long enough to have one really horrible nightmare.

I was chasing a dog that reminded me a lot of Henry – a little white furball with an attitude. I was after the bone in its mouth. The bone belonged to me. It was my big, stiff cock. My crotch was bleeding all over the place while I chased the damn dog.

Whenever Henry had a good lead on me, he'd hunker down and gnaw on the bone and I'd yell, 'Don't wreck it! You're gonna wreck it!'

But then he got away from me and I lost sight of him for a while. When I found him again, his mouth was empty but he had dirt all over his muzzle and paws. 'You *buried it*!' I yelled. He wagged his tail. So then I begged him to tell me where, and he grinned and swung around and pranced on ahead of me.

He led me straight to a graveyard. Then he vanished and I was all alone in the bone orchard without a clue as to where he'd planted my dick. I started looking. It was creepy. Tombstones everywhere. Weeds and tombstones and stunted, dead trees. And the worst part was that I noticed spooks sneaking around the graves, scurrying this way and that, ducking behind monuments. I don't know what they were supposed to be – zombies, maybe. I was afraid they might start coming after me.

Finally, I found a place where the soil looked loose and

dark. I started digging there, clawing away the dirt with my fingers. It was a fresh hole, all right. And pretty soon, I found what I was looking for.

So I thought, anyway.

I grabbed it and pulled.

It was attached to someone.

All of a sudden the ground crumbled and up sat a body all covered by dirt. The dirt started sliding off, and I knew this had to be Tit Ring showing up to haunt me. But it wasn't.

It turned out to be Jody. She was naked and grinning, and I still had hold of her cock. She said, 'Suck me, honey.'

I was awfully shocked that she had a dick. I mean, she's beautiful and has wonderful tits and she's almost too good to be true, but here I find her in a grave and she comes up out of the dirt and has herself some male equipment. Very damn weird.

And even weirder still is that I'm turned on by the whole thing. I've never done any of that perverted stuff, you know? That stuff was for Mitch and Chuck, not me. But I tell myself this isn't a guy, it's Jody. So I go ahead and open up and slide my lips down her rod, but all of a sudden it turns cold and hard. The way it feels in my mouth, I know it's a gun barrel.

I say, 'This isn't your cock.'

She says, 'No, but it's cocked.'

I'm thinking it's very clever of me to have wisecracks in my dreams.

But then the gun goes off and I wake up damn fast – before the bullet has a chance to reach my brain and kill me.

It's supposed to be very bad news if you get killed in a dream.

But I woke up in time. I'm pretty sure.

Woke up with a splitting headache and a sore face. The room was gray and chilly. I took my gun with me to the john.

I helped myself to some aspirin, then went to the kitchen and got a pot of coffee started. I didn't have any clothes on, so I was shivering. Have you ever noticed how a headache hurts a lot worse when you're shivering?

Once I was under the shower, the headache tapered off. There's nothing like a hot shower to take away the morning chill and relax you. The water made my face sting where the dog had bitten me, but it felt great otherwise.

When you're in the shower, you can't hear anything that's going on in the rest of the house. But you *think* you hear things. Like the telephone ringing, like footsteps and voices. It can get to you if you let it.

It can also add a little spice to your showering.

You've just gotta be logical about it and tell yourself you aren't hearing anything. I mean, the odds were very much against anyone turning up at the house at six in the morning.

After the shower, I put on a terry cloth robe that I found in Jack's closet. Jack is the father's name, by the way. Jack Fargo. His name is on magazine subscription labels, bills I saw in the kitchen, all sorts of things.

I took the wig with me, but didn't put it on. I just wanted to have it nearby as a precaution. I was in no mood to wear it, not with my headache. I didn't feel like getting dressed, either. For starters, it was too early in the morning to cope with Hillary's bra. Even though I get a bang out of the way I look in it, the thing makes me feel like I'm wearing a harness. Maybe it's too small. I'll have to try on the one I saw in Jody's drawer. Later.

For now, I'm happy just sitting here in the living room. The sofa is comfortable and I like the feel of Jack's robe. My first mug of coffee was great.

Time for a second. Back in a second.

Okay, I'm back. Ahh, this is the life.

Maybe I should make myself some breakfast.

That can wait. I don't feel like moving for a while.

Sooner or later, I'll have to move. Gotta figure out a way to find Jody and Andy. Or maybe they'll just show up on their own and save me the trouble of hunting them down.

What the hell, I've got till ten o'clock tonight. Plenty of time.

Right now, I want to talk some more about my adventures in murder with Tom and the gang.

I already told about Hester Luddgate, and about how we killed those two bike riders on our way up to Oregon. I guess I *didn't* get into how we killed the gal, or what else we did to her. Time's a-wastin', though. There's still a lot of ground to cover, so I'll just go on. Suffice it to say we had a merry few hours with the wench, and left her in no condition to tell the tale.

After that, Private and Clement were hooked. The four of us were on the road for a total of two weeks, and killed three more people for a grand total of five. One was a guy who was hitching his way to Portland. Then there were two gals whose car ran out of gas ten miles from the nearest town. Talk about stupid! Hell, they were too dumb to live. They weren't much to look at, but we had fun with them.

When Ranch and Minnow – God, Minnow's dead? That's what Tom said, but it's hard to believe. And it was Jody that killed him. I can see it, as a matter of fact. Her killing him. All she did was give me a tap with that bat of hers, and I've had a lump and a headache ever since. The headache comes and goes, to tell the truth. But it's probably from when she pounded me. If she really put some oomph into her swing, it's no wonder she dropped Minnow.

Anyway. Let me think. Oh, yeah. We got back from the trip and told those two, Ranch and Minnow, what we'd done and they went crazy. They acted like they'd been cheated out of all the excitement. They kept saying, 'Damn!' and 'Shit!' and 'No Fair!' and 'How could you do it without us?'

So that's when Tom said, 'It's no big deal. Let's go out and kill somebody right now. All of us.'

We were sort of having a party at Tom's place when he said that. It was the week after we got back from our Oregon trip, and we all had permission to spend the night. We were sitting around in his wreck room drinking beer and eating all sorts of munchies.

When Tom said that about going out and killing someone, I got so excited I almost couldn't breathe. Ranch went red in the face and began panting. Little Minnow started rubbing his mouth. Private mumbled, 'Oh boy oh boy oh boy,' and Clement bobbed his head, grinning like a dope.

All of us were hot to do it.

'What a bunch of sickos,' Tom said.

'And proud of it,' Private said.

'Have they taken the pledge?' Minnow asked.

For a while there, I didn't know what he was talking about. But Tom knew, all right. And he was ready. We all joined hands and did the oath, just the same as on the day when we buried Hester. The only difference was, this time there were six of us.

When we were done, Tom took us out to his garage.

The garage is off to the side and slightly behind Tom's house. It's huge, with six bay doors and room inside to hold at least that many cars. There are also a couple of normal doors and some windows. You can't see through the windows anymore, but you could on the night I'm talking about. It was later that we painted them black.

The garage wasn't air conditioned like Tom's house. It had been closed up all day, so it felt hot and stuffy. There weren't any cars inside except for the Mercedes. There was a lot of junk – tools and gardening equipment, things like that. But the garage was so huge that it was mostly empty space. It was almost like being in an aircraft hanger.

After we were inside, Tom told us to strip. Seems like we're always stripping, doesn't it? The thing is, bloodshed is a messy business, and you don't want to be stuck wearing gory clothes.

After we finished, Tom handed out black jumpsuits to all of us. He also gave us black socks and black sneakers. Everything fit, too. Which is strange. He'd found out our sizes on his own, without ever asking any of us. He only smiled when I asked him about it.

The jumpsuits looked great on us. They made us look like a skydiving club, or something. But they were awfully damn hot, especially while we were in the garage.

After we had our outfits on, Tom led us over to a corner where there were a lot of tools. He said, 'Pick your weapons, guys.' We helped ourselves to all sorts of nasty instruments: hammers, screwdrivers, pliers, hedge clippers, a sickle, a chainsaw, an ax. We also grabbed shovels and a pickax, though nobody discussed whether these were supposed to be weapons or tools for disposing of the body.

We piled all the stuff in the trunk of the Mercedes, then climbed into the front and back seats. It was pretty crowded in there. Tom opened the garage door by remote control. (Only the door for the Mercedes' section was equipped with an automatic opener.) Then we were off!

A team of six hunters prowling the night for prey.

I figured the plan was to drive around and search for a good target of opportunity. What we needed was a gal by herself in a fairly secluded place. You'd be amazed how easy it is. But that isn't what Tom had in mind.

He drove us to a house only about a mile from where I lived at the time.

Denise Dennison's house.

Minnow recognized the place, too. He sucked in a breath. 'You're kidding,' he whispered.

'You want her, don't you?'

'Sure. Yeah. But . . . You said we're gonna *kill* somebody.'

'That's the general idea.'

'Denise?'

Ranch laughed. 'It's the only way *you're* ever gonna lay your hands on her.'

'We'll do a lot more than lay our hands on her,' Tom said.

What an understatement that turned out to be.

It probably took us fifteen minutes to bust into the house. We were pretty quiet about it. We didn't remember to bring flashlights, so we just went ahead and turned on the lights each time we walked into a room.

We had no problem with the parents. We killed them before they could get out of bed. We did it fast without any fooling around. We don't do it that way anymore – we stretch things out so we can enjoy every dimension of their surprise and terror and pain and so on. We like to play with them for as long as we can. But we were new at it, that night in Denise's house.

We all got in on killing her mom and dad. With six of us working at once, it took about two seconds to wreck them both. It was really something to see. *Wham!* All of a sudden, they're nothing but spurting piles of demolished yuck.

We knew that Denise had a couple of younger brothers, but the next room down the hallway was hers. Its door stood open. We went in and turned on the light.

The switch made a lamp come on beside her bed. Even though it was bright, it didn't wake her up because she was sleeping on her side with her back to the lamp. The house had its air conditioning on. She was covered to the shoulders by a sheet.

Minnow sneaked to the foot of the bed and pinched the sheet and slid it down all the way.

Oh, man.

She wore a white nightgown, but it didn't cover much. What it *did* cover, you could see anyway because the fabric was basically transparent.

We just stood there and watched her sleep for a while.

You should've been there. I'll never forget the way Denise looked, or how I felt. I'd had the hots for her since junior high. So had some of the others. And now we had her at our mercy.

It was, to put it mildly, a magic moment.

A magic five minutes, more like it.

Then Tom snuck over alongside the bed. He had grass trimmers which looked like a big pair of scissors. He grabbed Denise's hair with one hand. At the same time, he caught her throat in the V of the open trimmers.

All of which woke her up.

Her eyes bulged.

'Don't make a sound,' Tom warned.

She shrieked, 'Dad!'

Tom partly shut the trimmers. Their blades broke her skin. She made a gasping noise at the pain and started to bleed, but didn't yell again.

We heard some voices and thumping sounds. Her brothers. They were on their way to the rescue. Which delayed things for Denise. Tom and Minnow stayed behind to keep her on the bed. The rest of us went into the hall and intercepted her brothers.

They were twins, blond and tan, about nine years old.

They looked like boy versions of Denise, only younger, of course. Very cute, if you're into that sort of thing. They were both wearing pajama pants that hung pretty low on them, and no shirts. Mitch and Chuck would've gone wild for these fellows, but they didn't come along and join up until a long time after this.

One of the twins charged at us waving a pocket knife. The other came at us with a baseball bat.

A couple of very spunky kids.

Spunky till Ranch cranked up the chainsaw.

Then they yelled and spun around and ran the other way. We chased them down. They didn't even make it out of the hall. Ranch got one with his chainsaw. I happened to be running beside the kid, going after his brother, and blood slapped me in the face like a wet rag. I couldn't even see where I was going. But I bumped into the back of the kid I was after, and shoved my screwdriver in. We both fell. I jabbed him a few more times while he screamed and thrashed around under me. Then Clement came along and caved in his head with a hammer.

You should've seen the hallway after that. What a mess.

We left the twins where they'd fallen. All we really cared about, now that they were out of our hair, was getting back to Denise.

She was still on the bed, Tom clutching her hair and holding the shears to her throat. But now she was lying on her back and Minnow was bending over her, busy pulling the torn remains of the nightgown down her legs. She didn't move at all except to sob and gasp for air.

Minnow blocked her view of us until he finished with the nightgown and stepped out of the way. Then she raised her head. Must've hurt, pushing her neck against the edges of the shears. But she did it anyway, and looked at us.

Seeing all that blood must've unhinged her.

Or maybe it was the sight of Ranch's chainsaw, which was pretty gory.

She went nuts. Nobody was holding her arms, so she grabbed Tom's hand and shoved the shears away from her throat. She even managed to turn them and poke Tom in the belly with them. They went into him far enough to leave a pair of quarter-inch scars. He yelled and fell backward off the bed.

Before Denise could do anything else, four of us pinned her to the mattress by her arms and legs. All she could do was twist and squirm. That left Minnow free to go first. So he took off his jumpsuit and climbed aboard. Must've been like a dream coming true for him. I mean, we'd all had the hots for her, but he'd been obsessed. For years. He must've thought he'd died and gone to heaven.

Ho ho. Now he *is* dead, thanks to Jody. Bet he didn't go to heaven, though.

Even if he'd been a regular saint for every other second of his life, the stuff he did to Denise for about fifteen minutes while we held her down bought him a one-way ticket to hell, that's for sure.

We basically didn't rush Minnow or anything, figuring he'd waited so long for a chance at her. Also, it was a fantastic turn-on to watch both of them.

By the time he was done, Denise was still alive but we didn't need to hold her down anymore.

Private went second, then Clement. Ranch went next, and showed a certain flare and originality – not to mention good taste – by licking her clean before getting down to real business. Then it was my turn. Denise didn't look like much by then. In a way, though, that made it even better. Mostly, I remember how slippery she felt.

Tom went last. His belly was bleeding pretty good from the way she had jabbed him. He was smiling, though. Denise was still alive when he started. He used the shears on her. She still had enough energy to scream, but we'd shoved a wad of nightgown into her mouth way before then, so not much sound came out. She was in a few pieces by the time Tom finished.

After that, we took quick showers so we wouldn't have to leave the house with blood all over us. We took our tools into the showers with us and washed them, too. Then we got dressed and took everything out to the car with us.

All of us climbed in except Tom. He said, 'Back in a minute,' and we had to wait while he went into the house. He was gone for a lot longer than a minute. Finally, he got in and started the car.

But he didn't pull away.

'What're we waiting for?' I asked.

'You'll see.'

Pretty soon, I saw.

Orange light through the living room curtains. Orange light that shimmered and shook and got brighter.

'Pretty good idea,' I said.

'Cremate the fuckers,' Ranch said.

'It's more to cremate the crime scene,' Tom explained.

Then we drove back to his place.

Chapter Thirty

It really ate up the time, telling all that.

If I tried to give you that much detail about everything, it'd take me for ever. Or at least longer than I've got.

My headache is gone. The aspirin must've kicked in. Also, I went ahead and made myself bacon and eggs after I got done telling about our fun and games at Denise's house. We had *some* fun there, didn't we?

I probably shouldn't have gone into so much detail. I might end up running out of time before I have a chance to tell everything else.

But our attack on Denise's house deserved some attention, since it was the first time we did that sort of thing. It was like a major event in the history of our little gang. A lot bigger, scarier and more exciting than just nailing one person we might find in the streets somewhere. It was like a quantum leap into a whole new dimension of mayhem.

The news media treated it that way, too.

They called it a 'Manson-style massacre'.

As to who had committed the atrocity, they didn't have a clue.

I think Tom's mother probably had a pretty good idea about who'd done it. But we didn't need to worry about her telling.

We behaved ourselves and began our university careers. Tom decided against Willamette because he didn't want to break up the gang. He went to Pepperdine instead. Ranch, Private and I went to UCLA, Minnow to USC and Clement to Loyola-Marymount.

Maybe we weren't angels, but we weren't dumb. Sure, sometimes we acted like dopes and goofed off, but that was just for fun. Underneath it all, we were smart enough to get into pretty good schools.

We got together sometimes over the next few months, but we didn't go out and kill anybody.

In November, my urges got the better of me and I nailed a coed in one of the UCLA parking structures. I raped her and used an electrical cord to strangle her. (Quiet, and not much blood to speak of.) This couldn't compare with hitting a house and doing a whole family, but it was better than nothing.

Anyway, we knew we couldn't hit a house very often. That sort of crime is just too big.

By the first week in January, we figured enough time had gone by. We all had time off for our winter breaks. Tom had recruited three new members. Somehow, he had a talent for picking guys with the right kind of urges and guts.

I wonder if there's something about Tom. Maybe he has a sixth sense about these things, or maybe he has a force inside him that switches people on. Serial killers are almost always loners. That's probably because there just aren't that many guys around who have the right mixture of necessary ingredients to bake that particular cherry pie, if you know what I mean. Sometimes you hear about two working together, but that's pretty rare. We started off with four, and worked our way up to *twelve*.

Unheard of, as far as I know.

So I guess we're 'history makers'. That makes me pretty important, being one of the charter members and also the guy telling the tale.

Also, I've been in on every kill done by the gang. (Not to mention that I've done more than a few on my own.)

I'm one of the only guys who knows it all.

Just call me the Boswell of the Krull Gang.

Better get back to the story. I got sidetracked about the new members Tom brought in.

They were Lawrence 'Dusty' Rhodes, Bill Peterson, and Frank 'Tex' Austin. Dusty is still with us, but the other two are toes up.

I already told what happened to Bill Peterson.

Tex caught it the third time he went on a house raid with us. That was in Reno, Nevada. (We got around, not wanting to foul our own back yard any more than necessary.) The wife happened to be in the John taking a leak when we made our entry. She took us all by surprise, but it was Tex that she killed. Jumped on his back and stabbed him in the neck about ten times with a little pair of toenail scissors. One of the stabs opened up his carotid.

Tex was our first member of the homosexual persuasion. By the time we found out, though, we all liked him so it didn't matter. Besides, he never messed with any of us. He saved it for the guys we met on our forays. Which worked out very nicely. He took special care of the fellas while we handled the babes.

Before he got killed, he brought in Mitch and Chuck. They were okay, I guess. I liked them fine, mostly, till Friday night when they were so useless going after Jody and Andy. And on top of which, the assholes ditched me.

In my book, they're *all* a bunch of assholes. The whole bunch.

They all deserted me. And now they're all ganging up on me over this Jody and Andy business. Guys I thought were my friends.

They're probably hoping I don't make the deadline, so then they can have their fun and games with Lisa.

Just for the record, Lisa doesn't know anything about our

little adventures. She knows I get together with the guys once a month and sometimes I end up staying out all night, but she always thought we were meeting at Tom's house to play poker and get drunk. She didn't like it, either. She's been trying to get me to quit.

We got engaged a couple of months ago, and the wedding is set for Labor Day weekend. Ranch is supposed to be my 'best man'. He's been talking about throwing me a bachelor's party where we take a sorority house – really plan ahead and go in there with some heavy artillery and take control of the place, then pick out the best looking babes for our entertainment.

I told him it sounded awfully risky.

He said, 'You only get married once.'

I think we really might have done it. Hell, it would've made more history. But everything's down the tubes, now. Even if I can manage to save Lisa, it'll all be over between us. And it's all over between me and the guys, no matter what. Even if they forgive me for screwing up, I can't forgive them for the way they turned against me.

I don't know how I'm going to get my hands on Jody in time for the deadline, anyway.

I've been trying to tell myself she'll come walking in the door any minute, but it isn't likely. Those dresser drawers of hers were just too empty. She must've taken enough clothes for a week or two. You don't do that, then come home the next morning.

God, I'd like to forget about Lisa and the deadline and all that shit, and just sit here and talk. I've never talked so much in my life as during the past couple of days. It's great. Telling about this stuff, it's like *being* there all over again. I can see it, smell it, taste it, feel it. What a turn-on!

What I'd really like to do is give the whole history in

detail. Maybe it could end up as a book. Call it, *The Incredible Krulls*. Har! No, that's an awful title. How about *The Sex-Cult Massacres*? I like that.

Maybe that can be my project if I get out of this mess alive.

Anyway, I'd like to just keep sitting here and really get into it, but . . . It'd be nice. It'd take my mind off shit, too.

But shit beckons.

In other words, I've got some calls to make. First, I'll give Tom a try. Maybe if I explain things, he'll give me a break. I know I can get my hands on Jody. I need time, though. Maybe a week.

He'll give me a week, my ass.

No way.

I could get down on my knees and beg, and he's the sort of guy who won't give me one extra minute on the deadline.

Well, screw that. I don't beg.

What I *will* do, though, is phone up my sisters. Depending on how things turn out tonight, Tom and the guys might go after them next.

This'll be real fun.

How do you tell your sisters that you had a falling out with some of your pals, and now those former pals might come along and torture, rape and butcher them and their husbands and children, so they'd better leave town for a few days or a month or the rest of their lives?

Talk about embarrassing, huh?

I wonder if they'll even believe me.

They're nine and eleven years older than me, so they never knew me very well. They were hardly ever around the house by the time I started getting into stuff with Tom and the guys. So they think I'm a sweet, quiet fellow. It might be awfully hard convincing them I'm mixed up in anything that could get them destroyed.

Maybe I should just wait a while before I call them. See how things go. If I can just get my hands on Jody . . .

No. I shouldn't have waited this long. It won't be any major deal if I let the guys nail Lisa – I mean, I do want to save her. But it's not like she's *family*, you know? I'm not even sure I *wanted* to marry her. But I can't let the guys get to my sisters.

Okay. Here goes. I'm gonna call.

I'll start with Dora, I guess. I get along with her better than I do with Sandy. Sandy's a real know-it-all.

Oh, man, I don't want to do this.

Here goes.

I guess I'll take the recorder along so I can tape my side of these miserable conversations for posterity.

The phone's in the kitchen.

This makes my stomach hurt.

Vhat duss not kill uss makes uss schtronker. Yah-vole!

I don't know my sisters' phone numbers by heart. Isn't that awful?

So, what's the number for directory assistance?

Five five five something, I guess.

Hey, what's this?

Folks! I see some numbers written on a pad here by the phone. They look suspiciously like a couple of long distance phone numbers.

Might these numbers provide a clue, perchance, to the whereabouts of Jody?

Fat fucking chance, Watson.

Eeeny meeny miney moe . . .

The bottom number it is.

Who knows what evil lurks . . .?

'Woops.'

For those of you listening, I just hung up. Can you guess who I encountered at the other end?

The police. The *Indio* police. That's Indio, California.

Be still, my heart. Whew! Be still, my ass. Have you ever noticed, when you're really scared, how your bowel area gets hot and tingly and feels like it's squirming around on you?

That's how I feel right now.

It's no picnic, making an innocent call and having a guy on the other end say he's the official answer-boy for a police department.

Who does the other number belong to, the fucking FBI?

I think I'll have another cup of coffee and give myself a couple of minutes to calm down before I try that one.

Okay. My bodily functions are slowly returning to normal.

Question. What is the number for the Indio cops doing on a pad by Jody's kitchen phone?

Answer. Somebody called them recently.

What I might do is make the call again, say I'm with the LAPD, wing it, see what I can find out. Terrific idea. No way.

Here's a little lesson in crime: don't mess with cops, avoid them.

If I call up and try to play games, the oink at the other end is gonna catch on and pull a cute stunt such as tracing the call. (You call some numbers, like 911 for instance, and your call gets traced *automatically*. They don't even have to stall and keep you on the line like in the movies. Bang, the computer gives them the address you're calling from. The miracles of modern technology.)

I'll try the other number.

If it belongs to cops of some sort, I'll say nothing and hang up.

Here goes.

The voice you're about to hear will be yours truly.

'Yes, Frank. This is Captain Duke Eastwood, LAPD ... Are you a mechanic there, or? ... Ah, I see. One of our officers gave us your number, indicated he might be heading out your way. The name's Fargo ... Uh-huh ... Oh, that's very good news! Excellent! We always hope these things will go that way. A kid that's actually been snatched just doesn't stand much of a chance, you know? ... Right, or they *do* get found. In a shallow grave. Terrible. God knows, I've seen enough of that. But we can count our blessings on this one, Frank. I'm just surprised Fargo hasn't passed the word to our end yet. What time did the boy turn up? ... Uh-uh ... Well, that's wonderful, wonderful. Now, do you know if he's on his way back with the boy? ... Really? What makes you think that? ... You can? From your window? Is it one of our black and whites? ... No, we don't use unmarked blue Fords. It must be his own personal car. Which motel is that? ... Uh-uh. I'll give him a call over there. Frank, I want to thank you for your cooperation. You've been very helpful. Have a good one, now.'

Do you believe it?

I don't believe it!

Oh man, oh man, oh man!

Okay, now what? I've gotta do some fast thinking. They're still at some motel called the Traveler's Roost across from the gas station – good old Frank can see Fargo's car in the lot.

It's eight-thirty now.

Thank God I woke up at dawn! And thank God I didn't ditz around any longer with the tales of our adventures!

Okay okay okay.

I've gotta make tracks for Indio.

And hope they sleep late.

Got an idea!

I *do* know Ranch's number by heart.

Come on, come on, answer. Be there!

'Yo! Ranch! ... Not too good, you wanta know the truth.

But a lot better than I was five minutes ago. Look, I know all about Lisa and everything . . . I know, I know . . . No, it's all right . . . Yeah, we're still pals. Now look, I know where the kids are. I'm going after them. You wanta come? . . . Ha! Thought so. Now listen up, the girl's old man is a cop, and he's with her. There's the three of them – the cop, Jody and Andy . . . Yeah, she sure is. *Better* than that, my man. Dusty was understating it. Wait'll you see her . . . That's the idea. Take her alive, play it by ear with the boy . . . I know, but who gives a shit what those two want? Now look, let's get Dusty in on this. I know he's got the hots for her, and a sharpshooter like him might come in real handy – case we wanta pop the old man or someone at long distance. So call him, okay? Just him, though. And tell him this is just between the three of us. We don't want everybody else trying to horn in on us . . . Tell him it's off if he pulls any stunts. I'm the only one knows where they are, and he wants her in a big way, so he'll go along with it . . . No. We'll take your car, so make sure it's gassed up and ready to roll. We've gotta be quick, or we'll miss them. I'll be over at your place in fifteen minutes.'

PART SEVEN

Checkout Time

Chapter Thirty-one

Jody woke up. The room was sunny. Rolling onto her side, she saw Andy on the other bed. He lay with his head turned away from her, his arms tucked under his pillow, his back bare down to where the sheet covered him. He'd gone to bed wearing Jody's robe, but he wasn't wearing it now. The sheet looked smooth over his rump and the backs of his legs.

Obviously, nothing underneath it except Andy.

Jody supposed she ought to feel embarrassed or angry. The room *was* too warm, though. She couldn't blame him for wanting to get comfortable. She might've slept in the raw, herself, if she'd been alone in the room.

Good thing I didn't, she thought.

As it was, her own sheet was down near her waist.

And she was still a little too hot. Andy probably felt just right, at least down to where the sheet covered him.

It sure was good to see him there.

No longer missing. Not kidnapped. Not dead. Safe and sound, and sleeping peacefully where Jody could see him.

With the white of sheets all around him, his tan looked dark. The color of a sandy beach in shadows. It seemed like the sort of tan that a kid should have halfway into a summer of swimming pools and lawn mowing and running around shirtless in the sun. But the tan should've been smooth and flawless. Instead, it was blotched with livid bruises, scuffed, scabbed and carved by small cuts that looked almost fresh.

As if he'd taken a bad spill off his bike, maybe tumbling

across the pavement for a while and then rolling down a hillside.

He *did* roll down a hillside, Jody reminded herself.

Just like me.

She realized that she felt fairly good.

Staying on her side, Jody wiggled slightly and flexed a few muscles. She found her body to be somewhat stiff and sore, but without any major pains.

So far, so good.

She pushed herself up on an elbow. *Not* go good. Especially her neck. After she sat up straight, though, her neck felt better.

She half expected to see Dad and Sharon at the table by the window. That's where they'd been when she and Andy had climbed into the beds at about three o'clock that morning. On the table stood a bottle with an inch of whiskey remaining. There were also some plastic glasses, empty cans of root beer and Diet Coke, and a couple of small packages of chips that they hadn't gotten around to eating.

The remains of their party.

She remembered how they'd all trooped down to the vending machines. A good stout wind had come up, so Sharon was struggling to keep her robe from blowing open. Dad had kept his eyes away from her, but Andy had watched her, even walking backwards part of the time.

The little creep, she thought, and glanced over at him.

He still seemed to be asleep.

She didn't think he'd caught any glimpses of what he shouldn't, but it hadn't been for lack of trying.

Oh, he wasn't even trying. Not really. He was just clowning around. Trying to impress me.

Is that what he was doing? she wondered.

Who knows? Maybe he's got a crush on Sharon.

Or maybe he sees her as a mother figure, or . . .

Not hardly. He was talking about Dad boinking her.

But where *is* she? And where's Dad?

Jody scooted slowly across her bed, holding the sheet to her waist and watching Andy. His face was still turned away. She couldn't hear him breathing because of the air conditioner (it's running, but is it working?), so she wasn't sure that he was actually asleep. He might roll over at any moment, wide awake.

But he remained motionless as she pushed away the sheet and swung her bare legs to the floor and stood up. The nightshirt unrumpled, but not enough. She grabbed its hem with both hands and stretched it lower. At mid-thigh, she let go. It unstretched a little, but stopped rising just in time.

Big deal, she thought. Who cares, anyway?

On the other side of the cluttered table, sunlight came into the room through a foot-wide opening between the curtains. Beyond the window, Jody could see the wrought iron railing of the balcony. Beyond that was a section of parking lot, some scrubby little trees, a road, and the Texaco station where Andy had made his escape from Uncle Willy.

She grinned, thinking about Andy up on the gas station's roof.

From up here, somebody might've been able to see him. But he'd kept low. And besides, it'd been dark, then. And the station was a pretty good distance away.

Jody leaned forward until the edge of the table pressed against her thighs. The table wobbled a bit, so she didn't dare put any more weight on it. From here, though, she could reach the curtains. She spread them farther apart. And spotted a man on the balcony, just to the right. He seemed to be standing directly in front of the door and close to the railing.

He wore his blue jeans and T-shirt.

Too hot for the chamois shirt, probably.

No shoulder holster. His Browing was tucked under the waistband at the back of his jeans.

Even with his face turned away, he looked like a thug.

That thick neck, those broad shoulders and bulging arms.

Sharon seemed to really like him, though.

They seemed to really like each other.

Jody couldn't see Sharon out on the balcony with him.

How long had Dad been out there?

And *why* was he out there, at all?

Maybe we aren't as safe as he's been pretending.

They can't find us here. How could they?

Ways. Who knows? There might be ways.

Jody let go of the curtains. As they swept down to where they'd been, she leaned away from the table and turned around.

Andy's hands were up, holding the pillow against the back of his head.

'Good morning,' Jody said.

He pressed the pillow down harder.

'Are you okay?'

She heard a soft, muffled, 'Leave me alone.'

She sat on the edge of his bed. The mattress sank slightly under her. She bounced on it a few times to shake Andy, figuring it might amuse him.

'Quit it,' he said from under the pillow.

Jody stopped. She noticed that her thigh was touching his hip and she could feel the heat of his body through the sheet. It felt good. Not exciting, like sometimes when she and Rob had touched. But good in a comfortable, close way.

'What's the matter?' she asked.

'Nothing.'

On the bumps of his spine just below the nape of his neck,

he had fine, golden fuzz. Jody traced it with the tip of her forefinger. She could just barely feel it. Andy squirmed a little.

'What're you doing?' he asked.

'Nothing.'

'Quit it.'

'Okay.' She bent down and blew. The wind of her breath bent the tiny hairs and sent a miniature wave crawling up the back of his neck.

One of his hands reached down, slapping at Jody but missing, then rubbing his neck.

Jody plucked the pillow off his head.

'Hey!'

She plopped it on her lap and clamped a hand on it.

'Give it,' Andy said, rolling onto his side.

'No way, Jose. And don't get any funny ideas about . . .' Her voice went dead when she saw his wet, red eyes.

He didn't try for the pillow. Instead, he turned onto his back and pulled up the sheet until it covered his face. 'Just leave me alone.'

'Can't.'

'Jodyyyy.'

'Hey, we're buds.'

'I knowwww.'

She reached out to him. The weight of her hand pressed the taut sheet down against him. Gently, she stroked his chest. 'You were fine last night,' she said. 'Weren't you?'

'Yeah.'

'What happened?'

'I don't know. It's when I think about them.'

Jody's hand glided up his chest. She pinched the sheet just under his chin and tugged it. Andy let go. The sheet slid down, uncovering his face, his neck and shoulders. He made a loud, wet sniffle. He blinked, and tears fell from the corners of his eyes.

'You'll get tears in your ears,' Jody told him.

'I don't care.'

She reached over his face and brushed the wet stream off his left temple. Then she bent down low and turned his head away slightly and stopped the other tear with her lips.

'Gosh, Jody,' he whispered.

She kissed the corner of his eye, then sat up.

Andy raised his head and looked past the end of the bed. 'Where's your Dad and Sharon?'

'Dad's standing guard on the balcony. I'm not sure about Sharon.'

Andy lowered his head onto the mattress. He sniffed. He lifted the sheet to his face and rubbed his eyes, then brought his arms out from under it and lowered them to his sides, pinning the sheet across his belly.

'Better now?' Jody asked.

'A little, I guess. Will you kiss me?'

'I just did.'

'I mean a real one. On the mouth.'

'Oh, sure thing.'

'Please?'

'You've got to be kidding.'

'Yeah.' He turned his head away. 'Sorry.'

'You're awfully young, you know, to be trying to get girls to kiss you.'

'I'm almost thirteen.'

'That's what I mean. You're too young for that stuff.'

'Mom used to kiss me.'

Jody's throat went thick and tight. Her eyes grew hot. Andy went blurry as he turned his face toward her. Bracing herself with a hand on the far side of his chest, she eased down and kissed his mouth.

After a moment, she started to rise. Andy moaned as if hurt, so she decided to kiss him a little longer. She hoped Dad wouldn't suddenly barge in. He'd be sure to get the wrong idea.

We're not making out. It's not like that.

She realized that her right breast was pushed against his bare chest. It had been that way from the start of the kiss, but she'd been feeling so sorry for Andy that she hadn't really given it much thought. She'd noticed some slight pain. She'd even known it was coming from the underside of her breast where she'd scraped it climbing the wall Friday night. But she just hadn't registered the idea that she was allowing her breast to press against Andy in such a way.

Terrific. I've never even let Rob get . . .

This is different, she told herself. It's perfectly innocent.

Perfectly. So why was she suddenly blushing so hard that she felt as if her face might burst into flame?

She started to push herself up. When their mouths parted, Andy said, 'No, don't.' He hooked an arm across her back.

Her breast hovered over him, almost high enough but not quite, her nipple poised against his chest, touching him lightly through her nightshirt. 'Let me up,' she whispered.

'Just a little longer?' he asked.

'Dad might come in. It'd blow everything if he thought we were messing around. You want to come and live with us, don't you?'

His eyes widened. 'Yeah. Do you think I can?'

'Not if Dad gets the idea you wanta . . . boink me, as you like to put it.'

This time, it was Andy who blushed.

'Which, by the way, is out of the question,' she told him. 'Now, let go.'

His hand dropped away from her back and Jody sat up. When she began to turn around, he raised his knees, making a small tent of the sheet that covered him from the waist down.

She glanced toward the window. Nobody's face was pressed against it, thank God.

Keeping Andy's pillow pressed to her lap, she got to her feet. She backed away from his bed.

As she stepped into her moccasins, she asked, 'Where's my robe?'

'What am *I* gonna wear?'

'What did you do with it?'

'Over here.' He rolled toward the other side of the bed, squirmed to the edge of the mattress and reached down, then flipped over, whipping Jody's robe through the air. At just the right moment, he released it. The robe sailed toward her, fluttering and falling.

She tossed the pillow at his face.

His smiling face.

And she caught her robe. 'Thanks,' she said.

'Thank *you*.'

She whirled away from him and swept the robe around her back and searched for the sleeves. Not until the robe was securely shut, its belt tied, did she face him again. She wiggled her fingers at him. 'See you later, alligator.'

He looked distressed. 'Where are you going?'

'Back to the other room where all my stuff is. You can go ahead and get dressed while I'm gone. Just wear what you had on yesterday.'

He wrinkled his nose. 'What if I smell?'

'What do you mean, if?'

'Ha ha, very funny.'

'Maybe we can buy you some stuff. I'll talk to Dad.'

'Okay.'

'Okay, see you.'

Andy suddenly looked forlorn.

'Hey, I'm not *going* anywhere, just down to the other room. I'll be back in ten minutes.'

'Okay. Hurry, okay?'

'I will.' She opened the door. Fierce heat and bright sunlight hit her like a blast. 'Jeez!' she gasped. Grimacing, she stepped onto the balcony. 'It's *horrible* out here.'

Dad, grinning, filled his lungs. 'Fresh, clean desert air.'

'You can have it.' She turned around and leaned back against the railing. Now, at least, she didn't have the sun in her eyes.

Dad was wearing his sunglasses. They made him look like a motorcycle cop.

'Have you been out here very long?' she asked.

'Long enough.'

'What does that mean?'

'It means I'm about ready to take a load off. This guard duty's for the birds.'

'Was it really necessary?'

'Nobody came along, so I guess not. So far. You never know, though. You just never know. It's when you least expect trouble that it sneaks up and grabs you by the . . . throat.'

'By the what?'

'You heard me. The throat.'

'Yeah.' She laughed. 'Where's Sharon, anyway? In our room?'

'That's where she *was*.'

'Where is she *now*?'

He raised his arm and pointed. Jody turned around.

321

'See that dirt road way out there past the Texaco?'

'Yeah.'

'Last I saw of Sharon, she was heading north. That was about half an hour ago.'

'What's she doing?'

'Running.'

'Running? You mean, for exercise?'

' "Gotta keep the bod fit." That's what she told me. I pointed out that it looked plenty fit to me, but that didn't stop her.'

'I don't want to *stand* in this heat, much less run in it. What is she, nuts?'

'Nuts ain't the word for her, honey.'

'Yeah? What *is* the word for her?'

'Mmmm. Phenomenal.'

'What do you mean?'

'Look it up.'

'I know what the word means. What do *you* mean?'

'She's an amazing specimen.'

'Specimen?'

'Of woman, of cop, of person.'

'Jeez, Dad.'

'You asked.'

'Wow.'

'Is Andy up yet?'

'Trying to change the subject?'

'Hope the little weasel kept his sheet on.'

'He did. He should be getting dressed right now. He's only got the stuff I gave him yesterday, though.'

'We'll pick him up a few things after breakfast.'

'Breakfast. Glad you brought it up. I'm starving.'

'How can you be starving, the way you stuffed your face last night?'

'That was only chips and junk.'

'Well, I hope you aren't starving *too* badly. God only knows when Sharon'll get back. And I'm sure she'll want to take a shower before we go anywhere.'

'Do you suppose she actually sweats?'

'I tell you what, sweetheart, I've been wondering about that myself. We'll just have to wait and see.'

'In the meantime, I might as well go get dressed.'

'Take your time. I have a feeling we won't be seeing Sharon for a while.'

Chapter Thirty-two

Jody hurried to the other room. After the outside heat, it felt cool and wonderful. The curtains were wide open, so she shut them.

In the dim, mellow light that came through, she saw Sharon's robe draped over the foot of Dad's bed. The bed that *had* been his, anyway, before he'd gone over to 238 last night. Sharon must've come back here to get some sleep while Dad stood guard. And brought her travel bag along with her. It was on the floor between the beds. So was her rifle case.

Jody glanced around, looking for any sign that her father had been in the room with Sharon.

Nothing.

What'd you expect, his jockeys on the floor? Real nice.

I just want Dad to be happy, she told herself. And Sharon's perfect. It'd be so great if they got together.

Yeah, but you're wondering if they did *it.*

No, I'm not. It's none of my business. Besides, they *didn't*. No way. Dad only met her last night.

Jody tossed her own robe onto the bed that had been hers before Andy's surprise arrival. Then she pulled off her nightshirt.

Wearing only her moccasins, she stepped away from the end of the bed so that she could see herself in the mirror above the sink counter.

'Horrible,' she muttered.

Her hair looked greasy in the dim light. Her bandages looked dirty. A couple were hanging partly off. In many places, her skin looked smudged with filth. She knew it wasn't filth, though. The dark areas were bruises and scrapes, and they wouldn't wash off.

Still, she wanted to take a shower.

Why not?

Andy'd taken a shower in 238 after downing a root beer and a ton of Doritos and Cheetos. He'd come out of the bathroom with a towel around his waist, holding its corners together at his hip because the towel was so small. That's when Jody had given her robe to him.

Before coming out, he'd removed all his bandages. Even the elastic Ace bandage for his knee. But he'd wanted that one on again, so Sharon had wrapped his knee with it while he sat on the end of the bed.

Losing the bandages hadn't seemed to do Andy any harm.

He'd looked sort of raw just after his shower. This morning, though, she'd seen everything above his waist and hadn't noticed any leaky wounds. She hadn't seen any blood on his sheets, either.

'We'll see how it goes,' she muttered.

In her travel bag, she found her shampoo.

324

Then she went into the bathroom and shut the door. She set her bottle of shampoo on the edge of the tub, spotted a small wrapped bar of Ivory in the soap dish, plucked a washcloth from its wire rack and made sure that one of the towels trapped in the same rack could be reached from the tub. After draping the washcloth over the faucet spout, she spread the bath mat on the floor.

She sat on the toilet. While she peed, she slipped her moccasins off and checked the bottom of each foot. The bandages had come unstuck last night, and she'd found them loose inside her socks when she'd gotten ready for bed. She hadn't bothered to put new ones on. Her feet looked as if they'd done just fine. None of the cuts or scratches seemed to be open. She prodded most of them with a fingertip. They felt tender, just slightly sore.

Which seemed to bode well for the rest of her injuries.

She slipped her feet back into the moccasins, returned to the tub, crouched and turned on the water. She adjusted the temperature, pulled the plastic curtain, and finally activated the shower. When water started splashing down, she left her moccasins on the bath mat and stepped in.

The hot spray felt wonderful.

Mostly.

On some of her injuries, it stung.

On the bullet wound just below her groin, it felt like acid.

She stiffened and grimaced, but after a few seconds the pain faded to where the 'scratch' beneath her soaked bandage felt no worse than a very bad sunburn.

She let out a long sigh.

That has to be the worst of it, anyway.

What's it like, she wondered, if you *really* get hurt?

Dad would know.

Dad would be an expert in that particular field.

Not to mention Mom.

Jody groaned.

I don't want to think about . . .

Or Evelyn, for that matter. Ask her how it feels to get a spear rammed smack through your middle.

'Oh, Jesus,' she muttered.

I've got to think about something nice, she told herself.

She picked up the soap and started to tear off its wrapper.

Think about something nice that doesn't have anything to do with all this.

Rob.

She pictured him in the driveway the first weekend after school ended. She'd been there by herself, washing Dad's car, and Rob had come along, surprising her. 'Could you use some help?' he'd asked. 'Sure. But you might get wet.' He'd smiled. A wonderful smile. Carefree, with maybe some mischief in it. 'A little water never hurt anyone.' After saying that, he'd taken off his shirt and joined in. Jody had never seen him without a shirt on. He looked so tanned and strong and smooth. She'd shot him with the hose. The water had turned his skin shiny.

Jody shaped the sodden soap wrapper into a ball and hooked it over the shower rod.

We're feeling better now, aren't we!

She turned her back to the spray and began sliding the bar of soap over her skin.

She smiled, remembering how Rob had flinched and yelped. The hose water *had* been awfully cold. She hadn't realized just how cold until he grabbed the hose away from her and she tried to run away and he caught her in the back.

She'd been wearing a big old loose shirt of Dad's over her white bikini. The icy spray from the hose had plastered the shirt to her back. Her squeal had started dogs barking all over the neighborhood. Then she'd made the mistake of turning around. She'd reached out with both hands, hoping to block the cold gush, but Rob had sent it in under her hands. As if by magic, it found the open space beneath the shirt's single fastened button and blasted the bare skin of her belly.

Right where the spear got me.

While her right hand glided the soap over her buttocks, her left hand moved toward the spear wound. The skin of her belly was slick and sudsy. She touched her navel, found the bandage down lower. The bandage felt like a small, wet rag.

She looked at it, then set down the bar of soap, rinsed her right hand and picked at the adhesive tape. The tape peeled easily off her skin. The underside of the gauze pad had a brown stain in the middle.

The wound itself was a dark slot that fit neatly inside a dime-size red area.

Not *very* red, she told herself.

And the little wound certainly wasn't bleeding.

She wadded the bandage and hooked it over the shower rod.

She liked having it gone.

They're no good wet, anyway.

So she searched out and removed every bandage until only one remained – the patch of gauze covering the bullet wound on her thigh. She decided to leave that one alone for the time being.

The tape from all those bandages had left tacky places on her skin. With soap on her washcloth, she carefully scrubbed the sticky areas. Then she soaped her whole body one more time, lathered up her hair with shampoo, and rinsed until her hair squeaked and she couldn't find any slippery patches on her skin.

Finally, she turned off the water. She skidded the shower

curtain to the end of the tub and stepped out. Dripping on the bath mat, she plucked a towel from the wire rack.

It was bigger than the washcloth, but not by much.

Threadbare, too.

Andy's must've been newer, she thought. The same size, but at least you couldn't see through it.

By the time she'd finished drying her head, the whole towel was moist. One more bath towel remained on the rack, but she needed to leave it for Sharon.

The towel wasn't really big enough to hold with both hands, so she draped it over one hand and wore it like a flimsy glove. Rubbing herself with it reminded Jody of drying Dad's car with his old chamois cloth. The day Rob had shown up.

It felt good to be thinking about that day again. A comfortable, safe place for her mind to be.

She remembered standing by a front tire, bending way over, stretching across the hood to reach as far as possible with the chamois cloth. Her thighs tight against the side of the car. The hood hot through her damp shirt. She'd thought that Rob was busy drying the trunk area, but suddenly his head had popped up just at the other side of the hood and he'd blurted, 'Boo!' Jody hadn't so much as flinched. 'Didn't I scare you even a little?' he'd asked. 'Afraid not.' He'd smiled and said, 'Drat,' then folded his arms on the car and rested his chin atop his right wrist. His face was about a yard away from Jody's, and slightly lower. Gazing across the hood at her, he'd asked in a very quiet voice, 'Do you mind if I watch?' Her mouth had suddenly gotten dry. 'I don't mind.' So then she had stayed stretched out on the hood, reaching and wiping with the chamois cloth while Rob had stared at her from the other side and she had stared at him.

She'd kept on rubbing the hood long after the hot metal was totally dry.

The car hasn't been washed since then, she realized.

I should ask Rob over when we get home.

When we get home. That's a good one.

We won't be staying away forever, she told herself. A week, maybe. Or two at the most. Dad's only got two weeks of vacation time, so we'll have to go back before that's up.

And when we get back, I'll ask Rob over. Tell him the car's dirty. Maybe wait and call him just before I go out to start washing it. This time, I'll wear the same bikini but I won't wear Dad's shirt.

Oh, yeah, right, sure thing.

She could hear it now. 'My God, Jody, what *happened* to you?'

Done toweling off her front, she leaned forward a bit and looked down at herself.

Her bikini would cover some of the damage, but not much. Not nearly enough.

I'll look fine in about a month, she decided.

If you live that long.

Oh, really nice.

You never know. They almost got you twice, so far. They aren't gonna give up until . . .

Jody winced when the towel lashed her back. She'd whipped it over her shoulder that way on purpose, but hadn't expected it to hurt quite so much.

Worked, though, she told herself. Took your mind off things.

With her other hand, she reached up behind her. She found the dangling corner of the towel. Holding each end, she struggled to dry her back.

The towel met a few tender places on its way down, but nothing that hurt *a lot*.

Finally, she decided that she was as dry as she was likely to get with this particular towel. She draped it over one shoulder, then scurried about the bathroom on a hunt for the soap wrapper and bandages that she'd tossed from the tub. After picking them all up, she took them to the wastebasket in the corner by the toilet.

She opened her hand to let them fall.

And glimpsed a torn, foil wrapper at the bottom of the basket.

A moment later, the jumble of adhesive tape and wet gauze and paper covered the foil square, concealed it.

Jody's heart was slamming. Her stomach felt tight, her legs weak. There seemed to be a tingling numbness in the middle of her head.

They *did* it, she thought. They really, actually did it.

It shouldn't make me feel this way, she told herself. I oughta be happy. Dad needs someone. Sharon's perfect for him.

No wonder he called her 'phenomenal,' he'd been in bed with her.

He'd boinked her.

Screwed her.

Jody's stomach hurt awfully bad. She lowered the toilet lid, sat on it and hunched over, hugging her belly.

This is crazy, she told herself. It's what I was hoping for, isn't it?

They don't even know each other.

They never met till last night after the guy shot me.

How long ago was that?

Jody didn't know what time it was now. Maybe ten in the morning? And they'd met at about eight last night, maybe. And then Dad had gone off again.

God, Dad, how could you? Always preaching to me about how I've gotta wait for the right guy, the guy I really love, and even then not to fool around till after I'm at least eighteen (but preferably twenty-eight) and I've been going with him for at least a year and make him get a blood test first and . . .

And Dad does it with a virtual stranger!

What if Sharon's got AIDS?

Dad's too smart to do a thing like that.

Jody had always thought so, anyway.

She could hardly believe he even *owned* a condom, after the way she'd heard him talk about the things.

'Don't think a condom will save you,' he'd warned her. They had both just seen Magic Johnson on the television talking about methods of practicing safe sex. 'Don't believe a word of it, honey. If the guy you're with is infected, a condom's about as safe as playing Russian Roulette. You've got one chance in six that the thing'll bust or fall off inside you. If that happens, getting pregnant will be the least of your worries. One in six, honey.'

How could he lecture me like that, and then go and do it himself!

Just couldn't help it, maybe, the way Sharon was parading around in nothing but that robe, and flirting with him all the time.

Probably her condom, too. She probably goes nowhere without a few dozen of the things, just in case she can find a horny guy to drag into bed with her.

The bitch.

Dad might be as good as dead right now, and all because of Sharon.

Jody blinked sweat out of her eyes. She pulled the towel off her shoulder and mopped her face.

Suddenly, she realized that she was drenched. Sweat was streaming down her body, tickling along the way. The toilet lid was slick under her rump.

Groaning, she got to her feet, slipped into her moccasins and hurried to the door. She pulled it open. The motion of the door swept cool air against her. It chilled her sweat. It felt wonderful.

'Oh,' she heard. At once, she pressed the towel to her groin and crossed an arm over her breasts. 'I'm sorry,' Sharon said. Jody spotted her then. 'Should've warned you I was here.'

Sharon was on the far bed. She hadn't bothered to move her robe out of the way. One of her feet was on it. Her shoes and socks were on the floor by the door. She still had on a pair of shorts and a T-shirt. She was lying on her back, arms resting at her sides, her knees up.

Jody said nothing. She felt strange, as if she were swelling up, as if her head might explode.

'Are you done in there?' Sharon asked. 'If you're not . . . I'm not in any big rush. I hear you're starving, though.'

'I'm done,' Jody muttered. She could hardly hear her own voice through the roar in her head.

Sharon sat up. She swung her bare legs to the floor, then peeled off her T-shirt. She wore a large, sturdy bra that looked very white against her skin. 'Hotter than blazes out there,' she said as she got to her feet. She wadded her T-shirt and wiped her face with it. 'Had to get the exercise, though. Especially after our little party last night.' She made a slightly nervous smile. 'I'll finish undressing in the John,' she said, and hooked her robe off the end of the bed. She held it over to the side, apparently to keep it at a distance from her sweaty body, and walked toward Jody.

Jody still stood motionless just in front of the bathroom door.

Sharon stopped in front of her.

'What's the matter, honey?'

'Don't you *honey* me.'

She frowned. 'What is it? What's wrong?'

'I know what you did.'

A corner of Sharon's mouth curled up. It reminded Jody of her father's smirk. It didn't show any amusement, though. It made Sharon look confused and wary. 'What in particular, Jody?' she asked. 'I do a lot of things.'

'I just bet you do.'

Suddenly, Sharon's mouth went straight. Her eyes narrowed. 'Quit playing games and tell me what's bothering you.'

'You know damn well.'

Sharon threw down the robe. She grabbed Jody by the shoulders. But didn't squeeze hard. Didn't shake her. 'Okay, Jody. Tell me. Right now.'

'You fucked him.'

Sharon's fingers tightened their grip. Then she seemed to realize what she was doing, and let go. Her arms fell to her sides. The look in her eyes made Jody want to turn away. It was as if she could see all the way to the back of Jody's head. 'I see. I fucked him. There are only two hims around here, so which one was it?'

'You know darn well.'

'Tell me.'

'Dad.'

'Wrong.'

'*Andy?* You . . .! He's only *twelve years old*! My God, what kind of depraved sex pervert *are* you!'

Sharon shook her head. She didn't look particularly upset, but she sure looked solemn. 'Well, I'm glad to know we don't have a *real* problem.'

'You don't call . . .!'

'I haven't *fucked* anyone – as you so delicately put it. Not recently. Not even *close* to recently. Certainly not your father or Andy. My God, Jody. I might not be as pure as the driven snow, but I don't go around jumping in the sack with guys I

333

just met – and I sure don't go around seducing *children*. What on earth makes you think I'd do something like that?'

'What I . . . I found *evidence* in the wastebasket.'

'Do you always go around looking in wastebaskets?'

'No! I was throwing out my bandages and . . . and I saw it.'

'What did you see?'

'The wrapper. The condom wrapper.'

Sharon narrowed her eyes. Her lips were a straight, tight line. She shook her head. 'I see.'

She stepped around Jody and entered the bathroom.

'Come in here, please.'

Jody followed her, watched her squat in front of the wastebasket and reach down. After searching for a couple of seconds, Sharon stood up and turned around. She held out the torn foil wrapper toward Jody. 'What does that say?'

Jody gazed at it, stunned. 'Oh, my God,' she muttered.

'Wrong. It says Alka-Seltzer. The booze and all those chips and things last night didn't agree with me.'

'So . . . you didn't . . .'

'No, I didn't. My God, Jody. Everything else aside, do you actually think your father would leave you and Andy unprotected so that he could sneak into my bed for a quickie?'

'Well . . .'

'He would *never* do a thing like that. Do you want to know what we did? After you two kids zonked out, he came over here with me and gave me a kiss at the door.'

'You don't have to . . .'

'We kissed, and it was very nice, but I didn't ask him in and he didn't invite himself in. He went back to the other room and planted himself on the balcony in front of the door and that's where he stayed. He wouldn't even let me relieve him. Said I needed my beauty sleep.'

'Your beauty sleep?'

'Yeah, my beauty sleep. I thought it was a really sweet thing to say.'

'I know.'

'Your dad's a sweet guy.'

'Yeah. I know. Oh, jeez, Sharon, I'm sorry. I'm so sorry.'

Sharon crouched and picked up her robe. 'Just don't jump to conclusions about me, okay?'

'I'm such an idiot.'

'You're fine, Jody. Now, move it or lose it, I've got a shower to take.' As Jody stepped out of the way, Sharon gave her upper arm a gentle squeeze. 'And don't worry, I won't say anything to your dad.'

'Thanks.'

In the bathroom doorway, Sharon turned around. She raised her eyebrows. 'We're friends?'

'You bet.'

'Good deal.'

Chapter Thirty-three

Her father was gone from the balcony, but Jody saw him as she walked past the window of room 238. He was at the table, in the chair Sharon had occupied last night, almost out of sight beyond the edge of the curtain.

She knocked on the door. Andy opened it for her. He'd gotten dressed. His hair was even combed, and still looked wet.

'Been waiting long?' she asked him.

'Yeah. What took you so long?' He shut the door after Jody was in.

'Things,' she said, and gave him a mysterious smile. She pulled the other chair away from the table and sat down. Andy dropped onto the end of the bed where she'd slept. Near the foot of the other bed was Dad's Mossberg shotgun. 'Where'd that come from?'

'It's been around,' Dad said.

'I thought you left it in the car.'

'It wouldn't do us much good there.'

She wondered for a moment what she'd done with her Smith & Wesson, then remembered sliding it under the front seat of the car just as they'd pulled into the Texaco station last night. It must still be there. The magazine and box of ammo, too. Unless Dad or Sharon had gone under there and taken them out.

Ask?

If she asked, she would get a firearms lecture.

So she decided to let it go. The gun was probably right where she'd left it.

It better be. If somebody broke in the car and stole it last night . . .

Not likely. The car was just down below in the parking lot, in plain view from the balcony where Dad had stood watch.

I shouldn't have left it there, anyway, she told herself. Major stupid move.

I'm being major stupid a lot lately.

Maybe it has to do with having people trying to murder you all the time.

'So, what're we doing now?' she asked.

'Now that you're here,' Dad said, 'we're waiting for Sharon.'

'Well, she's done with her shower. I heard the water go off just before I left and came over here.'

'Is your stuff all packed and ready to go?' Dad asked.

'Pretty much. Are we gonna leave, or have breakfast, or what?'

'Checkout time isn't till noon. That gives us almost an hour and a half. I think we might as well leave everything in the rooms and go have breakfast. We can load up the car after we get back, then make some final pit stops and be on our way.'

'On our way where?' Jody asked.

Dad smiled at Andy. 'That's just what we were discussing when you came along.'

'We're *not* going to Phoenix,' Andy told her.

'Thank God for that.'

'I suppose I'll have to phone Spaulding sooner or later,' Dad said.

'Don't hurry,' Andy suggested.

'He's been notified that you turned up – that'll do for the time being. I'll want to check with a few people and find out where we stand before I have it out with him. In the meantime, just consider yourself part of the family.'

Andy grinned. 'Can I choose which part?'

'Family pet,' Jody said.

'Ha ha. Is Sharon like part of the family, too?' he asked.

Dad shrugged. 'Guess so.'

Narrowing his eyes, Andy rubbed his chin like an old sage stroking his goatee. 'Let's say Sharon's my wife. You two can be our kids.'

'Get outa here,' Jody said.

Dad just shook his head. On his crooked mouth was a true smirk.

'How about it?' Andy asked.

At least he's not miserable and crying, Jody told herself.

'You'd have to ask Sharon,' Dad said.

'Maybe she's got a soft spot in her heart,' Jody said, 'for obnoxious pip-squeaks.'

'Then she must *love* you.'

'In your ear.'

'Children, children, let's try to get along.'

Just then, Sharon appeared on the balcony. She glanced through the window and raised a hand in greeting as she walked by.

'There's the little woman now,' Andy said, and hopped up to open the door. Swinging it wide, he bowed slightly. 'My dear, we've been expecting you.'

Sharon wrinkled her nose and looked from Jody to Jack. 'What's with *him*?'

'He's bonkers for you,' Jody explained.

Andy winced and went scarlet. 'I *am not*. I'm just kidding around. *Cripes!*'

Grinning at him, Sharon said, 'Nothing to be ashamed of, pal. Guys are always going bonkers for me.'

Jody turned so she could see her father. His face looked almost as red as Andy's.

'You do look very nice this morning,' Dad said. It sounded like a perfunctory compliment, but Jody had no doubt that he meant it. Meant it in a big way.

Sharon bobbed her head a bit and said, 'Thanks.'

She looked fresh and cool and ready for adventure. Her short-sleeved white blouse had epaulettes and pocket flaps and its top few buttons undone. The blouse seemed a bit large for her. It wasn't tucked in, and hung straight down from the front of her breasts so that it hid the top few inches of her shorts. The shorts were tan, loose around her legs, and very short. Their cuffs surrounded her thighs just below the hanging tails of her blouse.

Her legs were tawny and sleek. And they had muscles.

She wore white socks that came up just above her ankles. Her low-top British Knights looked brand new and brilliant white.

From her shoulder hung a brown leather purse.

Jody wondered if Sharon's pistol was in the purse. It might be there. Since her blouse wasn't tucked in, though, she might be carrying it in the waist of her shorts. Either in back or in front.

The way her blouse hung out in front, she could have *hand grenades* strapped to her belly and you'd never see a bulge.

Jody glanced from Dad to Andy. They were both watching Sharon – who wasn't even *doing* anything. Just standing there, hip out so she was mostly on one leg, her right hand hanging on to the shoulder strap of her purse, her left . . . maybe the guys were staring because of how the strap of the purse was pressing against Sharon's right breast.

Men. Jeez.

'So,' Sharon said. 'What's up? Do we check out now, or find a place to eat, or . . .?'

'I think we'll go and eat,' Dad told her. 'Checkout isn't till noon, so we've got all kinds of time.'

'Sounds good to me.'

'There's a Denny's just down the road.'

Jody expected him, next, to say, 'Let's walk. It's not all that far. The exercise'll do us good.' Before he could get the chance, she said, 'We'll drive, won't we? My feet are still sort of racked up, and Andy's got a bad knee. Anyway, I just took a shower. I don't want to get all sweaty and yucked up.'

'What the hey,' Dad said. 'We can drive.'

While he wrapped the shotgun inside their old blanket, Sharon opened the door and checked outside.

* * *

In the hot back seat of the car, Jody ducked down and slid her hand underneath Sharon's seat. The carpet felt gritty.

'What're you doing?' Andy asked.

She touched her pistol. 'Nothing.' She left it there and sat up straight.

Dad eased out of the parking space. 'Since we're not walking, we aren't limited to the Denny's. What-say we scout around and see if we can't find a local place?'

'Here we go,' Jody said.

'You can eat at a Denny's any time,' he explained as he backed out of the parking space.

'I know, I know.'

'Maybe we can find a McDonalds,' Andy said.

'Oh, you're dreaming,' Jody said. 'You and Sharon have gotta say goodbye to all the nice, reliable chain-food places you've come to know and love. You're traveling with Kong Fargo, now.'

Dad laughed.

'His life is a quest for culinary adventures.'

'We're on the road,' he said. 'Why settle for the same food we can get a few blocks from home?'

'I'm with you,' Sharon told him. 'It's not just the food, either. You get some local color.'

'And some local germs,' Andy said.

Jody laughed and nudged him with her elbow.

'Comedians,' Dad muttered.

As he steered past the Denny's, Jody said, 'Farewell to all that is familiar and safe.'

During the next few minutes, she came to see that Sharon was even better suited for Dad than she'd suspected. Sharon not only ignored the national chain restaurants, but even wanted to avoid local places that appeared reasonably normal. 'Aah, that joint looks boring,' she would say. Or,

'Too mundane.' Or, 'What kind of ambience is *that*?'

'You eat there,' Dad would add, 'and you won't even remember it by tomorrow.'

'We're gonna starve,' Andy said.

'Nope,' Jody assured him. 'Any minute now, they'll spot some dark, greasy dive that sports enough atmosphere to seem picturesque.'

Jody was the one who spotted it, though.

'Thar she blows.'

It was called Kactus Kate's.

'Good eye, good eye,' Dad said – a compliment he usually reserved for Jody when she chose not to swing her baseball bat at a bad pitch.

'That's a great sign up there,' Sharon said.

The sign suspended above the cafe's door was a six-foot Saguaro cactus that resembled a skinny green man with raised arms. Nobody had gone so far as to paint a face on the cactus, but it did sport a red sombrero tilted at a jaunty angle. The sign looked as if it had been cut out of plywood. It looked long overdue for a fresh coat of paint.

Dad swung to the curb in front of Kactus Kate's.

'We're really going to *eat* here?' Andy asked.

Jody nodded. 'Bet you're wishing you'd stayed on the roof of the gas station.'

'If it's really bad,' Dad said, 'we'll look for someplace else.'

'Don't get your hopes up, Andy. They're almost never that bad.'

Dad plucked the key out of the ignition.

'Maybe we shouldn't,' Sharon said, frowning at him. 'If the kids really don't want to try a place like this . . .'

'Jody just likes to hear herself complain. She gets a kick out of trying these places. Right, honey?'

Sharon looked around at her.

Jody shrugged. 'They keep life interesting, sort of. But then, so does a sharp stick in the eye.'

'What about you?' Sharon asked Andy.

'I don't know. We always used to eat at McDonalds or Burger King, or . . .'

'Are you willing to give this a try?'

'I guess so. Sure, why not?'

'Hey,' Jody said to him, 'what's the worst that can happen?'

'*That's* what I like to hear,' Sharon said. 'Let's go get 'em.'

Kactus Kate's had the decor of an Old West museum: walls hung with wagon wheels, rusty lanterns, branding irons, paintings of lonesome deserts and cliff dwellings, and framed, yellowing photos of the likes of Jesse James, Sitting Bull, Geronimo, Custer, Buffalo Bill, the Wild Bunch, Wyatt Earp, and Dad's all-time favorite gun fighter, James Butler Hickok.

Dad's eyes lit up when he walked in.

Sharon got excited when she found that she could order a breakfast burrito with egg and chorizo inside it.

Andy, studying the menu, muttered, 'All right!' when he discovered French toast made with cinnamon raisin bread.

For Jody, the best thing about Kactus Kate's was the waitress, a blonde in her twenties, over six feet tall, who chomped on chewing gum as she swaggered over to the table.

According to the plastic pin above her left breast, her name was Bess.

Now *Bess* is picturesque, Jody thought.

She wore snakeskin boots that reached up almost to her knees, skin tight blue jeans, a belt with an enormous brass buckle that showed a bucking horse, and a purple T-shirt decorated with a white fringe in a deep V down her chest. Both sleeves of her T-shirt were turned up, baring her upper arms. Her left arm looked smooth and unmarked. On her right, though, was the tattoo of a broken heart and the message, BORN TO BUST HEARTS AND BRONCOS. From the lobes of her ears dangled small, silver tomahawks.

After she'd brought over the coffee and hot chocolate, Sharon waited until she was out of ear shot, then said, 'I love that outfit.'

'You'd look great in it,' Dad told her. 'You might want to skip the tattoos, though.'

'Too late for that.'

Andy leaned toward her. 'What've you got?'

Sharon grinned. 'The chances of *you* finding out are slim to none.'

'Where *are* they?' Andy persisted.

'It, not they. And never mind. Drink your cocoa.'

Andy and Jody started to work on their drinks, biting and sucking their way through soft white piles of whipping cream before finding the hot chocolate underneath.

When Bess came back to take their orders, she squeezed Andy's shoulder and said, 'What's it gonna be for you, Sparkie?'

He blushed.

Maybe because the waitress had a hand on him. Maybe because she'd called him Sparkie.

Why'd she call him that? Jody wondered. Just to be colorful?

Andy stammered a bit as he ordered the French toast on the cinnamon raisin bread, and a side of sausage links.

That sounded good to Jody, so she asked for the same.

Sharon ordered the chorizo and egg burrito. Bess smiled at Dad and said, 'What'll it be for you, Sugar?'

'I'll try one of those burritos, too. Probably live to regret it, but . . .' He shrugged.

'You're gonna *swoon* for it. Swoon and drool. We got the best chorizo in five counties. It's all-fired ass-kickin' hot, though, so you don't wanta be sippin' coffee with it. Need a drink that'll cool down the fire, like a Pepsi.'

They all decided to have Pepsis with their breakfast. As Bess headed for the kitchen, Jody said, 'How's she for local color?'

'What a babe,' Andy said.

Sharon raised an eyebrow. 'Ass-kicking?'

'She might be a little far out in left field,' Dad said, 'but it sure is nice to be in a place where the waitress talks American.'

'Ooo, Dad. Naughty. You're such a bigot.'

'That's me.' He took a sip of coffee, then set down the mug. 'I wanta check out the pictures and things. Anybody else?'

'I wouldn't mind a closer look,' Sharon said.

The two of them left the table. Dad headed straight for the picture of Wild Bill, Sharon at his side.

'Is your father a Republican?' Andy asked.

'Nope, a fascist storm trooper.'

'You mean like a Nazi?'

She laughed. 'Yeah, only worse.'

'Those Nazis made lampshades out of skin. Real *human* skin. Did you know that? I saw this really gross book that this kid had at school. It showed all these *pictures*. They were so incredibly gross you wouldn't believe it.'

'You sound like you *loved* them.'

He shrugged. 'Well, they were pretty horrible in a way. But they were neat. Some of them showed all these women lined up to get gassed. The Nazis tricked them into thinking they were going in to take a shower, only the shower room was really this gigantic gas chamber. Anyway, none of them had on a stitch of clothes. I mean, you could see *everything*.'

'You *would* like that.'

He shrugged. 'A lot of them were sort of fat and ugly, but . . .'

'Jeez, Andy.'

'Yeah, okay. But anyway, this other picture showed a lampshade. It just looked like any normal lampshade, pretty much. It had somebody's tattoo on it, though. A bird. Some sort of bird, like an eagle or something. It looked like it was flying under the moon or the sun, but that was actually the guy's nipple.'

'That's nauseating.'

'Yeah, but it's kind of cool.'

'No it's not.' Jody stared at him. His parents and sister had just been butchered. How could he be *talking* about things like lampshades of human skin and naked women in line to be murdered, much less describing them with such *relish*?

And had he forgotten about the dead guy on the floor of his bedroom who'd been wearing *pants* made out of skin?

Pants. That's even worse than a lampshade. They hadn't been in some book, either. They'd been on a real guy in Andy's own bedroom.

And he's all excited about a picture of a lampshade?

That's crazy.

Maybe this is like denial, Jody thought. Or compensating, or something. One of those psychological things people do when they've gotten their heads screwed up.

'I'd sure like to see that tattoo,' Andy whispered.

'Knock it off about the lampshade, okay?'

'Not that,' he said. 'Sharon's. I bet it's on one of her boobs.'

Jody elbowed him fairly hard.

'Hey!'

'Don't talk about people's boobs.'

She saw Andy's eyes lower to *hers*.

'Cut it out!'

345

'Okay, okay! Calm down.'

'Anyway, that might not even be where her tattoo is. It might be on her butt, for instance.'

Andy frowned. 'That'd be an awful place for one.'

'I wouldn't want one *any*where.'

He leaned close and whispered, 'Maybe it's on her poon.'

'On her *what*?'

'You know, her *poon*.'

'No, I *don't* know.'

'Down there.' He pointed toward Jody's lap.

She whacked the back of his hand.

'Ow! That hurt!'

'Good. You oughta have your mouth washed out with soap.'

'You don't have to hit.'

'You'd just better not go around pointing like that again. Jeez! Somebody might've seen you.'

'Nobody's looking.'

'How would you like it if I pointed down at *your* you-know-what?'

Andy grinned. 'My peter?'

'SHHHH! We're in a *public place*. Now, stop it!'

'Okay.' He leaned close to Jody and whispered, 'Peter peter peter peter.'

'Idiot.'

'Poon poon poon poon.'

'What're you doing, turning into a five-year-old?'

He chanted, 'Poon and Peter sitting in a tree, f-u-c-k-i-n-g. First came . . .'

Jody clapped a hand across his mouth and held it there. 'Shut up! You're not funny.'

He nodded as if he wanted to assure her that he was very funny indeed.

'We'll see how funny Sharon thinks you are,' Jody said. Smiling, she lowered her hand.

Andy had quit smiling. His eyes searched the cafe until he spotted Sharon. She was standing beside Jack. They were both looking up at a painting of a moonlit desert.

'I think she'll be very interested,' Jody said, 'in your theories about the location of her tattoo.'

'Go ahead and tell.'

'I plan to.'

'I dare you.'

Jody grinned. The way her face felt, she was sure it must be a wonderfully *mean* grin. 'Sharon probably already *knows* what a poon is, don't you suppose? I mean, she's a cop. She's probably heard just about everything. But I bet you it isn't one of her favorite words. We women aren't usually very amused by dirty words about that particular place.'

Andy suddenly grimaced. 'You won't really tell, will you?'

'It'd serve you right.'

He was beginning to look desperate. 'Come on, Jody. You won't, will you?'

'Give me one good reason.'

'I don't knowwww. Because we're friends?'

When he said that, Jody's throat went tight. She hadn't expected that. She'd been angry, but she'd just started to enjoy taunting him. It came as a surprise to find herself suddenly on the verge of tears. 'Yeah,' she said. 'We're . . .' She couldn't say more, so instead she reached down and patted his leg.

'You're my best friend in the whole world,' he whispered.

She swallowed. 'Shut up, okay?'

'I promise, I'll never say peter or poon again.'

'Or fuck,' Jody muttered. And couldn't believe that she'd said it.

'I didn't say fuck,' Andy protested.

'You spelled it. Same difference.'

'Okay, I'll never . . .'

'Uh-oh, here comes breakfast. Cut out the dirty stuff.'

Bess walked toward them, carrying a huge tray loaded with plates and glasses of Pepsi.

'That's a neat tattoo on your arm there,' Andy said as she set the tray on a fold-up stand.

'Well thanks, Sparkie.'

'Do you have any others?'

'You bet.'

'Can I see 'em?'

Jody groaned.

Bess let out a bark of laughter. She grinned at Jody. 'Your brother here's sure a little pistol, ain't he?'

'Yeah.' Her face was burning. 'A pistol, all right. And he keeps going off by accident.'

Dad and Sharon came back to the table, but stood aside and waited until Bess finished setting out the breakfast. Then they slid into their booth.

'Anything interesting happen while we were gone?' Dad asked.

Andy gave Jody a nervous glance.

'Not much,' she said. 'How was the stuff?'

'Not bad.'

'You two should take a look around before we leave,' Sharon told them. 'Some of it's really neat.'

'I bet you'd really like the Apache squaw,' Dad said to Andy. 'Her photo's down at the far end near the restrooms.'

'Why would Andy like it so much?' Jody asked. 'Is she naked or something?'

'She's minus her nose.'

'She looks *awful*,' Sharon said.

'Lopping off a gal's schnoz was an old Apache punishment for adultery.'

'Those Apaches must've been loads of fun,' Sharon said.

As Dad laughed, Jody asked him, 'Why do you suppose Andy would think *that's* so great? Have you turned into a psychic?'

Dad shrugged. 'It's one of those guy things.'

'Remind me never to marry one,' Sharon said, and shoved a forkful of burrito into her mouth.

'The Nazis used to make lampshades out of skin,' Andy said, leaning toward her. '*Human* skin.'

'I'm so glad you shared that with us, Andrew.'

'He's so gross,' Jody said.

'Guys generally are,' Sharon told her. 'But they do have other characteristics that compensate for it. *Some* do, anyway. I'm not so sure about Andy.'

Andy blushed and laughed as if he'd been paid a major compliment.

Jody nudged him. 'That was an *insult*, you dork.'

'Language,' Dad told her.

'Language? *Me?* You should hear what . . .'

'Superb French toast,' Andy interrupted. 'I think it's the cinnamon bread.'

He and Jody stared at each other for a few moments.

I almost told on him, she realized.

She was glad that he'd stopped her in time.

She picked up her knife and fork, and began to cut into her French toast. 'So, what are we doing after breakfast?'

'I guess we'll go back to the motel and check out,' Dad said.

'Should we try to find a store first? Andy needs some new clothes.'

Dad glanced at his wristwatch. 'We'll have to see how late it is when we get done here.'

PART EIGHT

Simon Says

Chapter Thirty-four

Here we go. When I left off, last time, I'd just hung up the phone after a chat with Ranch. A lot has happened since then. A lot of blood has been spilled. Now, I've finally got some free time to talk about it all, so here goes.

Quick as I could manage after hanging up, I drove over to Ranch's. We took his Cadillac to Dusty's place and from there we headed for Indio.

We made good time, too.

But not good enough.

When we got there, I told Ranch to pull into the Texaco. He needed the gas, anyway, so he stopped at the self-service pumps and I got out to fill the tank for him.

Pumping the gas gave me a good chance to scope out the parking lot of the Traveler's Roost motel across the street. The bozo on the phone, Frank, had said he could see Fargo's car and it was a blue Ford.

Over at the parking lot, most of the spaces were empty. Only a couple of vans, a Jeep and three regular cars were still there. Not one of them was blue.

Hardly any wonder, when you figure it was almost eleven o'clock by then. Eleven's checkout time for most motels. So just about everyone had already hit the road – the Fargo clan included.

We'd missed them.

It made my stomach feel like hell.

But I had gas to finish pumping, so I stood there and kept at it.

I was still Simone, by the way. I wore my brown wig, since the platinum blonde from last night seemed too flamboyant for daytime and I didn't want to draw a lot of attention to myself. In the brown hair, I looked feminine but subdued.

My face had been horrid this morning (remember what that son-of-a-bitch Henry the dog did to me last night?), so we stopped in Desert Hot Springs and I sent Ranch into a drugstore for Band-aids and makeup. While we drove on, I fixed myself up. Just one large bandage was enough to cover the bites on my cheekbone (lucky for me that fucking Henry wasn't a Doberman), and I used makeup to hide the bruising.

I'd already gotten out of my bloody sundress before leaving Jody's house. I put on one of her T-shirts. Most of them looked like souvenirs from vacations or trips to Disneyland, but I managed to find a pink one that didn't have any pictures or slogans on it. Then I found a white pleated skirt.

I looked great in the outfit. Fresh and innocent and a lot younger than twenty-four, which is my real age.

Ranch sure noticed how great I looked.

It took me about fifteen minutes to drive to his place after leaving Jody's. When I got there and he opened his door, he said, 'Oooo, honey.' Then he grabbed me and hauled me up against him and squeezed one of my tits through the T-shirt. Ranch weighed about three hundred and fifty pounds. A lot of it was fat, but he also worked out with weights so he had plenty of muscle. It's a good thing I *didn't* have a tit inside that bra, or he would've mashed it. 'Well, shit,' he said when he noticed he was only squeezing tissue paper. 'What happened to my dream girl?'

'She's waiting for us in Indio,' I told him. 'And we're gonna miss her if we don't get our asses in gear, so put me down and let's go.'

He kidded around during the trip, pretending to flirt with me and reaching under my skirt. Actually, I'm not sure he was completely kidding. I think he sort of hoped or wished I'd somehow turn into the girl I looked like. You know how sometimes if you watch a movie that you've already seen, and maybe you don't like the way it ended last time, you keep sort of hoping and wishing the end will turn out different? If you really get into it, you can almost convince yourself that it *will* change. It was probably like that with Ranch. He had himself half convinced that I'd change into a female.

I think, honestly, that I was getting him a little horny.

Must be weird to be a gal and have that sort of power over guys.

Every once in a while, I had to tell him to knock it off. I even had to remove his hand from me a couple of times.

Dusty was in the back seat. He spent most of his time staring out the windows, and didn't notice the funny stuff. Or if he did, he ignored it. He was the sort of guy who never fooled around. He took every damn thing in the world seriously. In fact, he was basically a complete paranoid.

One of those survivalist nuts. He figured the world – or at least 'civilization as we know it' – would come to an end pretty soon. Like next week, you know? And he planned to be ready for it.

He even had a hideout/bomb shelter somewhere. He used to talk about it, but never told any of us where it was. He planned to go there and live through the big thermonuclear holocaust.

He was really hoping for that holocaust.

According to him, it was *on its way*. He could hardly wait.

You've never seen a guy as disappointed in your life as when the Soviet Union went down the tubes a couple of years ago.

What a pisser for poor Dusty!

It pretty much ruined his chances of ever seeing a mushroom cloud, and he was crushed.

But then we had that Rodney King riot in LA last year, so Dusty got his hopes back. He'd probably never get to enjoy a massive exchange of nuclear warheads, but a race war might be almost as good. So he pinned his hopes on that.

He started looking forward to an uprising by the blacks with the same sort of enthusiasm he used to have about nuclear war.

I think he dreamed of fighting off assaults from his secret hideout – dressing up in his Kevlar vest and helmet and camouflage suit, arming himself to the teeth and mowing down hordes of rampaging crazies.

The only times I ever saw him laugh or smile were when he was nailing someone.

A nut case, that's what Dusty was. But very good with his rifle, which was in the back seat with him.

Anyway, where was I?

The Texaco. Right. Pumping gas. In my nice brown wig and Jody clothes and all that. There were other people filling their tanks, and I got looks from a couple of guys, but nobody bothered me. Maybe because I had Ranch and Dusty in the car.

I was feeling sort of sick because we'd shown up too late.

Maybe if I hadn't bothered to change my clothes, or if Ranch hadn't wasted time hugging me on his front porch, or if we hadn't stopped at the drugstore to buy that stuff, or . . . Hell, maybe they left so early that none of that mattered.

What's done is done, right?

What counts is how you handle what's given to you.

Here's the thing: I'd told Ranch and Dusty that I knew where we could lay our hands on Jody. And of course I'd said she was in Indio. But I hadn't said a thing about any motel or what kind of car they were driving.

I left those things out just because I was playing the cards close to my vest, you know? I hadn't been planning to trick the guys.

But suddenly I *had* to trick them.

I couldn't just admit we'd shown up too late and blown our chance at Jody. Ranch might be okay about a thing like that, but there was no telling about Dusty. A very temperamental guy. He might flip his lid and kill me.

The nozzle clicked off, so I hung it up and capped the tank and went to the office to pay.

In LA, you have to pay for your gas before you pump it. That's because LA is full of assholes who'll drive off without paying if you give them half a chance. You know you've reached a civilized place when they let you pump first and give them the money after you're done.

I paid and went back to the car and got into the passenger seat. 'Let's go,' I said.

Then I gave Ranch directions just as if I actually had some kind of destination.

Every now and then, he'd ask where we were going. I'd say, 'You'll see.' Like it was a big secret.

A secret, all right. Even I wasn't in on it.

Dusty kept his mouth shut and watched out the windows.

We drove through a business area with a lot of shops and restaurants and so on. I looked at the people in the cars that went by, and I looked at the people on the sidewalks.

No Jody, of course. Big surprise.

There were a lot of blue cars. I glanced at who was inside, but didn't expect to spot Jody in any of them.

The truth is, I wasn't looking for her.

What I wanted was a reasonable facsimile. Someone Jody's

age and size, with golden hair and a good short haircut. Someone who could *pass* for her.

Ranch had never even caught a glimpse of Jody. He'd missed his only chance, which was when she ran past the master bedroom on Friday night. Right then, Ranch had been monkeying around with his back to the door.

Tricking him would be a cinch.

Dusty would be the problem. He'd gotten a good look at Jody through his rifle scope – such a good look that he'd seen what a knockout she is and told Tom we should try to take her alive so we could really have a chance to enjoy her.

Maybe Dusty could be fooled, though. Maybe he'd only gotten an *impression* that Jody's beautiful, and hadn't really seen her features in detail.

Fat chance.

Unless I could find an awfully good duplicate, Dusty would probably catch on.

There *were* some girls around, riding in the back seats of passing cars, walking down sidewalks with their families or friends, going into stores, even some pedaling along on their bikes. Something was always wrong, though. If they looked about the right age, then they were too fat or had the wrong color hair or wore glasses or were as ugly as dirt.

'Are you *sure* you know where we're going?' Ranch asked after a while.

'We're almost there,' I told him.

Hope springs eternal.

'Make a left here,' I said.

Ranch did it.

A couple of blocks later, I said, 'Take the next right.'

We were driving through a residential neighborhood with old stucco houses on both sides of the road. It was sunny and almost nobody seemed to be outside. Too hot, probably. We were fine in Ranch's car, though, with the air conditioning at full blast.

'Okay, a left at the next corner,' I said.

Ranch made the turn. Up ahead, the neighborhood thinned out. There were a couple of mobile homes. The only houses were far apart and crummy. From the look of things, we were at the edge of town and about to meet the desert.

'What're you trying to pull?' Dusty asked.

'Nothing.'

'So where the fuck is she? You don't know, do you? You're giving us some sort of fuckin' run-around here.'

'See the house with the pickup in front?'

It was about a hundred yards ahead and off to the right. It had a rusty mailbox at the edge of the road. The pickup looked brand new – forty years ago. All its glass was smashed out and it didn't have any wheels. The house didn't look much better than the pickup truck, but at least its windows weren't broken.

'You tellin' me she's in there?' Dusty asked. He didn't sound at all inclined to believe it.

'I'm not telling you shit,' I said. 'You'll see for yourself.' I said to Ranch, 'Stop by the mailbox.'

He gave me a funny look, like I'd lost my mind. 'You sure about this?'

'Sure as I *can* be. I got the address from an old friend. An old friend who just happens to be the LAPD lieutenant in charge of witness protection.'

Ranch looked surprised, maybe even impressed.

Dusty said, 'Gimme a break. A lieutenant with the . . .?'

'This is one of their safe houses. Wait here. I'll go in first. They've been told to expect a woman from Child Welfare Services, and I'm it.'

With that, I jumped out of the car and went for the house.

Sweat just popped out of me. It wasn't only because of the heat, either. I could feel Ranch and Dusty watching me. My ticker was pounding like a hammer.

I didn't know who was gonna be in the house.

Knew who *wouldn't* be, though. Jody.

The place looked like it might be vacant. No vehicle except for the useless old pickup. No signs at all that anyone was occupying the property – or taking care of it. The yard was nothing but dust and cracked earth and rocks and a few scrubby bushes. The outside walls were cracked, and big patches of paint had peeled off. The windows were so dirty that I couldn't see through them.

I stopped at the front door. It was shut and no sounds came from inside.

I knocked a couple of times, then stepped back and took a look around.

To the right, pretty far away, was an old mobile home up on blocks. It looked lived in, but there wasn't any car so I figured its people had driven off somewhere. This being Sunday morning, maybe they'd gone to church.

To the left was desert.

The houses across the road looked almost as run down as this one.

No matter where I looked, I couldn't see anyone watching me. That's if you don't count Ranch and Dusty in the car.

This was as good a place as any.

So I faced the door again, but just when I was about to knock some more, it swung open.

Which I wasn't expecting at all.

My stomach did a flip-flop.

I was in luck, though. The door'd been opened by a guy, and I knew how fine I looked.

Better still, he was a teenager.

Fifteen or sixteen, a little goofy looking with his flat-top haircut and the way his upper teeth stuck out. He wore a faded pair of blue jeans, and no shirt. He had a good tan, but he was husky and looked soft.

He sure wasn't what I'd expected to find in a place like this.

I'd expected it to be empty. Barring that, the likely inhabitant would've been a withered old hag or a filthy bearded hermit in bib overalls.

This kid was a pretty pleasant surprise.

And no doubt about it, I was a *great* surprise for him.

He stared out at me and blinked.

I said, 'Good morning. I'm Simone?'

'Hi.'

'I'm afraid my friends and I have gotten ourselves lost.'

'Yuh?' He leaned sideways and gazed past me.

'My husband and brother-in-law,' I told him. 'Men can be such dopes.'

He laughed once. It was more like a snort.

'Can you tell me how we might get back to the interstate?'

He squinted into space. 'Where?'

'The big inter . . . never mind. Maybe if I could have a word with your mother or father?'

'Ma's off at work. Ya know the Safeway market . . .?'

'Is your father home?'

'Naw, he's dead.'

'I'm sorry.'

'Aw, he was a shit. Just ask anyone.'

I smiled. 'Would it be all right if I come in for just a moment and use your bathroom?'

He blushed and his mouth dropped open.

'It's awfully embarrassing to ask, but this is a real emergency. We've been lost for a *long* time, and those two just got out a while ago and peed on some cactus. You fellas are so lucky that way.'

I gave his crotch a good, long look.

He cleared his throat. He rubbed his lips with the back of his hand. 'I reckon it's okay if ya wanta use the . . .' He shrugged, then stepped backward. 'C'mon in.'

I did.

In the immortal words of Bette Davis, *What a dump!*

Not only that, but it was hotter than blazes and it stank.

I shut the door. That took care of most of the light. Only a dim yellow glow came in through the filthy windows and curtains.

I set my purse on the floor and said, 'Did your mother leave you all alone?'

'Yuh.'

'Sure is hot in here,' I said.

'Yuh.'

Then I peeled off my T-shirt so I was standing there in my bra and skirt. With the light so lousy, I figured he wouldn't be able to tell that I was a fake.

'That's a lot better,' I said.

He said, 'Uhhh.'

'What's your name?' I asked.

'Henry,' he said.

Same as that fucking dog.

He just stood there when I walked up to him. He was a couple of inches taller than me. I put my hands on his chest and rubbed him. He was slippery. And he was starting to breathe *really* hard. I wonder why.

He gasped out, 'Didn't ya . . . wanta use . . .?'

'You're so handsome, Henry.'

I ran my hands up and down him. I even gave him a squeeze through the front of his jeans. He had a huge boner. Almost funny. I make a hell of a woman.

I pressed myself against him and hoped he couldn't tell there was only paper in my bra.

He seemed just as thrilled as ever.

More so, in fact.

He put his arms around me. He was huffing and rubbing himself against me.

I kissed the side of his neck, then said, 'I knew a dog named Henry.'

He didn't say anything, but sort of raked up the back of my skirt and pushed his hands under the seat of my panties.

'You don't bite, do you Henry?'

He went, 'Uhhh, naw.'

'*I* do,' I said.

I did.

Chomp, right in the neck.

The moment I got my mouthful, I twisted him sideways as fast as I could to turn the gusher away from me. I also shoved him. He stumbled and crashed against a wall and sank to his knees, grunting and whining.

I chewed while I watched him.

Maybe he should've been an art critic – he had excellent taste.

I didn't wait for him to die, but went off to find the kitchen.

Big nasty butcher knives look great when psychos go after people with them in the movies, and I'll admit that they do have their uses. I've had some fun with them, myself. But I wanted a nice, small knife that would be easy to conceal.

I found a very sharp paring knife.

The kitchen was at the back of the house. Its windows didn't have curtains, so there was some decent light. My chest and bra were splashed with blood, but there were only a few tiny spots on my white skirt.

I washed my hands. The sink was piled with filthy dishes.

Henry and his mother were apparently enormous slobs.

When my hands were clean, I took off my skirt. I draped it over the back of a kitchen chair. Some newspapers were piled on the table. I grabbed a page, tore it, and folded a small piece into a sheath for the paring knife. Hurrying out of the kitchen, I slipped the blade into the paper shield and pushed it up under the cross-strap at the back of my bra.

In the front room, Henry was still slumped against the wall.

I helped myself to his blood – he had no more use for it, but I did. I spread some on my chest and belly and legs, though I tried not to overdo it on my bra and panties. I intended to keep on wearing them, so the less they got bloody, the better.

After finishing with the blood, I pulled off his belt.

Henry'd been using the sofa for a bed. It had a bedroom pillow at one end. I shook the case empty.

With the belt and pillow case, I went to the front door.

Talk about nervous. I felt like crapping.

But I was excited, too.

I put the pillow case over my head, then looped the belt around my neck and pulled it tight enough to cinch in the bottom of the case. I let the end of the belt hang down my back.

I wasn't Simone anymore.

Now, I was Jody Fargo stripped down to her undies, bloody, captured alive by Simon, a pillow case covering her head so she can't see where she's going, a belt around her neck so she can't run away – but she *is* running away, or trying to.

I opened the door. Sunlight lit up the inside of the pillow case. I sort of half-lurched, half-stumbled out through the doorway, flailing with my arms, then flung myself backwards into the house again as if I'd been yanked by Simon at the other end of the belt.

What a farce, huh?

The idea was that I'd let them have a quick glimpse so they'd figure Jody was here and I was having fun with her. They were sure to want in on it – wouldn't be able to stand the thought that they were missing some action.

The idea sure worked.

By the time Dusty came charging in, I had the pillow case off my head and the knife in my hand. He got about two strides through the doorway, then tried to stop, then tried to back up fast and get away from me.

He'd been too eager. And way too careless.

You'd think such a paranoid would've exercised a little more caution than that. But maybe he figured his bullet-proof vest would protect him like magic. Or maybe he was so hot for the gal that he forgot to worry about running into trouble.

I punched the wadded pillow case into his face so hard it knocked his head back. I went in under his chin with my knife. Just drove its blade straight in through his windpipe and gave it a good hard twist before yanking it out. Then I real quick slashed the side of his neck and shoved him out of my way.

He was down on his hands and knees, busy dying, by the time my old friend Ranch showed up. I was off at the side of the doorway with my back to the wall. The first thing that came in was Ranch's Smith & Wesson .357 magnum revolver.

I hadn't counted on that.

He got off one shot, but it didn't come anywhere near me. He didn't even know where I was until it was too late. The gun went off because he jerked the trigger when I swung in from the side and stuck my knife into his right eye.

After that, he dropped the gun and slapped his hand to his face and fell to his knees.

I kicked him in the side of the head. He tumbled over, so then I crouched behind him and reached around and cut his throat.

Chapter Thirty-five

What a morning, huh?

But, boy, what a mess! You should've seen me. I saw myself in the bathroom mirror. I looked like I'd come out the loser in a food fight at Cannibal High.

So I climbed into the bathtub for a shower. Didn't even take off my wig, bra, panties, or shoes – they needed it as much as me. The only problem with that is what happened to the stuffing in my bra. All those tissues got turned into sodden muck. I had to take off the bra and scoop it out. Then the stuff clogged the drain, so the water started to rise.

Well, no big deal. I used plenty of soap on myself and my hair and undies, then rinsed off with hot water, then stood under cold water to cool myself down for a few minutes before climbing out.

There weren't any clean towels, wouldn't you know it?

Henry's mom must be a *real* loser.

I went into the only bedroom, which was hers, and dried myself with a clean sweatshirt I found in a drawer.

The sweatshirt was mammoth.

The mom's obviously a porker.

Her sweatshirt worked okay as a towel, but I knew that none of her clothes would even come close to fitting me.

Not that I wanted to wear her stuff, anyhow.

I went to get Jody's nice pink T-shirt, but it turned out to have blood all over it. I'd left it in the front room after stripping it off for Henry's benefit. Big mistake. That's where Henry, Dusty and Ranch bled on everything.

Jody's white pleated skirt had survived fine, being in a different room from where I'd done the killings. I took it off the kitchen chair and put it on. I still needed a top, though. Couldn't go around outside in just a bra and skirt.

Henry's clothes were in cardboard boxes in a corner of the front room. The boxes had gotten splashed pretty bad, but things at the bottom were okay. I found some sort of shirt that looked Hawaiian – a shiny thing with bright pictures of pink flamingos, blue water and green palm trees all over it. It was pretty big on me, but didn't look too bad. The way it hung down, its front covered the specks of blood on my skirt.

I checked myself in the bathroom mirror. My wig looked damp but otherwise okay. The bandage and makeup had come off my face, so my dog bite showed. I figured I'd take care of that later on in the car. My chest was flat. I decided to go for socks, this time, instead of tissue.

Basically, I looked pretty good.

I looked like a babe who'd maybe just come back from a day at the beach and was on her way to a luau.

I went to the mother's bedroom, found some socks in a drawer, and stuffed my bra with them. Then I picked up the sweatshirt that I'd dried myself with after the shower.

I used the sweatshirt to pick up Ranch's .357 and wipe the blood off it. Then I wiped the blood off my purse, opened it, and stowed the revolver inside. Dusty always kept a two-shot .45 Derringer in an ankle holster. I found it and stuck it into my purse. I put the little paring knife in there, too. You never know when you might want to make a slit.

My hands got messy taking out Ranch's and Dusty's billfolds and generally searching their pockets. Ranch didn't have keys, so he'd probably left them in his car. I wiped my hands on the sweatshirt, then put the billfolds into my purse.

The longer it took for cops to identify these guys, the better.

Burning the place down was a bad idea. I like to make fires. They're great for destroying evidence. Without one, though, the bodies might not be discovered for hours. That's what I wanted, so I couldn't torch the place.

In the kitchen, I washed my hands. Then I stripped down to my undies once more. Too bad I hadn't thought of this earlier and taken care of it before my shower. I left the shirt and skirt on the kitchen chair, out of harm's way, then found a big heavy butcher knife (of the sort preferred by psychos). On the stove was a skillet where somebody had fried up bacon within the past day or so. The bottom had a layer of old grease that had hardened and turned gray.

I took the skillet and knife into the front room.

The wooden floor made a good cutting board. I stretched out one of Ranch's hands and chopped off the end of his thumb. Then I gave it a toss into the pan. It made a soft thump. With the sweatshirt, I mopped most of the grease out of the pan.

That was to improve the sound quality.

So the rest of the thumbs and fingertips gave off nifty, ringing *poinks* each time they hit.

There's a fine line between taking time 'to smell the roses' and *wasting* time. I only needed to remove the finger and thumb tips from Ranch and Dusty. It would've been excessive to hack off Henry's, even though I was enjoying my work.

I took off his thumbs, just for the hell of it, then made myself quit.

Cops can do stuff with palm prints, so I peeled the skin off the fronts of their hands. Not Henry, this time.

As insurance against visual identification, I took most of the skin off Ranch's face, then Dusty's.

All the skin went into the pan.

In the kitchen, I put the skillet back on a front burner where I'd found it. Then I turned the burner on, went to the sink and washed again. There was nothing clean to use as a towel and I was tired of running around the house, so I shook my arms a few times then went ahead and got dressed.

By then, sizzles and crackles and pops were coming from the skillet. The patches of loose skin had turned dark and shriveled down to about half their original size. I used a fork to poke them over to one side. The ends of all those fingers and thumbs looked like stubby little sausages. They were browning up nicely except for the nails, which had curled oddly. Some of the nails had fallen off.

Have you ever noticed how sausages wiggle and shake once they get going good? Sometimes, they even roll over on their own accord.

These pieces of the dead fellas did that.

It'll be great to tell Jody about this. She might appreciate it to the extent that Dusty's trigger finger was in there, and so were the fingers Ranch used on Jody's little girlfriend, Andy's sister whatever-her-name-was, shish-ka-sister.

Jody wouldn't know about *that*, but I can make sure to tell her.

After a while, I forked out one of the fingertips. I chose one that had lost its nail (I mean, who wants to eat a finger nail?), then blew on it a few times and gave it a try. The pits. It probably could've been spruced up with salt and pepper, and might've been halfway decent marinated in teriyaki sauce.

But it was mostly bone, anyway. I'm afraid I can't recommend eating fingers.

Anyway, I kept the burner going until everything in the skillet was black and crispy. After that, I poured the excess grease over the dirty dishes in the sink, and hunted around for a bag. Henry's mom had a whole closet full of brown paper sacks from Safeway. I shook one open and dumped the tidbits into it.

Then it was time to go.

I took my purse and the grocery sack, and went out the front door.

It made me a little nervous, walking to the car in broad daylight after leaving three bodies in the house.

Nobody came along, though. No nosy neighbors' no cops, no nobody.

At the last minute, I had this awful fear that Ranch might've locked his keys inside the car. He'd done it a couple of times before, that I knew about. He'd also run out of gas on trips. I used to ask him if he'd been out to lunch the day they passed out the brains. He wasn't stupid, though. Just absent-minded.

Now he's *really* absent-minded.

Absent everything, more or less.

It turned out that he'd left the keys in the ignition. The car doors weren't locked, though.

I climbed in behind the wheel and set my purse on the passenger seat. I started to put the bag beside it, but saw dark brown spots where grease had leaked through the paper the way it does with fries or onion rings you might get at a fast food joint. I didn't want to ruin Ranch's seat upholstery, so I set the bag down on the floor.

Then I took off.

It was great to be back inside the car, tooling along the roads, the air conditioner blowing a chilly breeze against me.

About a couple of blocks from the house, I spotted a ratty old gray dog by the side of the road. I had an urge to swerve and hit him. That's what I like to do. But I was in a generous mood, so I stopped near him and put down the passenger window and tossed the bag out.

Pulling away, I looked in the rearview. The dog had already split the bag wide open. Its head was down. It was snapping up all that fresh, cooked meat.

This was his lucky day.

After getting rid of that evidence, I concentrated for a while on looking for a Jody substitute. Then realized I didn't need one.

Which is to say, not until tonight.

Killing Ranch and Dusty has changed a few things.

The good news is that there shouldn't be anybody at Tom's tonight who knows for sure what Jody looks like. Mitch and Chuck will be there. They got closer to her than anyone except me, but it was dark outside and mostly they never got a chance to see more than her back. With Dusty dead, I shouldn't have any trouble tricking the gang with a fake.

The bad news is that I'm fucked. With a lot of luck, maybe I'll be able to pull off the trade and get me and Lisa out of there alive. But they'll catch on to things, sooner or later. They'll find out I handed over a fake Jody and they'll figure out I killed Ranch and Dusty. Then it'll be hell to pay.

They'll hunt me down and kill me, sure as shit.

Unless I get them first.

Oh, man.

I can see it now, bust in there with a gun in each hand, blasting away like mad.

Suicide.

Forget it.

Hmmm. If I've got the element of surprise on my side . . .

after all, look how easy it was to handle Henry, Dusty and Ranch.

Who's gonna be there?

Tom, of course. They'll probably be in his garage, which is where we've been taking most of the dead bodies for the past few years. We've taken some live ones there, too. That's where they'll have Lisa.

If I know Tom and the guys, they've got her dangling by her wrists from a rafter. We've done it before. Ones we take alive, we sometimes keep them hanging for a couple of weeks and we pay them visits whenever we get the urge to fool around.

Funny to think about them having Lisa like that.

She's probably been hanging there since sometime yesterday, so the guys have had plenty of time with her. She was pretty upset when I talked to her on the phone last night. She sounded like she'd been roughed up and maybe felt up, but nothing real serious.

By now, I bet they've tortured and gang-banged her.

Which really pisses me off.

It's sort of like if they stole my car for a joy ride and crashed it on purpose into a wall, you know?

These guys who were supposed to be my friends.

Friends don't do that sort of shit.

I'll admit it gets me turned on, thinking about Lisa hanging there all naked and sweaty in Tom's garage. The guys going at her. A couple of them holding her legs up high and wide apart by the ankles while two other guys have at her, one going in the front door and one in the back. I can just see her twitching and shuddering. I can even *hear* how it'd sound. The rafter creaking up above them all. The guys grunting and gasping. Lisa whimpering, crying out. And a lot of wet, sucking noises.

They shouldn't be doing it to her.

To someone else, but not to Lisa. Not without my permission, anyway.

They're doing it to punish *me*, the bastards.

And they're loving it. I'm sure they've just been hoping and praying I'd screw up sometime and give them an excuse to grab her. Lisa hasn't got the greatest personality that ever walked the earth, but she has a great body.

It won't be so great after *they've* finished with it.

Even if I can save her, she'll probably have scars. That's if they didn't get carried away and amputate something.

She won't be any good to me if they've messed her up. But then, no big deal because they'll kill me first chance they get, anyway.

I'd damn well better *try* to kill them first.

It might not be as impossible as it sounds.

There'll be Tom. And Mitch and Chuck. That's three. Minnow makes four. No, wait. Minnow's dead. Jody busted his head in with her baseball bat, at least according to Tom.

Of course, I've only got his word for it.

Why would he lie? Maybe so I won't be expecting Minnow, and . . . I should've asked Ranch about him. Oh, well. Minnow *must* be dead, now that I think about it. He went off down the hall to look for more prey, but he didn't come back.

So that's three: Tom, Mitch and Chuck. Plus Clement Calhoun, and . . . and who else?

My God! There used to be twelve of us! Twelve! Of course, that was before Tex, Dale, Private and Bill got their tickets canceled.

Eight of us went into that house on Friday night. Minnow, Ranch and Dusty are down the tubes since then, and I'm not exactly one of the gang anymore. So there *are* only four of them.

If I go in with a gun in each hand . . .

No. One against four is extremely shitty odds.

I know!

What I do is go in with Jody – or a gal who'll pass for her. So it'll look like I'm keeping my part of the bargain. Also, I can hold her in front of me, use her as a shield.

Damn it! Why didn't I take Dusty's vest off him? That'd be the thing, go in there with a Kevlar vest under my shirt.

Shit!

It'd take me an *hour* to go all the way back to that house. I should've done some heavy thinking about the whole deal *before* I started shooting my mouth off into this tape recorder. Shit, the thing is like a . . . an addiction. The fucking *world* could be coming to an end, and I'd start the tape rolling so I could get in my two cents.

Shit!

I wasn't even to the freeway before I dug the thing out of my purse and . . .

Shit!

Okay, okay. Calm down.

What's done is done, right? Water under the fucking bridge. No way I can go back and get Dusty's vest. I'd have the *time* to do it, but for all I know the bodies might've already been found. Forget it.

Who needs a bullet-proof vest, anyway? Look at all the good it did Dusty.

Besides, it's not like the guys are gonna be waiting in there tonight to ambush me with guns. Mitch'll have his fucking saber, Chuck his ax, Clement his hammer and straight razor, Tom his Bowie knife. They'll have firearms handy, all right. We've got a real arsenal in the garage. But that stuff is for emergencies, so they aren't likely to have me covered if I walk in dragging along a sweet young thing so it looks like I'm playing along.

The problem is, I've got to find one.

Shouldn't be too hard. She won't have to be a dead ringer, or anything, now that Dusty's out of the picture.

Anyway, enough about all that. Time's running out, and there's no telling how busy I might get before the deadline tonight, so I'd better go ahead with the history of our little gang while I've got the chance.

Where the hell did I leave off?

I don't know. Did I tell about the time we went after Denise Dennison? That was our first house raid, and ... yeah, I already went into all that.

What about *after* Denise?

Geez, get a load of her!

Where was I?

Things were awfully hot around LA, so we drove all the . . .

Never mind.

I can't think.

It's this car I just passed. The girl in back looks just like Jody. I mean, maybe she's not the spitting image, but she's close – *very* close. About the same age. Cute face, very short blonde hair.

I'd been creeping up on the car for a pretty long time. A white Nissan Sentra. It was going just a little slower than me. I didn't want to get stuck behind it, though, so finally I swung over to the left and put some speed on. The idea was to race by, then get back into the slow lane.

Coming up alongside it, that's when I spotted the girl in the back seat.

Just when I'm trying to resume the history of our gang, I'm suddenly looking at exactly the gal I need.

Fuck the history.

I've slowed down now so that I'm going the same speed as the Sentra. It's about fifty feet behind me.

In the front seats are a man and a woman. They're probably her parents. The way things are these days, though, who knows? Nothing's the way it looks. Everything's twisted and odd.

It doesn't really matter who or what they are, though.

If they aren't her parents, big deal.

Just so they aren't a couple of undercover Green Berets or Ninjas or some such shit.

I don't think there's anyone else in back with the girl.

Just the three of them.

The girl's too good to lose. I've got to have her. It's just a question of how to do it.

They're close enough, if I stand on the brakes, they'll probably rear-end me. Maybe that's the way to go. They'd *have* to stop, or the driver could get into big trouble for hit and run.

It's risky, though. My Caddy is a lot bigger than their little heap, so I'm not likely to get hurt. But you never know *what* might go wrong. For one thing, you don't know how hard we might hit. Wouldn't it be great if I got them to pile into me, and both cars got put out of commission?

It's not likely, but it could happen.

Or what if the other guy loses control, maybe spins out, flips his car or gets broadsided by a truck or something? Naturally, I wouldn't pick a time when there's a lot of traffic around. Even still, they might crash and burn.

Forget staging a crash.

I want her alive.

Here's an idea. I could drop back and tail them. Sooner or later, they'll take an off-ramp. I can wait till they reach their destination, then figure out a safe way to snatch her.

Lousy idea.

They might not stop for hours. And when they do, it might be at someplace crowded.

This stretch of freeway is just about perfect. The traffic isn't real heavy, and there are long stretches with nothing on either side except desert.

Here's another idea.

I'll put some distance between us, then pull over and stop. Make it look like something's wrong.

I'm a gal, remember? And not a bad looking one, at that.

Let's see if the guy will stop for a damsel in distress.

Chapter Thirty-six

Oh yeah! Oh yeah! What a RUSH!

I was brilliant! Brilliant!

Whew! I'm out of breath. Hard work.

Wait'll you hear . . .

How do things look back there?

Fine . . . fine. Made a . . . clean getaway . . . looks like . . . Yeah. I go around this bend and . . . Yeah, can't see their car now . . . Home free.

Whew!

Gonna shut this off a minute and catch my breath.

All right, I'm back. Gotta tell you what I did. It worked great. I did like I said and sped up for a while to get out farther in front of them. While I was busy putting some space between us, I took the .45 out of my purse and shoved it down the front of my skirt. Not the best place to put it. For one thing, I couldn't get the barrel down far enough. The muzzle pushed right against my dick and I had this awful picture of the damn gun firing. But I worked on the problem and managed to get the barrel down into the crack between my thigh and nuts. Guys were never meant to carry guns in front like that.

The Derringer would've fit perfectly, by the way. But it only had a two-shot capacity, and I wanted more firepower than that.

By the time I got the Colt the way I wanted it, I was far enough ahead of the Sentra. Plenty of room to stop and climb out while it was still coming.

When you see somebody pull over in front of you, you *always* watch them. So I knew their eyes were on me. My plan was to hurry and put up the hood so it would look like I had engine trouble.

But one of those huge eighteen-wheelers rushed by when I climbed out. It must've just passed the Sentra, because I hadn't seen it before. The truck blew a gust of wind against me. I clapped a hand down on my wig to keep it from flying off. The blast of hot air whipped against me so hard that it jerked open a couple of buttons at the bottom of my shirt and flapped the shirt away from my belly. Which was no big deal except for the fact that it showed off the .45 that was stuck down my waist.

I hunched over and hugged my belly to hide the gun.

Just after I did that, the Sentra passed me.

Its brake lights were on. But only for a second. When they went off, I realized the guy wasn't planning to stop. He'd only slowed down as a safety precaution, and now he was ready to speed off.

Doing the quick hug to hold my shirt down is what gave me the idea.

I suddenly jerked and hunched down as if I'd been struck in the belly by a terrible pain. I staggered forward a couple of steps, then dropped to my knees beside the front tire.

Chivalry ain't dead.

The joker must've kept his eyes on me in his rearview mirror.

My knees no sooner hit the dirt than his brake lights came on again. He pulled off the highway and started backing toward me with his tires flinging up clouds of dust.

I saw the face of my sweet piece in the rear window. She looked very worried about me.

Glad to report that today's fall was a lot better executed than the one last night. This time, I didn't bash my knee. And fortunately there was no dog handy to bite my face. A few other cars and trucks were roaring closer. I didn't want any of them stopping, so I got to my feet and hobbled, still bent over and hugging my belly, but in a way that didn't look so drastic.

I had one hand *inside* my shirt, of course.

A few yards in front of me, the Sentra stopped. I staggered between the two cars and eased myself down till my rump came to rest on the edge of my hood. I tried to smile at my sweetie in the rear window. But I was supposed to be hurting, so my smile twisted into a major grimace of pain.

Oooo, I'm good.

Not only good, but lucky. Instead of just one adult getting out of the car to help me, they both did. A couple of very good Samaritans. Either that, or the guy came after me because I gave him the hots and the gal came along to keep an eye on him.

They looked like a real dynamic duo, both of them in their thirties, slim and trim and tanned, decked out in sunglasses, polo shirts, white shorts, white crew socks, and topsiders.

Maybe they were on their way through the desert to a distant marina for a day of yachting.

The man stopped a little short of me and asked, 'Are you all right?'

'Of course she isn't all right,' the gal said.

Obviously his wife. Nobody but a wife – or maybe a really overconfident fiancée – talks to a guy that way, as if he's a dope.

She put her hand gently on my upper arm. 'Is it your stomach?'

I bared my teeth and nodded.

And listened. Some major traffic was bearing down on us from the rear.

'Must've hit you awfully hard,' the man said. Actually, he was almost shouting. Because of the traffic noise, you could hardly hear yourself think. 'Was it something you ate?' he asked.

A semi roared by, and I could hear another on the way.

'I . . . I think I'm having a miscarriage,' I yelled.

'Oh, dear God!' the woman cried out. She squeezed my arm. 'How far along *are* you?'

'Six weeks.'

The next semi passed, throwing hot gusts of air against us. I suddenly doubled over.

'Jerry! We've got to take her to a hospital!'

'How are we gonna find a *hospital*?'

'We'll find one, don't worry.'

They both grabbed me. Holding me up, they hustled me over to the back door of their Sentra. Jerry opened it. He asked, 'Do you need anything from your car?'

I shook my head, then let out a whine.

'Have you got your car keys?'

'Yes!' I squealed.

The girl in the backseat scooted over to make room for me. I sort of tumbled in, and Jerry shut the door.

I was damn near ecstatic.

Never even *hoped* they'd invite me into their car.

Figured I'd have to kill them right out in the open by the side of the highway.

Jerry and his wife got into the front seats. Jerry was straight in front of me. He pulled down his shoulder strap and buckled it.

'What're we doing?' the girl asked.

'This woman needs a hospital,' her mother said. She was reaching up for her shoulder harness.

'So we're taking her to . . .?' The girl gasped when she saw the Colt come out of my shirt.

Very fast, I put two rounds through the back of Jerry's seat. As he pitched against his safety belts, the mother started to twist around to see what was happening. I dropped sideways, my shoulder on the girl's lap, jammed my muzzle against the back of Mom's seat and put two slugs into it.

The girl went ape, screaming and pounding on me. I pushed myself off her. Once I was sitting up, I bounced her head off her door window. The window cracked, but didn't break. She slumped, out cold.

All the windows were shut because of the air-conditioner, and it was so smoky in there you'd think we each had our own cigars. If you ask me, gunsmoke smells a lot better than cigar smoke. Love it. But I was afraid people driving by might worry if they saw all that smoke, so I put my window down to let it out.

Then I stuck the Colt down the back of my skirt. It went there fine.

Leaning forward, I checked out Jerry and his wife. The shoulder and lap belts had kept them both from going anywhere, but both of them had keeled sideways a little. They were still alive. They made some noises, but didn't fight me when I straightened them up.

I wanted them to look okay. That's how come I'd shot them in the backs when it would've been a lot more fun to pop them in their heads.

On the dashboard was a folded map. I had to climb halfway into the front seat before I could reach it. After grabbing it, I stayed up there and took a minute to check out the damage. Jerry and his wife looked fine, mostly, just as long as you didn't look any lower than about halfway down their chests. Lower than that is where the bullets came out, and what a mess.

Anyway, I unfolded the big map of California and propped it up against the steering wheel in front of Jerry. This way, all the folks speeding by would think these two had gotten themselves lost and pulled over to figure out where they were.

They were lost, all right.

Where they were going, though, a map wouldn't be doing them much of any good.

I watched them for a couple of minutes. Neither of them moved. They seemed to be unconscious, and they'd probably be dead pretty soon.

The girl was still slumped against her door. Her eyes were shut and her mouth hung open. She looked real good.

Not that she had a face anywhere close to Jody's. It wasn't ugly, though – just ordinary and a little cute. She looked about Jody's size, but maybe ten pounds heavier. Her tits and butt were bigger. She wore a short-sleeved red blouse and denim culottes.

Culottes. Doesn't anybody wear skirts anymore?

Gals must really be afraid that guys are gonna stick their hands up ... Am I repeating myself? Seems like maybe I already gave my theory on the paranoia of modern woman as shown by the fact they've gotta wear clothes with barriers between the legs.

I haven't got time to be repeating myself.

Anyway, I didn't go exploring under her culottes.

Instead, I undid a button in the middle of her blouse and slipped a hand in. She was wearing a bra, but it was the good kind that feels like it almost isn't there. I could really feel her through it.

You know the old saying, though: business before pleasure.

Anyway, that wasn't the greatest place in the world to start messing with her, what with two bodies in the front and cars speeding by all the time. So I let go of her.

I climbed out of the Sentra and strolled back to my car. After opening the trunk, I went to Jerry's door and pretended to talk to him. It took a while, but finally there was a big enough break in the traffic. That's when I raced over to the girl's side of the car, jerked open her door, dragged her out, picked her up, and hustled her to the trunk of the Cadillac. Tossed her in, slammed the lid shut, and still had time to spare. I walked back to the Sentra and shut its door, then got all the way back to my own door before the next group of cars and trucks came along.

Easy, huh?

It's easy if you happen to be me.

Like they say on the tube, 'Don't try this at home.'

Committing multiple murders is not something that should be tried by amateurs. It can be extremely hazardous to your health, resulting in possible imprisonment, injuries due to energetic victims and/or enthusiastic police, and on rare occasions death by gunshot or execution.

Hey, maybe the federal government should print that sort of warning on guns. 'The use of this weapon can be extremely hazardous' and the rest of it just like I said. To be fair, though, they'd need to also put it on knives. And on axes, arrows, chainsaws, hammers, baseball bats, plastic bags, ropes, cars . . .

Nah.

Hey, I've got a babe in the trunk of my car. What am I doing fucking around with word games when I could be fucking around with *her*?

Excellent point.

Maybe I'll try the next off-ramp, see if I can't find a good place where we'll have some privacy.

'Say hi.'

Nothing but a moan, folks.

We're coming to you right now, folks, from the backseat of my car. The engine's running and the air conditioner is going full blast, so it's nice and cool in here. Cool and comfy.

Nobody anywhere around.

'Just you and me, kid,' I told her.

Nothing from her.

She oughta be bubbling with joy that I finally took her out of the trunk.

Nasty in there. She must've been in it for about an hour.

Once I'd decided to stop, I got off the freeway and had to tool around for a long time before I got us onto a nowhere little road that looks very good and deserted. I even pulled off and drove back a ways and got us behind some boulders. If a car does come along, we'll be out of sight.

I'm a little worried about helicopters.

We're pretty far from where I left the Sentra, though. We oughta be okay here.

It's a damn good thing I found this place when I did. If my girlfriend here had spent much more time locked in the trunk with . . . with all that heat and bad air, she might've croaked on me.

She'd been out cold when I put her into the trunk. But she woke up later. Out in the boonies, away from all the traffic noise and everything, it was very quiet and I could hear her screaming in there.

Nobody to hear her but me.

I'll have to make sure she can't scream like that when we're back in LA. Real cute if she's doing it while we're waiting at a stoplight, or something.

She quit the screaming a few minutes ago.

By the time I hauled her out of the trunk, she was quiet and sort of blank. That's how she is right now. She's not unconscious, but she isn't really with us, either. Like she's in a trance. Maybe she's gone catatonic on me because of her recent misadventures.

'Is that it, babe? Or maybe you're trying to fake me out. Do you think you're safe if you're playing possum, is that it?'

Hear that? That was me slapping her face.

A medium-hard slap. I don't want to puff her up and wreck her looks.

She blinked, but that was about all.

She's pretty zoned out.

Hope I can bring her out of it. This won't be nearly as much fun if she's only half-present, you know? I want her *reacting*. I want her to jerk and flinch and jump and cry and beg and even struggle some. Otherwise, it just isn't the same.

'Is it? Hello? What's your name?'

I need my hands free, so I'm setting this on the floor. Can you still hear me? Hope so. No big deal if you can't. I just put in a new tape before I went to get her out of the trunk. There was still time on the one I took out, but I wanted a fresh one in so I wouldn't have to quit what I'm doing and change tapes. They each go for an hour. That should give us enough time. I can't do *much* to her, after all – she's gotta be alive when I take her to the guys tonight.

I don't want guns back here with us. Here goes Dusty's rifle into the front seat. Now my Colt. The knife and Derringer are in my purse, and that's still up there on the floor. Now there's nothing nearby that she can use on me – in case she *is* faking.

Of course, I might have to scramble if we have visitors.

Not expecting any, though. We're really in the boonies.

I've got her stretched out across the backseat, arms at her sides. She looks like she's taking a nap.

Now I'm unbuttoning her blouse. Mmm, yes.

'What's your name, honey?'

Spreading the blouse open. Ah-ha! A see-through bra. It's pale blue. Not very flattering. Makes her tits look sick.

Easy to rip, though.

Now they aren't blue anymore. Creamy and smooth, unbelievably smooth. The nipples are hard and sticking up.

Guess what. My panties are suddenly feeling too tight.

Ah, that's better.

Free at last, free at last!

Taking off my nice white skirt, too. Wouldn't want it to get messy.

Tossing them into the front seat. Out of harm's way.

I'm getting rid of her shoes and socks. For one thing, she'll look better without them. For another, her being barefoot will give me an edge if she somehow gets away from me and tries to make a run for it. I mean, the ground must be searing hot out there. Not to mention all the sharp rocks and thorny bushes, cactus and stuff.

Her socks are so sweaty you could *wring* them out.

Okay, here go her culottes. If she was wearing a skirt, I

could just push it up. She's making life difficult for me. Hard. At least she isn't wearing a belt.

Open goes the button. Down goes the zipper.

She's heavier than she looks. I'll have to really *tug* to get these out from under her. Umph! Ah! Guess what came down with the culottes. Her panties! They pulled out from under her rump, but then the culottes left them around her thighs.

They're blue like her bra.

I've got the culottes off her. Think I wanta see how she looks in the panties, though. Pulling them back up. There. Transparent, just like I thought. She doesn't have much hair. It's mashed flat, too. Reminds me of how you look when you make a mask out of a nylon stocking by pulling it down over your head.

The blue color makes it look like her snatch needs oxygen.

Hang on.

Hear that? Probably not. That was me ripping off her panties.

She looks a lot better without them.

That thump was the heel of her foot hitting the floor. Her left foot. Her right leg is still on the seat, but the left is hanging off the side.

The next sound you hear, folks, will be my mouth.

Not my voice, my mouth. If you get my drift.

Mmmmm.

'AAAAH! FUCK! OW! GIMME THAT, YOU FU . . .!'

PART NINE

Gunplay

Chapter Thirty-seven

'What if the car breaks down?' Andy asked.

Good question, Jody thought. They'd left the highway about ten minutes earlier, and now they were on a dusty road surrounded by miles of wasteland. 'I suppose we'll all die,' she said.

'The car isn't going to break down,' Dad assured them. 'And if it does, we'll just send Officer Miles running off to fetch a rescue party.'

'That's right,' Sharon said. 'I'll trot east till I hit Blythe.'

'How far's that?' Andy asked, his nose wrinkled.

'Not more than about forty miles,' Dad said, then added, 'as the vulture flies.'

'Very funny,' Jody said.

'We want to go shooting, don't we?' he asked. 'Well, this is how it's done.'

'I know, I know. But it's gonna be hot out there. We're gonna *cook*.'

'It'll be a blast,' Sharon said.

Jody leaned forward and jabbed her fist through the space between the seatbacks. Her fist connected with Sharon's upper arm, but not very hard.

'Hey!'

'Pun punch,' Jody informed her.

'What?'

'It's an old family tradition,' she explained. 'If you come

out with a really horrendous pun, you get a pun punishment punch. Which you just got.'

Sharon rubbed her arm. 'Somebody should've warned me.'

'Sorry,' Dad said. 'I'd forgotten all about it. It's actually a custom more honored in the breach than the observance.'

'*I'll* be sure to honor it from now on.' She grinned over her shoulder at Jody. 'Better watch out.'

'Oooo, I'm trembling.'

Sharon laughed.

'Girls, girls,' Dad said. 'Can't we all just get along?'

That got Sharon laughing even harder. Dad's right hand let go of the steering wheel. It crossed the space between seats – down low, maybe so that Jody wouldn't notice. But she did notice. She saw him grab Sharon's side just above the hip. The same place where he sometimes targeted Jody for a round of tickles.

Sharon, squealing, used her elbow to force his hand away.

The same way I do.

Andy gave Jody a look.

'Touch me,' she said, 'and I'll cut your hand off.'

He seemed to take that as an invitation or a challenge. Chuckling, he turned and reached for her. She was ready for the attempt. Surprised, though. She'd expected him to go for a side tickle or a thigh squeeze. Instead, his hand made straight for her right breast.

She stopped his hand an inch from its goal. Caught it by the thumb.

Andy yelped as she forced his thumb backward. 'I give,' he gasped. 'I give, I give.'

'Do I look like someone who cares?'

'Ow!'

Keeping her grip on the thumb, she drove his hand down

against his leg. He made sounds that were half-laugh, half-whine.

'You gonna behave?' she asked.

'Yes!'

Dad looked back at them.

'Just taking care of business,' she told him.

'Is she hurting you, Andy?'

'No. Ow!'

Sharon twisted around in her seat to see what was happening.

'Don't hurt him,' Dad said.

'I'm not.'

'Ow!'

'It's a *good* hurt,' Sharon said.

She and Jack both cracked up. Jody wasn't sure why. Andy looked perplexed, but his confusion became relief when Jody let go of his thumb.

'Thanks a heap,' he muttered. He gazed down at his thumb and made circles with it as if warming up for a hitchhiking contest. 'Guess you didn't bust it for me,' he said.

Jody almost gave him a pun punch for that, but decided against it. For one thing, she doubted that Andy was aware of his double-meaning. For another, drawing attention to a 'bust' pun would alert Dad that breasts were somehow involved in the backseat shenanigans. Not a good idea. Besides, she'd already inflicted a good dose of punishment on Andy; any more, and it might stop being fun for both of them.

In the front seats, Dad and Sharon had almost stopped laughing. They were smiling at each other, shaking their heads and taking deep breaths.

Jody noticed that the car had stopped, but she wasn't sure how long it had been that way.

'Are we here?' she asked.

'I just stopped because of all the . . .'

'This *doesn't* look bad,' Sharon broke in. 'No structures in sight. No other vehicles, either. And we can use that knoll out there as a backstop.'

'Yep,' Dad said. 'Looks just fine.'

Andy quit wiggling his thumb, and raised his head. 'Does this mean we have to get *out*?'

Dad shut off the engine. The air conditioner died with it.

'Fresh air!' Sharon blurted, and threw her door open.

Hot air gushed into the car.

Jody moaned, 'Oh my Gawd.' This was worse than she'd expected.

She waited for Andy to climb out, then got down on her knees and reached under the front passenger seat. She found her Smith & Wesson .22, its extra magazine, and the box of ammo. While she was getting up, Dad opened her door. He took out the Mossberg and Sharon's rifle case.

On the seat, Jody made sure her pistol's safety was still engaged. Then she shifted everything into her left hand and scooted sideways. Just before stepping out of the car, she used her empty right hand to give the bill of her cap a tug. The bill had been tilted high, but now she wanted it low enough to shield her face from the glaring sunlight.

She hadn't worn the cap to breakfast at Kactus Kate's, but she'd been wearing it ever since they'd checked out of the motel. She'd even worn it into the various stores they'd visited before leaving Indio, stores where they'd bought new clothes for Andy, snacks and sodas for everyone, and supplies for the target shooting. Dad normally would've made her take the cap off when they went into the stores. 'You aren't supposed to wear your hat indoors,' he always said. 'Not unless it's a cowboy hat.' He hadn't said that today, though. Jody'd known he wouldn't, known she could get away with wearing the cap, and had gotten a kick out of taunting him with it. He just *couldn't* complain. Because throughout all the shopping, a black and gold NRA cap had been perched on top of Sharon's head.

When Jody stepped out of the car, the sun pressed down on her. She could *feel* the weight of its heat on her shoulders.

'Is your safety on?' Dad asked.

She swiveled her eyes upward. 'Yes, of course.'

She followed him to the trunk. He opened it, reached in and lifted out the gun shop bag. The bag looked ready to split from the weight of so much ammunition.

'I'll set up the cans,' Sharon said. She went striding off, a sack of empty cans swinging by her side. Jody supposed there must be at least a dozen cans. In addition to the empties from last night's party – collected from the motel room wastebasket – they also had the cans from the sodas they'd drunk in the parking lot of the gun shop just before leaving Indio.

Dad and Andy both turned their heads to watch Sharon.

'Jeez, guys,' Jody said.

'Just wanta make sure she places the targets at the correct distances,' Dad explained.

'Oh, sure.'

As if to prove his sincerity, he called, 'Right there'd be good for a few.'

Sharon smiled over her shoulder, nodded, and took out a can. She squatted to place it on the ground. Jody supposed the guys were hoping she would bend over and give them a good view of the seat of her shorts. The way she squatted, though, her shirt tail covered it.

Dad stopped watching. He shut the trunk. Andy helped him spread the blanket over the trunk lid. When it was in place, Jody put her pistol on it. Then Dad set out the boxes of ammo. Four boxes, fifty rounds each, of 9 mm cartridges for his and Sharon's pistols. A single large box that contained several smaller boxes – a total of five hundred .22 caliber bullets for Jody's pistol. Five long flat boxes, wrapped in cellophane, containing twenty rounds each of .223 cartridges for Sharon's rifle. And two boxes, twenty-five per box, of 12-gauge shotgun shells with No. 000 buckshot.

'All we need now is a war,' Jody said.

'Are we really gonna *shoot* all this?' Andy asked.

'Not even close,' Dad said. 'We don't want to be out here in this heat for more than an hour.'

'Then why'd you buy so much?'

'Good question,' Jody said. She already knew the answer.

'You just can't have too much ammo,' Dad explained. 'It's like money.'

'It's the old storm trooper mentality rearing its ugly head,' Jody said.

Dad laughed, then gave her rump a swat.

They all turned around. Sharon was about fifty yards out, setting up the last few cans.

Dad picked up his stubby black shotgun. 'Put one on your head!' he yelled.

As Jody muttered, 'Jeez, Dad,' Sharon turned to face them and carefully set a can on top of her NRA cap. She threw a hip sideways. Weight on one leg, she bent the knee of the other. She raised both arms, palms turned up.

Like she's the sidekick for a carnival performer, Jody thought – the gal about to get knives thrown at her or hold a cigar in her mouth for the bullwhip man. All she needs is a skimpy costume that glitters.

'He isn't really gonna do it, is he?' Andy asked Jody.

'Sure I am,' Dad said.

'What're you waiting for?' Sharon called.

Dad licked the tip of his forefinger and stuck it into the air, pretending to test wind direction.

'Boy,' Jody said. 'You two sure are setting a great example for Andy.'

'Aside from the weapon not being loaded, I haven't once aimed it at her.'

'I know. But you shouldn't be clowning.'

'You're right.' To Sharon, he called out, 'Maybe later!'

She yelled, 'Chicken!' Then she took the can off her head, propped it among some limbs of a scrawny bush, and started heading in.

Dad grinned at Jody. 'You know, I would never actually *try* a stunt like that. Not with a shotgun.'

Sharon heard him and laughed. 'Nobody in his right mind would try it with *any* sort of gun.'

'That's how Mike Fink murdered his worst enemy,' Dad said.

'Mike Fink, King of the River?'

'Yup, the keelboat guy. It was a tavern wager. He was supposed to shoot a tankard of booze off the fellow's head, but he conveniently aimed too low and plugged him right between the eyes.'

'Very clever,' Sharon said. 'Made it look like an accident.'

'Not clever enough. Everybody saw right through it, and some pals of the dead guy ventilated Fink.'

'Dad's a fount of useless information,' Jody explained.

'No such thing as useless information,' Dad said.

'I know, I know.'

'Let's see what you've got,' he said to Sharon.

She unzipped her leather case and slipped out a rifle. 'A Ruger Mini-14,' she said, and passed it to him.

'Ooo, she's a beauty. Looks sort of like an old M-1.'

'Very similar,' Sharon agreed. 'Different caliber, of course.'

'I like that stainless steel' barrel and stuff,' Jody said. 'And the wood. The wood looks great. That black plastic you see all the time seems so . . . I don't know, cold and futuristic.'

'Is that why you hate my Mossberg?' Dad asked.

'I don't hate it. I just can't shoot it.'

'You'll have to try this one,' Sharon told her. 'Has a real nice feel to it.'

'It might be a good idea,' Dad said, 'for each one of us to try out everything. That way, if we *do* run into trouble, we'll all have at least a passing acquaintance with each kind of weapon.' He turned to Andy. 'Have you had any experience with shooting?'

The boy grimaced. 'I wasn't ever allowed to even have a cap gun. My parents didn't believe in it.'

Please, Dad, Jody thought. Be careful. Don't forget they're dead.

'A lot of people *don't* believe in guns,' Dad said. From the gentle tone of his voice, Jody knew she didn't need to worry. 'But guns aren't either good or bad, Andy. They're just tools. It's all in how they're used. If they're used properly, they can be a lot of fun.'

'Which you're about to find out,' Sharon told him.

'They can also be used to protect yourself and people you love,' Dad went on. 'I don't need to tell you about the evil people out there.'

Nodding slightly, Andy caught his lower lip between his teeth.

'The only time you ever shoot someone,' Dad told him, 'is if that person is a dangerous threat to an innocent person. Even then, you only fire if there's no other safe way to stop him. And always shoot to kill.'

Andy scowled. 'Shouldn't I try to just wound him in the arm or leg?'

'Never,' Sharon said.

'Jody?'

'What?'

'You tell him.'

She sighed. 'Always shoot to kill.'

'Tell him why,' Dad said.

'Because. If you go for an arm or leg, you might miss. And even if you do hit him there, the bullet might kill him anyhow. The purpose of shooting people is to stop them before they can do more harm. To do that, you need to put them out of commission. The only sure way to do that is to kill them.'

'And how do you do that?' Dad asked her.

She smirked at Sharon. 'I'm always getting this. The "drill". It really gets old.'

Sharon nodded. 'Let's get to the shooting. Andy, here's the whole deal boiled down: if you have to fire at someone, put as many slugs as fast as you can into his chest. Empty your gun into him. If you're a really great shot, forget the chest and go for the head.' She grinned at Jack. 'End of lecture?'

'Good enough for now,' he said. 'We oughta start him on the twenty-two.'

'But not yet,' Sharon said.

'What?' Dad asked.

'I think we'd better find out if Andy actually *wants* to learn how to shoot. He was brought up in a family that opposed firearms. If he has any sort of moral objections, it isn't our place to force him into . . .'

'You're right,' Dad said. 'I should've thought of that. Andy, how do you feel about it?'

'I want to shoot.'

'Are you sure?' Sharon asked. 'Your parents might not have wanted . . .'

'Maybe I could've saved them if I'd had a gun,' he said. 'Them and Evelyn.' His chin started to shake.

His eyes were hidden behind his new sunglasses, but Jody knew there had to be tears in them.

Sharon took a step toward him before she seemed to realize that she held the rifle in her hands. A helpless look crossed her face.

Jody put her arms around the weeping boy. 'It's all right,' she whispered.

He tried to push her away, but she hugged him more tightly. His sunglasses bumped her neck and fell off.

'It's all right,' she said again.

'Leave go. I wanta shoot.'

'You can't shoot while you're crying.'

'I'm not crying.'

'No, that's just your sweat soaking through my shirt.'

'Damn it!'

'Everybody cries,' Dad told him. 'You've got better reasons than most.'

'If you ever get done,' Sharon added, 'we'll turn you into a regular Annie Oakley.'

Andy choked out a sob that was partly a laugh. It gushed hot air against Jody's skin through the wet cloth of her shirt.

Chapter Thirty-eight

Dad picked up the small, stainless steel Smith & Wesson. Andy reached for it, but Dad said, 'Not so fast, pardner.'

'More lectures,' Jody muttered.

Andy shrugged. 'I don't mind.' He wiped his eyes one more time, then put his sunglasses back on.

'This kind of gun is a semi-automatic,' Dad explained. 'Which means you don't have to cock it between firing. After the first shot, it recocks itself over and over again until the magazine is empty. All you've gotta do is pull the trigger each time you want to fire it. That's what a *semi*-automatic does. A *full* automatic lets you fire just by holding the trigger back.'

'And they're highly illegal,' Sharon pointed out. 'Possession's a federal crime unless you've got the proper permits.'

'Which means,' Jody said, 'that only the bad guys are allowed to have them.'

Dad grinned. 'Very good.'

She dipped her head.

'Let's get back to the lesson.' He held up the twenty-two. 'A little on semantics. Most people will call this weapon an "automatic" or an "auto", but it's not. It's actually a *semi*-automatic. We just leave off the "semi" part to shorten the word and make things easier to say.'

'Easier, but inaccurate,' Sharon said.

'But almost everybody says it,' Dad added. 'Okay now, with an automatic or semi-automatic you've got two danger areas. One is the side port here.' He tapped it with his fingertip. 'Almost the instant you fire, the shell casing will be ejected. It flies out of here. It doesn't *fall* out, it flies out. Fast. The casings are brass and they come out hot. You don't want to be standing near the right side of someone who's firing, because it's easy to get hit in the face by the things.'

Andy looked skeptical. 'Can something like that really *hurt* you?'

'Might put out yer eye,' Jody said, trying to sound like an old geezer.

'Just keep your sunglasses on,' Sharon told him. 'Twenty-two shells mostly do nothing more than sting your cheek. But you get hit by a big one, it can hurt pretty bad and even cut you.'

'A flying shell isn't gonna be lethal,' Dad said, 'but any sensible person tries to avoid pain. So keep your distance from ejection ports. If somebody's firing a revolver, you don't need to worry about it. Revolvers don't spit out their spent shells.'

'Okay.'

'But it doesn't matter,' Jody added, 'because we don't have any revolvers with us.'

'It's worth pointing out, anyway,' Sharon said.

'Much obliged,' Dad told her. 'Now, the other danger area is in front of the muzzle.'

'Jeez, Dad. Isn't that just slightly *obvious*?'

'You've been known to get sloppy about it yourself, young lady.'

'*Me?*'

'Here's the thing, Andy. Everybody knows the muzzle is dangerous. It's where the bullets come out. But some people seem to forget about that when they aren't actually aiming and ready to fire. You've always got to be aware of where your muzzle is pointing – when you're walking with your weapon, when you're just holding it and doing nothing special, and *especially* when you're busy reloading it.' He turned his head to Jody. 'Paying attention?'

'Yes, Father.'

'Always assume there's a live round in the chamber and that it'll go off when you least expect it.'

'And,' Sharon said, 'make sure there *isn't* a round in the chamber when you don't want one there.'

'The main rule is . . . Jody?'

'Never point your gun at anybody you don't intend to shoot.'

'Very good.'

Sharon smiled at her. 'He really has drummed this stuff into you.'

'Tell her why,' Dad said.

'A safe shooter is a happy . . .' She suddenly felt cheap making cracks about it. 'He wants me to be able to protect myself and also to know enough so I don't get hurt by accident. It's sort of like when he made me take swimming lessons.'

Dad's head moved up and down very slightly. He whispered, 'That's right.'

Nobody else spoke.

Jody heard the hushed sound of a mild breeze. She heard chirps and clatters and buzzes from nearby insects. A few birds sang.

Then the plastic bag from the gun shop rustled as Sharon reached in. She came out with a handful of small cellophane packages. Inside each wrapper was a pair of bright orange foam ear plugs.

She passed them around. 'It'll get loud,' she told Andy.

They all tore open the wrappers and plugged their ears.

Then Jack took a deep breath and held the pistol toward Andy. 'Here you go, pal. It's loaded. Jody always keeps it loaded, a bullet in the chamber, the safety on. I know that sounds dangerous, but her main reason for having the gun is self-defense. If you need to shoot someone, you might not have time to fool around loading up. You've gotta keep it loaded so you can get off a shot fast. Any questions?'

'Not right now. Can I try it?'

'Yep.' Dad gave the gun to Andy, then guided his hand until the muzzle was pointing in the general direction of the soda cans. 'There's your safety. Push it down with your thumb. That's right. When you see the red dot like that, the safety is off and you're ready to fire.'

'Should I go ahead?'

'First make sure everyone's to the rear of your muzzle.'

Andy glanced from side to side. 'Yeah, they are.'

'Fine. Now, just point it at any of those cans . . .'

'One of those in the front,' Sharon suggested. 'A gun like that is for close range.'

'Right,' Dad said. 'Now pop a few rounds, see how it goes.'

The pistol jumped a bit and Jody heard a flat *bam!* through her ear plugs. A yard behind one of the soda cans, a plume of dust leaped off the ground.

Bam! Closer. Behind and slightly to the right.

Bam! Bam! Bam! Two more misses, but then the can hopped high, tumbling away, and fell to the ground at least a foot beyond where it had started.

'Wow!' Andy yelled. His head snapped around. He wore just about the biggest smile that Jody had ever seen on him. 'Did you *see* that! I did it! I hit it!'

Jody gave him a thumbs up.

'Good shooting!' Sharon called.

Dad said, 'You did it once, you can do it again. This time, line your target up in the sights. Put your front sight in the center of the rear sight's opening so that all three of the white dots form a straight row. Then make it look as if the target is resting on top of the front sight.'

Andy took his time with the next shot. When he fired, his bullet kicked up dust a yard in front of the can. The shot after that missed, too, but came close enough for the shock of its passage to shake the can.

'I think I'm better when I don't aim,' Andy said.

'It all takes practice,' Dad said.

Bam!

The can tumbled backward.

KRA-BOOM!

The unexpected blast, sharp and loud and shocking in spite of her ear plugs, made Jody jump.

The soda can hit the air like a punted football. It flipped end over end, flashing sunlight, getting smaller, and landed forty or fifty feet back.

Sharon lowered her rifle.

Dad grinned at her and said, 'Whoa, Nelly.'

Andy gaped at her, his mouth drooping.

'That's the difference,' Sharon said, 'between a .22 and a .223.'

'Jesus H. Christ on a crutch,' Andy muttered. 'Can *I* try it?'

'Everyone can try it,' Sharon said.

'Later, though,' Dad told Andy. 'I want you to stick with the .22 until you're more comfortable with it. Fire another hundred rounds or so. Jody, why don't you take turns with him? And show him how to change magazines, reload, whatever else he needs to know. Okay?'

'You hear that?' she asked Andy. 'I'm in charge.'

'This is *so* neat!'

'I know, I know. Now, the gun is empty. You know it's empty because the slide stayed back after the last shot you took. But put the safety back on, anyway. Always have it on when you're not firing.'

He pushed the lever upward until it covered the red dot on the side of the pistol.

'Good,' Jody said. 'Now it's my turn.' She pulled the spare magazine out of the pocket of her shorts. 'Gimme.'

'Can't I go again? If you let me, I'll let you go twice in a row.'

She thought about it for a moment. She remembered the look on his face right after he hit the can for the first time. 'Okay. You do two magazines, then I'll do two, and we'll work it like that. Here, give me the gun. I'll show you how to reload.'

Andy offered the pistol to her.

'Oh, great,' Jody said. 'Planning to shoot me in the stomach?'

He winced and turned the muzzle downrange. 'Sorry.'

'That's the sort of goof that gets people shot.' She saw her father watching. 'Right, Dad?' she asked.

'That's right. Glad you're paying attention.' Then he turned his attention to Sharon.

Sharon stood off to the side of the car, but near enough to reach her open box of ammo on top of the trunk. She was taking out long, pointed cartridges and thumbing them into a banana clip that glared like chrome in the sunlight.

'Jeez,' Jody muttered. 'Look at that.'

Andy looked. 'Holy smoke.'

Jody took the pistol from him. Careful to keep it pointing away from everyone, she pressed the release button. The slim black magazine dropped down out of the handle and into her palm. 'Ours are just a teensy bit smaller than hers.'

'No kidding.'

'Dad's gonna make me move up to a .38 one of these days. He thinks I need to have more stopping power. I've always tried to talk him out of it, but . . .'

'Why talk him out of it? It'd be *neat* to have a bigger gun.'

'Yeah, but I like this one. I don't wanta change.' She slipped the full magazine into the pistol and slammed it home with the heel of her hand. 'Watch me, not her. I'm making *you* do this next time.'

'I'm watching.'

'Okay. You've gotta make sure the magazine is all the way in and locked into place. Then you push this gizmo and the slide rams forward and chambers the round that's on top. Watch.' She did it. 'Now it's loaded and ready.'

'Except for the safety,' Andy added as he accepted the pistol from her.

'Right. You're learning.'

Her father, she noticed, had stepped over close to Sharon. They were talking softly as she fed more cartridges into the magazine.

'Should we go ahead and shoot?' she asked.

'Fire away,' Dad said.

'My can's gone,' Andy complained.

'Pick a different one,' Jody told him. 'Any of those four in the front.'

'Is there any special way I should stand?' he asked.

'Any way that feels comfortable. I prefer the Weaver stance, myself.'

'*What?*'

'Never mind. Spread your feet and crouch a little bit so you're good and balanced. Then just stick out your arm and shoot. If you want to really take careful aim, you can use your left hand as sort of a platform under your gun hand.'

'Like this?'

'Yep.'

'Here goes!' He squeezed off a shot. A can hopped straight up and dropped back to the ground. 'Hey!'

'Great!'

'I wish I could *really* send it flying.'

'The main thing is hitting it, not seeing how far you can make it fly.'

'Yeah, but this little peashooter might not even kill somebody.'

'It'll kill just as good as that big cannon of Sharon's.'

'Oh, yeah, right. Every day and twice on Sunday.' He fired again. This time, he missed.

'I'm not kidding. I happen to know that a lot of professional assassins use .22 caliber pistols. Like the secret Israeli hit teams that go after terrorists? They use them. At close range, a .22 is just as good as anything. And it's quiet enough so that it makes almost no sound at all when it has a silencer.'

He fired again, winging a can so that it fell over but didn't jump. Then he looked at Jody. 'Have you got a silencer for this?'

'You can't have 'em. They're illegal.'

'Guys on TV always have them.'

'Yeah, and guys on TV are always putting silencers on revolvers, too. TV is stupid about guns. They never get it right. After this out here, you'll spot crazy stuff every time you watch something.'

'Really?'

'Sure. Movies are like that, too, most of 'em. Just wait and see. Uh-oh.'

Andy fired and missed. 'You made me miss.'

'Sharon's about to go.'

Andy turned his head to watch.

'You don't have to stop,' Jody told him. 'I'm still waiting for my first turn, you know.'

'I don't want to miss Sharon.'

Sharon glanced over at them. 'Go ahead. I'll wait till you're empty.'

Andy emptied his gun with four quick pulls of the trigger. His first shot knocked a can spinning backward. The next three missed, but none by more than a few inches. 'Nuts,' he said.

'That was good,' Jody told him. 'If you'd been firing those

at a bad guy instead of at a little Pepsi can, you would've caught him in the chest every time.'

'Really?' He grinned. 'Hey, yeah, I bet you're right.'

'Everybody have your ear plugs in?' Sharon called. 'Okay. See that dried stump of wood sticking up, way out there? There, just in front of the hill?'

Jody spotted it. Not a very large target, and quite a distance beyond the farthest of the cans that Sharon had set out. To Jody, it appeared to be less than a foot high, and not much bigger around than her arm. It looked like the remains of the trunk of a small, dead tree.

'Do you see it?' Andy asked her.

'Yeah, do you?'

'Yeah, I think so.'

'Okay,' Sharon said. 'Here goes. I'm gonna let her rip.'

Taking a few steps back, Dad yelled, 'Rock 'n' roll!'

Sharon's gunshots hammered the air.

She seemed to be firing as fast as she could pull the trigger.

The brown stump shook and pieces flew off as the storm of slugs tore into it. Every shot seemed to chew off a hunk, then speed on and blast the hillside and throw a plume of yellow dust into the air.

Dad wasn't watching the target. His eyes were on Sharon.

Jody checked; that's where Andy was staring, too.

Watching her there, NRA cap turned backward so its bill stuck out behind her, the rifle jumping with each shot and throwing out flashes of brass as its muzzle spat fire and white smoke, her whole body absorbing the recoils that hit her with quick hard jolts and shook her shirt and made her thighs vibrate even though Jody knew her legs must be almost as solid as wood.

She does look great, Jody thought. No wonder the guys are staring like a couple of nuts. They're probably wishing they were on the other side so they could watch what the recoils are doing to her boobs.

The shooting stopped. The silence sounded huge. Sharon lowered her rifle and frowned into the distance.

'We're gonna have to call you Rambo,' Dad said.

'I guess I nailed it pretty good.'

'*You destroyed it!*' Andy blurted. He sounded very excited. 'Can I try it?'

'Maybe later,' Sharon told him. 'Right now you need to practice with the pistol.'

'One step at a time,' Dad added.

'But I want to really blast something.'

Jody shook her head. 'We've created a monster.'

Chapter Thirty-nine

Jack came back from the pay phone at the Arco station on the outskirts of Blythe. He climbed into the driver's seat. Pulling the shoulder harness across his body, he looked over at Sharon. 'Nothing.'

'Nothing at all?'

'Did you get through to Nick?' Jody asked from the back seat.

'Yup. Got him at home. He said to tell you hi.'

'They don't have *any* leads?' Sharon asked.

'They're checking out the components of the fire bomb that the shooter left behind in the Zoller house. Doesn't look promising, though. A mayonnaise jar full of gas, with one of those timers you can buy for turning on your lamps when you're on vacation. Common stuff. Zero chance of making any headway trying to trace stuff like that. There were also some shoe prints. The shooter stepped in blood and tracked it around the house. He's probably about six-foot-two.'

'Six-two and *bald*,' Jody said.

'Yeah,' Andy said. 'They were *all* bald.'

Dad nodded. 'If the shooter was one of the men from your house . . .'

'He *had* to be one of the guys from Andy's, didn't he?' Jody asked. 'Why else would he try to kill me?'

'He almost had to be one of them,' Sharon agreed.

'It's not a hundred per cent, though,' Dad said.

'And it's not for sure that he runs around bald all the time,' Sharon added.

'Yeah,' Andy said. 'Maybe he wears a wig all day, and only just takes it off when he gets together with the gang to go out and massacre people.'

'Anyway,' Dad continued, 'the shoes are a fairly good indicator of his size, at least. But they were a garden variety of Nikes you can buy in every mall in the country, so they're basically a dead end as far as making the guy.'

Sharon raised her eyebrows. 'If we *do* find him and get our hands on the actual shoes . . .'

'Yep. If we find him, we've got him.' Dad started the car. Before putting it into gear, he looked over his shoulder at Andy, then Jody. 'Keep your eyes open for a decent motel,' he said. Then he drove out of the filling station. After turning right onto the road, he glanced at Sharon. 'There were some fluids, too. You know.'

'Oh?' Her expression changed from surprise to revulsion. 'Oh,' she muttered. 'Yeah, I know.'

411

'Based on that alone, we're almost sure to get a conviction, but . . .'

'No idea who he might be.'

'None.'

'What about witnesses?'

'Nobody saw anything. Most of the neighbors were at a big barbeque at a house down the block when the guy tried to cap us. Get this one. The victims were invited.'

'You're kidding,' Sharon said.

'They RSVPd their regrets a few days before the party, claimed they had a previous commitment. The way it looks, though, there wasn't any previous commitment. The people giving the party have a German shepherd that apparently jumps up and slobbers all over everybody, and it's well known around the neighborhood that the wife – the gal who ended up dead – couldn't stand the dog. The party started at three in the afternoon, so if they'd gone . . .'

'Oh, wow,' Andy said.

'They wouldn't have been home when the shooter showed up.'

'The woman was pregnant,' Sharon pointed out. 'You can't really blame her if she didn't want to get mauled by somebody's pet.'

'It's just the irony.'

'Yeah,' Sharon said. 'Good old irony. The controlling force of the universe.'

'What?'

'Irony. The controlling . . .'

'I'd hate to think so.'

'Me, too. I can't help but wonder, though.'

'What are they talking about?' Andy whispered.

'Irony. Like God pulling nasty tricks all the time.'

'With everybody except the dog haters at this damn party,'

Sharon said, 'how come the bastard didn't break into an *empty* house?'

'Maybe he didn't know who was home and who wasn't,' Dad told her. 'It had to be a rush job – choosing which house, anyway. Once he was in it, he had plenty of time on his hands. They think he was ... with the woman ... for at least a couple of hours after he got there.'

'She was alive all that time?' Sharon asked.

'Maybe not the whole time.'

'I suppose nobody heard her scream for the same reasons nobody saw or heard ...'

'He stuffed something in her mouth.'

There was something about the way Dad said that. And there was something about the way Sharon looked at him.

'What was it?' Andy asked. 'What'd he use to gag her with?'

Dad shook his head.

Sharon twisted her head around and said, 'It doesn't matter.'

'Wow. It must've been something really *gross*.'

'Just drop it,' Jody told him.

'Do *you* know?'

'No, and I don't want to.'

'Let's just drop it,' Dad said.

Andy grimaced and sank lower in his seat.

Jody asked, 'Did Nick say anything about ... have they found out anything about the ones from Friday night?'

'You and Andy are still our best sources on that. Nothing new has turned up. Basically, we've got little or nothing to go on.'

'So what're we gonna do?' Jody asked. 'Just keep driving around and staying in motels forever?'

'It won't be forever,' Dad said. 'There's bound to be a break in the case before long.'

'I kind of like it,' Andy said.

'What if there isn't?' Jody asked. 'A break. What if they *never* figure out who did this stuff?'

'Let's just take things a day at a time, okay?'

'Speaking of a day at a time,' Sharon said. She cast an annoyed or frustrated look at Jack. 'Did you ask Nick about extending my time off?'

Dad nodded. 'They won't go for it. They're stretched so thin . . .'

'Damn it.'

'What's going on?' Andy asked.

Sharon frowned over her shoulder at him. 'I'm afraid I'll have to take off, tomorrow.'

'No!'

'She has to get back to work,' Jody explained.

'No! She has to stay with us!'

'I wish I could,' Sharon said. 'But look, I don't need to leave until tomorrow afternoon. So let's not worry about it, right now. We should make the most of the time that's left. How about it?'

Andy looked as if he were about to start bawling again.

'How will you get back?' Jody asked.

'Rent a car, probably. I hope this town has a car rental place.'

'I hope it doesn't,' Andy blurted. 'I hope you can't *ever* go back till we do.'

'Thanks, pal.'

'I want you to stay with us, too,' Jody told her. 'But I don't want you getting fired, either.'

Dad looked at Sharon.

'Keep your eyes on the road, Dad.'

He returned his attention to the road. 'Everybody should just cheer up,' he said. 'Nobody wants Sharon to go back

414

without the rest of us. But she has a job to do, and . . . anyway, maybe there'll be some sort of major break in the case and we'll all be able to go back tomorrow.'

'Fat chance,' Andy muttered.

'You never know,' said Jody.

'That'd sure be nice,' Sharon said. 'But I think we'd better not hold our breath. Let's just have the best time we can tonight, and worry about tomorrow tomorrow.'

'You can at least phone Nick again tomorrow, Dad. Before Sharon goes and rents a car. At least call him and make *sure* we have to keep hiding out.'

'Good as done, honey. In fact, I'll be phoning him every day till this is over.'

'I hope we find a motel pretty soon,' Jody said. 'I feel like I've been holding it forever.'

'Should've gone at the gas station,' Dad told her.

'Thanks, anyway. Gas station Johns are the pits. I can hold it till we get to a motel.'

'Let's make sure we pick one that has a pool,' Sharon suggested. 'I've had my heart set on diving into a nice, chilly swimming pool ever since we left Indio.'

'They probably *all* have pools,' Dad said.

'I think we should also hold put for a place with cable TV,' Andy said.

'If we hold out for too much,' Jody muttered, 'I'm gonna explode. It won't be pretty.'

PART TEN

Simon Says

Chapter Forty

Okay. Okay. If the fuckin' bitch busted it, I'm gonna make her wish she was never born.

Ho! Bet she already wishes that!

'Testing, testing – one, two. Testing, testing – one, two.'

Hey, bravo! It works. The way she whacked me in the head with the damn thing, I figured sure she must've busted it. But she didn't. That's the good news. The bad news is, the batteries got dislodged while she was pounding me, so the recorder shut off and missed out on all the fun and games we had. Would've made some very interesting listening, if you know what I mean.

Too bad for you.

Me, I didn't miss a thing. I was there.

The first thing that happened, she clobbered me three good ones on the side of my head with the recorder. That's when you heard me shouting. It must've been the third whack that killed the thing.

Before she did any more damage to me, I got hold of her wrist. With my other hand, I gave her a pinch that made her squeal and let go of the recorder.

She turned out to be a real squealer. A real screamer, too. And a fighter.

She was terrific.

All sweaty and slick and hot. The fighting made her breasts

419

jump around, and also made her squirm and slide around under me, rubbing me.

The best part was how her eyes bugged out each time I really hurt her. No, maybe that wasn't . . . the *best* part was when I gave her spasms of pain that made her clench up and grab me with her inside muscles.

It was great.

I called her Jody while I worked on her.

She never denied it.

Hell, maybe her name *is* Jody. I doubt it, though. It'd be too much of a coincidence. I might ask her when I take her out of the trunk. I'm sure she can't talk, but she might be able to nod yes or no.

Anyway, calling her Jody made it better. I called her that mostly when I didn't have a view of her face, and I pretended it was Jody under me. Sometimes it worked and sometimes it didn't.

What did work every time was telling myself I'd have Jody under me just like this – the *real* Jody – soon. Maybe in a day or two, maybe in a week. And the real Jody would be exactly like this, only better.

She'll have to go some to beat this gal. On a scale from one to ten, this gal was a nine.

Ho! Reminds me of our old Joy Scale. I'd forgotten all about that. For a while there, we rated every kill on the Joy Scale, but then we just sort of stopped doing it for no special reason.

The scale rates a combination of things, but mostly it takes into account how she looks and feels, plus how she responds to torture and rape and so on. (There was a scale for rating guys, too. It was started up by the fruits in our group. They called it the Joe Scale.)

As I recall, we originally made up the Joy Scale one night

when we were in Tom's garage. It was about a week after we did Denise Dennison and her family. Somebody – Minnow, I think – said that on a Joy Scale of one to ten, Denise rated a fifteen. We gave him a lot of shit about it. I mean, if a scale is from one to. ten, you can't go any higher than ten unless you're some kind of a witless dork.

Actually, we later broke our rules and gave one gal a twelve on the Joy Scale. That's because we all agreed that she was way far better than all the others. It's true she was older than a lot of our kills, but she was in a class by herself. Partly because of how gorgeous she was, but a lot of it had to do with how she acted – her terror and shame, the way she was so incredibly sensitive to pain, and how in spite of everything she seemed to relish every minute of the sex. She begged us to stop hurting her, but she was always hot to have us fuck her. She would go for three of us at one time. She was so incredible that we kept her alive in the garage for about two months before we finally killed her. That was a record. Later we stripped off all her skin.

We cured and tanned it.

Tom got first pick of which sections he wanted. He took the best parts for himself, of course.

But I got a good section, myself. We all got at least something – keepsakes to remember her by.

In the wreck room, we sat around and partied and made whatever we wanted to out of her hide. I won't get into what everybody made. For one thing, I don't have all the time in the world. For another, I might gross you out. Wouldn't wanta ruin your appetite, or anything. What *I* made, though, was a nifty little mini-skirt which I dubbed my Connie Kilt, after Connie Baxter who had kindly provided the material.

Anyway, that's about all I have to say about Connie, our one and only twelve.

It wouldn't be fair to say we gave her the twelve because she was Tom's mother. That'd be taking away from her. She deserved the twelve.

Let me think. That was about two years ago.

We haven't had a twelve since, and it was only a while after Connie that we sort of forgot about the Joy Scale.

Maybe Jody will be another twelve. Or higher.

Hell, maybe she'll be a major disappointment. I've built her up so high in my mind . . . There's something about her, though. Something. Just those few seconds with her on the grass Friday night – and then by the back wall. And being in her bed last night. And wearing her clothes. I don't know.

It's more than just how she looks. She has . . . a quality. A freshness. Maybe it also has to do partly with how spunky she was when we were after her.

Anyway, I can't wait till she comes back from wherever she's gone to.

I *have* to wait, of course.

Can't very well nail her when I don't know where she is.

I just hope she comes back soon.

I've gotta admit, there *is* something to be said for the joys of anticipation. Every time I think about how it's gonna be, I get a boner that doesn't quit.

From the feel of things, it's just as well that Jody *is* out of town for a while. I have some recovering to do.

I did take a nap after getting done with the girl. I needed it in a bad way. In fact, I needed it *so* bad that I actually conked out right in the back seat of my car, and right on top of her. A very stupid move. But I was too worn out to care. With me pinning her down, she couldn't go anywhere. Also, I figured she was in no condition to cause trouble. My main worry was that somebody might come along and find us, but that wasn't a big enough worry to keep me awake.

I zonked.

As far as I know, nobody came along and looked in the car while I was dead to the world.

If the girl woke up, she was smart or scared or hurt enough to behave herself. I mean, she could've taken out my eyes. Could've chomped my neck the way I did Henry back there in Indio. Could've done a lot of things to me.

But I woke up in no worse shape than I'd been in when I finished with her.

Except that I was pretty damn shocked to sit up and see how low the sun had sunk. I looked at the dashboard clock – 7:35.

Great, huh? Too bad I didn't sleep a little longer.

Maybe it *is* too bad, at that.

I mean, what if I'd slept another couple of hours? As it turned out, I got here with time to spare. Time to sit in the car and monkey with my recorder and get it working, with still plenty of time to play a little catch-up with my true-life adventure. And time left over.

Time to wait and worry.

But what if I'd slept longer out in the boonies? What if I woke up and there hadn't been enough time left to make it back here for the deadline?

Would I have come, anyway?

I mean, by 10:30 or so, Lisa probably would've been beyond saving. (If not dead, at least too messed up to be worth the trouble.) So why risk everything?

Well, as I guess I've already figured out, tonight doesn't really have much to do with saving Lisa. It has more to do with my own survival. If I don't take down Tom and the other guys, I'm as good as dead.

So here we are.

I'm parked by the side of the road about fifty feet from

Tom's front gate. I don't want him getting suspicious, so my plan is to wait until maybe five till ten before driving up to the gate.

That's about ten minutes from now.

There's a lot about the gang I didn't get around to telling. For one thing, maybe I should've made a list of the names of everybody we killed. I know most of their names, but . . . too bad. No time for that now.

A lot of things I could've told.

What I should've done is to talk while I was driving here. It was a pretty long drive, and I would've had time to get into a lot of stuff. The trouble was, I thought the bitch had busted my machine. It wasn't till I got here and had a while to kill that I took a look at it and saw it was just that the batteries had gotten knocked loose.

While I've still got a few minutes, I should mention what I did to the gal after I woke up. That's when we were still out in the desert and I'd just noticed how late it had gotten to be.

I was in too much of a hurry to bother with getting her dressed. Nobody was around, anyway. I just dragged her out of the car, both of us butt naked. She stayed asleep. Asleep or out cold, I don't know which.

After she was out, I put her down on the ground. You should've seen her. She looked great, sprawled out there. The sunlight had a beautiful, reddish look to it that made her hair sparkle like gold and gave her skin a soft, ruddy glow.

She was just gorgeous.

I hate to say it, but I might never see anything that glorious again ever. Maybe that's how come I want to spend some time talking about it, now.

Life has its moments of huge, miraculous beauty.

You want to pay attention when one of those moments comes along, and not miss it or treat it lightly. Because they don't come along very often. And someday, one of them will be your last.

Oh, man.

I suddenly have this awful feeling I'm gonna die in Tom's garage tonight.

If that happens, I'll never get my chance at . . . Guess it'll be very good luck for Jody Fargo, huh?

Anyway, I'm running out of time.

What I did after putting the gal on the ground, I went and took Dusty's rifle out of the trunk. Then I straddled her, my feet basically lined up with her tits. I raised the rifle overhead by its barrel and swung it down at her jaw.

As I swung, I shouted, 'FORE!'

The butt of the stock caught the side of her jaw, just the way it was supposed to.

It didn't knock her jaw flying, but it sure did knock it sideways.

Oh, shit, I'm running out of time.

I should've just thrown her back into the trunk after that, but like I said, she looked so great. I'm not one to miss out on life's occasional moments of splendor, so I got down and fucked her one last time. I could see her jaw swelling up even while I was pumping her. *Then* I threw her into the trunk. Then I got dressed and made tracks for Tom's place.

The reason I broke her jaw was to make it so she wouldn't say anything to Tom and the guys. The one thing I sure *don't* want is for her to deny she's Jody when we get in there.

Oh, man. Time to start moving.

Here we go.

If I don't make it . . . Shit, I had big plans for these tapes. They're all in the car, here. Maybe I should've dropped them off at my apartment, or mailed them to someone . . . I don't know. Too late for any of that, though.

I'm coming up on the gate. It's very well lighted and has a security camera. The monitor's in the garage, and so is the button they've gotta push to open the gate for me.

I'll open the window and put this on my lap till . . .

'Hi, guys. Right oh time, huh? I've got Jody in the trunk. She's alive and kicking, just like you wanted. And I killed the boy. It all went great!'

Okay, the gate is starting to swing open.

Here we go.

I don't *have* to drive through.

But I'm doing it. I mean, I'm sort of committed at this point.

I should *be* committed. This is a lunatic move. Suicide.

A real Gary Cooper move.

That's Cooper in *For Whom the Bell Tolls*, in case you're wondering, where he stays behind to cover the retreat – even though he knows it'll be his ass.

'I do this for you, Maria. You go, and I will go with you.'

Bullshit he goes with her. He bites the dust and turns into ant food.

Off to the side there, back in the trees, that's where we did Hester Luddgate.

I wish there was something I could *do* with these tapes.

Oh, well.

I'll just leave them in the car when we go in. Somebody will find them. Whoever happens to survive the upcoming epic, *The Gunfight at Tom's Garage*.

Produced, written, directed by and starring the great Simon Quirt!

If the wrong person finds these tapes, they'll never see the light of day. Guess I've *got* to survive, or at least make it so Tom and the other guys *don't*.

If I can save Lisa . . .

'Lisa, if you're listening to this, I want you to make sure these tapes aren't destroyed. I'm willing them to you. Take them to a lawyer, maybe. The cops should listen to them, but they might be worth something so make sure you keep all the rights. You deserve something out of this mess I got you into. Maybe a lawyer can put you in touch with an agent, or something. Maybe they can make a book or movie out of this and my exploits will be immortalized.'

Okay, I'm stopping here. Tom's mansion and the garage are just up the driveway. I can see them from here. Everything looks dark, which is normal.

The guys are probably waiting for me inside the garage.

Unless Tom has maybe sent Mitch and Chuck outside to cover me – or bushwhack me.

Oh, man.

This is it.

I'm gonna climb out of the car now, and haul Jody – or whoever she is – out of the trunk. My human shield.

Oh, man.

Four against one.

Great odds, if you happen to be the Terminator.

Oh, well. If I bite the dust, let it be said that I did what I had to do and didn't back down.

Talk to you again soon, folks.

Or maybe not.

Adios, amigos.

Where the fuck's a crapper when you need one?

PART ELEVEN

Home, Sweet Home

Chapter Forty-one

Jody tossed and turned and sometimes groaned. She knew she had only been in bed for forty-five minutes, but it felt like hours and hours.

She'd expected to fall asleep immediately. After all, she'd been very tired – drained – and this was not some lousy motel with a noisy air conditioner and a hard pillow. This was home.

Familiar, peaceful sounds came through the open window. So did a mild breeze that was almost, but not quite, cool enough to make her sit up and reach down past her feet for the top sheet. If she covered herself with the sheet, she might be too hot. This was just about right, sprawling here in her nightshirt.

Maybe if it weren't twisted around her like this – squeezing her, putting pressure on a few sore places, cutting off her circulation.

She sat up, pulled at her nightshirt and struggled to unwind it. When it was hanging loose, she lay back down. She folded her hands beneath her head. She could feel the rear of the nightshirt rumpled between the small of her back and the mattress, leaving her rump bare against the sheet. The hem in front was only slightly lower than her waist.

Felt just fine that way.

But it wouldn't do. Not with Andy in the guest room. Not that he was likely to sneak around in the middle of the night and spy on her.

You never know about him, though.

Pushing at the mattress with her heels, she raised her rump. She gave the hem of her nightshirt a tug to bring it down several inches, then lowered herself.

Better.

Not quite as cool and comfortable, but now at least she didn't feel so exposed, so vulnerable.

It isn't Andy that bothers me, she realized. It's *him*.

He was here.

Right here in my room. Looking around. Going through my drawers. Looking at my personal stuff. Touching things.

He took a nap in my bed, just like some warped version of Goldilocks.

He actually took my stuff and wore it!

God only knows what else he did when he was here.

She had a feeling that her father was keeping things to himself. A lot of things. She wished she could've listened to the tapes, herself.

'Be grateful you didn't have to,' Dad had said. 'I don't want you to *ever* listen to them. That goes for you, too, Andy.'

'What about me?' Sharon had asked.

'I wouldn't, if I were you. I wish *I* hadn't heard them, but I really didn't have much choice in the matter. My God, I knew there were a lot of sick, evil people out there, but ... these guys were monsters. And that Simon fellow ... thank God he's dead. Thank God they're *all* dead.'

Jody wished she *could* hear the tapes, though. Dad had spent most of the afternoon at the station, listening to them with Nick Ryan. He hadn't come right out and said so, but Jody supposed there must be at least five or six hours' worth of recordings by the nut.

Dad had definitely given them an abridged version when he got home.

He'd managed to compress the whole story into less than

an hour so that Sharon could hear it all before leaving to get ready for the start of her shift.

Closing her eyes, Jody could see him at the kitchen table. He had turned his chair around so that he could straddle its seat and lean forward, arms crossed over the top of its back. He'd told most of the story in a soft, calm voice, almost as if he were bored by it. Near the end, though, the upturned corner of his mouth had started to twitch sometimes.

The twitching had begun when he told about Simon breaking the girl's jaw with the rifle butt. 'He did it so Karen wouldn't be able to tell anyone that her name wasn't (twitch) Jody. After that, he put her back into the trunk and drove her to Tom's place. That's where he finished putting his story on tape. He left the recorder and tapes in the glove compartment of the Cadillac, then he apparently (twitch) took Karen out of the trunk and they headed for the garage.'

'He wanted to make it look as if he was cooperating, but he was armed to the teeth. He went in with an Army model Colt .45, plus a two-shot .45 Derringer and a Smith & Wesson .357 magnum revolver. He talks about all those weapons on the tapes, and they were also found in the rubble this morning.'

'We think he went in holding Karen in front of him. He said he wanted to (twitch) use her as a shield. But something must've gone wrong. Somehow, she got away from him. Maybe he had to let go of her so that he could have both hands free for shooting. Or she might've surprised him somehow, and made a break. Maybe she even got away from him after he'd sustained some wounds during the fight. If she recovers, she oughta be able to tell us exactly what happened. Her part of it, anyway.'

'However it all went down, Karen was shot once in the back (twitch) with a .45, probably by Simon. She (twitch) fell on the driveway a fairly good distance from the garage, so she didn't end up burnt (twitch) like the rest of them.'

'These guys were using candles and kerosene lamps to light the garage. To give the place atmosphere, maybe. But that's why the place went up. We think one of the lamps got hit by a stray bullet.'

'When the fire department arrived, the garage was totally engulfed. They couldn't send anyone in till after they'd knocked down the fire. By then, everybody inside was dead. A female was found suspended from a rafter (twitch) by chains, and had shackles (twitch) around her wrists. She was apparently Lisa. Whether she was still alive at the time Simon went in . . .' He shrugged. 'Either way, he didn't manage to save her.'

'God only knows what happened in there. One thing was pretty clear, though; Simon didn't shoot all of them before they got to him. There was some hand-to-hand fighting, and he got hacked up pretty good by a saber. He was found with two other guys on top of him, all three of them twisted together and charred black. The bodies of the other two men were found nearby. It looks as if Simon shot those two, and then got jumped by the pair who ended up in the heap with him. If Karen was in there, maybe she'll be able to tell us something about how (twitch) it all went down at the end. We'll also know more after the autopsies have been done on Simon and the others.'

As he'd said that, Sharon had pushed her chair back and stood up. 'I've gotta get a move on. Maybe you can fill me in on whatever else . . .'

'Will you come back here when your shift is over?' Dad had asked.

For a few moments, they'd stared at each other.

'Do you want me to?'

'Yup. Sure do.'

She'd taken a deep breath and raised her eyebrows. 'You *do* understand, Sergeant, what time that's likely to be?'

'Maybe I'd better give you a spare house key.'

Dad had left the kitchen with her.

When they were gone, Jody had glanced at Andy, expecting some funny looks or lewd cracks about her father and Sharon. But Andy sat motionless and silent, frowning at the table.

Soon, Dad had returned and resumed his seat. 'I guess it's about time we started thinking about supper. Do you like pizza, Andy?'

'Huh?'

'Pizza.'

'Let's not rush into things,' Jody had interrupted. 'I want you to tell us what else he said on the tapes. There must've been a lot more than you told us. I mean, you spent all afternoon listening to 'em.'

'I think I covered everything you need to know about.'

'I wanta know *everything* he said.'

'No, you don't. Now let's drop it and . . .'

'But he was in the *house*, Dad. He was in my *bedroom*. He was in my *stuff*.'

'I know. And I know it must seem creepy.'

'He was a *madman*. And a *pervert*.'

'I know, honey. I know. Look, if you feel nervous about sleeping in your bedroom tonight, you can sack out on the sofa.'

'The sofa's lumpy.'

'I know, but . . .'

'I want to sleep in my own bed. It isn't fair for him to take it away from me . . . ruin my own bedroom for me.' Even while speaking, she'd realized that she must sound awfully selfish and petty. Whining about her bedroom. Simon and that horrible gang had slaughtered Andy's whole family, butchered no telling how many other people . . .

'It's all right,' she'd said. 'I've just gotta get used to the idea and . . .'

'Maybe if we go into your room and give it a really good cleaning up . . .'

'We cleaned it while you were over listening to the tapes,' she'd explained. 'We cleaned the whole house, didn't you notice?'

'Not really.'

For the first time in a long while, Jody had felt a smile come to her face. 'Sharon'll be real glad to hear you didn't even notice. She worked her butt off.'

'I helped, too,' Andy had muttered.

'Those lab guys made more of a mess than . . . the guy.'

'Simon.'

'Yeah. Him.' She didn't need to be reminded of his name. She would probably never forget his name. But she didn't want to speak it. 'Anyway,' she'd continued, 'they left finger-print powder all over the place.'

Blinking like someone who'd just woken up, Andy had said, 'Could you tell me something, Jack? How come they wanted to look for his fingerprints here if he's dead?'

'It's because there'll be a major investigation into . . . everything. Even Simon's break-in here. Everything about him and his friends. We've gotta find out exactly who was involved, what everyone did and when.'

'Didn't you say he told the names of all the other guys?' Jody had asked.

'He did, but he might've left people out. Or he might've named people who weren't in the gang.'

'Like to get them in trouble?' Andy had asked.

436

'For whatever reasons. For all we really know, half of what he said on the tapes might've been lies.'

'Only half?' Jody had asked.

'Well, there's no question that he told the truth about a lot of it, honey. Things he said match up with what we know about . . . about what happened at Andy's house on Friday night, for one thing. And about Hillary Weston and her husband. About the homeless person he hit with his car in the alley on Saturday night. And those two men he shot in Hollywood so he could take their dog. About his . . . his visit to *our* house. Also about what he did to Karen's parents.' Another shrug. 'We don't have confirmation of his story about the triple-murder in Indio, but it's probably just a matter of time. Maybe that kid – Henry – lived alone and made up the story he told Simon about his mother being away at work. If it was something like that, it might be a while before their bodies are discovered.'

'When it comes right down to it, kids, we don't have any reason to believe he lied about anything at all. Every word on those tapes might very well be the truth. But even so, he only managed to tell a small part of the story. There are huge gaps. We need to fill in every gap and get the full picture of what these guys have done.'

Jody squirmed on her bed.

I don't care what the rest of them did. I just need to know about that pervert who was here.

What he said and what he did. What went on that Dad knows about from the tapes.

Must be pretty bad, or he would've told us.

But everything's okay now, she told herself. The guy is dead. They're all dead. They can't hurt me or anyone else ever again. It doesn't even matter that Simon was right here in my room and messed with my stuff and took a nap in my bed. We cleaned up really good. I won't wear anything he might've touched until it's been through the washer. Sharon already changed the sheets . . .

Remembering, Jody began to feel a little squirmy.

It had been weird about the sheets.

At the time, she'd been so upset and worried that she hadn't noticed just *how* weird. The main thing, then, was that a stranger, a killer, might be lurking somewhere in the house.

No sooner had Dad unlocked the front door and stepped into the living room than he'd filled his hand with his Browning. 'Company,' he'd whispered.

It *isn't* over, Jody had thought.

She'd felt such relief earlier when she'd thought it was all over.

On the car radio on their way to breakfast, they'd heard the news report. A mysterious fire at the Hollywood Hills mansion of someone named Thomas Baxter. Six charred bodies discovered in the burnt garage. The sole survivor, a nude teenaged girl showing indications of a severe beating and sexual assault, found outside the garage with a bullet in her back. Suspicions that this incident might be related to the house fires and disappearances that had occurred Friday night in the Avalon Hills section of Los Angeles.

After hearing the news report, nobody in the car had cared any longer about trying to find an example of Blythe's more colorful or picturesque restaurants. They'd stopped at a Burger King, and Dad had rushed to the pay phone.

And he'd returned to their table with a weary, satisfied look on his face. 'Nick says it's over, folks. He wouldn't go into details, but he says it looks like the people who died in that garage . . . they're the ones who murdered your family, Andy. We can go home.'

But home had been visited.

Somebody had eaten breakfast in the living room, had left a dirty plate and cup and silverware on the coffee table.

Sharon, crouching, had inspected the breakfast remains. 'I think this stuff's a day or two old,' she'd said.

But she'd spoken in a whisper.

'If anyone's here,' Dad had whispered, 'we'll find him.'

And they'd begun to search. Guns drawn.

Sharon had been first into Jody's bedroom. She'd gone in, pistol ready, while Dad had stayed with Jody and Andy in the hallway.

She'd come out with Jody's bedsheets bundled in her arms. The look on her face had been grim, maybe a little disgusted. 'He was in there, but he's gone. We might as well get started on the cleanup, huh? I'll just throw these in the washer. He got some blood on them.'

'He was in my *bed*?' Jody had blurted.

'Do you know where the washing machine is?' Dad had asked Sharon.

'In the garage, right?'

'Right.'

And he'd stood there – they'd all stood there – while Sharon carried the sheets up the hall to the garage.

After her return, they had continued and finished their search of the house.

Then Dad had made a phone call to Nick Ryan to report the break-in.

Then the investigators had arrived. After a few words with them, he'd left for the station to find out what Nick had on the killers.

Later, after all the investigators had left, Jody and Andy had helped Sharon clean up the messes. Once again, Sharon had been first into Jody's bedroom. And her first act, there, had been to put a fresh set of sheets on the bed.

What the hell was it with my sheets?

Blood is evidence.

Why would Sharon toss sheets with evidence on them into the washing machine instead of leaving them on the bed for the lab guys?

Unless she's some sort of cleaning fanatic.

But Dad LET her do it.

Dad knew better for sure.

He would NEVER allow evidence to be ruined like that.

Jody suddenly suspected why they'd done it. Moaning, she curled onto her side and hugged her belly.

The bastard might've left blood on the sheets, as Sharon had claimed. But that wasn't all. That couldn't be all. He must've left other stains, too.

She squirmed. She felt horribly hot.

Could I get pregnant from something like that?

Don't be an idiot.

Anyway, these are clean sheets.

But Sharon didn't change the mattress pad. What if the stuff had soaked straight through the sheet? Then it'd still be down under me on the pad.

This is stupid, she told herself. There's a clean sheet between me and his stuff.

And then she thought, If they think I'm gonna sleep on this bed after that degenerate butcher shot his wad all over it, they've got another damn think coming!

She rolled over fast, swung her feet to the floor and stood up.

Chapter Forty-two

Jody plucked her top sheet off the bed, wadded it into a bundle, and clutched it against her chest. Then she picked up her pillow and crept to her door.

The hallway was dark.

She walked slowly, her bare feet silent on the carpet. After a few steps, she could see the door to her father's bedroom. It was open. Dad had gone to bed just a little while after Jody and Andy, so he was probably asleep by now.

It doesn't matter if he's awake and hears me, she thought. I'll just tell him I decided to sleep on the sofa, after all. It was his idea in the first place.

As she neared his open door, she heard the growling noises of his snores.

Good. She wouldn't have to explain anything.

But sneaking past his door, Jody almost hoped he would wake up. Though glad to be spared a questioning, she didn't care much for the idea that he was asleep. It was as if he had gone away, abandoned her.

She suddenly felt sure that Andy was asleep, too.

It's like they're not even here.

It's like they left me by myself.

Stupid, she told herself. They're *supposed* to be asleep. That's what night is for. It's no fault of theirs that I'm screwed up and wide awake.

Soon, she found her way to the living room. She stopped and studied the area ahead. The dim glow that seeped through the draperies – a faint mixture of milky gray from streetlights and moonlight – revealed shapes of chairs, lamp tables, the sofa and the coffee table in front of it.

Black shapes.

Black, or almost black.

What if I go over to the sofa and somebody's there!

Cut it out, she told herself. Nobody's on the sofa. Nobody's in the whole house except me and Andy and Dad.

'And I'm not too sure about them,' she whispered.

Immediately, she wondered who might have heard her say that.

Someone stretched out on the sofa, maybe. Or someone sitting right over there in Dad's easy chair.

This is stupid, she told herself. I'm too old to be spooking myself with this sort of nonsense. Nobody's here.

Just to make sure, she readjusted her bundle, freeing her right arm. Then she stepped over to an end table, reached out and turned on a lamp.

The sharp light stung her eyes.

Squinting, she turned around in a complete circle. Twice.

See? Told you there was no one here.

She turned off the lamp. As she stepped between the coffee table and sofa, her bare right foot crunched something into the carpet. Something small and brittle like a crumb of toast.

This is where he ate!

And I'm gonna sleep here?

I can't. No way.

Nose wrinkled, she stepped away from the sofa.

This is bad, she thought. What am I gonna do, avoid every place he might've been?

Just the places I'm sure of.

Crazy.

It's not crazy! He was a filthy degenerate and a butcher! Not to mention he came on my bed. Who knows where else he might've . . .

Where do you think you're gonna sleep? she wondered.

She halted. Her heart was pounding very hard.

Just calm down, she told herself.

It isn't fair! He wrecked everything! My own bed. The sofa. The whole damn house! It'll never be the same. It'll never feel clean or safe or . . .

'Knock it off,' she muttered. She didn't like hearing her voice in the silence, but decided that she would talk anyway. 'Okay? Just calm down. Everything's fine. Okay. Now, think. Where can you sleep? Where *wasn't* he?'

In the car.

I'm not gonna sleep in the car, she thought. There has to be someplace else. Come on, where?

They'd found evidence of his presence here in the living room, in the kitchen, in the bathroom, in Dad's bedroom, in Jody's, even in the garage.

Face it, she thought, he was probably everywhere.

He hadn't disturbed the guest room, so far as they'd been able to tell. Of course, that proved nothing. It only meant he hadn't rearranged or taken anything, or made a mess.

Too bad Andy's in there.

Anyway, who's to say the guest room's bed is any better than mine? Who knows where the guy . . . ?

The trundle bed!

Yes!

Jody headed for the guest room, delighted by her success in discovering the perfect place to sleep. On rollers underneath the main bed and hidden by a draping quilt, the trundle was completely out of sight.

Not a chance in hell the dirty bastard laid a finger on it.

Yes!

She was glad to hear her father snoring as she halted near his open door.

Might be a trifle difficult to explain why I'm sneaking to Andy's room in the dead of night.

Turning away from his door, she looked into the bathroom and considered whether she needed to pee. Not badly.

Better take care of it, she told herself.

So she slipped inside and eased the door shut. With the Barney Rubble nightlight glowing beside the sink, she didn't need to turn on the overhead lights. She set her sheet and pillow on the counter, raised her nightshirt, and sat down on the toilet.

Good thing I made a pit stop, she decided after a while.

Must be that Pepsi.

When it came time to flush, she almost didn't. The sound might wake up Dad. She could just lower the lid . . .

But she suddenly realized that the sound of a flushing toilet was exactly what she needed.

If Dad hears that, he'll know why I'm up roaming around.

Yo ho ho!

He'll think I'm on the way back to my room, and never suspect the awful truth!

Grinning, Jody flushed the toilet. Then she gathered up her pillow and sheet. She strode boldly out of the bathroom and up the hallway toward her bedroom.

When she stopped at her bedroom, she realized that she wasn't sure whether or not her father had been snoring as she'd left the John.

Doesn't really matter, she told herself.

She took one step into her bedroom, found the doorknob, and pulled the door toward her.

She didn't shut it all the way; that might arouse suspicion. But she didn't want to leave it standing wide open, either. Not with Sharon coming over later. Sharon or Dad might happen by and notice that her bed was empty.

Leaving the door slightly ajar, she headed for the guest room. She walked slowly, rolling her feet from heel to toe even though that made it worse on places that were still sore from Friday night.

Every few steps, she stopped and listened.

The house was very quiet.

Jody's breathing and the thudding of her heart were the loudest sounds around.

This end of the hallway seemed awfully dark.

Jody had seldom walked it in the middle of the night, but she couldn't recall it being this dark before.

The guest room door must be shut, she thought.

Usually, it was left open and light from the room's windows stretched out into the hallway. With that door shut, and certainly no light coming in from the door to the garage, Jody could see nothing at all in front of her.

She shut her eyes.

It made no difference in what she saw.

Wonderful, she thought, and opened them again.

Blackness.

She halted. She sidestepped to the right until her arm bumped softly against the wall.

I can't have very far to go, she told herself. Let's not freak out over a little darkness.

This is more than a little.

No big deal, she told herself. Just turn around, and you'll be able to see again.

She turned around.

And there was light. Dim light, but vastly better than nothing. And Barney Rubble in the bathroom seemed to give off a *very* healthy glow, considering that it had only one tiny little bulb and it was plugged in so far from . . .

. . . from the door . . .

445

. . . which was swinging shut, squeezing out the glow from Barney . . .

. . . squeezing it down to a slice . . .

. . . killing it.

'Oh, Jesus,' Jody whispered.

She backed away, arm rubbing the wall until she bumped a jutting edge of wood.

The door frame.

One more step, and the guest room door was beside her. She shifted the sheet and pillow to her right arm. With her left hand, she gripped the doorknob.

She didn't turn it, though.

She stood there, struggling to breathe, staring down the hallway.

It wasn't my imagination, she told herself. The door did shut.

Maybe Dad shut it. Maybe he's in there, right now.

That has to be it.

He woke up. I probably woke him up when I flushed the toilet. And he figured since he was awake anyway he might as well go ahead and take a leak.

That's gotta be it.

Far down the hall, a dim yellow slice of light appeared and slowly thickened.

Jody sucked a quick breath.

She twisted the doorknob, shoved her shoulder against the door, and lurched into the guest room. She shut the door fast, but took care not to let it bump. Leaning back against it, she panted for air.

That had to be Dad in the John, she told herself.

But what if it wasn't?

Peering into the darkness, she tried to see Andy. The curtains, usually left open, were shut. Only enough light filtered in to let her see vague, blurred shapes. She could barely make out the bed underneath the window. She couldn't actually see Andy in it. Holding her own breath for a few moments, she heard *his* breathing.

What if this isn't Andy?

What if Andy's dead and this is that dirty – Simon – pretending to be asleep?

The bastard can't be here and also down by the John, she told herself. Especially figuring he's DEAD. This has to be Andy.

Find out. Turn on the lights.

But if she turned on the lights, a bright strip at the bottom of the door would show in the hallway.

Simon'll see it.

A coldness seemed to clamp Jody's insides.

This is suddenly an awful lot like Friday night, she thought. And Friday night when I came out of the room with Andy, everyone was dead.

Dad's down there right across the hall from the John.

She muttered, 'Not this time.'

She tossed her pillow and sheet to the floor, whirled around, jerked open the door and rushed into the hallway. Nothing. Darkness. Everything looked normal. The light from Barney Rubble was a distant glow as dim as mist. No light came from her father's room.

She swept down the hall, moving as quietly as possible but moving fast. So fast that she could feel a breeze against her bare skin, feel the nightshirt drift against her thighs and belly.

So far, so good, she thought.

She rushed into her own bedroom and hit the light switch. As brightness stung her eyes, she half expected to see a hairless, half-naked madman leap at her with a hunting knife.

It didn't happen.

She jerked open the drawer of her nightstand and snatched out her Smith & Wesson.

On her way to the door, she thumbed the safety off.

She rushed down the hall to her father's room. Halting just outside his door, she listened.

And heard the slow growl of his snoring.

Thank God!

She crept through the doorway, slipped sideways, and nudged the switch with her elbow.

Nobody stood over Dad's bed, poised to strike him dead.

Nobody appeared to be in the room, at all, except Jody and her father.

He lay sprawled on his back, hands folded under his head, wearing his good blue pajamas. He had no sheet on top of him. The shirt of his pajamas was unbuttoned and hung open.

One of his snores turned into a moan.

Jody killed the light and slipped out of the room.

She crossed the hall and was about to check the bathroom when its door began to swing shut.

The door moved very slowly, blocking out the glow from Barney Rubble.

Oh my God!

She felt as if her heart had been dropped from a roof.

But she didn't let that stop her.

She raised her trembling left hand. The door bumped softly against it.

With her right hand, she aimed at the center of the door.

She had fired at enough boards, out shooting with her dad, to know that her .22 would punch straight through such a door.

Don't shoot till you see who it is, she warned herself.

She waited, expecting a strong thrust.

For a few moments, the door pushed gently at her hand. Then it eased away, stopped, and began coming back.

What's . . .?

She thumped it with the heel of her hand.

It swung away.

Swung away silently without knocking into anyone behind it.

Jody slapped the light switch, rushed in and whirled around, ready to fire.

The door had come to a stop against the far wall. Nobody could possibly be hiding behind it.

From where Jody stood, she could see into the bathtub. Nobody in there, either.

A sudden movement, off to the side, sent shivers crawling up her skin.

She gasped and jerked her head in that direction.

And saw the pale yellow curtains rising, full of wind, away from the open window.

Wind.

A gust, not a maniac, had been toying with the door.

To make sure, she half-shut the door. Feeling the warm breeze against her back, she stepped aside. A moment later, the door swung slowly until it bumped against its jamb.

The joke's on me.

She felt too shaken to laugh.

Talk about paranoia, she thought. Any other time, I would've figured it out right away.

She had taken a shower that evening after they'd returned from the Pizza Barn. The shower had steamed up the bathroom. As usual, she had opened the window to let in some fresh air.

And open it had remained.

Just to play things safe, she stepped over to the window and checked its screen. The screen was hooked in place, as it should be.

One big, fat false alarm.

She thumbed her pistol's safety switch upward to cover the red dot.

Then she approached the sink.

The girl in the mirror above it looked sweaty and haggard and a little wild. Her short hair was a tangled mess, wet loops glued to her forehead and temples. Her eyes seemed partly frantic, partly amused. Beneath them were half-moons of glistening speckles. A mustache of wet dots gleamed above her lips. The wide neck of her nightshirt drooped off her right shoulder.

Should've gotten a smaller size, she thought.

She'd bought it at a store in Indio while Dad was helping to pick out some new clothes for Andy. Nothing special about it. It had no cartoon characters or slogans. She'd bought it because she hadn't wanted to send Dad outside Saturday night to take her Pooh nightshirt off the clothes-line, and she'd packed an old white nightshirt to take on the trip. But the white one had turned out to be embarrassing: too tight, too short and too thin. This one hung loose almost down to her knees. And it was pink, so you couldn't see through it.

The only problem's the neck, she thought. *Way too big.*

She looked at her bare shoulder.

Bet Rob wouldn't mind seeing me in something like this.

She rolled her shoulder. The neck of her nightshirt slipped father down her arm, and now she could see the top of her right breast.

He'd go crazy.

Who knows? she thought. *Maybe someday . . . or some year.*

I'll call him tomorrow. Ask him if he wants to help me wash the car. And I'll be out there in my bikini . . .

Oh, yeah, right. No doubt, the sight of all my bruises and scabs would be a real turn on for him.

I'll call him, anyway. Maybe we can get together and do something. My face is okay. I'll just have to keep my shirt on for a while.

She gave herself a haggard smile.

God, it's been so long. He must wonder where I've been. Hope he's missed me as much as I've . . .

She suddenly realized that she hadn't actually missed Rob very much.

I *missed* him, she told herself. I thought about him a *lot.* So what if I didn't *long* for him and pine away. I did have a few other things on my mind.

Including Andy.

The little pain in the butt.

Jody switched the pistol to her left hand, turned on the cold water, and bent down over the sink. With her right hand, she scooped water to her mouth.

As she drank, she thought about Andy.

He was bound to wake up and get cute with her.

No matter what, I'm gonna sleep in that trundle bed. Even if it means I've gotta tie the little squirt up, or . . . Real nice. Tie him up. His whole family's dead, and he's got nobody except me. But he's gonna try something. He'll want me to hold him, or something.

It won't kill me to hold him.

Just so long as he doesn't try to get grabby.

She remembered yesterday morning in the motel, holding him while he'd cried.

That had felt sort of good, really. Comforting him, knowing how much he needs you, even knowing that you were getting him a little turned on.

Not that I was *trying* to turn him on. It was just the circumstances, being on the bed, him with nothing on except his sheet and me in only my nightshirt, and the way he felt.

It might be that same way tonight, except that we'd be in a dark room with nobody likely to walk in on us.

Oh, man.

She turned off the faucet. The way she was bent over the faucet, the mirror gave her a view straight down the hanging front of her nightshirt.

If I bend down to pull out the trundle bed, and Andy's watching from the front . . . I can pretend I don't know where he's looking.

Real nice, Jody. Why play games? Just shuck it off and the hell with it.

Grimacing at her reflection, Jody straightened up.

She took a deep breath. She was trembling. She shook her head.

How can I even *think* about messing around with Andy?

He's not your brother, you know.

Yeah, I know that. But aside from being a twelve-year-old kid, he's also annoying as hell. I can hardly *stand* him half the time, so why would I want to fool around with him?

Maybe because you love him.

I don't. Not that, way, anyhow.

Jody told herself that. She wasn't certain that she believed it.

But she was suddenly certain of one thing: she wouldn't be returning to the guest room tonight.

I have to, she realized. My pillow and sheet are in there.

Okay. That's okay. I'll just go in and grab them. Maybe Andy won't even wake up. I'll just sneak out again, and find somewhere else to sleep. Maybe on my bedroom floor. I can get my sleeping bag out of the closet . . .

Oh, yeah? You took it to sleep over at Evelyn's house, remember? It's all burnt up.

She wished she hadn't thought about that.

I'll just sleep on my floor without it, she decided.

She opened the bathroom door.

The man in the hallway grinned at her.

She didn't have time to move.

She didn't have time to thumb off her safety, much less bring up the pistol and fire it.

She didn't have time to cry out.

Chapter Forty-three

Jody had time only to see him.

A man about her own size, the top of his head bristly with short whiskers, his eyes atwinkle with glee in a face that looked feminine and might have been very pretty except that one side of it was so wrecked with bruises and runny wounds. She got the impression that he was naked.

Even as she caught her first glimpse of him, she wanted to call out for help and she wanted to shoot him.

Before she had time to do either, he slammed a fist into her belly.

Jody folded at the waist.

As she sank to her knees, she saw that he wore a mini-skirt. It was nearly the same color as his skin. A hunting knife was sheathed at his hip. On his feet were white socks and blue sneakers.

He stepped on her left hand, pinning the pistol down and mashing her fingers. The pain wrenched her mouth open. She had not breath to cry out.

Crouching in front of her, he grabbed her hair and jerked her head up. 'Hello, Jody,' he whispered. 'I'm Simon. Remember me?'

She didn't try to answer. All she could do was fight to suck air into her lungs.

But she remembered him, all right.

'We're gonna have some great fun,' he whispered.

He took his foot off Jody's hand and pulled the pistol out from under her throbbing fingers. Then he stood up, lifting her by the hair.

Pivoting, he swung her across the hall and pushed her backward into her father's bedroom.

She choked out, 'Dad!'

The overhead lights came on. Simon's right arm was out, the barrel of the gun at the switch.

Now the barrel was swinging toward Jody.

He shoved her.

Stumbling away, falling, she watched him aim at a point above her head.

Bam Bam Bam Bam! Bam Bam!

In the midst of the gunshots, she heard her father cry out.

Then she struck the floor – rump, then back, then head.

Simon, beyond her feet, had stopped firing. White smoke curled up out of the muzzle. The pistol's slide was back.

It's out?

There could've been two more rounds. Andy had been last to load the magazine. He must've quit at six.

He shot Dad six times, oh my God, oh my Jesus, no!

Simon dropped the pistol. He pulled the knife from its sheath. 'One down, one to go.'

One to go?

Does he mean me or Andy?

Maybe he doesn't know about Andy.

Simon shook the blade at her. 'Stand up.'

As she got to her feet, she turned around to see her father. She glimpsed him sprawled on the mattress, motionless, his pajama shirt open, blood everywhere.

'No!'

She spun and threw herself at Simon.

His knife was out, waiting for her.

She didn't care.

She expected it to push way deep into her belly, and she wondered how it would feel.

At the last moment, she hunched down slightly and rammed him with her shoulder. Simon grunted. He fell backward through the doorway and crashed to the hall floor, Jody on top of him. The impact jolted her. But she didn't feel any horrible sickening pain, didn't feel a blade buried in her anywhere.

Underneath her, Simon chuckled.

'Knew you'd be like this,' he said. 'Feisty. A real scrapper. Love it.'

She tried to push herself up, but he clamped an arm across her back and held her tight against him. When she tried to kick, she found her legs trapped between his legs.

She felt a tug down by the side of her left thigh. Then came a ripping sound.

So that's where the knife is.

Where's Andy?

Go on ahead and cut the thing to ribbons, you bastard.

'ANDY! ANDY! RUN FOR IT!'

'Shut up!'

'GET OUT OF THE HOUSE! HE'S HERE! HE'S HERE! YEOW!'

'Shut up, or I'll stab you again.' Simon rolled and hurled her aside. He scrambled to his feet and raced up the hallway toward the guest room.

How does he know . . .?

'HE'S AFTER YOU!' Jody shouted. 'GET OUT THE WINDOW! HURRY!'

Simon snarled over his shoulder at her.

She propped herself up with an elbow and looked down to check the damage.

There was plenty of light from the open doors on both sides of the hallway.

Her nightshirt had been slit up the side almost to her armpit. Simon had stabbed her just below the hip. The half-inch wound sent blood trickling both ways, down to her groin and down the slope of her buttock.

She struggled to get up, and was on her knees by the time Simon slammed open the guest room door.

A moment later, light spilled into that end of the hallway.

'You little shit!' she heard Simon yell.

Eyes on the guest room's doorway, Jody got to her feet.

I could get away!

Instead, she dashed for the guest room. She was surprised that she could run so well. Her left leg looked strangely healthy, striding out bare and sleek, but pain from the stab wound radiated down to her toes and all the way up the back of her neck.

How bad'll it hurt if he really *stabs me?*

If?

When's more like it.

So what?

She was almost to the guest room door when Simon lurched out in front of her.

He was not splattered with blood.

He clutched the front of Jody's nightshirt, swung her, and slammed her hard against the wall.

'Neat play,' he muttered through his clenched teeth. 'But it isn't gonna help you.'

'He got away?'

'Doesn't matter. I've got you. You're mine.' He jerked her away from the wall. Using the clump of nightshirt like a handle, he rushed her down the hall. She stumbled sideways. Though Simon was no larger than Jody, he seemed far stronger. He didn't even seem to be *bothered* by her struggles.

In her father's bedroom, he threw her to the floor.

He went to the bed, grabbed Dad by one arm and dragged him sideways.

On hands and knees, Jody cried out, 'Leave him alone!'

Dad tumbled off the edge of the mattress and struck the floor.

'You dirty fucking bastard!'

Simon came at her, grinning. 'That's what I like. Spirit. Give me hell, honey.'

Jody started crawling backwards.

She saw that Simon had an erection. It stuck straight out, propping up the front of his mini-skirt, terribly big and stout, the slot at its tip glistening.

He's gonna stick it in me.

That big, awful thing.

'Cops,' she gasped. 'They'll be here in a minute.'

'Oh, I doubt it. Bet I've got at least ten. And that's *after* Andy calls. First, he's gotta get to a phone that works – find a neighbor to let him in? We'll have *plenty* of time.'

He clamped the knife between his teeth to free his hands, rushed Jody, grabbed hold of her upper arms and hoisted her up. He swung around. He drove her backward. He hurled her down on the bed.

She bounced on the mattress and slid on the warm goo of her father's blood.

Taking the knife from his teeth, Simon knelt on the end of the bed. He leaned forward and grabbed her ankles. As he pulled her toward him, he spread her feet apart. Kneeling between them, he tugged at a Velcro fastener at the side of his skirt. He tossed his skirt to the floor. He still wore a leather belt and knife sheath.

He crawled between Jody's knees. He flapped the loose front of her nightshirt out of the way, bent over and resumed cutting it.

Jody listened for sirens.

She didn't hear any.

She heard only her own rough heartbeat and breathing, and the whispery sound of Simon's knife slicing the fabric beneath her arm. Then came a quiet giggle and a blast of pain that made Jody buck and whimper.

He'd stabbed her armpit.

'Was it good for you?' he whispered.

'Fuck you,' she gasped.

'Oh, no. Fuck *you*.' Instead of continuing to cut her nightshirt, he put the knife between his teeth and grabbed the neck of the garment with both hands. He jerked. As the fabric split in front, he tugged it off her shoulders and down to her knees. There, he was in the way. He crawled backward until he was past her feet.

Where he had to be kneeling at the very end of the mattress.

Jody raised her head. She saw him pull the bunched rag of nightshirt off her feet and toss it aside.

She spread her legs. She raised her knees. She pushed at the mattress with her heels and slid herself a few inches toward the head of the bed.

She was careful not to move far.

Simon grinned. He took the knife out of his mouth. 'Where

do you think *you're* going?' he asked, and began to crawl toward her.

'Leave me alone,' she gasped.

'You're so beautiful. This is gonna be so great.'

She drew her knees up and farther apart.

Simon's gaze latched on where she knew it would. He moaned. He licked his lips. He leaned toward her. 'Oh, this is even better than . . .'

Jody shot her legs forward. Her feet clapped against his shoulders. With a yelp, he tumbled backward and vanished off the end of the bed. He thudded to the floor and grunted.

Jody rolled fast to her right, to the side of the bed that didn't have her father on the floor. Even in her rush to save herself, she didn't want to step on him. She didn't want to *see* him, not all bloody and dead.

Her feet hit the floor. As she stood, she saw Simon on his back past the end of the bed. He was propped up on his elbows, gaping at her. He had the knife in his right hand. He shook its blade at her. 'Which do you want first, babe? This – or *this?*' He thrust up his hips.

I'll never get past him!

Then she seemed to hear her father's voice. *Never say never, kid. Go for it. Go for broke.*

She went for it. Hurling herself forward. Dashing alongside the bed, teeth gritted against the pain of her old and new wounds. Pouring on the speed. Seeing the surprise on Simon's face.

Surprise and joy.

He rolled to intercept her.

She leaped high.

The knife got her in the back of the leg, in the crease behind her knee.

She cried out. When she came down from her leap, her

left leg folded. She slammed the floor. The rug scorched her as she slid.

Gotta have the knife!

Squirming, she reached back to pull it from her leg. Her fingertips found only the raw gash.

She twisted around and saw Simon crawling toward her. The knife was still in his hand.

'*FREEZE! DON'T MOVE A MUSCLE OR YOU'RE DEAD MEAT!*'

Andy!

Jody looked up and saw him standing in the doorway only a few feet in front of her. He wore the pale blue pajamas that Dad had bought for him in Indio. He held Jody's .22, its muzzle aimed beyond her.

He hadn't escaped out the guest-room window, after all.

Must've hidden somewhere.

Couldn't run away and leave me to this bastard.

Came to save me.

To save me with an empty gun.

The Smith & Wesson in Andy's hand was the same pistol that Simon had used on Dad.

Simon had dropped it – almost in the same place where Andy now stood – after running out of ammo.

But its slide was forward as if it were loaded and cocked.

Andy's arm stiffened, 'I said FREEZE! I mean it! I'll shoot!'

'Not with *that*, you won't.'

'You wanta bet?'

'Fire away.'

Andy shook his head. 'You just want me to waste my ammo.'

'You don't *have* any ammo,' Simon said. 'Have you ever seen Jody naked before? Look at her, Look at her lovely legs.' Hands clutched her ankles. 'Wouldn't you like to do this to her?'

Andy watched, his eyes very wide, his mouth open.

Jody twisted her head around and saw Simon, on his knees, sink down and kiss the calf of her left leg. He kissed it only once, then began to lick up her blood. He worked his way higher, his tongue darting out and stroking her. It felt slimy. She supposed a snail would feel like this. Or a slug. A leech, a blood sucker.

When he came to the back of her knee, he sucked hard on the gash.

Jody flinched and swung her head around and looked up at Andy.

The boy seemed transfixed.

'Don't *let* him!' Jody gasped. 'Shoot him!'

Right. Shoot him with an empty gun.

'You'd like to do this, too, wouldn't you?' Simon asked, his voice soft and sweet. 'Look at her lovely ass. Mmm.'

Jody felt him kiss one buttock, then the other. Then his tongue slid down her crack.

'For God's sake, Andy!'

The front of Andy's pajama pants now jutted out.

'Don't *let* him. Please.'

'Stop,' Andy said. He didn't sound as if he meant it. His voice was a quiet monotone. 'You'd better stop, mister.'

Simon bit her right buttock.

The pain was odd and familiar. She knew it from sliding into bases. A pain that hurt but also made you feel like giggling. She felt a thickness in her throat. Tears blurred her vision. She lowered her head and started to cry.

Simon's teeth clamped her other buttock.

Bam!

She jerked. Simon's teeth released her, this time without biting.

Jody blinked tears from her eyes and raised her head.

Andy had the pistol pointed at Simon. She twisted her head around.

Simon, on his knees between her legs, was straightening himself up from the waist. His hands were by his sides. The knife was in the sheath hanging from his belt. He had a surprised look in his eyes. His face was all bloody – the tip of his nose, his lips and cheeks. Blood even dripped off his chin.

He's shot through the mouth!

Wait, she thought. No. He couldn't have been shot through the mouth. Not with my butt in his teeth.

Then where . . .?

Nowhere, that's where.

If he'd been shot, he probably wouldn't be grinning.

His front teeth were bloody.

'Told you it was loaded,' Andy said. He didn't sound so strange, now. Almost like normal, but not quite. 'I was here before. I was here when you had Jody on the bed. That's when I got the gun. But it was empty, so then I had to go to Jody's room for the other magazine.'

'Very clever,' Simon said. 'You know, I could use a smart young man like you. We could team up. How would you like that? Just imagine.'

'*Shoot* him, damn it! What'd you do, fire a warning shot? You should've blown his head off!'

'I was afraid I'd hit you,' he mumbled.

'You won't hit me *now*! Shoot him! He killed my dad! He killed *your* mom and dad. And Evelyn. He . . .'

'That isn't true, Andy. I'll take some blame for shooting Jody's old man, but he didn't give me any choice. It was a pure and simple case of self-defense. As for *your* family, I had nothing to do with it.'

'That's a lie!' Jody blurted. 'We *saw* you. You're one of the guys that chased us. You had me on the grass.'

'I'm not saying I wasn't there,' Simon explained. 'But I was there to *stop* the others. I wanted to *prevent* them . . .'

'Liar!' She swung her head around and looked up at Andy. He still had the pistol aimed at Simon. He was frowning. He looked befuddled. The front of his pajamas still stuck out, but not so far as before. 'Don't listen to him, Andy. He's trying to mess up your head.'

'The fact is, I *killed* the men who murdered your family. Did you know that?'

'And you know *why* he killed them, too,' Jody said. 'He didn't do it for *you*. It had nothing to do with that.'

'But I *did* kill them, Andy. I made them pay. I killed every last one of them.'

'Shoot him, damn it!'

Andy shook his head. 'I wanta know where he took the bodies, first.'

'Whose bodies?' Simon asked.

'My mom and dad and sister.'

'I didn't take them anywhere. I was left behind to deal with you and Jody. But I know what was *usually* done with bodies. I know where we buried the parts we didn't want anymore. I can take you there. Not if you shoot me, though.'

'Do it!' Jody blurted.

Andy again shook his head. 'I wanta know how he did it, too.'

Simon grinned. 'How I did what, *amigo*?'

Jody shoved at the floor to push herself up.

Simon gave her rump a single, hard spank. The swat landed where he'd bitten her. The blast of pain made her whole body spasm. She gave a huge gasp. She was suddenly limp on the floor, panting for air, weeping.

God, Andy! Andy! Are you gonna let him do that to me?

'You didn't have to do that,' Andy muttered.

'She was interfering with us. Sometimes, you have to be a little rough with these bitches. You know? And do you know what else? They like it. Turns 'em on. Now. What else is it that you want me to explain?'

'You were supposed to be dead. That's how come we came back. So how . . . one of the burnt guys wasn't you, huh?'

'*Five* of the burnt guys weren't me.' Simon sounded very cheerful.

'Who was it that was supposed to be you?'

'Guess.'

'I don't wanta guess. And I don't want you hurting Jody anymore, either. So just don't move. Talk, but stay still or I *will* shoot you.'

'Wouldn't you like to have Jody turn over? Wouldn't you like to see . . .?'

'Shut up. How did you trick us?'

'How much do you know?'

'Sergeant Fargo heard your tapes. He told us all about them.'

'Did he? I knew he was rambling on and on about *something*, but . . .'

'What do you mean? You were *here*?'

'In the attic. Sitting quiet as a mouse. Ever since . . . oh, some time before sunrise this morning.'

'You were here all day?'

'Oh, yes. Sitting up there in the dark and the heat, all by my lonesome, all day long and into the night.'

'How'd you get in the house?'

He chuckled. 'Why, I came in through the kitchen window. The same way I entered when I paid my first visit. Pretty smart, don't you think? Nobody even *considered* the possibility that I might be in the house *today*. Did you?'

'They all said you were supposed to be dead.'

'Just as I planned it. You see, I was very careful to point out on my tapes that there would be *four* fellows in the garage. You didn't hear the tapes, though. Right?'

'Right.'

'If you *had* heard them, you might remember a point soon after I left Indio – and before I kidnapped my fake Jody – when I mentioned wishing I'd thought to grab Dusty's bullet-proof vest.'

'Didn't hear about that,' Andy said.

'Well, it's there. Now, here's one of my little tricks. Paying attention? Just after talking about how I wished I'd taken Dusty's vest, I turned off my recorder. And I found a freeway exit. And I turned around and drove all the way back to Indio. I went straight back to the house where I'd killed Dusty and Ranch and the kid.'

'Henry?' Andy asked.

'Right. Henry. Henry the kid, not Henry the hound. Well, everything was just the way I'd left it. Only hotter and stinkier.' He chuckled. 'Anyway, here's what I did. I took Dusty's bullet-proof vest – which I later wore underneath my shirt when I went into the garage to kill Tom and the rest of them. Not only that, but I also took Henry's body out to my car and locked it in the trunk. Right in broad daylight. Very risky, very exciting. A little risk spices things up, you know – makes things tastier. Risk is the mustard on the hot dog of life.'

'He was in my trunk all the way back to LA. But he had some company after I grabbed the girl. You should've seen her, Andy. She sure didn't enjoy being shut up in the trunk in the dark with that boy. Talk about freaking out! You should've heard her screams! When I pulled her out to fuck her in the desert, she was all covered with blood and shit from the kid. It was incredible. I'd probably have to give her a ten, when it comes right down to it.'

'Of course, she wasn't anywhere near as hot as our Jody here. Have you ever seen a better-looking girl than our Jody?'

'Don't talk about her like that.'

'It turns you on.'

'Does not. Shut up. What happened at the garage?'

'Oh, it was choice. It was *choice*, Andy. First off, I made sure the tapes were just right – really hammed it up so it'd look like I went in expecting to bite it. And of course I never mentioned one word about wearing Dusty's vest or having an extra stiff in the trunk. The whole idea was to trick the cops into thinking I was dead along with the other guys. So you'd come back to LA. Not *you*. Jody. It was all for Jody.'

'I wanted her, pure and simple. Well, maybe not quite so *pure*, huh? But I *had* to have her, that's the thing. She's spectacular. So gorgeous and sweet . . . and innocent. But you know that, Andy. You want her as much as I do, don't you?'

Andy didn't answer.

Jody *knew* the answer.

Andy wanted her. She had no doubt at all about that.

Yeah, he does. Sure, he does. But he's not like this guy. He's just a kid, a horny kid. He wants me, but he won't go for this sort of stuff.

Not Andy.

'This gal was naked, the same as Jody. Only like a dumpy version of her. She wasn't any dog, but she wasn't a fox, either. You know? What do you say we turn Jody over? I *know* you wanta see what's up front.'

'Don't,' Jody said. She didn't look up, didn't move at all, just lay stretched out, arms crossed under her face, and spoke her word at the carpet.

She hoped the small protest wouldn't cause Simon to smack her again.

She waited for the blow.

'She doesn't need to turn over,' Andy said.

'A little later, maybe.'

'You went in the garage with Karen in front of you for a shield?'

'Was that her name, Karen?'

'Yeah.'

'Hmm. Anyway, yes. And they were waiting for us. Mitch opened the door and stepped back to let us in. I had my left arm across the gal's neck. Karen? My right hand was behind her back, where the guys couldn't see it. I had a .45 automatic in it. And I had Dusty's magnum shoved down the front of my skirt. And like I said, she was naked. Not that Mitch or Chuck could give a rat's ass – couple of fruits – but I knew it'd perk up Clement and Tom.'

'Soon as we were in the garage, I spotted Lisa. My fiancée? She was hanging by her wrists. You could see they'd done a few things to her. She had a lot of welts and stuff . . . clothes pins clipped to her nipples . . . They'd shaved her, burnt her with cigarettes. Matter of fact, they'd done a *lot* to her. A lot of really cool stuff. Pissed me off. But they hadn't done any real mutilations, you know? They'd had fun with her, but they hadn't totally fucked her up.'

'When she saw me come in, she gave me this really nasty look. Like I was to blame, or something.'

'Anyway, I told the guys that this gal I had was Jody. She couldn't claim she wasn't, since I'd busted her jaw back there in the desert. Then I said I had Andy's body out in the trunk of my car.'

'Me?' Andy muttered.

'Sure, they wanted you dead. And I *could've* killed you, Andy. I had my chances. I had you and Jody both in my rifle sights when you were at that motel in Indio.'

'You did?'

467

'Sure. But I didn't fire. I liked you, so I decided to give them Henry's body instead of yours. Anyway, everything went along slick as snot. When I told about having you in the trunk, Mitch and Chuck were all set to go out and get you. The thing is, they were pretty sure to know Henry wasn't you. These guys were with me Friday night, chasing you and Jody around. They hadn't seen you up close, but they weren't likely to be fooled by this kid in the trunk, who was pretty big and husky. So I figured I'd better go into action while they were still in the garage.'

'I gave that gal Karen a shove, sent her flying. She hadn't even hit the floor yet before I had guns in both my hands. Man, I took those suckers *totally* by surprise. They didn't know whether to shit or go blind. None of 'em even got their hands on a weapon. I just blew them all down. It was choice, Andy. Took me about two seconds, and all four of 'em were spread out dead on the floor. Not even Eastwood could've done a sweeter job on those asswipes.'

'But then I've got this bitch Karen making a run for it. I was out of ammo. So I went chasing after her, meanwhile digging into my shirt pocket for my Derringer. I hadn't used it yet, so it had two shots in it. I missed with the first shot, so then I waited until I was right on her heels. She was way out on the driveway by then. I plugged her smack in the back. Man! It was great. You ever kill a gal, Andy? It's a trip. Nothing like it. You'll see.'

'You didn't kill her,' Andy said.

'Shut up,' Jody said.

'What do you mean, I didn't kill her?'

Jody raised her head. Andy still had the pistol aimed toward Simon. He still had a jut in the front of his pajama pants, too. 'Don't say another word, Andy. Do you want him to go and try to finish . . .?'

Simon swatted the back of her head.

'Hey!' Andy blurted.

'Come on, let's do her!' Simon clutched Jody's upper arms and pulled, hoisting her off the floor. As she came up onto her knees, they skidded on the carpet until she bumped his body. He hooked his left arm across her throat and jerked her tight against him.

'Look at her, Andy. Look at her.'

He didn't need any urging. His gaze was already fixed on Jody's breasts.

Simon's right arm reached around in front of her. Reached all the way across to her left breast. Cupped its underside. Squeezed it.

Jody tried to struggle, but quit when he tightened his chokehold.

'I'll hold her still for you,' Simon said. 'Come here and feel her. Have you ever touched a tit? Come here. See how sweaty and shiny it is? Come here. Touch. It's all slick and hot and springy.' Simon squeezed it a few times quickly. 'You want to do that, don't you? How would you like to kiss it? How about sucking it? You could suck this baby into your mouth, fill your mouth with it, flick the nipple with your tongue, *chew* on it. Wouldn't you just love to chew on it, Andy? Suck and chew while you shove that cock of yours way up . . .'

'You're strangling her. Quit it.'

The arm across Jody's throat eased off slightly. 'Sorry. You're in charge, Andy. You're *totally* in charge. I'll do anything you say. Consider me your servant. I'll hold her still while you do anything you want. Okay?'

Keeping the pistol aimed at Simon's face, Andy used the back of his other hand to rub his lips. His eyes had stayed locked on Jody's breasts except for a few times when they glanced lower. From the moment she'd been pulled to her knees, he hadn't looked once at her face.

'Come on, Andy,' Simon said. 'There's no reason to hold off. Nobody'll ever know about this. You've got a magnificent boner, there. You don't wanta let it go to waste, do you? How would you like to have Jody suck on that for you? Easy as pie. Just drop your PJs and take two giant steps forward. She'll be happy to open up wide for you. Show him how you open up wide, Jody.'

She clamped her teeth together.

'Is that any way to behave?'

Simon twisted her nipple. Her mouth sprang open.

Andy fired.

Chapter Forty-four

Jody and Simon both cried out in pain through the crack of the gunshot. Abruptly, Simon quit twisting her nipple. His left arm jerked hard against her throat.

It had to be a head shot.

With his chin on Jody's right shoulder, his head was the only part of Simon that wasn't shielded.

He'd been shot, so he *must've* been hit in the head.

But instead of falling away behind her, he slammed her forward straight at Andy's legs. Andy gasped. Jody threw her arms out to catch herself. Her hands pounded the floor. She tried to prop herself up but Simon's weight on her back was too much for her. Her arms buckled. He drove her down hard against the floor as he scurried over her.

Why wasn't Andy still firing?

Afraid he'll hit me?

'Shoot him!' Jody gasped. 'Shoot! Shoot!'

Simon's shoe scuffed her cheek.

Raising her head, she saw him plow headfirst into Andy's stomach. Though lifted off his feet by the blow, Andy kept hold of the pistol.

Its muzzle was pointed at Jody.

It swung toward Simon's side as Andy was rushed backward out of the bedroom.

'Shoot him!' Jody yelled.

Simon slammed Andy against the hallway wall and the pistol dropped to the floor.

Jody scrambled for it.

Eyes on Simon.

And couldn't believe her eyes.

No!

Andy, pinned against the wall by Simon's forearm across his throat, bucked and twitched as Simon's other hand punched the hunting knife into his belly again and again.

Blood washed out over Simon's thrusting hand.

Jody slapped her right hand down on the pistol.

Simon, whirling around, kicked her in the forehead.

'Wake up, babe. Wake up, now. It's all over. Everything's fine.'

Jody felt soft, moist lips against her mouth.

She felt a bed beneath her back.

Opening her eyes, she saw that it was Andy kissing her.

Had it been Andy's voice?

She wasn't sure. But it was definitely Andy kissing her.

This isn't right, she thought. He shouldn't be kissing me like this. He's only twelve and . . .

And I saw Simon kill him.

No, that must've been a nightmare, because this is Andy for sure.

Something funny about him, though.

About the way his weight was pressing down on her. Something not quite right about that. And something very *wrong* about how a whole lot of drips were splashing her just below her neck.

Her mind seemed fuzzy, though. Dull and numb.

Before she could figure out anything at all, Andy's lips stopped pressing against hers. She watched his face glide away. As it moved, so did the drips. They pattered lower on her chest, down between her breasts.

And then she saw the hands against the sides of Andy's head, the raw and stringy stump of his neck.

Gimme a break, she thought.

Can't be.

But it is, oh yes. It sure is.

Then she heard herself start to scream.

She thrashed and squirmed. Someone was sitting across her hips. And someone had tied her down. Her arms and legs were spread wide, stretched out toward the four corners of her father's bed, bound at the wrists and ankles.

When she ran out of breath, she screamed again.

Andy's head moved aside and Simon grinned down at her.

Andy's bullet hadn't missed him. It had cut a bloody furrow straight back from the corner of Simon's right eye and across his temple, then knocked a hole through his ear. A fraction of an inch more to the right, and it would've missed him completely. A fraction more to the left would've put the bullet into his eye and killed him.

Even as Jody kept on screaming, a part of her mind remained rational enough to consider what a close shot it had been.

If Andy's aim had been just *slightly* better . . .

If he'd fired a few more rounds yesterday . . .

'Hey!' Simon yelled. 'Quiet! What do you wanta do, wake the dead?'

When she didn't stop screaming, he shoved Andy's neck down against her mouth. It was wet and spongy except for the bone of the spinal column that scraped against the edge of her lower teeth. The neck muffled her scream. And then the draining fluids choked her.

Simon lifted the head and smiled as she coughed.

'He was *so* hot for you,' Simon said. 'Missed his chance, though. I was gonna let him all over you. He would've had the time of his life, the stupid fuck.' Simon turned the head around and brought it close to his face. 'You stupid little fuck! You *blew* it! You were too fuckin' *dumb* to live!' Then he twisted sideways and hurled Andy's head. It crashed against the bedroom wall, bounced off, and thudded against the carpeted floor. It left a bright red smudge on the wallpaper.

Simon held his open hands toward Jody's face.

They were gloved with blood.

'You ever seen so much blood? Whose do you figure it is? Your Dad's? Andy's? Mine? Yours? Like a multiple choice test, huh? Answer's gotta be *E*, all of the above.' He turned his hands over. 'A little blood from everyone, don't you think? Sort of a party mix.' A grin spreading his mouth, he lowered his hands to Jody's breasts.

From the feel, he might've been rubbing lotion on her. His hands were slidy and sticky. They circled, caressed, patted, squeezed and tugged.

They made wet snicking sounds.

He was watching his hands at work. As he watched, he writhed against Jody where he sat on her.

And he moaned.

She raised her head off the mattress. Glimpsed his hands playing her breasts, painting them scarlet. Started between them at his stout penis pointing toward her face. The way it jutted out from down where their bodies met, it almost looked as if it had sprouted from her own groin. But it moved slightly from side to side, even though she was lying still, and she could feel the furry sack of Simon's scrotum rubbing her.

She saw the knife sheathed by his right hip.

No way for her to reach it, though. Not as long as she was tied this way.

Just let it stay where it is.

Just let him leave it there, and not use it on me.

Are You up there, God? Listening? Fat damn chance of that, after what happened to Dad and Andy. But if You . . .

Never mind.

Screw it.

Everybody's dead but me, anyhow . . .

Simon let go of her breasts. Hands on the mattress by her sides, he eased himself down and swirled his tongue around her right nipple. He licked it clean. Then he went at the rest of her breast, his tongue thrusting and sliding, taking the blood off her like a dog lapping up honey. He did it feverishly, gasping and groaning, slobbering. Soon, all the blood was gone from that breast, leaving it shiny with his spit.

He raised his head and grinned at her.

He had a ring of red around his lips.

Then he spread his mouth wide open – wider than seemed possible – and lowered it back down onto the breast. He sucked hard. His mouth felt like a horrible, toothed vacuum cleaner. She could feel her breast stretching, going in deeper and deeper.

And she felt the head of his penis shove against the lips of her vagina.

He's gonna bite!

He's gonna wait till he's got that horrible thing of his in me, and then he's gonna bite off my boob and . . .

– SNICK-CLACK –

A familiar sound. A great sound.

It came from very close by.

Just to her left.

Jody jerked her head to the left as Dad's face rose up beside the bed. Bloody. All bloody except for the whites of his eyes and the teeth exposed by his snarling lips.

His face rose up past the edge of the mattress. His shoulders followed. And his shoulders were followed by the short black saviour of his pistol-grip Mossberg shotgun. The muzzle glided forward over Jody's left breast and stopped an inch from Simon's gouged, raw temple.

As Jody saw this, she felt Simon's mouth loosen its sucking hold on her breast.

His penis quit trying to prod its way in.

A low, whispery voice said, 'Turn your face away, honey.'

She followed orders.

The mouth very quickly released her breast. 'Hey, man, don't shoot. I . . .'

KRA-BOOOOM!!!

Along with the enormous punishing wonderful noise came a hot blast, a gust that flung Jody's hair and blew like a quick, mean sandstorm against her chest and neck and upturned cheek.

With her head turned away, she couldn't avoid seeing the shower of mess from Simon's head. A red spray. Chunks of bone. Gooey lumps. Most of it hit the wall more than five feet past the side of the bed.

Simon's gore completely covered the smudge he'd put on the wall by throwing Andy's head.

Jody watched it drip.

Better to watch it drip than to catch a glimpse of Simon. The blast had knocked him tumbling. He was about to flop off the edge of the bed. Jody could see enough, even with her eyes on the dripping wall, to know that he was face up and that his face was some sort of monstrous ruin.

She would rather not add that to the long list of things she had seen tonight and would never forget.

So she fixed her gaze on the splattered wall for another moment, until he'd dropped out of sight.

Even before he struck the floor, she turned her head to the left.

To see her father.

But he was gone.

Chapter Forty-five

'Dad?' Silence. 'Dad?'

'Honey?' His voice was no more than a whisper. 'You okay?'

'Sort of.'

'I got him, didn't I?'

'You sure did.'

'Thought so. The recoil . . . knocked me back down.'

'I thought you were dead.'

'You and me both, hon. Till you screamed. Sounded like a . . . damn banshee.'

'Are you okay?' In the midst of asking that, her voice broke upward. Tears flooded her eyes and she began to blubber. Her body shuddered as she cried.

She struggled to stop. Her father on the floor beside the bed might be dying. If she cried through his final seconds of life . . .

'I love you,' she sobbed. 'Dad?'

'Quit it, would you? You're gonna get *me* bawlin', and I . . . that's gonna hurt.'

'Okay.' She sniffed. It sounded loud and wet and slurpy.

'Christ, hon. Blow your nose.'

'Ha ha.' She didn't care that she couldn't blow her nose, but the tears made her eyes and cheeks itchy. She tried turning her head, hoping to rub the side of her face against her shoulder. The way her arms were stretched out, though, her shoulder was beyond reach. She turned her head the other way. Couldn't get to that shoulder, either. 'He's got me tied down so I can't move.'

'Yeah. Saw. The bastard. Was it *him*? Simon?'

'Yeah.'

'Supposed to be dead.'

'The body wasn't him. It was the kid he killed in Indio.'

'Huh? How . . .?'

'He faked us out. Some of the stuff on the tapes were lies. Andy got him to explain most of it before . . .'

'Andy? Oh, my God. Forgot about . . . Where is he?'

Here and there, Jody thought. And was shocked that her mind could tease her with a sick word game.

Might've made Andy laugh, though. Here and there.

'Simon killed him, Dad. He's dead.'

Dad was quiet for a few moments. Then he muttered, 'My God. I'm sorry, hon. I'm so sorry.'

'Yeah. Well . . . He . . . he had chances.'

'Huh?'

'All kinds of chances,' Jody said. 'Chances to get away. Chances to kill Simon. All kinds of chances. He . . . sort of screwed up all of them. One way or the other. It . . . didn't have to . . . turn out this way. And I guess I blew it, too. If only . . .'

'Don't,' Dad said. 'No point. What's done is done. The thing is . . . are you all right?'

She snuffled. 'Probably a lot better than you.'

'Hope so. God, honey.'

'I'm okay. Really. He stuck me with a knife a few times and they hurt like hell, but I think he just did it to hurt me, not . . . I don't think any of them are very deep.'

'Where'd he get you?'

'In the armpit. The hip. And the back of my leg. You know, right behind the knee. In the crease there. That one *really* hurts.'

'Bet it does.'

'Yeah. And, oh yeah, he bit me in the ass. Where'd he get you?'

He didn't answer. Instead, he asked, 'Did he . . . did he rape you?'

Jody felt herself blush.

Blushing seemed very strange at a time like this, but there was definitely a feeling of embarrassment, plus a sensation of heat rushing to her skin. Weird. Almost funny, considering.

'Jeez, Dad,' she muttered.

'I'm sorry. But . . . did he?'

'I don't think so.'

'You don't *know*?'

She focused down there. She forced some muscles to flex. 'Doesn't feel like it,' she said. 'I mean, I'm not sure what it's *supposed* to feel like after something like that, but ... I'm pretty sure he didn't.'

'Thank God,' Dad murmured.

'What about you?' Jody asked.

'I'm pretty sure he didn't rape me, either.'

'You don't *know*?'

She heard him laugh once, then groan. '*Jesus*, honey.'

'It only hurts when you laugh?' she asked.

'Hell, it hurts no matter what.'

'Are you bad?'

'I've always been bad.'

'Now who's making the cracks?'

'Okay. I'll stop. Where ... were we?'

'Where did he hit you?'

'Easier if I tell you where he didn't.'

'Dad.'

'Sorry.'

'It must be pretty bad, or you wouldn't be down there on the floor.'

'Good point. On the other hand ... how bad can it be ... if I'm conscious ... and chatting with you?'

'You *weren't* conscious, though.'

'Nope. Out like a light. One of 'em caught me in the noggin.'

'Oh, God.'

'It's not so bad. Went through my hand first. By the time it hit my head ... My *hand* isn't in such great shape, but ... Two wounds for the price of one, huh?'

'What about the others?' Jody asked. 'He shot you six times.'

'That many? Damn.'

He went silent.

'Dad?'

'Doing an inventory.'

'And?'

'Don't know, honey. Only got five holes here. And the one . . . got me twice. Guess he missed a couple of times.'

'How could he miss at that range?'

'Trying for head shots? That'd figure. Bastard thought he was hot . . . stuff.'

'He did awful good.'

'Till he ran up against me.'

'Guess he didn't shoot you in the ego.'

'The one place he missed.'

'You aren't gonna die, are you?'

'What time is it?' he asked.

'I don't know.'

'Sure hope Sharon comes . . . straight over after work.'

'She will.'

'She better.'

'She's in love.'

'Think so? With me?'

'Definitely.'

'Yeah?'

'And you know it.'

'She's some gal, huh?'

'A phenomenon.'

'Yep. Exactly.'

'You're pretty good, too.'

'Yep.'

'A phenomenon.'

'I sure pulled *your* butt out of the fire.'

'Just barely,' Jody said.

'Barely's just fine. I'll . . . settle for it.' Suddenly, he gasped as if surprised by a new stab of pain.

'Dad?'

'Oooo.'

'Are you okay?'

'Not very.'

'Oh, God. Can you last till Sharon gets here?'

He didn't answer.

'Dad? *Dad!*'

'Do you hear that?'

'What?'

'I think I hear a siren.'

Jody strained her ears.

And she heard a siren.

And the distant, faint cry of it was growing louder.

'Maybe somebody heard the shots,' she whispered.

They both went silent.

After a few seconds, Dad whispered, 'Is it coming here?'

'Sure sounds like it.'

Not far away – near enough to be on the street in front of their home – brakes shrieked and the siren died.

Jody heard two doors thud shut.

'Let's have a great big cheer for the good guys,' she said.

'Hope they've got strong stomachs,' Dad said.

'Yeah. What if Sharon's first through the door?'

She expected Dad to make a crack. *She'll have to clean it up.* Or, *Hope she doesn't get any on us.*

Instead, he said, 'That'd be great.'

'Yeah,' Jody said. 'Guess it would be.'

Midnight's Lair

One day, feeling oh so brave,
I went walking in a cave.

Now, I fear, I can't get out.
I'll die in here, I have no doubt.

I'll mold and turn to slimy bone
Here where the sun has never shown,
Where I'll die in darkness all alone,
Here in my tomb of ancient stone.

Remember me, before you dare
To Journey into midnight's lair.
Remember me, and what I write:

'Here lies one who loved the light
But he was curious and brave –
He went walking in a cave.'

'The Explorer'
Allan Edward DePrey

1

Darcy Raines, standing at the bow with her back to the group, grabbed a spike jutting from the cavern wall and stopped the boat. Keeping her grip on the spike, she turned sideways.

Kyle Mordock stared up at her. The first of the boat's bench seats was vacant. He sat on the second, next to a young couple holding hands. *His* seat.

Every day since Darcy began working as a guide through the cavern two weeks ago, the kid had shown up for at least one of her tours. There were other guides but he never went on their tours, just Darcy's. He always stayed close to her, usually managing to get the same seat for the boat ride, the one directly behind her, the one with the best view – not of the cavern, but of Darcy. He rarely spoke. He simply watched her with his tiny, feral eyes.

Now, he was staring at her rump. The way Darcy stood, sideways with one foot propped on the bow, her trousers were drawn taut against her buttocks. She could feel Kyle's eyes.

A fifteen-year-old lech.

Boss's son or not, she thought, I'll have to do something about this nonsense before he drives me nuts.

Tom stopped the second boat behind Darcy's, and nodded for her to start.

'End of the line, folks,' she said. 'Everybody out.'

There were murmurs and quiet laughter from many of the people on the boats. Several glanced from side to side as if prepared to follow her orders, then caught the joke and laughed more loudly than the others.

'You go first,' called a man in the second boat.

'Actually, the water is only about waist-deep in the Lake of Charon at this time of the year, though the level rises considerably higher in the spring with the seepage from melting snow and rain. But I wouldn't recommend taking a dip. The water is about fifty degrees.'

She glanced at Kyle. He was staring at her face. She turned her head away, and nodded towards the rock wall in front of the boat.

'This barrier,' she said, 'marks the end of the portion of the cavern that's accessible to the public. The wall was constructed in 1923 by Ely Mordock. Originally, it was possible to explore the entire length of the cavern – just over a mile. For a number of years, Ely led parties into the cave through its natural opening on the steep slope of the hillside near the eastern border of his property. The trip was an all-day, difficult hike, and not for the timid. In those days, they didn't have the walkway or lighting. Ely supplied waders, picnic lunches and torches.'

'But his dream was to make the wonders of the cavern accessible to the general public, not just a hardy few, so in 1921 he began construction of the elevators. The shafts were sunk 150 feet to provide an entrance at what had previously been the far end of the cavern. When those were completed, work was begun to install the lighting and walkway.'

'It was then that tragedy struck. On June 12, 1923, Ely and his wife, Elizabeth, were roaming an area somewhere between here and the natural opening when she slipped and fell into a deep chasm.'

An elderly woman muttered, 'Oh dear.'

'Ely lowered himself into the chasm on a rope, but the gap

into which his wife had fallen seemed bottomless and he was forced to abandon any hopes of saving her . . . or of retrieving her body.'

'He was grief-stricken, and determined that the chasm would never claim another life. So he sealed the cavern's natural opening, and built this rock wall as a permanent barrier to prevent anyone from entering the hazardous eastern half of the cave. In effect, that entire part of the cave became the tomb of Elizabeth Mordock.'

'That was over sixty years ago,' a man called from the second boat. 'Aren't there any plans to re-open that end?'

Darcy shook her head. 'Ely's will stipulated that the barriers should never be breached. His descendants have chosen to abide by his wishes.'

'Seems like a waste,' the man said.

A husky teenaged boy in Darcy's boat raised his hand as if he were in school. She called on him. 'What does that wall there do to the stream?'

'Good question. The wall restricts the natural flow of the River Styx. Before it was built, there was no Lake of Charon.'

'So, it's like a dam,' the boy said.

'Exactly. The river in this part of the cavern was only a few inches deep before the wall was built, and people could stroll through here instead of having to go by boat. In fact, portions of the original walkway are still intact below the surface.'

'How come the whole cave doesn't flood?'

'Ely was smart enough not to block the opening completely. He left a space near the bottom of the wall to allow water to run out. Any other questions before we head back?'

'I have one,' said a young woman two rows behind the boy. 'With the cave closed up like this, where does the air come from?'

'Originally, there were three elevators down from the

surface. After Ely blocked off the natural opening, one of the elevators was converted to a ventilation shaft. Fresh air is circulated from the surface, and that has the additional benefit of raising the cavern temperature during the summer months. It still may feel a little chilly to some of you, but the natural temperature of the cavern would be about fifty degrees Fahrenheit, like the water, if it weren't for the warm air from the shaft. That brings it up to about sixty.'

'If there aren't any more questions, we'll head back now. Before you know it, you'll be up top again and sweltering.'

Her comment was greeted by the usual chuckles and moans.

Someone said, 'No rush.' But there weren't any more questions.

'You may have noticed,' Darcy went on, 'that the first row of seats in each boat was left vacant. That was no oversight. We've got this whole thing *planned*. It's a lot easier to turn *you* around than the boats. So, I'd like those of you in the first occupied row to stand up carefully, do an about-face, and plant your bottoms on the seats we so conveniently left vacant for you.'

Following her instructions, the three people at the front of each boat stood, turned around, and sat down.

That included Kyle Mordock. Darcy was glad to be freed from his constant stare. Soon, she would be at the opposite end of the boat from him.

One row at a time, as she gave the word, the rest of the tourists reversed their positions by moving to the seats in front of them. There were seven benches in all. It didn't take long.

'Okay, now comes the fun part for me and Tom. If those of you on the left will scoot towards the centre, we'll perform our daring feat.'

'Drum roll, please,' said Tom.

Near the middle of Darcy's boat, a girl of about seven had her elbow on the gunnel. Darcy smiled at her and waved her in. Her mother pulled her out of the way.

Darcy let go of the spike. 'If Tom and I are very lucky,' she said, 'we may reach the other end of the boat without getting wet.'

The only guide to fall recently during this manoeuvre was Dick Hayden. He'd done it last week, on purpose as a treat for the tourists, and vowed he would never try that stunt again. When Darcy saw him step out of the elevator forty-five minutes later, his clothes were sodden, he was shivering and his face was blue. He came down with a cold, and missed three days of work.

Darcy knew of nobody falling into the cold water by accident. The walk to the other end of the boat might look tricky, but she considered it a cinch.

Arms out for balance, she stepped onto the gunnel. Though it was wider than her foot, she walked it as if it were a tight-rope. She saw Tom performing a similar act along the side of the other boat.

He disappeared.

Darcy felt as if her vision had been switched off.

She saw black.

Great time to lose the lights.

People gasped.

She wobbled, trying to keep her balance.

'SHIT!' From Tom.

Then a thud, a heavy splash.

Worried voices. 'Did he fall? . . . He fell! . . . Oh, my God!'

'Quiet!' Darcy yelled. 'Everyone stay seated!' She clawed at her side, snatched the flashlight from her belt, switched it on and swept its beam to the second boat. Tom wasn't there. Fear squeezed her chest.

'Tom!' she called. No answer.

Her pale beam darted over the water along the port side of the boat.

It's only waist-deep! Where is he?

She saw the blunt top of the stalagmite known as Satan's Buoy jutting from the surface less than a yard from Tom's boat.

He'd been next to it when the cave went dark.

That thud.

Oh Jesus!

Darcy pointed her flashlight at the gunnel in front of her feet and rushed along it. The passengers in both boats were silent, an audience captivated by a strange show. At the stern, Darcy raised her flashlight overhead and kicked out. The leap carried her out past the squared corner of Tom's boat. Frigid water sprayed her face, wrapped her legs, seized her groin like a hand of ice. Her feet hit the bottom. They started to slide. She hooked her left arm over the edge of the boat and caught herself.

Her flashlight probed the water. She could see the bottom under its bent beam.

Tom was not beside the boat.

Turning, she swept the light over the surface on both sides of Satan's Buoy.

'Maybe he's *under* the boat,' someone said. 'I think I heard a bumping . . .'

'Take this.' Darcy thrust the flashlight at the nearest passenger. It was pulled from her hand.

She took a deep breath. Her lungs felt shrunken. Ducking, she slipped an arm under the metal hull. She thrust herself down. The chill water seemed to squeeze her head. It soaked through her jacket and blouse and bra. It gripped her skin.

Her eyes were open, but she saw nothing.

She waddled through the shallow water under the boat, the back of her head and shoulders rubbing along its hull, her arms waving, searching.

Her right hand swept against something round. Tom's head? She curled her fingers in, the middle finger finding a small ridge, the two on either side touching marblesized . . .

His eyes. They felt *open*.

Darcy flinched and jerked her hand away. Then she reached out, arms spread to avoid his face. She found his shoulders, clutched his jacket with both hands, and dragged Tom sideways.

Clear of the boat, she straightened up. There was a splash as someone jumped into the water behind her. She jerked Tom, and he burst to the surface. The flashlight found his face. His head was tilted sideways. Water spilled from his mouth.

His open eyes were rolled upward, only the whites showing.

'Let's get him into the boat.' It was the man who'd jumped into the water. He waded past Darcy, wrapped his arms around Tom's chest, and walked backward, pulling the limp body to the stern of the boat. The beam of the flashlight stayed with them. 'Hang onto him.'

Darcy hugged Tom to her chest. She felt his face against her cheek, felt his whiskers. He didn't seem to be breathing.

What if he's dead?

The man grabbed the side of the boat, thrust himself up, and climbed in. Bending over, he grabbed Tom beneath the armpits. As he started to haul the body up, Darcy released her hold. She clutched Tom's rump and lifted. He surged out of the water. For a moment, her hands were pinned between his buttocks and the gunnel, his open legs caught under her elbows. She slipped her hands free and raised her arms. His legs flew up and he dropped backward into the boat.

Darcy threw herself against the side in time to see the man lowering Tom onto the vacant bench. As she boosted herself up, the flashlight beam skipped from the man to Tom. She glimpsed the bloody right side of Tom's head. Then, the man was straddling him and bending down. Someone reached for Darcy, grabbed her upper arm, and gave her a helpful pull as she squirmed over the gunnel. She sprawled across that person's lap, slid off, and squeezed between his knees and the leg of the man on top of Tom.

'I know first-aid,' she said.

The man ignored her. His hand was around Tom's throat. Then he dug fingers into the mouth.

'Got a pulse?'

He nodded. His fingers came out, stringed with saliva. He tipped Tom's head back and blew into the open mouth.

He knows what he's doing, Darcy thought. Thank God.

She struggled to her feet and turned around. The flashlight was now in the hand of a young woman in the first seat. The woman kept it on Tom and the man.

Darcy heard a confused noise of voices all asking questions at once. She raised her hands for silence.

'I'm sure all of you are wondering . . . Tom fell when the lights went off, and I guess he hit his head on that stalagmite near the boat. But we have him now, and a gentleman's giving him artificial respiration. I think he'll be all right.'

'You're to be commended for your prompt action,' said a voice in the darkness.

There were mutters of agreement, scattered applause.

'The important thing now,' she said, 'is for all of us to remain calm.' She was shivering badly. She wrapped her arms across her chest. 'We've apparently had a power failure. I'm sure it's temporary, though, and the lights will come back on shortly. In the meantime, there's no cause for alarm. We're perfectly safe here. Hell, a cave is just about the safest place in the world to be, no matter what's going on topside.'

I shouldn't have said that.

The swell of murmurs had an uneasy tone.

'I'm not saying that anything has happened up top,' she added.

'What's the power source?' someone asked.

'Generators inside the complex.'

'This happened before?'

'Not that I know of. But I'm new here. Kyle!' she called. 'Have the generators gone down before?'

'Nope. Never.'

Shit.

'Something happened!'

'War,' someone muttered. 'A nuclear . . .'

'Don't be an ass,' Darcy snapped. 'It's probably just some kind of simple breakdown. They'll have it repaired in no time. So let's not upset everyone by making outlandish guesses about the . . .'

From behind Darcy came choking sounds. She twisted around. The man was rising quickly, turning Tom onto his side as watery vomit gushed and splattered from his mouth. It sprayed the pants of the woman holding the flashlight. Tom kept on heaving. Then he was coughing and groaning.

He's okay, Darcy thought.

But she felt no relief.

That jerk and his nuclear war.

My fault, she told herself. I probably put the idea in his head. Earthquakes and nuclear war. How a cavern's the safest place you can be. Maybe I'll knock that out of my spiel from now on.

But what *did* happen up there? Something sure as hell killed the power.

She thought about her mother, who had come to visit and was staying at the hotel directly above the cavern. What if there *was* a disaster?

'What about the elevators?' asked a voice from behind her.

She looked over her shoulder. 'They'll be out, too. But as I said, I'm sure the power will be restored shortly.'

'Terrific.'

'We're trapped,' somebody whispered nearby.

'I'm sure,' Darcy said, 'that we'll all be out of here in time for lunch.'

There were quiet voices, people discussing the situation, comforting their spouses and children, probably sharing their concern with friends and strangers.

Darcy turned again to Tom. He was standing up, coughing, pressing a folded handkerchief to the side of his head. The man held him steady with a hand on his shoulder.

'How are you doing, pal?' she asked.

He answered with a groan.

'Bad?'

'Shit warmed over,' he muttered.

It was good to hear his voice. Darcy's throat tightened. She ran a hand over the wet hair on top of his head. 'We'll get you out of here quick as we can.'

He looked up at her. The woman with the flashlight was smart enough not to shine it in his eyes, but the halo of its beam illuminated his face. His features seemed slack, eyelids drooping and mouth hanging open. 'What's . . .?'

'Power went out.'

He sighed, and that triggered a coughing fit.

The man on the bench beside him stood up next to Darcy. 'Why don't you stretch out?' he suggested to Tom. 'We'll find something to cover you up.'

'He can have my jacket,' said the man who had pulled Darcy into the boat.

She eased Tom down. He raised his feet and rested them on the gunnel. Soon, there were three jackets and a sweater on top of him.

'You look good and comfy,' she said.

'We should get him to a hospital as soon as possible,' said the man beside her. 'He's probably got shock and a mild concussion, but the head injury . . . you never know.'

Darcy looked at him. He was a big man, tall, with a broad face and wide shoulders. He wore a sweatshirt. 'Thanks for all the help,' she said. 'Are you a doctor?' He looked more like a football player than a doctor.

'I worked as a hospital orderly while I was going to law school. And I was a policeman for a couple of years. Maybe there is a doctor down here.'

With nearly forty tourists on the boats, there should be at least one doctor. Darcy turned her head around and asked.

No such luck.

'Well, it was worth a try.' She held out her hand to the man. 'I'm Darcy Raines,' she said, even though she had introduced herself to the entire group at the start of the tour.

'Greg Beaumont.' He wiped his hand on a leg of his jeans, reminding Darcy that it had been slick with Tom's saliva. She didn't care. She squeezed the big hand when he raised it.

'Thanks again,' she said. 'I don't know what I would've done.'

'You were doing just fine. But I'm glad I could help. Now, we'd better see what we can do about getting out of here.'

'We *can't* get out of here,' she whispered. 'The elevators are the only way, and . . .'

'We'd better at least go though some motions,' Greg said. 'These folks have been pretty good so far, but they're gonna start losing it.'

In the darkness behind them, a child began to cry.

2

They *will* start losing it, Darcy thought. But nobody was likely to get hurt as long as they stayed in the boats. The lights were sure to come on, sooner or later.

There was only one flashlight, unless Tom's still worked. In spite of the walkway and railings that led from the dock to the elevators, herding all these people through the darkness would be tricky. The walkway curved, sloped, had some stairs. A few falls were almost inevitable. And what about Tom? What if he couldn't walk under his own strength? He'd have to be helped along, or maybe even carried.

All to reach a pair of elevators that wouldn't function anyway, until the electricity was restored. At that point, the lights would be on. Why not just wait here, and make the return trip after the cavern was once again brightly lit?

What if that's hours from now?

What if that's tomorrow?

What if that's never?

The thought made Darcy feel tight and sick inside, and

she realized that everyone on the boats must be wondering the same thing, feeling the same stirrings of terror.

She suddenly remembered Lynn's group. Had those people been trapped down here, too? Maybe not. They'd passed Darcy, heading back, quite a while before the blackout.

The tours were scheduled to overlap, each taking an hour and a half. So Lynn's group should have reached the top at about the same time as Darcy reached Ely's Wall.

It would have been close. Maybe they made it, maybe not.

A hand squeezed her forearm. She looked at Greg. 'Even if we've got nowhere to go,' he whispered, 'we ought to go through the motions. Better than just waiting here and letting everyone's worries build up.'

'I think you're right,' she said. 'But we can't pull the boats along on those wall spikes the way we got here. It's tricky enough when you can see what you're doing.'

'Tow them?' he suggested.

'It's either that, or everyone wades. I'll take this boat and lead the way. Are you up for a dip, or should we call for volunteers?'

'I'm already wet.'

'Thanks.'

'No problem.'

Darcy faced the passengers. Many were speaking to one another in hushed voices. The child who had been crying was now sobbing quietly. The talk faded when the flashlight lit Darcy's face.

'First, Tom seems to be doing a lot better. I want to thank those of you who gave up your wraps to help keep him warm. I'm very pleased with the way all of you have been acting in the face of this situation, which I'm sure will be over soon. While we're waiting for the lights to come back on, Greg and I are going to hop back into the drink and take the boats to the dock. I'm sure everyone will feel a lot better once we're on dry land.'

'Then what?' someone asked.

Before she could answer, Greg said, 'Let's just take this one step at a time, people.' He patted Darcy's back, then leaped off the boat.

Darcy followed. The cold of the water was a shock, but it didn't seem quite as bad as before. She held onto the gunnel. 'You with the flashlight?'

The woman looked at her.

'What's your name?'

'Beth.'

'You've been doing great, Beth. Thanks. Now, just aim the light forward so I can see where we're going.'

'Fine.'

Darcy waded around the corner of the boat. She clutched its metal rim with both hands and leaned backward. It slid sluggishly toward her. She began walking, and it picked up speed. Once it was moving smoothly, she guided it away from the cave wall.

The chill water climbed her body. She gritted her teeth when it wrapped her breasts.

Think warm thoughts, she told herself.

You'll bake when you get out of here. They won't expect you to take down any more tours today. You'll have the afternoon off. Go to the hotel pool with Mom and stretch out on a lounge.

If you do get out of here. If there's still a hotel. If there's still a Mom.

Damn it, nothing's happened up there!

Then why aren't the lights on yet?

'How's it going, Greg?' she called to stop herself from dwelling on the awful possibilities.

'No problem.'

She looked over her shoulder. The beam of the flashlight slanted through the darkness, making a shiny patch on the water several yards ahead. 'Aim it up, Beth.'

The light lifted. Near the dim end of its reach was the dock, a wooden platform stretching along the far side of the cavern. Maybe eighty or a hundred feet off.

'Just a few more minutes, everyone,' Darcy said.

'Let's lift our voices in song.' That was Greg. Darcy smiled. A few of the passengers laughed. A woman in her boat actually began to sing 'Darcy, tow the boat ashore.' More laughter. Nobody joined in the song, and her voice trailed off after the first 'hallelujah'.

Darcy stepped into emptiness. Her other foot slipped off its hold. Gasping with alarm, she sank to her chin before she could pull herself up. She hung on. The boat carried her backward. She felt her legs rise up beneath it, her knees lightly bumping the hull. The boat slowed. A voice from its other end said, 'Look out, there.'

'What the . . .?' Greg.

Darcy's boat shook, lurched forward a bit.

'You okay?' she called.

'No problem.'

'He almost got squashed,' said a woman.

'It's okay,' Greg said. 'You run into trouble?'

'I ran out of bottom,' Darcy answered. She lowered her feet. They found rock. 'It's okay, now,' she said, and tugged at the boat. It inched forward again. 'Watch out for the hole, Greg.'

'Yeah. No sharks down here, I hope.'

'We're the only wildlife.'

'A fucking comedy team,' a voice said.

'Watch your language, mister,' Darcy snapped. 'There's kids down here.'

'Big deal.'

'Mister!' Darcy warned.

'Up yours.'

'Dad, stop it.' A boy. Darcy imagined he must be the kid, thirteen or fourteen years old, wearing glasses and a hooded red sweatshirt – the kid who'd walked the tour beside the man with the sour face. The kid who got his arm yanked roughly when all he wanted to do was pause for a second to look at Indian Face rock, and Darcy had wanted to smack his creep of a father.

This had to be the same pair.

'. . . speak to me that way,' the father muttered threateningly.

'Ow, don't.'

'Knock it off back there, Slick.' The voice of a different man.

'Mind your own business, you old fart.'

'Hey!' Darcy yelled.

'Okay, pal.' Greg. 'You're the fellow in the Peterbilt cap and cowboy boots. You're gonna shape up right now.'

Silence.

Must be a real shock, Darcy thought, the creep hearing himself described by someone who couldn't even see him in the dark.

She looked over her shoulder again. The flashlight still pointed at the dock. 'Pretty soon, now,' she said.

Only about forty feet to go. Though the boat didn't seem especially difficult to tow, Darcy was starting to hurt. Her arms seemed all right, just a little heavy, but her back muscles, especially behind the shoulder blades and all the way down her spine, were hot and sore and felt as if they were bunching into knots. Her buttocks ached. So did the backs of her legs.

This is what happens, she thought. You hit twenty-one, the body goes. All downhill from here on.

She smiled.

Deke the Creep had grabbed her in the parking lot of Sam's after the party last month, tried to steal a kiss from the sloshed birthday girl, and she'd tossed all over him. The look on his face! Then *he'd* tossed, missing her as she whirled out of the way. The story went all over campus. They started calling her Barfin' Darcy with the Kiss of Death.

Thank God the semester ended soon afterwards.

By fall, she thought, it'll be ancient history.

By fall, *I* might be ancient history.

Her stomach knotted.

We'll be all right.

Forget lounging by the pool. I'll spend the afternoon soaking in a bathtub in water so hot it'll steam up the mirror. Then go with Mom to the cocktail lounge. Have a double something. Anything but beer. Maybe a Maitai. Maybe Greg will be there.

I wonder how he looks in the light.

He's older, but not very. Under thirty.

Darcy must have seen him before the blackout, but she couldn't remember. She wondered if he was alone.

He'll probably leave, anyway, once we're out of here. Everyone does. If people stay in the hotel, it's usually just for the night *before* they take the tour. After they've seen the cavern, they take off, either heading home or for the next place of interest marked on their vacation maps.

I won't let him get away, she thought. Not, at least, until I've bought him a drink.

Maybe he's with his wife.

I'll buy her a drink, too. We'll *have* to celebrate when we get out of this mess.

We *will* get out of this mess.

Darcy kept looking behind her, A few yards from the dock, she walked her hands across the boat's edge, moved herself around it's corner, and shoved. The boat eased away. 'Watch out behind,' she said. 'We're slowing.'

The boat slipped along in front of her. She was between its side and the dock. As it settled in the water, she clutched its gunnel with both hands and leaned away, her back muscles on fire with the effort. The boat moved slowly towards her.

A man at the front, the one beside Beth who'd helped Darcy aboard and was first to offer his jacket for Tom, sprang up and leaped to the dock. Beth followed him with the flashlight. Darcy watched him as she pulled the boat. He rushed over the planks, sat down quickly to her right and stuck his legs out straight.

Darcy let go of the gunnel. She turned away. The boat mudged her back, but she didn't need to worry, now, about being squeezed against the dock. The man held the boat off with his feet while she thrust herself up and scrambled clear.

They knelt side-by-side, pulled the outstretched arms of passengers, brought the boat in closer, then grabbed the gunnel and worked the boat forward alongside the dock.

'Everyone stay seated,' Darcy said in a breathless voice. 'Wait till both boats are secure.'

Beth and two other passengers disregarded the order and jumped out. Just as well, Darcy thought. Beth provided light for the man and woman, who were getting to their knees farther up the dock and reaching out for her boat. Once they had it, Beth hurried forward and held the light on Greg's boat.

Greg waded to the other side and pushed the boat close enough for Darcy and the man to take over. They brought it in against the dock and three passengers, including

Kyle Mordock, hopped out and began trying its lines to the posts.

As Darcy got to her feet, she saw Greg in the gloom near the far end of the boat, climbing from the water. She went to him.

'So far, so good,' he said.

'I'll buy you a drink when we're out of here,' she told him. 'A nice hot steaming mug of coffee.' He pulled off his sweatshirt, held it at arms' length, and began to wring it out. He was a pale blur above the darkness of his jeans, but Darcy could see that his shoulders were hunched up with the cold. She heard water patter on the boards. 'You want to go back and get the passengers organized?' he suggested. 'I'll be along in a minute.'

'Sure,' she said, guessing that he wanted to wring out his pants.

He turned away and walked farther into the darkness.

Darcy's own clothes were sodden and cold. She thought of the grotto near the other end of the dock.

She faced the boats. The passengers were already stepping out. She made her way through them. 'Greg and I want to rest and dry off for a couple of minutes. Then we'll all take a hike for the elevators. In the meantime, everyone stay here and try not to fall in the lake.'

There were a few laughs.

The seat on the forward boat where Tom had been was empty. She found him standing on the dock, held steady by the man who'd helped her with the boats. His head was hanging. He still pressed the handkerchief to his wound. 'How're you feeling, Tom?'

'Guess I'll live,' he muttered.

'Thanks for the help,' she told the other man. 'Are you Beth's husband?'

He nodded. 'I'm Jim. Jim Donner.'

'You've been a lot of help, Jim. Beth, too. I appreciate it.'

'Hey, we're all in this together.'

'You want to look after Tom till I get back?' she asked.

'Sure thing.'

She reached for the flashlight clipped to Tom's belt, pulled it free, and thumbed the switch. A white beam darted out. Its brightness made her realize how weak and yellowish the other flash had become.

With a glance over her shoulder to make sure no one was following, Darcy hurried over the boards and reached the concrete walkway. A few yards farther, she found the stone stairs, rushed up them and entered the grotto.

It had been the size of a small, round closet when Darcy first saw it two weeks ago. Now, it was slightly larger. Near the entrance was a wheelbarrow loaded with chunks of limestone hacked from the walls. A pickaxe was propped against the side of the wheelbarrow.

Cubby Wales, Ethan Mordock's handyman, had been down here during the weekdays, enlarging the grotto. Once it was big enough, Ethan planned to install a chemical toilet for the convenience of the tourists.

Too bad this is a Saturday, Darcy thought. Would've been nice to have another able-bodied employee on hand.

She set the flashlight on the wheelbarrow's piled rocks, pointing away from her. Its beam spread out against the side wall, filling the small enclosure with light.

As fast as she could, she took off her shoes and socks. The floor was gritty under her bare feet, so she spread her jacket and stood on it. She kept her back to the entrance as she removed the rest of her clothes. Though the garments were sodden and cold, she felt worse without them. The chilly air of the cave seemed to seep into her damp skin. She crawled with gooseflesh and her nipples felt hard and achy. Her jaw muscles were sore from clenching her teeth together.

For a while, she stood there shivering, hunched over slightly, legs clamped together for warmth, and briskly rubbed her hands over her nubby skin. That didn't seem to help much.

With a palsied hand, she lifted her panties off the wheelbarrow handle, balled them up and squeezed. Water spilled through her fingers. When she couldn't force out any more drops, she shook the flimsy garment open. Hopping from foot to foot, she stepped into the leg holes, and drew the panties up. They were damp, but much better than before. The snug cling of them felt good.

Not good enough. She was still shuddering with cold as she leaned forward and pulled her trousers off the wheelbarrow. She struggled to slide the belt put of the wet loops, and then emptied the pockets, dropping her change purse, keys, comb and handkerchief onto the jacket at her feet.

She twisted a long, blue leg of the trousers into a tight club and water splattered the tops of her feet. Gathering up the other leg she began to wring it out . . .

. . . and flinched at a quiet, scraping sound behind her. A footstep? She whirled around.

Kyle stood in the opening.

She jerked her trousers up to cover her breasts. 'Damn it,' she snapped. 'Get out of here!'

In the dim glow from the flashlight, she saw Kyle form a narrow smile. 'I thought you might like to have this,' he said, holding his jacket towards her. 'It's dry,' he added.

'Thanks.' Her voice shook. She clamped the pants against her breasts with a forearm, and took the jacket with her other hand.

'Let's see if it fits,' he said.

'I'm sure it will.'

'Oh, come on.'

'You've already seen me, Kyle.'

'Not on purpose. I just came over to do you a favour.'

'And I appreciate it. Now, please go on back. I'll be along in a minute.'

His grin stretched wider. 'Do you want my pants?'

Darcy shook her head. 'Your jacket's plenty. Thanks.' She was about to suggest again that he leave. Instead, she asked, 'Do you have any idea what happened to the lights?'

'Maybe someone switched them off.'

That possibility had never occurred to her. She'd assumed, from the start, that the lights had gone off because of a power failure. If they were only turned off, then the elevators could still be working.

'Glad I asked,' she muttered.

'But I don't think that's it,' Kyle said. 'I think it's the generators. I mean, who'd turn off the lights?'

Darcy shook her head. 'I don't know. Anyway, thanks again for the jacket. See you later.'

He turned around and vanished into the darkness. The sound of his footsteps faded.

Wouldn't surprise me, Darcy thought, if he sneaks back for a second look.

Weird little creep.

Take it easy on him, she thought. He brought me the jacket.

Just an excuse to take a peek. I should've figured he'd do something like that.

She turned her, back to the opening, held the pants between her legs, and got into the jacket. It was a windbreaker of synthetic fabric that felt weightless. It was slick and cool

506

against her skin. Tucking her chin down, she bent over slightly to watch her trembling hands struggle with the zipper. And noticed how her damp panties clung like transparent skin.

She felt sick.

The bastard couldn't have seen more if I was naked, she thought.

Damn him!

At last, she fitted the zipper together. She slid the tab up.

And sighed, moments later, when she felt how the jacket seemed to trap her body heat.

At least I got the jacket out of the deal, she told herself.

Would've been better to freeze, though, than have that shit lay his eyes all over me.

Darcy continued to shake as she finished wringing the water from her pants. But the tremors weren't from the cold – she shook with fury and humiliation.

Bad enough he saw my breasts.

Maybe he didn't notice the other.

Fat chance. He's short and he was standing below me. He saw, all right.

She stepped into her pants and pulled them up. After filling the pockets, she worked the belt through the loops and buckled it. She squeezed the water from her socks, pulled them on, and stepped into her shoes.

It felt good to be dressed again. Though she was still wet and cold from the waist down, the jacket gave her enough warmth to make the discomfort seem minor.

She debated what to do with the remaining clothes. She certainly didn't want to put them on. She could bundle up the bra and blouse inside her jacket and take them with her, but that seemed like too much trouble. I'll just pick them up the next time I'm down here, she decided, and draped the jacket over the wheelbarrow handle.

* * *

When Kyle reached the bottom of the stairs, he took a few more steps to make Darcy think he was going away. The tourists were still gathered on the dock. Their bodies blocked most of the light from the other flash. He watched until he was sure no one was approaching him, then turned around and returned, walking slowly and rolling his feet quietly from heel to toe.

He stopped at the bottom of the six rock stairs, and gazed up at Darcy.

She had the jacket on. Her back was toward him. Her head was down, and she seemed to be trying to fasten the zipper. The jacket wasn't quite long enough to reach her hips. It left a band of bare skin above her low, brief panties.

Though her back was in shadow, he could see a hint of the darker, curving crease between her buttocks.

She zipped up the jacket, then started wringing out her pants.

Kyle stared at her long, slim legs, at the smooth mounds of her rump.

He wished she would take off the jacket and give him another look at her front. He wanted more than anything to see her breasts again. For just an instant, while she was turning around before, he'd seen them in the light. They were pale and the nipples were sticking out. Then, she'd covered them and her front had been in shadow.

She *might* take the jacket off, he told himself. She might go to get into her bra and shirt again. But she wouldn't have to turn around to do that.

Worth sticking around for, though. If she only turned sideways a bit, he'd at least get a glimpse.

Amy Lawson was nothing next to Darcy.

She's all yours, Dad had said.

What if he could do Darcy the way he'd done Amy?

Kyle had had that thought many times before, but now it was almost too much for him.

He rubbed the back of his hand across his dry lips. His heart was thundering. His erection, pushing hard against the front of his jeans, felt as if it might explode.

Do Darcy the way he did Amy.

Get her into Room 115.

She'd have to ride the chute, after. But that was okay.

3

It was a week ago, Friday, that Amy Lawson checked into the Mordock Cave Hotel. Kyle first saw her when she entered the restaurant for supper. It was his job to seat the guests as they arrived.

She came in alone. She appeared to be about Darcy's age, but wasn't nearly as beautiful. Her hair was long and brown, not short and golden. She was inches shorter than Darcy, with bigger breasts, but also a bigger waist and rump, and her calves below the hem of her dress were on the heavy side. She appeared to be stout rather than fat, but Kyle much preferred Darcy's slender shape. Her face was pleasant, though, and looked rather pretty when she smiled at him.

'May I see you to a table?' he asked.

'Please. Thank you.' Her eyes betrayed the usual amusement at realizing that a boy Kyle's age was acting as host. He didn't bother to explain himself. This woman would simply assume, as they all did, that he was a relation of the owner.

'Will you be dining alone?' he asked.

She nodded.

He led her through the dining room to a table for two which had a nice view of the gardens. He pulled out a chair for her. Her scent was sweet and cloying.

'I like your perfume,' he lied.

She smiled over her shoulder at him. 'Thank you. It's Rose Blossom.'

'Very nice.' He was glad Darcy didn't use a sickening perfume like that. He'd stood close to her in the elevators. She had a faint, fresh smell that made him think of a morning breeze.

'A waitress will be along in a minute to take your order,' he said. 'I hope you enjoy your meal.'

'Thank you very much.'

Kyle returned to his station by the entrance, hoping Darcy would show up. She had come in Monday night with that other guide, her room-mate, Lynn Maxwell. It made him ache, now, remembering how she had looked striding into the restaurant. Her sleeveless dress was white with blue flowers, the blue in the dress matching her eyes. The light tan of her skin seemed tawny next to the white, and the dress floated against her as she walked. Kyle made believe he was under it, watching the airy fabric caress her skin.

After Monday, Darcy hadn't come into the restaurant. Kyle supposed she only dined here that night because it was her first time at the hotel and she was celebrating. He found out later that she had started going into town with some of the other guides. It was the usual thing. A room at the hotel came with the job, but the employees had to pay for their own meals and the Cave Chalet was too expensive. They'd be eating up their wages if they didn't head into town for hamburgers or pizza or whatever.

Besides, the guides liked to get away. They didn't go to town just for the cheap food, but to have fun. From hearing their talk over the years, Kyle knew that they went to movies and bars. Some of them tried to pick up townies if they didn't have one of the other guides to mess with.

Not Darcy, though. Kyle could tell from the way she acted towards the male guides that she wasn't letting any of them get her. She was friendly to all of them, but there was no one special.

And she wouldn't do it with townies.

Lynn probably did. But Lynn was a slut.

Kyle doubted that Darcy would show up tonight. Especially since this was Friday. The guides *always* went into town on Friday nights. But each time the door swung open, his heart quickened until he saw who was entering.

By eight o'clock, he'd lost all hope.

Darcy had gone into town, all right, and would probably be out till midnight – or even later.

How about tonight? he thought. He began to tremble slightly. It was always exciting to enter a guest-room with the pass key and have a look around. He'd been tempted all week to try Darcy's, but he couldn't leave the restaurant until 8.30 and by then he was afraid the guides might come back from town and he'd be caught. This was Friday, though. He could do it tonight.

I will! I'll do it!

Waiting for 8.30 became an agony. His heart raced, his mouth was dry, his clammy hands trembled. Only twice did new guests arrive for dinner, and he was grateful each time for the interruption that briefly distracted him from dwelling on what lay ahead.

Darcy's room. Her clothes. Her personal things. The bed where she slept. The bathroom where she'd been naked in the tub.

He couldn't stand the waiting.

At twenty minutes after eight, he left the door and crossed the foyer to the cashier's booth. 'Minnie?' he asked in a pained voice. The scrawny little woman, leafing through a stack of bills, looked up at him. 'I'm not feeling real hot. Do you mind if I go now? It's only ten more minutes before . . .'

'You do look a mite puny, hon. You go on ahead. Your daddy won't never be the wiser on my account.'

'Thanks, Minnie,' he said, and made his way slowly to the door, hanging his head and holding his stomach just to make it look good.

Outside, he straightened up. After the air conditioning of the restaurant, the evening felt warm. He took a deep, trembling breath, and started along the walkway towards the hotel. His father would be manning the registration desk, so Kyle entered the side door at the end of the west wing and trotted up the stairs to the second floor. The corridor was deserted; his footfalls were quiet on the thick carpet. As he passed the main stairs at the halfway point, he saw a middle-aged couple on their way up. He slowed down. Glancing back, he saw them reach the top and turn the other way.

At the door marked 210, he looked back again. The people were near the far end of the corridor, the man unlocking a door. A moment later, they were gone.

Kyle listened. No sounds came from behind the door. Just to be safe, however, he knocked. If Darcy or Lynn should answer, he'd say that Dad had sent him to look for Tom, who sometimes watched the desk for him. Did they know where Tom might be?

Nobody answered the knock.

He dug a trembling hand into the pocket of his slacks and pulled out his key case. The keys clinked together, loud in the silence, as he fumbled for the right one. At last, he had it. He pushed it into the lock, turned it, gently twisted the knob, and eased the door open.

He saw no one, but he left the door open while he crept forward far enough to see through the alcove on the left. Nobody in the bathroom.

The girls were gone, all right.

He stepped back to the door and shut it.

I'm in!

He leaned against the door and took deep breaths, trying to calm himself. The curtains at the other end of the room were open. The wooded hills in the distance were gloomy with dusk. If Kyle didn't waste time, he'd be able to get by without turning on any lights – except in the alcove and bathroom, which didn't have windows.

He rubbed his sweaty hands on his slacks, and pushed himself away from the door. The alcove had clothes hanging along one side. He would give them a look later. And the bathroom. He moved on.

The twin beds were both made, but a little rumpled. Clothing was scattered on top of the nearer bed: blue pants lying flat with the legs draping the edge, a white blouse lying in a heap, a white bra. The pants had a wide waist. The bra had broad straps and enormous cups. Lynn's. So that must be Lynn's bed.

Because of the difference in the girls' sizes, Kyle had no trouble figuring out which drawers of the built-in bureau contained Darcy's clothes. The bottom drawer held sweaters, a sweatshirt, a couple of heavy shirts. They were all neatly folded. He lifted them, glanced at each, but took none of them out.

The middle drawer was more interesting. There, he found slips, pantyhose, a couple of T-shirts, a pair of faded blue shorts and a bright yellow jersey. He picked up the jersey and let it fall open. It was a nightshirt. It had slits on each side. Kyle held it against his body. He was shorter than Darcy. On her, it would hang only part-way down her thighs, the open sides leaving her bare to the hips. He could see her wearing it, the light fabric showing all her curves. He imagined how it would tremble over her breasts as she walked. Bending down, her rump would show, and if she reached for something high, the nightshirt would rise up and he'd be able to see between her legs.

The thoughts made Kyle hard.

He folded the nightshirt and placed it carefully into the drawer. Satisfied that it looked the same as when he found it, he slid the drawer shut and opened the top one.

Here were panties, brassieres, socks and two swimsuits.

One of the suits was bright blue and backless, the other a white string bikini. Neither had stains, and they both smelled clean. Kyle supposed that Darcy had packed them fresh and hadn't used the hotel pool yet. He'd checked it a few times on Wednesday and Thursday, her days off, hoping to see her there. Now, he knew that he hadn't missed her. He would keep a watch on the pool. Sooner or later, she'd show up.

Most of the bras were white with a lacy fabric for the upper half of the cups, narrow straps, and two fasteners in the back. But one was black and strapless. It was stiff along the bottom. It would hold her breasts underneath, and leave them bare on top. The other two bras were flimsy, shapeless things. One was pink, one blue. They fastened in front with a hook and eyelet between the cups. Holding them up, Kyle could see right through them and the wispy fabric felt slick against his face. The pink one smelled faintly of Darcy, that fresh early morning scent of a breeze blowing through the woods.

Kyle bent over to ease the pressure of his erection pushing against his pants.

He put the bras away.

He looked at the stacks of brightly coloured panties.

He was breathing hard, gasping. He was almost past control. If he didn't stop now, he'd mess himself for sure.

He slid the drawer shut.

I'll come back, he thought. Some other time. See the rest of it then.

On his way back to the door he glanced at the bathroom. He'd badly wanted to see the tub. Darcy, was naked when she was in there.

Next time, he told himself. Next time, I'll see everything.

Right now, he had to get out before he burst.

He was in the corridor, pulling the door shut, when the sound of voices made him turn his head.

Out of the elevator near the main stairway stepped an elderly couple. And his father.

Dad had suitcases in each hand.

He glanced at Kyle, then turned away and led the couple towards the west wing.

Kyle felt sick. He went through the fire door, sat down on a stair and hunched over, clutching his knees.

Now what'll I do? He saw me. Shit, oh shit.

What were you doing in that room?

Maybe he didn't see me.

He looked right *at* me. Maybe he'll forget about it.

Fat chance. I've gotta have an excuse. Darcy phoned from town, said she couldn't find her purse, and wanted me to see if it was in her room? That won't work. How could I get the call? Dad would've been at the switchboard.

Dad doesn't *know* why I was there. He might think I wanted to steal something. That'd be better than the truth, anyway. But maybe he'll guess the truth.

I've gotta have a story!

How about if I say I was out back and thought I saw someone in the window? I knew Darcy and Lynn were gone, and thought somebody'd broken in, so I came up to check.

Okay? That's not bad. Okay, that's what it'll be. He might believe it.

The best thing to do is go see Dad right away. Tell him the story. That's what I'd do if I really had seen someone in the window.

Kyle sat on the stair, unable to move.

Dad'll never believe it. It never worked, trying to lie to him. He always knew the truth. Like he was a mind-reader, or something. He'll know what I was doing in there. He'll think I'm perverted.

Better not to say anything, Kyle decided. That way, at least, I won't get it for lying. Just wait and see what happens. See what he asks.

Kyle finally got to his feet and went downstairs. He pushed through the metal door. Feeling numb and shaky, he headed for the lobby.

Please, he thought, let Dad not be there.

Kyle's father was behind the registration desk and looked up at him as he approached. Nobody else was around.

'You have some business in 210, young man?'

'Darcy wanted to borrow a couple of my speleology books,' he said, and wondered where *that* idea had come from. 'I just took them up and left them for her.'

He nodded.

He believed it!

'Business pretty brisk at the Chalet tonight?'

'About the same as usual,' Kyle said. 'It was pretty full.'

'Glad to hear it.'

'Guess I'll go watch some TV, okay?'

'Go on ahead. I'll let you know if I need you.'

Kyle stepped around the end of the registration desk and opened the door to their rooms. He went straight to his bedroom and shut himself in. Immediately, he slid two of his speleology books off the shelves and hid them in the space behind some other volumes. Not that Dad was likely to check. But when you make up a story, you have to follow through with the details.

Once the books were concealed, Kyle felt a lot better.

He turned the television on, and sat in the middle of his bed.

He was too uneasy to follow the shows. Part of the time, he worried about Dad finding out the truth. (He's gonna. No, he won't. What if he asks Darcy about the books? What if he just *knows*?) Part of the time, he got past the worries and took himself back into Darcy's room. There, he lifted her things from the drawers, looked at them and touched and smelled them and dreamed of how they would look on Darcy.

Later that night, with the lights off, he sat propped up in bed and stared at the television and thought about the next time.

Next time, maybe he would take off his clothes. Maybe try on some of her things. (If he stole a pair of her panties, would she notice they were gone?) Maybe he would lie down on her bed, stretch out naked on the same sheet she slept on. In the bathroom, maybe he'd find a towel Darcy had used after a bath or shower. It might still be damp. A towel that had rubbed her body all over.

Someone shook Kyle's shoulder. He woke up, startled, and

rolled onto his back. His father was leaning over the bed, face grey in the fluttery light from the television. The screen was fuzzy, the way it looks after a station has signed off for the night. Kyle glanced at the digital clock on his bed table. Two thirty-six.

'What's wrong?' he murmured.

His heart sped up. He knew what was wrong. Dad knew he hadn't been in Darcy's room to leave books for her.

'Get dressed and come with me,' Dad whispered.

This was strange; if Dad meant to give him a lashing, or even just a lecture, he'd do it here, wouldn't he? Maybe he had some other kind of punishment in mind.

Maybe he plans to make me face Darcy! At this hour?

'Where are we going?'

'Do like I say.'

Dad didn't sound angry, but Kyle heard a tremor in his voice. Was he scared about something? Excited?

Kyle climbed out of bed. His clothes were draped on a chair. With his back to his father, he dropped his pyjama pants and put on his jockey shorts. He started to step into the good slacks he'd worn for hosting at the Chalet.

'Not those,' Dad said. 'Put on some grubbies.'

Why?

He didn't ask. He went to his closet, and got into jeans and an old shirt. Then he put on socks and jogging shoes.

Dad led the way. The lights had been dimmed in the deserted lobby. The hotel was silent. Kyle felt as if the building itself were asleep.

Dad said nothing.

They walked down the corridor of the east wing, even walked past the door of 115, the final guestroom.

We're going to the stairs, Kyle thought. *He is taking me up to Darcy's room.*

But Dad stopped at the very last door before the corridor's end. It was unmarked. In the past, Kyle had tried to unlock it. This was the one door he'd found in the entire hotel that didn't open to the pass key.

Dad had told him, long ago and more than once, that it was a storeroom.

He's gonna lock me in!

You like sneaking into rooms so much, spend some time in this.

Dad took a leather key case out of his pocket. It was the one Kyle had given him for his last birthday. He unsnapped it. On one of the metal clips were two matching keys, one that looked shiny and new. He tugged the new key loose, and held it up in front of Kyle's eyes. It shone like gold in the dim lights.

'I had this made for you on your fifteenth birthday,' he whispered, still in that same tense voice. 'But I saved it till I was sure you were ready.'

'Ready for what?' Kyle rubbed his sweaty hands on his jeans.

'I saw you coming out of that room tonight, I figured it was time.'

'I didn't do anything.'

'Oh, I got a pretty good idea what you were doing. Used to do it myself. Then one day, my Daddy gave me one of these.' He handed the bright new key to Kyle. 'Go on, open her up.'

Kyle's hand shook so badly that the point of the key scraped the lock face. His father took his hand, held it steady, and guided the key in. Kyle turned it. He opened the door.

He glimpsed red curtains, an easy chair. Then Dad nudged him forward, followed him inside and closed the door.

The small room was dark except for a faint glow coming in around the edges of the curtains. A hand on Kyle's shoulder guided him, turned him.

'Now, don't yell or anything,' Dad whispered.

Silently, the curtains parted.

Kyle's mind reeled. His heart hammered. His breath rushed out.

He was standing no more than two feet from a window – not a window, exactly. It had to be a two-way mirror. A full length mirror like those on the bathroom doors of all the other units. This one, however, was obviously not on the bathroom door. It was set into the wall.

On the other side of the glass was a guest-room.

Room 115.

Its lights were on.

On the bed was the woman he'd seated at the Chalet, the one with the rose blossom perfume.

The bed covers lay heaped on the floor and she was squirming on the sheet.

'Name's Amy,' Dad said. 'Amy Lawson.'

She was naked.

A wide band of white tape covered her mouth. Her hands were tied together with clothes-line, arms stretched over-head and secured to the wrought-iron bedframe. Her legs were spread far apart, tied at the ankles to the corners of the frame.

Kyle stared. He had never seen a real woman naked. Pictures in magazines, but never the real thing.

This was better than anything he had ever imagined.

Her struggles to free herself made it even better. She was rocking, twisting, arching her back, pulling at the ropes. Her big breasts bobbed and swayed. Her skin was shiny with sweat. It looked dark and polished from the sun, pure white where a bikini had kept the sun away. There were faint, reddish patches on her breasts and shoulders and thighs. Dad, Kyle thought, must've made those.

Dad, for sure, had done the number on her face. The face

had been pounded pretty good. A cheek was red and swollen, and one eye was swollen almost shut.

'I always put the best-looking babes in 115,' Dad whispered. 'Sometimes, they're just for looking. This one checked in by herself. When they do that, sometimes they get the treatment. What do you think?' he asked.

Kyle muttered, 'Neat.'

He gazed at the writhing woman, hardly able to breathe. He felt trapped inside his jeans, his rigid penis threatening to ejaculate. It was the way he'd felt in Darcy's room just before he rushed out.

But some of the urgency drained away as his father eased him aside. The man crouched for a moment, then stood up and twisted a pair of latches near the top of the mirror's frame. Just below the latches were two metal handles. Dad gripped them and pushed the mirror outward. Stepping over a foot-high section of wall he entered the room, carrying the mirror in front of him.

'Come on in,' Dad said.

Amy made quiet whiny noises.

Kyle stepped into the room.

She stopped squirming. She watched him with wide eyes.

Dad propped the mirror against the wall near the opening to the secret room. Then he put a hand on Kyle's shoulder. 'She's all yours, son. I'll be back in an hour.'

Dad went out through the regular door.

Kyle stared at the naked, sweaty body.

This can't be happening, he thought. He felt as if his father had taken him by the hand and led him into a dream – an amazing, erotic dream that was too wonderful to be true.

It's not a dream, he told himself.

I'm really here.

And I've got an hour.

As fast as he could, Kyle took off his clothes.

4

In spite of her humiliation and anger at being seen half naked by Kyle, Darcy was glad to have the jacket. From neck to waist, at least, she felt warm.

Greg met her just before she reached the dock.

Now, if *he'd* been the one to show up at the grotto . . .

I'm sure feeling lively, she thought, and smiled at him.

'How's it going?' she asked.

'Not bad. There's a fellow with Tom who said he'd stick with him on the way out.'

'Okay, good. How would you like to take up the rear and keep an eye out for stragglers?'

'Fine.'

'I'll get the other flashlight from Beth. Here, you take this one.' She gave it to him. 'It's the stronger of the two. It should be good enough to keep things fairly bright for everyone.'

'We ought to count noses before we start out.'

Darcy nodded. Then she faced the group and called for attention. 'In just a minute,' she said, 'we'll start for the elevators. But I want to give you some instructions first. Most of you came down here with friends or family. I want you to stay close to those you came with. Hold hands or something so you don't lose each other. Any of you who came alone, step up to the front right now, and we'll make sure you get a partner.'

Several people started working their way forward. They gathered in front of Darcy. One was Kyle. Four of the others looked around, formed pairs, and introduced themselves to their new companions.

'Why don't I be your partner,' Kyle said to Darcy.

'That'd leave somebody out,' she told him. 'Who's still alone?' she asked.

A girl raised her hand.

A blonde with a pony tail. She looked fifteen or sixteen. Darcy wondered what a girl that age was doing on the tour without her parents. 'What's your name?' she asked.

'Paula Whitmore,' the girl answered.

'Okay, Paula. Do you want to pair up with this young man?'

She looked at Kyle, smiled and nodded. 'Sure. If it's all right with him.'

He shrugged and said, 'I'm Kyle.'

'Okay,' Darcy said. 'It's you two, then.' She felt guilty about sticking Paula with Kyle. It seemed like a dirty trick, just a way to keep the jerk off her own back. Hell, she told herself, it's only natural to pair them up. They're the same age and everything. And Paula could have objected. The girl might actually enjoy having a male escort.

Darcy turned her attention to the rest of the group. 'Okay, now. Does anyone *not* have at least one partner?' Nobody responded. 'Once we start out, I want each of you to be responsible for three things. First, stay beside your partner. Second, keep track of the people directly in front of you. If it's too dark to see them, keep a hand on one of them. Third, pay attention to the people right behind you. Don't leave them behind. There's no hurry.'

'With a flashlight at each end of the group, there should be at least a little light. Some of you have matches, lighters, and cameras with flashes. If necessary, use them. But don't waste them. The trip will probably take about an hour, and we really don't know how long we'll be in the cavern before electricity is restored. I think we should try to get by with the flashlights, and save the matches and things in case we need them later on.'

'If anyone has trouble along the way, call out and we'll stop immediately. Any questions?'

'Couldn't we make torches or something?' It was the voice of the boy who'd asked about the damming effects of Ely's wall.

'I guess we could,' Darcy answered, 'but I don't think it's really necessary. The flashlights should be enough to keep us in light until we reach the elevators.'

'Are there any bats down here?' asked a woman near the back.

'No. Bats used to inhabit the cavern, but they didn't last long after Ely Mordock sealed the natural opening. The same goes for cave rats and other wildlife. So you don't need to worry about running into any nasty critters down here.'

'Well, thank goodness for that,' the woman said.

'Any more questions?'

'We gonna stand around here all day?'

Greg swung the flashlight across the group and found the face of the man in the Peterbilt hat. Squinting against the glare, the man turned his head away.

'Any *other* questions?' Darcy asked. When no response came, she said, 'Let's have Tom at the front here.'

He came forward, walking slowly, Jim and Beth Donner on either side of him. Darcy was glad to see that they weren't holding him up. A belt was wrapped around his head to hold cloth pads against his wound.

'I'm going to lead the way,' Darcy announced. 'Greg will take up the rear. He has a flashlight, and he'll keep an eye on everyone.'

'You'll need this,' Beth said, and gave her flashlight to Darcy. It seemed only about half as bright as the one Greg held, but it was still strong enough to do the job.

Greg put a hand on her shoulder; it felt big and warm through the jacket. 'Whenever you're ready,' he said, speaking quietly. 'I'll stay put and count them as they go by.'

'Great,' she told him. She faced the others. 'Everybody ready?'

'*Head 'em up, move 'em out!*' The kid who'd asked about torches. Darcy was starting to like him.

She turned around, then raised the hand with the flashlight high overhead, swept it down, and started walking. The wooden planks of the dock creaked under her feet, and rumbled as those behind her began to move. A few strides took her to the concrete walkway.

She kept the beam aimed low, lighting the area just ahead of her feet. Soon, she spotted the steps to the grotto on her right. The encounter with Kyle forced its way into her mind. She felt herself blushing.

The little creep's probably thinking about it right now.

Kyle, watching the dim shape of Darcy beyond the three people in front of him, saw her head turn. The grotto's over there, he thought, and felt a warm stir in his groin as he remembered the way she'd looked.

Nothing on but her panties, and he could see right through those.

He'd been in her room three times, so far, and now

he'd seen her nearly naked. The next thing was to *get* her.

Put her in 115.

Dad won't let that happen, though. She's a guide. She's not like Amy Lawson, someone you can just get rid of.

There must be a way.

The girl beside Kyle suddenly stumbled and grabbed his arm. Steady again, she muttered, 'Sorry,' and released her grip.

'It's all right,' Kyle said.

'I'm such a klutz sometimes.'

'Maybe you should take my hand,' he said, so polite, as if he were hosting at the Chalet.

She put her hand in his. It felt warm. Kyle looked at her. He couldn't see much, just that she was wearing glasses. But he remembered what she looked like. Even though he'd kept his eyes mostly on Darcy during the tour, he'd checked out all the other females. This one had blonde hair in a pony tail, and was kind of pretty in spite of the glasses. She was wearing a white blouse, an open white sweater, a plaid skirt with pleats, and knee socks. Kyle recalled that she had big breasts for someone so slim.

He noticed, now, that she smelled good. Not fresh like Darcy or flowery like Amy. It was an aroma that made him think of cotton candy.

'Where are you from?' she asked.

'Oh, I live around here.' He decided not to tell her that his father owned the place. 'How about you?'

'I'm from Santa Monica, California.'

'You're a long way from home.'

'We're visiting my uncle in Albany. My dad's brother. We rented a car so we could explore around for a few days.'

'You and your parents?'

'Just my dad and me. My mom died three years ago.'

'Oh, I'm sorry.' He wasn't sorry. He didn't even know the girl's mother. But it seemed like the right thing to say.

She squeezed his hand. 'That's okay. What about you?'

'Mine ran off with somebody.'

'So you live with your father, just like me.'

'You live with my father?'

She laughed quietly. 'Silly.'

'What are you doing down here without him?'

'He's got claustrophobia.'

'You're kidding.'

'No, honest.' The way she sounded, Kyle guessed she was grinning.

'And he brought you to a cavern?'

'Well, I saw it in the guide book and I said it sounded neat. So here I am. He's probably shitting bricks, if you'll pardon my French.'

'Shit ain't French.'

She giggled, and the pale blur of her right hand darted up to cover her mouth. When it lowered again, she said, 'You're weired, Kyle.'

'I'm not weird. Shit's English. It's in Chaucer. Past tense is shat. He shat a brick.'

Stifling more giggles, she bumped her shoulder against Kyle. 'That's *awful.*'

The woman just in front of them, who was walking beside Tom, looked over her shoulder. She said nothing. A moment later, she faced forward again.

Kyle gave her the finger.

Paula bumped him again.

This isn't bad, he thought. She likes me. Maybe I can cop a feel before we get out of here.

* * *

Carol Marsh flinched as Helen put an arm around her back.

'You're shaking like a leaf,' Helen said.

'I'm freezing, that's all.'

'You should've paid attention. I warned you it would be chilly down here.'

Yes, Helen had warned her. Helen was full of advice. She was thirty-six, only five years older than Carol, but she treated Carol like a child. Too many years in the classroom with kids short on common sense.

She'd been that way since Carol started at George Washington Elementary School. Carol's first day on the job, the more experienced teacher took her under her wing. And kept her there ever since.

The mother-hen treatment never bothered her much until this trip. Being in Helen's company day after day, night after night, Carol had started feeling smothered and annoyed by the treatment.

By now, the fifth day of their vacation, she had it up to her nose with the constant advice and the underlying assumption that she was incapable of running her own life.

This morning in the hotel room when Helen had said, 'You're not going on the tour in *that*, I hope,' she replied, 'I don't see anything wrong with it.'

It was a yellow sundress.

'Well, at least put on a sweater. You don't want to catch a cold.'

'It's ninety degrees outside.'

'We'll be a hundred and fifty feet below ground in a chilly, damp cave. And the guidebook . . . Let me get it.' *She's going to read me a lesson.* Helen found the booklet, opened it to a map she had used to mark her place, and read, ' "Mordock Cavern, while warmer than many similar caves in summer due to its unusual ventilation system which circulates air from

528

the surface, nonetheless remains chilly. Those wishing to take the tour in comfort are advised to wear sweaters or light jackets.'"

'I think I'll live,' Carol said.

'Well, it's up to you, of course.'

'Yes, it is.'

Now, Carol wished she'd chosen a different issue for her small rebellion. The cool of the cave had felt good for a while, but soon it began bothering her. She'd been shivering ever since the lights went out. She suspected that the shivers had less to do with the temperature of the cave than with fear. Whatever the cause, however, warmer clothes would have improved the situation.

Her sundress didn't cover much. It was cut low in front and back, sleeveless and short. The fabric was so light it seemed to float around her, barely touching her skin. It let the air in. Wonderful in hot weather. Not so great down here.

Helen's arm felt warm and good on her back. She put her arm around Helen.

Felt the thickness of her friend's cable-knit sweater.

I wonder if she'd let me wear that for a few minutes.

No way am I going to ask, Carol told herself.

We'll be out of here before long.

She looked up. Light from behind brushed the shoulders and heads of those in front of her. Its glow lit the stick grey wall of the cave to the right. She saw a ruffled slab of flowstone that the guide, Darcy, had talked about on the way in.

We're more than halfway back to the elevators, she realized.

Helen suddenly seemed to stiffen. Her hand pressed more tightly against Carol's side.

'Are you all right?' Carol whispered.

'I'm sure . . . we're not actually trapped.'

'No, of course not. It's just temporary.'

'Perhaps they had to send to town for an electrician. That might take a while.'

'They won't leave us down here, Helen.'

'I understand that. I'm certain we'll be out of here in a matter of hours, at most.'

'Probably,' Carol agreed. 'I really don't think anything *serious* happened up there.'

'A short circuit, something of that nature.'

'Can you believe that cretin suggesting there'd been a nuclear attack?'

'I suppose it is a possibility. It's *always* a possibility.'

'But remote,' Carol said. 'This is bad enough without dreaming up catastrophes.'

Helen patted her side.

They walked in silence.

Carol forgot about the cold. She struggled against an awful feeling of loss. What for? she thought. There certainly wasn't any goddamn nuclear war. Probably.

Even if there was, I don't have any family. If everyone got wiped out, I'd lose a few friends. Helen's probably my best friend, and she's safe down here with me.

Isn't that fine? No one to lose. No husband, not even a lover. No child. You're thirty-one, and you've got nothing. You blew it with Derek, you blew it with David. You wanted your space.

You'll have all the space in the world if it's been levelled.

'Carol?'

'Huh?' she asked, glad to have such thoughts interrupted.

'I left my insulin in the hotel room.'

'Are we almost there yet?'

Wayne Phillips looked down at his daughter. Katie was walking between him and Jean, holding a hand of each.

'Almost where?' Wayne asked.

'Don't be dumb, Daddy. The elevator.'

'We'll be there in fifteen minutes or so, I think. If the monsters don't get us.'

Katie jerked her hand away and punched his hip. 'Mommy, tell Daddy to stop. He's talking about monsters.'

'Really, Wayne, I don't think this is a good time for that sort of thing.'

'You're right. Besides, I haven't seen any. Yet.'

'Daddy!'

'He has monsters on the brain,' Jean said.

'And a good thing, too,' he told her, 'or we wouldn't be able to afford this fine vacation.' It made him feel good to think of the $7,500 they'd just received, the first half of the $15,000 advance for his new novel, *Lurker in the Dark*. The other half was due in nine months or on publication, whichever came first.

'I'll get a book out of this, for sure,' he said. 'What a terrific premise. Forty people trapped in a cave.'

'Didn't we see an Irwin Alien movie like that?' Jean asked.

'That was a disaster movie. This'll be horror. There's something *nasty* in the cave. Something that creeps out of the darkness and . . .'

'Stop it, Daddy. I don't think you're funny.'

'I'm not trying to scare you,' he protested. 'I'm just thinking out loud.'

'I wish you'd think to yourself.'

Seven years old, he thought, and she's already giving orders to men.

She's scared.

She loves spooky stories and horror movies, but this is getting to her. This is the real thing. No zombies or madmen or scuttling aliens (not yet), but we're in just the sort of place they might really go for, and she knows it.

And so do I.

There's no one down here but us, Wayne told himself.

And he suddenly remembered the clay people from one of those Flash Gordon serials he used to watch on television. It was the same story that had the forest people, those freaky folks with the wild hairdos who swung through the trees – and got either Flash or Happy with an arrow from one of their weird little crossbows.

Good God, Wayne thought. I *used* the forest people.

They'd shown up as the Krotes in his second novel. Until now, he'd never realized the connection.

So how about the clay people? he wondered. They were every bit as frightening as those creeps in the trees. They kind of looked like mummies. They were *in* the walls of the caves. You couldn't see them at all. They were just part of the rock (or clay) until they decided to move around, and then they sort of unblended and lurched along.

A *lot* like mummies. Maybe that's what made them so creepy. And the fact that they could be anywhere. You lean against a wall of the cave to rest, and maybe you're leaning against one of *them* and the next thing you know it grabs you.

They turned out to be good guys, Wayne remembered. Getting turned to clay was punishment for screwing up. It wasn't Ming doing it. Some babe. Some evil queen or princess.

Pretty far-fetched. Maybe you could get away with stuff like that in 1938 or whenever, but not today.

Still, it is a spooky concept.

All around us. Right in the walls. After we pass by, they materialize – grey, misshapen creatures of the cave. They're hunched over. They don't walk so much as shamble. And they start to stalk us.

Something snatched Wayne's hand. He jerked rigid and sucked a harsh gasp.

His hand had been snatched by Katie.

She started to laugh.

'You scared the bejabbers outa me,' he whispered.

Katie laughed even harder.

He knew that giving Dad a good scare, even if done by accident (like this time), was seen by Katie as one of life's genuine joys. It ranked right up there with talk of boogers, barf, butts and farts.

With tastes like that, he thought, she'll end up preferring to read Stephen King instead of her dear old dad.

Wayne noted that the couple ahead of him were carrying on a conversation – and not likely to hear his whispered words. 'You scared me so bad, I think I blew a hole in my unders.'

'Turn them into a Hershey factory?' Katie asked.

'Who *have* you been reading?'

'She's been listening to *you*, dear,' Jean informed him.

'And me a Nestlés man.'

Calvin Fargo had long ago lost track of the number of broken bones in his body, but he suspected he could count them up now without much trouble if he had a mind to. Each of the old fractures seemed to be clamouring for attention. The dank chill was doing it.

Calvin had been a stuntman for over thirty years, spent a good part of that time in the saddle, and bit the dust in more than a hundred movies. He'd been trampled by horses and cattle, been run over a few times by stage coaches and buckboards (and by a chariot in the remake of *Ben Hur*), taken falls off balconies, roofs and bluffs. It all added up to more fractures than a human has bones.

The hand-carved mesquite walking stick with its brass stallion-head handle had been a gag gift on his fiftieth birthday. Busted up as he was back then, he could still get around on his own two feet without the help of a cane. But it came from Yakima Canutt, who was not only his old pal but also the greatest stuntman of all time, so Calvin cherished the cane and took it with him everywhere – even if he didn't need it.

Today, he was mighty glad to have the help.

But the cane was enough. He sure didn't need Mavis trying to keep him up.

'Leave off my arm, there, sugar,' he said when he realized she wasn't just holding his arm, but lifting on it. 'I don't need a woman tugging at me.'

'Don't be such a chauvinist, honey.'

'I'm sure the lucky one,' he said. 'Married to the only gal in the country still talks like a sixties issue of *Cosmo*.'

'Oh, quit your complaining.'

'Then you quit dragging on my appendage.' She stopped helping him along, and merely held onto his elbow. 'Much obliged.'

'Pride goeth before a fall.'

'Shitfire! Now she's into scripture!'

He heard Mavis chuckle softly. 'You old coot. I don't know why I put up with you.'

''Cause I'm the hottest cocksman north of the Rio Grande, that's why.'

'Shhhh. Someone's gonna hear you.'

'Let 'em hear. Tell the truth and shame the devil, as you're so fond of saying in between calling folks chauvinists.'

'You're certainly cantankerous today.'

'Pissant called me an old fart.'

'Well, you shouldn't have interfered.'

'A man can only take so much, watching that son-of-a-whore bullying his boy. He's damn lucky I didn't lay into him.'

'You just forget about laying into anyone, Calvin Fargo.'

'Got no right to treat his boy that way. Your children, they're the best thing you get out of life . . .'

'Well, thank you very much.'

' 'Cept, of course, for a good horse, old boots, a warm place to shit, and a tight . . .'

'Don't you *dare* use that word in public.'

He laughed. 'Shitfire, honey, I just wanted to include you in, that's all.'

Mavis squeezed his arm. 'Your compliment is duly noted. Just don't go announcing it to the world.'

The walkway ended, and Darcy stepped onto the rock floor of the area known as the cathedral. She raised her flashlight. Its beam wasn't strong enough to reach the far end of the chamber, but she knew that the elevators were just ahead in the darkness.

The area seemed deserted.

'Hello?' she called.

No answer.

So Lynn and her group had made it to the top before the power failure. Lucky for them.

We've been pretty lucky, ourselves, she thought.

She could hardly believe that the trek had gone so smoothly. There'd been no shouts of alarm. Apparently, no one had tripped or strayed from the route or panicked.

She turned around and walked back. Greg's light was a beacon, held high and shining down on the tourists, sweeping from side to side, up and down.

'We've made it, everyone!' she called.

Her announcement was greeted by subdued applause, a few cheers and a whistle.

Facing forward, she spotted the elevator doors at the faint, far end of her light. She walked toward them.

5

Leaning between the elevator doors, rump against the rock wall, Darcy asked, 'Any trouble?'

There were murmurs. Nobody spoke up.

'I want you all to stand still for a minute. Greg's coming up, counting noses to make sure we didn't lose anyone.'

She switched off her flashlight to save whatever dwindling juice might still remain in its batteries, and watched Greg move through the people.

What if we did *lose someone?*

Unlikely. Possible, though.

I'd have to go back and search.

Greg walked up to her. 'They're all here,' he said. 'Thirty-eight, including you and me.'

'I'd say we pulled that off rather smoothly. Thanks for all the help.'

'Am I dismissed?' he asked.

'Do you have someone to go back to?'

'All by my lonesome.'

'Then stick around, why don't you, and help me hold up the wall.'

'I won't be needing this.' He handed the flashlight to Darcy, then took his place against the wall close by her side.

Darcy raised the flashlight. 'Okay, folks,' she said, 'the tricky part's over. All we have to do, now, is sit tight and wait. Obviously, none of us knows the reason for the power failure. I don't think that speculating on it will do anyone much good. Let's just look at it as an irritating fact of life – like a traffic jam.'

'I don't want to raise any false hopes,' she continued. 'It may be a while. God knows, I never expected it to last this long. The important thing to keep in mind, though, is that we aren't in any danger. None at all.'

'If you get cold, snuggle up with someone. We have plenty of water. As for food, I can't promise that we won't get hungry. But nobody is going to starve. I can't imagine that we'll be down here for more than a few hours. It may be just a minute before the power is restored. They know we're down here, and I'm sure that getting us safely to the top is the major priority right now.'

'Why don't you all sit down and make yourselves as comfortable as possible? If you want to smoke, go on ahead. I'm going to turn off the flashlight in a minute to conserve the batteries, so it will be totally dark in here, and I'm sure a few glowing cigarettes would be welcomed by everyone.'

'If anybody needs to go to the bathroom, call out and either Greg or I will come to you with a flashlight. The important thing is for nobody to go wandering around in the dark.'

Darcy played her flashlight over the people until everyone was seated. Then she turned it off. For a few moments, there was silence. Darcy heard her own heartbeat and the quiet whisper of the River Styx. Then came a few soft voices.

'Black.'

'Christ on a crutch.'

'Can't see my hand in front of my face.'

'Are you there?'

'Is that you?'

Darcy spoke up. 'Unless you've been in a cavern before, probably most of you have never experienced this kind of darkness. This is a total absence of light, darker than any night. As an experiment, a man once left a roll of film exposed in a cavern for two weeks. When the film was developed, it was found to be completely blank.'

'Living creatures that have adapted to cave life are usually blind and without any pigmentation due to the lack of light.'

'Which reminds me – though your are adjusting to the darkness, you won't be getting any night vision. There has to be a small amount of light for that, and there is none.'

Darcy stopped talking. There was silence. Then the voices started again. She thought it sounded like a classroom when the teacher was out, a dozen or more quiet conversations going on at once, creating a steady murmur.

Here and there, matches or lighters flared. They fluttered in front of faces with cigarettes or cigars clamped between lips, and formed pools of light throughout the group. Darcy saw that everyone was seated. Most were in small clusters of two or three. The brightness didn't last long. Then the chamber was dark except for half a dozen spots of glowing red.

'Guess I'll sit down and make myself comfortable,' she whispered.

She sat on the stone floor and crossed her legs. Something bumped her knee.

'Sorry,' Greg said.

'It's okay.' She reached out and touched his leg. He was

beside her. Before she could bring her hand back, he took hold of it.

'Do you mind?' he asked.

Darcy answered by squeezing his hand. 'It's nice to have a friend in the dark.'

'Or any other time.'

'How'd you end up here?' she asked.

'One of my secretaries told me about it. She got married in the Bridal Chamber.'

'Recently?'

'Six years ago.'

'I wasn't here, then,' Darcy said.

'No kidding. You would've still been in diapers.'

She laughed softly. 'Thanks a bunch. I'm not *that* young.'

'Let me guess, then. You look about eighteen, but the way you've been handling yourself, you act about thirty. Add them up, divide by two, we get your true age of twenty-four.'

'Nifty gimmick, but you're three years high. What kind of law do you practise?'

'Some criminal, mostly personal injury defence. And I do the usual odds and ends – probate, divorces . . .'

'Like it?'

'It's exciting. Though not as exciting as being trapped in a cavern.'

'This is a thrill I could do without.'

'This wouldn't be so bad,' Kyle whispered, 'if it weren't so cold down here.'

'I don't think it's so bad,' Paula said.

Neither do I, Kyle thought. But he made his voice shake as he said, 'That's because you've got a sweater. I wasn't cold, either, when I had my jacket. I gave it to Darcy.'

'The guide?'

'Yeah. I figured she needed it more than me – after being in the water.'

'That was a sweet thing to do.'

'Sweet, but dumb.'

'Want to wear my sweater?'

'Maybe if I just put my arm under it. That'd help.'

'Sure, okay.'

He trembled as he slipped his hand beneath her sweater, but it had little to do with the chilly air. Paula's back felt warm through the thin fabric of her blouse. She wore a bra with a wide strap.

Kyle moved his hand across her back and curled his fingers into the warmth of her armpit.

'Just don't tickle,' she warned.

'I won't.' He uncrossed his legs and scooted closer until he felt his hip against her.

Paula put her arm on his back. 'Is that a little better?' she asked.

'A lot.' He could feel the soft warmth of her breast pushing his side.

'For me, too.'

This isn't too bad at all, Kyle thought. She's no Darcy, but she's okay.

And cooperative. So far.

With the hand that was under her arm, he could reach her breast.

Don't try it, he warned himself.

You spook her and you'll blow it.

It's so dark in here, I could do anything. Anything at all, as long as Paula stays quiet.

He would need to keep her quiet.

Kyle patted the pocket of his jeans and felt the knife inside. Moving his hand over a bit more, he gave his erection a gentle squeeze through the heavy denim, felt a surge of pleasure, and imagined sliding it into her.

Then imagined the lights coming on suddenly.

Forget it, he warned himself.

Even if he had all the time in the world and could somehow find his way around the entire cavern, there was no place to get rid of the body. There'd be a search as soon as they got out of here, and she'd be found.

Only one way to have Paula – she has to go along with it.

'Just for the fun of it,' Darcy said. 'The pay's not good, but this is pretty interesting for a summer job.'

'What's your major?' Greg asked.

'You tell me. You probably have a theory.'

Greg laughed softly. 'Majoring in tour guidance?'

'Yeah, sure.'

'The obvious, of course, is geology.'

'Wrong again.'

'That was an observation, not a guess.'

'So, what's your guess?'

'Psychology.'

'Oh, come on. Only fruitcakes go into psychology. You think I'm a fruitcake?'

'No, your head seems pretty well screwed on. How about phys-ed?'

'Now I'm a jock. Thanks.'

'Jocks are air-heads, right?'

'You got it.'

'But they're also physically fit and graceful, so you shouldn't consider my guess to be an out-and-out insult.'

'Okay, I won't.'

'How about a clue?'

' "It is an ancient Mariner, and he stoppeth one of three." '

'Seamanship.'

Darcy elbowed him.

'Archery?'

She looked at him with surprise. There was nothing to see. 'You do know your literature.'

'I wonder if someone down here recently murdered an albatross.'

'Not me,' Darcy said.

'We could ask around. All this might be punishment for some kind of transgression.'

'Right.'

'As a matter of fact, I'm serious.'

'You don't sound serious.'

'I find it intriguing. You take life, a lot of nasty business goes on.'

'I'll buy that.'

'It all comes down to one of three things,' Greg said. 'About fifty per cent is crap that just happens, nobody's fault, just God or Mother Nature or Fate or Chance dropping on you like a ton of bricks. The other half of the bad stuff is caused either by human evil or ignorance. Evil and stupidity are about equal.'

'Nifty theory.'

'I think so. Now, you take our present situation, I figure the odds are fifty-fifty that we're victims right now of somebody doing what he shouldn't.'

'Twenty-five per cent that somebody shot an albatross.'

'Right.'

'So where does that leave us?' she asked.

'Right where we were before I started my lecture.'

'Except I'm wiser, now.'

Greg laughed softly.

'And we're a few minutes closer to getting out of here.'

'I sure hope so.'

Darcy didn't like the sound of that.

'Have you thought about . . .?' He stopped.

'What?'

'You said, yourself, we don't know what happened up there. We've been assuming that, whatever the problem is, it'll be fixed before long. But what if it's not? I think we have to . . . consider the possibility.'

'Great. Thanks. I've been trying like hell *not* to consider that.'

She felt Greg let go of her hand. He stirred beside her. Then his arm went across her shoulders, and she leaned against him.

'I figured to give it a couple of hours,' she whispered.

'Then what?'

'Then, we get our asses out of here.'

'That's what I like, a woman of action.' She thought she could hear a smile in his voice. 'But how do you plan to accomplish this feat?'

'With great difficulty.'

When Paula began to sniff, Kyle thought she had a runny nose. Then he wondered if she might be crying.

'Are you okay?' he asked.

Her voice trembled as she answered, 'Not very.'

She *is* crying.

'What's wrong?'

'I'm just . . . so scared.'

'Hey, there's nothing to be scared about.'

'It's so dark. Why aren't the lights on yet? What's taking so long?'

'They'll be on pretty soon,' Kyle said. He hoped not. It'd be just fine, he thought, if the lights stayed off for hours. Maybe we could even spend the whole night down here.

He liked the blackness. He liked the feel of Paula, and wanted more. The moment the power came back on, that would end it with her.

'Maybe you should try to take a nap,' he whispered. 'It'd pass the time.'

'I don't think I could sleep.'

'My butt's already fallen asleep.'

Paula made a loud, wet sniff. 'Mine, too.'

'Let's try lying down. Even if we can't sleep, it'd be a lot more comfortable.'

'All right.'

Kyle took his hand out from under her sweater. He felt her hand on his shoulder as he lay down. The chill of the cavern floor seeped through the back of his shirt. He rolled onto his side.

'This isn't all that comfortable,' Paula whispered.

'Here.' He touched her hair, then slid his arm under her head. He put his other arm around her back. 'Is that better?'

'Yeah.'

Paula's hand found his side just below the ribcage. But she didn't move any closer to him. Their bodies were apart.

A couple more inches, Kyle thought, and we'd be touching. She's probably worried about that.

He could feel her shaking.

'Cold?' he asked.

'A little.'

He scooted himself closer. Her breasts pressed against him. He felt their warmth, and the warmth of her belly and thighs. Instead of moving away, Paula tightened her arm around his back and she squeezed him to her body. She sighed. 'This is nice,' she whispered.

'Yeah.'

'You feel so warm.'

'You, too.'

He wondered if she could feel his hard-on. She must. It was pushing right against her. But she didn't try to get away from it.

Maybe she likes it, he thought.

He'd never messed around with a girl his own age, never even taken one out, but he knew guys who had and sometimes they bragged about scoring. Unless those guys were lying, there *were* girls who put out.

Maybe Paula's one of them.

Even if she's not, Kyle was pretty sure that a lot of girls her age would let you do other stuff – everything *but* that.

He slid his hand down her back and rested it on her hip. Her dress was a soft fabric. He moved his hand over it, feeling the curve of her rump.

Her head moved. Kyle felt her face against his. Her lips brushed over his cheek, then found his mouth. She kissed him. It wasn't a noisy smack like he got on the cheek from his aunt and grandmother. It was a soft, quiet suck on his lips, and afterwards her mouth didn't go away.

Nobody had ever kissed Kyle this way.

She was a girl his own age, kissing him because she wanted to.

She must like me, he thought.

He pressed his lips against hers. He was hard and aching and wanting Paula more than ever. But there were new feelings: amazement, gratitude and tenderness.

This must be what it's like, he thought, to have a girlfriend.

But she'll go away when the elevators start up.

It isn't fair.

I'll still have room 115, he told himself. And I'll still have Darcy.

But I won't have Paula anymore.

He felt a tightness in his throat.

Even if she does like me, she'll go away.

The hell with her.

Keeping his mouth on Paula's, he twisted enough to make room between their bodies, and closed a hand gently over her breast. She made a small gasp and stiffened.

'Kyle, don't,' she whispered.

'It's all right.' He moved the sweater out of his way. He squeezed her breast through the blouse and bra. 'Nobody can see anything.'

'What if the lights come on?'

So it was okay with her; she just didn't want to get caught. 'If they do, I'll stop.'

'I don't know.'

He covered her mouth with his lips. She was breathing hard and trembling. He fumbled with buttons, opened a way in her blouse, and slipped his hand inside. Some of her breast wasn't covered by the bra. He caressed its smooth warmth. She moaned into his mouth, a moan that seemed partly desire and partly protest. Then Kyle pushed his fingers under the bra. She flinched and squirmed.

'No, don't.'

'It won't hurt anything,' he said, digging deeper into the yielding flesh until his fingertips found the rigid post of her nipple.

She yanked his hand away. She held it motionless by the wrist. 'I told you no, Kyle.'

'I thought you liked me,' he said.

'I do. But . . . you're going too fast. I've never let anyone . . . There are people all around us.'

'I don't see any.'

'Silly.' She squeezed his wrist. Then she guided his hand

through the blackness and placed it on her breast. He felt the blouse. 'Outside my clothes, okay?'

'But your skin is so smooth and nice.'

'Kyle.'

'Please?'

'Do you promise to leave my bra alone? And not go below the waist?'

'I promise.'

'Okay.'

She released his wrist.

Kyle unfastened the other buttons, then slid his hand inside her blouse.

Pretty soon she'll let me undo her bra, he thought. Pretty soon, she'll let me do everything.

'She took your car?' Darcy asked.

'And my stereo and VCR and all the cash in the house.'

'That's awful. After everything you did for her.'

'Well, she was such a mess,' Greg said. 'I was pretty upset for a while, but I was relieved, too. It was no kind of relationship. Once the shock wore off, I realized how lucky I was to be rid of her.'

'Did you love her?'

'I don't know. I thought so. At first, anyway. She was very attractive and vulnerable, and she needed me. There was certainly a strong element of sexual attraction. But putting up with her . . .'

'It must've been terrible.'

'On top of everything else – her fits of rage and jealousy and all the rest – she tried to commit suicide twice, and one night I woke up and found her holding a butcher knife to my throat.'

'Good Christ.'

'She said I'd put a radium bulb in the bedside lamp to poison her chromosomes.'

'I don't know how you could live with that kind of thing.'

'It wasn't easy. I kept hoping she'd get better. But she'd come back from the clinics and be fine for a while and then it would all start up again. I felt totally trapped. I really wanted her out of my life, but she was so dependent on me – I knew she'd go off the deep end if I tried to throw her out.'

'Why did she finally take off like that?'

'I don't have any idea. As crazy as she was, maybe she decided I was plotting against her. Maybe she met someone at one of the bars. I just don't know. I'm just thankful that she left.'

'Do you think she'll come back?'

'She's been gone more than a year, now, so I doubt it.'

'And you haven't been . . . involved with a woman since she left?'

'No. And it's been wonderfully peaceful.'

'So, you've let your experiences with Martha turn you off completely to . . .'

'Not turn me off, just make me careful. The last thing I need is to get messed up with another emotional crip – what's that . . .?' His voice stopped.

Darcy tensed.

Greg's hand tightened on her shoulder.

She listened. The sound came from behind her – from the elevator shafts? A far-off, skidding rumble that reminded her of a subway train approaching a station. It grew louder, louder.

Greg's hand darted under her armpit. Her other arm was grabbed and she felt herself being lifted, hurled forward through the blackness with Greg at her side until they stumbled over people who yelped with alarm.

Greg, on Darcy's back, pressed her down onto a squirming body.

She heard the roar, shouts and screams, a tremendous crash.

Greg rolled off her. Raising her head, Darcy saw that she was sprawled on top of Beth Donner. The woman's face glowed with fluttering yellow-orange light. She had a look of terror in her eyes.

'Sorry,' Darcy muttered. 'You all right?'

Beth nodded.

Darcy pushed herself up. She looked over her shoulder.

Into the flames.

The elevator on the left, its wooden doors blasted apart, was a closet of fire.

Darcy squinted into the burning, twisted wreckage of its car. She saw no bodies.

That's something, she thought. At least . . .

There came another roar.

Another crash.

The doors to the second elevator burst apart in a spray of slabs and splinters.

6

That morning, after coffee and a sweetroll from the snackbar, Chris Raines walked with her daughter to the area beyond the giftshop where people were standing in line to buy tickets for the tour.

'You sure you don't want to come down for another look at the wonders of the cavern?' Darcy asked.

'I don't think so. But maybe tomorrow. I suppose I should see it once more before I take off.'

'What'll you do with yourself all day?'

'I'm sure I'll think of something. Sit around and relax, I suppose. This *is* my vacation.'

'If you get really bored or something, you can always drive into town.'

'Maybe later on. I'll stick around long enough to have lunch with you, though.'

'Fine. Whatever. See you.'

'Have fun.'

As Darcy walked towards a doorway beyond the ticket booth, several of the men waiting in line turned their heads to watch her.

My kid, Chris thought, and felt the familiar stir of pride and concern. Darcy had always been beautiful. When she was a child, it had been women who seemed to make most of the comments: store clerks, people waiting in supermarket lines, strangers passing on the sidewalk. Later, the women stopped remarking on her beauty at about the same time that boys and men began to notice her. And stare. And often get awkward. Chris's male friends, after meeting Darcy, rarely failed to say, 'She's going to break a lot of hearts.'

She probably did, too. But never on purpose, as far as Chris knew. The girl accepted her beauty, realized it was nothing more than a lucky accident, and never let it go to her head, never dumped on people because she considered them inferior.

It was Darcy's own heart that ended up broken, so often, when she let herself fall for guys who turned out to be creeps.

Comes with the territory, Chris thought. All the men want

you, but so often it's the wrong kind who comes along with the right moves. God knows, she'd had to struggle with that, herself, all her life.

Darcy's father was a prime example.

Don't ruin a lovely day by thinking about him, she told herself, and started walking quickly through the tourist centre. She opened a door at the front, and entered the hotel lobby. On her way to the stairs, she glanced at the registration desk. Ethan Mordock was there.

Speaking of creeps, Chris thought.

Fortunately, he was on the telephone with his back turned.

The man had been perfectly polite and friendly the few times she'd spoken with him, but he had that look in his eyes. Like a vulture inspecting its next meal. He might be looking at your face and chatting about the weather, but you always had the feeling he cared more about the colour of your panties.

A real sleaze.

And Darcy's boss.

Chris hurried up the stairs, and felt a little relieved once she turned at the landing and knew she could no longer be seen by him.

She had warned Darcy about the guy. 'I'd keep my guard up around him, if I were you.'

'Oh, he's all right.'

'If you don't mind a man undressing you with his eyes.'

'Depends on the man.'

'Very cute. I'm serious.'

'Don't worry, Mom. He's not my type.'

'Is he married?'

'Interested?' Darcy asked, that glint in her eyes.

'Right. I'll run right down and throw myself into his arms.'

'He'd probably go into cardiac arrest.'

'I take it he's not married.'

'I've heard his wife ran off with someone a few years ago.'

'Well, just watch out for him.'

'Don't worry. He starts any trouble, I'll give him the ol' one-two and knock his lights out.'

The kidding around, Chris knew, was simply her daughter's way of dealing with the problem. The warning had been heard and accepted.

And probably wasn't necessary in the first place. Darcy was a sharp kid. But a little motherly advice never hurt.

Chris searched her shoulder bag as she made her way along the corridor. She found her room key, stopped at the third door from the end, and let herself in.

With the door shut, she turned the latch.

Don't want Ethan the lech coming in with a pass key while I'm undressing, she thought.

The pits to think he can let himself into any room that suits his fancy.

Good thing Darcy has a roommate.

Chris wondered if they used the inside latch. They certainly should.

Remember to mention it at lunch.

Oh, Mom, you worry too much.

The man is probably harmless.

I latched my door, she thought, and I'm sure I'm not nearly as tempting to a man like that as Darcy is.

She suddenly remembered Arthur, one of her boyfriends. Oh, that bastard, that bastard. She hunched over, hot and sick, no longer in the hotel room but home and waking up in her dark bed and wondering where Arthur had gone and looking for him and finding him in Darcy's room, crouched over her bed, touching her while she slept.

Darcy, only sixteen.

Thank God she didn't wake up. She never found out about that disgusting episode.

Days later, she asked, 'What happened to Arthur? You dump him?'

'He was a shithead.'

That grin. That glint in her eyes. 'Hey, I could've told you that.'

And no man, not one, ever slept over again.

Chris looked at herself in the mirror. She was bent over, her face red, as if she'd taken a punch in the belly. She straightened up.

She took her clothes off.

And felt stupid gazing at her reflection.

But it helped.

'Not bad for an old bag of thirty-nine,' she said. Then she got into her swimsuit.

Hank Whitmore looked up from his paperback when the woman entered the pool area. He watched her stride past the end of the pool and choose a lounge chair on the far side.

The scenery, he thought, has taken a definite turn for the better.

She was a tall, slender blonde, probably in her early thirties. As Hank watched, she removed her long white shirt. Her swimming suit had thin straps that formed an X on her back. Except for those, her back was bare to the top of her rump. Shiny white fabric hugged her buttocks.

Hank pursed his lips.

And Paula felt sorry for me, he thought. Poor Dad has to wait around for an hour and a half with nothing to do.

The woman turned slightly and bent over to drape her cover-up on the back of the lounge. Her side was bare all the way down to the hip. Though the suit clung to her breast, it didn't quite reach far enough. The very base of her breast, where it just began to rise from her chest, was left exposed.

Hank forced himself to look down at his book.

No better than a peeping Tom, he thought.

But my God, what a gal.

He looked up again.

She was facing the pool, maybe considering whether to go in for a dip. A couple of kids were splashing around in the shallow end.

Hank wished she would take off her sunglasses.

Her face – what he could see of it – looked just as fine as her body.

She took them off.

Even at this distance, Hank could see the blue of her eyes.

Christ almighty, he thought, I'm in love.

He looked at her left hand. No wedding ring. No ring at all, on either hand.

Her only jewellery was a thin gold chain around her left wrist.

She's not wearing a wedding ring and she's alone.

That doesn't mean she's available, Hank told himself. Maybe she's got a boyfriend who'll be along in a minute.

A gal who looks like this simply cannot be unattached. It's against the laws of nature.

Maybe she's gay.

There's a cheerful thought.

Maybe she's a hooker.

Now there *is* a cheerful thought.

Hank had never been with a prostitute. Not even in Viet Nam, which amused his buddies no end. Over the years since then, he'd frequently toyed with the idea – some were absolutely gorgeous and he knew that they'd do just about anything – but they were so *experienced*. somehow, he'd always been sure he would commit a blunder and end up totally humiliated.

The woman on the other side of the pool was now sitting on her lounge, spreading suntan lotion on her sleek legs.

Hank looked at his wristwatch. He still had more than an hour before the tour ended.

He thought about his money. He had close to two hundred dollars in his wallet, plus five hundred in traveller's cheques. And he'd heard that the classier hookers often took credit cards.

I could do it.

Jesus H. Christ.

He was trembling badly.

To spend an hour in bed with someone like that . . .

He'd always dreamed of having a really beautiful woman. Just once in his life.

What if she's got AIDs or something?

He'd noticed condoms in the hotel shop.

Go for it, man. You may never get another chance like this.

Hank folded his book shut, forgetting to mark the place. He got to his feet. His legs felt shaky and weak. He began to walk.

What'll I say?

What if she's *not* a hooker? As great as she looked, she was awfully old to be in that line. Weren't most of them supposed to be teenagers?

Who knows.

Nothing ventured, nothing gained.

Oh God, I must be out of my mind.

He walked around the end of the pool.

The woman was leaning back, spreading lotion on her arms.

Whatever you say, Hank told himself, don't sound like a jerk.

He stopped beside her lounge.

'Excuse me,' he said.

She looked up at him.

Say something.

'I'm Hank,' he said.

Hello, Hank. Fuck off.

She smiled. It was a fine smile, nothing superior about it. 'Hi,' she said.

He rubbed his hands on his shorts. 'I've got an hour or so to kill.'

'That's a terrible thing to do to an hour.'

'Kill it? Yeah. Well, I guess I'd rather make the most out of it.'

'Reading's a good way to do that.'

She'd noticed him with the paperback. Had she also noticed him staring at her?

The book won't go away,' Hank said.

'And I will?'

'Good chance of it. Are you with someone?'

'My daughter's down in the cavern.'

Hank realized, with mixed disappointment and relief, that she undoubtedly was not a hooker after all. So much for fantasies. But they both had daughters in the cavern. That gave them something in common. Though he wouldn't be getting her into bed, at least he could pass the time with her and enjoy the view. 'Really? My daughter's down there, too.'

'I'm Chris,' she said. She lifted her hand toward him, then hesitated. 'Oh, it's all yooked . . .'

Hank took her hand. It was moist and slick with suntan lotion. 'Nice to meet you, Chris. I'm Hank.'

'I know. Feel free to pull up a seat, if you like.'

'Thanks.' He grabbed a nearby lounge and set it next to Chris's – at an angle so he could look at her without twisting his head halfway around. 'How come you're not taking the tour?' he asked.

'I went yesterday.'

'Didn't your daughter go with you, or . . .?'

'She's a guide. I'm staying here at the hotel for a couple of days, just visiting.'

'Your daughter's a *guide*? They use kids?'

'Everybody's someone's kid.' She laughed softly. 'Don't worry, your daughter is in good hands. Darcy's twenty-one.'

'Gee, you must've been ten when you had her.'

'And then some,' Chris said, her face taking on a red hue. 'What about your daughter? How old is she?'

'Paula's sixteen.'

'She went down alone?'

'I'm not big on caves. She wanted to see it. I didn't think I should deprive her of the experience just because I wasn't interested.'

'That's pretty neat of you,' Chris said. 'Most parents wouldn't do that.'

'Most parents would see the cave with their kid.'

She frowned slightly. 'If you feel that way about it, how come you stayed behind?'

'I figured maybe I'd latch onto some fabulous babe by the pool.'

Oh shit, why did I say that!

Chris laughed.

'As a matter of fact,' he said, 'I've got a touch of claustrophobia. I don't do real well in tight places.'

She looked interested. 'Were you always that way?'

'Something I acquired in the service.' He felt his heart speeding up. 'Do you have any phobias?'

'Getting a splinter in the eye.'

'Ow!'

'Fortunately, it's never happened. But I'm careful about walking close to shelves. Libraries make me very nervous, which is something of a handicap.'

'Why is that?'

'I'm a researcher. I freelance at it. Basically, that means I do the dirty work for lazy writers. How about you?'

'I teach.'

She raised her eyebrows. 'You don't look much like a teacher.'

'You don't look much like a researcher.'

'Because I don't wear glasses and wear my hair in a bun?'

'Among other things.'

She blushed again. 'If you're a teacher, it must be PE.'

'Me, a jock?'

'You obviously work out a lot.'

'I do body-building to work off the tension of the job.'

'So what *do* you teach?'

'Driver's education.'

'Oh shit, you're kidding.' She slapped a hand across her mouth as she started to laugh.

My turn to blush, he thought as he felt his skin heat up.

'I'm sorry. It's just that . . . driver's ed. In high school?'

He nodded.

'It's just . . . I can't picture you. My driver's ed teacher was such an incredible old fart. His name was Deederding and he looked like one. He had this high, squeaky voice. And a nervous tic.' She demonstrated the tic, twitching her left cheek.

God, she was cute doing that!

'Deederding. He was so awful. But there's nothing intrinsically funny about being a driver's ed teacher. I shouldn't have laughed.'

'As a matter of fact, there's plenty intrinsically funny about it. Most people do laugh. They picture a nervous nilly cringing and covering his eyes.'

'I'm sure you're not like that.'

'I do cringe a lot. I rarely cover my eyes.'

'Where are you from?' she asked.

'Santa Monica.'

'You're a long way from home.'

'Where are you from?'

'Da Big Apple.'

Hank felt a tug of disappointment. *We're from opposite sides of the country. I'll never see her again. Today is it. Probably.*

'My daughter's a student at Princeton. She's here on a summer job. I hadn't seen her since spring break . . .' Chris lowered the back of her lounge. She lay down and folded her hands behind her head. 'If you're planning to stick around,' she said, 'why don't you bring your stuff over? No point in taking up two places.'

'Right,' Hank said. 'Save my seat.'

She smiled.

He got up and started making his way around the pool.

She likes me, he thought. *Man, why couldn't this happen back home? Why couldn't she be from Santa Monica or Brentwood or some place? Just my luck. I have to be three thousand miles from home when I meet a gal like this.*

Not only gorgeous, but nice. And she likes me.

And we'll be leaving in an hour.

Shit.

Who says we have to leave? The thought struck him hard, knocking him breathless. His heart thudded.

We could stay here tonight. All I have to do is check us in, if they've got any vacancies. Paula wouldn't mind. Cancel out on Cooperstown. She wasn't all that eager to see the Hall of Fame, anyway. Stay here tonight. Maybe take Chris and her daughter to dinner. Who knows what . . .?

Maybe Chris wouldn't want to do that.

Ask. Nothing ventured, nothing gained.

Hank pulled his shirt off the back of his chair and picked up his book. He walked back around the pool. When he reached the lounges, he saw that Chris's eyes were shut. He sat down and looked at her.

She's shut me out, he thought.

Probably thinks I'm a nuisance, after all. Was just being nice, did her bit for the sake of politeness, and now she wants to be left alone.

So much for my grand schemes.

At least with her eyes shut, she can't see me looking at her.

So Hank looked. She was smooth and tanned and her swimsuit hugged every curve and hollow and mound. But he took little pleasure from the view. His hopes had been smashed, and he felt only loss.

You never stood a chance, he thought.

She's gorgeous, and you're a nonentity.

The tip of her tongue slid out and wetted her lips.

He could *feel* those lips.

You never will.

'If you aren't in any big hurry,' Chris said, 'maybe you and your daughter could join us for lunch.'

Chris woke up. She hadn't meant to doze off. Turning her head, she saw that Hank's lounge was empty. Except for his book.

He'll be back, she thought.

She wondered how long she'd been out.

Maybe the tour's over and he went to get his daughter.

She didn't want to move. The sun felt like a hot, heavy blanket. But she needed to use a toilet, and this was as good a time as any.

Sitting up, she mopped her damp face with a towel. Then she put on the oversized white shirt, buttoned it, and stepped into her sandals. She left her suntan lotion and sunglasses on the lounge to show that she would be back. She picked up her shoulder bag.

No need to return to the room, she thought. She could use the ladies' room in the hotel lobby.

Just ignore Mordock.

The lech.

Walking toward the doors, she smiled. How come Mordock's a lech and Hank isn't? He couldn't take his eyes off me. So what's the difference?

Hank's sweet.

Mordock's a sleazebag.

You can't get much more different than that.

Chris pushed open one of the glass doors. Entering the lobby, she saw Hank at the registration desk. He reached into a rear pocket of his shorts and took out his wallet.

What's he doing?

Checking in?

Because of me?

Good Lord, she thought. She entered the ladies' room and went to one of the stalls. She set her bag on the shelf. She draped her shirt over the door. The toilet looked clean, but she pulled a paper seat cover from its dispenser, tore out the inner sheet, and set it in place. While she was peeling her swimsuit down, an end of the paper slipped and dropped into the water.

'Damn,' she muttered, and brushed the rest of it into the bowl.

She got a new cover, put it down, and sat quickly.

So Hank is checking into the hotel, she thought. In a way, it was almost alarming. But nice, too.

Maybe it has nothing to do with me.

Of course it does. We hit it off, and he decided to stick around for a while to see what develops.

What can develop? He lives in California.

Maybe he's hoping for one night.

Sorry, buster, but if you think I'm going to hop in the sack with you . . .

Santa Monica wouldn't be such a shabby place to live.

You don't even know the guy. Hardly.

He's checking in.

God almighty.

Finished, Chris stood and pulled her swimsuit up. She slipped the straps over her shoulders, turned around and balanced on her right leg while she stepped on the flush lever with her left foot.

The toilet water started to go down, then didn't.

Great, Chris thought. Plumbing problems. She wondered if she should mention it to Mordock.

Let someone else. I'm not talking to that guy if I can help it.

She put her shirt on, slung the bag strap over her shoulder, unlatched the stall door and stepped out.

Hank. He checked in.

Smiling, she shook her head.

The guy really has nerve. Of course he does – he's a driving instructor.

And Darcy was afraid I might get bored.

She stepped to a sink and twisted a faucet handle. Water

trickled out. She tried the other handle, but still no more than a thin stream ran from the nozzle.

Forget it, she thought.

She went to the door and reached for its handle.

And the roar of gunfire pounded her ears.

7

The man behind the registration desk handed the credit card back to Hank and gave him a room key with a big plastic tag. 'Checkout time is eleven a.m.,' he said.

'Thanks.' Hank, turning away, stopped abruptly to stare at the man striding through the lobby doors.

He was about twenty, fat and wearing glasses. His face was scarlet, dripping with sweat, and his cheeks jiggled as he walked. Clamped between his teeth was a lighted cigar.

He carried a bucket in each hand.

The buckets were full. Liquid sloshed over their rims as the man lugged them along.

Hank smelled the pungent stench of gasoline.

'Holy shit,' he muttered.

'Outa the way,' the man said in a high, girlish voice.

Hank backed away from the desk.

The man walked towards it.

The hotel man looked stunned. 'I told you, fella . . .'

'Fuck what you told me, Mordock.'

Hank kept backing away.

The guy with the cigar set one of the buckets on the floor. He lifted the other and swung it with both hands.

The amber liquid surged out, splashing the face and chest of Mordock who shut his eyes and mouth tight as the flood hit him.

'What did you do with her?' the fat man asked. He took the cigar from his mouth and tapped ash onto the counter.

Mordock, dripping gasoline, squinted at him with one eye and shook his head wildly. 'I told you, nobody named Amy Lawson ever checked in. I showed you the cards, I never heard of her. Put that cigar away! Come on, mister!'

'She was here.'

'If something happened to her, it wasn't my fault. I had nothing to do with it.'

'Then why'd you get rid of her registration card?'

'I didn't. I tell you . . .' Suddenly, Mordock had a revolver.

Hank threw himself at the floor. The first shot crashed in his ears an instant after he hit. He saw the fat man flinch and toss the cigar like a dart. Mordock kept blasting as the cigar sailed toward him. The slugs pounded the fat man. Some came out his back, puffing out his white shirt and throwing sprays of blood. Another caught his face. The back of his head flew open.

Mordock got off his last shot, which seemed to miss, just as the cigar touched him off.

He was a torch. The fat man was shot apart.

They faced each other for a moment – two dead men.

The fat man fell forward. His chest hit the edge of the counter. His knees folded. As he dropped, the edge caught his chin and knocked his head back. He tumbled sideways. His shoulder struck the bucket of gasoline on the floor and overturned it.

Mordock started screaming.

Hank pushed himself to his hands and knees. An arm went around his back.

'Hank! Hank!'

Chris was crouched beside him.

Staring at Mordock, he got to his feet.

The man was shrieking and flapping his arms. He was all ablaze, his face bubbling.

He vaulted the counter.

'No!' Hank shouted.

Mordock's feet came down on the belly of the fat man. He stumbled off and fell to his knees, igniting the puddle of gasoline from the second bucket. He squealed, got to his feet, and ran for the doors.

He left flaming shoeprints on the carpet.

He crashed head first through the glass door on the left, fell flat on the concrete just outside the hotel, and lay there.

Chris was already running towards him. Hank chased her, caught her by the shoulder, and pulled her to a stop.

'We've gotta help him!'

'Forget it. He's finished.'

'What'll we do?'

A drop of water splashed the side of Chris's nose and slid off.

Hank looked up. The ceiling sprinklers had been set off, but they weren't showering water down – they were dripping. He couldn't believe it. 'Crazy son of a bitch must've turned off the water.'

He whirled around. The area surrounding the registration desk was an inferno, flames climbing the wall behind it, engulfing the counter, lapping at the ceiling, spreading over the carpet.

He spotted a pair of pay phones near the restroom doors. They were clear of the fire, for now. He grabbed Chris's hand and pulled her towards them. 'Got any change?'

'I think so.'

They reached the phones. She dug into her bag, came out with a change purse, opened it and took out a quarter. 'You call,' Hank said. 'I'll be right back.'

As she lifted the handset, Hank dashed for the tourist area. He pulled open a glass door. There must have been nearly a hundred people in the huge room: wandering the gift shop, standing at the snack bar, sitting at tables, waiting in line for the next tour to start.

'Give me your attention!' he yelled. A few people looked at him. Others continued about their business. 'There's a fire in the lobby! Everybody get out! Stay calm, you've got plenty of time.'

People started shouting, 'FIRE!'

Couples grabbed each other's hands. Parents clutched children, picked up the small ones. Everybody began to rush for the exits along the side and rear of the room.

There were plenty of exits.

They'll be all right, Hank thought.

At the rear of the room, two elevator doors slid open.

A tour group returning from the cavern.

'Thank God,' Hank muttered. He ran for the elevators as they began to empty.

It's too early for Paula's group, he thought. No, it's not. She's here. Please!

He scanned the people leaving the elevators. Must've been thirty of them. He couldn't spot Paula.

He was nearly there when a fire alarm began its deafening honk.

The guide, an attractive young woman, turned to her group

and raised her arms. 'Everybody stay calm!' she shouted. 'Follow me. We'll be outside in a few seconds.'

Hank reached them. 'Paula!' he called. 'Paula!'

Not there.

Clamped with fear, he rushed to the guide. 'Are you Darcy?'

She shook her head. 'I'm Lynn. Darcy's down below. What's going on?'

'Fire in the lobby.'

'Oh, wow.'

'Take 'em out,' Hank said.

Lynn started leading her bunch away.

Hank rushed past them.

The alarm went silent. The lights went off. He threw himself into one of the elevators and pushed its 'down' button. Nothing happened, he pushed it again and again.

Not going anywhere, he realized. Power's out.

Something seemed to collapse inside him.

Paula.

My God.

He told himself she would be safe down in the cavern.

Safe, maybe, but trapped.

Chris. Her girl's down there, too.

Chris, holding the glass door open, gazed into the tourist area. The huge room was deserted except for a few people in a bunch near one of the side exits. And Hank.

Hank was running towards her.

Chris stepped through the doorway. Hank stopped in front of her. He looked grim. Chris took hold of his arms. 'What's wrong?'

'Paula and Darcy are still in the cavern. The other group got out just in time, but they're . . . the elevators . . .' He shook his head.

Chris felt a numbness spread through her.

'I'm sure they're safe,' Hank told her. 'The fire can't get to them. It's just that . . . I don't know how they'll get out. Did you get through to the fire department?'

His voice seemed far away.

'Chris? The fire department?'

Darcy can't get out.

'Chris!' He grabbed her shoulders, shook her. The fog in her mind seemed to lift. 'Did you get the fire department?'

'The phones were dead.'

'How . . .? The crazy bastard must've cut the lines.'

'But I found the fire alarm. I broke the glass, and . . . that'll bring the fire department, won't it?'

'I don't know. I doubt it.'

Chris felt warmth on her back and looked over her shoulder. Flames danced beyond the glass door. They hadn't reached the door yet, but they were close.

'Come on,' Hank said. 'Let's get out of here.'

'Shouldn't we . . . there might be people in the rooms.'

'They would've heard the alarm.'

Chris nodded. The alarm hadn't lasted long, but it had made a terrible clamour. Nobody could have slept through it.

'What about a deaf person?' she asked.

'Do you know of a deaf person staying here?'

'No, but . . .'

'If we ran around knocking on doors, he wouldn't hear that, either.'

'No. Yes. You're right.'

Hank put an arm around her shoulders and guided her diagonally across the room to one of the side exits. Outside, Chris squinted in the brightness. She started to search her handbag, then remembered that she had left her sunglasses beside the pool.

Hank pulled her along, rushing her farther away from the hotel. People were wandering around. There were a lot of cars. She realized that she was on the main parking lot behind the complex.

So disoriented, she thought. Gotta pull myself together.

They stopped.

'My car,' Hank said. 'Want to get in?'

She shook her head.

'Wait here, Chris. I'll check around. Maybe someone has a car phone or CB.'

He hurried away. Chris, watching him, leaned back against the side of the car. And lurched off it, gasping, as the sunheated metal seared her buttocks through the thin fabric of her swimsuit.

She rubbed herself.

She realized what she was wearing.

Swell, she thought. My clothes are in the room.

She looked at the hotel. From out here, no one would ever guess the conflagration inside. The only sign that anything might be wrong was a thin screen of grey smoke rising into the sky on the far side – probably pouring out the lobby door that Mordock had smashed.

Chris wondered if she could get to her room.

I'm not going back in there.

Besides, the corridors might be filled with smoke.

No great loss, she told herself. My clothes, but . . . oh, Darcy. Darcy had a whole steamer trunk full of things.

As long as *she's* all right . . .

Chris remembered seeing the stuffed kitten, Snow, on Darcy's bed that morning. Snow. Santa had given her Snow when she was four.

Tears suddenly flooded Chris's eyes. She lowered her face into her hands and wept.

* * *

A family outing. A goddamn parade. Daddy held the little kid
on his shoulders for a better view.

'You got a car phone?' Hank asked the man.

The man glanced at him, said, 'Sorry,' and pointed. 'See
there, Andy? See the fire in the window?'

Hank hurried on. A few of the tourists were in their cars
and driving slowly through the lot, trying to leave. But most
were standing around to watch the fire.

Hank flinched as something burst. He looked at the
hotel. Black smoke was rolling through a second floor
window near the middle, probably just above the lobby.
The noise he'd heard must have been the window pane
exploding.

He glimpsed claws of flame in the smoke. They curled up
the outside wall.

Someone squeezed Hank's wrist. An old woman in round
spectacles smiled up at him. Her thick lenses were like
magnifying glasses; made her eyes huge. The whites were
yellow and webbed with red. 'How did it start, duke? Y'see
how it started?'

He shook his head.

'My land, ain't this the berries?' Her hand shook his wrist
as if she were demanding an answer.

'Yeah,' Hank said. 'The berries.'

'She's goin' up in smoke. Wouldn't you say so, duke? Goin'
up in smoke.'

'Right. Excuse me.' He freed himself from the woman's
bony grip and hurried away.

Not far ahead, a young man and woman were sitting on
the hood of a Jeep Wagoneer. They both wore cowboy hats.
They both had bottles of beer. Clamped between the knees of
the woman was an open bag of potato chips.

'Have you got a car phone?' Hank asked. 'A transmitter of some . . .'

'Nope,' the guy said. 'What's the trouble?'

'We've got to report the fire.'

'It hasn't been *reported*?'

'I don't think so. We tried to call right after it broke out, but the phones were dead.'

'Shit, that fucker's gonna burn to the ground.'

As he said that, his eyes went wide. Hank whirled around in time to see a section of the roof cave in. Seconds after the crash, a galaxy of glowing embers floated up through the smoke. Flames began to chew the ragged edges of the crater.

'Take this, pal.' The man gave his beer to Hank. 'Come on, Luce,' he said, and leaped off the hood.

'What?'

'We're gonna lay rubber outa here and report this bitch before the whole fuckin' place goes up.'

Hank clapped him on the shoulder, then waved some bystanders out of the way to make room for the Jeep to back out of its parking space.

Once out of the lot, it picked up speed.

No matter how fast it goes, Hank thought, it couldn't reach town in much less than twenty minutes. Then it might be another twenty minutes before the first fire truck could arrive. At best.

Maybe, somehow, the fire's already been reported.

But Hank doubted it.

He continued his search for someone with a car phone or radio transmitter.

Standing on the bumper of Hank's car, Chris spotted him near the far side of the lot. He was wandering among the spectators, stopping briefly and moving on.

'Looking for someone, honey?'

She nodded, and glanced down at the man. He wore a blue T-shirt and jeans. His T-shirt read, SAVE A TREE, EAT A BEAVER. His eyes were inspecting the merchandise.

Chris realized her shirt was open. She started to button it.

'Aw, now.'

'Don't bug me, okay?'

'I happen to have a fully equipped bar over in my trailer. You look like a martini might do you a world of good.'

'No, thank you.'

'Some fire, isn't it? I hear a couple of folks got cooked. They say there's more than a hundred trapped in the cave.'

'Including my daughter. Get outa here.'

'Well, excuuuuuuse me.' He turned away. As he walked off, Chris heard him mutter something that sounded like, 'Tightass cunt.'

She flinched at the roar as another section of roof collapsed. The fire was spreading more rapidly to the right – to the east . . . in the direction of the cave elevators.

A man with a home video camera crossed the driveway at the front of the parking lot. He stepped over the curb and made his way closer to the burning complex.

A young woman in a guide uniform rushed up behind him. Thick, reddish-brown hair. She had to be Lynn, Darcy's room-mate.

She grabbed the man by the arm, spoke to him, turned him around and walked him back into the lot.

Chris leaped down from the bumper. She hurried forward, weaving between parked cars and spectators, scanning the area ahead, trying to spot Lynn.

And found her near the front.

'Lynn!'

The girl turned to her. For a moment, she looked confused. Then she raised her thick eyebrows. 'Oh, Darcy's mom, right? Hey, you know, I'm sure Darcy's just fine. I mean, there's no way in the world the fire's going to get down in the cavern. She's totally safe, you know?'

'I have to talk to you.'

'Sure. Shoot. You got any idea where Mordock is? He ought to be helping with the crowds, you know?'

'He's dead.'

Lynn's eyes went wide. She didn't appear bothered by the news, just surprised. 'No fooling? Dead? Ethan? The owner?'

'That's right. He's been dead from the start. You've got to help me, Lynn.'

'Sure. Just name it.'

'Darcy's trapped.'

'Yeah, I know. The pits, but like I say . . . I mean, I wouldn't wanta be stuck down there myself, but it's safe, you know?'

'How is she going to get out?'

Lynn shrugged. 'I guess the elevators.'

'The place is burning to the ground,' Chris pointed out, trying to keep her patience. This girl seemed incredibly dense. How could she be a guide, like Darcy? 'In a little while, there won't *be* any elevators.'

'Well, yeah, I guess not. But the shafts, they'll be there. They aren't going anyplace. So the fire department can maybe lower ropes or a basket or something.' As if reciting, Lynn added, 'The shafts are a hundred and fifty-three feet deep.'

'That's pretty goddamn deep.'

'I'm sure the fire department will have a way to get to them. Don't you think so?'

'I suppose.'

After the fire's cold, Chris thought. After the rubble has

been cleared from the shafts. 'Are there supplies down there?' Chris asked.

'You mean like food? Nothing like that. There's plenty of water, though. You shouldn't worry about it, really. I mean, I can't imagine they won't be out in a few hours. By tomorrow, anyhow.'

'I took the tour, yesterday,' Chris said. 'Darcy talked about a natural opening to the cavern.'

'Yeah, but that's all blocked off.'

'With a rock wall like the one on the inside?'

'I guess. I've never seen it up close.'

'Do you know where it is?'

'Kind of.' She pointed to the east.

'Come with me.'

'You've been there?' Hank asked.

The girl shrugged. 'Well, see, I wasn't what you might say actually *there*.' A voluptuous ditz, Hank thought. 'I mean, I saw it from the other side of the valley. Tom – that's the guy who helps with the boats down in the cavern – he's down there, too, you know.'

'What about him?' Hank asked.

'Well, it's just that Tom's the one that showed it to me. We were on this dirt road over across from it. So I couldn't see it too well.'

'But you know where to find it?'

'I think so.'

Hank opened the passenger door of his rental car. 'How about climbing in. I'll drive us over there.'

'Gee, I don't know. I'm sort of like on duty, you know, and I really don't know . . .'

'Is something more important,' Chris asked, 'than getting those people out of the cave?'

'Well, I guess not. But you can't get in. Like I was saying, it's all walled up.'

'We'd better take some tools along,' Chris said. 'A pick or something.'

'You'd need lights, too,' Lynn told them. 'Really, you oughta just wait for the fire department. They'll get everybody out.'

'Eventually,' Chris said. She looked at Hank. 'What do you think?'

Hank gazed past her at the blazing hotel. The entire east wing was now engulfed, so the area housing the elevators was already being consumed.

'The fire department isn't even *here* yet,' he said. 'By the time they get this thing out, there might be a ton of rubble covering the elevator shafts. They'll have to bring in heavy equipment to clear all that away.' He turned to Lynn. 'How far is it through the closed part of the cave to that other wall?'

'About half a mile. But it's dark and there aren't any walkways or anything. I mean, it'd be the pits, you know? And there's that chasm somebody might fall into like Elizabeth Mordock. I don't think . . .'

'We could probably get to them in a couple of hours,' Chris said.

'Depending on the walls,' said Hank.

'Really, you two, I don't see what the big hurry is. The fire department can take care of it. They'll get 'em out.'

'It's our daughters down there,' Hank said.

'But they're safer staying where they are until the fire department can . . .'

'How do you know that?' Chris asked her.

'Well . . .'

'What if something's gone wrong down there?'

Hank felt a sudden tug of fear. 'What do you mean?'

Frowning, Chris shook her head. 'Maybe somebody's been hurt. If they don't already know they're trapped, they'll find out pretty soon. People might panic. There might be arguments, fights. God only knows. I just think, the faster they're out of there, the better.'

'Same here,' Hank said. 'Let's go for it.'

8

'On the bright side,' Greg said, 'we've got light and heat.'

After the initial confusion, nearly everyone had stood up and approached the blazing remains of the elevators. Darcy stood with the others in a semi-circle, Greg at her side. Some held out their hands as if to warm them at a bonfire.

A man said, 'Who's got the marshmallows?'

His little girl frowned up at him. 'You're not funny, Daddy.'

'How in God's name do we get out of here, now?' a woman asked.

Darcy didn't care about that. Not at the moment. Staring into the flames, she could only think about her mother.

Something awful had happened up top. A fire, maybe an explosion. Maybe a nuclear blast like the man had suggested so long ago.

Mom's all right, she told herself. Please. She has to be.

Greg put his arm around her. 'Don't worry,' he said.

'My mother.'

'I'm sure she's fine. She probably had plenty of time to get away.'

'What do you mean?'

'It wasn't anything sudden,' he said. 'Whatever happened, it must have started when the lights went off. It took all this time before the elevators dropped, so the whole place didn't go up at once.'

Darcy thought about that. Greg was right. Obviously, the entire complex hadn't been destroyed in some terrible cataclysm. The fire must have started a distance away and spread until it consumed the elevator housings. So people had time to get away. Maybe Mom was okay. Maybe she wasn't even in the hotel when it happened.

Darcy looked at Greg. 'Thanks,' she said.

He nodded. His broad face was ruddy in the firelight, his eyes shining. Steam was rising off the front of his sweatshirt. Darcy rested her head against his shoulder.

The heat from the fires was almost too much. She had thought for a time that she would never be warm again. But now her face felt as if it were being seared. Her skin was stinging under the snug heat of her trousers. The touch of the windbreaker against her breasts was painful. Sweat trickled down her sides.

She turned around, and sighed with relief as the hurt faded and her back began to warm up.

Someone sidestepped through the fluttering light and moved in front of her. The man in the Peterbilt hat. 'You're supposed to be in charge here,' he said. 'What are you gonna do now?'

'Just take it easy,' Greg told him.

'I'll get us out of here,' Darcy said.

Those nearby, who heard her over the other voices and the

windy noise and snapping sounds of the fire, stepped in closer and looked at her.

'Gonna get us out, are you? How do you figure that?'

He spoke to Darcy as if this were all her fault.

'Cool down, slick.'

'Butt out,' he snapped.

The old man's head moved forward on his long neck. His scalp was hairless except for a white fringe over his ears. His eyes were small and squinty, his nose a beak. He looked to Darcy like a bald eagle about to rip off the bastard's face.

'Don't let him rile you, Calvin,' said the buxom woman at the old man's side – maybe his daughter. She tugged his arm. He pulled it free.

'Yeah, Calllllvin,' mocked the man in the truck hat. 'Don't want you having a heart attack.'

'Low-life son of a whore, you best start minding your manners, or . . .'

'Or what, Calllllvin?'

'All right, now!' Greg's voice shot out. 'We've got enough trouble without fighting among ourselves. Darcy said she's going to get us out, so why don't we listen to her?'

Those nearby gathered in closer. Others, farther off, continued to talk among themselves.

'LISTEN UP!' It was the fat boy.

The voices went silent. Darcy stepped past the scowling man, patted the shoulder of his son, and made her way into the cool shadows a distance from the fires. Turning around, she found that Greg had stayed with her. She held up her arms.

The people faced her, their backs to the blazing elevators.

'Obviously,' she said in a firm voice, 'it's a lot worse than we thought. The area above us is burning.'

'Tell us something we don't know.'

'Would you *please* hush?' A woman's voice.

'What'll we do?' Another woman.

'We're going to die.' More of a whiny squeal than a voice.

'Nobody's going to die,' Darcy said. 'I still think that rescue is possible from the elevator shafts, but that'll take a lot longer than we imagined. And since we don't know what's going on up there, I think it would be foolish to do nothing but wait. There is another way out.'

'The natural opening.' It was the fat boy's knowing voice.

'That's right,' Darcy said. 'Just before the lights went out, I was showing you Ely's Wall and telling about how he closed off the other half of the cavern. There's a pick axe near the dock area. With that, I'm sure we'll be able to break through the wall. From there, it's only about half a mile to the natural opening. We'll take the pick axe with us, and knock out the wall at that end. Then we'll be home free.'

'Fuck. Should've done that in the first place.'

'Yeah, we'd be out by now.'

'Let's do it!'

Back-lit by the fires, the group seemed to Darcy like a band of villagers eager to begin a foolhardy errand. Movie extras. Faceless dark forms gesturing and mouthing brave words. A hunting party, a lynch mob, peasants working themselves up to go chasing the Frankenstein monster.

'What're we waiting for?'

'Let's haul ass!'

'EVERYBODY SHUT UP!' Darcy shouted.

The noise faded to mutters.

'It won't be a picnic. We've got one good flashlight and one that's nearly dead. Beyond Ely's Wall, there will be no walkways. There is also the chasm that Elizabeth Mordock fell into. In other words, the terrain will be rugged and dangerous. If we all try to go trooping through there, most of you will be doing it in darkness.'

'Here's my suggestion. I think that no more than six of us should try to go out that way. One flashlight should be enough for a group that small, and we'd be able to keep track of each other. Everyone else, can wait here, where there's warmth and light. Once we're out, we'll make sure the rest of you are rescued as quickly as possible. You'll either be lifted out through the elevator shafts or a rescue party with plenty of good lights will come in from the natural opening and guide you out. Either way, you won't be in here much longer than those who go in the first group with me. But you'll be able to leave in a lot more safety.'

'I'll give you a while to think about it. Decide whether you want to stay here or go with the escape party. I recommend you choose to stay here unless you've got a very good reason not to. After you've had a chance to make up your minds, I'll pick my group from those of you who want to leave with me.'

'Guess that leaves *me* out,' muttered the Peterbilt man.

'That's right,' Darcy said. Raising her voice, she announced. 'You've got five minutes.'

'I absolutely must be one of the six,' Helen said to Carol.

'I'll stick with you.'

Helen shook her head. The lenses of her glasses reflected fire. She lifted a hand to Carol's cheek. 'You're so sweet. But there's no need for you to risk life and limb. Besides, look how you're dressed.'

'I know how I'm dressed,' Carol said. The heart from the burning elevators felt wonderful, and she knew she would regret leaving the warmth. 'Hell, the fires aren't going to last for ever.'

'I'll leave you my sweater.'

'I'm going with you. If they'll let me.'

'Stay. I'd stay, myself, if it weren't for this damned diabetes. I just can't take the risk of waiting any longer than necessary. The hotel must have burnt.' She shook her head. 'I'll have to go into town, I suppose.'

'We'll both go, Helen.'

'It might be terribly dangerous. You heard what the guide said. There won't be a walkway. And that chasm. It sounds just horrendous. I wouldn't be able to forgiver myself if you came along on my account and . . . something happened to you.'

'Nothing will happen. Besides, what makes you think I'd want to stay behind? I don't know, any of these people. You're my best friend. Even if you are a pain in the ass sometimes.'

Helen made a sound that was more like a sob than a laugh, and embraced her.

'I'd sure like to see what's on the other side of that wall,' Wayne said.

'Don't be ridiculous,' Jean told him. 'It wouldn't be any different than what's on this side.'

'Except it's been closed up for about sixty years. And it's where Elizabeth Mordock died.'

'Daddy, don't be so disgusting.'

'Might be haunted,' he said.

'There's no such things as ghosts,' Katie told him.

'Who says so?'

She slapped his arm.

'You hit me one more time, young lady, I'll knock your block off.'

'Mommy.'

'Don't speak to her that way, Wayne. It's not funny.'

'That's right.'

'She shouldn't go around hitting me all the time.'

'You shouldn't tease her about ghosts.'

'Who's teasing?'

'If you really thought Elizabeth Mordock's ghost might be lurking in the other side of the cave, they couldn't *drag* you there. You're the biggest chicken I know.'

Wayne laughed. She was right, of course. 'Well,' he said, 'it's quite obvious that I can't go with the first group and leave you two alone. We'll get to see the other end of the cave sooner or later, anyway.'

'I don't want to,' Katie said.

'It's either that, or we'll have to be lifted out with ropes or something. Personally, I'd rather take my chances with Elizabeth's ghost than get dropped.'

'Goddamn it, Wayne!'

'I reckon you'd rather stay here by the fire,' Calvin said, smiling and patting Mavis's considerable backside.

'Don't tell me *you* want to go.'

'I don't aim to leave you behind, that's for sure. Minute I'm gone, old slick'd take it into his head to give your ass a poking.'

'Calvin!'

He laughed.

'It's not at all funny.'

'Don't fret. It ain't about to happen. I'll be right here and see to it. 'Sides, I reckon his pecker's so teeny he'd never find it in the dark.'

'Why don't you quit harping about him? Honestly, Calvin, you act like such a baby sometimes.'

'Which is it, a baby or a chauvinist?'

'Both.'

'You sure do take pleasure in insulting a man. Not that I hold it against you. It's just the way you gals are. No sooner you get married than you turn into a shrew.'

He saw the corners of her mouth turn down. Now I've gone and done it, he thought. 'Shitfire,' he said, 'don't take it personal.'

'How am I supposed to take it? You as much as said you wished you hadn't married me.'

'I said no such thing, May. You're just fine, you're just fine.'

'You called me a shrew.'

'Well, you *are* a shrew. But like I say, it ain't your fault. You're just a woman, and that's a natural part of the equipment. It comes with the wedding band.'

Now, she was weeping. In the firelight, Calvin saw shiny tears rolling down her cheeks.

'Oh, damnation,' he muttered. He clamped his cane between his knees, and put his arms around her. 'I'm sorry, sweetie-pie.'

'You should be.' She squeezed him tightly. He felt the cane move. 'Is that *you*, Calvin?'

'If I go,' Paula asked, 'will you come, too?'

Kyle went tight and cold inside. 'You don't want to go, do you?'

'My dad . . . I'm scared he might've gotten hurt. And even if he's okay, he must be awfully worried about me, I've just got to get out of here as fast as I can.'

'If your father were here,' Kyle said, 'I bet he'd want you to stay and wait for a real rescue.'

'Why?'

'Because he wouldn't want you to take a chance like that. It'll be . . . really bad on the other side.'

He wished he could tell her how bad. He wished he could tell *Darcy* how bad, and talk her out of breaking through the wall.

At first, after the elevators fell, Kyle had been stunned to realize that the trouble was more than a simple power failure. The whole complex up top must be burning down: the hotel, the tourist area with its gift shop and snack bar, his own room – and worst of all, room 115.

The loss of 115 *hurt*. To think that it was gone before he'd even gotten another chance to use it.

He told himself, Dad'll rebuild the place. He'll make another room just like 115. It will be the same, and some day I'll be running the new hotel and I'll pick who I want to put in there.

The thoughts of rebuilding made him feel a lot better, but then Darcy started talking about escape through the other end of the cavern, and Kyle felt a rush of dread that turned his legs soft and he'd held onto Paula to keep himself steady.

He couldn't let them do it!

If they broke through Ely's Wall . . .

How could he stop them?

Warn Darcy. But what could he tell her without revealing the truth?

There had to be another way.

Get rid of the pick axe. Without that, they wouldn't be able to smash through the barrier.

The pick axe must be in the grotto where Darcy had changed clothes. Kyle hadn't seen it there, but his eyes had never left Darcy. Still, that's where it probably was. Cubby Wales had been working to enlarge the grotto and must've left his tools behind.

While Darcy continued speaking to the group, Kyle imagined himself finding the pick axe and hurling it into the Lake of Charon. They'd never find it there.

He would have to sneak away. Maybe whisper to Paula that he had to take a leak, then hurry to the grotto. Without any light. (Follow the railing.) But it would take so damn long. They were bound to notice he was gone. When they got to the grotto and the pick axe wasn't there, Darcy would know he was the one who took it. Then, after they found the pick axe (they'd make him show where he threw it), they'd break through the wall anyway.

They'd find what was there.

Maybe not.

But if they did, they'd realize that Kyle knew about it – otherwise, why did he ditch the pick axe?

I can't do anything, he finally decided. I can't let on that I know. Then, whatever happens, I won't get the blame.

If there was some way to stop just Darcy . . .

Don't think about it, he told himself. You can't do anything. Maybe she'll be all right.

But now Paula wanted to go along, too.

Kyle took Paula by the hand and led her away from the others. 'I have to tell you something,' he said. They walked towards the darkness. The heat from the fires faded. 'I don't want anyone else to know this, so you've got to promise you won't say anything.'

'What is it?'

'Do you promise?'

'Sure,' she said. Her voice trembled slightly.

'It's who I am.' He stopped. He looked back. They were far from the rest of the group. He put his hands on Paula's shoulders. 'I'm Kyle Mordock.'

'You mean like Mordock Cavern?'

He nodded. 'My family owns all this. My dad, actually.'

'Oh Kyle, I'm sorry. Maybe it's . . . just a small fire.'

He shrugged. 'Doesn't matter. It's all insured. Dad has lots of insurance. We'll rebuild. But the thing is, it has to be a secret that my dad's the owner. If the others find out, they might . . . you know, cause trouble. They might blame me.'

'Doesn't Darcy know?'

'Yeah, but that's different. And I don't think she's told anyone. Do you know what a scapegoat is?'

'Sure.'

'I'd be the scapegoat if it got around. That's why Darcy's keeping it a secret. The thing is, I've lived here all my life. My dad and I, we've got rooms in the hotel. So I know a lot about the cavern – maybe more than anyone. I know some things the guides don't know.' He eased Paula closer to him. He felt the soft push of her breasts against his chest. 'The other part of the cave . . . a certain area behind Ely's wall . . . used to be an Indian burial place. I've read Ely's diary. When he closed it up, all the bodies were still there. A whole lot of them. And he even wrote that he thought it was spirits of the dead Indians that pushed his wife into the chasm. That's stupid, of course. I mean, I don't believe that, myself. But the corpses of all those Indians . . .' He shook his head. 'I get the creeps, just thinking about it.'

'Aren't they buried?' Paula whispered.

'They're just . . . like lying around. Some are sitting up, some leaning against the walls. At least that's what Ely wrote.'

'Jesus.'

'That's how come I don't think you really want to go along with the others. Me, I don't want to set foot on the other side of Ely's Wall. I don't want to see those things.'

'Me neither,' Paula said.

'You'll stay, then?'

She nodded, her hair tickling Kyle's cheek.

'If we're lucky,' he said, 'we'll get rescued through the

elevator shafts. Then we won't have to go through that place at all.'

'Oh, I hope so. Jesus. Shouldn't we tell the others?'

'We can't. They'd find out who I am, and . . .'

'Okay,' Darcy called, 'those of you who want to go along with me, step forward and I'll make the final selection.'

Paula looked over her shoulder at the others. Then her arms tightened around Kyle.

Darcy was glad to see that there weren't many volunteers. For most of the people, remaining here with the light and heat of the elevator fires was apparently far more attractive than venturing into the chilly darkness, into an unknown and dangerous section of the cavern.

Greg volunteered, as she expected he would.

So did Jim and Beth Donner.

Tom.

A young man and woman who were holding hands. The woman wore a maternity dress in the style of a sailor suit.

A white-haired, obese man who was smoking a cigar and appeared to be at least sixty years old.

A pair of lean, matching men in plaid shirts and goatees. They appeared to be about forty.

A couple of women, one rather stiff looking in a sweater, blue slacks and glasses, the other looking innocent and vulnerable and wearing a sleeveless sundress that must have kept her in shivers until the fires came down.

No Kyle. That was a nice surprise. Maybe he'd dumped Darcy for that girl – Paula. She felt a small stir of guilt, once again, for pairing Paula with Kyle.

Might not be such a good idea, she thought, leaving them here together.

Hell, I'm not a chaperone.

She looked at the people gathered in front of her. 'I'm afraid I won't be very democratic about this. Tom, I want you staying here. For one thing, you shouldn't be exerting yourself. For another, I want you to take charge of the group that stays behind.'

'Either way's fine with me,' he said.

Darcy turned to the pregnant woman. 'There may be a lot of rock climbing in the darkness. I don't want to worry about you falling.'

'I'm perfectly capable of . . .'

'I'm sure you are. But you're staying unless you've got some kind of overwhelming reason to get out fast.'

'You're not being fair.'

'I'm being practical. You're staying here.' She turned to the heavy man with the cigar. 'You, too.'

'You're the captain,' he said.

Darcy smiled. 'Thanks.' She scanned the others. 'Greg, I want you to come. Jim and Beth – you've both been a lot of help, so you're welcome to join us . . . though God knows why you'd want to.'

'I miss the sunlight,' Beth said.

'And we have dinner plans,' said Jim.

'Well, you're in.' Darcy looked at the remaining four. 'I only want to take two more, and I think men . . .'

'I have to go with you,' said the woman with the glasses. 'I'm a diabetic. I left my insulin in the hotel. I need to follow a special diet and I didn't expect to miss lunch. I'm afraid that if . . .'

'Okay. You're in. Both of you.' She turned to the matching men. 'Sorry, fellows.'

'It's quite all right with me,' said one. 'It was all Brian's idea, and I'm sure I would much prefer to stay cozy and snug by the fire.'

'You're such a sissy,' said Brian.

'You wouldn't have me any other way.'

Darcy raised her voice. 'Okay, my group is ready to go. I'll be leaving Tom in charge here with one of the flashlights. We'll be as quick as possible. For all I know, you people might be out before we are. In any case, you won't be in here for more than a few hours.'

'Any questions before we go?'

There were no questions. A few people wished them good luck. Someone said, 'Break a leg.'

'We'll try to avoid that,' Darcy said.

Crouching, she rushed to one of the blazing elevators. The heat pressed against her. She squinted into the debris, then grabbed a broken length of plank. She backed up, pulling it out. Its end was burning. It would make a fine torch for as long as it lasted, and postpone the time when she would need to use the flashlight.

Greg, hurrying past her, found a fiery brand for himself.

Jim did the same.

Those staying behind stood in silence as Darcy, her torch held high, led her small group into the darkness.

9

'You don't get me going in there,' Lynn said as Hank pulled out of the parking lot. He glimpsed the burning hotel in the rear-view mirror. 'I mean, Elizabeth Mordock's *body* is in there.'

Chris looked over her shoulder. 'You don't have to go in. All we want you to do is show us where the place is.'

'You won't be able to get in.'

'We'll get in,' Hank said. He glanced at Chris. 'We have to make a detour into town, first. There's a shopping centre. Paula and I stopped for doughnuts this morning. I think it had a hardware store.'

'Yeah,' Lynn said. 'Andy's. I've been there a few times. They've got all kinds of stuff.'

Hank slowed the car to round a bend, then picked up speed again. The trees along the roadside flashed by in a blur of green.

Where the hell are the fire trucks? he wondered. Then he thought, who needs them? If they'd shown up in time to save the elevator area . . . The way it's going, we'll reach the girls before the fire even gets knocked down. That's if the fire department shows up at all.

Maybe they were busy at another call.

Maybe that guy in the Jeep changed his mind about reporting it.

Doesn't matter any more. We'll get the girls out.

Hank shuddered.

I can't go into that cavern.

He imagined the darkness, the walls closing in on him, suffocating him.

I can do it, he told himself. I'll have to do it. I can't send Chris in alone.

'Are you okay?' Chris asked.

'Does it show?'

'I'm just worried about Paula.'

'I've told you,' Lynn said from the back seat. 'Everybody's safe down there. What won't be safe is leading that whole bunch out through the bad end of the cave. I mean, I don't think you know what you're doing.'

Hank sped around a curve, saw a stop sign ahead, and hit the brakes. As the car slowed, he checked the main road. Nothing in sight. He rolled past the sign, swung onto the road and floored the accelerator. The car shot forward, pressing him into the seat.

'What do you suppose that was all about?' Chris asked.

'Back in the lobby.'

'And Mordock being dead?' Lynn wanted to know.

'A guy came in with buckets of gasoline and a cigar,' Hank said. 'He was upset about some woman he thought had been a guest at the hotel. Apparently, he thought Mordock had done something to her. He doused Mordock with gasoline, and Mordock suddenly started busting caps.'

'Started what?' Lynn asked.

'Shooting at him. The guy tossed his cigar, and *poof.*'

'Man,' Lynn murmured.

'What did he think Mordock did to her?' Chris asked.

'Made her disappear. I guess this guy had talked to Mordock about it before. He seemed sure that the gal had checked in, but Mordock must've shown him the registration cards to prove that she hadn't. Her card wasn't there. That's what convinced the guy that Mordock was behind her disappearance.'

'He must've been crazy,' Chris said.

'The gal was probably his sister or wife or something.'

'I wonder what Mordock did with her.'

'Who says he did anything?' Lynn argued. 'Just because some guy accuses him . . .'

'The man seemed absolutely certain she checked in. She'd probably phoned him from the hotel.'

'I had Mordock figured for a sleaze,' Chris said. 'But it's hard to imagine he actually . . . do you suppose he killed her?'

'I bet the guy with the gas thought so.'

'Ethan wouldn't do that,' Lynn said. 'He was a nice guy.'

'I got the feeling he was *too* nice,' Chris told her. 'At least as far as pretty women were concerned. I noticed you didn't seem very upset when I told you he was dead.'

'I don't care about him one way or the other. I mean, it's too bad he got killed and everything. But I don't think he was some kind of a lunatic going around murdering his guests like that guy in *Psycho*. That's nutty. And I don't think it's nice to dump on him now that he's crumped.'

'Somebody got rid of that woman's registration card,' Chris pointed out.

'Assuming she did check in,' Hank said.

'I have a feeling she did.'

'So do I.'

'That doesn't mean Ethan had something to do with it,' Lynn persisted.

She sure is sticking up for him, Hank thought. Maybe she'd been involved with him. Possible. It couldn't have been a very serious relationship, though, or she'd be more upset about his death.

None of my business, he decided.

As his car bore down on the rear of a station wagon, Hank swerved across the centre line. In an instant, he passed the station wagon. He swung back into his lane. The wagon shrank in the rear-view mirror.

'If anybody was nuts around there,' Lynn said, 'it was that kid Kyle.'

'Who's he?' Chris asked.

'Ethan's kid. Wouldn't surprise me much if *he* tried messing around with a guest. I wouldn't put anything past him. Spooky kid. He *really* had Darcy going crazy.'

'He'd have access to the registration cards,' Hank said.

Chris turned around on her seat and looked back at Lynn.

Her left knee touched the side of Hank's leg. He glanced at her smooth thigh. It was draped by a corner of her shirt. The bottom of the shirt was open. Between her legs, the swimsuit was narrow and tight. Hank didn't allow himself more than a glimpse before forcing his eyes back to the road.

'What did he do to Darcy?' Chris asked.

'Not much. I mean, he had a . . . he was interested in her. He kept going on her tours and staring at her. You'd be surprised how many guys on those tours get *very* interested in us. I don't know, maybe it's the uniform. These teenage guys, you can almost see their mouths watering. You just . . . it's flattering, you know, and nothing much ever . . . they take the tour and go away, you never see them again. But not Kyle. He's always around. And he's Ethan's son, so Darcy wasn't real eager to tell him to fff . . . bug off.'

'This Kyle . . .' Chris's voice stopped. Her head snapped towards the front.

'It's about time,' Hank said, hearing the sirens. Slowing down only slightly, he eased the car to the right. The side tyres rumbled on the gravel at the edge of the road.

The sirens blared louder, louder, and a police car shot around the bend and flashed past, lights whirling. Next came the red car of the fire chief. Then an emergency rescue van, a pumper truck, a hook and ladder. They roared by and the noise faded. Hank swung back onto the road and pressed the accelerator down. 'Nothing that'll get our kids out,' he said. 'They'll need a bulldozer, probably. Maybe a crane.'

Chris nodded. Her face was grim. She turned her head to look at Lynn in the back seat.

Hank glanced again at her inner thigh, the clinging swimsuit. He felt a warm rush of arousal and guilt.

Keep your damned eyes on the road, he told himself.

'You said this kid, Kyle, went on her tours.'

'Yeah, and he'd just gaze at her. It was like he had a crush on Darcy. Only with him, "crush" doesn't seem like the right way to put it. It seems too . . . I don't know.'

'Innocent?' Chris asked.

'Yeah. I mean, he's only like fifteen but he doesn't come across as innocent. He's pretty spooky for a kid.'

'Was he on the tour this morning?' Chris asked.

'Yeah, he was. We passed, you know? Darcy's was taking her bunch in, and mine was on the way out. Yeah, Kyle was right behind her.'

'Great,' Chris muttered.

She looked at Hank. He met her worried gaze, shook his head, and put his hand on her leg. He felt guilty about that. I'm just comforting her, he told himself, and kept his hand there. 'I'm sure it's all right,' he said.

She put her hand over his.

'Yeah,' Lynn said. 'He's not gonna . . .'

'You just told me you wouldn't put anything past him,' Chris reminded the girl.

'Well . . .'

'Chris,' Hank said, 'there are over thirty people down there.' Including Paula, he thought. Paula. The same age as the kid, and alone.

Kyle had access to the registration cards.

Kyle could have made that other girl disappear.

Paula's trapped down there with him.

But it's Darcy he's got the hots for. And there are all those other people. He wouldn't try anything.

'Darcy can take care of herself,' Chris muttered as if trying to reassure herself.

Ahead was a traffic light. It was red. As Hank slowed down, he saw the shopping centre beyond the intersection. The sight of it should have been a relief. Instead, Hank felt his stomach knot.

We're that much closer.

When we leave, we'll be heading for the cavern.

I'll be okay, he told himself.

Like hell.

As long as Paula's okay, that's all that counts. And Darcy. If that fucker's messed with them, he'll pay.

The light turned green.

'You two go on ahead,' Chris said as they walked across the parking lot. 'I'll go to the sporting goods store and meet you back at the car.'

'They've probably got flashlights at Andy's,' Hank said.

'I need clothes. If they have a Coleman lantern, I'll pick up one of those and some flashlights.'

'If you really plan on going into the cavern,' Lynn said to Hank, 'you should have a sweatshirt or something. You'll be cold in that.' She fingered the front of his knit shirt.

'I'll pick up something warm for you,' Chris told him. 'I'd already planned on it.'

He reached into the back pocket of his shorts and took out his wallet.

'Forget it,' Chris told him. 'You take care of the pick or whatever.'

Lynn went along with Hank, which suited Chris fine. She hadn't cared much for Lynn from the moment Darcy introduced her yesterday. The girl had struck her as being not only a little vague, but irresponsible. And back in the car, the way she'd taken Mordock's side when anyone could see that the guy was a creep – he's dead, Chris reminded herself.

And maybe his son's as bad as he was, or worse. The kid had a lech for Darcy.

I can thank Lynn for that cheerful information.

The girl had seemed to savour telling her about it. A juicy bit of gossip.

Hey, guess what. You think Ethan was a creep, you should get a load of his son. Oh, and by the way, he's hot for your daughter and he's in the cave with her. God only knows what he might be up to. I tell you, I wouldn't put anything past him.

Just what I wanted to hear.

Then she's running her fingers down Hank's chest.

Not only a twit, but a flirt.

Chris entered the sporting goods store. The air inside was cool on her bare legs.

A man standing in the checkout line stared at them.

Big deal. Hasn't he seen legs before?

She grabbed a shopping cart and rolled it through the aisles until she came to the sportswear section. She found warm-up suits in her size, picked a blue one and dropped it into the cart. She found a plain grey sweat-shirt for Hank, then changed her mind and chose a warm-up suit for him. After all, she thought, he's not only wearing the shirt Lynn seemed so fond of touching, but shorts. Surprising that Lynn didn't give those a stroke, while she was at it.

Remembering the stares of the man in the checkout line, Chris picked up a pair of jogging shorts for herself. Then she headed for the shoe department, and threw some white socks into her cart.

As she scanned the shoe display, a young man with a moustache and the heavily muscled body of a weight lifter approached her. 'Can I help you with something?'

'I'd like a pair of running shoes. White. Size six.'

'Have a seat. I'd better measure. It's very important, particularly with athletic shoes, to have a perfect fit.'

'I'm in a hurry. Size six will be fine. Regular width.'

'If you say so.' He sounded slightly reproachful. 'Any particular style or brand?'

'Something like this,' she said, pointing out a white Reebok on the display wall.

'Excellent choice.' He lifted the sample and inspected it.

'May I help you?' asked an older man approaching from the side.

The one with the muscles held the shoe towards him. 'We'd like a pair of these in size six, regular width.'

'Certainly.' He disappeared into the storeroom.

'You don't work here,' Chris said.

'I hope you won't hold it against me. My name's Brad.' He made a smile which he obviously considered charming.

'You have a foot fetish?'

'Legs, and so on. Oh, don't look so annoyed. You're flattered, and you know it.'

'Give me a break.'

He arched an eyebrow. 'You're a very beautiful woman.'

'Thanks. But I'm also very busy.'

'Are you alone?'

'Not as alone as I'd like to be.'

'Ha! I like a woman with a good sense of humour.'

The batwing doors swung open and the salesman came out with two shoeboxes in his arms. 'You might want to try these, first.' He gave her the box on top. 'They're six and a half. Reebok sizes run fairly small.'

Chris sat down. She felt the chair's vinyl upholstery against the backs of her legs. Both men stood in front of her, watching as she bent over and slipped into one of the shoes. 'Feels fine,' she said, and took it off.

'You'd better try it with a sock on,' Brad suggested. He stepped to her shopping cart, took out the athletic socks, and handed them to her.

'Thanks,' she said, wishing he would disappear.

She pulled a sock on, then stepped into the shoe again.

'How's that?' asked the salesman.

'Good.'

Squatting, he began to lace the shoe. The bald top of his head was sunburned and peeling. He tied a bow, then squeezed the sides of the shoe, its toe. He nodded. He murmured, 'Mmm-hmm, mmm-hmm.' Chris couldn't see his eyes. But she thought she could feel their gaze like oiled fingers sliding up her thighs.

I never should've come in here dressed this way, she thought.

The salesman tipped his head back and smiled up at her. 'They seem all right to me,' he said.

'Maybe you should try walking in them,' Brad suggested.

Right. Let's have a parade! 'These fit fine. I'll take them.'

'Would you like to wear them now, or . . .'

'No.' As the salesman reached down to remove the shoe, she brought her foot up. She propped it on her knee and quickly removed the shoe and sock. While the shoe was being boxed, she slipped into her sandal and stood up. She was glad to be standing, glad to have the shirt draping her thighs.

'Will there be anything else?' the salesman asked.

'I'll just look around, thanks.' She put the socks and shoebox into the shopping cart, and headed away.

Brad stayed at her side.

'Don't you have something better to do?' she asked.

He grinned. 'If I did, I'd be doing it.'

Chris steered the cart into an aisle between displays of camping equipment. She found a Coleman lantern and lifted its box into the cart. Brad lifted a one-gallon tin of fuel.

'Want this?' he asked.

'Thanks,' she muttered.

'Going on a camping trip?'

'Something like that.' Beyond the end of the aisle, backpacks were hanging on the wall. She chose a small red one.

'That won't hold much,' Brad informed her.

Ignoring the comment, she added it to her collection.

She came to the flashlights. Some were as long as her forearm, others no larger than a pencil. Some had casings of ribbed metal, some of rubber, others of red plastic. She decided the plastic ones would do fine. She counted them as she placed them into her shopping cart.

'Going out with a girl scout troop?' Brad asked.

Eight. That was all they had, but there were metal ones the same size so she began putting those into her cart.

'That's a lot of flashlights.'

She looked at Brad.

He raised his eyebrows.

'There are about forty people trapped in Mordock Cavern. I'm going in with a friend to get them out.'

He looked her in the eyes. 'You're shitting me.'

'Right. I figure I need twenty lights.'

'I'll get the batteries for you.' He checked a flashlight package. 'Size D,' he muttered, then sidestepped, bent over, and began picking up Everready twin-packs. 'How did it happen?'

'A fire in the main complex. The elevators are gone.'

'So how're you planning to get in?'

'The natural opening.'

'That's blocked off.' He dumped a handful of batteries into the cart, and crouched to get more.

'My friend's buying some tools.'

Brad whistled softly. 'Going into Lizzy's Tomb,' he muttered.

'Is that what they call it?'

599

'Around here. Wow. How come you're doing it?'

'My daughter's trapped.'

'Jesus.' He added more batteries to the growing pile. 'Isn't that a job for the police?'

'Probably. But we're doing it.'

'You and who else?'

'Hank. His daughter's trapped, too. There's a guide, Lynn. She's going to show us . . .'

'Lynn Maxwell?'

Small world, Chris thought. But it didn't come as much of a surprise to learn that a girl like Lynn was known by a pushy young man like Brad. 'You know her,' she said.

'A friend of a friend. If Lynn's showing you the way, who's the guide in the cave?' He frowned. 'It isn't Darcy Raines?'

Chris's heart thumped, and she felt heat rise to her face. 'Yeah, Darcy.'

'Shit. Better her than Lynn, though.'

Chris stared at him. 'What the hell do you mean by that?'

'She's got it all over Lynn. She's really got her act together, you know? If I had to get trapped in that damn cave, I'd want her to be the one in charge. I don't want to insult anyone, but Lynn's a flake.'

I'm starting to like this guy, Chris thought.

He dropped another handful of battery packs into the cart. 'Okay, that makes twenty pairs. Have you got twenty flash-lights?'

She nodded. 'How do you know Darcy?'

'Seen her around. I took her tour. We've had drinks together a couple of times. I take it you know her.'

'I know her.'

'Look, if she's stuck in the cave . . . Could you people use an extra hand?'

'You want to come along?'

'I'd like to help.'

Chris stared him in the eyes. He met her gaze for a moment, then looked away.

'Hey, I'm aware I was acting like a creep a little earlier. I was just fooling around. I'm not always like that.'

'God, I hope not.'

He let out a short laugh.

'Yeah, you can come with us. An extra body might come in handy.' Chris picked up a plastic lantern. 'Want to get me a six volt battery for this?'

'Sure. Hey, since we're going to be partners in this adventure, how about telling me your name?'

'Chris Raines.'

Smiling, he held out his hand. As Chris shook it, he frowned. 'Raines?'

'Darcy's old lady.'

'Now I *know* you're shitting me.'

Lynn folded her arms across the back of the passenger seat, and said, 'It's sure taking her a long time.'

'She had more to buy.'

'You interested in her?'

'We just met,' he said.

'So? You are, aren't you? Interested in her.'

'Some reason I shouldn't be?'

'No, I'm not saying that. Just curious. She's not too bad looking for a woman her age. She must be up there pushing forty, don't you think? I mean, Darcy's twenty-one, so . . .'

'You're so interested, why don't you ask her?'

'None of my business.'

That's right, Hank thought, and wondered what was going on with Lynn. She'd started acting pretty chummy while they were in the hardware store. When they'd returned to the car, Lynn had waited by the passenger door and given him a sharp glance when he opened the door to the back seat for her. Now, she was trying to run down Chris.

He supposed it was nothing more than Lynn feeling like a third wheel and wanting to usurp Chris's position.

Too bad Lynn's necessary at all, he thought.

Well, she'd claimed she wouldn't go into the cavern. If she didn't change her mind about that, she'd be out of the way before much longer.

'About time,' Lynn said.

Hank looked through the side window and saw Chris leave the sporting goods store. A man in jeans and plaid shirt walked beside her, pushing a loaded cart. Just outside the store, Chris stopped and spoke to the man. She reached into the cart, took out a pair of red shorts, and stepped into them.

'Miss Modesty,' Lynn muttered.

Hank felt a small pull of guilt, wondering if he was the reason she'd bought the shorts.

Once the pants were on, Chris scanned the parking lot, spotted the car, and started forward. The man with the cart stayed with her.

'Gee, that's Brad what's-his-face. God's gift to women. Too bad, Hank.'

Ignoring the remark, he climbed out and went to the rear of the car. He had the truck open before they arrived.

'Hank,' Chris said, 'this is Brad.' As they shook hands, she explained, 'We met in the store. He knows Darcy.'

'I'd like to come along and help, if it's okay with you.'

'Fine.'

Quickly, they put the warm-up suits, lantern and fuel, and a bag that was heavy with Tropical Chocolate bars into the trunk. The flashlights and batteries were dumped onto the back seat next to Lynn. Chris took her shoes and socks into the car with her.

Brad got into the back with Lynn. As they greeted each other, Hank drove out of the parking lot. Chris slipped her sandals off and started to put on her socks.

'I figured it couldn't hurt,' she said, 'having another man along. Especially when it comes to breaking through those walls.'

'Yeah. It'll help.'

When her shoes were on, Chris turned around. 'Hand up some of those batteries and flashlights,' she said.

Chris, Lynn and Brad loaded the flashlights while Hank drove as fast as he dared towards Mordock Cavern.

10

'I wonder if they're at the wall, yet,' Paula said.

'It's too soon,' Kyle told her. He wished she hadn't mentioned the wall. He didn't want to think about that.

Darcy's group had no sooner started off than Kyle began to regret his decision not to sneak away while he had the chance and dispose of the pick axe. So what if they figured out he'd been the one who got rid of it? No big deal. They weren't crazy, they wouldn't do something like torture him to make him tell where he'd put it. They'd be pissed, but so what? If they couldn't find the pick, they'd have no way to get through the wall.

It's too late for that, now.

But not too late to stop them.

If Dad was here, *he'd* stop them. No way would Dad let them break in there.

I'm just a kid.

If I try to stop them and they go in anyway, they'll know I'm involved.

Just forget it, he told himself. Play dumb. Dad'll catch the blame. Nobody's going to think I had anything to do with it. I'm just a kid.

With Dad out of the room, Amy changed. She stopped struggling against the ropes binding her to the bedframe. Some of the terror seemed to fade from her eyes. They met Kyle's eyes and seemed to plead with him. The noises coming from her taped mouth were no longer frantic grunts and moans; they were soft sounds, each rising at the end like a question.

Naked, Kyle stepped to the end of the bed.

He saw Amy glance at his erect penis, then lift her gaze to his eyes. Shaking her head slowly from side to side, she made humming noises. There were no words, but Kyle knew that she was trying to talk him out of it.

It would be interesting, he thought, to find out what she has to say.

Interesting to hear her beg.

He crawled up the bed. Her legs were wide apart and he could put it right into her – just get a little lower and it'll run right in. But there was plenty of time for that, for everything, and he wanted to hear what she had to say.

He climbed over her thighs and sat down. He felt her pubic mound pushing against his rump, felt a moist pad of hair against his skin. Her torso gleamed. Her breasts rose and fell as she panted for air.

Amy was holding her head up, staring at him and humming, 'Mmmm. Mm? Mmmmm?'

Kyle leaned forward. The head of his penis prodded him above his navel. He reached towards Amy's breasts, realized the feel of them would probably make him lose control, and placed his hands on the slick hot skin above them.

You could fingerpaint on her sweat, he thought.

He looked into her eyes. 'You want to say something?'

Her head jerked up and down.

'I'll take the tape off your mouth,' he said. 'But if you scream or make any loud noises, you'll be sorry. Real sorry.'

Amy nodded some more.

'Besides,' he added, 'it won't do you any good. The room's soundproof.' He didn't know that, but it wouldn't surprise him. Dad had gone to a lot of trouble fixing up this room. 'Nobody'd hear you but me, and I'll hurt you bad.'

Kyle slid a fingernail under a corner of the tape, picked, caught the tape between his thumb and fore-finger and ripped it from her face. She winced and flinched. The flinch felt good for Kyle.

'Let me go, okay?' she whispered. 'You're just a kid. You don't want to . . .' Her chin started to shake. Tears made her eyes shine. 'That man hurt me a lot. He . . . he did bad things to me.'

'He's my dad.'

'But you're not like him. I can see that. You're a good boy. You don't want to get into something like this. Untie me, okay? Untie me and help me get away. I'll give you anything you want, and I'll never tell on your father. I promise. Okay?'

'What'll you give me?'

'Anything.'

'I want to fuck you.'

'Okay. That's okay. That's fine. Untie me, and I'll make it real good for you. It'll be the best, okay?'

This is terrific, Kyle thought. She'll make it good for me. She wouldn't give me the fucking time of day if I didn't have her like this, if we met on the street or something.

She'd been nice to him at the restaurant.

But he could just imagine the look of scorn in her eyes if he had dared to ask her for a date.

Don't be ridiculous. Get lost.

They were all like that – all the pretty ones, anyway. School was full of them. Lovely, slender, laughing girls you could never have. They looked right through you. You were a sub-species, a lower form of life, best ignored. Don't feed it, maybe it'll go away.

'If I let you go,' Kyle said, 'will you marry me?'

That one threw Amy. For a moment, she looked confused. 'Sure. Of course I will. I was engaged, but I broke it off. You're a handsome young man. I . . . I'd love to be your wife.'

'Will you let me kiss you?'

She nodded.

Kyle put his hands on the mattress and bent down. He felt her nipples touch his chest. He kissed her mouth. At first, it was shut tight. Then, as if she decided she'd better make this good, she opened her mouth. Her lips writhed against his. She sucked on his mouth and moaned as if consumed with passion.

Kyle caught her lower lip between his teeth, bit into it and sat up fast, tearing it off. Amy's eyes bulged. Blood gushed over her teeth. Kyle slapped a hand across her mouth in time to muffle the scream.

He blew out the lip. It shot onto her face and stuck beneath her left eye, clinging there like a fat slug.

Keeping her mouth covered with his left hand, he used his

right to punch the side of her head. His pounding fist crashed against her cheek, her temple, her eye, then her cheek again. When he took his hand off her mouth, she didn't try to scream. She just coughed, spraying up blood.

He grabbed the pillow case and shook it until the pillow dropped out. Then he stuffed an end of the cloth into her mouth. He crammed more and more in until her mouth was full. He flapped the rest of the case up so it hid her face.

She kept coughing, but the sound was quiet. Each cough made her body jerk under Kyle, made her breasts jump and sway. He scooted backwards and pressed his face between her breasts, smelled her sweet rose perfume and her sweat, felt her breasts patting his cheeks as she squirmed and coughed.

It was too much. He wasn't even in her yet, and it was too much. One knee was between her legs but the other was still outside and he wanted to be *in* her but her breasts were buffeting his face, whapping his cheeks, and he grabbed them and squeezed and she squealed into the cloth and he clamped himself to her thigh and slid against it, gasping and pumping.

When he had his breath back, Kyle got to his hands and knees. He looked at the clock on the nightstand.

He'd been with Amy less than fifteen minutes.

Plenty of time left, he thought.

Time for everything.

But it went by so terribly fast.

Kyle heard a soft whistle. He looked over his shoulder. Dad was standing near the wall. Apparently, he had entered the same way as before, through the space left by the mirror. He was shaking his head, grinning. 'Guess it *does* run in the family.'

'Do I have to stop?' Kyle asked.

'There'll be other nights. Right now, we've got to clean up and take care of business.'

Kyle crawled off the bed. He stood and looked down at himself. Most of his skin was smeared with blood.

'You really did a number on her,' Dad said.

'Yeah.' He wasn't embarrassed by the remark. He felt as if he'd been expected to do a number on her, and had fulfilled some kind of unspoken obligation.

'I'd ask if you enjoyed it,' Dad said, 'but I guess that goes without saying.'

'When can I do it again?'

'We'll discuss that later.' He came over to the bed and gazed down at Amy's sprawled body. 'What'd you cut the ropes for?'

Kyle shrugged. 'She was out cold.' Or dead, he thought. 'I didn't see any harm.'

'Was she unconscious before you took the tape off her mouth?'

'Well, no. But she didn't scream or . . .'

'Did she have anything interesting to say?'

Kyle grinned. 'She said she'd marry me if I let her go.'

Dad snorted. 'That's a good one. Amazing what they'll come up with.'

'You talk to them sometimes?'

'Not so much anymore. After a while, they all sound pretty much the same. They beg and whine. They offer you money, sex – which is a yuck considering you're going to get that anyway.' He reached down and pressed fingertips to her wrist. 'Still has a pulse,' he said after a few moments.

'Really?' Kyle was surprised.

'That's all right. It's better not to kill them.' He looked at Kyle and raised an eyebrow. 'You're a lot like your grandfather. He always left a real mess. I'm not that much into savaging the bitches. Just use enough force to subdue them, you know?'

Kyle felt heat rush to his face. 'I'm sorry. I just . . .'

'No, it's all right. If you like it that way, fine. It's a matter of personal taste. But you're going to have to replace the sheets and things out of your own pocket.'

'Okay.'

Dad nodded toward the bathroom. 'Now get in there and take a shower, son. Make it quick, but get all the blood off. Be sure to get it out from under your nails.'

'What are we going to do with her?'

'Nurse her back to health and give her a bus ticket to Omaha.'

'What?'

'You'll find out. Take your shower.'

Kyle stepped into the bathroom. On the metal shelf over the sink were Amy's toothbrush, a small tube of Crest, a bottle of roll-on deodorant, a hairbrush with a clear pink plastic handle and quite a lot of wispy brown hair tangled in its bristles.

What are we going to do with all this stuff? he wondered.

What are we going to do with *her*?

She isn't even dead. Weird. He'd felt sure she was dead before he even took the pillow case out of her mouth.

Dad says it's all right, though. Dad knows what he's doing. He's done all this before, plenty of times – enough times to get tired of listening to them.

Kyle leaned forward and studied his face in the mirror above the sink. He looked for a difference in his eyes. They seemed pretty much the same as usual. He wiggled his eyebrows. The skin on his forehead felt stiff because of the partly dried blood. He smiled. His whole face felt stiff. A single, short curl of hair clung to the blood near the corner of his mouth. He left it there, and turned away from the mirror.

A bath-towel was hanging on a bar to dry, but a clean one remained neatly folded, clamped in place on the wire rack.

The bath-mat was draped over the side of the tub. He spread it onto the floor and stepped on it. It felt damp and cool.

A wash-cloth had been left hanging over the cold water nozzle. A small, plastic bottle of shampoo stood on an edge of the tub. In the soap dish was one of the tiny white bars provided by the hotel.

Kyle picked up the wash-cloth.

Amy had used it, rubbed herself all over with it.

He pressed the thin, damp cloth to his face, breathed through it, sniffed it. It smelled faintly of soap, nothing more.

But he was flooded with memories of his last time in Darcy's room, the feel and aroma of her wash-cloth, the cool dampness of her bath-towel against his bare skin.

He turned on the water, washed his hands under the spout, then pulled the knob to make the shower come on. He stepped into the tub and pulled the curtain shut.

The heavy, hot spray of water felt good. The blood seemed to melt off his skin. It slid down him, turned pink around his feet and ran towards the drain.

As he soaped himself, he imagined Darcy tied to the bed in the other room. If it had been Darcy instead of Amy tonight, it would've been even more incredible. In a way, it *had* been Darcy. Once the pillow case hid Amy's face, he'd been able to fill his mind with the slender, beautiful guide. That made it better, but he'd known all along he was just pretending.

If it had been Darcy tonight, he thought, it'd all be over now.

I don't want it to be just an hour with her.

Days, weeks.

It'll never happen, he realized, sinking inside. But getting her for a while, maybe for a whole night . . . that could happen.

Something to shoot for.

Wearing soap lather like a suit of white foam, Kyle shampooed his hair. He rinsed, then checked his fingernails. They looked clean.

He turned off the water, slid back the curtain, and stepped onto the bath-mat. He pulled the clean white towel off the wire rack. He dried himself. When he was done, he held the towel open in front of him and checked both sides. It was still white.

His clothes were in the other room. He wrapped the towel around his waist. It was just large enough to meet at the hip. When he tucked the corners together, the side of his leg was left bare.

When I run this place, he thought, the guests will get bigger towels. No wonder we get rated so low.

He stepped out of the bathroom.

The bundle on the bed looked like a cocoon. Amy had been rolled up in the sheets, which were tied around her with ropes. The white sheets were soaked through with blood.

Dad, standing at the foot of the bed, was shaking open a plastic garbage bag.

'What should I do?' Kyle asked.

'Just watch. I'll show you everything. Next time, you'll do it all and I'll supervise. You'll be doing it by yourself one of these days.'

Kyle stepped over to his pile of clothes. The towel came loose as he walked, and he held it up, wondering why he bothered; he'd been naked in front of his father only a little while ago. It seemed different, now. He tucked the towel together and it stayed in place until he had his briefs on. Then he let it fall. He watched his father and continued to get dressed.

With the plastic bag open, Dad crawled onto the bed. He started to slip it around Amy's wrapped feet. 'All you missed,' he said, 'was tying the sheets around her. I already checked the bedspread and blanket. They're all right. They were off the bed before you started working on her.' He lifted the bundle, pulled the bag up to Amy's waist, then went for another bag. He put that one over Amy's head, drew it down so it overlapped the top of the other bag, then started binding them together with duct tape. Before climbing off the bed, he slapped the plastic mattress cover. 'This saves our mattress. We'll come back afterwards, mop it off, do a final cleanup.'

He went into the bathroom. Kyle watched him wash his hands, then gather up everything Amy had left behind, including the small bottle of shampoo on the edge of the tub. He brought her belongings out, and put them into her suitcase. 'One rule,' he said. 'We don't keep anything except cash. Nothing that can connect us to her.'

He wandered the room, collecting all of Amy's possessions and adding them to the suitcase. When he found her handbag, he took out the wallet and removed a handful of bills. He stuffed them into his pocket. Then he took out a key case.

'She drove in, so we've got a car to deal with. First thing in the morning, Ralph Dexter'll take it off our hands. He's been taking care of the cars for years, never asks any questions. He's got a garage, paints 'em, changes licence plates, does the whole nine yards, has some kind of connections so they end up being sold out of state. We've never had any trouble with the things getting traced back to us.'

Kyle shook his head, amazed. 'You've really got it . . . set up.'

'Had a lot of practice,' Dad said. He shut the suitcase and snapped its latches. 'It started with Ely, and we've been doing it ever since.'

'And getting away with it,' Kyle said.

'We've had a few close calls. Your grandfather got busted

once, but they dropped the charges. No evidence. That's part of the trick, don't leave any evidence. But the main trick is this: don't arouse suspicion.'

Dad wandered the room, making a final inspection, then picked up an ashtray, sat on a corner of the bed and lit a cigarette. 'I've been averaging about one a month for almost twenty years, now. I did it sometimes before then, but when your grandfather had his stroke, I took over the whole thing from him. Do you know how many women that makes?'

Kyle shook his head. He felt tired, excited, too dazed. by it all to fool with maths.

'It makes about two hundred forty. That's give or take maybe a dozen. And I've never been busted. It's because I'm careful, and you've got to be careful too. You'll be doing all this by yourself, some day. For the time being, I'll show you the ropes, we'll share, take turns, that kind of thing.'

Kyle nodded.

Dad blew twin streams of pale smoke out his nose. 'It all comes down,' he said, 'to who you put in this room. You want them to be young and good looking, right? Where's the thrill of doing a gal looks like she's been whapped with an ugly stick? But there's a lot more to it than that.'

'You're working the registration desk, a gal comes in. If she's not alone, obviously you forget it. The nice thing is, the cavern's an attraction that pulls in all kinds, and we get some women who are travelling alone. Not a whole lot of them, but enough so you can pick and choose.'

'Okay, she's someone you wouldn't mind putting it to and she's alone. Is she married? Check her rings. If she's married, forget it. She fills out the registration card. Does she live nearby? Normally, they don't, or they wouldn't be checking into the hotel. But pay attention to where they live. Go for the ones who live out of state.'

Dad crushed out his cigarette. 'Take Amy. She comes in alone, she's a little hefty but cute. No wedding or engagement ring, and she's from Ohio. I talk to her a little bit, just acting friendly. Find out she's had a falling-out with her financee, a guy who's a little nuts and likes to knock her around. She's on her way to Manhattan, planning to start a new life without him. Saw the hotel sign as she was driving by, decided to spend the night and see the cavern tomorrow. Probably hoping to run into a nice young man in the process.' Dad grinned. 'And she did, huh? Two nice young men.'

Kyle chuckled.

'The point is, I got to know her some. Enough to find out nobody has an idea she's stopping here for the night. That means, when she turns up missing, nobody is going to come around here asking questions. She's perfect. So I check her into 115. See this?' He took a folded card out of his shirt pocket. 'It's her registration card. I burn it, no record she was ever here.'

Dad stood up. He set the ashtray on the bureau, and turned to Kyle. 'That's how it's done. You want to find a gal who can't be traced to the hotel. That's ninety-nine per cent of the trick. The other one per cent is making sure you don't get caught in the act. No big problem with that. Grab her suitcase.'

11

Kyle picked up the suitcase. His father lifted Amy's wrapped body off the bed and slung it over his shoulder in a fireman's carry. 'Another rule to remember,' Dad said as he started to walk under the burden. 'Don't bite off more than you can chew. Don't kill more than you can carry. It's not easy, lugging these bitches around.' He stepped through the opening left by the mirror.

Kyle followed him.

'Normally,' Dad said, 'I'd put her down on the chair here while I make sure the coast is clear. You go ahead and check, though.' He nodded towards the storeroom's door. 'Take a peek in the corridor and stairwell. Nobody's going to be wandering around this time of night, but it pays to be careful.'

Kyle set down the suitcase and opened the door. The long, dimly lighted hallway looked deserted. He stepped out and rushed the few feet to the firedoor. He pushed it open, glanced up and down the stairs, listened for a moment, then hurried back to the storeroom. 'It's okay,' he said, picking up the suitcase again.

He held the door open and was surprised by the speed with which his father crossed the open area to the fire-door. Kyle shut the storeroom door, made sure it was locked, then hurried to the stairwell.

Dad was already at the bottom, pushing the exit door.

He's taking the body outside?

He knows what he's doing, Kyle told himself. Must.

Kyle trotted down the four stairs to the bottom, and followed his father through the door.

The Cadillac was there, its trunk already open.

Dad bent over. The body flopped off his shoulder and dropped into the trunk. The car rocked slightly under the impact. He took the suitcase from Kyle and swung it in beside the body. Then, he lowered the trunk lid and pressed it down firmly so it latched with barely a sound.

Leaning back against the trunk, he folded his arms across his chest. 'That wasn't so hard, was it?'

'We're right out in the open,' Kyle whispered.

'Are we? Take a look around.'

Kyle didn't need to take a look around; he'd been here countless times. They'd carried the body out the fire exit at the end of the hotel's east wing. Their car was backed up very close to the door, but . . .

Dad pointed at the hotel. 'No windows on this end,' he said. 'It was planned that way. Hedges over there,' he added, pointing to the other side of the driveway. Then he pointed out the rows of thick, tall bushes on either side of the exit door. 'And these,' he said, 'are in the way of anyone who might happen to wander onto the driveway from either the front or the back. So we may seem to be out in the open, but this particular spot is pretty well sheltered. If you're going to be seen by anyone, he has to be right on top of you.'

'What if that happens?'

'It never has, so far.'

'But . . .'

'I've always figured, if someone saw me, I'd kill him.' Dad reached behind his back, under his hanging shirt-tail, and pulled out a revolver. 'Insurance.' He slipped the gun back into place. 'Come on, let's get going.'

They climbed into the car. Dad started the engine, and drove with the headlights off until they rounded the first bend. There, trees along the roadside stood between them and the hotel. The headlights came on, pushing bright tunnels into the night.

'Where are we going?'

'Not far.'

'Have you got a special place where . . .?'

'Very special.' Dad pulled onto the dirt road at the cattle crossing. He climbed out, removed the padlock and chain from the gate, swung the gate open, and came back. He drove slowly forward. 'You know the story of Ely's Wall,' he said.

'Sure.'

'Well, it's a pile of horseshit. Elizabeth didn't fall down any chasm. Ely found out she'd been screwing around with their handyman, a guy by the name of Arnold Winston. So after the elevators were installed, he blocked off the natural opening and took her into the cavern. He tied her up down there. *Then*, he built Ely's Wall. Sealed her right up in that section of the cave, alive and well.'

'Holy shit,' Kyle muttered.

'Ever read *The Cask of Amontillado*?'

'Sure,' Kyle said.

'Well, Ely was a big fan of Mr Poe. It just tickled the hell out of him, walling up that hot-pants bitch of his.'

The car stopped in the middle of a stand of trees. Dad killed the headlights, then pressed the button on the dashboard that released the trunk latch. 'Come on,' he said.

They went to the trunk. Dad handed the suitcase to Kyle. He lifted the body out, swinging it over his shoulder.

Side by side, they walked through the trees. Kyle heard the far-off hoot of an owl. The only other sounds were their footsteps crunching over the forest floor, their breathing. The trees blocked out most of the moonlight. Except for a few speckles and patches of brightness, they walked in darkness.

Finally, Dad stopped near a cluster of rocks. He leaned forward. Amy's body dropped to the ground. Dad leaned back against a boulder, and sighed. 'Put down the suitcase and come here,' he said.

Kyle set it down. As he approached the vague shape of his father, he saw the man swing an arm out, thumb pointing behind him as if he were hitching a ride. 'Take a look back there, but watch your step.'

Kyle moved carefully around the side of the boulder. He saw a narrow patch of black on the dark ground. 'I don't . . . what's there?'

'The chute, son, the chute.'

Kyle shook his head.

'What it is, it's a sinkhole. It's like a natural chimney, drops right down into the closed part of the cave. What Ely did, once he had Elizabeth sealed up down there, he tricked Arnold into coming out here, banged him one on the head, and dropped him down the chute. Ely's idea of justice. His wife wanted Arnold, now she could have him. Forever.'

'Wow,' Kyle said. 'Fixed them, didn't he.'

'Maybe a little better than he ever expected.'

'What do you mean?'

Quiet laughter came from Kyle's father. Strange laughter. It made a chill crawl up Kyle's back.

'They didn't die. Neither one of them. That chute, it goes all the way down, but not *straight* down or the fall would've killed him. It's like a slide – part of the way, at least. Ely, he comes back a few days after he dropped Arnold down, and he yells into the hole just on the chance Elizabeth's close enough to hear. And she answers. They both do. They shout up to him, begging for him to let them out. So what does Ely do? He starts bringing them food and throwing it down the chute. Not much. Just enough so they don't starve. He wants them to stay alive, you see. Alive, but trapped forever down there. In the darkness. In the cold. Together.' Again, Dad let out that weird, crazy laugh.

'He brought them real delicacies. Table scraps, at first. Bones. Raw meat, sometimes. Whenever he showed up, they'd be waiting at the bottom of the chute. He'd tease them. He'd call, "Hungry down there?" And they'd beg him for food, and he'd make them say, "Pretty-please." He really put them through a routine. I'll show you his diary. It's pretty amusing stuff.'

'Anyway, he was out driving one day and found a cat that'd been hit by a car. So he scooped it off the road and took *that* to them. He knew they'd eat it. They'd *have* to eat it, or starve. When they found out what he'd tossed down for them, they shrieked and yelled curses. Well, that really tickled Ely. So he started to bring them every kind of disgusting thing. He got hold of snakes and lizards and tossed them down the hole. He trapped rats for their supper. Sometimes, he'd throw them a loaf of bread, but he'd piss on it first. He even shot dogs and waited for them to get ripe before throwing them in.'

'He really did all that?' Kyle asked. He felt a little sick, but at the same time he admired the lengths that Ely had gone to for his revenge.

'Sure did,' Dad said. 'And enjoyed every minute of it. After a while, though, Elizabeth and Arnold changed their tune. They stopped saying "pretty-please."' Dad started laughing. Kyle, unable to stop himself, joined in.

Finally, Dad wiped his eyes and sighed. 'Anyway, it started getting a little spooky. He'd hear them laughing down there. And they'd call up, asking him to come a little closer. They'd say they had something for him.'

'Wanted him to fall in the hole?' Kyle asked.

'Sure.'

'Sounds like they went nuts.'

'Totally bonkers. But Ely kept coming around and bringing them stuff. Then one day, a pretty young gal showed up at the hotel. She'd been on the road, didn't have any money, asked for a place to stay the night. Ely'd been without his wife for a couple of months, by then, and he was feeling pretty horny. So he used his pass key on the gal's room that night, let himself in, and had at her. She tried to fight him off. He ended up strangling her. When he was done, he brought her out here and gave her a ride on the chute.'

'And they ate her?' Kyle asked. 'That's how it started?'

'Yep. Ely got into the habit. And when his son, your grandfather, got old enough to appreciate the situation, he got initiated and kept the practice up, and passed it onto me.'

Kyle shook his head. 'But they must've died. Elizabeth and Arnold. I mean, that was like sixty years ago, or . . .'

'I imagine they did,' Dad said. He stood up and stepped around the rock. He got on his hands and knees at the edge of the hole. 'Soup's on!' he called. 'Hello! Room service!'

Quiet sounds floated up. Moans, giggles, voices.

Kyle cringed. He felt as if he had spiders in his hair.

The voices, barely audible, made no sense. But they sounded gleeful.

Kyle looked at his father and shook his head.

'I come out here a couple times a week,' Dad said. 'Bring them a little something. And I listen. I figure there's six or eight of them down there. Sometimes, I've heard babies crying.'

Kyle crawled backwards away from the hole and couldn't hear the sounds anymore.

Dad stood up. He brushed off his knees. 'Come on, let's give Amy a ride.'

He picked her up, carried her to the black opening, and dropped her in. The garbage bags hissed and crackled. There were quiet bumps and thuds. Then silence.

'Suitcase, too,' Dad said. 'Keep the folk well-dressed.'

Kyle dropped the suitcase into the hole and listened as it skidded down.

Crouching, Dad cupped his hands to his mouth and called into the blackness, 'Dig in, folks! Get it while it's hot!'

12

Jim's torch died. When Darcy's dwindled to glowing embers, she dropped the smoking remains of the board to the walkway. The middle of Greg's plank still burned. He held it low in front of him so the fire could climb the wood towards his hands.

The flames wobbled and flapped like a bright flag.

'They should give torchlight tours,' said Carol, who was walking just behind her. 'It's a lot more ... interesting this way.'

' "May you live in interesting times," ' Helen said.

'An old Chinese curse.'

'I think it's nice.'

'You won't think it's so nice,' Helen told her, 'when that one goes out.'

'Greg's won't go out,' Darcy said. 'He's bearing the magic torch.'

'Right,' Greg said.

She put an arm across his back. His sweatshirt was cool and damp under her hand, but she felt his warmth beneath it. She moved closer to him, walking with her hip against his hip, the side of her breast pressing his upper arm.

She knew the others were looking at her. But she didn't care.

It's just Carol and Helen and Jim and Beth, she thought. Though Helen seemed a bit stiff, possibly even prudish, Darcy didn't mind showing some affection for Greg in front of these people. They were little more than strangers, but they were special. They were her team.

She had felt good, almost buoyant, ever since leaving the main group at the elevators. It was as if she had been set free. Kyle had been left behind. So had the man in the Peterbilt hat. And more than two dozen strangers who'd been depending on her to keep order and calm their fears and save them. The relief at being away from them all was huge.

It was like starting home after a bad party.

Or, she thought, more to the point, the senior dance. Very much like that. Her final year in high school, she had been class president and in charge of organizing the entire function – decorations, refreshments, entertainment. And when Mike Wakefield spiked the punch, she got plenty of heat from the adults. They'd blamed her, even though she'd had nothing to do with it. The other kids thought the dance was a great success, but Darcy hadn't been able to relax and enjoy a single moment of it, and the evening became a real ordeal after the liquor was discovered in the punch. Then she left with her date and two other couples and the pressure was gone. She went wild. She shouted and twirled around the parking lot like a mad woman. She talked her friends into driving out to the river and they all went skinny-dipping. She'd never felt so carefree, so daring. She swam under a bridge, leaving everyone behind except Steve, her date. They embraced in the warm water. Then she led him ashore and found a moonlit clearing. Though she'd gone steady with Steve for months, though she knew that she loved him, she had never allowed him to go all the way. That night, dripping from the river, she lay down on the cool grass and raised her arms towards him.

Darcy remembered it all as she walked alongside Greg in the fluttering glow of his torch. Always before, her memories of that night had been tainted by thoughts of their break-up, the letter Steve sent during her first spring at Princeton. Now, she felt none of the usual pain. Steve was part of the past, and Greg was with her and she felt the same sense of relief and daring that had possessed her after escaping from the senior dance.

The springy feel of wood under her shoes pulled Darcy out of her revery. She was on the dock. She stopped. 'I forgot the pick,' she said. 'Do you want to go back with me and get it?' she asked Greg. She wondered if he could hear the tremor in her voice.

'Sure.'

She unhooked the flashlight from her belt and turned it on. 'We'll be back in a few minutes,' she told the others.

Greg gave his torch to Jim. Beth, Carol and Helen formed a circle around the small flame as if it were a campfire.

Back on the concrete walkway, Darcy said, 'We walked right past it. Stupid. I was daydreaming.'

'About getting out of here?' Greg asked.

'Not exactly.' She played her flashlight beam over the shiny limestone wall to the right, and spotted the grotto entrance. Taking Greg's hand, she walked closer. Her mouth was dry. Her heart beat fast. Though her mind flashed a reminder of her earlier encounter with Kyle at the grotto, she wasn't bothered by it. What happened with Kyle didn't matter. Not at the moment.

Greg, at her side, she climbed the stone stairs.

They entered the grotto. The pale beam of the flashlight illuminated the wheelbarrow, the pickaxe leaning against its side, her blouse and bra draped over one of its handles.

'This is where I changed,' she explained.

'And became what?'

She turned to Greg. Smiling, she shook her head. Then she looked down and began to hook the flashlight to her belt. As the metal clip slipped into place, Greg put his hands on her shoulders. He eased her forward, and she wrapped her arms around him and tipped back her head. He kissed her. It was a gentle, tentative kiss at first. Then his lips parted and Darcy stroked them with her tongue and their mouths joined, pressing hard and sucking. His hands roamed her back.

This is crazy, she thought. The others are waiting.

Let them wait.

Her hands went under Greg's sweatshirt. His skin was damp, but warm. His tongue filled her mouth. She squirmed against him, rubbing herself on his firm body. His hands moved up and down her sides, caressing her through the thin fabric of the windbreaker. She wanted them inside, wanted them on her skin.

His mouth pulled away from hers. 'We'd better get back,' he muttered.

'I know.'

'The others.'

Nodding, she dropped her hands to her sides. He was right. No matter how much she wanted this time with Greg to last, it wouldn't be fair to make the others wait. 'Duty,' she muttered.

'After we get out of here . . . maybe we can spend some time together.'

'That would be nice.'

'A lot of time.'

'I think I'd like that.' She put her hands on Greg's hips. 'I think I'd like that very much.'

He lifted a hand to the side of her head, he fingered her hair, her ear, her cheek. 'I want to be with you in the sunlight.'

She kissed his palm. Then Greg drew her to him and for a moment their mouths met.

His breath was warm on her lips when he said, 'Let's bust outa here.'

'As fast as we can,' Darcy said.

They turned away from each other and went to the wheelbarrow. Greg hefted the pickaxe and swung it onto his shoulder. Darcy touched her blouse and bra. They were wet, very cold. She considered putting them on, not because she saw any use for them, but because she was tempted by the idea of taking off her windbreaker in front of Greg. Even if she kept her back to him . . . She imagined him stepping up behind her and putting his arms around her, his big hands closing over her breasts. She felt warm and snug in the windbreaker. The bra and blouse would feel awful. Worth the discomfort, though. Worth it to stand in front of him, bare to the waist, and have him touch her. She would turn to him, and he would gaze at her, and then he would bring her up against him . . .

Greg reached out and squeezed a sleeve of the blouse. 'Yuck,' he said. 'You're not thinking about putting these on, are you?'

She shrugged. She blushed, but her face was in shadow so she was sure he didn't notice.

'You'd freeze. You'd better forget it.'

And she blushed even more as she plucked the front of the windbreaker away from her belly and said, 'It's just that I feel so naked in this.'

'You're not. It's perfectly circumspect.'

'I bounce when I walk.'

'Not much,' he said, 'and very nicely. You don't want to put those things on. Come on, let's go.'

They turned toward the opening, and Darcy undipped the flashlight from her belt. 'You've been watching me bounce.'

He laughed softly. He patted her rump. He said nothing.

They trotted down the stone stairs. Darcy saw the others waiting on the dock, still clustered around the tiny fire of the torch in Jim's hands.

It's over, she thought. And it's their fault.

Don't blame them, she told herself. They're simply part of this, the same way Greg is part of this.

And this is just fine.

Though Darcy ached with a mild feeling of loss because she could no longer be alone with Greg, the ache was mixed with a sense of fullness, of wonder.

She felt *so* close to him.

It's almost as if we made love, she thought.

We *did* make love. That's exactly what we were doing in there. Just didn't have time to finish.

We'll finish when we get out of here.

After I find out about Mom. Mom's all right. She has to be.

Entering the glow of the torch, Darcy switched off the flashlight and put it on her belt. 'All set?' she asked.

'That ought to do the job,' Jim said, nodding towards the pickaxe.

'It will,' Greg said.

Darcy led the way past the first boat and stopped beside the other. 'Okay, everybody in.'

Greg lowered the pickaxe carefully into the boat. He and Darcy held onto the gunnel while the others climbed in. Carol and Helen took seats in the middle, Jim stood near the bow so the torch would be at the front. Beth sat down behind him.

'Go on and get in,' Greg said. 'I'll tow it to the wall.'

'Maybe I should try pulling it along on the spikes.'

Greg shook his head. 'If it was too dangerous before, it's too dangerous now. I don't want you catching one of those things in the face.'

'I could try,' she said, though she knew he was right. Even under normal conditions with the lights on, the method of propelling the boats forward by grabbing the spikes along the cavern wall was hazardous. It required a firm stance, good balance, and frequent ducking to save your head from jutting rocks. Attempting it by torchlight, or even with the flashlight, would be foolish. But she hated the idea of Greg going into the water.

'I'll have to get wet again, anyway,' he said, 'when we reach the wall.'

'But . . .'

'You can just enjoy the ride, this time.' He stepped out of his shoes. Putting a hand on Darcy's shoulder to steady himself, he peeled off his socks. 'I'm not going to get my clothes wet, this time,' he said. He pulled the sweatshirt over his head and gave it to her. Then he opened his pants, pulled them down his legs and shook them off. He was wearing white briefs.

Darcy looked at the women in the boat. Only Carol was watching Greg.

Darcy stepped forward to block her view.

Greg gave the pants to Darcy, then squatted and put his shoes on his bare feet. While he was retying them, Darcy crouched and picked up his socks. She pressed the bundle of clothes to her chest, and put a hand on his back. He was shaking. 'Are you sure . . .?'

'No problem.' He stood up. He grinned at Darcy in the faint, shimmering light, then clapped his hands once, pivoted away from her, and trotted up the dock. Just past the bow of the boat, he dived.

He sprang off the dock, stretched his arms out beyond his head, and the dim shape of his body flew low over the Lake of Charon. He hit the surface almost flat. Water splashed up, droplets glinting in the torchlight.

Darcy shuddered. She could *feel* the terrible shock of cold.

Greg came up, swam in a circle, and stopped in front of the boat. 'Are you all right?' Darcy asked.

'It's . . . invigorating.'

'I'll bet.'

'Nice dive,' Jim said.

As fast as she could, Darcy untied the boat. She climbed in next to Jim and knelt, looking down at Greg. The boat began gliding forward.

His arms and shoulders were shiny in the torchlight. His hair, flat against his head, looked oiled down. His face was beaded with water. His eyes were fixed on Darcy. His lips were peeled back, showing his teeth in a rigid grimace.

Darcy covered his hands with hers. They felt as if they'd been dipped in ice water.

He winked at her. 'Don't look so miserable,' he said. 'It's not bad. Doesn't even feel as cold as before.'

'When we get to the wall,' Jim said, 'it'll be my turn. You've done enough already. I'll knock the hole through that wall.'

'Well, don't try and deprive me of my chance to warm up swinging the pick. I'm looking forward to it.'

'We can all take turns,' Beth said.

'But me first,' Greg insisted.

'It's a man's job,' Jim said. From the tone of his voice, Darcy knew he'd made the remark to tease Beth.

Beth rose to the occasion. 'Oh yeah, bub? How'd you like a fat lip?'

'Apologize, Jim,' Greg said as he pulled the boat along. 'Don't get us in trouble with the broads. We're out-numbered.'

'Broads?' Darcy asked. She grinned.

'We can take 'em,' Jim said.

'Maybe in a fair fight,' Greg told him. 'But dames don't fight fair. They bite, pull hair . . .'

'Do this,' Darcy added, and leaned out over the bow and pressed a hand down on top of Greg's head. His head went under. The cold water wrapped Darcy's hand to the wrist. Immediately, she felt bad. Her throat tightened.

Stupid! Not funny at all!

'That wasn't necessary,' Helen said.

'Score one for the females,' Beth said.

Jim was laughing.

'Is he all right?' Carol asked, worry in her voice.

Greg was still under. Then his head bobbed to the surface. His eyes crossed and he spouted water from his mouth. The thin stream arched over the front of the boat, splashed Darcy's chin and ran down her neck. Yelping, she clutched her throat, but not before a few drops made their way inside the wind-breaker. They slid like melted snow down her warm skin, and she slapped a hand between her breasts to snuff the drops as if they were burning embers.

Greg looked up at her, a silly grin on his face.

Darcy leaned out over the water, the metal gunnel pressing into her ribs. She took Greg by the ears and pulled him gently closer and kissed him on the mouth. 'That's for dunking you,' she whispered. 'Forgive me?'

'No need to forgive you – I got even.'

She settled back, holding his hands again.

The boat moved along, silent except for occasional murmurs of water lapping the hull. Jim held the torch low. Its charred end almost touching the water beside Greg. The broken plank burned near its middle, the flames clinging to one edge like fingers trying to hold on. The light given off wavered, faded and grew and dimmed again as the flames struggled. Surrounding the fire was a faint golden aura that shimmered on Greg's wet skin, spread a dim layer of bright-ness on the water beside him, and hung in the air like a mist. Darcy could barely make out the wall of the cavern to her right, almost beyond the reach of the glow. Though she thought she knew every inch of that wall, the squirming light and shadows gave it an alien appearance that she found somewhat unnerving.

Don't let it get to you, she told herself. Just the same old wall.

It looked *alive*.

Goosebumps crawled over her skin.

This is ridiculous. Your mind's doing a number on you. She reminded herself of other times she had felt this way: getting into the car after a scary movie and feeling that someone might be crouched on the back floor; reading late at night and suddenly afraid to look at the window, certain a face is pressed against it; taking a bath and hearing a faint noise somewhere in the house; getting out of bed and walking to the bathroom and suspecting that one of the shadows along the way might lurch out and rush at her. Nothing more than the mind playing tricks, teasing, making shivers.

Darcy wanted to force her gaze away from the wall, but she was afraid *not* to watch it.

'I think this little lake has grown since the last time,' Greg said.

His voice erased Darcy's anxiety.

She looked down at him. She slipped her fingers around his wrists. 'We must be almost . . .'

Black descended. Someone behind her gasped. Jim muttered, 'Shit.'

Where the torch had been, there was a vague patch of red. It moved upward. Darcy heard a puffing sound. The red brightened. A tiny flame licked the darkness, then sank. The puffing sounds went on – Jim blowing on the embers. The crimson glow swelled and faded, but with each breath it weakened.

'For Godsake,' Helen whispered. 'Darcy, don't you have a flashlight?'

'It's all right,' she said. She plucked the flashlight off her belt and turned it on. The beam shot into the blackness, pale and cold after the mellow light of the torch. The bright disk at its centre caught the edge of Satan's Buoy, no more than two yards behind Greg's back.

'You'd better watch where you're going,' she said.

He glanced over his shoulder. 'Woops.' He sidestepped, turning the boat so it would pass between the small jagged island and the side of the cavern.

'That's where Tom fell,' Beth said.

'Yeah, that's the place.' Darcy raised the flashlight. It made a tunnel of brightness through the black, and stopped at the barrier of Ely's Wall.

Today, it seemed more like a door than a wall – a door of rocks and conrete.

Darcy supposed that Ely had chosen this particular spot

631

for his barrier because nature had nearly done the job for him. The cavern seemed to end here except for the fissure that would have provided a passageway before it was closed off. The gap must have been no more than a yard in width.

There had been no Lake of Charon before the wall. The river had probably been a shallow stream here, just as it still was on the other side of the dock where the cavern was higher. Darcy imagined that the water had not even reached the tops of Ely's shoes as he crouched and cemented the first rocks into place.

Though he'd left a narrow gap at the bottom, the wall had restricted the natural flow of the River Styx. About four feet of his handiwork was now below the water. The visible portion looked like a three-foot square.

That's where we'll break through, Darcy thought. Don't want to mess with what's below the water line, or we'll have the lake pouring into the other side.

'Where do you want me to park this thing?' Greg asked.

'Might as well put it all the way up,' she told him.

He stepped out of the way, held onto the port gunnel, and eased the boat forward until it gently bumped to a stop.

'Okay,' Darcy said. 'I'll secure it.' She asked Jim to move back, then picked up the bow line, stepped in front of him, and tied the rope around a spike jutting out of the water at her shoulder level.

– The spike she'd been holding while she delivered her story about the origin of Ely's Wall to the tourists.

It seemed like days ago.

She remembered being annoyed by Kyle's lecherous gaze. Wonder how Paula's getting along with him, she thought.

'How about some light?' Greg asked.

She turned around, keeping one hand on the spike, and

aimed the flashlight high so it wouldn't shine in Greg's eyes as he reached up and accepted the pickaxe from Carol.

With the pick held overhead like a soldier's rifle, he waded alongside the boat, past Darcy, and took a few steps to the left. He stopped in front of Ely's Wall and looked back. 'This'll just take a minute,' he said, smiling.

'Hope so,' she told him. 'Try not to smash things up below the water.'

'Aye-aye.' He faced the wall, lowered the pick, lifted it over one shoulder and swung. The blade struck with a deafening metalic clamour that made Darcy flinch. A knob of rock flew off the wall and splashed in front of Greg. Darcy's ears were still ringing when he slammed the pick into the wall a second time.

'*Jesus.*' Carol's voice.

'Loud enough to wake the dead,' Beth muttered.

Greg pounded the wall again and again, striking it high near the area where Ely's rocks met the cavern's smooth, ancient limestone. Chips flew. Chunks fell and thumped the water. Most of his blows seemed directed at the mortar filling the spaces between the rocks. Sometimes, entire blocks came off, hitting the water with such force that Greg's face was sprayed.

As the opening grew, Darcy expected to see the darkness of the cavern on the other side. Instead, she saw another layer of rock. Greg kept hacking and prying at the outer wall until the opening was large enough to crawl through – if there hadn't been the second layer.

Breathing heavily, he rested the pick on his shoulder. He shook his head and turned around. 'That Ely ... didn't fool around. Wonder how thick he *made* the damn thing.'

'Why don't you climb aboard and rest up?' Jim suggested. 'I'll take over for a while.'

633

'Think I'll take you up on that.'

As he returned to the boat, Jim began to undress.

Darcy took the pick from Greg. It was warm where his hands had been clutching the haft. The boat wobbled as he climbed over its side. He stood up straight and folded his hands behind his head and panted for air.

Jim, stripped down to his boxer shorts and shoes, sat down on the gunnel and lowered himself into the water. 'Whoa! Damn!'

'Start swinging that sucker,' Greg told him, 'and you'll be toasty in no time.'

Darcy handed the pick down to Jim. He carried it to the wall. Beth holding the light on him, he began to smash at the inner layer of rock.

Darcy turned to Greg. Helen had apparently given her sweater to him. He was using it like a towel. Picking up his bundle of clothes, Darcy stepped over a seat. She stood at his side, facing him, watching as he bent over and ran the sweater down his legs. When he swung the sweater behind him to dry his back, Darcy set his clothes down. 'I'll get your back,' she offered, speaking loudly to be heard over the clank of the pick.

He gave the damp sweater to her, and turned around. She mopped his back. Crouching, she rubbed his buttocks, then his legs.

'What do you know!' Jim called.

Looking over her shoulder, Darcy saw a patch of blackness in the wall. He'd broken through.

'Thank God,' Helen muttered.

The clamour started again.

'Won't be long, now,' Beth announced over the noise.

'Then the *real* fun will start,' Greg said.

Darcy patted his rump. 'You mean this isn't the real fun?'

Though she was still drying his legs, he turned around. His groin was at her eye level. She glanced at the bulging front of his briefs, then lowered her eyes and began to rub the sweater on his thighs. He put a hand on her head, he knew, just as she did, that he had already dried the fronts of his legs.

She looked at Carol. The woman's head was turned. Her eyes were on Jim.

Darcy slid the sweater up one of Greg's legs and, as if by accident, touched the back of her hand to the damp underside of his pouch. He flinched slightly.

'Your shorts are sopping,' she said.

'Is that so?'

She rubbed them gently, a single layer of the sweater between her open hand and his briefs. She curled a hand under his scrotum, slid her palm up the underside of thick, rigid penis, then stood up, smiled at him and said, 'All done.'

'Glad it's dark in here,' he said close to her ear.

'Something you wouldn't want the others to see?'

'How about handing me my pants?'

'Don't you think you should get out of those yucky, wet shorts?'

'Oh, I don't think so. Maybe some other time. My pants, please.'

'I like you better without them.'

'This is a hell of a time for you to get horny.'

'Me?' Darcy asked. 'You're the one with the . . .'

'All right!' Jim called. 'That should do it!'

Darcy looked around. He was holding the pick at his side, stepping close to the wall.

The hole in front of him was about two feet across and nearly a yard high – plenty large enough for them to crawl through.

The bottom edge of the gap was just above the surface of the lake. Jim's chest pushed against it as he leaned forward to peer into the darkness.

'What do you see?' Beth asked.

'Surely you jest.'

The flashlight's beam was at such an angle that, even had Jim not been in the way, it wouldn't have penetrated the opening.

Jim said, 'It's just as black as . . .' He staggered backwards a step and Darcy glimpsed a thick, pale shaft protruding from his mouth. It came out and Jim started to slump.

An arm darted through the hole, clutched his hair, and yanked him forward. His head went into the darkness.

Beth started to scream.

Darcy gazed, stunned, as Jim's body slid up out of the water and disappeared through the opening in Ely's Wall.

13

When the sound of the first clank reached them, Kyle heard snatches of conversation from those gathered in front of the elevators.

'All *right*.'

'They made it.'

'They're starting in.'

Kyle felt a shiver of dread, and pressed Paula more tightly against his side.

The sounds went on. Nobody spoke now. Everyone seemed

to be listening to the quiet metallic clanking that came ringing up the tunnel of the cavern from Ely's Wall. The distant clamour, though faint, was distinct through the soft crackle and pop of the elevator fires.

Maybe something will happen, Kyle told himself. Maybe the pick handle will break and they'll have to quit and come back. Maybe the wall's just too hard, and they won't be able to break through it.

He couldn't convince himself.

He remembered the giggles, the moans, the mad hushed voices he'd heard coming up from the chute. Six or eight people down there, Dad had told him.

Crazy people. Living in the blackness, nothing to eat except what was dropped down the chute to them.

Amy Lawson. They *ate* her.

And now, no matter where those crazies might be within their sealed length of cavern, they had to be hearing the pick as it clashed against the wall.

He could see them moving blindly towards the noise.

Maybe they won't go towards it, he thought. They might not understand what's going on. Maybe they'll be frightened, and hide. Maybe they'll stay hidden the whole time, and Darcy and her bunch will never even guess they're around.

It could happen that way.

Soon, the far-off pounding ceased.

Paula turned her head and looked up at Kyle, the firelight flashing on her glasses. 'They must've gotten through,' she said.

Kyle heard others.

'They did it.'

'Didn't take long.'

'The thing was probably old and falling apart, anyway.'

Kyle, feeling as if his bowels were being squeezed, let go of Paula and sank to a crouch.

Then the pounding came again.

'Damn.'

'They were probably just taking a rest.'

'Maybe they busted through, but only just decided they oughta make the hole bigger.'

'Whatever, it won't be long now.'

'Shhh. I can't hear.'

'Who gives a hot fuck if you can hear?'

'Cool out, Slick.'

'Up yours, Callllvin.'

The pounding stopped again. So did the voices of those clustered with Kyle around the elevator fires.

Kyle's guts felt knotted. Paula, standing beside him, brushed her hand through his hair. And suddenly clenched his hair as the shrill of a scream floated in from the distance.

Heart slamming, he sprang to his feet. Paula released his hair. He gaped at her. She looked stunned.

The scream went on and on.

Nearby, a girl made terrified whiny sounds.

'It's all right, honey.'

'Jesus H. Christ,' someone muttered.

'What'n hell's going on?'

Kyle *knew* what was going on. The crazies beyond the wall hadn't hidden, they'd attacked. He felt as if snakes were squirming up and down his back.

The screaming stopped.

Though no one had moved from in front of the fire, nearly every head was turned, facing the darkness. The whining kid, a girl of about seven, was clutching her mother.

Tom said, 'I'm sure everything's all right.'

'Like hell it is.'

A man who stood with his hands on the shoulders of the frightened girl said, 'Maybe we'd better ... some of us should go and find out what happened. They might need help.'

'I'm with you, pardner,' said the old cowboy, Calvin.

'Sure does sound like they might've run into a spot of trouble.' That was the fat old guy who'd volunteered to go with Darcy in the first place.

'Count me in,' said the man with the pregnant wife.

'Oh, no you don't,' she protested. 'You're not going anywhere.'

'But ...'

'I think we should all stay here,' Tom told them. He fingered the bandaged side of his head. 'A bunch of you go running off into the dark ... I don't know. I think we should stay together. Since we don't know what happened ...'

'One of the gals probably just got spooked.' That was the guy Calvin always called Slick. 'Saw a bat or something.'

'There aren't any bats,' Tom pointed out.

'Could've been anything. These bitches'll shriek their heads off at the drop of a hat.'

One of the thin men in the matching goatees said, 'I think we should go and investigate, nonetheless.'

'Well just go ahead,' Slick said. 'Swish on down there.'

'Redneck trash.'

'I'll "redneck" you, you goddamn butt-fucker.'

'Dad, you shouldn't ...'

Slick backhanded his son across the face. The kid stumbled backward. The father of the little girl caught him before he fell.

'Hey, buddy, that's no way to act.'

'Wanta make something of it?' He brought up his fists.

The other guy rubbed his hands on his jeans and lumbered toward him.

'Wayne, don't!'

'C'mon, c'mon.' Slick flapped a hand, beckoning to him.

'He's mine,' said the goateed man, stepping in the way of Wayne.

'I'll take y'both. C'mon, c'mon.'

'Stop this!' Tom shouted. 'I'm in charge here, and I won't have you people . . .'

'Shut the fuck up.'

The gay guy pushed Wayne back, then turned to face Slick, who grinned and kissed the knuckles of his right fist, then cocked the fist back, ready to smash the man.

And didn't see Calvin beside him.

'Hey there, you son of a whore. Didn't I warn you?'

Slick whirled to face Calvin.

He was still whirling when the wiry old cowboy jabbed with his walking stick. The brass end of the cane flashed golden in the firelight. It sank into Slick's belly. Whoofing, Slick started to double. Calvin let go of the cane with one hand, took a single step forward as Slick was buckling, and smashed a fist into the side of the man's face. Spittle flew from Slick's mouth and his head snapped sideways. The blow sent him stumbling towards an elevator. People gasped. He fell inside the car, and yelled as he crashed down on burning debris. Sparks flew up around him.

The two men with goatees rushed in, grabbed him up by his jacket, and dragged him out.

His hat was gone, his hair on fire.

The man he'd called a 'butt-fucker' slapped his head and snuffed the flames.

They let go of him. He dropped to his knees, sobbing, and clutched his smoking scalp.

'Should've let the low-lifer burn,' Calvin said.

Slick's son threw himself down and hugged the whimpering man. 'Dad?' he asked. 'Are you okay? Dad?'

Slick shoved the boy away.

'You're some kinda work,' Calvin said, and bashed the guy's head with his cane.

Slick crumbled and lay still.

'You old fool, you've killed him!'

'Don't get yourself all riled up, May. I didn't kill the sidewinder, though it might've been a boon to humanity if I had.'

A few people applauded.

Calvin tipped his Stetson to them.

The guy who'd put out Slick's burning hair crouched down, felt his pulse, and nodded. 'He's not dead.'

'Ah,' said his friend, 'but I should think he'll have a frightful headache.'

'His brains needed a good scrambling,' Calvin said. 'I reckon he'll be better off for it.'

The old fat guy handed Calvin a cigar.

'Much obliged.'

'Fellow's nothing short of a bum,' the fat man said, turning away from Calvin and addressing the whole group. 'He had a good point, though, about the scream. Could've been pretty much anything made one of those ladies haul off and scream her head off like that.'

'You're right,' Tom said. 'I think we ought to just stay here. It might've been nothing, so we shouldn't get upset and go off on a wild-goose chase. If they've had a real emergency and they need help, I'm sure they'll send someone back here to let us know.'

If anyone's left alive, Kyle thought.

What *did* happen? he wondered. There were four women

641

in Darcy's group, but the screaming had all been done by just one. Maybe it had nothing to do, after all, with the crazies behind the wall.

Maybe they got through to the other side without being attacked.

Or maybe the others didn't get a chance to scream.

Or they might have all gone silent, hoping to hide in the darkness as the crazies came scurrying through the hole. Even now, a mad hunt and struggle could be going on in the Lake of Charon.

When it's over . . .

The crazies won't go back into their side of the cave. They'll head this way.

Kyle led Paula aside. He felt the heat from the fires fade, the cool air seep through his clothes. Standing in the shadows, he whispered, 'I want to sneak away from this bunch. They're going weird, you know?'

'Just that creepy guy.'

'But look what Calvin did to him. He could've killed the guy. Everyone's real nervous, starting to act crazy. I think we'd be a lot safer if we made ourselves scarce until help gets here. Who knows what they might do next, do you know what I mean?'

Paula nodded. 'You think someone else might start trouble?'

'Yeah, I do, and the longer we're trapped down here, the more likely it'll get. The fires are going down. Before long, they'll be out. It'll be dark again, and cold. Everyone's already nervous, but pretty soon some of them are going to start panicking. When that happens, there might be some *real* trouble.'

'So you want us get away from them and hide?'

Kyle took both her hands in his, and stared into her eyes.

He realized that his fear of those from the other side of Ely's Wall had been pushed aside by feelings of eagerness, almost excitement.

They won't get me, he thought. Not a chance. This'll be good, really good.

Hiding with Paula. Away from the others. In the dark.

'I'm just thinking about you,' he said. 'I probably wouldn't bother, just for myself, but . . . Another thing is, I don't like the way some of these guys have been looking at you.'

'What do you mean?'

'Like they might want to . . . I don't know, maybe I just worry too much. But when it's dark again and no one can see what anybody else is doing, people might try things. Stuff they wouldn't normally do. I'd try my best to protect you, but . . . I just think we shouldn't stick around. It'll be better for both of us if they don't know where to find you.'

Frowning, she shook her head. 'You're afraid someone might want to . . . molest me?'

She's buying it, Kyle realized. She believes me.

'Maybe I shouldn't have brought it up,' he continued, 'but yeah, that's crossed my mind. Nothing would surprise me.'

'Who?'

'The one that got knocked out was giving you funny looks.'

'Yug.'

'Both those guys with the goatees, they've been checking you out, too.'

'But they're homos, aren't they?'

'If they're homos, why have they been staring at your breasts?'

'Have they?' She wrinkled her nose.

'Yeah. And the old guy that gave the cigar to Calvin.'

'You're kidding,' Paula whispered.

'But the one I'm really worried about, it's that gal with

Calvin.' Kyle wrinkled his own nose and made himself sound disgusted. 'I can almost see her drooling when she looks at you.'

'Oh God. A lizzie?'

'Haven't you seen any of these creeps giving you the eye?'

She shook her head.

'I'm not saying they'll actually try something, but once it's dark . . .'

'So you think we should hide,' Paula said.

'Yeah.'

'Where'll we go?'

He nodded toward the darkness. 'Over there. On the other side of the River Styx. They'll never find us over there.'

Neither will the crazies, he thought. That was the main thing. He wanted to get alone with Paula, but more than that, he wanted to be hidden if those from behind the wall should come. He was sure they'd take the walkway if they left the Lake of Charon. The walkway followed this side of the stream, and would lead them straight to those waiting near the elevators. With or without Paula, he intended to be hiding on the other side of the stream when they arrived.

But with her would be so much better.

'Okay?' he asked.

'Okay.'

Taking his time, he led Paula around the outer rim of the group. No one seemed to notice. Most were facing the fires, as if they feared the darkness and hoped to deny its existence by keeping it behind them.

But there were about thirty of them. For a while, Kyle hovered at the rear of the group, trying to make sure that no one was watching. Then he stepped backwards drawing Paula along with him.

After four silent steps, they were well into the darkness.

Even if someone should look now, eyes accustomed to the brightness of the firelight probably wouldn't be able to spot them.

Kyle turned around. Paula stayed at his side. Arms around each other, they moved quietly away, deeper into the dark.

'Can we stay in sight of the fires?' Paula whispered.

'Sure.' He'd already planned on that. He hoped to see what would happen when the crazies showed up. Though he'd warned Paula that the fires would soon burn out, there was enough broken wood inside the elevators to keep the flames going for quite a while yet. With any luck, the fires would last long enough for him to watch the mayhem.

From a safe distance.

Kyle stopped and looked over his shoulder. The clustered people were dark silhouettes against the light of twin fires, forty or fifty feet from where he stood. Taking that distance into account, Kyle figured he must be very close to the railing that bordered this side of the stream.

He led Paula slowly forward, reaching out with one hand until he touched the cold, moist metal of the railing. 'Here we are,' he whispered. 'I'll go first.'

He squatted low and ducked beneath the railing. When he was clear, he turned around and felt for Paula. He found her shoulder. She rose up in front of him.

'This is so weird,' she whispered. He saw the vague shape of her head turn, and he guessed that she needed to comfort herself by looking back at the firelight. 'What if they find out we're gone?'

'Big deal. You think they'll come looking?'

'I just wonder if we should be doing this.'

'Do you want to go back?'

She was silent.

She's not going back.

645

'I guess not,' she finally said.

Kyle took her hand. 'Well, if you change your mind, fine. Just tell me. I'm not forcing you into anything.'

'I know.'

'I'll go first. Stay in back of me, and hold on.' He turned around. Paula curled her fingers over his shoulders, and he began making his way down the embankment, knees bent, arms out for balance. He could see nothing in front of him. The rock slope felt smooth and somewhat slippery under his shoes. Instead of taking steps, he scooted without lifting his feet.

When he judged that he must be near the stream, he stopped. He slid a foot forward and tapped a few times with his toe. Hearing no splashes, he moved ahead a little farther and tried again. This time, he heard a soft liquid patter when he tapped.

'We have to wade across,' he whispered. 'It's only a few inches deep, but out feet'll get wet. I'm going to take off my shoes and socks.'

'Okay,' Paula said. 'Me, too.'

They sat down beside each other on the slope. Kyle pulled off his running shoes, peeled his socks off his feet and stuffed them inside the shoes. Paula, he remembered, wore a kilt and knee socks. Without the socks, her legs would be bare.

Bare all the way up to the panties she must have on beneath the kilt.

He suddenly pictured Darcy in the grotto, naked except for her panties, clutching her trousers to her breasts. The panties were wet. They were glued to her.

The memories made him hard.

Then came a hollow ache as he realized he would probably never see Darcy alive again, never get a chance to touch her or squeeze her or taste her, never ram her with his cock or make her bleed and squirm and cry out like Amy Lawson.

Others might get to do it. The ones who dwelled beyond the wall. But not Kyle.

They'll cheat me out of it, he thought.

But I've got Paula.

'Okay,' Paula said.

Holding both his shoes in one hand, Kyle stood. He took her arm, and helped her stand up. She stayed at his side as they eased forward and entered the water.

She made a hissing sound. 'Christ, it's cold.'

'Yeah.' His feet felt numb to the ankles. The streambed was gritty as if a thin layer of sand and gravel had been sprinkled over its rock floor. He lifted a foot out of the water, took a small step and set it down carefully. Then he did the same with his other foot.

What if I make her fall? Kyle asked himself. So it looks like an accident. Then her clothes will be all wet and I can get her to take them off when we reach the other side. I'll tell her she can wear my pants, and . . .

If she falls, she might yell. The others will hear her, and come looking.

Forget it.

There'll be plenty of time to work on her. He'd had her blouse open just before the elevators fell, it shouldn't take much to get her bra off, and after that, who knows?

His foot came down, finding rock instead of water. 'Here's the shore,' he whispered. 'I'll go first. Get behind me and hang onto my belt.' He released her arm and her fingers pushed under the back of his belt. Crouching, he felt the rocks ahead and began to move forward up the embankment. His shoulder bumped something, probably one of the stalagmites he'd often noticed along this side of the stream. He stepped around it.

He'd looked across the River Styx countless times, and had even explored over here on several occasions. He knew that the area was cluttered with speleothems that would provide wonderful hiding places, but he couldn't recall the exact details and the dark was disorienting.

He felt his way along like a blind man stumbling through a maze.

And stepped on something soft.

He crouched, stroked the cool cloth surface, and realized what he was touching. 'There's a blanket here,' he said.

'Geez.'

Kneeling, he crawled on the blanket. It was doubled over, giving it a double thickness. It seemed to be about a yard wide and six feet long. When he reached its far end, his sweeping hand crushed a slick, springy mound that he guessed might be a pillow. He explored it with his fingers – and realized it must be a sleeping bag in a stuff sack. He picked it up and heard a muffled clank of glass. Reaching down, he found a bottle. It was heavy. Liquid sloshed inside. He twisted off the cap and sniffed. There was a pungent odour of alcohol. Though he didn't know much about such things, he guessed that it must be a bottle of Scotch or Bourbon.

'Pretty neat,' Paula whispered from behind him.

'There's a sleeping bag.'

'You're kidding.'

'And a bottle of booze.'

'Really?'

He turned around on his knees and eased the bottle in her direction.

'I can smell it,' Paula said.

'Take a sip. It'll warm you up.'

'I don't know.'

'I won't tell.'

'Where'd it come from?'

'Right here.'

'Is this stuff yours?'

'Sure isn't.'

'You took us right to it.'

'Glad I did, too. But it isn't mine. I didn't even know anything was here.'

'If it isn't yours, where'd it come from?'

'God, I don't know. Somebody must've . . . maybe it's a make-out place.' Turning his head, he saw only black. He reached out. Just past the edge of the blanket was a barrier of rock. Rising, he saw the distant shapes backlit by the elevator fires. 'This is great,' he said. He sat down again. 'Think I'll give it a taste.'

'Maybe you shouldn't. If you don't know whose it is . . .'

'Must belong to somebody who works here. Maybe Tom. Maybe he comes over here with one of the guides.' Darcy? he wondered. Had she spent time here with Tom, hidden among the rocks, drinking and fucking?

He imagined her naked inside the sleeping bag, writhing and gasping, but not with Tom. It was Kyle in the bag with her, squeezing her breasts, thrusting deep into her wet heat.

Maybe they would sneak down here at night. Or even hide here during the day, out of sight as tours went by.

Not Darcy, though.

Probably Lynn. Lynn and Tom.

Lynn was such a slut, he wouldn't put anything past her.

'You think it's sanitary?' Paula asked.

'Sure.' He lifted the bottle to his lips, and tilted it up. The liquid took a moment to reach his mouth, so he figured the bottle was about three-quarters full. He sipped. Some kind of whisky, all right. He swallowed and the heat rushed through him. Shuddering slightly, he said, 'Good. Try some.'

He held the bottle out and felt it being taken from his hand. There came a quiet sloshing sound, then 'Whoo.'

'Like it?'

'It's all right.'

'Want to get in the sleeping bag?'

She was silent for a few seconds. 'I don't know. I don't think so.'

'I'll get it out, anyway. We can sit on it.'

'Okay.'

He opened the drawstring, pulled out the sleeping bag, and spread it over the blanket.

They sat on it, side by side in the darkness. Kyle wrapped an arm around Paula's back. She snuggled against him. He heard her take another drink. Then she nudged his chest with the bottle. He found it, and drank.

'Wouldn't it be something,' Paula whispered, 'if we both got smashed? We'd go staggering out of here, blasted out of our gourds.'

'Sounds like a good idea.'

'I was just kidding.'

'Have you ever been drunk?'

'No. How about you?'

'Me neither,' Kyle said. 'But this seems like a good time to try it.'

'I don't know. You wouldn't try any funny stuff, would you?'

'No. Promise. No funny stuff. Cross my heart and hope to die.'

14

Beth, screaming, had leaped off the boat while her husband's legs were still in the air. The soles of his shoes vanished through the hole at the same instant water flew up from Beth's splash.

'No!' Greg shouted at her.

She lunged through the chest-high water, left hand swiping the air in front of her, right hand waving the flashlight. The beam jerked and jumped over the cavern wall, jittering all around the hole.

She hadn't taken two steps before Greg swung Darcy out of his way and threw himself off the boat. Darcy staggered. The edge of the seat caught her behind the knees. She dropped backwards, grabbed a gunnel, pulled herself up and twisted onto her side in time to see Greg hook an arm around Beth. His other arm reached out. He grabbed her forearm as if he feared she might lose the flashlight. The woman struggled against him, trying to pull free.

'Jim! Jim! Come back!'

'Stop it!' Greg snapped. 'Beth, he's gone. Let's . . .'

The back of her head struck Greg's chin. Darcy heard the thud, heard his teeth clash together, saw his head jerk. He dropped backwards. As he went under, Darcy pushed herself up and crouched to dive and glimpsed something off to the side.

Pale movement.

She looked and saw Beth wading. The flashlight beam skittered all over the wall, not settling on the hole but flicking across it. And as it skimmed past the hole, Darcy glimpsed someone coming out head first.

651

For an instant, she thought it was Jim coming back. (Just an hallucination, seeing him stabbed through the mouth and yanked into the hole.) He was okay after all. Now, he was coming back.

It wasn't Jim.

No *way* was that hairy, bearded thing Jim!

Seeing Greg come to the surface, she dived. In midair, she heard Helen squeal and Carol say, 'Oh Jesus God!' Then she hit the water. The cold swarmed around her, but it didn't matter. She was still underwater when her hand pushed against Greg. His hip. She stood and grabbed his arm as he began to wade towards Beth. He was shaking his head, apparently still dazed from the blow.

She turned and moved with him.

Beth, a yard in front of them, made a *whoof* and began to double over. Then she was hurled up. One of her kicking feet brushed Darcy's forehead. She was hoisted above the lake, writhing and flapping, a dim bearded shape rising up beneath her. Not touching her. Throwing her high and over his head with something knobbed at the end like the handle of a baseball bat (a bone?). As she tumbled over him, he jerked the weapon out. The flashlight, still in Beth's hand as she somer-saulted, lit the weapon – a bone, more than a foot long, sharp at one end, ashimmer with blood.

Beth hit the water behind the man.

The flashlight went down with her. It stayed on, but the cavern suddenly fell dark. As dark as a moonless night, but not black. Darcy could almost see Greg blend with the man. She heard grunts, growls, splashes, and felt the water churning against her body. She was knocked aside as Greg stumbled backward. The two men went under.

She waded toward the flashlight. It lay on the bottom of the lake, its beam pushing a short tunnel through the water.

Ducking down she grabbed the cylinder. She brought the flashlight up in time to see a person crouched on the edge of the hole in Ely's Wall.

Another one?

Her stomach went cold and tight.

The stranger's arms were out against the sides of the hole. Darcy's eyes were drawn to the thin bone it held in one hand. Something shiny at its end.

Scissors.

Toe-nail scissors?

They were somehow fixed to the end of the bone, their tiny blades forming a point for the bizarre weapon.

Long hair hung over the stranger's face. The face looked dead white. The teeth were bared with a snarl. Pointed teeth. In the instant before it sprang at Darcy, she saw that it wore a blood-smeared white turtleneck sweater. Jeans.

Large breasts swayed inside the sweater as the woman leaped from her perch.

Darcy swung the flashlight.

A jolt went up her arm as the head of the cylinder smashed against the woman's face.

The light went out.

The body hit her, driving Darcy backwards and down. The water closed over her. Though she expected a savage assault, no hands clutched at her, no scissor points dug into her flesh. She realized, vaguely, that the blow from the flashlight must've stunned the woman. She rolled out from under her. Wrapped an arm around the head. Got to her feet and pulled the head up out of the water and, hugging the wet face to her cheek, hammered the head with the flashlight. With each impact, the face jerked against her.

She heard the sounds of Greg's struggle off to her side.

One last blow.

Five.

Then a sixth for good measure. Then she let go of the woman's head. The body slid down against her. She kneed it away, turned sluggishly in the water and waded toward the gasping, choking, splashing noises.

Heard quick whispers to her left. Helen and Carol.

A heavy thud and spatter in the lake behind her.

A *third* invader from behind Ely's Wall?

She heard herself whimper. Don't worry about more, she told herself. Worry about the one Greg's fighting. Thank God they're still at it.

She neared the turmoil.

Heard splashes off to the side. Had Carol and Helen left the boat?

Something rammed her thigh. She reached down into the water and grabbed an ankle. She felt a sock under her fingers. Greg wasn't wearing socks. The foot kicked out of her grip.

Not wanting to lose the flashlight, she stuffed it under the elastic bottom of her windbreaker, then reached down again. She clutched a trouser cuff. (Greg was in his briefs.) Face in the water, she climbed her hands up the leg to the inseam. Drove an arm deep between the legs and rammed it up hard into the crotch. The legs clamped on her arm. She felt the body shudder. Pulling her arm free, she clawed at the man's rump, hooked her fingers into the back pockets of his pants, and tugged, trying to get him off Greg.

The flopping, bucking body came with her as she stumbled backward.

She heard a swoosh of water. Coughing. Greg must have come up.

'Got him,' she whispered.

Greg didn't answer. He kept coughing.

'Where *are* you?' Carol's voice.

'Go for the dock!' Darcy yelled. 'Get out of here!'

'Which way?'

How can I answer that?

'Just go! And be quiet! There's more of them!'

The body jerked forward. Darcy yanked the pants pockets, trying to keep it back, then realized that the sudden movement hadn't been the attacker's doing. Greg must be pulling on him. So she relaxed her grip and felt the body dart forward and up. Her fingers slipped out of the pockets.

There was another thumping splash behind her.

Another savage entering the lake?

Soft swashing sounds of someone wading or swimming back there.

Other such sounds ahead of her.

A yelp of fright from the front.

'It's me, just me.' Helen's voice.

'Thank God.'

Reaching out, she clutched thick, oily hair. She fumbled under her windbreaker for the flashlight, planning to beat the man with it. But the head rammed violently back against her hand, then went down.

'Okay,' Greg gasped. 'Okay.'

Darcy moved towards the sound of his voice, so close in the blackness. The submerged body was in the way. It sank lower and slipped away as she walked over it with her knees. Then her arms were around Greg. She pressed herself against him, felt his heaving chest, his wet cheek, his warm breath brushing her ear.

There were soft liquid swooshing sounds behind her, in front of her. And breathing sounds. Whimpers nearby, probably from Carol or Helen.

Darcy, herself, was shaking violently.

She flinched rigid as she realized that someone was very near, approaching her back.

'Hold your breath,' Greg whispered.

He pulled her down.

She crouched. The water closed over her head. Greg eased her away, but held onto her arm. He turned her, pulled her. She left her feet and he towed her along. She felt the chill water streaming over her body. He couldn't be doing this and swimming. She supposed he was wading, squatted low to stay beneath the surface.

This will work, she thought. We're leaving them behind.

As long as we stay under, they won't find us. They can only go by what they hear.

We should've told the women to do it.

Darcy began to need air. She fought the need, but soon her lungs ached. Then they burned. She wondered if Greg was going up for breaths, if he'd forgotten about her.

Then he pulled her to a stop. She felt a hand press her mouth. He raised her slowly. When her face was out of the water, he removed his hand. She sucked air into her lungs, but tried to do it quietly.

She expected Greg to submerge her again quickly. He didn't, though.

They stood motionless, holding each other.

Darcy heard her own breathing and the quick thumping of her heart. She heard Greg's too. And a few quiet patters as drops of water fell from them. Nothing else.

It was as if all movement in the Lake of Charon had ceased.

It was as if they were alone in the lake.

What's going on?

She wished she could hear the others.

Maybe Carol and Helen are swimming underwater, she thought. Maybe everyone is.

Or maybe they're all standing motionless, just like us. Carol and Helen hoping their silence will save them. The others hoping for a sound that'll give us away so they can home in on us and nail us.

Suppose the attackers have left? Went back through their hole to the other end of the cavern?

We got two of them. Maybe didn't kill them, maybe did, but that might've taken the starch out of the rest.

No. We weren't under long enough. They wouldn't have had time to get back through the hole.

Greg touched her chin, which she took as a signal to submerge again. She filled her lungs. His fingers were still on her chin, so he knew when she nodded.

They went down slowly, silently.

Greg towed her through the water, just like before.

She sensed that they were moving toward the dock. That had to be, or they would've run into one of the cavern's walls before now.

If we can just get to the dock!

With just a little headstart on the pursuers, they'd be all right. From the dock, they could find the walkway and follow its railing back to the main group. They'd be safe there. Those horrible things wouldn't dare . . .

Things? People.

But they looked and acted like mindless savages, seemed less than human.

What the hell were they doing behind Ely's Wall? Did they *live* there?

That's crazy. Nobody could survive in . . .

Unless there's an opening somewhere. If they had a way in and out. Not supposed to be an opening, but maybe. Who knows?

Killed Jim and Beth.

Hope Carol and Helen are okay.

We're okay, that's the main thing.

Darcy felt a nudge of guilt and she wondered if she might be punished for her selfishness and she thought, Please God, let Carol and Helen be all right.

Greg's hand covered her eyes, then slid lower and pressed her mouth. She nodded. She put her feet down and let him guide her to the surface.

The cavern was no longer silent.

Loud splashing. But far away. Behind them.

And suddenly a high terrified voice whining, 'No! No! Leave me be! *Please!* MY GOD!'

It was Helen. Her voice went silent. The splashing continued, but with less frenzy.

They got Helen, Darcy thought. Oh Christ, they got her.

Feeling Greg's hand on her cheek, she took a deep breath and nodded. They went down again.

Greg's grip on her arm was tighter than before and he seemed to be towing her faster.

Because of what happened to Helen, she thought.

Why are they killing us?

We broke through Ely's Wall. If we'd stayed at the elevators ... It's my fault. Jim and Beth and Helen, they'd be alive if . . .

Shit, I had no way of knowing. Who could have known we'd be *murdered*?

They must have heard us pounding, and gathered on their side of the wall, just waiting.

Thank God it was Jim who broke through. Jim, and not Greg. It would've been Greg if there hadn't been a second layer of rocks.

Poor Jim, though. *Jesus*. That bone. Right into his mouth. And Beth. In the stomach.

The water carried a hollow, ringing thump to her ears. It came from beside her. From Greg's side. Though alarmed and puzzled for a moment, she quickly understood the meaning of the sound: Greg had gone up for air and struck his head on the hull of the boat that was tied at the dock.

It better be that boat he hit, she thought. If it's the *other* boat, we're in deep shit.

Her grim humour surprised Darcy. It came from relief, she supposed, from knowing that they had found the dock.

Greg pulled her forward, then lifted her.

Before, when they came up for air, they had both remained crouched so that only their heads were exposed. Now, Darcy stood up straight. The water was as high as the undersides of her breasts. She put a hand on Greg's shoulder. He released her other arm, and she reached out to her left. As she expected, her fingertips found the metal side of the boat. The boat, she knew, had been moored snugly against the dock. Raising her arm, she felt the rough wooden planks above her head.

They'll never find us here, she thought. We're under the dock with the boat blocking the way. If they get this far, they'll go around the boat. They'll run into the dock, and they'd be more likely to climb onto it than to search beneath it. If we're quiet, they'll never find us.

You brought me here, Greg. Somehow, you got us here.

We'll be all right, now.

She knew they were coming, could hear the soft liquid sounds of their approach. But they were still some distance away.

She slipped both arms around Greg and hugged him tightly.

They stood in the blackness, embracing. They were both trembling and breathing hard, and she could feel the thud of his heartbeat through his chest. The barrel of the flashlight was pressed between their bellies. After their breathing calmed, he slipped a hand under Darcy's windbreaker and pulled the flashlight out. He gave it to her. She clipped it to her belt, out of the way. For a moment, she considered opening the zipper and spreading the front of the windbreaker. It would be so good, so comforting, to feel him against her bare skin. But she didn't do it. Because those from beyond Ely's Wall were wading nearer and nearer. She pressed herself against Greg, and listened.

And heard a slurp behind her.

Jesus no!

Greg went rigid.

He stopped breathing. So did Darcy.

Someone was under the dock. It seemed impossible, but Darcy had heard the slosh. So close behind her! And it wasn't her imagination. Greg had heard it, too.

If we don't make a sound . . .

Something touched her right shoulder. Flinching, she pushed her mouth against Greg's shoulder to stifle a gasp.

Her shoulder was patted, squeezed. Her hair was stroked.

She heard a faint sigh.

Carol?

Darcy let go of Greg. His arms loosened around her. He, too, must've guessed the intruder's identity. Darcy turned slowly, careful not to disturb the water. Her hands, below the surface, found fabric. She remembered the sundress Carol had been wearing, and moved her hands higher and felt the armholes. She touched an armpit, a breast, the low neckline of the dress. She slid her hand up the side of the neck, and stroked the woman's wet cheek. She felt eager nodding.

And heard a quiet sob.

Curling a hand behind the neck, she drew Carol against

her. The woman hugged her. Greg, moving silently to Darcy's side, put his arms around them both.

Carol shook as she wept, and her breath made hitching sounds.

The others were very near. They seemed to be in front of Darcy and over to the right, approaching the dock – probably somewhere just beyond the bow of the boat.

Fearing they might hear Carol, Darcy brought a hand up and pressed the woman's face against the side of her neck to muffle the ragged breathing sounds.

She heard a soft bump, followed by an 'Uh!' Someone must have bumped the edge of the dock.

'What?' A whisper. A woman's voice.

'Hit something.' A man.

Christ, Darcy thought, they can talk.

Patting sounds on the wood. 'I know what this is. It's the pier where they keep the touring boats.' That was a woman. She had to be one of those from the other side of the wall, but she was familiar with this side.

Who the hell *are* these people?

There came a whush of spilling water. A sudden thud as if a heavy object (a person) had been thrown onto the dock. Darcy flinched. Carol jerked rigid and sucked hard on the side of her neck. Darcy felt Greg's grip tighten on her shoulder.

Then there were sloshing sounds, dribbles, thumps and scurrying sounds.

They're climbing onto the dock, Darcy thought. Thank God. They're not going to search under it.

She listened carefully. From the sounds they made boosting themselves up and clambering onto the platform, she guessed that there were at least four of them. Maybe five.

They didn't leave.

Darcy wanted to hear them walk way, but they seemed to be going nowhere. She guessed that they were sitting down. They'd left the water about six feet ahead of her, and had come no closer. She heard water dribbling onto the surface of the lake, probably spilling off their bodies and falling through the cracks between the planks.

They're so damn close, she thought. But not so close that she could hear their breathing. And they can't hear ours, she told herself.

'Let's we leave her for later,' the woman whispered, 'and go after the others.'

Someone laughed as if it were a stupid suggestion.

'I mean it. If they reach the elevators, they'll go up and tell about us. They'll tell what we did. People will come down with guns, and . . .'

A smack. A whimper.

'Okay,' the woman muttered.

Darcy heard quick, soft popping sounds. Things clicked on the wood, skittered along. Something plipped into the water.

Buttons, she thought.

Leave her for later. They weren't leaving her for later. Somebody had just ripped open her blouse, making buttons fly.

That first loud thud before the others climbed onto the dock. It *had* been a body hitting onto the dock. Beth or Helen, more likely Helen since she was the one who'd been caught a few minutes ago.

Carol, apparently coming to the same conclusion, squeezed herself more tightly against Darcy.

The sounds continued. Darcy wished she could cover her ears and free herself from the knowledge of what was happening above. But she heard thumps as limbs were lifted and dropped, the rasps of fabric, the tinkle of a buckle, the skid of a zipper and she could *see* them up there in the black, kneeling in a circle around the body, stripping off its clothes.

They're going to rape her, she thought.

She wondered if Helen was dead.

She heard sighs and moans, quiet chuckles. She wondered if any of the moans came from Helen.

No, Helen's dead. Must be.

If she isn't, how can we just stand down here, hiding, while they rape her?

What if Greg decides to go to the rescue?

The way he was clutching Darcy's shoulder, she guessed that he might be considering it.

Then came a wet, ripping sound.

Another and another.

Something began to patter the water in front of Darcy.

Blood?

Then came rhythmic squishes, moans, moist sucking – the sounds that people might make with mouths full of meat.

Chewing.

15

With the rubble cleared away, Hank crawled over the rock slab. The water running around his hands and knees, though less than an inch deep, felt like ice. Cool air blew softly against him as if the small hole in the hillside was the open door of a refrigerator. He was bare to the waist, sweaty from wielding the sledge hammer under the hot sun, and the breath of the cavern chilled his wet skin.

Goosebumps scurried up his back as he put his head into the cave.

His body blocked out most of the sunlight. All he could see in the dim shadows was more of the shallow, narrow stream.

He crawled farther, until he was completely inside the cave. The cold wrapped around him. The dark pressed in on him. His heartbeat quickened. Though he couldn't see the walls or ceiling of the cavern, much less *feel* them, he sensed them shrinking, closing in on him, suffocating him. The air was being squeezed from his lungs.

Water swirled around his hands as he rubbed the stream-bed. That's solid rock, he told himself. It felt like concrete. This cave's been here thousands of years, maybe millions. It isn't about to fall in on you.

It's solid rock. It's a cavern. It's safe.

'Yoo-hoo, Hank,' Lynn called from behind him in a sing-song. 'What are you doing in there?'

What *am* I doing in here? he wondered.

Testing myself? Giving it a little try to see if I can take it?

I'll take it, no matter what. Paula's at the other end of this darkness, and I'm going to get her out.

'Is everything okay?' Chris asked.

It was good to hear her voice.

'Fine.'

Fine, like having a pillow pressed against your face by someone trying to cancel your ticket.

Hank began crawling backwards. He wanted to rush, to free himself from the oppressive tightness, but forced himself to move slowly.

Then he was free. He filled his lungs. He sniffed the piney

air of the hillside. The sunlight clothed him with wonderful heat.

As he stood in the water, gasping, the others stared at him. He saw concern on Chris's face, confusion on Brad's, and a strange, rather leering smile on Lynn's as her gaze roamed down his body.

'What's wrong with you?' Brad asked.

'Closed-in places. I don't like them.'

'You've got claustrophobia?'

'But only a touch of leprosy.'

'Well,' Lynn said, 'what do you know about that?'

Brad arched an eyebrow and rubbed one of his bulging pecs. Like Hank, he had stripped off his shirt during their labours to smash through the wall. He had the body of a Mr Universe contestant, and his sweaty skin gleamed in the sunlight as if slicked with oil. Hank suspected the man's chest didn't itch, that he was rubbing it simply to draw Chris's attention to his amazing proportions. But she was looking at Hank, not Brad.

'Maybe you should wait here,' Brad told him, and Lynn nodded in agreement.

'I'll be all right.'

'What if you're not? Suppose we get in there and you have some kind of panic attack?'

'Don't worry about it.'

'I think you should stay here,' Lynn said.

Of course you do, Hank thought. You'd like nothing better than to get me alone.

He suspected that the girl was less interested in seducing him than in defeating Chris. Some kind of a competitive thing that had little to do with desire, a lot to do with ego.

Earlier, when they parked the car on the dirt road across the small valley, she had climbed out and tied her jacket around her waist and proceeded to unbutton her uniform blouse. There was nothing under it but skin. She didn't take the blouse off. Instead, she lifted its front and knotted the tails just under her breasts. From the glances she gave Hank, the show was for his benefit, not Brad's.

When it came time to distribute the equipment for the hike to the cavern, she insisted on carrying the backpack full of flashlights and candy bars. She faced Hank while she put it on. Her struggle getting into the straps made her blouse spread apart and one side fell away, baring her left breast for a while before she noticed the problem, said 'Woops', and covered it.

Hank might have been amused by such ploys, but he sensed Lynn's rather malicious intent – and Chris was a witness to every display. Though Chris didn't complain, Hank caught her frowning slightly, sometimes shaking her head, and she'd even rolled her eyes upward as if asking the Lord for mercy when Lynn so accidently exposed the breast.

Chris stayed at his side as they hiked across the narrow valley and up the hillside to the cavern. Lynn, continuing with her tactics, walked a short distance ahead of them, swaggering and waving her rump, often walking backward to give Hank a view of her half-naked, bouncing breasts. Whenever she faced him, she spoke to Hank as if Chris and Brad weren't there. She told him about Tom. 'He's a nice guy,' she said, 'but we weren't, you know, serious. I mean, he's not all that mature.' She asked if Hank was still married. He said, 'No.' She asked, 'So what happened to your wife?' A dark place swelled inside him. 'She died.' And Lynn said, 'Woops.' And he thought, you are a little shit. But Chris looked at him with tenderness in her eyes and said softly, 'I'm sorry.'

Now, Lynn wanted him to stay behind with her while Chris and Brad went into the cavern.

Not a chance, he thought.

Even if he didn't need to go in for Paula, it would take more than claustrophobia to make him remain behind with Lynn. He wanted nothing to do with her.

And he didn't want Chris and Brad to be thrown together.

Though Brad was more subtle than Lynn, he'd obviously taken a fancy to Chris. He would be very glad to have Hank stay with Lynn. Then, he'd have Chris all to himself in the dark cavern.

'Frankly,' Brad said, 'your condition might endanger the rest of us.'

'Frankly, bullshit.'

'Chris, maybe you can talk sense into him.'

Chris glanced at Hank, her brows drawn together. Then she looked at Brad. 'Hank's already talking sense. It's his decision. I'm sure he's aware of his . . . limits. If he thinks he can make it, he should give it a try. I want him with us.'

'So what am I supposed to do?' Lynn asked with a whine in her voice. 'Stay here all by myself?'

'Or go back to the car,' Hank suggested.

That got a quick grin from Chris.

Lynn, pursing her lips in a pout, tipped her head to one side. She folded her arms, squeezing her breasts together and lifting them. 'So I just get left out?'

'Come with us if you prefer,' Chris told her.

'Maybe I just will.'

'It's up to you,' Hank said.

'Come on with us,' Brad urged her. 'Why not?'

She nodded briskly. 'I think I'll do just that.'

Great, Hank thought. Shit.

'That's good,' he told her. 'You can carry the back-pack. You've very accomplished at that.'

She wiggled her eyebrows, grinned, and said, 'You bet.'

While Hank and Brad had taken turns smashing through the layers of rock and concrete with the pickaxe, sledge hammer and wedge Hank had bought at the hardware store, Chris had fuelled the Coleman lantern, and lighted it. Now, crouching beside the hissing lantern, she picked up the fuel canister. She slipped it into the backpack and took out four flashlights. Putting them down, she lifted the pack and offered it to Lynn.

Lynn squirmed into the straps. Though she stretched and squirmed more than necessary, her blouse didn't spread open quite as much as before and she failed to expose either of her breasts entirely. When the pack was on, she modestly tightened her blouse's loose half-knot.

A corner of Chris's mouth curved up as she watched the girl. 'Aren't you going to wear your jacket?' she asked.

Lynn patted the sleeves tied at her waist. 'I have it if I need it.'

Chris glanced at Hank. She looked as if she might start laughing. 'Up to you,' she told Lynn.

'That's right. I mean, it's boiling out here. It's going to feel nice in the cavern.'

Even as she spoke, Brad was pulling his knit shirt down over his head.

'Why don't you take my shirt,' Hank told him. 'I won't need it.'

'If it fits,' Brad said.

Hank tossed it to him, and Brad put it on over his own shirt. His arms fit into the short sleeves, but he was unable to button it across his massive chest.

'Nothing a diet wouldn't cure,' Hank said.

Brad whuffed out a laugh.

Sitting down on the hillside near the cave entrance, Hank pushed his feet into the warm-up pants Chris had bought for him. As he drew them up over his shorts, he watched Chris step into her pants. She left her red shorts on. Balancing on one foot, then the other, she pulled the pants up, and her slender bare legs vanished inside the baggy garment. Instead of taking off the oversized white shirt she'd worn as a cover-up, she tucked it in. Her fingertips pinned the cuffs against her palms to keep the sleeves from climbing her arms as she slipped into the warm-up suit's jacket. Like a kid, Hank thought. Just how a kid does it.

She left the front of the jacket open.

Getting to his feet, Hank put his jacket on. It clung to his sweaty skin. He pulled up the zipper, stuffed a flashlight into a side pocket, and lifted the sledge hammer.

'Are we going to take the hammer *and* the pick?' Brad asked. He already had the pickaxe resting on his shoulder.

'I guess just one or the other,' Hank said. 'Might as well make it easy on ourselves.'

They decided to leave the sledge hammer and wedge behind. Brad insisted on being the one to carry the pickaxe. Hank lifted the lantern by its wire handle. 'I guess we're all set,' he said, and a tremor passed through him as he turned toward the dark opening of the cave.

He entered first, on his knees and one hand, the lantern held out before him. The twin mantles glared silvery-white and produced an amazing amount of light. He saw the stream stretching out ahead of him until it was engulfed in darkness. The walls around him formed a low, narrow tunnel. Though the ceiling was several inches above his head, he felt it pressing down on him, squeezing the breath out of his lungs. His heart hammered. He gasped for air. But he kept crawling.

'You all right?' Chris's voice. Close behind him.

'Yeah,' he managed.

He heard a clank, apparently the head of the pickaxe bumping a side of the cave.

They're all behind me, he thought. Blocking the way out. Jesus.

A vice was tightening around his chest. He heard a ringing in his ears. He made high-pitched wheezing sounds each time he sucked air into his shrinking lungs.

A hand rubbed the calf of his right leg. Chris. 'God,' she said, 'it's really bad for you. Do you want to go back?'

'No,' he gasped.

The hand went away, and he kept crawling. Though the cave seemed to be crushing him, he could see that it was growing larger. A short distance ahead, the walls and ceiling seemed to vanish. He scurried forward, sprang to his feet, and rushed on to make room for the others to come through behind him. Then, stopping, he raised the lantern high.

The ceiling, jagged with stalactites, was probably thirty feet above him. The walls to his right and left were barely visible at the far extremes of the lantern light. Surrounded by columns and stalagmites, he felt as if he were standing in a forest of rock. The formations gleamed and glistened and cast deep shadows.

'How are you doing?' Chris asked.

He turned around and watched her stand up. The legs of her pants were wet from the knees down. She rubbed her hands on her thighs. She looked wonderful.

'Better,' he said. He *was* better, though he hadn't realized it until now. He still felt trapped under the weight of the hill, he still struggled to breathe, but he was no longer wheezing and his heart had slowed down somewhat. It no longer slammed inside his chest as if trying to smash through his ribcage. 'It's not . . . so tight,' he said.

Chris stepped closer, and he swung the lantern out of the way. She put her arms around him, pressed her cool cheek against his. And the vice on his chest loosened just a little more. He curled his free hand over the firm soft mound of her rump. Squeezed it. Then moved his hand up her back as Lynn crawled out of the tunnel's mouth.

The girl stood up and staggered toward them. Her blouse was untied. Her breasts, half covered by the hanging fabric, bobbed and swayed. They stopped moving a moment after she did. Smirking at Hank, she shook her head.

As Brad came up behind her, she fastened a button at her waist, then a second one a few inches higher.

Hank lowered the arm that was wrapped around Chris. She kissed his cheek, then turned around. Hank could still feel the warmth her body had left on him. Too quickly, the cold seeped in.

'How are you doing?' Brad asked.

'Better.'

'You sounded terrible back there.'

'Well, it's not so bad now.' But it seemed to be getting worse now that Chris was no longer holding him.

'Good.' Brad's head tipped back and swivelled. 'This is incredible,' he said. 'You realize, we're the first people to set foot in here since . . .'

'1923,' Lynn supplied, and looked pleased with herself.

'Man,' Brad went on. 'Just think of it. It's awe-inspiring. I've been hearing about this end of the cave all my life. To think that nobody but us . . . *nobody* . . . has set foot in here during all that time. Hell, my grandfather was a *kid* in 1923. Incredible.'

'Incredibly creepy is what it is,' Lynn said. She looked around. Her lip was curled up. 'I mean, this is where Elizabeth Mordock bit the big one.'

Chris, who'd stepped around behind Hank while the others were talking, took hold of his left hand. The tightness in his chest eased slightly. He looked at her and smiled.

He gulped a few quick breaths, then said, 'We might as well get going.'

She kept her grip on his hand as they turned around.

'Up the middle of the stream?' Chris asked.

'The River Styx,' Lynn informed them.

Scanning the lighted area in front of him, Hank saw that the stream itself was lower than its banks and free of obstructions. All the stalagmites and columns and other rock formations, which seemed to surround him, were actually off to the sides of the narrow waterway.

'It'll be a lot easier if we stick to the stream,' he said, and began walking, Chris at his side.

'I wouldn't mind getting my feet out of the water,' Lynn said. The beam of her flashlight poked in among the cones and pillars on the high ground to the right. Hank glimpsed the far wall of the cave, probably thirty feet beyond the shore of the stream. Lynn's light swept to the other side. More of the same. 'Forget it,' she muttered.

Prefers wet feet, Hank thought, to climbing around in all those shadows.

Can't blame her.

'Creepy as shit,' she said.

'I'd thought you might be used to the cavern,' Brad told her.

'Yeah, right. The *lighted* side. Where there's for christsake a *sidewalk*. And where there isn't any god-damn *stiff*.'

'I don't think we'll run into the stiff,' Brad said. 'It's supposed to be at the bottom of a chasm.'

'Yeah, well, it's here just the same. I don't have to *see* it to know it's here.' She splashed up behind Hank, appeared at his side, and wrapped her fingers around his upper arm. The arm carrying the lantern.

'I need this for myself,' he said.

'Sure.' She let go, but stayed beside him.

The stream was really too narrow, Hank soon realized, for the three of them to walk side by side. Though Lynn often nudged him, he refused to give ground and force Chris over. Let Lynn be the one crowded against the bank. Maybe she'll get tired of it.

When they came to a thick truck of rock on the stream's edge, Lynn turned sideways to squeeze by. Her backpack hissed against it. Her left breast rubbed against Hank's upper arm. 'Excuse me,' she said, and edged out in front of him. The rubbing had brushed the blouse off her breast. Her nipple, jutting out like a fingertip, nearly touched the lantern's glass chimney. Hank quickly swung the lantern out of her way, though it crossed his mind that he might've let her get burnt as a lesson.

Saying 'Woops,' she covered herself.

'Maybe you should stay up in front of us,' Hank said. 'Or go back with Brad.'

'Yeah,' came Brad's voice. 'I'm all alone.'

'Too bad, so sad.' Sidestepping, she grinned at Hank. Her pack hit another stalagmite. Yelping, she twisted around and flopped facedown into the water.

Chris groaned. Brad started to laugh.

Hank, pleased but worried, said, 'Are you okay?'

Gasping, 'Oh shit, shit, *shit*!' she pushed herself up to her hands and knees. Chris hurried forward, clutched her arm, and helped her up. 'God *damn*!'

Lynn turned around. Hunching over and shivering, she looked down at herself and shook her head.

'Did you hurt yourself?' Chris asked.

'Yes! No.' With a whine in her voice, she added, 'Shit, I'm soaked.'

Her dark hair was matted across her forehead. Her face dripped. Her blouse was dark and clinging to her chest and belly. The front of her pants hugged her legs.

'Let me carry the backpack,' Chris offered. She held it while Lynn squirmed out of the straps.

Brad came forward and stopped beside Hank. He was still chuckling. 'Fall down go boom?' he asked.

'Eat my shorts.' She plucked the blouse away from her skin as if its touch were repulsive. Then she opened the two lower buttons and took it off.

Brad whistled.

'You don't have to watch,' she said. She used the dry back of her blouse to wipe her face, her arms, her chest and large pale breasts, her belly and sides.

Though Hank watched, the sight of her stirred no desire. She had a fine body, he couldn't deny that. But he felt embarrassed that she had stripped like this in front of Chris. He was annoyed, too. Her fooling around, acting the tease, had led to an accident that might've been serious, an accident that *was* delaying their progress through the cavern, postponing the moment when he would reach Paula.

'Hold this,' Lynn said, and handed her blouse to Chris. Making no attempt to cover herself, she staggered toward Hank. 'The lantern,' she muttered. Hank was holding it down at his side. He raised it as she approached with outstretched arms.

'Careful,' he warned her.

She stepped close to it, and looked as if she might hug the glowing lamp to her chest. She sighed. 'Ah. Ah, that feels good.' Her head tipped back. She shut her eyes. Her mouth hung open. She might have been standing under a shower, luxuriating in its hot spray. She took long, deep breaths. She began to rub her breasts.

'For the love of Christ,' Hank snapped.

Her eyes shot open.

'Put on your jacket and let's get going.'

She gave him a hurt look. 'I was just trying to get warm.'

'You're getting me downright hot,' Brad said.

She scowled at Brad, then pulled apart the sleeves of the jacket tied at her waist. Backing away from the lantern, she put the jacket on. She tugged its zipper up to her throat and said to Hank, 'There, are you happy now?'

'Can we go?'

Chris, coming up behind the girl, met Hank's eyes. She shook her head, grinned, and tapped Lynn on the shoulder.

Lynn took the wet blouse from her. 'What are you smiling about? You think this is real funny?'

'I'm just happy for your boobs,' Chris said. 'I'm sure they're a lot warmer now.'

'Hardy har.' Lynn tied the sleeves of the blouse at her waist. 'You're a real laugh riot. I don't know what I'm doing here anyway.'

'You don't have to stay,' Chris told her.

'Oh, you'd like that, wouldn't you.'

'You're holding us up,' Hank said.

'I *fell*! Or doesn't that mean anything to you?'

'I'm sorry you fell, but . . .'

'Do *you* want me to leave?'

Here's my big chance, Hank thought. Say yes, and she'll probably go.

To his amazement, he realized that he felt sorry for her. She was somehow like a kid, a troublesome brat, but a brat who was starved for attention, approval, even love.

Don't go soft, he told himself. She's a pain in the ass, and this won't be the end of it unless you get rid of her.

'Well?' she asked. 'Just say the word, and I'm out of here.'

'I don't know. Will you behave?'

'Behave? Are you shitting me? You sound like my old man.'

'I believe,' Brad explained, 'that Hank is asking you to stop acting like a bitch in heat.'

'Spare me, huh?'

Chris put a hand on Lynn's shoulder. 'You don't want to go back alone,' she said.

Lynn stared at her. No smart remark came out.

'Let's get moving,' Hank said. 'Take the lantern, Lynn. You can lead the way, and the thing'll help warm you up.'

Nodding, she took the lantern from him. She turned around and began walking upstream, her shoes making soft splashes. Brad followed, the pickaxe resting on one shoulder. Chris put her hand in Hank's. They walked up the stream behind Brad.

They were in shadows. Though Hank could see the brightness ahead, the dark seemed to be pressing in on him. Sometimes, when Lynn passed a bend in the stream and high rocks blocked the light, he felt the cavern shrinking. His heart hammered. He struggled to breathe. When the brightness bloomed ahead of him again, the pressure receded slightly.

He wished he hadn't given the lantern to Lynn.

At least she's out of our hair, now, he told himself. Then he realized her annoying antics had been such a distraction that, for a while, he'd forgotten he was in the cave.

I ought to thank her, he thought.

Ought to hurry on ahead and catch up with the little twit and encourage her to start flaunting herself again.

'Do you smell that?' Chris whispered.

He sniffed the dank air. Though he'd been inhaling it,

often frantically, from the moment he crawled into the cave, he hadn't given any thought to its smell. Now, he did. And detected faint odours he hadn't noticed before. 'My God,' he muttered.

'It smells like . . . faeces. And rotten meat.'

'Must be . . .' He fought for breath. 'Animals. Must live in here. And die.'

The hooch was suddenly on top of him, crushing him. Not just the hooch, but his gunner, Willy Jones. Blackness. A stench of shit. He knew Willy was hurt, felt the blood running all over him. It didn't take long to realize Willy was dead. But he couldn't move, couldn't get out of the blackness, couldn't get out from under the body. Which started to rot.

'Hank? Hank!'

Chris was in front of him, shaking him, then clutching him tight to her body as he shuddered and wheezed.

Light came. As he began to recover, he saw Brad and Lynn in front of him, staring with alarm.

'I'm okay,' he gasped.

'You're in no shape to go on with this,' Brad said.

'Maybe we'd better all turn back,' said Lynn.

'No. Got to . . .'

'It's all right,' Chris whispered close to his ear. 'You're all right, now.'

'What set him off?' Brad asked.

'We were talking about that odd smell.'

'Yeah, what *is* that smell?' Brad asked. 'I just started noticing it, myself.'

'Death,' Hank muttered.

Chris rubbed his back.

'Can't be nothing dead in here,' Lynn said, sniffing the air. 'It's all closed up.'

'So what's the stink?' Brad asked her.

She shrugged. 'Does smell a little like shit, I guess. But that's impossible.'

'Not just shit,' Brad said. 'It's like there's a rotting carcass.'

'Elizabeth Mordock? Maybe we're close to that chasm.' Lynn, still sniffing, started to look around as if searching for it.

'She's been dead sixty years,' Brad said. 'She's got to be nothing but bones by now.'

'Maybe we'd *better* get out of here.'

Brad looked at Hank. 'You going to flip out again?'

Flip out.

Hey, this guy's flipped out.

Well fuck, wouldn't you?

That's what they'd said, the Marines who pulled him out. Pulled him out after an eternity that had actually lasted three days – the time it took to recapture the base camp after it had been shelled by the NVA and overrun.

'I didn't flip out.' Hank told Brad. 'You don't know what the fuck flipping out is.'

He felt Chris go rigid, as if shocked to hear the hard words spew out. He stroked her hair. Some of the tension went out of her body. She ran her hands down to his hips. 'You okay?' she asked.

He nodded. 'Let's keep going.'

They parted, and he saw Lynn shaking her head. 'Not me. No way. This is getting too damn weird. I mean, you're throwing fits and ... and it *doesn't* smell right in here. It didn't smell like this before, and that means something's up ahead and I mean it must be dead and stinking, whatever it is, and I don't want to find out. No thanks. It's not like they even *need* to get rescued. If you don't get to them, they're just gonna get taken up in the elevator shafts so what's the point anyway? It's stupid. So from here on, you can just count me out.' She thrust the lantern toward Hank. He took its wire handle. 'Adios.' She turned her flashlight on, and stepped forward as if to pass between Hank and Chris.

'Wait,' Hank said.

'You're not going to talk me out of it, this time. Huhuh. I'm getting bad vibes about this place, *real* bad. So you guys enjoy yourselves.'

'Hold on. Chris, maybe you'd better go with her. Brad and I can go on ahead, if he's still willing.'

Brad nodded.

'I'm not leaving,' Chris said.

'I don't need an escort,' Lynn said. 'I'm a big girl.'

'I'm staying with you, Hank.'

'Something's very wrong about all this,' he told her.

'I know.'

'This part of the cave is supposed to be closed up. Isn't it, Lynn?'

'It was till we knocked through the wall.'

'No other way in or out?'

'Not supposed to be.'

'Well, something has been decomposing in here.'

'And taking dumps,' Lynn added.

'It's turning nasty,' he said to Chris. 'I've got . . . bad feelings, myself.'

'Well, I'm going with you.'

'Bye.' Lynn stepped between them and started to run.

Looking over his shoulder, Hank saw her dashing down the middle of the stream, the beam of her flashlight jumping around the rocks. Then she disappeared around a bend. The sound of her splashes faded.

'Let's stick close together,' Hank said.

Holding the lantern out ahead of him, very aware of Chris

gripping his other hand, he started walking. Brad stayed close behind them.

Though Hank still had some trouble breathing, he felt as if all his senses had been put on alert.

There was danger here.

Danger that he could feel, that he could smell in the subtle foulness of the air.

The cave no longer squeezed him. He wasn't in a cave, he was in the jungle, on patrol. He didn't know what to expect, so he expected anything.

And therefore he, didn't gasp, didn't even flinch, at the sight that made Chris suck in a harsh breath and hurl herself against him and clutch him like a thrown cat.

Brad came up beside them, took a step ahead of them. He brought the pickaxe down, holding it level with his chest as if prepared to use it as a weapon. Turning slowly, he looked from side to side. 'Jesus,' he muttered. Hank heard *him* labouring for breath. Then the big man doubled over and vomited.

A stalagmite to the right of the stream had been clothed in a transparent pink nightgown. Arms of bone hung from the sleeve holes. A gleaming white skull was perched on the blunt top of the effigy. The bodice of the nightgown bulged, but not with breasts. Through the sheer fabric, Hank saw a pair of fleshless heads. Someone had stuffed small, human skulls into the gown. Infant skulls.

Chris shook and whimpered against him. He stroked her back with his free hand. Bart was still hunched over, heaving.

Near the effigy, on a lower clump of rock draped with glossy green satin, was a ribcage. A skull inside it seemed to be peering out through bars.

He saw a pelvis beside it with skeleton fingers reaching through its cavity.

He saw fleshless legs, apparently standing on their own, joined at the top to a gape-mouthed skull.

Hank had seen carnage before. He'd seen hideous desecration of corpses. But never anything done with such perverse artistry – the creations of a mad sculptor.

And we're in his gallery, Hank thought.

The glow of the hissing lantern revealed more than a dozen samples of the maniac's work.

And one sculpture, to the left of the stream, far worse than the others.

It wasn't bare bones.

This is the sight, Hank suspected, that had turned Brad's stomach.

A woman. Young. Lashed to a column by a belt around her throat so she appeared to be standing. Long brown hair, neatly brushed, hung to her shoulders. From the look of her face, she'd been beaten, maybe before her death. The body had no arms, no breasts. Most of the skin, from the neck down, was gone. Her torso appeared to have been hollowed out.

She wore blue jeans. From the way they sagged, there was little left of her legs except bones. But the bare feet were intact.

Something about the feet.

Hank realized that they were on the wrong sides of her body. Her legs had been reversed.

'I don't believe this,' Brad muttered. He was facing Hank, but still bent over slightly. 'I don't believe this,' he said again. 'It's . . . it's . . .' He shook his head and squeezed his eyes shut.

'I bet,' Hank said, 'it's Amy Lawson.'

16

The chewing went on. There were sighs, moans, sounds of tearing flesh, crackling gristle. Sometimes, Darcy heard small splashes as if inedible pieces had been tossed into the lake. She wanted to duck below the surface to stop herself from hearing the horrid feast, but she didn't dare move. She stood in the black, hugging Greg and Carol, waiting.

Then came whispers.

'Take her back?'

'Get the others. Take 'em all back. Save 'em up.'

'We don't have to go back.' The woman's voice. The one who had known about the dock and tour boats and elevators. 'We're free. We can get out, maybe.'

'Topside?'

'Yeah, topside.'

'No topside.'

'Where're your balls?'

A sharp smack. The woman gasped.

'Coward,' she said in a shaky voice. 'You're afraid of the Mordock.'

'I fear no one.'

'Then come with me. We'll leave the world. We'll kill the Mordock and live in the sun. It's wonderful up there, you'll see. But we've got to go now. We've killed topside people, and they'll hunt us with guns if we don't get out now.'

There was silence for a few moments. Then the man spoke. 'We go. We kill the others. We take them back to the world, save them up.'

'But you don't under . . .'

Another blow. This one didn't sound like a slap; it might have been a fist striking her face. She grunted. A moment later came a thud as if her head had struck the flooring of the dock. She moaned for a few moments, then squealed from a new silent hurt, and started to whimper. Squealed again. Gasped. 'No, don't. Please. I'm sorry.'

'We go,' the man said.

Darcy heard sounds of movement, then footsteps that passed directly over her head and kept going. The woman still whimpered.

'Lana.'

Moaning, she began to move. There were rubbing sounds, creaking wood, soft bumps. Darcy pictured her rolling over and getting to her knees. Then the woman was up and walking.

Darcy listened to the footfalls on the planking. Soon, she could no longer hear them.

My God, she thought, they've actually left. They're on the walkway now, heading away.

Carol, who had been rigid in Darcy's arms, began to shake and sob Darcy stroked her hair. She felt Greg's arm loosen its clamp across her back.

'Okay,' he whispered. 'We're all right.'

'Was that Helen?' Carol asked, her voice quiet and trembling. 'Do you . . . think that was Helen?'

'I think so,' Darcy said. 'It could've been Beth, but I don't . . .'

'They ate her. They ate her, didn't they?'

'That's what it sounded like,' Greg admitted.

'Eeeeeeeeeee.'

'Carol, stop it.' Darcy shook her.

'Eeeeeee.'

Darcy pinched the ridge of her ear.

683

She gasped and stopped making that crazed sound.

'Greg, what'll we . .?'

'She was such a prude,' Carol said. 'Frigid, you know? Wouldn't have anything to do with men. They stripped her. Did you hear them strip her? Boy, would she be pissed. Her stepfather used to fuck her, that's why.' Carol's voice came out in a breathy rush. She sounded as eager as a town gossip. 'Hated men. Thought I was dirty 'cause I liked 'em. Not that I was promiscuous or anything, God knows, but all the time she was warning me, you know? Don't let 'em touch you. Don't let 'em touch you. Boy, she sure got touched. Did you hear them strip her? I bet she didn't like that, not one little bit.'

'Carol.'

'Such a prude. Always changed in the bathroom, you know? And I'd go to change and she'd go away. Like it was a big sin, you know, to take off your clothes? God, and they just stripped her naked, didn't they. Tore her clothes right off.' Carol began to squirm, rubbing her pelvis and breasts against Darcy. 'Bet they felt her up, too. Touched her all over. Didn't fuck her, though, did they. Didn't sound like it. They could've, could've all taken turns, you know, and really . . .'

Darcy thrust the clinging, writhing woman away from her body and pressed her shoulders down, submerging her for a few seconds. Carol came up coughing, and began to weep.

'I'm sorry. God. I'm . . .'

'Calm down, okay?' Darcy said. 'And be quiet.'

'They ate her. They ate *Helen*.'

'Shhh.'

'What're we gonna *do*?'

'We'd better not stay here,' Greg said, sounding calm. 'They'll probably come back.'

'Oh God.'

'The way they headed,' Darcy said, 'they'll run into the others.'

'Then they'll probably turn back.'

'Do you think so?'

'They aren't about to go up against a group like that. They're only – what, four of them?'

'I'm not sure,' Darcy said. 'Four or five, I think.'

'They wouldn't go up against thirty.'

'I don't know. God knows what they'd do. They might try. If it's dark when they get there, they might try anything. If the fires are out, they could sneak right in. Nobody'd even know what was going on.'

'So what do you want to do?'

'I'm responsible for those people, Greg. I've already lost three, and . . .'

'It's not your fault.'

'If we hadn't tried to go through . . .'

'It's not your fault.'

'I don't want any more to die. We have to do something.'

'Okay.'

'Go after them?'

'No!' Carol cried.

'I guess we'd better. But not . . .'

'No, please! They'll eat us!'

'Wait here,' Greg said.

'What?'

'I'll get the pickaxe. If we catch up to those bastards, I want to have something to use on them.'

'Can you find it in the dark?'

'I hope so. It was right at the wall before the shit hit the fan.'

'Okay. But hurry.'

He let go of Darcy and brushed against her back.

'Don't leave us,' Carol begged.

'It's all right,' Darcy told her. 'He won't be gone long.'

'What if they come back?'

'We'll just be real quiet.' She turned her head toward the sloshing sounds of Greg's movements. 'Be careful.'

There was a quiet slurp, then silence. Darcy guessed that Greg had gone down to pass under the boat. Moments later, she heard him come up. From the quick noisy splashes, she guessed that he was swimming.

'He'll be back pretty soon.'

Darcy felt Carol embrace her. Remembering the way the woman had squirmed against her earlier, she was tempted to push her away. But there was no hint of erotic frenzy this time. Carol simply hugged her like a terrified child. So Darcy held her and listened to Greg splashing through the lake.

If he finds the pickaxe, she thought, he won't be able to swim back with it. He'll have to wade. That would take a while.

The longer it takes, the less chance of catching up with those savages. They already had a headstart.

Better if we don't.

She felt a stir of guilt. There were kids among the tourists. The little girl, the fat boy, Paula, the son of that creep in the trucker hat. Kyle.

Big loss if they nail Kyle.

That pregnant woman.

Quite a few men, though. Maybe the men would be able to handle the situation. But if the elevator fires are out . . .

Confusion. Nobody knowing what's going on, who to fight. There could be a slaughter in the darkness.

I don't have to wait for Greg, she thought. I could go on ahead and try to warn them.

She imagined herself being grabbed along the walkway, thrown down. She felt hands ripping at her clothes. *Tore her clothes right off . . . Touched her all over*. Felt the hands on her bare skin. Coming from every direction. Clutching, probing. Fingernails digging in. Then teeth. Teeth sinking into her arms and thighs and belly and breasts. Felt them tugging ripping. Heard the wet sounds of chewing.

It happened to Helen, it could happen to me.

Go off by myself, try to warn them, it really might happen. You owe them a try.

Not my life. God, no.

Enough of a try, waiting for Greg and going after them with the pick. We'd stand a chance that way. Won't help anyone if I run on ahead and get nailed.

'Ugh!' The splashing stopped.

Carol stiffened.

Darcy wanted to call out, but she feared that she might be heard by the savages. No telling how far they'd gone, and sounds could carry a long way in the cavern.

Then she heard Greg resume swimming.

Maybe he'd run into a body, she thought. A nasty surprise like that could've made him gasp and stop short.

Three bodies in the lake. Maybe. The woman who threw herself at Darcy, the guy who killed Beth, and Beth. All floating around near Ely's Wall.

'He must be just about there,' Darcy whispered.

She felt Carol nod, the woman's face sliding against her cheek.

The sounds of the swimming stopped.

Carol, tight against Darcy, rammed her backwards, breath exploding out, fingers digging into her back. Darcy felt a hot stab. She went down, Carol on top of her, pinned to her. Darcy jammed a hand between their bodies. Felt the slick shaft joining them: it jutted out of Carol and entered Darcy just below her ribcage on the right. As she clutched it, the shaft was driven forward. It started to penetrate deeper. She twisted away, shoving at Carol, and felt the point rip free of its hole and skid across her skin.

Then she was clear. She rolled and rolled through the water, trying to put distance between herself and the attacker.

She burned where the point had entered her. It hadn't gone in very deep, she thought, or it wouldn't have pulled out so easily. Half an inch, maybe less.

A bone weapon like the other guy had used on Beth?

Must've speared Carol through the back.

Darcy's side bumped a wall. Rolling, she pressed herself to the rocks and held herself motionless. Currents stirred against her. She heard splashing nearby, and wondered if the attacker was still with Carol. She needed air. Hoping the sounds of the turmoil would cover any sounds she might make, she eased herself upward until her head broke the surface.

As she took a shallow breath, she heard splashing nearby. Harsh breathing. Grunting sounds. The savage still wasn't approaching her.

More splashing in the distance. Those sounds had to come from Greg. He knew there was trouble, was swimming back.

A sigh under the dock. Then quiet sloshing.

He's coming for me.

Darcy held her breath.

If he can't hear me, he can't find me.

Her heart thudded. Her wound pulsed fire.

He seemed to be heading straight for her.

Maybe he hears my heart.

Smells my blood.

Pressed flat against the wall, she felt the flashlight pushing into her side. Greg, she remembered, had slipped it into the pocket of her windbreaker. She eased it out.

What now? she wondered.

Whirl around and try to bash him with it?

If he's got that pointed bone . . .

Darcy still didn't know what to do, but the wading sounds were little more than a yard behind her, now, she let herself drift backward away from the wall, then brought the flashlight out of the water.

Toss it over to the side, the way guys always did in the movies to mislead the bad guys?

That's the movies.

Might work, though. Might make him think I'm over there.

Not gonna stake my life on a goddamn movie trick.

Darcy spun around, jumped, felt herself rise out of the water to the waist, tucked her chin down hoping her head wouldn't hit the underside of the dock, heard herself growl like a furious dog, and threw the flashlight straight ahead with all her strength. The sound of the impact would've come at once if she'd been on target. It didn't. She twisted her body. As she splashed onto her side, she heard a ringing clamour and realized the flashlight must've struck the side of the moored boat.

Going down, she kicked her way toward the bottom, stroked once hard, then let herself glide forward hoping she was off to his side, hoping to slip past him before he had time to react.

An explosive splash. Something rammed between her legs, searing an inner thigh. She clamped her legs together. Trapped it. Crossed her ankles. Twisted. Felt an instant of resistance. Then it was loose and the momentum of her turn rolled her over. She reached down. Grabbed the pointed end of the bone as her face came out of the water.

She sucked air.

She got her other hand on the shaft.

Then lost hold as her forearm was yanked. She kicked and writhed as the attacker tugged her to him. He jerked her upright. She felt his breath on her face, smelled its fetid stench. She drove a knee up. It struck him, but the blow seemed to have no effect. He clutched the front of her jacket. His other hand hooked her groin. He grunted, and Darcy was hurled upward. The top of her head slammed the floor-boards of the dock.

Pain burst through her. She saw bright flashes. Heard ringing in her ears. Smelled the odd, metallic odour she vaguely remembered from times she had bumped her head at the ice skating rink.

Greg, she thought, Maybe Greg . . .

Through her daze, she realized she was soaring again toward the underside of the dock. She flung her arms up. Her fists were battered between her skull and the planks.

He lowered her again.

Darcy opened her numb fingers. Reached out. Grabbed hair. Pulled and drove her head forward. Her wide open mouth found flesh. She bit. Her teeth sank in, and the man bellowed. She bit down as hard as she could. Something came off in her mouth. His nose? He was yelling, staggering backward, still clutching her jacket and crotch. She spit the flesh out.

They both went down.

Darcy squirmed lower, tearing at his hair, forcing his head back. Her mouth found the side of his neck. She burrowed in, biting and ripping, and suddenly felt as if a garden hose had been thrust into her mouth, hot water gushing from its nozzle.

Got him, she thought.

Took out the carotid.

Jesus.

His clutching hands jerked against her, fluttered away.

She shut her mouth, but didn't release him. Still clinging to his hair, she wrapped her legs around him. Together, Darcy and the savage rolled slowly beneath the surface of the lake. She felt his body jump with spastic shudders, felt the warm current throbbing against her face. She needed air. Her lungs ached. But she stayed with him until he went limp.

Then she shoved him away and stood up, gasping.

She heard splashes nearby.

'Greg?'

The splashing stopped. 'Darcy? My God, what's going on?'

'Nothing. Anymore.'

'Are you okay?'

'Not exactly.'

'Oh God. What happened?' From the quiet sloshing sounds, he was wading toward her.

'He got Carol.'

'Oh, no.'

'He . . . stayed behind, I guess. Waited till you were far enough away. Then he . . . I think Carol's dead. Carol?' she called.

No answer. She hadn't expected one.

'What happened to him? Where is he?'

'Around here someplace. Belly up.'

'You killed him?'

'Yeah.'

'I shouldn't have left you two. I shouldn't . . .'

Darcy reached out and touched Greg. He moved in against her. His arms went around her. She squeezed herself tight against him and winced at the pressure against the wound below her ribs.

'Did he hurt you?'

'Here and there. I got . . . poked a couple of times.'

'Stabbed?'

'He had one of those pointed bones. Like the guy who got Beth.'

'Oh Christ. Where'd he get you?'

'It's no big deal,' she said. Her thigh wound didn't hurt much. It felt as if a path had been scraped along her skin. The other wound hurt plenty. It might have had a hot coal stuffed inside it. Her head had a dull ache from striking the dock.

'We'd better get out,' Greg said, 'and patch you up.'

Darcy shook her head. 'We've gotta get moving. Those others . . . they'll reach the group.'

'I didn't bring the pickaxe. I found it, had it in my hands. Then I heard something going on over here. All I could think about was getting to you as fast as I could.'

'As cavalry charging to the rescue,' Darcy said. 'you leave a lot to be desired.'

He laughed softly, then kissed her mouth. 'Thank God you're all right.'

'To the extent that I am.' She eased away from Greg. 'I'll find his weapon. It's down around here someplace.' Holding onto him with one hand, she lifted each of her feet and pulled her shoes off. She gave them to Greg. Then she wandered slowly, searching along the bottom with her feet. She felt sand and gravel through her socks. Stones, slabs of rock.

She heard Greg moving around nearby, and guessed that he had joined in the search.

'A femur?' he asked.

'I didn't see it, but I think so. It was long enough to go through Carol and stab me.'

One of her feet snagged something soft that wrapped around it. Raising her knee, she untangled her foot. The thing was fabric. She explored it with her hands, and moaned.

'What?'

'Carol's dress.' She remembered the splashing she'd heard just after the attack and before the savage came for her. The grunts and hard breathing. He'd stripped the sundress off Carol. What else had he done to her?

'God,' Darcy muttered, and hurled the dress away.

'Maybe we'd better give it . . .' His words broke off with a gasp.

'What?'

'Another . . .' Slurps of water. 'Found your . . . *Jesus!*'

'What is it?'

'His face, it's . . .'

'Yeah.'

'You did that?'

Darcy felt heat rush to her face as if Greg had discovered a nasty secret about her. 'He was trying to kill me,' she said.

'You really . . .'

'Would you stop fooling with him?'

'Sorry. I didn't mean to . . .'

'Just stop, okay?'

'I want to see if he's got anything that might . . . Yeeuh.'

'If that's his throat . . .'

'No.'

'I tore it out, that's what I did. What was I supposed to do?'

'Hey, it's okay. I'm not . . . you did great. I'm just glad you were able to do it.'

'Then it'd be nice if you'd quit going yick and yuck.'

'I got a handful of the guy's dick.'

'What?'

'I was trying to check his pockets. Hasn't got any.'

'He's not wearing pants?'

'Or anything else.'

'God.'

Shouldn't come as any red-hot surprise, she told herself. Not after finding Carol's dress.

He probably stripped off his clothes before he even attacked.

Naked the whole time because he knew he was going after two women.

Naked when he got Carol, naked when he grabbed Darcy and smashed her head against the dock, when she bit his face and neck, when she straddled him and wrapped her Jegs around him, when he jerked against her in his death throes.

Standing rigid in the water, she wrapped her arms across her breasts and squeezed her legs together tight.

She heard Greg sloshing around nearby, heard his breathing.

She knew she should keep looking for the weapon, but she couldn't force herself to move.

'I think I've found it,' Greg whispered. A moment later, he said, 'Yeah, here it is. Christ, it's a bone, all right. Ball joint at one end. The other end feels like it's been broken off. Pretty sharp. Darcy?' He waded closer. 'Darcy, you okay?'

She shook her head.

'Darcy?'

'I want it to go away.' Her voice sounded strange to her – high and pinched. 'Greg? I can't . . . It's . . . I want it to go away. I want it all to go away.'

17

'Lucky Lynn,' Brad said. 'She got to miss all this.'

'Never seen anything like it,' Hank muttered.

Chris eased away from him, but kept a hand on his arm and stared at his chest. 'Let's get out of here,' she said.

'I'm with you,' Brad told her. He was standing close behind Chris, but she didn't turn around to look at him. If she did that, she would see the sculptures of bone, the ravaged remains of the woman. 'Seemed like a good idea, going through this end, but . . . this is bad shit. We'd be nuts to go on.'

'I didn't mean leave,' Chris said, keeping her eyes on the front of Hank's warm-up jacket. 'I want to keep going, get away from . . . If it stops. Maybe it doesn't stop, but . . .'

'You're kidding, right?'

'I want to get to Ely's Wall.'

'Hank?'

'I'm not turning back. I don't know what's going on down here, but my kid's on the other side.'

'Yeah, okay, but what's on *this* side? That's what I want to know – what I *don't* want to know. I mean, some kind of maniac's been messing around down here. I don't want to meet him. Hugh-uh. We're talking real sicko. This isn't something you fuck with. You want to end up like these poor stiffs, some kind of cave decorations? Not me.'

'Well, leave me the pickaxe,' Hank said.

'Are you out of your mind? Do you want to get yourself killed? Want to get Chris killed? Come on, man! What about Chris? She won't go on without you.'

'You should go back with Brad,' Hank said. 'He's right. I can go ahead and get to the girls. It doesn't have to be both of us.'

'I'm going with you,' Chris told him. 'And I think we should stop talking about it and get moving.'

'What if I turn back?'

'You won't. But if you do, I'll go on without you.'

'She wouldn't be able to break through the wall by herself,' Brad said.

'Don't count on it,' Chris told him.

'Okay. Well, I'm not going to stand here and argue. You two want to be heroes, fine.'

Chris took the Coleman lantern from Hank. Brad handed the pickaxe to him. 'I'll be waiting outside. Good luck.' He gave Chris's arm a brief squeeze as he stepped past her. She watched him over Hank's shoulder. He was only visible for a moment before vanishing around a bend in the stream. The splashing sounds of his footfalls faded.

'You're sure about this?' Hank asked.

She looked into his eyes, and nodded.

Hank smiled. 'More guts than brains.'

'Goes for both of us.'

Hank lifted the pickaxe. He held it in front of his chest with both hands – as if it were a rifle, Chris thought.

She lowered her gaze to the water in front of her feet, and turned around.

It wasn't good enough. Her peripheral vision picked up the grim sentinals on either side of the stream.

She walked fast. Hank stayed at her side.

'Christ,' Hank muttered. 'They go on.'

She could see that. But the horrors weren't distinct, just vague shapes at the edges of her view.

'Like running a goddamn gauntlet,' Hank said.

'Who could've done this?'

'Nobody in his right mind.'

'Do you think he knows we're here?'

'If he's here, he probably knows. I'm sure he would've heard us pounding to break out the wall. But I can't imagine . . . Nobody could *live* in here. There's got to be a hidden entrance. Whoever it is, he probably brings his victims in, does his thing, and leaves.'

'Ethan Mordock?' Chris said.

'My God, of course. If that . . . mess back there was Amy Lawson . . .'

'Even if it wasn't. Mordock owned the hotel, the cavern. He had access – not just to the cavern, but to guests at his hotel. And its pretty obvious he was involved in making Amy Lawson disappear.'

'The guests check in,' Hank said, 'but they don't check out. Some of them, anyway.'

'Probably young women who check in alone. And they wind up down here.'

'Could've been going on for years.'

'And Mordock's dead!' Chris clutched Hank's arm and turned her face to him. She saw the same knowledge and relief that he was probably seeing in her eyes. And beyond his head, a fleshless skull wearing a green pillbox hat with a ragged red feather.

She winced and lowered her gaze.

They started walking again.

'If it was Mordock,' Hank said, 'we don't have to worry about getting jumped by some lunatic.'

'Thank God. It's bad enough without that.'

'We'd figured it out a little sooner, Brad might've stuck.'

'Who needs him,' Chris said.

They rounded a bend in the stream.

'Mordock was creepy,' she said. 'I could tell, just the way he'd look at me and Darcy, that he wasn't right. But . . . God, I never would've guessed he'd be capable of this kind of madness. It's hard to imagine *anyone* taking bodies and . . .'

'Speaking of which, I don't see any around. I think we left them behind.'

Chris looked up. The pale glow of the lantern revealed a forest of stalagmites and columns on either side of the stream. Rock, clean and glistening, bare of body parts. She sniffed. The foul odours remained, but seemed less oppressive than before. 'Situation's improving,' she said.

'I think we'll have to reach the wall before long. Which brings up another matter. I'm starting to wonder if we should bring the people out this way.'

Chris had seen them lined up to wait for Darcy's tour to begin. She remembered there had been women, several children. 'There were kids,' she said.

'Mine's one of them. I don't want her to see Mordock's handiwork. My God. She can be a pretty gutsy kid, but I wouldn't wish that on anyone. She'd be seeing it the rest of her life.'

'I don't want to see that stuff again, myself.'

'We'd better figure something else.'

'Once we get to them, maybe it won't matter getting them out right away. I mean, the main thing is to get to Darcy and Paula. Once we're with them and know they're all right, maybe we can just wait along with them.'

'Yeah. The fire department'll get everyone out sooner or later.'

'I wouldn't care even if it took a day or two, as long as I'm with Darcy.'

'And we've got the candy bars,' Hank reminded her.

'Yeah. Nobody'll starve.'

Chris suddenly felt as if an awful weight had been lifted.

There was no longer the prospect of the return trip.

She and Hank would stay on the good side of the cavern with their children and the tourists, and eventually be hoisted up the elevator shafts by the fire department or some other rescue agency. She would not have to walk again among Mordock's dead.

'Maybe we can find the other opening,' Hank said. 'The one Mordock used.'

Her relief started to fade.

'I don't want to go exploring, do you?'

'Well . . .'

'I think we should just join up with the others and . . .'

'What's that?' Hank nodded to his right.

Chris wasn't sure she wanted to look.

'Over there by that big clump of rock.'

He sounded curious, not disgusted or wary, so Chris looked. Running along the floor of the cave, almost beyond the glow of the lantern, was a slot of darkness that appeared to run parallel to the stream.

'A crevasse?' Chris asked. 'Maybe it's that chasm Elizabeth Mordock fell into.'

'Want to take a look?'

'No. Let's just keep moving, okay?'

'Maybe the hidden entrance . . .'

'One of us might fall. Besides, I don't care about any hidden entrance. If I see daylight, *then* I'll care. Otherwise, let's not take any detours, okay?'

'I suppose you're right.'

They kept on walking.

'Since when did you become a cave explorer?' Chris asked. 'And what ever happened to your claustrophobia?'

'Thanks for reminding me. I'd forgotten all about it.'

'How can you *forget* to be claustrophobic?'

'I'll ask my shrink if I ever go to one.'

'You're not having any symptoms at all?'

'Very mild, maybe.'

'Must've gotten shocked out of you.'

'Could be.'

'All those awful bodies, and . . .'

She saw daylight.

'Good Lord,' she whispered.

A pale hazy glow far ahead in the blackness beyond the reach of her lantern's illumination.

'What do you know about that?' Hank muttered. 'You said if you saw daylight . . .'

'That's what I said. And I meant it. Geez, this is getting better and better.'

They continued to walk in the stream, but Chris kept her eyes on the distant light. It seemed to fill an opening about the size of a doorway in an area she guessed must be near the right-hand wall of the cavern. Sometimes, it vanished as rock forms blocked her view. Then, it would reappear and look closer then before.

She hoped the stream might lead directly to it.

But when they came abreast of the dim glow, it was still off to the right. They stopped and stared at it.

'Do you want to wait here while I check it out?' Hank asked.

'You've got to be joking.'

'Well, I'd better lead the way.' He lowered the head of the pickaxe into the water and propped its haft against the slope of the embankment.

Chris gave the lantern to him.

He climbed the bank. Chris lifted the pickaxe, swung it

over one shoulder, and followed him. When he looked back, he said, 'I thought we'd leave that behind.'

'We might not want to search for it,' she told him. 'Besides . . .'

'What?'

'I just think we should hang onto it. You never know.'

'Want me to carry it?'

'*And* the lantern?'

'Well, we could trade.'

'I'd rather have you go first. I'm all right with this thing.'

Hank shrugged, and resumed walking. Chris stayed close behind him. They took a winding route, skirting rock formations that rose from the cavern floor to block their way. The area of pale light grew. Chris saw that it did come from an opening in the wall of the cavern.

Hank stopped at the opening. As he leaned forward and swung the lantern through it, Chris peered over his shoulder.

The chamber in front of them appeared to be about twenty feet around. Its floor was heaped with clothing: dresses, blouses, sweaters, undergarments, slacks, nightgowns and robes, even a few jackets and coats. All seemed to be women's clothes. Near one wall, Darcy saw a pile of grooming articles: hair-driers, brushes and combs, curlers, tubes of toothpaste and brushes, sanitary napkins. An open suitcase to the side of the pile was filled with glittering jewellery like a pirate's treasure chest.

'Must be stuff that belonged to his victims,' Hank whispered. 'Makes sense. He'd have to do something with it. Wouldn't want those things lying around the hotel if anyone came snooping.'

He stepped into the chamber. Chris followed. Her feet sank into the heaped clothes.

The clothes of dead people.

She shivered.

Hank's head tilted back. Chris, too, looked up.

The daylight came from above, drifting down like a pale mist through a chimney-like orifice in the ceiling of the chamber. Standing directly beneath the hole, Chris couldn't see the sky. Though the tunnel obviously led to the surface, she guessed that it must curve along the way.

The ceiling of the chamber was at least twice Hank's height.

'You might get in and out this way,' he said, 'but you'd need a rope. Won't do us much good.'

'Do you think this is Mordock's secret opening?'

He shrugged. 'Could be. Maybe if he had a rope ladder.'

'Let's go back to the stream, okay? This place gives me the creeps.'

Hank said, 'Okay,' and stepped backward as if trying to get a better angle on the ceiling hole – and stumbled.

Chris gasped, fearing the lantern might ignite the thick layer of garments on the chamber floor, but Hank landed on his rump and kept the lantern high. 'You all right?' she asked.

He nodded. 'Come here.'

She waded through the clothes.

'Hold this.'

She took the lantern from him. 'What?' she asked.

'Want to see what I tripped on.' He got to his knees and began digging, flinging aside skirts, bathrobes, pantyhose.

'Maybe you'd better not,' Chris said.

He snatched up a wadded blouse, exposing a bare foot and ankle. Chris stiffened. Shivers squirmed like cold worms over her skin.

More bodies, she thought.

Bodies under us. I might be *standing* on one!

Hank touched the ankle, then jerked his hand back fast.

He looked up at Chris. His eyes were wide, his mouth hanging open.

'Let's get out of here,' she whispered.

His head shook slowly from side to side, and he began to toss more clothes out of the way. He uncovered another foot. Shins. The legs of the body were side by side, but slightly apart. He exposed the knees.

'Hank. Please. I don't want to see it.'

'This one's alive,' he said.

And it bolted upright through a cascade of clothes, shrieking.

A girl with wild blonde hair. Eyes squeezed shut. Lips curled back, baring pointed teeth. Chris shouted a warning. Even as the word 'Look' burst from her throat, she saw the girl swing a white blade-studded stick at Hank's face, saw his open hand whip sideways at her face, heard a thud and a clash of slamming teeth as the edge of his hand drove beneath the girl's chin. The blow snapped her head back. The scream stopped. Chris's voice, yelling 'Out!' resounded through the silence. She finished her warning while the girl flopped towards the mat of clothes. Hank rammed an open hand against the girl's chest and jerked his other arm up close to his side as if about to blast his knuckles through her throat.

He didn't deliver the blow.

He knelt there, poised for it, and didn't move.

The girl lay motionless.

'Hank?'

He took a deep breath, then reached over the sprawled body and picked up the weapon. He held it up, inspecting it.

Not a stick, Chris realized. A bone. Maybe an arm bone. Its upper half bristled with razor blades that appeared to be imbedded in grooves.

Hank hurled the weapon away. It clattered against a wall of the chamber, and dropped silently onto the floor of clothes. Then, he looked down at the girl. 'What was she doing here?' he muttered. 'And with a thing like that?'

'Maybe . . .' Chris realized she was panting for air. Her heart was slamming. 'We . . . could ask her.'

Hank didn't answer. He began tossing aside more clothes to uncover the girl.

She wore a blue satin negligee with spaghetti straps. One of the straps had fallen, and the white, blue-veined mound of a breast was exposed.

The negligee was taut against her rounded belly.

'Pregnant,' Chris whispered.

The girl looked no older than fourteen or fifteen.

Chris stepped over her and lowered the lantern close to her face. Her eyes were open, but rolled up so that only the whites showed. Her mouth was shut.

Hank opened the girl's mouth and fingered down her lower lip. Her pointed teeth were scarlet with blood from her broken gums. 'Do you believe those teeth?' Hank said.

'I . . . feel like I'm going crazy.'

'We had this thing figured out wrong. There's a lot more to it than Mordock bringing his victims down here for fun and games. Those teeth . . . she's pregnant . . .'

'I don't get it.'

'Neither do I. Let's get going.'

'We can't just leave her. Shouldn't we try to wake her up and . . .?'

Hank gave the girl's chin a small push. Her head flopped toward Chris. Her ear was bathed with blood.

'What?'

'She's dead,' he explained.

Chris felt herself go numb. She heard her voice, distant and strange, say, 'No. She can't be. All you did was hit her once, and . . .'

'Sometimes, it only takes once.'

'But . . .'

'I'm sorry, Chris. I'm sorry you had to see it.' He stood up and faced her. 'She was just a kid, and pregnant, but she was coming at me with a weapon. You don't fool around when that happens. You get just as dead from a kid. Come on, let's get out of here.'

She stood there, staring down at the body.

At the girl's distended belly.

'I killed her, okay? I murdered her and her baby. Those are the breaks. She shouldn't have tried . . .' He suddenly rushed past Chris and the quickness of his movement broke through her daze of shock and regret and she wondered if he'd seen someone *else* rising out of the piled clothes. She twisted around.

Hank, near the wall, snatched up the girl's weapon. He raced back with it, kicking up blouses and skirts.

'What are you . . .?'

'Keep an eye out. God knows, there might be more of them.'

He dropped to his knees between the girl's legs. Clamping the bone in his teeth, he gripped the hem of the negligee and tugged. The fabric split up the middle, baring the dead girl's pubis and belly.

'What are you *doing*?'

He took the bone from his teeth. As he plucked out one of the razor blades, he muttered, 'I don't *know* what I'm doing.' Then he slashed the girl open. Coils of guts spilled out, steaming as they met the chilly air. Hank lifted them out in heaps and dumped them aside.

Chris staggered backward. The pickaxe fell off her shoulder.

She knew, now, what Hank was trying.

No killer.

Wonderful.

And she also knew that her head was spinning and the light from the lantern was dim and she was seeing a blue aura around Hank as he disembowelled the girl and slashed with the razor. She carefully (wobbling) set the lantern down on the soft clothes and stumbled backward away from it before sliding down into darkness.

'Wake up. Come on.'

She opened her eyes.

Hank was kneeling beside her, a bundle in his arm. 'It's a boy,' he said. 'Seems to be all right. She must've been pretty close to . . .'

'You got it out?'

'All yours.' He set the bundle down between her breasts. Chris felt its warmth. It was moving. She parted the sweater that was wrapped around it and saw a pudgy face with half open eyes.

'God,' she whispered.

'You're not much of a midwife,' Hank said, 'but at least you didn't set the place on fire.'

Chris put her arms gently around the baby.

'Come on,' Hank said. 'Let's get going.'

18

'Lemme ha' s'more,' Kyle said, slurring his words as if he were drunk. Paula pressed the bottle against his belly. He took it, raised it to his mouth and upended it. Whisky sloshed against his pinched lips. He made swallowing sounds, then sighed, said, 'Goo' stuff,' and gave the bottle back to her.

'Through the teeth 'n over the gums, watch out, stomach, here it comes.' He heard Paula drink. 'Good for what ails you,' she said. 'That's what my dad says, "Good for what ails you."'

'Your dad drink a lot?'

'Yaaah, he's not a boozer. That what you mean? He's not a boozer, but he drinks. Has a couple 'fore dinner, but just on weekends. *Used* to be a boozer. Cause of Vietnam, Mom said. Then he smashed up the car with me 'n Mom in it. That was the last time he ever got sticko.'

'T'zat when your Mom got killed?' Kyle asked.

'Naw. Nobody got hurt. I was like two years old. I don' even remember the crash. Mom, she had a urinism.'

'A what?'

'A uri . . . *ane*urysm. A blood vessel in her brain. It just blew and she keeled over.'

'Geez.' Kyle put a hand on her knee. She was sitting beside him on the sleeping bag with her legs crossed. Earlier, he had unzipped the sleeping bag, spread it open and brought its end up to cover their legs. Paula's knee was warm. He slid his hand to the hem of her kilt, and patted her thigh.

He heard Paula take another drink. 'Leas' it was quick, y'know? Better'n cancer or shit like that. Or AIDs. Jesus.

Freaks me out, start thinking about shit like AIDs. 'Nough to make you *stay* a virgin.'

'Me, too. It's too damn dangerous.' He realized he had forgotten to slur his speech, but decided it didn't matter. Paula was sounding pretty smashed – probably too smashed to notice. He'd taken a few swallows, at first, but had only pretended to drink once he realized the control he would have over Paula if he could get her sloshed.

'You never . . . did it?' she asked.

'Nope.'

Amy Lawson, he thought, and suddenly felt hot and squirmy inside. What if Amy Lawson had it?

'How'd your mother die?' Paula asked.

'She didn't. She ran off with some guy.'

'Oh yeah, tha's right. Ran off.'

'Bitch.'

'She visit?'

'She doesn't visit, doesn't even send me a fuckin' Christmas card.'

'Tha'sa pits.'

'Haven't heard shit since the day she ran off. Four years. Didn't even say goodbye. Just left a note in the typewriter saying she was sick of wasting her life in "Hotel Boondocks" and she was going away with some rich guy who'd checked in the day before. Said if she never saw me or Dad again, it'd be too soon. Bitch. Hope *she* got an aneurysm.'

'Oh, Kyle. I'm sorry.'

'Yeah, Well. So much for mothers.'

He heard the bottle clink softly. Then Paula twisted herself towards him, her knee nudging the side of his leg. He slid his hand farther up her thigh, and she didn't protest. He felt the softness of her breast against his upper arm. Her hand found his face and stroked it. The way she leaned on him, he couldn't have stayed sitting if he'd wanted to. He didn't want to. He let himself drop backward onto the sleeping bag and felt her smooth skin slide under his hand as she straightened out her legs. He felt her other thigh on the back of his hand. Felt the slick fabric of her panties. Heat.

I didn't even do this myself, he thought. Just an accident. *She* did it stretching out like that.

God.

A delicious current seemed to surge from her body into his hand and up his arm – sizzling through his whole body, stealing his breath away, making his heart race, swelling his penis to a stout rod.

Then her fingers gently wrapped his wrist and pulled his hand away from the silken fabric, away from the heat, and guided it out from under her skirt.

Okay, he thought. Okay, don't want to spook her.

He put that arm under her head and rolled onto his side. Paula kissed him, but there seemed to be no passion in it. More like a goodnight kiss she might give her father. Then she lay still except for a hand slowly caressing his back.

Kyle slipped his hand under the front of her sweater and cupped her breast through the layers of blouse and brassiere.

'Le's just hug, okay?' she said.

He rubbed her breast.

'C'mon, don't.' Her protest was feeble, lazy. 'Le's just snuggle.'

He'd had her *blouse* open before the elevators fell. Now she didn't even want him touching her through the clothes. The booze was supposed to loosen her inhibitions, maybe even make her horny, but here she was acting as if she didn't want to mess around at all.

Maybe she had too much, Kyle thought.

Maybe she's going to zonk out.

Yeah.

'If that's what you want,' he whispered. He let go. Sitting up, he drew the top of the sleeping bag over Paula. Then he lay down beside her and covered himself. Paula squirmed closer, pressing herself gently against him.

'Cozy,' she whispered.

'Yeah.'

Kyle didn't move again until, from the deep slow sounds of Paula's breathing, he was pretty sure that she was asleep.

She moaned slightly but didn't wake up when his fingers curled over her breast.

He found the top button of her blouse. He was about to unfasten it, but changed his mind. If she woke up and her blouse was unbuttoned, she would know what he'd been up to. He moved his hand down. Her blouse was untucked. He reached beneath it. Her blouse was roomy inside. He fondled both breasts, listening for changes in her breathing.

She's totally out of it, he thought.

Fantastic.

Carefully, he slid a bra strap off her shoulder. His hand fitted easily under the loosened cup. He held her bare breast. The skin was so warm, so smooth. He fingered her nipple. She squirmed a little, but didn't wake up.

'I don't like this,' Katie whispered. 'Not one little bit.'

'There's nothing to be afraid of, honey,' Jean told her.

'Darkness isn't my favourite thing.'

From where Wayne Phillips sat with his family, he could see into both elevators. The flames in the elevator to his left had died out a while ago. Those in the other elevator had burned longer, but the last of them had just fluttered out. Now, there were only red, glowing embers.

Darkness isn't my favourite thing, either, Wayne thought.

The embers gave off some light, but not much. Only enough to see vague shapes.

Pretty soon, he thought, even that will be gone. It'll be black as a pit.

'Look on the bright side,' he said, as much to still his own uneasiness as to comfort Katie. 'I'll make a book out of this and we'll get a lot of money. Then we'll go to Disney World.'

'Oh, sure.'

'Honest. Have I ever lied to you?'

'When you said there was a bone-cruncher living under my bed that was gonna chew off my foot. When you said about the troll under the house. When you said there was Madman Murray sneaking to our front door every night and trying to come in. When . . .'

'Those weren't lies.'

'Don't start, Wayne.'

'They were just stories.'

'A story is a lie,' Katie told him.

'Not exactly.'

'It is, too.'

Wayne sighed. 'Anyway, I'm not lying about Disney World. I'll write a really scary book about all this, and we'll get piles of money and go to Disney World. It's a promise.'

'We'll hold you to it,' Jean said.

'Make sure you take them to the Epcot Center.'

The woman's soft voice didn't startle Wayne, but he was surprised by the discovery that someone was sitting so close to them. Close enough to hear every word. 'Yeah,' he said. 'We'll go there, too.'

'It's not to be missed.'

'I've heard it's very good,' he said.

Right behind me. Christ. I'd better watch my language.

'Does anyone object if I smoke?' she asked.

Several nearby voices urged her to light up at the same time Wayne said, 'No, go ahead.'

He heard quiet sounds, probably the woman searching inside her handbag. Then came a crinkle of cellophane. He looked over his shoulder in time to see a tiny spray of sparks as the match snicked across the striking surface. The matchhead flared. The sudden brightness stabbed Wayne's eyes. He squinted. Around the brilliant flame was a tremulous, yellow-orange aura that illuminated not only the woman with the cigarette in her lips but a few other people seated nearby.

The woman, well over fifty years old and probably tipping the scales at three hundred pounds, wore her grey hair in a Buster Brown cut and glasses as round as her face. She was wrapped in a cable-knit shawl. Her faded dress reached only to her knees. Her calves, the size of hams, were encased in 'knee-high' hose, the tops of which sank into her flesh and were overhung by tyres of blubber.

A real looker, Wayne thought.

Her handbag rested on the tilted platform of the dress stretched taut across her thighs. She dropped the matchbook inside. With a flick of her wrist, she shook out the flame and vanished.

All that remained was the glowing tip of her cigarette.

Wayne thought of the Cheshire Cat. This woman's cigarette was like the cat's smile, staying behind after the rest was gone.

I'll have to use that in my book, he thought. The Cheshire Cat bit.

She would make a good character. A minor character, but sufficiently grotesque to make the readers uneasy. Cook up a nasty ending for her.

Wayne turned away from her and gazed at the embers inside the elevator cars.

What kind of nasty ending? he wondered. You're jumping the gun. Haven't even figured out what's nailing the people. They're trapped in the cave. Something or someone starts ripping them off.

What if that gal has evil powers? She's a sorceress, warps the minds of the people trapped down here, turns them against each other? I can use the bit with Calvin tearing into that asshole. God, I could pretty much use that whole scene just the way it happened.

But that's just the start. Really bad shit starts to happen.

Maybe the fat gal's doing it with her magic, or maybe its the evil in all these people coming to the surface because they're tired and frightened. Is it black magic or human nature causing the mayhem? Really play that up, and you'll give the thing some depth, it'll look like more than just a cheap horror novel.

Throw in some scapegoat stuff. They blame the fat gal, call her a witch, burn her at the stake – burn her in one of the elevators.

Shit, this is really shaping up.

Wayne grinned.

'How's it going, Katie?' he asked.

'I'm not having a very good day.'

'Nobody is, honey,' Jean told her.

'Oh, I'm starting to have a pretty good day,' Wayne said. 'I think this little cloud has a silver lining that's going to make us all very happy.'

'Bug squat,' Katie muttered.

'I'm feeling a chill, Calvin.'

'So's everyone else, I suspect. Do you want to move closer

to the elevators? They've got good beds of coal built up, probably giving off considerable heat if we hauled ourselves near enough to feel it.'

'Oh, I don't know. It's so dark. We'd trip over people.'

Calvin wondered why she had even bothered to complain about the chill if she wasn't willing to put herself out some to get warm. Just for the sake of hearing herself talk, more than likely. 'Want me to lay on you?' he asked.

'Shhhh. People will hear you.'

'I reckon I could warm you up right quick.'

'*Calvin.*'

Grinning, he patted her thigh. 'Don't you worry, hon, I won't do nothing to embarrass you.'

'A little bit late for that.'

'Shitfire, here we go again.'

'You like to've killed that man.'

'I'd *like* to've killed that man, truth be known.'

'You don't mean that. Calvin, you'd burn in Hell for eternity.'

'Mavis, darling, any God that'd send a man to burn in Hell for eternity 'cause he rid the world of a misbegotten son of a whore like Slick over there – well, I reckon he can just take his Pearly Gates and . . .'

'Don't you dare say such a thing! Lord, you'll get yourself in Dutch for sure.'

' 'Fraid He'll send down a bolt of lightning to . . . CHRIST!' Calvin blurted as a blast roared in his ears and he thought, *Holy jumping Jesus, I'm a dead man!*

But others were yelling, too, over the deafening noise.

Calvin felt a cold mist on his face. Drops of water pelted him.

The roar seemed to come from the elevator car several yards in front of him. The red glow in its centre was blotted out. Around the blackness, sparks and embers exploded upward and died. In seconds, every trace of light from inside the elevator had been obliterated.

The noise faded, then came again.

A fire hose, Calvin thought. They must've shot a gusher straight down the shaft. Now the fire in the other elevator was being doused.

A few moments later, the roar diminished, then ceased altogether.

'Yuh, I'm drenched!' someone complained.

Another voice muttered, 'All over me.'

The darkness seemed heavy with char-smelling steam.

Here and there, people clapped and cheered.

'All *right*!'

'Won't be long, now.'

'Took 'em long enough.'

'Apparently,' someone said, 'there wasn't any Third World War up there.'

'Never thought there was, jerk-off.' That was Slick's voice. Calvin shook his head. The fella'd taken a whooping and got his hair burnt off, but it hadn't straightened out his disposition.

'Can't wait to sink my teeth into a thick, juicy sirloin.'

'I wanta wrap my lips around a bottle of Molsons.'

'I'm gonna reacquaint myself with my old pal Jack Daniels.'

'All I want's a long, hot bath.' That was a woman, of course.

'If I never see another cave, it won't be a moment too soon.'

'Oh, don't be such a downer, Brian. It's been a marvellous adventure.'

'HELLO, THE CAVERN.' The voice boomed through the darkness, silencing everyone.

A bullhorn, Calvin thought.

'This is Chief Richmond of the Pleasant Valley Fire Department. Is anyone there?'

In the quiet following the announcement, Calvin heard footfalls. Then crunching, soggy sounds. Someone, he figured, was stepping into one of the elevators. 'Hello up there!' Sounded like Tom.

The tinny, amplified voice said, 'The fire has been extinguished, and we're making preparations to evacuate you people. Will anyone require medical assistance?'

'We're all okay,' Tom called.

'My ass,' Slick said. 'I been . . .'

'Shut up,' someone told him.

'Who said that?'

'How many are trapped down there with you?' Chief Richmond asked.

'About thirty,' Tom replied. 'How long'll it take to get us out?'

'We'll have you out as soon as possible. Heavy construction equipment has been requested. We need a bulldozer to clear the area up here. Then we'll execute the evacuation by means of a crane. In the meantime, I want you all to adopt a sit-tight policy and stay clear of the elevator shafts. Any questions?'

'How come I don't see any light up there?' Tom called.

'The elevator housing is still intact. It's burnt out, but . . . I've just been informed the equipment is arriving. Again, stay clear of the shafts and wait for further instructions.'

'Ask him to lower us a few flashlights!' someone said.

'Yeah!'

'Chief?' Tom yelled. 'Chief Richmond?'

No answer.

'Shit.'

'No big deal,' Tom said. 'We'll be out of here before long.'

Calvin felt Mavis squeeze his hand. 'Well,' he said, 'I reckon the fun's about over.'

Kyle, squirming and gasping and wanting to roll Paula over and stick it in her (so what if she wakes up), jerked his hand out of her panties when the silence was smashed. Her fingers, curled loosely around his erection where he had put them, wiggled a little. He quickly took her hand away and held it.

Paula sighed and moaned.

The noise faded. So did the voices and shouts of alarm.

Maybe she won't wake up, after all.

Then the roar swelled again.

Paula said, 'Huh?'

'It's all right,' Kyle whispered.

The noise stopped. People spoke, but their words were indistinct.

'What's going on?' she asked.

Did she mean the sounds? Or was she aware of what Kyle had done to her?

She can't know, he told himself.

He'd slipped the bra strap back onto her shoulder before pushing his knee between her legs and lifting the front of her skirt and sliding his hand inside her panties. Nothing had been unfastened or removed.

But maybe she could tell that her clothes had been fooled with.

Could she feel where he had touched her?

Did she know, somehow, that Kyle's hand wasn't what she'd been holding a few seconds ago?

'I don't know what's happening,' he said. 'Some kind of commotion over by the elevators.'

Paula moaned.

Any second, the accusations would start.

'God,' she mumbled. 'My head.'

A hollow, distant voice said, 'Hello the cavern.'

'What's that?'

'I don't know.'

'See what's . . .' She let go of his hand, and moaned as she sat up.

Kyle stayed with her, holding her arm in the darkness. They stood up and turned to the sounds of the voices. As they listened, he touched his penis. It was still big, sticking straight forward, but not as rigid as before so he was able to tuck it back inside his jeans. He left the zipper open. In spite of the voices from the elevator area, Paula might hear if he pulled the zipper up.

Kyle heard Tom call out something about flashlights.

Other people spoke, but their words were too faint to understand.

He and Paula stood silently. The voice of Chief Richmond didn't come again.

'So I guess they're getting us out,' Kyle finally whispered.

'Do you think we should go back now?'

'I bet it'll still be an hour or so before they start taking people out.'

'Yeah?'

'I think we should just wait here.' Kyle told her.

'If we go back now, maybe we can sneak in and nobody'll find out we were gone.'

'Who cares if they find out?' Kyle said.

'Well, yeah. They don't know me.'

'Besides, we haven't done anything wrong.'

Sounding a little bit amused, Paula said, 'They'll probably think we were over here screwing around.'

Man, she doesn't have a hint.

'Well,' he whispered. 'If they're going to *accuse* us of it, maybe . . .'

'Ho ho ho. Right. Want me to barf in your face?'

'Just kidding.'

'God, I never should've drunk all that.'

'Maybe we'd better have some more. They say it's supposed to help.'

'Thanks but no thanks. Maybe someone over there has some aspirin I can borrow.'

Kyle stepped behind Paula and began to rub her neck and shoulders. 'Mom used to do this for me when I had a headache,' he said. Gently, he pulled the sweater down her back. Then he resumed the massage.

She sighed.

'Feel good?'

'Mmmm.'

He kneaded the sides of her neck, moved his hands over her collar and squeezed her shoulders. Her skin felt smooth and warm through her blouse. He wished there was nothing between his hands and her skin.

Just wait, he told himself. Pretty soon.

She began to sway back and forth. As if she were half asleep, or maybe mesmerized.

Kyle continued to hear voices from those near the elevators. He didn't even try to understand what was being said. He didn't care. And Paula seemed oblivious to everything except the rhythmic rub and squeeze of his hands on her neck and shoulders.

He half expected her to slump into his arms.

Leaning forward, he lifted her hair out of the way and kissed the side of her neck. She moaned. She didn't tell him to stop.

Kyle slid a hand over the top of her shoulder and opened the top button of her blouse.

She said nothing.

He unfastened the next button down, feeling her breast under his wrist.

'Hey,' she murmured.

'It'll be better this way,' he said and slipped the blouse clear of her shoulders and went on with the massage. She seemed a little rigid at first, but soon she was limp and swaying again.

Kyle slipped the bra straps out of his way.

Now her shoulders were sleek, warm skin and he knew that the hanging straps left her bra loose and if he wanted he could slide his hands right down into the cups.

His mouth was dry, his heart racing.' He lowered a hand, plucked the front of his jeans to free his straining penis, and went back to rubbing her.

He eased forward. The soft wool of her kilt brushed the underside of his shaft.

He slid both hands over the shoulders and down her chest.

Paula flinched and grabbed his wrists, stopping him before he reached her breasts. 'Hey, come on,' she whispered.

'What'll it hurt?'

'Kyle, no. Besides, I'm getting cold.'

'Please?'

'I think it's time we'd better go . . .'

'YEEEEAH!'

It didn't come from Paula. It came from the darkness ahead.

'What the hell . . .?'

'LET GO OF ME!' the woman cried out. 'WHAT DO YOU WANT?'

'What the fuck's going on?'

'Oh sweet Jesus, *he's dead*! Somebody . . .'

'HELP! HELP!'

Kyle trembled with terror and joy.

720

Paula stood rigid, squeezing his wrists. 'God,' she whispered. 'What's happening!'

'Don't know.'

Kyle knew. He knew, all right.

The crazies had arrived.

Those he'd heard mumbling and tittering when he went out in the night with his father to give Amy Lawson a ride down the chute – the wild, demented progeny of Elizabeth Mordock.

They'd poured through the hole in Ely's Wall, just as he'd feared when the earlier scream came floating up the cavern.

They'd probably slaughtered Darcy's group.

Now they were falling upon the others.

He heard shouts of confusion and alarm, shrieks, *laughter*.

He pressed himself against Paula's back. Her body was stiff and trembling. Her hands, still clutching his wrists, shook as if she were seized by a spastic frenzy.

This is it, he thought.

They're here.

The arrival of the crazies meant there was no longer a need to be sneaky, no longer a need to waste time in futile efforts to seduce Paula.

She's mine.

Whatever I want.

Same as if we were in 115.

Do her any way I please.

They'll blame it on the crazies.

'It's all right,' he whispered. 'We're safe over here. We've just got to be quiet till it's over.'

Paula kept on shaking.

'If you make any noise,' he said in her ear, 'they'll come for us.'

She moaned.

'They'll kill us if you make a sound.'

'I . . .'

He wrenched a hand from Paula's grip and pounded it into her belly. Her breath blasted out. She folded. A soft thud. Her head hitting the stalagmite? She stayed bent and didn't fall. Maybe holding onto the rock.

Kyle clawed the blouse down her back. Feeling through the darkness, his left hand found the nape of her neck. He squeezed it, holding her down, and ran his right hand down her back to the bra strap. A quick tug popped the clasps.

Still clamping her neck, he tugged the waistband of her kilt. Something snapped. The kilt loosened. He jerked it down her rump, let go and slid his hand over the slick fabric of her panties. He snatched the panties down. Her buttocks were firm and smooth. He stroked down the centre.

Was blocked by her legs, squeezed tightly shut.

He dug his fingers into the crease between them and brought his knee up against the backs of her thighs to force them apart.

As he pushed and felt them open, his hand at the back of Paula's neck was grabbed, yanked sideways. Taken by surprise, he lost his grip. The clutching hand pulled him forward. He fell against her. She twisted sideways. He slid off her back, onto the blunt top of the rock that scraped his ribcage and rammed his left armpit.

Something pounded the other side of his chest. Though the blow didn't hurt much, it jolted him, started him rolling away from Paula. He raked his right hand through the black, hoping to snag her hair or flesh or clothes, but found only empty air. Then his back hit the steep side of the stalagmite. He skidded down. At the bottom, he flipped himself over and lurched to his feet.

He heard Paula.

In spite of the bedlam from across the stream, he heard her.

Her quick, shaky gasps. Her sobs.

Nearby.

Moving.

He moved toward her, felt the soft mat of the sleeping bag under his feet and knew where he was.

Paula was off to his left.

Heading for the stream?

Is she *nuts*? Doesn't she know what's going on over there?

Just doesn't care. Just wants to get away from me.

Kyle hurried after her, feeling his way through the dark, guided by the sounds of her terror. He waved his arms in front of him. Tripped, stumbled, but stayed up. Heard Paula splashing in the water not far ahead of him.

He rushed down the embankment. Kicked a rock and yelped with pain and flew headlong through the darkness. He landed flat in the stream. The cold water exploded under him. Though his foot burned with pain, he scurried up and heard Paula gasping and whimpering nearby. He lunged toward the sounds, reaching out for her.

And caught a handful of fabric.

Her blouse?

It tugged at his arm. He lost his balance and fell forward, but kept his hold on the blouse, hoping to pull her down on top of him.

As he dropped, the weight of her pulling body went away. He hit the water. He pushed himself to his hands and knees. All he had was her empty blouse.

He got up and staggered after her.

Tossed the blouse away, dug a hand into the tight wet pocket of his jeans and brought out his knife.

Pried the blade open.

They'll blame it on the crazies.

Paula wasn't splashing anymore. From the sounds of her ragged breathing and sobs, Kyle realized she had reached the other side and was scurrying up the embankment.

Gotta nail her quick.

Before she gets to the railing.

Or we'll be running straight into *them.*

A part of Kyle's mind warned him to forget Paula.

Not worth it. Christ, no. Go back and hide before they get you!

But he wanted her. Wanted to tear her down and rip her and chew her tits and fuck her.

He scrambled up the slope.

Heard a soft ringing sound.

Paula was at the railing!

Moments later, Kyle's wavering left hand struck the railing. He grabbed the cold metal, ducked beneath it, and rushed on through the utter darkness.

If I nail her right now!

He grabbed a fistful of hair and jerked it. The body came against him. He drove his knife into her back, pulled it out, struck again.

And again.

She flinched and shuddered each time he rammed the knife into her back.

He felt hot blood pouring over his hand.

She slumped against him, twitching.

He found her throat and slashed it open.

19

Chris gently tucked the baby's face against the crook of her neck when they found the body.

Hank set the pickaxe aside. He wouldn't be needing it; someone had already knocked a hole through Ely's Wall.

He crouched over the body. It lay sprawled on its back off to the side of the opening, away from the strip of water that slid through the narrow gap below the remaining portion of the stone wall.

It was a man. His hair was neatly trimmed. He was clean-shaven. He wore nothing except pale blue boxer shorts and shoes. His gaping mouth was full to the lips with blood. His cheeks and chin and neck were painted with it. Hank pressed his hand to the man's neck. The blood felt tacky and the skin beneath it still retained some heat.

'He hasn't been dead very long,' Hank said. 'Probably less than an hour.'

'I know him,' Chris muttered.

'What?'

'I mean, I don't *know* him. I saw him this morning. He was waiting for Darcy's tour to start.'

'God almighty.' He looked up at Chris. Her face was contorted, nose wrinkled, lips peeled back, eyebrows pinched together. Her eyes looked feverish, a little wild.

'What's . . .?' She shook her head.

'I don't know. Somebody killed this guy. If he was on the tour . . . and he's on this side of the wall . . .'

'Did they try to get out this way?' Chris asked.

'And maybe turned back when this one was killed. Or maybe he was alone,' Hank said.

'Who *killed* him?'

'The girl, maybe.'

'Or . . . or maybe there are others. Others like her.'

And if so, Hank thought, where are they?

Where's Paula? What if she was with this guy and . . . She's all right. God, please. She's all right.

He felt as if icy hands were squeezing his heart.

'We've gotta hurry,' he said.

Turning away from the body, Hank braced a hand on the sill of the wall and leaned through the hole. He held the lantern out in front of him.

He expected to find the narrow, shallow stream on the other side. Instead, there was a lake, its still surface for yards around him shiny in the lantern light.

He saw two bodies floating face-down, their heads and legs below the water.

One wore a white sweater (Paula had put on her white sweater, telling him that the guide book warned of the cavern's chilly temperature) and Hank felt a twist of panic before he realized the body wore some kind of black pants, not a kilt.

The other body was dressed in a plaid shirt and blue jeans.

Though the heads of both bodies were submerged, he could see their floating hair through the clear water. Long hair. The hair didn't necessarily prove that these were women, but their hips seemed to flare out and their rumps looked female.

Women, all right.

But neither one was Paula.

And neither wore a guide's blue uniform.

'What do you see?' Chris asked.

'They're not our kids,' he said outright to save her even a moment of wondering. 'Two dead bodies. Female.'

'My God. You're sure . . .?'

'Darcy wore one of those uniforms like Lynn?'

'Yes.'

'That's what I figured. She's not one of them.' He saw a square-cornered, metal boat a short distance to the left. Bundles of clothing rested on seats. 'And there's an empty boat. There's a lake over here.' he added.

'The Lake of Charon,' Chris said.

'What's it doing here?'

'Ely's Wall dammed the stream. They take you over the lake on those boats.'

From his perch on the edge of the wall, Hank could see inside the boat. He didn't see any oars or motor.

How big is this lake?' he asked.

'I don't know, it's maybe fifty yards to the docks. It's not very deep, though. I think Darcy said four or five feet.'

That was about the depth he would've guessed from the look of the rocky bottom, but he knew that the clear water could distort his perspective and the lake might be considerably deeper than it appeared.

'I guess we take a dip,' he said.

He climbed through the hole, sat on the wall's edge and lowered his legs into the lake. Holding the lantern high, he scooted forward and dropped. The water wrapped him to the chest. Its chill squeezed his breath out. 'Uhhh.'

'You all right?'

'Colder than a witch's . . . nose.'

Turning around, he saw Chris appear in the opening. 'Just a minute,' he said. He waded to the boat. Draped across a seat near the front were a plaid shirt and blue jeans similar to those worn by the dead woman. Propped against

727

the seat was a four-foot length of board, the upper half of it burnt black. Another pair of pants rested on a seat near the middle. He saw a grey sweatshirt there. And a green sweater (not Paula's).

Hank set the lantern on one of its seats, then returned to the wall and reached up. Chris handed the baby to him. He held the small, squirming bundle against the side of his face.

Chris crawled onto the edge of the hole. As she positioned herself to jump, she stared past Hank – a look of revulsion on her face. Then she glanced down, and leaped. She entered the water with a small splash. Her eyes went wide and she gritted her teeth.

'Nippy, huh?'

'Gawd.' She waded to him, moving stiffly.

'You okay?'

She responded with a stiff nod.

'You want the baby or the lantern?'

'Baby,' she gasped.

Hank passed it to her. She nuzzled the infant against her cheek. It made quiet cooing sounds.

She stayed at Hank's side as he waded back to the boat.

'That piece of wood there,' he said. 'Looks like they used it for a torch. See the clothes? Must've been at least two men in the boat. And those women.'

'And Darcy,' Chris muttered. 'She would've been with them.'

'Maybe not.'

'She's the leader.'

'She might've stayed behind. But even if she was here . . . whoever belongs to the second set of clothes must've gotten away. Probably others did, too.' He lifted the lantern off its seat. 'The whole group might've been here.'

'It takes two boats to hold everyone.'

'Well, the other boat doesn't seem to be around. Maybe the rest of them got away in the second boat.'

'Maybe.' Chris sounded doubtful.

'Wonder where the oars are,' he said.

'Aren't any,' Chris told him. 'Spikes in the walls. When I was on the tour yesterday, Darcy stood up and . . . pulled the boat from spike to spike.'

'Weird.'

'It's how they do it.'

'Why don't you climb aboard, I'll push.'

'Don't you think . . .? Quicker if we walk.'

'Probably, but . . '

'Let's hurry.'

'Yeah.'

They walked, staying close to the side of the boat so Chris wouldn't have to pass near the bodies. Hank would've liked to take a look at them and see how they were killed, but he refrained for Chris's sake. Besides, she was right. They had to hurry. Every second might count.

Someone, he was sure, had come through the hole in Ely's Wall and murdered at least three of those who had approached in the boat.

Someone, perhaps, who had lived in that strange nest with the girl he'd killed.

He thought about how she had attacked him for no reason. With a weapon of bone and razor blades.

He thought about her teeth, filed to points.

Some kind of savage.

What the hell was she doing there?

Did others live in that place?

Was one of them responsible for the hideous display of human remains they'd found along the banks of the stream?

How *many* are there?

Where are they now?

He heard only the sounds of his breathing, Chris's breathing, quiet gurgles and coos from the baby, the soft sloshing sounds of their own movement through the lake.

He wished he *did* hear others.

Savages coming toward them out of the darkness.

Let them attack.

At least I'd know they're here and not chasing down Paula somewhere.

'I'm scared, Hank.'

'Yeah, me too.' He put a hand on her back.

'What if Darcy and Paula . . .?'

'I'm sure they're all right.' Sure I am, he thought. He was only sure of his hope. He knew that hope wasn't enough. You hope for the best, you hope *against* the worst, but what he'd learned during two tours in Vietnam was that the worst could happen and often it pushed beyond the boundaries of what he had hoped against, pushed into the black territories of the unthinkable.

But hope was all he had, so he clung to it.

'Even if they were here,' he said, 'it doesn't mean . . . How many people were on the tour?'

'Thirty or forty, I guess.'

'That many couldn't have been . . . And we've only seen three bodies.'

'So far,' Chris said.

Seconds later, as if to shrink the hope, they found another body. Chris saw it first, gasped and flinched back.

This body didn't float. It hung spread-eagled in the lake a couple of feet below the surface. Like the two women, its long hair was spread out, drifting around its head like a strange seaweed.

'A man,' Hank said. Stepping in front of Chris, he reached down into the water and grabbed the man's hair. It felt thick and greasy. He lifted. As the head came up dripping, he turned the face toward him.

One glimpse, and Hank knew that this was not a man from the tour.

Bushy eyebrows. A heavy black beard. Skin so white it may never have been touched by sunlight. Pointed teeth.

When Hank was a boy, his father used to frighten him with tales of the Wild Man of Borneo. He'd loved the stories and begged for more, though sometimes the Wild Man stalked him through nightmares.

Staring at the face of this dead savage, Hank felt as if he'd slid back into his childhood.

Shivers crawled up his back.

'The Wild Man of Borneo,' he muttered. 'In the flesh.'

'It's one of them?' Chris asked in a small, high voice.

'Just like the girl.' He plunged the head down into the water and pushed. The body glided away, feet first. Hank rubbed his hand on the leg of his warm-up pants. When he finished, it still seemed coated with an oily film.

They started walking again.

He kept his hand underwater, kept rubbing it on his leg.

He wished he had a bar of soap.

Forget about it, he told himself. So the guy had dirty hair. Real big deal. You were up to your wrists in a dead girl's guts ten or fifteen minutes ago.

But this. Such a little thing.

Like finding a stranger's hair in your soup.

'I wonder how many others . . .' Chris said. She was looking around.

Won't even see the ones submerged like that guy, Hank thought. Not till we're right on top of them.

Those with enough water in their lungs would stay below the surface, he knew, until they started to decompose and the trapped gasses popped their bloated carcasses to the top.

'At least he was on the right side,' Hank said.

'They might be all around us,' she whispered.

'The more like him, the better.'

'It's . . . almost worse than the other place.'

Hank knew she meant the madman's gallery. She was right. There, you could see the things.

And there, it had never crossed Hank's mind that one of the corpses might be his own daughter.

She could be here.

No!

She's fine. Darcy's fine. Others had been killed, not our girls. The horror stops there. It has to.

Hank, like Chris, scanned the surface of the lake.

And then, near the far reach of the lantern's glow, he saw the dull gleam of a square-cornered boat. A few steps more, and a dock came into view.

Chris moaned.

She saw it, too – another body. This one lying flat on the floor of the dock.

Cold dread seized Hank.

They waded closer.

A woman's body. Naked. Torn up.

Faceless in the distance and dim light.

She seemed taller, thinner than Paula, but . . .

Clothing lay scattered beside her.

A white sweater and blouse and kilt? A blue uniform?

He just couldn't see!

Chris began to weep.

Hank lunged forward, leaning into the chest-high water,

trying to run. The water pressed against him like hands holding him off. But he waded closer and closer, leaving Chris behind.

The clothing.

Those were blue slacks in a pile beside the body's hip.

Not Paula's kilt. But pants like Darcy's.

Oh God, no!

'Chris, stay back!'

'What?'

He trudged past the bow of the boat, rammed the lantern down on the dock, and thrust himself out of the water. On hands and knees, he crawled to the side of the corpse. The flesh gaped with deep wounds as if chunks had been chewed out. The left arm had been torn from its socket and partly devoured.

The face was intact.

A face frozen in a rictus of horror.

A face that had never been beautiful – not tike Chris, not tike Chris's daughter *must* be.

And it was the face of a woman who must have been pushing forty.

Hank let out a long, trembling sigh.

He looked over his shoulder. Chris was yards away, a dim shape in the faint glow that reached her from the lantern.

Hank was pleased; she'd done as he asked and stayed put.

'It's all right,' he said.

It's all right? The woman's dead. They ate at her. And it's all right?

'Not one of our girls,' he explained.

Chris nodded and started forward. Not wanting her to see how the body had been ravaged, Hank slid the severed arm against its side. He covered the body from the waist down with the slacks, then spread the blouse over the torso. He didn't try to hide the face.

Crawling to the edge of the dock, he reached down. Chris handed the baby to him. From the slow sound of its breathing, he guessed it was asleep. He marvelled that the child could sleep through a situation like this.

Lucky kid, he thought. Doesn't have the foggiest idea what's going on.

Probably thinks Chris is its mother.

Chris boosted herself up and scrambled onto the dock. She looked at the corpse. She sniffed and wiped her eyes. 'Why did you cover her?'

'She's . . . partly eaten.'

'They *ate* her?'

'Must've worked on her for a while. And I think . . . too much was gone for one person to have done it. I'd guess there must've been a few of them.'

'Aw, Jesus.'

'In a way, it's looking better.'

'How can you *say* that? They . . .'

'That guy on the other side of the wall, he hadn't been dead very long. An hour at the most. Then, some kind of struggle took place here at the lake. That used up some time. Then, those bastards didn't go straight after the survivors. (If there were survivors, he thought.) They stuck around for a while and had themselves a meal. So they probably don't have much of a headstart on us.'

'You think we might have a chance of catching up with them?'

'We might,' he said, though that was almost too much to hope for.

He picked up the lantern. They got to their feet and started walking quickly up the dock.

'Another thing in our favour,' Hank said. 'They probably don't have any light, and we do. That means they won't be able to move as fast as . . .'

He went silent.

Out of the darkness ahead came faint, human voices shouting and screaming.

We're too late!

Darcy trotted through the black, one hand on Greg's bare shoulder, the other hand gliding along the metal bar of the railing.

The belt around her midriff was starting to slip. Before they left the dock, Greg had wrapped her with the belt to secure her folded handkerchief against her wound. She had argued against taking the time necessary to apply the makeshift bandage, but he had insisted.

'If you lose so much blood you pass out on me,' he told her, 'it'll slow us down even more – I'd have to pick you up and carry you.'

'It's not bleeding that much.'

'We aren't going anywhere until you're patched up.'

'Okay,' she said.

And so, standing on the dock in the utter darkness, Darcy opened her windbreaker and took off her belt. She dug her sodden handkerchief out of the front pocket of her pants and gave it to Greg. She felt his fingers gently exploring her skin. Winced as he touched an edge of the wound.

'We've already lost so much time,' she whispered.

'A couple more minutes won't make that much difference.'

'Might make all the difference.'

'Face it, Darcy, we're not going to catch up with them.' He placed the handkerchief against her wound. 'Hold that.' She did. She gave the belt to him. 'They've got too much of a headstart,' he said. 'They'll reach the others before we're even halfway there. And when they realize how many they've got to contend with, they probably won't attack at all. They might just watch for a while, or they might turn back. And run into us.'

'We've gotta go after them.'

'I know.'

'So many are already dead.'

The belt encircled her body, just below her breasts. Greg touched her fingers. 'Got it,' he whispered. Then he tightened the belt. It closed around her like a tourniquet and she hissed at the pressure on her raw flesh. 'If it's too loose, it won't do any good.'

Darcy nodded and then realized how foolish it was to nod in such a darkness. 'It's okay.'

She felt for him and found his shoulders and pulled him against her. In an instant, his cold skin turned warm where it met her chest and breasts and belly. She felt the rise and fall of his chest, and beating of his heart.

Greg stroked her hair.

If we go, Darcy thought, *he* might be killed.

'If we can't overtake the savages,' she said as she held him, 'at least we might be able to call out and warn the others that they're coming. If we're even too late for that, we can join in the fight.'

'You've done enough fighting,' Greg told her.

'We might save lives. Even if we save just one . . .'

But what if it costs Greg his life?

Maybe we shouldn't go.

'Whatever we do,' Greg said, 'there's no point in staying here.' He eased away from her. For just a moment, his hands moved lightly over her breasts. Then they found the sides of her face. He drew her forward, kissed the side of her nose, then her mouth.

'Ready?' he asked.

'Yeah.'

Darcy heard a quiet snap. 'What was that?' she asked.

'Elastic. I took the bone out of my shorts.'

She laughed and couldn't believe she was laughing. 'You actually . . . had that thing in your *underwear*?'

'Right in there with the other bone.'

'Uh.'

'Let's move.'

Her laughter died.

Greg led the way, Darcy keeping a hand on his shoulder.

Somehow, they managed to walk the length of the dock without falling into the lake. When the concrete walkway was under their feet, he guided Darcy to the left until they reached the railing. With its metal bar to follow, Greg picked up speed.

'Faster,' Darcy said.

Soon, they were jogging through the total darkness.

The belt remained in place until she began breathing hard. Each time she exhaled, it slipped down a bit. Now, it hung around her waist and she felt warm trickles of blood sliding down her belly.

It won't kill me, she thought.

We must be at least halfway there.

Halfway.

'Greg?'

He stopped.

'Let's try yelling. We're close enough, they ought to be able to hear us if we yell out a warning.'

'You think so?'

'Sound carries a long way in here.'

'All right. But it'll give away our position. As soon as we do it, let's get off the walkway. Don't want those . . .'

'Yeeeeah!' The far-off cry of a woman.

Other voices too faint to distinguish.

Then, 'Let go of me! What do you want?'

A chill spread up Darcy's back.

'I didn't think they'd really do it,' Greg whispered.

Someone screamed.

20

The black air shook with shouts and screams.

Katie started to cry.

'What's happening?' Jean whispered in a frantic voice.

'An attack,' Wayne whispered. 'Some kind of . . . I don't know.'

He heard growls, gasps, thuds, even laughter. And the crying of his daughter.

The three of them had sat there and kept silent until a few moments ago, as if, like Wayne, Katie and Jean understood that the silence was their protection, a shelter that hid them from the invaders. Now, the girl's crying threatened to give them away.

'Katie,' he said. 'Don't. Shhhh. Please, honey.'

If they hear us, they'll get us!

Who? Who's *doing* this?

When it began (a minute ago? five minutes? seemed to be going on forever) he'd thought it was a joke – someone taking advantage of the darkness to throw a fright into a girlfriend or wife. Then someone cried out, 'Oh sweet Jesus, *he's dead*!'

and Wayne knew it wasn't pretend. In seconds, he was engulfed by cries of alarm and pain.

It'll stop soon, he'd told himself.

It'll just fade out and end, like the Los Angeles earthquake when he was a grad student there back in 1972. When the earthquake hit, he'd known he was going to die, but he'd done nothing, just sat there on his bed, and it had gone away.

It'll be like that. If we just sit real still and don't make a sound, it'll stop and we'll be all right.

But it wasn't fading. It was swelling, growing, getting worse.

Wayne felt as if he'd been sucked into the plot of one of his own grim novels.

And thought, those are books. What *is* this shit!

She's got to stop crying!

Reaching into the dark, he touched Katie and she yelped. 'It's all right, honey,' he whispered. He stroked the side of her face, reached beyond her and felt Jean. The girl must be sitting on her mother's lap, just as she'd been before the fires in the elevators died. 'Don't worry. Nothing . . .'

'Don't let them kill us, Daddy.'

What can I do? he thought. I'm a goddamn writer. I'm no Chuck Norris.

A fucking wimp.

'Daddy.'

'Lie down and keep quiet and don't move,' he said. 'Both of you. Jean, get on top of her.'

Then he twisted himself around, turning straight into an explosion of blood that slapped his face and stung his eyes and filled his mouth.

Got the fat lady, he thought.

They're close. Fucking close. We're next!

The blood kept spraying his face. He crawled into it. His hands met the woman's thick calves. Her legs were still crossed, but jumping as if she'd been plugged into a socket. Wayne slapped a hand down on her dress. Found the handbag. Hissed and ducked aside as a thread of fire streaked down his ear and cheek. But kept the handbag and tore it open and dug inside and grabbed the matchbook.

With palsied fingers, he plucked out a match and struck it.

For an instant, there was a bloom of light.

He glimpsed the woman sitting in front of him, bouncing and twitching. Her eyes were rolled back. Her slashed throat spat blood. The blood doused the match but before the darkness dropped over his eyes, Wayne saw a crouched figure lurch past his side.

Toward Katie and Jean!

He bit down on the matchbook and sprang forward, slamming the fat woman onto her back. Her head thumped the rock floor. Kneeling on her soft, shuddering body, he found her shoulders, found her cable-knit shawl, tore it off.

'WAYNE!'

Katie screamed.

He scurried backward, balling up the shawl. Whirled around. Struck a match and saw in the shuddering glow of the flame his wife huddled on top of Katie (did as she was told, for once) and a man crouched over her back ready to slash with a straight razor.

A man – a teenager? – with a face as white as bread dough, wild, tangled black hair and a bushy beard. He wore a quilted pink bathrobe trimmed in lace, its front soaked with blood.

As the match flared, he squeezed his eyes shut and turned his head away.

He seemed stunned by the light.

Then his other hand flew up to cover his eyes and he started to slash down at Katie but the shawl in Wayne's hands was already a ball of fire. As the blade whipped down, Wayne dived at him and shoved the blazing garment into his face.

He shrieked. Wayne smashed him backwards, landed on top of him, rolled clear, thrust himself up to his hands and knees and jerked his head toward the light.

The attacker, beard and hair afire, squirmed on his back and kept screaming as he struggled with the flaming shawl. It seemed to be tangled in his arms. By the time he flung it aside, the sleeves of his robe were burning. He lurched to his feet. He twirled and flapped his arms, then lurched past Jean and started to run. He dashed past sprawled corpses, past bodies huddled in terror, past someone lying prone who darted out a hand and tripped him. He stumbled, fell, shoved himself up and staggered onward.

Maybe hoping to reach the stream, Wayne thought.

He was still running when Wayne crawled over to Jean and Katie. 'Are you okay?' he gasped.

'Yes,' Jean told him. 'Yes.'

'Did you get him, Daddy?'

'You betcha.'

As Kyle slashed her throat, blood gushed over his hand. He let go of her hair and stepped backwards away from her shuddering body. A moment later, her head struck the rock floor of the cavern.

He clamped the pocket knife between his teeth and moved forward. Her blood splashed his pants, his jutting penis. When he was beyond the spray, he turned toward the place where she must be lying, and knelt.

Scooted on his knees until they bumped against her. Reached down and touched her bare leg. Her shin. It was trembling.

Still alive. Fuck her fast while she's still alive and shaking.

Before they *show up*.

He crawled over her and got between her legs.

Behind him, the chaos went on. The mad sounds of struggle and slaughter.

Kyle's whole body quivered with terror and need.

The crazies were back there, doing their number, and no one knew he was here with Paula. He was invisible. He could do whatever he wanted with her. No one would ever know.

They'll blame it on the crazies.

He slid his hands up her shaking thighs, slipped them up beneath her damp skirt.

Skirt?

What's . . .?

Pulling his hands out from under it, Kyle reached higher and touched more wet fabric. A blouse? He squeezed the soft mounds of her breasts through the cloth. From the feel of them, she wasn't wearing a bra, but . . .

Where the hell did she get the clothes?

He'd stripped off her kilt and panties before she broke away from him. Her blouse had come off in his hand when he grabbed her crossing the stream.

Paula's naked.

This isn't Paula.

He remembered the pursuit through the darkness. He'd been right behind her. She was just out of reach when he got past the railing, and he'd stuck out his arm and clutched her hair . . . *someone's* hair.

Nailed the wrong person.

I'll never get her now, he thought. And then he thought, who cares?

He tore open the blouse and filled his hands with the big, warm breasts. Then, he shoved the skirt up her legs and felt for her panties. She wore none.

Great.

Who is *she?*

Who cares.

Kyle folded the knife and slid it into his pocket. Bending down, he rubbed his face on her breasts. He kneaded one of her breasts and took the other into his mouth and sucked it in deep.

There was a high shriek. But not from the woman. From somewhere behind him.

Big deal.

Another tourist bites the dust.

He bit this one, and felt blood swell into his mouth.

The shriek got louder.

Then there was light.

Orange, fluttering light.

Kyle thrust himself up, suddenly alarmed, and was about to look over his shoulder when someone with a burning head and flaming robe tumbled to the cave floor beside him.

No more than a yard away.

He felt the heat of the flames.

He thought, *Christ, now everyone can see me!*

The crazies can see me!

He started to get up.

And saw the face of the woman he had killed.

The face was shiny red.

But he knew that face, though he hadn't seen it in years.

His mind tilted.

Whimpering, he climbed off the body of his mother and ran for the darkness.

Calvin, standing on the debris inside an elevator car, watched the man in flames run through the group and fall just this side of the railing. A kid next to the burning body climbed off someone and ran away.

Other matches suddenly flared as folks from the tour followed the first guy's example. In the glow of the matches, Calvin saw people pull off sweaters and shirts. They started the garments on fire. In seconds, the area in front of the elevator was ashimmer with light.

Plenty of folks were down – some playing possum, he suspected, some killed.

If we'd stayed put, Calvin thought, we'd be in the thick of it. Maybe toes up, our own selves, by now.

But when Calvin had realized it was trouble and not just foolishness, he'd hussled Mavis through the dark and got her into the elevator. There, they were safe on three sides. Blocking the entrance, he'd whipped his cane from side to side until the fires started and he saw that nobody was coming at him.

He made out four trouble spots.

A gal that was bare-ass naked and didn't appear to have a weapon was being tackled by one of their people while the pregnant lady squealed like she was dog-bit.

A gal decked out like the queen of the ball in a satin gown was bent spraddle-legged over the fat man, skewering him in the guts with something that looked like a bone while he bellowed and bucked. Calvin no sooner glimpsed her than the two gay fellows hit her and took her down.

Takes care of her.

Over to the right, half a dozen folks were tumbling around, wrestling each other and yelling. They were starting to break it up, though. Calvin guessed that the light let them see they were only fighting others from the tour.

Just a few yards to his left, Calvin saw his old friend Slick in trouble. The kid was riding the back of some bearded yahoo in drag who had his knees on Slick and planned to ream the son of a whore with a good-sized pair of scissors. It was just the kid hanging onto the fellow's wrist that kept him from polishing Slick off.

Calvin leaped out of the elevator, hobbled over to them, and swung his stick.

The brass horse's head bashed through the yahoo's teeth.

He flopped backwards onto the kid.

Using his cane like a golf club, Calvin teed off on the fellow's nuts.

The kid got clear, snatched up the scissors, and rammed them into the joker's chest.

Calvin stepped back and looked around.

He didn't see any more trouble spots.

The bunch that had been fighting each other had calmed down.

The gay fellows were on their feet and taking turns kicking the gal that wore the fancy gown.

The bare-ass gal was on her knees, talking and nodding to the guy who'd tackled her. He was taking off his shirt for her.

Peculiar, Calvin thought. She one of ours?

He took another look around. Sure enough, the attack was over.

Now, folks were keening over their dead, tending to the wounded.

Calvin limped back to the elevator. He stepped through the debris and wrapped his arms around Mavis. She hugged him hard.

'Next time you want to see a cave, May,' he whispered, 'get yourself a picture book.'

Darcy heard quick footfalls and gasping, sobbing sounds – someone running toward them through the darkness.

Greg halted in front of her. She tightened her grip on his shoulder.

They stood motionless and silent.

The sounds came closer, closer.

Someone from my group? she wondered. Or one of them? Almost on us!

Greg made a sudden twisting move – swinging the bone weapon? It whooshed. His shoulder jerked at the same moment Darcy heard a soft thump. A grunt.

She couldn't see a thing, but from the sounds Darcy guessed that the bone had struck the person – not his head but maybe his arm. He was staggering off to the side, falling, hitting the concrete walkway.

Greg lunged in that direction, and she lost his shoulder.

'No! Please!' A frantic voice. Familiar.

'Greg, wait. I think it's Kyle.'

'Kyle?' Greg asked.

Darcy bumped into Greg's back and put her arms around him. She rested her open hands on his belly. She felt him breathing hard. In spite of the chilly air, his skin was moist with sweat.

'Darcy?' the boy gasped.

'Yeah.'

'Alive. You're alive.'

'Are you all right?' she asked.

'It's . . . murder. Murder.' He sobbed. 'They're all being murdered. I got away and ran for it.'

'Did I hurt you?' Greg asked.

'Just . . . I guess I'm okay.'

'We're going on ahead,' Darcy told him. 'You can come with us or stay here.'

'No!'

'I'm sure you're safe here,' Greg said.

'Don't go! They'll kill you.'

'There're only three or four of them,' Darcy said.

Greg added, 'Maybe even fewer, by now. I can't imagine our people aren't fighting back.'

'But they're . . . they're crazies. They're insane. 'They're killing everyone!'

'Just calm down, Kyle. Greg, let's get going.'

'Wait! No! I'll come with you! Don't leave me here!'

'Can you get up?' Greg asked.

'Yeah. Yeah.'

Darcy heard moans and shuffling sounds as Kyle struggled to rise. She stroked Greg's belly. He wasn't breathing so heavily now. It felt good, holding onto him, and she didn't want to let go.

'Where are you . . .?' Kyle asked.

'Here,' Greg said. 'You're right in . . .'

'This you?'

'Yeah.'

MY HAND!

Darcy blasted her breath out.

Her arm jumped away from Greg's belly, trying to get her hand safe, wanting to free it from the sudden molten pain but the pain stayed.

She whirled around, doubled over with agony, went to clutch her wound and her left hand knocked against something protruding from the back of her right. Scalded by a fresh raw surge of pain, she flicked her hand. Whatever it was flew out and clattered onto the walkway.

Dropping to her knees, she thought, *A knife! He stabbed me. Tried to stab Greg but my hand . . .*

She heard sounds of a struggle.

Greg'll take care of him.

Stabbed me! Kyle . . . tried to kill Greg!

She rocked back and forth, pressing her pierced hand to her thigh, feeling the blood soak through her pants.

The fighting went on. She heard blows being struck, grunts and gasps.

Her arm shook, vibrating the hand against her leg. The pain seemed to fade a little, but she couldn't stop the shaking of her arm. She held the hand with her left, and that seemed to help. The pain faded to a dull throb, a throb that was only slightly worse now than her hurt from the pointed bone.

That's two from the bone, she thought. The one below her ribs, the other on her left thigh.

The leg wound's nothing, she thought.

But Christ, Christ, I'm being ruined piece by piece.

She *buzzed* with pain.

And began to weep.

Kill him, Greg, she thought. Kill the bastard!

Vaguely, she realized she no longer heard the sounds of their fighting. Just someone panting for air.

'Greg?' she asked. She sobbed. 'Greg, you get him?'

The breathing sounds came closer.

Something brushed across the top of her head, then patted it. A hand. She started to reach up for it with her good hand. A blow crashed her forehead.

Darcy's back slammed the walkway. Her head hit the concrete.

A weight dropped onto her hips.

She lay there, stunned, dimly aware that hands were moving over her, unzipping her windbreaker, opening it, touching her breasts, squeezing them, pinching her nipples but not so much that it hurt through the vagueness.

Not Greg. Greg wouldn't.

Kyle.

He must've hurt Greg.

The thought that Greg may have been injured blew through the fog in her head, cleared it a little.

She tried to move, but couldn't.

Gotta . . . pull myself together.

She felt wetness on her right breast. Kyle's mouth. Pulling, sucking.

She heard his moans.

His mouth pulled at her other breast.

The fuck, she thought. *It's what he's always wanted.*

His mouth went away.

His hands smeared the saliva on her breasts, then slid down her body and she jerked rigid when he touched the wound.

'What's this?' he whispered.

He dug a finger in and Darcy squealed and he laughed.

Shuddering, she felt him tug the belt wrapped loosely around her middle. Then he let go of it. He opened the button of her pants. Slid the zipper down. Started to tug.

The fog was gone. The bright bolt of pain when he'd stuck his finger into her wound had blasted away the last of it. Her head was clear.

She wondered where the knife was.

Had to be out of reach. It had fallen beside her, and then she'd been knocked backward. Had to be way down by her feet.

Kyle's weight wasn't on her.

She felt her pants jerk out from under her rump, felt the cold concrete.

Kyle pulled off one of her shoes, then the other.

With her left hand, she unbuckled the belt.

Her feet were lifted. The cuffs slid over them. The pants slid down her legs.

The belt was out from under her.

Kyle forced her legs apart.

749

She felt his trembling hands glide up her thighs, hissed at the pressure against the torn skin down there. He didn't dig into that wound – more interested in what was higher up.

He rubbed Darcy through her panties.

Then his fingers hooked the thin elastic band and she sat up, reaching for him with her gashed and burning right hand. He yelped when it touched him. Flinched rigid.

Her hand was on his shoulder.

'Kyle,' she said. Her voice came out as thin and frail as a tattered rag. 'Don't. Don't.'

'You're mine,' he said. 'All mine.' He made a strange laugh. 'They'll think the crazies . . .'

'You're . . . not one of them. You're just . . . a kid. You don't want to . . .'

One of his hands went away from her panties and found her breast in the darkness.

'Leave me . . . alone.'

It rubbed. It squeezed.

Darcy punched out.

With her left fist.

With the belt buckle clutched tightly, frame down against palm, the metal prong jutting out between her middle finger and ring finger.

Punched through the darkness at the place where his neck should be.

Felt her fist pound against him.

He squealed.

Somewhere behind Darcy, a baby began to cry.

Hank heard a sharp, high squeal. The baby in Chris's arms, apparently frightened by the harsh sound, started wailing.

'Wait here,' he whispered.

Started to run.

Chris didn't wait, she ran at his side.

He dashed around a bend in the walkway.

The glow of his lantern lit a woman with wild blond hair straddling a teenaged boy. She wore a blue nylon jacket. Panties.

The kid had short black hair, no beard.

One of us.

And the gal was killing him. She had him by the ears, was lifting his head up and crashing it down against the concrete. Again and again. His head made soggy thuds each time it hit.

Too late, he thought. Kid's a goner.

As Hank ran, he dipped to the side and let go of the lantern. Its metal base skidded, but the lantern stayed upright.

He sprinted toward the woman.

She kept bashing the poor kid's head down.

Hank saw another body – a big guy sprawled motionless on the concrete beyond the two.

Naked except for jockey shorts.

One of the guys from the boat?

She got him, too?

Had help from the others, probably.

The big guy moved, raised a knee.

Least he's not dead.

The woman turned her head. She looked at Hank through tangles of damp hair. She let go of the boy's ears and twisted around to face him.

Quick kick to the chin.

Her jacket hung open. He saw her breasts, her flat belly.

This one's not pregnant.

Blood all over her belly, a nasty wound just below her ribs. Blood spilling from her right hand. A gash on her thigh.

Took a licking, this one. Took a licking and kept on ticking.

He saw confusion in the blue eyes peering at him through the tangled hair.

Great eyes.

Familiar eyes.

But eyes of a savage, a cannibal.

For the kid.

He shot his foot at the point of her chin.

'NO!' Chris yelled.

21

'I thought she was one of them,' Hank muttered.

Chris held her daughter tightly, and couldn't stop crying.

'Mom,' Darcy said, 'you're hurting me.'

She was crying, too. So was the baby Chris had handed to Hank after he'd come so close to killing Darcy. That kick . . . it would've broken her neck.

If Chris hadn't yelled.

If Hank hadn't been so quick, so good, that he was able to turn even in the middle of that deadly kick and blast his foot through the air beside Darcy's ear.

'Mom.'

'I'm sorry.' She let go of Darcy.

Darcy turned around and went right into the arms of a big man who wore nothing but his underwear. He stroked her hair, her back.

'What'd he do to you?' Darcy asked the man who held her.

'Don't know. My head hit something. Thought I had him, and then . . . Are you okay?'

'That's a good one,' she said, and sobbed.

'You saved my life,' he told her.

'Guess so. My hand'll never be the same.'

'I love you, Darcy.'

Who is this guy? Chris wondered.

Hank patted her shoulder. She turned to him, and he gave the baby to her.

'Paula,' he said.

That was all he had to say, and Chris's gladness and relief shrivelled.

Darcy turned away from the other man. 'Paula?' she asked.

'My kid,' Hank said.

Darcy's mouth twisted, but no words came out.

'What?'

'She was . . . they were together,' Darcy said, and nodded toward the body of the teenaged boy.

'Is that Kyle Mordock?' Hank asked.

She nodded again.

Chris saw pain come to Hank's eyes.

He picked up the lantern and started to run.

Chris rushed after him. We're leaving them in the dark, she thought. She had the backpack loaded with flashlights, but the baby was in her arms. She couldn't leave the pack for them. But she heard them following.

Please let Paula be all right, Chris thought as she ran. *Darcy's okay, thank God, hurt but okay and it wouldn't be fair if Hank lost Paula*.

From the darkness ahead came sounds of wailing.

It's bad up there, she thought.

But Hank is so good. He'll nail anyone in our way. He'll get us to Paula.

Please God, let Paula be alive.

Hank's a good man. He's killed, but he had to. He doesn't deserve to lose her.

She quickened her pace. The infant in her arms, no longer crying, tugged at Chris's ear.

She caught up to Hank.

Side by side, with Darcy and Greg not far behind, they raced through the cavern. Ahead was blinding tragedy or joy for Hank. No matter which, Chris would be with him.

Either way, she told herself, we'll be together.

That should count.

The anguished cries grew louder, but Chris realized that no screams, no shouts of alarm came from the darkness beyond the glow of Hank's lantern.

Was it over? Had the beasts from the bad end of the cave been beaten, killed? Or had they only retreated? Were they coming this way?

Dashing around a bend, she saw light ahead. The shimmering light of half a dozen small fires. She saw people standing near the fires, adding shirts and sweaters to the flames. Others milled about as if lost. Some huddled together in small groups. More than a few were sprawled on the ground. Of those who were down, some lay abandoned. Others were being tended to by people crouched beside them. Still others were being held, wept over, mourned.

Faces jerked toward the brilliant glare of Hank's lantern. Chris heard startled gasps, quick shrieks, shouts of warning. Hank came to a sudden halt. She stopped beside him and took hold of his arm.

'PAULA!' he yelled.

Silence fell over the group.

A few men began to approach, slowly, hunched over as if ready to do battle.

'PAULA?' he called again.

And a small, wary voice answered, 'Dad?'

From behind a shirtless man standing with a woman near the far end of the chamber stepped a girl. A girl with thick long hair that glowed auburn in the firelight. A girl in a plaid shirt that was much too large for her, its cuffs flopping below her hands as she walked, its tails draping her bare thighs.

'Dad!' Her voice boomed out, now glad and eager, and suddenly she was running, dodging the survivors in her way, and Hank was passing the lantern to Darcy and rushing forward to meet her.

Hank stopped. His daughter didn't. She slammed into him. Chris heard the soft impact, and tears blurred her vision as she saw Hank spin, crushing the girl against him.

Darcy refused an ambulance. She stood in the wet debris at the top of the elevator shaft, a blanket clutched around her body, and watched the cable roll off the squeaking reel of the winch. It should almost be to the bottom by now. But it moved with terrible slowness.

She had intended to be last out. It was only right, since she was the leader. First to be hoisted from the cave were the injured. Then the others, one at a time, had strapped themselves into the harness and been raised to the surface until only Darcy and Greg remained below. The Coleman lantern had run out of fuel. They stood together, only the beams of their flashlights warding off the darkness.

Greg had insisted that she go before him.

Just as well. Duty or not, she hadn't liked the idea of being alone down there with only a flashlight. Alone except for the corpses.

A voice rose faintly from depths of the shaft. 'Got it.'

'He's got it,' repeated the fireman kneeling at the other side of the opening.

Darcy heard the winch clank, reversing.

The cable began moving upwards slowly.

She imagined Greg, snug in the harness, starting to rise. Stepping closer to the edge, she peered down into the shaft. The faint light of dusk faded a few yards below the rim, and she saw no more than the cable creeping upwards.

'*Yeeyahhh! NO! God!*'

Darcy's breath slammed out.

The cable jerked, quivered, swayed.

'GREG!' she yelled. Flinging her blanket off, she leaped. She caught the rising cable, clenched it between her legs, started to slide down. The cable felt like fire against her stabbed hand, her torn thigh.

Snapping 'Shit!' the fireman grabbed her. He tore her from the cable, swung her clear of the shaft and wrestled her backwards as she struggled to free herself. 'Calm down,' he grunted. 'Christ, you nuts?'

'Greg!'

Twisting free of the man, she scurried over charred rubble to the edge before he caught her around the thighs, hugged her rump to his chest, stopped her.

She waited, gasping, staring down the hole.

Out of the darkness below came Greg, his head down, his body hunched over in the harness.

Darcy heard him moan.

He rose out of the shaft, naked except for his underwear, groaning and clutching his right calf. Blood was spilling from beneath his hands.

The fireman released Darcy. She lurched up, grabbed Greg and pulled him away from the mouth of the shaft. As she clung to him, others freed him from the harness.

She held him while he was carried to the grass and put down.

Paramedics pried his hands away pried from his blood-slick leg. Darcy glimpsed a torn patch of skin hanging off the back of his calf.

His small toe was gone.

'Aw geez,' Darcy murmured. 'What . . .?'

He shook his head. His face was pale, sweaty, twisted with pain. 'Bit me. Came outa . . .'

'They were *dead*,' Darcy blurted.

'Others. Two of 'em. Maybe three. Not the dead ones. Others. Don't know where they came from.'

'They'll be taken care of,' said someone behind Darcy. Looking over her shoulder, she saw a big lawman crouching, staring down at Greg. He met her eyes, then rose to his full height and turned away. 'Clement! Groves! Baker! Standish! Get the pumpguns, we're going in the hole. Move it! We got some mopping up to do!'

Darcy leaned over Greg. With her uninjured hand, she stroked the cool slickness of his forehead. 'You're going to be all right,' she whispered.

'You, too.' He tried to smile. His chin trembled.

'I'm gonna be fine,' Darcy said.

'Me, too.'

She eased down, feeling the mild evening breeze on her bare legs, feeling it seep through her thin panties, knowing she was being watched by firemen and paramedics, by survivors and spectators and even her mother . . .

. . . but not by Kyle . . .

She didn't care what they saw.

On her knees, she sank down over Greg. She felt his breath on her lips. 'You're mine, now,' she whispered.

'I'm missing a goddamn toe.'

'It was my favourite, too.'

'You love me anyway?'

'You bet,' she said, and covered his mouth with her lips.

The Richard Laymon Collection Volume 2

Richard Laymon

THE WOODS ARE DARK

In the woods are six dead trees. The Killing Trees. That's where they take them. Innocent travellers on the road in California. Seized and bound, stripped of their valuables and shackled to the Trees. To wait. In the woods. In the dark . . .

OUT ARE THE LIGHTS

The Vampire movie came first, then the story of the Axeman. This was the horror movie series to end them all. Cinema buffs admired the grainy, amateur camera work – it suggested the action was the real thing. But it couldn't be – could it?

'If you've missed Laymon, you've missed a treat' Stephen King

'A brilliant writer' *Sunday Express*

'This author knows how to sock it to the reader' *The Times*

0 7553 3169 9

headline

The Richard Laymon Collection Volume 3

Richard Laymon

NIGHT SHOW

When he was in high school Tony Johnson locked school beauty Linda Allison in a haunted house for the night. Now he has moved to Hollywood determined to break into horror movies and he's forgotten all about her. But Linda is a girl with vengeance in her heart – and she certainly hasn't forgotten him . . .

ALLHALLOW'S EVE

The Sherwood house has been deserted since the horrific killing of a local family in the sleepy town of Ashburg. When invitations to a mysterious party to be held there are sent out nobody is particularly surprised – after all *everyone* wants to party in a house of death on Allhallow's Eve.

'If you've missed Laymon, you've missed a treat' Stephen King

'A gut-crunching writer' *Time Out*

0 7553 3170 2

headline

The Richard Laymon Collection Volume 4

Richard Laymon

BEWARE

Elsie doesn't normally shut shop early, but neither is it normal for meat cleavers to fly through the air by themselves, or for Elsie to wind up on the meat counter neatly wrapped and jointed. Something very strange is happening in the small town of Oasis and everyone had better . . . BEWARE!

DARK MOUNTAIN

It was supposed to be a peaceful escape for the two families camping high in the California mountains. But they made the mistake of camping at Mesquite Lake, home to two of the wilderness's most terrifying inhabitants: an aged hag with gruesome powers and her depraved son whose unnatural lusts even she cannot control . . .

'If you've missed Laymon, you've missed a treat' Stephen King

'In Laymon's books, blood doesn't so much as drip as explode, splatter and coagulate' *Independent*

0 7553 3171 0

headline

Coming soon in the **Richard Laymon**
Collection and available from your bookshop
or *direct from his publisher*.

FREE P&P AND UK DELIVERY
(Overseas and Ireland £3.50 per book)

Volume Ten:
Savage & In the Dark   £7.99

Volume Eleven:
Island & Quake   £7.99

Volume Twelve:
Body Rides & Bite   £7.99

TO ORDER SIMPLY CALL THIS NUMBER

01235 400 414

or visit our website: www.madaboutbooks.com

Prices and availability subject to change without notice.